ISBN 978-1-332-24908-4
PIBN 10304106

AMERICAN

BEE JOURNAL.

EDITED BY SAMUEL WAGNER.

"———To Us, both field and grove,
Garden and Orchard, lawn and flowery mead,
The blue-vein'd violet, rich columbine,
The wanton cowslip, daisies in their prime,
With all the choicest blossoms of the lea,
Are free allowed and given."

PARLIAMENT OF BEES, JOHN DAY, 1607.

VOLUME VII.--1871-72.

PUBLISHED BY
SAMUEL WAGNER, WASHINGTON, D. C.
1872.

INDEX TO VOLUME VII.

AMERICAN BEE JOURNAL.

A big frog story 233.
A few apiarian devices 36.
A lady beginner's notes, No. 2, 14.
A well assumed moral indignation 249.
Age of the honey bee 25.
Albany Co., N. Y., bees in 110.
Alleghany Co., Md., bees in 64.
Alley, Mr., business transactions of 62, 75.
Alley's rejoinder 61.
Amateur 15, 38, 76.
American hive 58.
Apiarist or apiarian 111.
Are artificial queens inferior to natural? 227, 267.

Basswood beats the world 228.
Bees, the "coming" 77.
Bees, an hour among 78.
Bees in college 116.
Bees, the yellow and the black 68.
Bees, improvement of 130.
Bees, death in winter depository of 264.
Bees without brood 132.
Bees, to prevent robbing among 136.
Bees, weight of the honey 97.
Bee feeders 20, 159, 254.
Bee hives, 120, 155, 253.
Bee orchard, a 131.
Bee culture, nomenclature in 50.
Bee keeping in the West 65.
Bee keeping and patents 8.
Bee-keepers' conventions.
- Central Illinois Association 48.
- Central Iowa Association 244.
- Chautaugue Co. (N. Y.) Association 108, 283.
- Michigan Bee-keepers' Convention 101.
- Tennessee Apiarian Society 190.
- West St. Louis Co. (Mo.) Association 160.
- The Southern N. York and Northern Pennsylvania Association 2.

Bee stings, cure for 18, 118.
Beginner, notes from a 51.
Beginner, first report of a 140.
Berlepsch on movable frames 172.
Bethlehem, Iowa, report from 161.
Breeding, in-and-in 51.

Canada, encouraging report from 56.
Chloroform and "blunders" 216.
Cincinnati, bee keeping around 19.
Comb, to prevent the breaking of 188.
Comb for new swarms 202.
Comb guide, the triangular 236.
Correspondence 22, 45, 46, 47, 48, 70, 94, 95, 117, 142, 189, 234, 254.
Corresponding hives and queens, 185.
Crippled bees 87.
Cross-bred bees 149, 219.
Cursory remarks and observations 156.

Debeauvoy's hive 197.
Drone production 49.
Dronings 148.
Dried cow dung as a fumigator 268.
Dysentery in bees 251.
Dzierzon theory, test of the 118.

Editorial 21, 45, 69, 93, 94, 116, 141, 151, 152, 158, 165, 166, 167, 168, 211, 237, 261, 283.
Eggs, non-hatching 96, 119, 133, 145.

Fertilization, non-flying 177, 268.
Fertilizing queen bees 88.
Fertilizing queen bees in confinement 252.
Foul brood 124, 125, 126.
Foreign bee journals, review of 258.
Frames, claims on 41.
Furman on Gallup 259.

Gallup's new style hive 12.
Gallup upon H. A. King 256.
Grimm, A., gets a blowing up 226.
Glycerine balsam 44.

Hartford, Wis., report from 191.
Hazen's patent hive 7, 240.
Hives, plain box 58.
Hives, how to make supers 154.
Hives, supers and nucleus 204.
Hive, proposed improved 192.
Hives at the Indianapolis convention, 225.
Hive controversy 9, 39.
Honey, balsam of 31.
Honey bee, the age of 25.
Honey boxes, proper size of surplus 59, 136.
Honey cask, timber for 183.
Honey dew 15, 49.
Honey district, inquiries for a good 17.
Honey extractor 35, 154.
Honey extractor and strainer combined 60.
Honey, extracted 79.
Honey in comb or extracted 154.
Honey poisonous 80.
Honey, production of 105.
Honey resources from a strange quarter 115.
Hrusclhka and the Italians 13.
Huber's unedited letters 241, 265.

Illinois, report from 55.
Imported queens 236.
Indiana, bee notes from 32, 91.
Investigating, modes of 17.
Introducing queens (see queens).
Iowa, another beginner in 92.
Iowa State Fair 106, 107.
Iowa, notes from northern 161.
Iowa, the season in 231.
Italian bees, on pure 232.
Italian vs. black bees 247.
Italian bees not working in boxes 152.
Italian bees at Cleveland convention 232.
Italians in supers 209.
Italian queen bees, purity of 10.
Italian queens, color in 263.

Kansas, letter from 34.
Kentucky, notes from 18.
Kentucky and Tennessee bee-keepers 126.

Le Roy, (Ill.) report from 139.
Lessons of the past season 159.
Linden and buckwheat 116.
Louisiana, bees in 243.
Lucknow, Canada, bees at 215.

Maine, a moan from 139.
Malt as a bee-food 271.
Melextractor 131.
Michigan, a trip to 103.
Michigan, the winter in 251.
Minnesota, letter from 18.
Mitchell & Co. reviewed 193.
Monarda Punctata 209.
Movable comb hives 57.
Movable frames 169, 170, 172.

National Society of Beekeepers 203.
New Boston (Ill.), report from 138.
New Jersey to New Hampshire, from 62.
Non-flying fertilization, 177, 210.
Notes of a beginner 182.
Novel bee dress 203.
Novice 3, 6, 26, 51, 74, 99, 121, 179, 198, 235, 256, 274.
Nucleus hives 242.

Observations and reflections 137.
Oil region, the season in the 162.
Over-stocking with bees 175.

Parricides 7.
Patent hives 40.
Patents and patent hive inventions 81.
Patent hive deceivers 82.
Patent honey boxes 215.
Personal 213.
Pratt's Hollow (N. J.), report from 185.
Prindle & Green hive 56.
Purity, test of 89.
Puzzle 164, 210.

Queens 226.
Queen, an ill-treated 98.
Queens, breeding 12.
Queens, fertility of 58, 67.
Queens, raising 14, 85, 100, 122, 123, 239.
Queens raising on the outside of the hive 14.
Queens, on introducing 10, 11, 43, 92, 95, 96, 98, 150, 167, 185, 201, 269.
Queens, natural, hardy and prolific, 44, 86, 112, 206, 278.
Queens, raising large reserve 73.
Queens, rearing artificial, and their value 146.
Queens, drone layers from virgin 186.
Queens, winter-bred 191.
Queens piping 44.
Queens, my experience with hybrids 230.
Queens and corresponding hives 185.
Queen nursery, "Novice's" 6.
Queen cells, a lage number 16, 273.
Queen cells and their contents 86.
Queen killing, 87.
Queen progeny of a failing queen 125, 150, 152.
Queen bee laying in a queen cell 129.
Queen bee, the instinct of 200.
Queen mothers 147.
Queen nurseries 242.
Queenless colonies, on introducing young queens to 1.
Queenless colonies saved 29.

Side opening hive wanted 228.
Six months of disaster 261.
Stocks in summer, removal of 231.
Sugar syrup for wintering bees 252.
Swarms, combs for new 202.
Swarm, why the bees did not 84.
Swarm, products of a 202.
Swarms condensing 269.

Temporary bee room 210.
Tennessee, a trip to, and back 30.
Tennessee, a cheer from 32.
Tennessee, the honey region of West 63.
Tennesseean, experience of a 63.
Thomas' hive improvement 40.
The twin hive as a non-swarmer 200.
Tomato honey 5.
Triumph hive described 205.
Transferring bees 115, 181, 275.

Upward ventilation 202.
Useful suggestions 157.

Wagner, Samuel, death of 211, 237.
Wasps, new mode of destroying 240.
Wayne Co., Ohio, bee notes from 64.
Wax, how to utilize 133.
West, bee-keeping in the 65.
West Virginia, letter from 34.
Wintering bees 199, 254.
Wool in the apiary 26

INDEX TO CORRESPONDENTS.

Abbe E. P. 124, 157; A Beginner 64, 182; Adair D. L. 253; Alley H. 11, 61, 100, 150; Amateur 15, 38, 76; Anderson J. 42, 78; Argo R. M. 43, 149, 156, 210, 239; Austin C. N. 33; Avery G. 264.

Bailey F. M. 66; Baker W. 247; Barclay G. W. 65, 106; Barbour B. J. 62, 248; Barnard A. 6, 17, 137; Bassett G. H. 84; Bason W. F. 17, Benjamin J. E. 114, 183; Bennett A. 200; Bickford R. 29, 133, 138; Biglow C. H. 14; Bingham T. F. 233; Bishop A. T. 139; Bohrer G. 103, 132, 204, 225, 232; Brewer F. 17; Briggs E. L. 115, 200; Brown A. L. 86; Burgess G. T. 143.

Cameron N. 34, 143; Chapman A. 84; Collins H. T. 36; Cook A. J. 50, 251; Condit J. W. 158, 216; Cole S. W. 154; Cramer J. W. 158, 216; Crathorn F. 125; Criticus 111; Crowfoot Bros. 191; Curtis Joel 67.

Dadant C. 80, 86, 116, 197, 207, 259; Dadant C. P. 269; Davis J. 137; Davis W. J. 148; Dawborn C. 41; Doolittle G. M. 10, 151, 153; Drone B. J. 19; Duffield J. 261; Dzierzon 49.

Enthusiastic 55; Enquirer 252.

Fearon G. F. 185; Flory J. S. 14; Fortune J. P. 203; Fox S. Bevan 227; Furman W. H. 260.

Gallup 12, 30, 59, 122, 163, 186, 191, 200, 202, 207, 215, 226, 228, 231, 238, 242, 253, 254, 256 269, 276, 282; Gastman E. A. 202; Gardner J. 208; Green J. W. 57, 89; Grimm A. 129, 132, 146, 153, 155, 164, 177, 186, 216; Grimm Miss Kate 53.

Halifax 2d 40; Hamlin T. B. 67; Hazen J. T. 143, 270, 167; Henderson W. P. 13; Hester M. C. 32, 92; Hewett M. 152; Hollingsworth Mrs. L. 35; Howe G. 244; Hulman T. 51, 131; Hunt D. C. 240.

James 60; Jerard G. W. P. 115, 124, 210; Jones D. A. 56.

Kellogg, W. M. 273; King E. A. 92; King W. R, 126, 179, 206, 252.

Langstroth L. L. 1, 175, 193, 213, 217, 223, 236, 242, 244, 249, 263, 267, 268; Lathrop 58; Lattner P. 231; Lee Sage 20, 48; Leuchart 145; Lindley J. W. 161; Liston E. 83; Livingston P. 185; Long G. B. 271; Loud S. W. 184; Lucas G. L. 230; Lunderer B. 75.

Mahin M. 130, 149, 181, 201, 251; Mansfield W. D. 168; Marvin J. M. 105, 209; McClay J. 209; McKernan J. S. 76; McLane J. L. 12; McNitt E. 119; Menzel Prof. A. 25; Millet D. C. 60, 75; Miner H. D. 57, 125, 126, 226; Miller C. C. 95; Miller R. 184, 270; Moore J. P. 228; Morgan Mrs. K. A. D. 54, 183; Muth C. F. 201.

Nesbit H. 10, 192, 210; Novice 3, 6, 26, 51, 74, 99, 121, 179, 198, 235, 256, 257, 274.

O'Neil M. A. 159; Osborn H. N. 42; Old Fogy 68.

Palmer Bros. 138; Parmely E. 16; Peabody J. L. 18; Phelps H. H. 65, 183; Pickering J. 189; Pohilman E. 98; Price J. M. 44, 112, 278.

Querist No. 2 90.

Rigg J. 107; Rowel S. 18; Rusticus 140, 160, 204.

Salisbury A. 85, 244; Scientific 8, 59, 80, 157; See H. 23; Seay J. W. 134; Sesaye 82, 275; Silsley G. S. 39, 58, 113, 140, 167; Smith A. J. 138; Smith C. T. 90, 162; Smith T. 9; Snell F. A. 55, 96.

Taylor W. P. 41; The Smallest Novice 63; Tillerghast 66; Townley J. H. 180.

Vogel 98.

Walter J. N. 66, 83, 271; Weeks C. 67; Wheeler G. T. 44, 136, 229; Widener C. E. 96; Winfield J. 92; Wixom H. W. 135; Wilson M. 152; Wright G. A. 77; Wright W. D. 110; Wolcott J. L. 264; Wolf W. 133; Woody T. H. B. 37, 88; Wors E. J. 16; Worthington D. W. 15, 35, 79.

AMERICAN BEE JOURNAL.

EDITED AND PUBLISHED BY SAMUEL WAGNER, WASHINGTON, D. C.

AT TWO DOLLARS PER ANNUM, PAYABLE IN ADVANCE.

VOL. VII. **JULY, 1871.** No. 1.

[For the American Bee Journal.]

On the Introduction of Young Queens to Colonies that are Queenless.

Some ten years ago, I was led to suspect that the ordinary statements of Huber and other eminent apiarians, with regard to the antipathy of bees, under all circumstances, to change queens, was incorrect. Eminent writers have supposed that it would not be safe to introduce even a queen cell to a colony until twenty-four hours had elapsed after the old queen had been removed.

In experimenting with Italian bees, shortly after their introduction to this country, I soon ascertained that this was an entire mistake, and that queen cells could be safely introduced, under ordinary circumstances, immediately after the removal of the queen.* This led me to experiment further in the same direction. Supposing that perhaps the hatching of a young queen in the colony might reconcile them at once to her presence, I introduced to queenless colonies cells, the lids of which were being gnawed open by the young queen. In some instances these queens hatched in less than five minutes after the cells were inserted, and I found them to be unmolested, although the hive had been unqueened but a few moments before their introduction.

I now began to suspect that there might be something in the young queens themselves, either in their actions, or in their odor, or their voice, or want of voice, which made the bees indisposed to disturb them. Therefore, after unqueening the hive, I introduced just hatched queens at once, and found them almost invariably well received. The bees would occasionally seem to manifest some surprise at their presence, and probably, if they could have spoken their feelings in words, would have said inquiringly—"does your mother know you are out?"

If the queens were too young, they were sometimes dragged out of the hive, just as imperfect bees are removed by workers. I next discovered that, in many instances, these young queens could be put upon the very comb where the old mother was, and yet be undisturbed by the bees. In order to test this matter more thoroughly, after introducing a just hatched queen and finding her well received, I would place upon the same comb an unfertile queen several days old. The bees would at once attack her furiously, confine, and speedily destroy her. It would seem, therefore, that under ordinary circumstances, young queens which have not yet attained their proper color, and perhaps the power of piping, may be introduced at once to queenless colonies. I have availed myself of this discovery largely, in breeding Italian queens: it being a common practice with me as soon as the queen of a nucleus has laid a suitable number of eggs to test her purity, to cage her, and at once introduce a queen not more than five or six hours old. It may be that it would be safe to introduce queens even a day old, but my practice has been to select for this purpose such as had very recently hatched. When the young queen thus introduced becomes fertile, and has laid a proper number of eggs, I cage her in turn and introduce still another. And thus I am able, with one nucleus, to accomplish in queen raising, as much as is ordinarily done with two or three.

Occasionally I have known the workers to destroy these young queens, if not immediately, still within a few hours after their introduction. I do not, therefore, recommend the practice above described to those who have very few queens, nor would I risk a young queen which I valued very highly. But, as under ordinary circumstances, the breeder has often more queens than he knows what to do with, he can easily dispose of them in the way above described.

In order, at times, to secure a suitable number of queens for this purpose, I have been accustomed to condense into one colony a very large number of queen cells of about the same age, inspecting the colony about every hour in the day, and removing queens as fast as they hatched, and before they had an opportunity to destroy each other or the other queen cells. These same combs may be returned at night to their proper nuclei.

The expert will know how to avail himself of the plans which I have suggested, and how to modify them to suit his circumstances.

L. L. LANGSTROTH.

Oxford, Ohio, June, 1871.

* Instead of the circumlocution of saying—removing a queen from a hive, or giving a queen to a hive—I propose to use as more definite terms, the words, *unqueening a hive, or queening a hive.*

[For the American Bee Journal.]

BEE-KEEPERS' CONVENTION.

Interesting Discussion in Relation to Bees.

REPORTED BY ROSWELL R. MOSS.

The special meeting of the Southern New York and Northern Pennsylvania Bee-Keepers' Association met at the City Hall in Elmira, April 19th, and was called to order at 11 o'clock A. M., by I. V. Mapes, President. In the absence of the Secretary, Mr. A. D. Griswold was elected Secretary *pro tem.* The Convention remained in session two days, during which the following questions were discussed :

Wintering Bees in-doors or out—Which is the Best?

Mr. Chase, of Allegheny county, had wintered heretofore in-doors, but did not like it; started on summer stands last winter with 102, and now has 98.

Mr. A. D. Griswold built a house at one time to winter—bees would get uneasy, and discharge their fæces about the entrance of the hive. One winter he left the bees out, with more satisfactory results. Now uses a double hive with double walls, and finds that the bees leave the hive as frequently as in single walled; finds the double walls proof against the heat of the sun in summer, and new swarms are less liable to leave the hive. Has a neighbor who wintered in-doors, and was much discouraged.

Mr. J. Hadsell likes an even temperature for bees; thinks they do best in a house cellar, well ventilated, about 25°; if much above that bees become uneasy, and are apt to discontinue work; has had good success the past winter; has lost some, but attributes the loss to foulbrood.

Mr. D. C. Knight, of Allegheny, has wintered with the best success in a house in such a winter as the last. Bees fly frequently and become chilled and lost. Must not be too warm nor too many stocks in a house, as there is a good deal of animal heat in a swarm; thinks a house better than a cellar. Should be without a floor, as a step would jar the stocks; and must be well ventilated.

Mr. John Rowley wintered his in a cellar; thinks they used less honey than they would if left out doors, but finds the comb mouldy; does not know the reason, as it was dry and well ventilated. Put in fourteen stocks.—From one hive that he had out-doors, all the bees left during one of the recent warm days.

Mr. Moore has wintered both in-doors and out; wintered well out-doors by shading the entrance to keep bees from flying.

Artificial Swarming.

Mr. Hadsell has had good success by dividing the frames and putting into a new hive, leaving the queen in the old hive, transferring some young bees and setting near an old stock, some of the bees of which, on returning from work, would enter the new hive.

Mr. Griswold has had some experience in artificial swarming, but has no desire to practice it. If he did, would take the queen from the old stock and place it in a new hive on the old stand. The bees on returning and finding her, would be willing to remain, and commenced building comb, while the old stock would raise a new queen.

Mr. Moore has had good success with the method described by Mr. Griswold.

Mr. Knight has done nothing with artificial swarming; thinks they are more profitable to remain in stock until they swarm naturally. He then puts two or three young swarms together, thus getting a good deal of surplus honey.

Mr. Chase has tried both natural and artificial swarming, and thinks the natural will do for him, certainly, if surplus honey is his object.

When is the best time to put honey boxes in the hives?

Mr. Griswold thinks it desirable to put one box on as soon as the bees will put honey in it, and as often as they will fill it; wants to get all they will make of box honey before the bees commence swarming. On new swarms, waits a few days until the queen gets established below. This prevents her going up and remaining in the box.

Mr. Hadsell puts the boxes on as soon as the hive seems full of bees.

Mr. Moore concurs, and thinks the bees will not get the swarming fever as soon as they would if not supplied.

Mr. Chase finds it quite a trade to know when it will do to put on bees to get the most honey. He uses the American hive, and puts one tier of boxes immediately on a new swarm; raises them when half or two-thirds full and puts empty ones under them, raising the under one as soon as the upper ones are full. Leaves the empty or unmarketable ones on all winter, which the bees will fill as soon as they are able, by which means he gets the greatest amount of surplus honey.

Mr. Knight put boxes on old swarms as soon as the bees commence to stay about the entrance of the hive. On young swarms, puts the boxes on before he hives the swarm; is not bothered by the queen going into boxes, probably on account of his making the new swarms strong by doubling.

What is the most profitable size for honey boxes?

Mr. Chase has made about thirty thousand boxes for sale, of several sizes; finds a box with four glass sides, two of them four by five, and the other two, five by six inches, small posts, the best. The glass is secured by small tins; tops and bottoms of wood; weighs about one pound, and will hold about three and a half pounds honey—two combs. This size sells best in New York.

Mr. Hadsell sells in Elmira; has had bad luck sending to New York. Makes boxes to fit the top of the hive, which he fills with small panes to weigh about three or four ounces. When filled will weigh two and a half or three pounds gross. Buys back the frames, which he prefers to new ones, for five cents.

Mr. Coke thinks for this market the small frames described by Mr. Hadsell the most salable. Probably for New York it would ship best in Mr. Chase's small boxes.

Mr. Denson finds that the small boxes are best for New York, as the honey will not get dusty; thinks the best form is a single comb box with two glass sides, weighing from four to five pounds. This is considered very aristocratic.

Mr. Knight uses a six inch tube, four glass sides, three combs in a box; has taken such to New York, and they looked and sold better than any he saw there. While in the city he saw at Mr. Thomas', at Washington Market, a sample of small frames which he would not buy, as it was accessible to ants, flies, &c. Thinks that while a greater amount of honey could be obtained in large boxes, yet on account of the better prices received per pound, that in small boxes will make the larger returns in the gross amount of money received.

Best antidote for bee stings?

Mr. Griswold keeps ammonia for the use of visitors. Once when stung himself so as to feel sick at the stomach, he eat a large quantity of honey which relieved him. Others recommended Ray's Salutifer, kerosine oil, an application of spittle, salt, or wet earth or dry or chewed plantain leaves. Several made the statement, that bee stings would after a while, so inoculate the system as to render it less liable to the effects of the poison.

How high from the ground should the hives be placed?

Mr. Hadsell prefers to set them low. From four to six inches from the ground. Bees when heavy laden can get back when they fail to reach the lighting board, if a slanting board is set for them to climb up.

Mr. Knight prefers to have them low as possible without danger from moisture—from ten to twelve inches—for the reason given by Mr. Hadsell. It is easier, too, to take out the surplus honey than having them higher.

Mr. Chase places his on a stand of boards with two inch cleats, thus making the hive three inches from the ground. Puts planing mill shavings on the ground around the hive.

What is the proper distance to place hives apart?

Mr. Griswold thought they should be placed at such a distance, that the bees may not quarrel from mistaking their home, and so the queen may not be lost when returning from the bridal trip from the same cause. If covering a good deal of ground, it is more trouble to manage. If the hives are of different colors, two or three feet will do.

Mr. Knight would have the hives of different colors, and five or six feet apart.

What can we provide in the way of pasturage for bees?

Mr. Griswold has grown Alsike, but the result was unsatisfactory. It might have been owing to white clover being in blossom at the same time. Thinks buckwheat good.

Is there any superiority of Italian over native bees?

Mr. Knight had one Italian queen given him in swarming time. The swarm was cleaned out in the fall. Has dealt in honey gathered by Italians; it is not of as good quality as that of the common bee, probably owing to their gathering from poorer flowers. If they gather enough to more than make up the difference in price, they may be more profitable than the common bee.

Mr. Griswold obtained queens from two noted importations; found the bees unnecessarily quarrelsome, stinging when unprovoked. Not having got any in condition to sell, he had not had a chance, nor does he feel disposed to talk about their good qualities. Of those he had, he soon got rid.

To prevent robbing, it was said that a noxious smell, as of kerosine or coal tar, would keep robbers away, while the other bees would endure it rather than leave their home, but it was thought best to keep the colonies strong; and with weak ones to contract the entrance according to their weakness.

Mr. Denson asked if the use of the melextractor is advisable?

Mr. Knight said it would be if the honey could be sold, which it has been difficult to do, such honey being a drug upon the market.

Mr. Coke has not found strained honey a very valuable article. Any one undertaking the process of working sugar, can make an artificial article that is difficult to distinguish from genuine, and people seem to be afraid that honey offered as strained may not be all right.

Mr. Knight's strained honey sold at ten cents, when his box sold at thirty cents.

Mr. Coke has been experimenting with strained honey to prevent it candying, but has not arrived at a satisfactory result; thinks he may yet. Has restored candied honey by heat, but thinks it darkens its color.

[For the American Bee Journal.]

Novice.

Dear Bee Journal:—We have so many things to say, just now, June 8th, that we hardly know where to begin.

Our bees are not as strong nor as busy as we had expected to have them by this time, and indeed we cannot tell why, either. During fruit blossoms many of the stocks hung out on their hives, and, to keep them strong, we fed them on coffee sugar and water for two or three weeks, daily. Yet several severe frosts during that time, and quite a drouth since, rather checked brood raising; and we feel sure that we have not now as many bees as we had a month ago. Many of the old bees were lost during cold, high winds, and we have got to look to the now rapidly "rising generation."

Last season we had over half a ton of honey from locust tree blossoms by the last of May, but these were a failure this year. Only a few trees blossomed, and those the bees did not notice.

Our first honey was from hickory tree blossoms—much of it—which gave it so dark a hue that we emptied all our hives, June 6th and 7th (over four hundred pounds) to make room for pure white clover honey, which comes in now pretty well. On the night of the 6th, we had a very heavy, long rain, and as we were very busy, we commenced removing honey early next morning, but were surprised to find the bees—especially the *full blood Italians*—very cross; robbers in abundance, and no bees at work until afternoon, although the day before everything had been tranquility. Why was this? Did the rain wash out all the honey from the clover, so that the bees had to wait for more to be secreted, or were they lazy? It did not seem to us that they even went to look whether there was honey to be had, or not. We were advised to mount the "Railroad Car" (we have really got a railroad car in our apiary to save "sore backs,") and deliver an address to them on the sinfulness of being idle and unthrifty.

The June number is full of good things, but why in the world is there no more said of results of experiments with non-flying fertilization? Has anybody succeeded? (As we hear no response, we shall have to think that all have utterly and miserably failed, as we have.) We have tried all plans given, and some that were not; in darkness, and in light; and light for thirty minutes at two o'clock P. M.; in large cages, and in small; with one drone and with a dozen; with brood, and with no brood; with queens from five days old to twelve. And yet all the satisfaction we ever had was in letting out queen, drones, and all, after the queen was ten days old; whereupon one drone did pursue the queen round and round, in circles larger and higher, until we nearly twisted our neck off in trying to follow them, and stretched our eyes so wide that they have scarcely "got level" yet. We presume that the pursuit is still kept up, with the same alacrity, as we have never seen queen—she was a fine one—nor drone since.

A few days after this we heard most positively that a bee friend had succeeded, and was raising queens "all right," for $2.00 each. We did not sail our hat (we have a new one now, and our better half won't allow it,) but sailed ourselves, *via* horse and buggy, quickly, ten miles to the scene of action. Well, he hadn't succeeded, but—was going to. He had with much pains made a lot of very neat cages, but as he had been successful in raising only about half a dozen Italian drones for every dozen queens, was in a quandary until we gave him since a whole box full of drones—and all the faith we have left.

Mr. Langstroth's sawdust pile only lost us our clept virgin queen, as we felt sure it would, from former similar experiments. If the queens cannot fly, they go "a-foot" and, with us, always away from the hive.

We do *so earnestly* hope that, side by side with this article, some record of success will be given; for since we have recognized the many advantages that are to accrue from success, we feel as though we must succeed. Trusting that the Creator has provided some means of attaining it, as Mr. Langstroth says, we leave the subject.

We regret that a description of our queen nursery did not reach the editor in time for the June number, as we have full faith that it will be a great acquisition. We think that, with it, there will be no trouble in getting laying queens from a single hive every two days at least, thus:

After a stock has started as many queen cells as it will, cover them all with cages as directed, and insert fresh brood. More cells will then be built, as we have repeatedly demonstrated. Cage all these as before, and so on. When the first queen has hatched, let her loose, after covering all the cells. When you see marks of fertilization, or she begins to lay, remove her and let out the next in age. By watching the hive constantly, we are not sure that a queen might not be fertilized any hour, when drones are very plenty. Ours have been fertilized very speedily. In a locality where there are no black drones, we think two dollars, each, would be a great remuneration. The bees will continuously raise queen cells, if supplied with brood, if they have none but caged virgin queens.

On page 269 of the June Journal are some questions for Novice. We are always pleased with questions asked through the Journal, as it indicates that our experience or opinion is regarded as of some weight by *some one* at least.

Our frames are, inside measure, 16½ by 8½ inches. Ten above and ten below. Although the upper story is broader, we prefer inserting only ten frames, as we want as *thick* comb for surplus as can be handled. Taking out frames of comb two inches thick, full of honey, makes us perfectly happy, unless the wire cloth should be so poorly supported in the extractor, that the combs all break down; and then we usually vibrate to the other extreme of perfect misery, until all is made whole again.

Distance across frames (or hive inside) below 14½ inches, above 16 inches. We use the old triangular guide, because our frames were so made; but as we now always have all combs built between two good ones, we should not care much about it.

We never had any honey get really sour; although a little, taken out last year when it was *very* thin, looked much like it, and tasted a little that way, but became much thicker by keeping. We always leave the combs till nearly ready or partly sealed.

We have never scalded any honey, only when it had candied.

Our glass jars were only closed with corks, and were not air-tight.

We are now putting our honey in barrels, for the present. We have been offered fifteen cents per pound for it in that shape; but as that is not more than first-class syrup sells for, we have hopes of getting considerably more. Twenty cents would be as good or better than putting it in jars at twenty-five.

Mr. Quinby challenges Novice, or any one else, to specify where or when he had intimated that L. L. Langstroth was not entitled to his patent and the benefits he should receive for his invention. If we do not word it right, we think the idea is conveyed.

Well, Mr. Quinby, if the public have misunderstood you in that matter, we are most heartily happy to hear it, and hope you will correct the erroneous view of your position they have taken from your writings.

We, among others, certainly did think, on reading that same appendix, that the obligation you were under to Mr. Langstroth, for the invention there mentioned, was but faintly felt or recognized by you.

And in your later edition, where you mention the hive that embodies nearly all that is valuable of the Langstroth hive, do you anywhere give him credit for what *he did do?* And when you say, in a note, that no one need write you asking if the hive you advise infringes on Mr. Langstroth's patent, are we not right in presuming that you do not consider or care whether it does so or not? In short, whenever or wherever you speak of movable comb hives, is it not to be inferred that you do not feel any friendly interest in Mr. Langstroth's success in disposing of his invention? We need not tell you that your position in the matter has perhaps greater weight with the bee-keeping community than that of any other apiarian.

We owe to you, too, a great debt of gratitude for your "Mysteries Explained," when we were all in the dark; and, oh, how very happy we should be to see our two great pioneers in our favorite science, Langstroth and Quinby, laboring side by side towards one common end. Even now we need your help. Vainly have we looked for something from Quinby on non-flying fertilization. Cannot his practical common sense aid us?

If we have quoted anything amiss or wrong from Mr. Q.'s last book, we hope it will be excused, as it was burned with the Quinby hive; but the general impression that the public have received, is too-often mentioned and quoted to be a mistake.

On page 227, something is said of the yield of honey from the 5,051 hives of the bee-keepers at the Convention in Cincinnati. We then thought, from what we could learn, that perhaps the greater part of those hives were old box hives that had much better been left out of the statement. The yield, Mr. Quinby mentions, was less than seventy-five pounds to the hive; and we have several apiaries here in Ohio, of considerable size, that gave last year twice that amount—that is, with the melextractor.

Two queens in one hive reminds us of a little incident. We have sometimes told our assistant that she would see queens where there were none; and one day she declared she had found the queen of a hive when we had her on another frame; we were about laughing at her, when a glance for ourselves convinced us that she really had a queen too, and a laying one. The frame this queen was on was carefully set in the upper story of the hive, and placed, perhaps, a yard or two from the old hive, while we occupied ourselves, about ten minutes, in preparing a cage for the young one. A lady visitor just then coming in, we mentioned the circumstance, and proposed to show her the young queen. As the stock were pure Italians, no bees had left the frame, and on looking on both sides and seeing no queen, another laugh came in, for sure enough no queen was there. We suggested that our glance had been so hasty we were both mistaken, for if there had been a queen, *where was she?* So the hive was closed up, but it was no use arguing with a woman; she saw her, she KNEW she did. We suppose our lady readers know *that* settled it.

It was so near dark then, that we did not look again (just to please her) until next day, when lo, behold there indeed was her "ladyship," close beside her royal mother (one of Grimm's best), assisting in that highly important and maternal duty of laying eggs, as a dutiful daughter should do. We were so much pleased with the idea of an extra laying queen (it was in April) that we did not hear distinctly some remarks about "being positive," "theory," and "practice."

Well, the young queen "just fitted" a queenless hive, and after proper ceremonies was received very graciously. Next day, on looking for eggs, we were much chagrined to find that our volatile young majesty was off again, leaving no clue (nor eggs). In answer to the suggestion that she had "gone to see her mother again," we with sage wisdom replied that "laying queens *never* left their hives only under the swarming impulse."

"Just look and see, for the fun of it!" Like a woman for all the world! But, as we found her there, on the same comb with her mother again, we shall be obliged to be less positive, in future, in regard to laying down rules in bee-culture. This time we put the old queen in our queenless hive, where she sedately dispenses justice (or eggs), much to the satisfaction of all parties, especially

NOVICE.

P. S.—We are now reminded that there *may be* two laying queens in every hive we open, in spite of all the arguments and theories we can bring forward.

P. S. No. 2.—Why was the extra queen raised? The old one is all right. She came from Mr. Grimm last fall. Cannot some Yankee study up the conditions, so that we can make them do it at pleasure?

About one year ago, we found an extra queen in a hive, which we used elsewhere; and the old one did not fail, nor was she replaced until late in the fall.

[For the American Bee Journal.]

Tomato Honey.

To each pound of tomatoes allow the grated peel of a lemon and six fresh peach leaves. Boil them slowly till they are all to pieces, then squeeze them through a bag. To each pound of liquid allow a pound of sugar and the juice of one lemon. Boil them together half an hour, or till they become a thick jelly. Then put it into glasses, and lay double tissue paper over the top. It will scarcely be distinguished from real honey.

[For the American Bee Journal.]

Novice's Queen Nursery.

Get two pieces of wire cloth about three inches square, cut a small square out of each of the four corners, so as to make two square boxes, with sides three-quarters of an inch high, when they are turned up. Ravel out the wires on each side half their depth, so that the boxes can be pressed into a comb deep enough for the projecting ends of the wires (like a row of needles) to reach the bottom of the cells. Now push one into a comb over a queen cell, and the other on the opposite side of the comb, so that the ends will just meet, and your que n when she hatches is safe, even if the bees cut clear through the comb, as they may do to get at her. Bees enough will hatch inside the cage to take care of her, and you can thus cage all the queen cells in a hive, without cutting a comb, and when removed your comb is uninjured.

When the first hatched queen is five days old, she may be let out until she commences to lay, then remove her and release the next in age, and so on until you have used all, or they are ready for artificial fertilization on any of the plans mentioned.

In this case the queens are always at hand, on the comb where they were hatched, with warmth and young bees, and no places to get fast or to die otherwise. You can put on the cage in less time than to cut out cells, and if on the edge of a comb all the better, as a small corner of comb will serve to hold them, the cages, in place, if they match exactly, which they should do.

We visited a "brother Novice" yesterday, who last season took nine hundred (900) pounds of honey from six Italian stocks, besides increasing them to twelve. We were much pleased with his apiary, appliances, &c. Of course his yield made a sensation in that neighborhood. His great secret of going so far beyond every one else, was that he had read the Journal *over and over until he had it at his fingers' ends.*

He got his Italians as premiums for twelve subscribers to the Journal, and has the combined experience of the leading bee-keepers of our country. Nothing seems to have escaped him that is of any value, and he has energy enough to put what he learns in practice *at once.*

He told us that he had spent the *whole summer* of 1869 in learning to raise queens, and did not get a drop of honey; but we told him the knowledge he had acquired was worth more than tons of honey. He uses the Gallup form of hive.

We told him he had omitted one duty, viz.: *to write* for his treasured Journal, and we shall look for something from him soon. If we have spoken extravagantly, it is because such men are very scarce about here, and we fear they are in other places too. Of course he used an Extractor, and says he never wants any more boxes under any consideration.

One more item. Our assistant has a stock of undeniable hybrids (all her own), and opens them, on an average, to see the queen, &c., *about eight times a week,* (at a rough guess, remember,) and they are the quietest and best tempered bees in our apiary, and certainly as good workers. Remember this, ye who complain of hybrids, and claim that bees should not be "overhauled" so often. The stock that gave us last season three hundred and thirty pounds was opened *invariably* when visitors desired to see Italians at work.

In regard to expedition, if we cannot take fifty pounds of honey from a hive and shut it all up in less time and with less labor than the same amount can be taken off in boxes, and the bees all got out, call us forever

NOVICE.

[For the American Bee Journal.]

Reply to Novice.

MR. EDITOR:—In the June number of the Journal, pages 267–8, Novice, in further explaining himself on the Eureka hive, &c., thinks that in my article in the May number, page 263, I misunderstood him in his remarks on page 206. I *mean* to be understood right, and carefully examine what I do write about. What we both wrote on those occasions is now before the public, and of its judgment I will not complain.

From what Novice has to say on pages 267–8, it appears to me that he has but partially understood me. I hope he will *carefully* read my article again. Having carefully read over a number of times what N. has to say in his last article, and also read what he there refers to, I hope I understand him this time, and wish to make a few remarks concerning it.

Novice's principle, as now laid down, seems to be that our surplus honey must be obtained *in frames* rather than in *boxes.* Now, if that is the best for him, at the head of apiculture, with his tact and knowledge, does it prove that it would be the best for *us,* little folks, before we better learn the trade? And must the best hive for obtaining surplus honey, be struck from existence, simply because it is a box hive—leaving us without one stepping stone between the foot and head? It is the ignorant that need knowledge, and I contend that they should have a chance to obtain it gradually. Now, if Novice will allow us no intermediate steps between "the little and the great," he is evidently in fault. If I were here to introduce for sale the two-story Langstroth hive, with the melextractor (as they need to go together), and also the Eureka hive, I believe I would sell ten of the latter to one of the former. Why? Because the *frame* is so far in advance of what bee-keepers here have practiced, that they are discouraged about trying it. Not so with the latter. Having been used to obtaining honey in boxes, this is not so far ahead but that they would try it, and be benefited. Mr. Hazen has therefore filled a very important link in the chain, and is much to be honored, at least, for his invention. I believe the use of the Eureka hive would be an advance in bee-keeping beyond anything I see practiced around here. So let us have it. Let those that can do better, do it. Fair criticism as to merit and demerit of hives is good, but without showing a fault in a hive, simply slurring it, is not good. When Novice says, speaking of Mr. Hazen's hive, "were his patent hive ventilated, we fear it would present a sorrier show than even Mr. King's American hive," is he not slurring? When he says Mr. Hazen's articles were published as "*bona fide facts*," is he not slurring? Please give us the facts, if we have them not, and do not give us slurs.

Novice asks, "What has Mr. Hazen invented, or what has he done to further bee-keeping? Answer—what part of his hive was invented and patented by him, I know not, but I do know that he has advertised and described a hive of which he claims to be the inventor, known as the Eureka hive, and the boxes are small, and so made that, when filled, they will show off in the best manner. They are so made and arranged in the hive that, if there is honey to be had and bees to make it, they will surely put it in, and in large quantities. The hive also is so arranged that a large number of boxes can be applied at one time—sufficient to keep the bees at work during one honey season, without overhauling. This comes to us as the doings of Mr. Hazen, as an advancement in bee-keeping. We hope a grateful public will honor him, and we hope this is a sufficient answer to N.'s questions, without mentioning what else he has done.

Speaking of Mr. Hazen's "scattering his articles through the press," Novice says—"Their tendency has been to discourage all real progress or improvement, *with no other design* (the italics are mine) than to advertise indirectly his non-swarmer, as he claims it to be." Is not that a hard saying? Can anybody believe that it can be *all* truth? While all that has been pointed out as against it is, that it is arranged so as to get surplus in *boxes*, rather than in *frames*.

Now I want to talk a little about how it looks to us little folks to follow Novice's way. In the first place we must lay aside our present hives and get the Langstroth, with right to use; then a melextractor; and then, for the want of experience, we should probably make a failure for some years. Then, too, I think Novice has somewhere told us (though I do not see it now) that "we must not mind any quantity of stings, not even a dozen an hour." "*I pray thee have me excused*," many will say, as well as myself. But N. further tells us how to get our honey in frames without extracting it. Simply fill in the otherwise box space with frames. Such frames would not be so convenient to keep from flies and get to market in good condition, as the boxes, and yet if they were small would cost more than the boxes. In getting honey in frames for market, I will leave the public to judge if it is not behind the box system.

What I have so far said has been in connection with the idea that a larger *profit* may be realized, by an expert, with frame hives than with box hives. But does anybody know that while of late there has been great improvement in the quantity of honey obtained from frame hives, there has also been from box hives? while the latter bears the better price.

With my best wishes to all bee-keepers, and my thanks to all who have imparted the information on the subject that they possess. I close.

Bangor, Me., June 6, 1871. ALONZO BARNARD.

[For the American Bee Journal.]

Hazen's Patent.

MR. EDITOR:—A correspondent of your Journal writes:—"Nothing certainly could give us *more pleasure* than to learn that Mr. Hazen has made a larger profit from his bees than we have from ours. We rejoice at any one's success with bees; but not in selling the public patent rights for something which they have already. What has Mr. Hazen invented, or what has he done to further bee keeping? Mr. Hazen has for the past six years, or more, scattered his articles through the press, so carefully gotten up that they were innocently published as giving *bona fide facts;* and yet their tendency has been to discourage all real progress or improvement, with no other design than to advertise indirectly his Non-swarmer, as he claims it to be."

This is something like shooting poisoned arrows in the dark, for the writer does not give us his name or place.*

His implications are that Mr. Hazen is fraudulently selling a patent to which he has no right, and pressing the sale by falsehoods, innocently published by the press as *bona fide facts.*

I should take no notice of these remarks, or make any reply to them, did I not think proper to give a short answer to the question—"what has Mr. Hazen invented?" And this would hardly seem necessary to any who have the back numbers of the Bee Journal, with an illustration of the Eureka hive. The three important parts of the hive are the central apartment for breeding and wintering the colony. This, in the medium sized hive, occupies a space of six or more inches wide, eighteen inches deep from front to rear, and sixteen and a half inches high. Comb frames, or bars with side guides, or simple bars, may be used at the pleasure of the operator. If judged necessary from the size of the sheet, a centre guide may pass from the centre of the bar down to the bottom of the hive. Upon each side of the breeding apartment is a chamber for boxes, six inches wide in the clear, eighteen inches deep from the front to the back of the hive, and sixteen and a half inches high. This height is reached by three courses of boxes one upon another, each box five and a half inches high. These boxes are placed with their inner end within three-eighths of an inch of the naked comb, with such apertures at the top and bottom of the box as the operator pleases. This leaves a chamber, eighteen inches square and six inches deep, at the top of the side boxes and breeding apartment, which we call the top chamber. This is the central or breeding apartment.

When the side boxes are removed, we come to the naked comb on both sides of the breeding apartment. On each side we then place a board, eighteen inches long and sixteen and a half inches high, which we call movable partitions. They reach just as high as the top of the breed-

* Novice's real name and residence are, nevertheless, as well known to bee-keepers generally, as those of Mr. Hazen, and it is hardly fair to charge him with shooting *in the dark*.—ED.

ing apartment. Then, with a board or ventilator, or cloth, cover the top of the breeding apartment, and they are doubly enclosed for winter.

My claim allowed me was the combination of the central apartment, the movable partitions, and the side surplus honey boxes—arranged in the manner described.

If this hive and arrangement of boxes and movable partitions was never seen before, I don't know but this may be an answer to the question—"What has Mr. Hazen invented?"

With reference to side surplus honey boxes, as inviting the labor of the bees, I will state—if you will venture to publish my statement as *bona fide*—I have within a few days examined my hives, and have found bees at work in the side surplus boxes, from one to nine boxes in a hive, and yet not in one of the top boxes. I see a reason for it that is satisfactory to me. I place small pieces of guide comb on the underside of the top of the bar at the end next to the bees, and an entrance directly to it. The bees can almost and sometimes quite reach from the comb in the central apartment to the piece of guide comb in the box; whereas they must travel five inches—the whole height of the box—to reach it in the top box.

I have sometimes by accident placed the guide in the outer or distant end of the box and had the box neglected entirely. With a fixed partition between the box and the box that they must pass through to reach, they will be much less likely to begin to store honey at all in the box. This is one important advantage in movable partitions, that they can be taken away and bring the surplus honey boxes square up to the sheet of comb.

I must close this short article.

JASPER HAZEN.

Albany, N. Y.

[For the American Bee Journal.]

Bee-keeping and Patents.

DEAR JOURNAL:—The April number came to hand in due time, freighted as usual with numerous ideas which encourage the novice in bee-keeping, to press forward and emulate the example of those whose experience places them in the advance rank of apiculturists. We like to meet on the pages of the Journal the names of Quinby, Novice, Gallup, and many other true bee-men; and would like to testify our appreciation of their services to the bee-keeping fraternity, by a good, long, strong shake of the hand.

On page 208 I see a very disinterested account of a honey emptier. I use something similar, but Mr. Davis and I will not quarrel about it, for my machine is non-patented also. I hope Mr. D. hasn't a patent hive behind his extractor, to pop up like Jack in the box, when we "address him by letters with a stamp."

If every bee-keeper would use his brains and his mechanical genius (if he has a little of both), he could devise and make his own hives and other appliances during the long winter evenings and other leisure hours. I have but little confidence in those who use your columns as a grindstone to grind some of the gaps out their axes. Their patent traps and long columns of figures would look much better on the last page of the Journal. I claim that such persons are not true bee-keepers. They are patent right salesmen, and keep bees, or pretend to keep them, as a means through which to advertise their wares. Their stock in trade generally consists of a small model hive, printed circulars, *farm rights*, and a smooth tongue. The proper way to meet these men, is for the intelligent bee-keepers to insist upon a trial of their hive for one year. In nine cases out of ten they will not send you a full-sized hive. If they do, of course the hive merits your careful consideration. Bee-keepers should bear in mind that a complicated hive, with many fixtures and moth traps, &c., will prove a curse to his apiary, if he introduces it there.

The hive nature provides, is a hollow tree. Let bee keepers follow out the idea, and study simplicity in construction. Frames can be fitted into a simple box hive. Top storing or side storing cases can be attached to it, if desired. The hive of our grandfather's days, with the *real modern improvements*, is far better than those bearing the high-sounding titles of palaces, &c.

To protect our swarms from the ravages of the moth, we have learned to keep our stock strong. So, to keep this pestiferous, swindling horde of patent right moths form our apiaries, let bee-keepers become strong in bonds of union, in every State, county, and town, throughout our broad land. Then when an invention comes before our Committee on New Inventions, its merit, if it has any, will soon become known to all, with no danger of being swindled, unless a bee-keeper likes the idea of being humbugged, as a great many seem to do now-a-days.

Come, bee-keepers, wake up everywhere, and form societies for the interchange of views and co-operation with our National Convention.

On page 263, Mr. Beckwith discourses upon "My Patent Bee Hive," and Mr. Langstroth's claims as inventor of the movable frames. This is a subject that interests every bee-keeper, and upon which we want more light. I devise and make my own non-patented hives, and my neighbors are adopting my plans. I make a frame as simple as it can be made, by nailing together four pieces of lath. Now, if I am infringing upon Mr. Langstroth's patent, I want to know it, and am willing to pay him for the right to use the frame. As I understand it, the frame was used in Europe, and was public property to any one who chose to use it in this country before Mr. Langstroth procured a patent. My idea of his patent was that it covered some peculiarity of construction of the frame. As Mr. B. says, "we want to know just what inventors claim."

SCIENTIFIC.

Hartford, N. Y., May, 1871.

☞ The movable frame as given to us by Mr. Langstroth, nor in any other practical shape, was not in use in Europe or anywhere else, before he invented it. The case will shortly come up before the courts for decision, and we, therefore, refrain from saying more on that point now. The *Huber hive* is not a *movable* frame hive, in the sense of term as used by modern bee-keepers; nor was it intended to be so by its inventor. It is simply an *observing* hive, long since superseded in use as such. No apiarian would for one moment think of using it in practical bee culture, as a movable comb hive, nor was it ever called so till Mr. Langstroth himself happened to dub it so. The *Debeauvois* hive, too, was an impractical structure that never was or could be introduced into use. So utterly was it a failure, that Mr. Hamet, the author of several treatises on bee culture, and editor of the "Apiculteur," has become so strongly prejudiced against movable frames, as to denounce them as involving an impracticable idea—believing, apparently, that as the French inventors have failed in their efforts in this line, no others could ever succeed. —Ed.

[For the American Bee Journal.]

The Hive Question Again.

I dislike to ask permission to occupy the columns of the Journal again with this subject; but as Mr. J. H. Thomas has asked me a number of questions, either with a real desire to have me answer them, or to try to puzzle me and make my statements appear confused, and has made a garbled quotation of my language to make it seem contradictory, I feel it due to myself to reply, and will try to be brief.

Mr. T. makes a very evasive reply to my statement about the combs breaking down, being careful not to say whether his hives were in the sun or not. To prove that they will not break down in his hive, he says they do not break down in the ordinary box hives, some of which contain larger combs than his. Now, ninety-nine out of a hundred of all the box hives I ever saw had cross-sticks in them, to support the combs and prevent them from breaking down; and I cannot but believe that such has been the case with those in his country. His modest allusion to superior knowledge, I let pass for what it is worth.

Referring to my experience in wintering, he asks: "Were both the tall hives and the shallow ones ventilated *exactly* alike?" No. The ventilation with the Thomas hive, with a hole in the bottom board three inches square, covered with wire cloth, is a peculiar feature of that hive (or *was*, as it has been changed lately), recommended, I suppose, for its "scientific principle." The shallow hives did not have this, and their entrances were left somewhat larger than in the Thomas hive. The top ventilation and covering were as near alike as I could make them.

"There was a large number of dead bees in some of the tall hives. Was this carelessness, too?" No, not that I am aware of, or I would have so stated, for I had no object in view except to state the facts.

"Was it a fact that they contained far more old bees than the other hives!" It was not.

"Why should tall hives mould more than shallow ones?" This question should be in this form: Why did *the Thomas hives* mould, &c.? and even then I must confess that it puzzled me. At one time I thought that that hole in the bottom board had something to do with it; but I hardly think that is satisfactory.

"How is it that Mr. S. says: 'I have no hives patented or unpatented,' while the next paragraph commences with: 'I have made a hive,' &c.?" Mr. Thomas has here deliberately quoted only a part of a sentence, to make me appear inconsistent. That kind of garbling won't win. I said plainly, "I have no hives, patented or unpatented, *to sell*." Is there anything inconsistent with that, and my making a hive for my own use, and recommending it to others? I have neither time nor inclination to go into the hive manufacturing business.

"How is it that Mr. S. has made a tall hive, —frames 14 inches deep," &c. I did not say my frames were fourteen inches deep; the comb in my frames is just twelve inches deep, though I call it a tall hive. The hive I made was gotten up in the winter, before I was aware of the result of the wintering. My experiment only showed that the bees wintered better in the shallow hive than in the Thomas hive. But it does not follow from this that a tall hive, made upon a different principle, is not better for wintering than a shallow one. I admitted the correctness of the theory in regard to the advantages of wintering in a tall hive, and made one moderately tall to secure those advantages, and for the purpose of making it better adapted to placing surplus boxes at the sides,—as I still wished to retain the advantages claimed for this last feature, I have no cause yet to change it. But with Mr. Langstroth's plan I am now nearly satisfied that the shallow ones will winter just as well as the tall ones. Of course I do not consider one experiment conclusive.

I cannot accept Mr. Thomas' proposition to try and beat what his hive has done in St. Catharine's, or anywhere else. No test of hives can be made except upon the same grounds. When one kind of hives give three times as much surplus as another kind, in the same apiary, under the same circumstances as near as possible, for a successive number of seasons, I can very soon decide which is the best for that apiary. If Mr. T. can afford to stick to the tall hive and top box and remain behind the times, while H. A. King & Co., who have so long been the advocates of the same, have, in their latest issues, shortened their frames, put on a second-story of frames, and made arrangements for side surplus boxes; and such extensive manufacturing establishments as the "National Beehive Company," at St. Charles, Ills., have to give their attention almost exclusively to making two-story hives, to supply the demands of progress in this direction (see Bee Journal, vol. VI., page 160),—to say nothing of the many individuals who are doing the same,—I am sure I have no right to complain.

I have no desire to make "a thrust at the Thomas hive without good grounds;" nor do I wish to injure it or its maker in any way. In my dealings and correspondence with Mr. T., I have found him prompt and obliging. But I hold that in the investigation of this subject, whatever experience we may have that we believe will tend to its development and advancement, should be given without fear or favor, regardless of whose personal interests may be affected by it.

THADDEUS SMITH.

Pelee Island, Ontario, Feb. 4, 1871.

[For the American Bee Journal.]

Purity of Italian Queen Bees.

The purity of Italian queen bees has been, and still is, the question in which every queen breeder and the majority of those keeping bees are interested. The country is full of what are called pure Italian queens, and queen breeders are advertising queens warranted pure, prolific, &c.; and, right in the face of all these queen raisers, Mr. Langstroth, who has heretofore advertised the same, says: "There is every reason to believe that the Italian bee is itself a hybrid." How is this? and what does such a warrant amount to? What are we to understand by this purity, if all Italian bees are hybrids? A mulatto is not pure African, neither is he pure white. So with the Italian queen. if she is a hybrid. We must give up and call all Italians mongrels, or else we must call them pure. I am for calling them pure.

I have had considerable experience with Italian bees, and have raised lots of queens. I have also had queens from different breeders, and some were the simon pure; but the majority of them were hybrids, and some not as good as that. A good many writers will tell you that if a pure Italian queen mates with a black drone, some of her workers will show the Italian blood, and some will be entirely black. This I do not find to be so. It may be, as Quinby says, that my bees are contrary. I never yet had a pure queen fertilized by a black drone, that ever produced a worker bee with less than two yellow bands. If I had a queen that had mated with a black drone, and she should produce any black bees, I should be inclined to doubt the purity of her mother. In the American Bee Journal, vol. V., page 83, Querist asks: "The present standard of purity of Italian bees is the three yellow stripes on the worker; but is that a proper test?" I answer, No. I have had queens from a hybrid mother, which were nearly black, which mated with a pure Italian drone, and produced workers which no man could tell from the simon pure. A queen to be pure must produce workers with three yellow bands; yet she may produce such, and not be pure. Therefore we want an additional test, and that is this: *The queen, besides producing workers with three yellow bands, must duplicate herself*; in other words, *her queen progeny must be exactly like herself*, allowing a little for the season.

One of the best queens I ever saw, and as good a one as I ever had, produced queens exactly like herself, and nearly half of her workers showed *four* yellow bands, as they stood on the comb. You could scarcely be aware of their temper, they were so peaceable. There are a great many queens sent out as pure, that are not fit to breed from; though the inexperienced will be satisfied with them, as they do not know the difference, and part Italian is better than none. I received four queens from a certain breeder last summer, which were certainly impure, for nearly one-half of the queens raised from them were black. Yet he advertised his queens as pure. If a queen has the slightest dash of black blood in her, it will show in her queen progeny, although her workers may look well. Black bees are not Italians, and coal is not chalk; but humbugs are plentiful in some localities, and so with impure Italians. In some places pure Italians can be found; in others, Italians can be found to be bogus mongrels, and the bogus are the most numerous.

One word to those who wish to purchase queens. I would say, get a queen that produces all three-banded workers, uniform in color. The drones should also be uniform in color, and the queens from all duplicates of herself. Then you will get a queen worth having; and anything short of this will be dashed with black blood. Such a queen cannot be raised short of eight or ten dollars. Therefore, if you purchase a cheap queen, you must expect a cheap article. We do not raise coarse wool sheep from fine, if both mother and sire are pure Merino; but if there should happen to be a dash of Southdown blood in them, it will occasionally show itself by brown spots on the face and legs. So with Italian bees. If there is any black blood in them, it will show itself in the way of occasionally a queen being dark, or, perhaps, some of the workers will not show more than two yellow bands. Then comes in the humbug cry, "She has met two different drones, one black and one Italian, and is producing bees after both drones. Queens that produce bees after two drones are as scarce as white crows.

In conclusion, I would say, with Rev. E. L. Briggs, in the August number of the Journal: "Then let the price be kept up at paying figures; but send out no queens for breeding purposes but such as are fully up to the standard of excellence; and those who delight in handling this wonderful insect, may not only have the most beautiful, but the gentlest, the largest, the most fertile, and the most industrious honey bees known to the world.

G. M. DOOLITTLE.

Borodino, N. Y., April 8, 1871.

[For the American Bee Journal.]

Introducing Queens.

MR. EDITOR:—On page 233 of the Journal, vol. VI., you give a process for introducing queens, without removing the old queens, &c., and request those experimenting to report.

In 1869, I was very unfortunate in introducing queens in almost every way. I tried all the modes I had read of, and lost at least two-thirds. After losing five out of seven *imported* queens, that cost me a round price, too, I set to work to devise a plan to procure some brood from the remaining two, in case they should be killed, and invented the same trap you describe, or *Queen's Castle*, as you term it, excepting that I made the sides, bottom, and top of thin boards. I put in this a comb of hatching brood, put the queens in, and as fast as the young bees hatched out, the queens filled the cells with eggs. I watched them very closely for a few days, and was delighted at the prospect, as I thought, of safely introducing my last two imported queens. After six days, I concluded to release one, but first looked over all the combs for eggs and queen cells. I saw none, as I had removed the old queen ten days before, and concluded all was right. I lifted out the *Queen Castle*, took out the frame containing the new queen, set it in the hive gently, and thought I had succeeded with *one* at least; but next morning, I found her dead at the entrance. On further examination, I found a young unfertile queen, that had hatched from a small cell that I had overlooked.

Just here I will say to beginners, when looking for queen cells that you wish to cut out, shake or brush all the bees from every comb that has brood in it, or you will sometimes overlook queen cells that the bees are clustered on.

On the seventh day, I took out the other and last of seven imported queens, and to be doubly sure there were no queen cells or young queens in the hive, I shook off all the bees, examined the combs, and then *run* the bees to see if there was any queen among them. I found none, and set the queen at liberty, as the former. All went well for two days, when I found her in a cluster of bees, almost dead, with one of her antennæ pulled off at the first joint, and she died in a few hours.

Last season, 1870, to gratify the curiosity of my assistant, I put five queens in these castles, and lost four out of the five.

You state it is alleged that queens so introduced are invariably accepted, and the old queen of the colony, or any fertile worker, discarded, &c. If so, why do they not discard the queen when a queen is placed in a hive in a cage? I have, for several years, been in the habit of preserving queens that I had no immediate use for, by putting them in cages and suspending them between the brood combs of any hive that has a fertile queen laying eggs; and have left them so sometimes for two or three months. Last summer I had nine queens so preserved at one time, in one hive, for two weeks, with the queen laying eggs all the while.

On page 231, Mr. Grimm gives his experience in introducing queens. In his first case, had he set the queens at liberty, and closed the entrance so that only one bee could pass at a time, it is my opinion that he would have saved all his queens. I introduce queens as per instructions of Mrs. Tupper, and failed only in one case out of a great many,—and that failure lay to the queen having been taken from a swarm that had settled. I think the queen still had the swarming impulse, swarmed out, and was lost.

Let not what I have here said prevent others from trying the Queen Castle, as many may succeed where I failed. In the early spring, or in the swarming season, I usually succeed in every way; but later in the summer, I find it more difficult. H. NESBIT.

Cynthiana, Ky., April 11, 1871.

[For the American Bee Journal.]

Introducing Queens.

As this is the season for introducing queens, perhaps a few suggestions at this time will not be amiss. Many of the readers of the Journal know that my favorite method for introducing is the use of tobacco smoke. In my opinion all that is necessary is to scent the bees and queens alike, and there is no trouble. Of all the methods that I have seen in print, I think there is none so good as the tobacco smoke. A few days since I introduced eight queens safely into very full stocks of bees, and was only a little over an hour about it from the time I commenced to look for the old queens. I did it in this way: I gave the bees tobacco smoke to keep them quiet while I was hunting out the black queens. They were all in movable comb hives. All the bees that were on the combs were brushed into a box about a foot square. The Italian queen was put in with them. Then, with my fumigator, I commenced to smoke them and shake them about in the box, so that all would be smoked alike. When they began to look as though they were daubed with honey, (and I presume they were, as the smoke seems to make them vomit,) they were then turned on the frames, the cap put on, and the hive left quiet for a short time, until they were somewhat recovered from the effects of the smoke. Many of them will cluster in the cap, if the colony be a large one and the weather is warm. Should they do so, they are to be shaken down in front of the hive, and left to run in at their leisure. The honey board is then put on, and no one could tell, from the appearance of the bees next day, whether they had been meddled with or not. Nearly all the queens I introduced in this way were accepted by the bees.

The bees left in the hive should also have a good quantity of smoke, but not near so much as the bees the queen is put with. A pint of bees is enough to put the queen with. If this operation is performed when forage is scarce, care must be taken that other bees do not rob them. Just before sunset is a good time to introduce queens in this way.

The honey harvest bids fair to be a poor one here in New England. The apple blossom was light, and white clover is nearly dried up, as we have had no rain for quite five weeks, and no prospect of any at present.

The weather was so cold during the first part of May, we could not raise queens, as the bees would not make cells. We have had some very hot and some very cold weather for the season. Our first queens were sent out May 29th.

Those correspondents who wrote us, and do not give the name of the State in which they reside, must not expect answers. We have received several letters of this kind within a few weeks. One man sent us $2.50 for a queen. He did not sign his name to the letter, or give the name of the State, and yet was in a great hurry for his queen.

H. ALLEY.

Wenham, Mass., June 8, 1871.

[For the American Bee Journal.]

Queen Breeding.

MR. EDITOR :—As it is some time since I contributed aught to the columns of the American Bee Journal on the subject of bee-culture, may I be allowed a short space for a few remarks, on the very important and interesting question of the relative value of naturally and artificially raised queens.

Generally, naturally raised queens, or queens reared when the bees are preparing to swarm, are more prolific and longer lived than forced queens. In searching for a cause for this, we find that when a queen is forcibly abstracted, at an unnatural time, the bees, in order perhaps to shorten the cessation in breeding as much as possible, hasten the process of queen construction by taking a larva several days old. By this means they are enabled to secure a queen in from ten to twelve days, which is from four to six days of a gain on their natural period of incubation. Other things being equal, the hive has a properly developed female bee, every way qualified to perform the maternal duties of the colony, several days sooner than if started from the egg, as is the case in natural swarming.

Now, the fact that such queens are generally shorter lived than those that are longer in maturing, needs no explanation to those who are familiar with the principle in nature, that the life of a being is in the ratio of the time intervening between birth and puberty. Our domestic fowls, for example, will arrive at puberty in one year's time, and their ordinary life time is five or six years. The same is true of the ewe, while the cow and the horse that are two and three years in maturing are two and three times longer lived. Man himself is no exception to this rule. The same principle holds good in the vegetable kingdom. The quince, or the pear on quince root, will bear fruit in three or four years, and will decay and die in from fifteen to twenty years; whereas the pear on its own root will require from eight to ten years to arrive at bearing condition, and its life will be prolonged accordingly. The apple is subject to the same law; some varieties bearing much sooner than others, while their lives are proportionately shortened.

From the foregoing facts it will appear natural enough why a young queen sixteen days in process of development should live much longer, and be every way more profitable, than those forced into premature maturity, to fill the unexpected interregnum. We have succeeded in rearing queens from the egg, by a plan which we have not seen developed elsewhere, which enables us to determine the very day that the young queens are ready to emerge from the cells. The importance of securing the proper development of the queens from the egg, at a time when they can be taken from the hive all at once, is certainly an item of some moment, if we consider only economy of time and labor. The plan is simply this: We deprive a full colony of its queen at a time when forage is abundant. In four or five days afterwards, we take and destroy all the queen cells that have been constructed. We then introduce a pure queen from which we wish to breed, and allow her to remain in the hive two or three days. Then we abstract her a second time. The previously deposited eggs being too far advanced to be available for queens, the recently deposited eggs are used by the bees for that purpose; and, as these cannot vary *in theory* more than two or three days in the time of their issuing, we find that *in practice* there is not even *a day's* difference. If we allow sixteen days for the natural period of development, since the eggs have subsisted for at least two days in the hive, the queens must issue in fourteen days, nor need we expect them any sooner. A practical example of this method last fall demonstrated the truth of this theory, where we took thirteen queens from a hive, barely giving us time to cage them, as they consecutively cut themselves loose from their cells.

The honey season proper set in here on the 22d instant (May), by the blooming of the locust, and it gives promise of a profusion of honey. Out of four days' bloom our bees have had three and a half, and the promise of three or four more. It is impossible for an apiarian to estimate the bloom of the locust too highly. We count one day properly employed, in this extraordinary forage, equivalent to three in white clover bloom. If we were not favored with this remarkable tree in our vicinity, we would unhesitatingly pull up stakes and pitch our tent in a region where the atmosphere is perfumed by its delicious fragrance.

JOHN L. MCLEAN.

Richmond, Ohio, May, 1871.

[For the American Bee Journal.]

Gallup's New Style of Hive.

MR. EDITOR :—Gallup has been foolish enough to get up a bee-hive. Now, I am not going to find any fault with a two-story Langstroth hive for the extractor, yet I did not like the idea of having to take off the upper story in order to get at the lower one, so in the hive I got up, I have obviated that difficulty. I wish to say to all who use my old style hive, that I use the same kind of frame in my new one. I have made seven and put bees in them all. One contains thirty-two frames, and the others twenty-six each.

We find out as well as others, that in order to have the full benefit of the extractor, we must have a large quantity of comb ready built, and we do not wish to vary our style of frame in the least. We wish to get our most prolific queens into the large hives, and want to set them to work to the best advantage. And if we desire to manage the queen on the non-swarming plan, we want a hive that we can do it in. We frequently want to exchange a swarm of bees from a large hive to a small one; and a small swarm can be accommodated in our large hive.

In running a large apiary, we consider it an advantage at present to have different forms of hive, but all with the same frame. In fact the advantages of our hive are too numerous to even think of, let alone mentioning in one article.

Any one enclosing one dollar will get a full description, so that any mechanic can make the hive; and that is as cheap as I can afford it, as I cannot spend my time for nothing. The hive is covererd by the Langstroth patent, so that any one using it should own a right to that patent.

Those using my old form of hive can make one of the new on trial, and move a swarm, frames and all, into it immediately. The hive is a good-looking one, and is calculated to winter on the summer stand. But small swarms can be placed in the old form of hive, and wintered indoors. There is no humbug about this hive, so send on your dollar and get a description. The cry comes to me from every quarter, inquiring about hives, and I might spend nearly all my time describing the hive; but this I cannot afford without pay.

The season bids fair to be a good one. My bees commenced swarming on the 14th instant. There has been a heavy honey-dew for the past few days. Red raspberries and white clover are coming into bloom. The weather is hot and moist, which favors the secretion of nectar, and urges forward the swarming. In fact the swarming mania is up to the full standard. We had two or three weeks of cold rainy weather, that set the black fellows back early in May; but the Italians kept up their reputation, for the continued breeding up to the full capacity.

E. GALLUP.

Orchard, Iowa, May 26, 1871.

[For the American Bee Journal.]

The Hruschka, and the Italians.

MR. EDITOR:—I procured a honey extractor this spring, and the way it slings the honey is a *wonderment* to the natives. With the old woman in the sitting room running her sewing machine, the slinger going at full speed in the room adjoining, and the old fashioned churn dasher in operation near by, I tell you it sounds like business at our house.

But this honey slinger don't belong to the deparment of poetry in bee-keeping—it is work and trouble. No trouble to turn the gearing, and no mistake about the honey coming out easily and nice too; but to get it uncapped, if capped—to get the everlasting, ever sticking, and never leaving Italians off the comb is one trouble, and not the least one either. Smoke them off on one side, they move over to the other; and undertake to brush them off, you then and there get up an issue. It takes experience, intelligent experience at that, and withal

"For care and trouble set your thoughts,"

with the Italian bees and the Hruschka machine. But I feel a good deal like the old lady, who had raised seventeen children (mostly boys and girls,) and then bought a kettle, and didn't know how she did so long without it! I am pleased with the machine.

The Italians swarmed earlier this spring by ten days than the native brown or black, although much weaker in numbers early in the season. Their hives are generally clearer of the moth-worm. They will not submit to as rough handling as the blacks, without using their sting. On cold days, when opening a colony of blacks, you are saluted with a general buzz, and they raise themselves up on their fore legs as high as their length will permit, yet after a few moments they will submit to almost anything the operator desires. Not so with the Italians, for as soon as they are exposed in cold weather to the light, they go for your eyes. I have frequently opened hives of blacks without the use of smoke, and not in the least irritating the colony. I have never attempted to open a full colony of Italians, without about a pint wanting to sting. To keep them quiet, I have to use smoke, every few minutes repeat, and double the dose. I have yet to find them the peaceable creatures some persons proclaim them to be. Italians are not given to robbing, as the black bees are. Their nature and disposition are to gather stores from legitimate sources. They care but little for broken honey, when anything can be collected from blossoms. It has been repeatedly stated, and I can add my testimony, that they go through the winter with half the number of consumers as the blacks. My Italians became so reduced in numbers last winter, that I was fearful that the cold snap in December would freeze them, but they went through all right.

Some dealers in and breeders of Italian queens claim more superiority for the Italian bees, than they are entitled to. I believe them a superior bee in many respects, but do not subscribe to all I see in their praise.

In searching the hive for the queen, says one dealer, "you can more easily find the Italian, for she is perfectly yellow and can be readily discovered." Introduce an Italian queen to a black colony, and for the first three or four weeks I agree with you. But wait three or four months, until the colony is fully Italianized, and it is just as easy to find a black queen (which, if aged, nearly always has a red cast) amongst black bees, as it is to find a yellow queen amongst yellow bees. Some persons claim for them that, their proboscis being longer, they can gather the sweets from red clover. There are red clover fields in abundance near my apiary, and I have yet to see an Italian bee visiting the blooms, except in the latter part of the month of September, or in October, when, on account of cool nights and dry weather, or other causes, the blooms are dwarfed and diminutive; and then the blacks as well as the Italians are foraging. At this season of the year, the humble or bumble bee, is the only bee I can find on red clover.

WM. P. HENDERSON.

Murfreesborough, Tenn, June, 1871.

I have often seen wasps and hornets at work on the grapes in my father's vineyard, and in others, but never saw a bee attack a sound, ripe grape.—C. SCHROT.

[For the American Bee Journal.]

Raising Queens.

My experience agrees with that of most bee-keepers, that we can raise better queens in full colonies than in small nuclei.

I select a populous stock, containing a queen that I wish to breed from. After removing the queen, when queen cells are capped, or a few days before they are hatched, I cut them out and place them in nuclei, or take a 1½ inch board, make it same size of the frame in the hive, and bore 1¼ inch holes through this board, tack on one side wire-cloth, covering the other side with the same, but in pieces about 1½ inch square, and cover the holes after putting one sealed cell in each.

Remove one of the frames in the hive, and put this board into the hive near the centre. If done early in the season, the cells will hatch as well as if left on the comb.

I have had good success this way, having as many as twelve or fifteen queens in at one time. They were fed by the bees, and sometimes there has been a fertile queen laying in the combs at the same time. These queens can be kept here till a nucleus is prepared for them, or some other disposal is made of them.

I do not claim that this idea originated with me, for I think the same principle has been recommended before. I think Dr. Davis's nursery has some of the same features. My first experience with this method was two years ago.

C. B. BIGLOW.

Perkinsville, Vt., May, 1871.

[We have been using a nearly similar device, for the same purpose, four or five years past. It is a rectangular block, or piece of pine plank, 1¼ inches thick, and only about two-thirds as long as the frames in our hives, and is screwed fast to a top bar equi-distant from its ends. The block is perforated by fourteen holes bored *through* with a brace bit. These holes are 1½ inches in diameter, and are lined on the inner surface with a glazed card board. Within them are inserted cylinders of card board, slightly smaller in diameter and 1½ inches long, with removable wire gauze caps fitted to each end. These are intended for queen cages; and when queen cells for hatching, or queen for preservation, are put in, the block is suspended in a strong colony, between two combs of maturing brood, when practicable. Any cage containing a cell or queen may be readily taken out or inserted, at pleasure.—ED.]

[For the American Bee Journal.]

Queen Raising on the outside of the Hive.

A somewhat novel circumstance occurred in my apiary last summer, showing how strongly the instinct to replace a queen upon the throne, pervades a colony when her majesty is destroyed.

In looking over a colony of black bees for the queen, I noticed in one frame a portion of drone comb, containing drone larvæ in different stages. I removed it; and, in cutting it out, cut with it a few cells containing worker larvæ and some cells filled with honey. I placed it reclining against one corner of the projecting ends or portico of a Langstroth hive from which it was taken, that the bees might take out the honey, (I feared no robbers then.) At the same time I took out the queen, and next day put in a sealed Italian queen cell. I neglected taking the piece of comb away for several days—a week or more. I had previously destroyed all the queen cells that had been started in the hive. Noticing one day a number of bees on said piece of comb on the outside, I took it up, brushed off the bees, and there was a beautiful sealed queen cell, in which was a living queen!

J. S. FLORY.

Fayetteville, West Va.

[For the American Bee Journal.]

A Lady Beginner's Notes.—No. 2.

DEAR BEE JOURNAL:—Like everybody else who embarks in a new enterprise, we are fond of talking about our successes, and the encouraging aspect of things generally, in our particular line of business.

Is industry contagious? Guess not, or else the case of the man who was so indolent that his bees would not work, would have been reversed.

Well, we are determined that our bees shall not catch the idle in this quarter. The 18th of March we added six swarms to the four we told us, and then we had eight swarms in box hives. We had movable frame hives waiting to receive them, but the cold weather compelled us to put off transferring till the 27th.

We'll confess, in a whisper though, we *did* begin before that, and the first move we made was a mistake—gave the bees too large a dose of smoke, and consequently they were in the same condition we would be, under like circumstances. —Couldn't get them up into the drum box, drum we ever so vigorously.

When we began to work right, we got so interested and excited that fatigue and bee-stings were forgotten, till four swarms had taken possession of their new homes. Wonder if all beginners know how much better strips of cane are than strings, for holding combs in the frames? They are easily and quickly put on, with very small tacks; and the bees let them alone till the proper time for cutting them off.

Bad weather prevented our opening the hives till the fifth day after transferring, when we found combs all repaired and fastened to the frames, corners filled with comb, and in several places three and four inches square of new comb, already filled with honey.

If any one has a more encouraging report for the 1st of April, let him stand up. We are using two kinds of movable frame hives, and when experience shall entitle us to an expression of opinion already formed, we'll talk of their relative merits.

Our enthusiasm on the subject of *extracted* honey found quite a cooler the other day. We were visiting a thriving town in southwestern Missouri—(the place, too, where we expected to find a market for almost any amount of honey;) and while talking about honey, our hostess informed us that, a short time before, she had bought a jar of white clover honey and as an article of diet she thought it about equal to varnish! Honey in the honey comb for her, after that! We found the jar contained liquid thinner than any strained honey we ever saw, and about the color of New Orleans molasses. As to flavor, we could only taste something very like anise, certainly not honey. Said stuff is labelled "*White Clover Honey*," with the name, street, and number of a firm in Philadelphia.

We have a good many thoughts about the unprincipled men who can stand ready with impositions of every shape, but can only say—"there be land sharks and water sharks," and people who would eat extracted *honey* will do well to keep said "sharks" in mind.

SUE W.

Pacific, Mo.

[For the American Bee Journal.]

Amateur, No. 1.

DEAR JOURNAL:—We are of the number of those spoken of by NOVICE, who will drop everything to look over the Journal whenever it arrives. I have been reading it for some time, but have not all the back numbers. Wish I had. Send them along, Mr. Editor, if you can supply them, and I will "foot the bill."

I do "go for" everything on the subject of bees; and now I am "going for" Novice,—in no other way, however, except in "that contention or emulation, rather, of who can best mark and best agree." I have read with interest everything that he has written in the Journal since I have been taking it (two years past), and have received some very valuable hints from him; and as he is but a novice, I hope he will not be offended at "a few small talk."

Well, I wonder what kind of knife that is he has. What, Novice advertise a honey-knife! Yes. Well, here is *mine*, any one can make for himself, out of an old handsaw, by cutting it with a cold chisel, about an inch and a half wide and twenty inches long. Grind both edges sharp, put a handle to it, and you have the best honey-knife ever made,—far ahead of the Peabody. I don't know about Novice's, as I never saw one. But it will accommodate itself to any irregularity of the comb, being very thin and limber.

Well, I suspect Novice uses the Peabody Extractor. It is a good one, but mine is as good. It is a little improvement on Novice's first,—using a wooden frame for the gauze, instead of the wire frame. I like it much better than to have another vessel for the honey.

I wonder how Novice manages extracting when the robbers are troublesome? That has troubled me not a little; but I have a preventive now, in the way of a *wire house*. That is, a frame six feet by eight, and seven feet high, covered on all sides with wire gauze, with a door covered with the same material. The top is of dark calico, to keep off the sun, &c. This house I can move about my apiary, to suit my own convenience. Last year I had to take my frames of honey to the house to get away from robbers. This is too much labor, besides too hot work in a close room, shut up to keep out the robbers. This wire house is as cool as out of doors in the shade. To carry my honey frames from place to place, and to hang them on when examining a stock, I use a rack long enough to hold twenty frames. When full, I take it into my wire house, remove the honey, and return frames to hive.

That troublesome thing of raising queens. I wonder how others manage that. This is my plan: Hive or transfer a strong colony into a hive two feet long, with two rows of small frames, six inches wide and six inches deep, for the nucleus boxes. This hive will hold about thirty of these small frames, and when full, it is an easy matter to keep your boxes in running order from them. Have your queen cells started in strong stocks, and when nearly ready to hatch, transfer them to the nucleus boxes. Put these boxes into the same wire house. I have ten boxes in mine. Distribute them as best you can; they will not interfere with your work, nor with each other. When the queens are old enough, they will come out in their natural way, and mate with your pure drones, which you must see are taken care of in some of the small boxes. This does not interfere with nature at all, and is a sure plan of fertilizing by any drone desired. So far as I have tried it, I have not had a single failure. They all,—queens, drones, and workers,—seem as well satisfied as if they had the whole world for a home, except when you introduce new occupants, who are restless for a while. Of course, you must put feed into the house, so that all may have plenty.

This is ahead of any plan I have ever yet seen recommended, and I claim that the arrangement will not fail when properly managed. I have never heard of the plan before, nor seen it suggested anywhere, and hope others will try it, as the arrangement is not patented,—nor will it be, I suppose.

A more speedy way is to raise the queens in a nursery, and when they are four or five days old introduce them to queenless nuclei,—being careful, however, lest you have them destroyed.

Wishing for more light on our pet subject, and hoping all will try to improve, is the sincere desire of an

AMATEUR.

[For the American Bee Journal.]

Honey Dew.

On the fourth of this month I noticed that the leaves of a young chestnut tree in front of our house were covered with honey dew, on which my bees were hard at work; indeed, they are still working on it, although we had a hard rain yesterday, which I hoped would have washed it off. I say *hoped*, because the bees seem to be so demoralized by finding honey in such unusual places, that they will hardly allow me to use my extractor; perfect swarms of them getting on the machine, and into the honey after it is extracted.

The honey is beautifully clear, and of good consistency. On examining the tree, I found the under side of the leaves covered with small green aphides, about the size of a large flea and of very much the same shape. The "dew" was evidently voided by the insects; there being none of it on the under side of the leaves and no aphides on the upper side, as there would have been had they been eating the "dew." I have since heard that the trees for several miles around us are full of it.

We have had one of these long dry spells of weather so favorable to insect life, which, coming so early in the season has, I suppose, caused a great increase of the aphides, and consequently a very general honey dew.

DANIEL M. WORTHINGTON.

St. Dennis, Md., June 13, 1871.

[For the American Bee Journal.]

A Strange Occurrence.

MR. EDITOR:—I have a question to ask you or some of the readers of your valuable Journal, which is this:—

On the 7th of this month, June, a swarm of Italian bees issued from one of my hives, and lit on a pea vine in the garden, near the ground. I took a hive there, which had been painted about three weeks, after inserting three frames of brood, bees and all, to give the swarm a start, —it being an afterswarm. When I set the hive there, about the half of the bees went in themselves. About this time, I observed that they were taking the "blind staggers," as I thought. They would crawl around, drag their hind legs on the ground for a few minutes, and then expire. While the bees were crawling in, so many of them died before the entrance, that I had to scrape them away to give the others a chance. After all were in, I put the hive on the proper stand, well ventilated. Next morning, to my great surprise, I found more than half the bees were dead, and among the dead ones I found the queen, which was a virgin. Now, if any of your readers have experienced anything of this kind, I wish they would tell the reason why, and oblige

E. J. WORST.

New Pittsburgh, Ohio, June, 1871.

☞ The mortality here was probably caused by the paint, though a better judgment could be formed if we knew what kind of paint was used, and whether any was applied to the interior of the hive.—The symptoms resemble much those given by the Germans as attending what they call the "*Toll-krankheit*,"—a bee disease of which, fortunately, we have no experience or knowledge.—ED.

Eager youth and greenhorns are prone to fancy that the surest way to get upon a pedestal is to push somebody else down. But there is room for all who are at all worthy of conspicuousness; and the bustling booby, as well as the contriving knave, is sure to sink to deserved oblivion at last, despite of awkward efforts or cunning schemes.

[For the American Bee Journal.]

Large Number of Queen Cells.

I have seen several statements of large numbers of queen cells found in a hive, though less in number than in my own knowledge. My desire is not to bring before your readers a larger story or exceptional cases; but to show that the number of cells depends much upon circumstances. Three or four years ago, I received some imported queens for Mr. Langstroth. The choicest one I put in a single frame observing hive, and after a few days forwarded her in a small box to Oxford, Ohio. Mr. Langstroth had requested me to send eggs to Mr. Cary, at Colerain, Mass. I sent him the frame. The following day he had a swarm issue, which he deprived of its queen, and gave it the frame, placing the hive on the old stand. In due time he found forty-eight (48) queen cells. This number would not have been made, if the frame had been given to the swarm as it was; but by cutting the comb irregularly increased space was given for the formation of cells, which induced the bees to build a greater number—a fact well known to old queen-raisers.

Another case. Last season I noticed an unusual commotion about one of my hives, and saw three young queens run out within a minute. I then decided I would cut out cells and give them a queen from a nucleus, and was surprised at the number of cells I found. In all examinations I carry a box to save wax scraps, and dropped in the cells as I cut them out. Some of the queens emerged in my hand, and when I had finished there were a number of queens crawling about the box and trying to kill each other. On counting I found one hundred and nineteen (119). This was a hybrid Egyptian swarm; but I think under similar circumstances, the same number—if not more—might be obtained from any other strong colony. This hive had been made up the year before from combs taken from several stocks, and places favorable to the formation of queen cells were much increased by irregularities in the combs, that would not be found in a hive under ordinary circumstances—that is, where the combs had been built as they stood. The queens were as large and active as when a smaller number are raised. The strength of the colony and the state of the honey harvest also influence the number of cells which will be formed. EHRICK PARMLY.

New York, April, 1871.

Velocity of Insects during Flight.

M. E. Marcy has made some curious investigations on this subject. The result of his experiments, allowing, in regard to accuracy, from a variety of disturbing causes, was to show the following number of beats per second, for the wings of each insect. The common fly, 330; the drone, 240; the bee, 190; the wasp, 110; the hawk moth, 72; the dragon-fly, 28; and the cabbage butterfly, which is inaudible, nine beats per second.

[For the American Bee Journal.]

Modes of Investigation.

Mr. Editor :—I believe I have never intruded upon your columns, notwithstanding I am the possessor of over a hundred colonies of bees, and have made the study and practice of bee-culture a specialty for several years past. To commence, will say that, thus far, my experience is that the greatest difficulties new beginners labor under arise from the conflicting opinions given as facts in the books and papers ; and the only safe way to succeed and to avoid becoming discouraged is to "make haste slowly." Then, after hearing what others have to say on the various subjects under discussion, apply the test of reason to such assertions as are not backed by established facts, and, if up to the standard of probability, further test by experiment. By this course one can at least claim the right to an opinion of his own ; and by comparing notes much useful practical information may be collected.

Among the unsettled questions of the day, the following will be put to the above tests again this season by me, and the results noted for future reference :

First.—Artificial impregnation of queens by confinement.

Second.—The Italian bees as compared with blacks.

Third.—The use of empty combs given to new swarms, compared with no combs furnished.

Fourth.—Artificial swarming compared with natural ; and

Fifth.—To which side of the drone question I belong?

At present, I acknowledge my scepticism in the first, and doubt its utility or even practicability.

The second, doubtless, will not maintain the standard given it by many, yet am favorably impressed with the Italians and expect *satisfactory* results. I am an advocate of the empty comb system, whenever combs can be procured. Even cell bases are better than no start at all, in my opinion. As to artificial swarming, I believe the best and only way to make it a success, is to do it long before the natural swarming season ; otherwise nature's plan is best. At least this is my opinion. Am warm on the third proposition.

F. Brewer.

Waynesville, Mo., May 8, 1871.

☞ Another question which our correspondent could place in his curriculum for the summer might be this—Is it well or wise to accept Ayres' or Hostetter's almanacs, a *smedical periodicals*, and look to them for disinterested and useful information in hygiene?

Nothing is wanting but good hives, good pasture, cleanliness, and attention to insure a rich reward to those who engage in bee culture ; but training is quite as necessary to the full comprehension of the occupation, as it is in the trade of a carpenter or shoemaker.—Mrs. Griffith.

[For the American Bee Journal.]

More Light Wanted, &c.

Mr. Editor :—For information's sake I would, through your Journal, like to have a little more talk with Mr. A. Grimm. In the May No. of Vol. VI., page 243, he has kindly furnished me and the public an answer to my question whether "the allowed superiority of the Italian bees over the black bees was a *natural quality*, or only the result of improvement." He affirms it to be a natural quality, and cites as proof that for the last four years he has bought all the black colonies in his neighborhood (to get them out of the way), and brought them home. "Treated them exactly like the Italians, they have, nevertheless, in every instance, fallen greatly behind in productiveness." This is not quite definite enough. When he says that the black bees received the like treatment with the Italians, we presume he means after they were received by him. We wish to ask him if, before he bought them, they had been cross-bred with black bees of other apiaries, or even with other hives in their own apiary? Whether, in breeding them, pains had been taken to breed from the most prolific queens, and also from the greatest workers? (This has been done with the Italians, not to mention other improvements.) If not, his comparison is between *un*improved black bees and *improved* Italians. Of course it does not touch the merits of this question. Either both must be unimproved, or each receive the same improvement, and then the comparison will be just.

From accounts in the Bee Journal, I believe that most of the Italian bees in this country have been much improved (for which I am heartily glad). I believe the black bees capable of as much improvement (which they have not received) ; and when they have received it, they will not be inferior to Italian bees.

Alonzo Barnard.

Bangor, Me., May, 1871.

[For the American Bee Journal.]

Inquiry for a Good Honey District.

Mr. Editor :—Having become wearied with professional life, I was induced by the various representations through the journals, and books on apiculture, to give bees some attention. And after several years' study and attention, with the *rights* and *agencies*, and the *use* of the most approved inventions and facilities, I have become greatly attached to my new vocation, and would be greatly obliged to the numerous contributors, or any one of them, who could direct me to a locality where I can certainly, without feeding, receive an average yield of forty or fifty pounds of nice box honey, per hive, and without endangering the lives of my colonies.

I have now twenty colonies at the home apiary, which have given off but one swarm (Italian), and no box honey yet ; and I have deliberately concluded that it is no use in trying to make bees pay in this place. Hence. I am very anxious to hear where I can certainly do as well as many who contribute to your Journal.

It is far from my wish to discourage any one in this interesting and instructive science; but I love *truthful* representations, and unless I can hear of a better locality than this, I am sure to discredit most who make such boasted representations through the Journal.

Let me have the locality where I can realize half the success of the many who crowd your pages, and oblige

W. F. BASON.

Haw River, N. C., May 23, 1871.

[For the American Bee Journal.]

Cure for Bee Sting.

MR. EDITOR:—I am sorry to hear of death caused by a bee sting, when there is a remedy so simple. Mr. Gallup first spoke of it in the Journal, and it has been tested in our own family with perfect success.

One year ago I was working with hybrids, very near the house. They were very cross, and the day was exceedingly hot. My mother-in-law went to the cistern for water, and one of the bees attacked her and stung her on the head—probably on a vein. She was very warm at the time, and immediately felt a prickly sensation from head to foot; and some large red spots made their appearance all over the body. My wife advised a wet sheet pack, which was applied. She remained in it somewhat over half an hour; then got up and felt no more ill effects from the sting. It certainly will cure if applied very soon after being stung. If you think best, please publish this.

J. L. PEABODY.

Virden, Ills., June 6, 1871.

[For the American Bee Journal.]

Notes from Kentucky.

MR. EDITOR:—Thinking a few notes from this part of the country may be acceptable, I may try my hand.

Our bees to-day (June 6th) are gathering honey more briskly than at any time this season. Owing to the heavy frost that did so much damage in this section, our locust bloom was cut off, or very much shortened. The 19th of May was the first day bees generally gathered at all briskly.

Notwithstanding the unfavorableness of the season, we have a colony that threw off a *very fine* large swarm on the 17th of April. Upon examining the stock to see what it meant, we found brood in all *ten* cards of comb in a Langstroth hive. Where there was no brood there was honey. The outside comb contained a good deal of *sealed honey*. This swarming was from a month to six weeks earlier than common. At present, with about two hundred stocks, we have had only ten or twelve swarms. Swarming seems to have commenced slowly at last.

I think the "*Hruschka*" will be of great service in giving queens more room to lay, and perhaps in taking honey from stocks that show too much disinclination to store in boxes. We hope, from present appearances, to have a good honey harvest. Comb honey is most in demand in this section. We sell some extracted honey now and then. We shall barrel up the honey from the machine this season (when we get it), and feed or sell it, as we think best.

We say, do not let any one that wants much honey, fail to *feed his bees in the spring*.

Will Mr. Quinby not tell us where to obtain the indestructible combs he somewhere speaks of? We would be glad to hear what *he* himself *knows of them*—price, and how to get them.

I must close this scrawl, with many wishes for the success of our Journal, I remain

A SMALLER NOVICE.

Lexington, Ky., June 6, 1871.

[For the American Bee Journal.]

Letter from Minnesota.

MR. EDITOR:—Not seeing any correspondents in the Journal from these parts, I thought I would try my hand. If you do not find my communication worth publishing, you can burn it, and no offence will be taken.

We had a pretty early spring. Bees commenced swarming the earliest I ever knew them, the first Italian swarms I heard of coming out on the 22d of May, and the first black swarms about the last of that month.

I played smash with my apiary last year, in my attempts to Italianize; and it will take all this summer to get up to where I ought to have been last fall. I set out thirty-three swarms, many very weak, and have lost three queens this spring. My strongest Italians swarmed June 9th. I think my black bees have not yet commenced preparations to swarm. I shook out six black swarms last Saturday, using surplus Italian queens. After shaking out two swarms about noon, the Italians were attempting to rob, so that we had to stop operations and use smoke to drive away the robbers. While puffing smoke at the entrance of one of the hives containing a new swarm, I saw a large black queen on the alighting board. Supposing that she had just come out of the hive, I poked her back, and next morning found her dead on the alighting board, close to the entrance of the hive, surrounded by a cluster of bees. I thought it strange that they should kill their own queen, next morning I examined the hive and found no eggs; gave them a queen cell. Yesterday, on examining again, I found the queen cell destroyed and an old black queen and eggs present. *Question*—Had two queens been in the hive all winter? If not, where did the extra queen come from? The same night (Saturday), after shaking out the other four swarms, I found I had not got the old queen with the new swarm, although I had shaken all the bees I could from every comb in the brood chamber. Would an old queen leave her hive and enter another, without being accompanied by a swarm, and that too when there were no queen cells started?

One of my neighbors has disposed of all his Langstroth hives and uses the American. He thinks they are far ahead of the Langstroth. He does not use the extractor, and has never sold much box honey—having made his profits by selling swarms. When that plays out, as it must in a few years, and he has to depend upon surplus honey for profits, he will probably begin to see some of the disadvantages of his system.

Another neighbor bought two Kidder hives, because he could get them cheap—$1.50 each. He thought he would like them better than any other. I saw one the other day. I find it more trouble to handle the frames of the empty hive than it is to handle the frames in a Langstroth hive when full of combs and bees.

I heard, the other night, of a way to prevent after swarms without destroying the queen cells—namely, put the new swarm on the old stand and remove the old hive to a new stand. I do not know where the idea originated, but it comes to me from Mr. J. H. Locke, of Clearwater, who, I understand, practiced it all last summer without a failure.*

S. ROWELL.

Silver Creek, Minn., June 14, 1871.

* This is a common practice among bee keepers who use the old box or basket hive, and is generally successful.—ED.

[From the Cincinnati Ruralist.]

Bee-keeping around Cincinnati.

There are several old bee-keepers about Cincinnati, old fogies and progressives, some who know too much to learn any more, some who like to improve at reasonable speed, and some who are so fickle-minded that they adopt every new thing that is called an improvement, and, wasting all their time in experiments, never come to any profitable result. New beginners, like new converts to religion, are generally most zealous, and are full of new inventions. On a visit to one lately, who had just obtained a Langstroth hive with a swarm in it, I found him seriously considering how he would put on the upper box a pair of cast-iron handles. Thinking that upon some occasion he might wish to use it upside down, he was at a loss how to place them, whether right side up or the contrary. I asked him if he could not lift the box without handles. O yes, he said, but he wanted to have it handy both ways. Perhaps he will patent it.

This reminds me that Dr. J. W. has at his drug store a model of an apparatus, which is a most astonishing remedy for the *Behemoth.* When the chickens go to roost at night, their weight on the perches puts into movement a system of levers and slides which closes the entrances to all the bee-hives, and then Mrs. Moth can't get in without she goes in before roosting time. This is patented. Mr. W. can tell something about it, and maybe sell rights.

One of our oldest bee-men is Mr. T., who came here many years ago from New York, I think. He has long experience, and perhaps knows as much about bees as any man can know by keeping them in the old boxes. He has, I believe, always refused to adopt the frame, but has been a successful manager. I have been lately told that he is, at last, about to adopt both the frame hive and the Italian bees. I expect to hear shortly that he is thinking about a honey slinger. Although he has been in the business thirty years, to my knowledge, and sold, I suppose hundreds of swarms, his stock has entirely run out, and he is ready to begin anew in a better way.

Another old fogy about here, Mr. D. L. S., has had bees in the family ever since he was born, and he is now sixty-five or seventy years old. If you visit his place you will see two stands, containing perhaps one hundred boxes each, another empty and turned into a chicken house, and an old out-house containing one or two hundred more. In 1868-9 he lost about seventy swarms—all he had. That could not be helped, as almost every bee-keeper suffered more or less by the unusual condition of things that season. He afterwards sent five hives up into the centre of the State, and got them filled with Italian swarms. Unfortunately, he sent his old style of hives, and more unfortunately still, he will not study them. He is afraid of bees after being acquainted with them all his life. A friend and myself went out to see his Italians and examine his hives, but we could not get him nearer than about thirty feet from the hives. He stood there with his hands in his pockets, ready to run. The first bee coming towards him started him.

He gets his honey by driving up a hired man to take off the boxes. He is a hopeless case. H. G. of Clifton, is a white horse of another color. He began about twenty or twenty-five years ago with an old rattle-trap of a non-swarming and dividing hive, or something of that sort, which I believe was given to him by its former unsuccessful owner. Being of an inquiring turn of mind, and every way fitted for the study of bee-ology, he has kept up with all the improvements, bought and tested many contrivances, some of which turned out to be the reverse of improvements, until some ten years ago he came across the Italian bees and the Langstroth hive. He personally visited Mr. Langstroth at Oxford, and bought of him his first queen. He has many of her descendants at work. He has not made a money making business of bee-keeping, but after selling and giving away thirty or forty swarms, losing in '68-9 sixty-five swarms out of seventy, selling and giving away about fifteen since, he has fifteen or twenty on hand. He knows pretty much all that is known about bees. He might perhaps find out something by taking the *American Bee Journal;* but in a general way you may say of him, that what he don't know about bees is not worth knowing. If you want to talk bee to him you must not consume more than an hour each day, for his brother looks upon bees with much disfavor, and (*his hobby being fishing,*) thinks that time spent in talking about or working with bees is worse than wasted. With him *fishing* is the only sensible pastime.

J. L. is another old fogy, living beyond Brighton. He has had some bees perhaps twenty years in old style boxes. He has the best pasture for bees in this part of the country; but after going as high as twenty swarms on hand at once, he has at length dwindled down to two. He always gets the first honey and first swarms, and this year has taken off, by the 10th of May, fifty pounds from his two hives; yet with all his advantages, he has dwindled down to two swarms. He at last shows signs of vigor, for he begins to inquire for the Langstroth hive, &c. With improved means and his excellent pasture, he might be the most successful bee-keeper about here.

The honey locust* is now in bloom (May 13,) and has bloomed for some days, but many in low grounds were nipped by frost three weeks ago, and the yield of honey may be small from that source. In this neighborhood this is one of our chief dependencies, and the only good one till the white clover comes in some weeks later.

Those who have only two or three swarms, especially in the old style hives, will use boxes for their surplus honey. But those having five or six, or more, with frames, would do well to inquire about, if they do not buy, a melextractor. There are several kinds advertised, and all are efficient; but of course there are preferences. A few days ago I saw Mr. Langstroth and one of his acquaintances, the oldest and the youngest bee-keepers of the neighborhood, at the tin-shop of Mr. Stevenson, on Main street above Fifth, examining a melextractor or *honey slinger*, as Mr. S. has properly named it, which embodies some improvements not yet adopted by others. Mr. Langstroth expressed himself so much pleased with its plans, and requested Mr. S. to send him one as soon as he could. Mr. Langstroth seems to be recognized as one of the chief, if not *the chief*, bee cultivator and hive improver of the country. The Honey Slinger, or Rusher, as it might be called from the name of its inventor (Hruschka) is, I believe, a German invention in its principal features. All the different kinds made here are only variations from the original, and some perhaps are improvements. As I never saw a description of the original, I cannot say. Most bee-keepers have seen the cuts of those made in this country advertised in the bee journals, and should make themselves acquainted with their different features and general use. The produce of each swarm may be increased two to four fold by the use of the Slinger. The extracted honey should be put up in such jars of one, two, or four pounds each, as may be used for putting up fruit after the honey is used up. The idea of chawing up a comb to get the honey out, thus making a melextractor of your teeth or gums, is about played out and might as well be discontinued.

B. I. DRONE.

* We presume that the *Robinia pseud-acacia*, and not the *Gleditschia triacanthus*, is the tree here spoken of.—[ED.]

The sweet sap that exudes from vegetable pores, and which is accumulated in the nectary of flowers, serves alike to sustain the bee and to render the seeds of plants fit for germination.

[For the American Bee Journal.]

Still Another Bee-Feeder.

As quite a number of bee-feeders have been described in the Journal, we thought we would give another—believing it to be the best ("of course.")

We use the Langstroth hive. On the underside of the honey-board we tack a piece of cotton cloth, six or eight inches square. A hole of suitable size is made in the honey-board, through which to pour in the feed. The cloth is allowed to sag a little, or the honey-board can be cut out a little, where the cloth goes on.

With this feeder we can feed at any time, without disturbing the bees; placing the food where it should be, directly over the cluster. It is simple, costs but little, and is easily made.

Our objections to the Hershey feeder, and the like, is that it tends to divide the cluster. Bees do not cluster around their honey, and why should they around other food.

We have tried a feeder recommended by Mr. Quinby, but the bees did not come up through the honey-board in cold weather; and besides, it gave more air space than is needed when we are feeding.

☞ No patent on this!

LE SAYE.

June 1, 1871.

[For the American Bee Journal.]

ONE MORE ON THE LIST,

and one more lady with "bee on the brain." I became afflicted with this malady in April, 1870, while assisting in transferring twenty-four colonies from the box hive to the movable frame hive, and now, May 10th, 1871, finds me still studying the "busy bee"—for the more I learn the more I want to know. I think the hive an inexhaustible fountain of mysteries, one into which I feel myself incapable of entering, except by the light and aid of others; but should I discover anything in after years, that had escaped the eyes of others, I shall be only too glad to communicate it to all bee-keepers. I am a young lady (not yet old enough to vote), and finding more to interest me in the "hive," than in the "school-room" as a teacher, I have turned all my attention in that direction. I have attended one "Bee Convention," and hope to meet with my friends at Cleveland.

I shall be glad at any time to welcome you to my home and apiary. Very truly,

(in) EARNEST.

☞ The lady has omitted to give us her address, and the postmaster who mailed her letter managed to make his official stamp perfectly illegible. May ample success in bee culture serve to unravel the mystery, long before the "vexed" and perhaps vexatious question of female suffrage receives its quietus, *pro* or *con*.

In the hive bee the maternal instinct exhibits itself as an energy diffused through a multitude of individuals.—*Shuckard.*

THE AMERICAN BEE JOURNAL.

Washington, July, 1871.

VOLUME SEVENTH!

☞ We commence another volume of the Journal with a still growing subscription list, though one yet short of what is needed for the adequate support of such a publication, unsustained as it is, and ever has been, by profits derived from the sale of humbug patent hives. We believe it is generally conceded that the last volume is an improvement on its predecessors, and we design that the present shall be a further advance in usefulness and interest. As the most efficient means of fostering our efforts in that direction, and securing satisfactory results, prompt renewal of subscriptions and payment of arrearages are respectfully solicited.

☞ Shortly after making the discoveries as to the safe introduction of young queens to queenless colonies, as stated in an article in the present number of the Journal, Mr. Langstroth communicated them to us by letter. We trust that restored health will enable him to be a frequent contributor to the Journal henceforward.

Dr. T. B. Hamlin, of Edgefield Junction, Tenn., President of the Tennessee Apiarian Society, who has long been actively engaged in bee-keeping, has issued a "*Practical Treatise on Improved Bee-culture*," adapted to the wants of the South, and designed principally to aid beginners. It is a neat and convenient manual, and its instructions, so far as we had leisure to examine them, are brief, simple, and plain.

☞ We have received from the composer, Mr. Karl Merz, of Oxford, Ohio, the music of "*a Bee Song, a quartette for mixed voices.*" We must beg, however, to let others judge of its merits, for as Shakspeare has it, "there's a vice in our ears" which wholly disqualifies us for criticising sounds and tunes, crotchets and quavers.

"Our destiny severe,
Though ears she gave us two! gave us no *ear*!"

The Wise Man has remarked—"Is there anything whereof it may be said, See! this is new? It hath been already of old time, which was before us." The history of bee-culture furnishes some queer illustrations of this. We have lately obtained an old German treatise on bees and bee-culture, which is really quite a curiosity and a treasure in its way. It was originally published in 1568, by Nicholas Jacob, a Silesian bee-keeper, whom the Baron of Barlepsch regards as "the greatest apiarian of his day," and is substantially an older work than that of Butler, which was first issued at Oxford, in 1623. It was reprinted at Gorlitz, in the Upper Lusata, in 1601, by John Rhambow, and republished in 1614, with modifications and illustrations by Caspar Hœffler, whom Berlepsch calls "the greatest bee-master of the 17th century." This edition was soon exhausted, copies were so scarce that none could be got from the booksellers, and the Rev. Mr. Schrot of Langen-Leube, in Saxony, borrowed one from a friend, which he copied with his own hand. At the instance of many bee-keepers, he re-arranged the work, and published it, with additions and illustrations, in 1659. This continued to be, in Germany, the leading and most popular work on bees, for nearly two centuries, the last edition of it having appeared in 1753. The copy which we have, is of the third edition, printed at Leipzig in 1700. It is a duodecimo volume of 347 pages, besides title, dedication, prefaces, and index.

Among a number of modern contrivances and manipulations anticipated in this book, the now celebrated comb guide figures quite prominently, being mentioned already in the original work by Jacob. "I mould," says he, "several pieces of soft wax in a longish form, like small tapers, and press them fast in the hive above. This is done not merely that the young bees may the more easily attach their combs, but principally to induce the bees to begin building by rule, not setting the sheets of their work crosswise [irregularly] but lengthwise [straight]. This is a good plan, and not to be disregarded." The experienced bee-keeper will readily see that a piece of soft wax thus moulded and extended would necessarily assume, when pressed by the fingers to the ceiling of the hive, the form of a triangular elevation, ridge or edge. It could not well take any other shape under such manipulation; and thus we have the triangular comb-guide clearly anticipated by more than three hundred years! Mr. Langstroth promptly abandoned his claim to the invention when he ascertained that John Hunter had long ago suggested the device. Clark's patent is invalid on other grounds, but can any one suppose that it could be sustained for a moment, in the face of such clear evidence of the use of guides in the olden time?

Again. The process usually called "Schirach's discovery" of the art of raising queens from worker larvæ, was known to, described, and recommended by Jacob, in 1568. When a colony is suspected or known to be queenless, his advice runs thus:—"As they have honey enough and no brood from which young bees are raised, I cut away three of their combs; then go to a strong colony and cut out two combs having plenty of brood in the cells, taking pieces about a span long and broad. The brood must not be sealed, but be young, fresh and small larvæ. Take along also the adhering bees. Insert these pieces of comb in the queenless colony in place of those removed, fixing a comb of honey before, near the brood, and an empty one in front of that. The honey will soon cause the bees to fly; they will then cover the brood, and the young bees obtained from the strong stocks, have brought with them the natural qualification, by divine impartation, to labor and produce a new queen in about fourteen days."

Here we have, in pretty accurate detail, the whole art and mystery of artificial queen raising, as it was practiced two centuries before Schirach was born. By the way, Schirach never claimed as a discovery, that which has been so generally ascribed to him. He professed to have found the practice in use among the Lusatian peasantry, and to have merely tested it and recommended its adoption, after bringing it to the notice of bee-keepers and naturalists. Huber mentions these trials as "Schirach's beautiful experiments;" and so, we think, does Bonnet, in his "*Contemplations de la Nature.*" The term "discovery," as applied to them, was first used in the caption of one of Huber's letters, and is undoubtedly an error.

And then, too, in this old book, we find a full description of the surplus honey boxes, which are regarded by some apiarians as a recent invention. A minute account is there given of them, illustrated by a cut, which shows that these boxes were not placed on top, but applied laterally, and the special reasons for this arrangement are clearly stated. Those who wish for swarms are advised not to apply these boxes "till the swarming season is over, because the smaller the hives are then kept the more disposed are the bees to fill them rapidly;"—otherwise apply them early, to "avoid the necessity of deranging the combs in the main hive, and keep the bees from becoming indolent." These "small surplus boxes may at times, also, serve for hiving small swarms."

Unquestionably surplus honey boxes are not of recent introduction, even in this country. They were used and recommended by Col. Fenwick, in Virginia, by Mrs. Griffith, in New Jersey, and by Drs. Thatcher and Smith, in Massachusetts, years before Weeks of Vermont tried to make a *hobby* of them.

☞ To an inquiring correspondent we would say, "to prevent bees from working on fruit," gather it before it is dead ripe and attacked by birds, wasps, and hornets. Plenty of *mischievous children* in the neighborhood is, also, commonly an efficient preventive; and "children of larger growth" are ofttimes serviceable in the same way.

CORRESPONDENCE OF THE BEE JOURNAL.

TOWANDA, ILLS., May 17, 1871.—Our Bee-keepers' Association for this section of the State is a *success*. At a meeting the 1st of this month, we had a pleasant and instructive discussion on various topics interesting to bee-keepers, at this season of the year. One member said, that as he examined his stocks when taking them out of the cellar last February, he found one that had a perfect queen cell. He looked for the queen, but could not find her. Later in the month (Feb. 25th), he found that the young queen had hatched out. Having no drones, he supposed he would have a drone-laying queen. Following up his examinations, he found no eggs until the first of this month (May). I saw him the other day, when he told me his young queen had a large quantity of worker brood ready to hatch. Thus, it seems, she went from the 25th of February to the last of April, before she was impregnated. What will the doctors say to this? Maybe Dr. Gallup can answer.

The season is very dry, and many are losing their bees for want of timely feeding. S. C. WARE.

BORDER PLAINS, IOWA, May 22.—My bees are breeding fast, but have not gathered any honey yet, over their immediate wants, though some are preparing to swarm. G. M. DALE.

NASHVILLE, TENN., May 27.—We are blessed with an abundant crop of white clover, and the largest yield of honey we ever had. Dr. P. W. DAVIS.

EDDYVILLE, IOWA, May 27.—Bees are doing very well here. I have had several swarms. Hoping the Bee Journal may soon come semi-monthly, yours, E. T. WALKER.

LIGHT STREET, PA., May 29.—Bees are doing pretty well here. Had an Italian swarm, April 30th,—early for this latitude. H. H. BROWN.

WILLOW BRANCH, IND., May 29.—My bees are doing a big business in the way of increase this spring. I had twenty-four stands, all nice, to start with this spring. Wintered fine in the Langstroth hive, Italianized last summer, and now have thirty-six at home, besides two that I sold. The increase is mostly by natural swarming, notwithstanding I have been making heavy drafts on them to raise queens, as I had the only Italian bees within ten miles of where I live. Black bees are not swarming yet, though my Italians commenced doing so nearly three weeks ago. I expect to get lots of honey this season, but do not expect to get within gunshot of Novice, as I have too much else to attend to, to use the honey-slinger this season. I am transferring and Italianizing bees in various parts of this county, and have introduced eighteen queens this spring. I have been successful in every case, except one,—which, I think, is doing pretty well for a raw hand. My mode is to scent the bees well with sweetened water, scented with peppermint, either sprinkling the bees with it or the combs, or in the mass as they are run into the hive; then sprinkling the queen with it also, put her in with the bees, and all is well, provided you have taken the old queen away. I would say, further, that the queens that I bought and those I raised last year, so far as I know, were all what Mr. John M. Price would call artificial queens, and they all came through the winter right. And the way they are increasing this spring makes them good enough for me, Mr. Price to the contrary notwithstanding. JONA. SMITH.

WALPOLE, N. H., June 3.—We are having dry weather, but favorable for bees. White clover is coming out, and I have a few very populous colonies that are taking advantage of it. J. L. HUBBARD.

WINCHESTER, VA., June 6.—The bees about here have gathered very little honey, up to this date. It has been so very dry that the white clover, of which there was a very large quantity, has yielded very little honey. I have heard of very few swarms, no black swarms, and only two or three Italians. J. F. BROWN.

WESTFIELD, N. Y., June 8.—Will the bees swarm? My bees (Italian) commenced swarming May 10th, and swarmed as follows: May 10th, one swarm; 12th, one; 15th, one; 18th, two, both second swarms; 20th, three, two were thirds and one a first swarm; 21st, one second; which was the last, notwithstanding I have twenty-five other stocks equally strong.—Now for the secret. The first half of May was very cold; about the time my bees commenced swarming we had frosts, which froze ice as thick as common window glass (apple trees in bloom), and soon after my bees commenced throwing out the drone brood; and about the 20th, many of my strong stocks began a vigorous attack on the drones, and kept it up for several days. Bees had nothing to work upon that was of much account for nearly two weeks, and I was obliged to feed my new swarms. Forage has been plenty for about a week, and the weather very warm,—the thermometer ranging from 80 to 92 in the shade. H. B. ROLFE.

MARSHALL, OHIO, June 9.—The bees in this section of country have not swarmed yet, and I think will not this season. They have stored but very little box honey. C. J. DICK.

TOLONO, ILLS., June 12.—I wintered seventy-two stocks on their summer stands, and all came through all right. All but ten were in framed hives. I lost three this spring, however, in consequence of their losing their queens. While the trees were in bloom, about the 1st of April, the bees did well; but after that time, it became very dry, and for six or eight weeks they did nothing. I fed all my weak swarms last fall; but, for fear they would not have enough, I gave the weakest one or two boxes of honey. They did not touch it until late this spring. White clover came on the 15th of May, but gave no honey till we had rain. Now it is wet enough, and bees are doing well. I have heard of only two swarms yet, and think I shall not have any before the 20th of June. My bees are nearly all Italian. Last year was the poorest year I ever knew in this county. We have two hundred colonies in this village. DR. H. CHAFFEE.

GALESBURG, MICH., June 13.—I am over seventy years of age, and have kept bees over forty years. I have taken your Bee Journal one year, and have learned more about bees in that one year than in all my lifetime before. L. BURDICK.

BUFFALO, N. Y., June 17.—Bees in this section have wintered well, and are doing well so far. MRS. WM. HARRIS.

[From the Crawford (Pa.) Journal.]

Artificial Swarming of Bees.

MR. EDITOR:—As I have been requested to give, through the columns of your paper, our method of swarming bees artificially, with your consent, I will proceed to do so. This method of swarming or dividing bees is based upon the well known fact of the bees being able to rear themselves a queen from any worker larvæ, under five days old. Any worker egg or larvæ, which, under ordinary treatment would have produced a worker, is so changed by the peculiar food which they (the bees) supply the young grub, that instead of twenty-one days being required to perfect the insect, it takes but sixteen. On the other hand, the duration of her life is much prolonged. As a worker, she would not live to exceed six months, usually not more than from six to eight weeks in the honey season; as a queen, she will live, if healthy, from three to four years—in rare cases—five years. Why this is so is one of the unexplained mysteries in the physiology of the honey-bee, which has puzzled far wiser heads than mine.

Of the many methods of dividing or swarming bees, I will give but one or two. One of the most common, and at the same time requiring the least skill, is to divide a full stock into two equal parts. To illustrate: Take the Langstroth hive, which contains ten frames; we will call the parent stock No. 1, and the empty hive which is to contain half the combs and bees No. 2. Now, for the process. To subdue or quiet your bees for handling, use dry bark—oak is best. Put two small pieces together, light one end of it, and you will be surprised to see how easily your bees are subdued by the smoke. Set your empty hive along side of the one you wish to divide, containing five empty frames. Remove the upper box or cover and the honey board. Give the bees a few puffs of smoke, which will drive them down among the combs; proceed to loosen the frames and remove five of them to your empty hive. Be sure and notice which hive is in possession of the queen. Spread the combs in the hive in which she is, and insert your empty frames, first a full and then an empty one, thus alternately, till your hive is full. To the queenless hive give no frames until they are in possession of a young queen, which will be from twelve to sixteen days. The reasons for so doing I will not take the time or space to explain here (any one will find this fully explained in Langstroth on the Hive and Honey Bee). Take No. 1 and set it about two feet to the right of the old stand, and No. 2 as far to the left, or right, as the case may be. Notice the hives for a day or two. If one seems to be getting more than its share of bees, move it still farther from the old position, and the other as much nearer. If your hives are alike in shape and color, put some distinguishing mark on the hive that will soon be in possession of a young, virgin queen, for bear in mind, the queen must make at least one, usually several, excursions from the hive in search of a drone before she is capable of fulfilling her functions as the prolific parent of the whole colony. When the young queen leaves her cell, proceed to fill up the hive as above described. If this division of stock is deferred, as it should be, until the season of natural swarming approaches, the old stock may be in possession of queen cells nearly mature. By giving the queenless hive a comb containing a sealed queen cell, it will greatly facilitate our operations.

The above method is little, if any, superior to natural swarming, only that by dividing our bees we make the increase of our colonies a sure thing, provided we succeed in getting a fertile queen in each colony.

We will now describe our favorite method of swarming bees. If we can anticipate or assist nature in her works, I think we are justified in interference. If we cannot do this, or work in accordance with the unchangeable laws by which bees, as well as all animated creation are governed, we had better not interfere. About three weeks before we wish to swarm our bees, we remove the queens from three or four of our most prosperous colonies, by taking a comb on which the queen is seen, with all the adhering bees. Place this comb in an empty hive to one side. Insert a division board to economize the heat in our little colony. Confine the bees to the hive by tacking a small piece of wire cloth over the entrance. Set the hive containing this small colony, which we will now call a nucleus, wherever you wish it to remain for the season. On the evening of the fourth day remove the wire from the entrance, and allow the bees to fly. A great many will return to the hive on the old stand, but enough will remain to care for the queen during her temporary absence. On the eighth day, after the removal of the queen, give the hive a thorough examination, to see how many queen cells you have at your disposal. The ninth day, for every queen cell that can be removed without injury, form a nucleus, minus those in possession of the old queens. Be very careful when forming those miniature colonies that you do not remove the queens from the old stock. Confine the bees as above described, and liberate on the evening of the fourth day. On the tenth day proceed to cut out the queen cells. In doing this it is best to cut round the cell an inch or more, so as to avoid cutting into them. Be very careful not to jar or jam them in any way. Cut a like place in the comb of each nucleus, just large enough to receive the cell, and hold it in place. Put the cell so it will hang in the same position it did before removal. Take the old queens from the nucleus (giving each of them—the nuclei—a cell), and restore them to the old hives from which you have removed the cells. To do this, confine them in what we call a queen cage, made by taking a piece of wire cloth, (No. 10 is a very good size for this purpose) and bend it round your finger and press one end together. Confine the queen by stopping up the opposite end with a paper wad. Put the cage through the top bars of the frames in the centre of the hive, and leave her there confined for forty-eight hours, at the end of which time she is usually well received. By carefully removing the paper from the end of the cage, if the weather has been favorable, nearly all your nuclei will be found to be in possession of a fertile queen, by the time the white clover comes into blossom. This is the time we swarm our bees, so they will have ample time to fill their hives, and if the season is favorable, store a nice lot of surplus honey. Two or three days before swarming our bees, if any of our nuclei have not bees enough, we strengthen them by taking a comb or two from some of our strongest and most prosperous colonies, and shake or brush the bees from the comb a foot or so in front of the nucleus we wish to aid. The old bees will return to the parent stock. The young bees never having flown from the hive, knowing no other home, will enter the nucleus. When we wish to swarm our bees, we take a set of empty frames to any hive that is strong in numbers, which we will call No. 1. Open the hive and smoke the bees as above described. Lift out the frames one by one till you find the queen. Set the comb on which she is seen to one side, with all the adhering bees; then shake or brush the bees off of the rest of the comb in front of the hive. Proceed in this way till you have all the bees in the front of the hive on the old stand. Take the comb on which the queen was seen, place it in the centre of the hive with all the adhering bees, and fill up the space on either side with your empty frames; now, take the No. 1 brood combs to one of your nuclei, No. 2. Remove the division board, place the comb of the nucleus in the cêntre of the hive and fill up the hive with the combs taken from No. 1, these combs containing brood in all stages of development, from the egg to the fully developed bees just emerging from their cells. No. 2 will soon be almost as populous as hive No. 1 before the removal of the combs. The bees in No 1 remaining on the old stand are not confused by a change of position, and will proceed to build comb in every respect like a natural swarm. We have had swarms, made in this way, store 75 pounds in boxes, besides an abundance for winter needs.

By the above method of artificial swarming, we avoid the trouble, vexation and delay, to say nothing of the danger of introducing queens to strange bees, as each colony retains possession of its own queen respectively. Some may say, "I fail to see where this last method of swarming is superior to that first described." Patience, friends, and I will endeavor to explain wherein it is superior. In natural swarming the first or prime swarm leaves about the time the queen cells are sealed over. Eight days after the cells are closed up the young queen is ready to leave her cell. It is usually from five to six days before she leaves the hive in search of a drone, and from two to three days after this, if successful, before she begins laying eggs, making fifteen days at least that the parent hive is without a laying queen, to say nothing about the delay caused by after swarming and bad weather. A prolific queen will lay from two to three thousand eggs per day, but we will put it at the first figures of two thousand per day, making an increase of thirty thousand bees, a very large swarm, which, if the season is favorable, is equivalent to thirty pounds of honey, at a very modest estimate; selling our honey at 25 cents per pound (often 30 to 35), it amounts to $7.50 over and above what we would have secured had we let our bees swarm naturally. Thus you see it pays us for our extra trouble. Our bees began swarming the 12th of this month. Who can beat this, this season? If any man who reads this has a more successful method of swarming bees than I have endeavored to describe, I for one would be happy to hear from him. HENRY S. SEE.

Evansburg, Pa.

Vigilance and neatness are for ever in requisition, and the care of bees, like all other profitable business, cannot be pursued to any advantage unless it receive daily and minute attention.

// AMERICAN BEE JOURNAL.

EDITED AND PUBLISHED BY SAMUEL WAGNER, WASHINGTON, D. C.

AT TWO DOLLARS PER ANNUM, PAYABLE IN ADVANCE.

VOL. VII. AUGUST, 1871. No. 2.

[Translated for the American Bee Journal.]

The Age of the Honey Bee.

BY PROF. A. MENZEL.

Like the greater number of domestic animals and cultivated plants, we find the honey bee a companion of man already in the earliest periods of history. The most ancient records mention her presence on the islands and coasts of the Mediterranean and the Black Sea, and speak of her as being almost universally diffused in the interior of the continents of Europe, Asia, and Africa, so far the travels, the trade, and the military expeditions of the ancients extended—as in Egypt, Syria, Greece, Italy, Gaul, Germany, Thrace, Sicily, &c. Everywhere, too, is the honey bee spoken of as indigenous in those countries, and nowhere in the annals of antiquity are we told that this highly useful and interesting insect was transferred from one country to another by human intervention or instrumentality.

Still further back, in the dim dawnings of history, partly in the era of the sagas, we are assured of the existence of the bee, by the accounts given us of the already general use made of honey, the product of the unwearied gathering and storing impulse of this insect—a product at once aromatic, refreshing, and invigorating, and which, in connection with milk, has ever been regarded as an evidence alike of the fertility of the soil and of the happy condition of the human family in those early days—the Golden Age. In the mythology of the Egyptians, Greeks, and Romans, the bee occupied a distinguished place, and it is significant of the intimate relations which must at one period have subsisted between the earliest civilized nations, that common popular faith in each of them held that the honey bee originated from the putrefying carcasses of oxen, and that the name of the sacred bull of the Egyptians is perpetuated in the Latin word *apis*. The first traces of bee-culture, also, are found everywhere back in the saga period. Thus in Spain, the Cunetes, dwelling near Tartessus, ascribed the invention of the art of procuring honey to their ancient fabulous King Gargoris, while the Greeks and Romans attributed this merit, as well as that of first placing bees in prepared habitations, and domesticating them, to their gods or the descendants of their fancied deities—to Dionysos or Bacchus, the son of Zeus and Semele, or to Aristæus, the son of Apollo and the nymph Cyrene—regarding Thessaly as the scene of these important improvements.

Again, yet further back in prehistoric times, from which no written records, reports, names, or dates survive, but of which remains of weapons, implements and utensils, of buildings and building materials, of garments and personal ornaments, of animal and vegetable comestibles, and of human bones, furnish intimations of the state of civilization among the inhabitants, we find unmistakable indications that the honey bee was then already very commonly and extensively cultivated. From the stone age and the period of the Helvetian pile structures, utensils of clay, regularly perforated, and more or less well preserved, have come down to us, which, according to the judgment of the best antiquarians, were used in draining honey from the comb, in the manner still practised by the peasantry in many districts of Switzerland—though others incline to think they were used in the manufacture of cheese. The fossil organic remains frequently found in the same localities, point out conclusively the same classes of plants and animals which are found at this day still in intimate connection with the life and habits of the honey bee.

And again, still further back in the abysm of time, in those remote eras in the progress of the development of the earth, which preceded the elevation of the Alps, and which by their various remains of fossil organisms, demonstrate that a subtropical climate, with a medium temperature of 66° once prevailed in what is now Switzerland. In the upper miocene we find beside the petrified remains of various flowering plants, of honey-producing or honey-loving insects, and of enemies of the bee and her products, belonging to other families of the animal kingdom, a fossil honey bee also of that special family of which only one variety has ever been cultivated—namely the *apis mellifica*. The only specimen of the honey bee in a fossil state hitherto found, occurred in the insect-bearing stratum of the quarries of Oeningen. It was first recognized as an *apis* by Prof. Heer, from the nervures of its wings, and named *apis adamitica* by him, as it differs in this respect from the *apis dorsata* Fabr., besides being somewhat smaller. On the other hand, it is larger than the *apis Indica*, and the *apis florea;* but is intimately connected with the *apis mellifica* and may rightfully claim to be regarded as the forerunner if not progenitor of the latter.

Thus we find the honey bee existing geologically as an inhabitant of our earth ages before the appearance of the human race, living doubtless as now in orderly communities, laboring for a common purpose, and leading her wonderful life in all its interesting relations with the industry, the love of order, the neatness and loyal devotion to the queen, the brood, and her associates, which still distinguish her. Then, as now, no doubt vigilant and courageous in conflict, feeling and expressing pain or pleasure, and causing herself to be respected among her foes by her envenomed sting; storing up honey for herself and others, and forming cells artistically from self engendered wax. Nothing warrants us to assume any changes in her instincts and habits, since her corporeal frame, adapted to her inclinations and impulses, has undergone no change in the twenty-two centuries which have elapsed since the time of Aristotle, when she was already universally diffused—being invariably the same, whether in the genial clime of the tropics, or exposed to the severer temperature of the rigorous north.

☞ We purpose furnishing for the Journal shortly a translation of Prof. Menzel's account of bee-culture among the Greeks in the days of Aristotle, and among the Romans in the time of Virgil—to which the foregoing article may be regarded as preliminary.—[ED.

[For the American Bee Journal.]

Novice.

DEAR OLD BEE JOURNAL:—Here we are, on the 8th of July, revelling in a flood of honey again. Perhaps not quite equal to last year, but after all very well, as we have just made up about two tons, after having begun to think that we were going to have our first "*bad season*"—such a one as Gallup had, for instance. No swarms have issued in this vicinity, and probably will not now, although some of our neighbors have had their new Langstroth hives standing ready for more than a month, putting on no boxes for fear it might prevent swarming, yet neglecting the simple operation of transferring, because it was some trouble.

Locust blossoms were an entire failure here, as we have said before, and white and red clover yielded very little honey until about the 20th of June. We had empty combs for the upper stories for about one dozen hives only, and were anxious to have combs built for the balance as speedily as possible.

We delayed comb-building considerably by opening the back ventilators to many of our hives early in June, presuming the weather would continue warm, which it certainly did not; and we now think, from careful observation of the matter, that we shall hereafter only use the back ventilators when the bees cluster out and show symptoms of being in need of more air. In fact, we begin to think that no ventilation, more than removing the entrance blocks is ever really necessary, if other matters are properly arranged. Certainly it was so this season.

Mr. Langstroth recommended grass for brushing the bees from the combs, but we find that two or three large asparagus branches, or the tops entire, suit us best. Tie them together so as to make a large brush, and simply rolling this in the hand against the comb will remove every bee—even full blood Italians. We prefer to shake the bees on top of the frames, when they will allow it to be done; but when they will not, we shake them off in front of the entrance. Some of our full-blood Italians are as quiet and peaceable as one could wish, until we attempt to shake them off, which they resent as a decided insult. Of course there is no difficulty if a little smoke be used, but we dislike to go to the trouble, and by studying the peculiarities of each queen's bees, we are enabled to get along with almost the entire sixty-five hives, without resorting to any smoke at all.

We have tried smokers and many smoking devices mentioned in the Journal, but it seems to us they all consume too much time. A chunk of very dry rotten wood, and some matches in a particular pocket, will get up all the smoke we ever want, and that very quickly. Such a piece can be laid in some safe place, and will keep burning an hour or two, so that a little blowing starts it sufficiently, and we find very little smoke answers with the Italians. We very often take all their combs away when they "won't be good," and after they have bemoaned their loss a little while, give them back the combs, and they will be as thankful as can be.

In place of Mr. Langstroth's virgin queen introduced, why not cage the cell and leave it caged, queen and all, until she is seven or eight days old, then destroy the old queen, release the young one, and you will not have your hive without a *laying* queen more than forty-eight hours. We think failures will not be greater by this method than by his, if as great.

Mr. Barnard's "Reply to Novice," if we are right, amounts to this, (that is, that part of it which may be of benefit to the bee-keeping world, and we do not wish to encumber the Journal with useless controversies,) that there are hives better suited for the masses, or, we will say, "old style of bee-keepers," those who do not wish to "bother with" their bees, nor study the subject. Now, as our assertion will not be proof in this matter, we can only present the subject, and wish the readers of the Journal, each and all, to decide the matter for themselves.

We thank Mr. Barnard for the complimentary way in which he has spoken of us, but would much rather he would let us be little folks, too, and stand by his side. What we have done is not at all difficult to do, as a dozen steady farmers around here will tell you, if they also would only write.

In regard to "slurring," please read all Mr. Hazen has written in the back numbers of the Journal, and see what the summing up of them all—even the last one included—is.

"What has Mr. Hazen invented?" If the readers of the Journal can make out from Mr. Hazen's answer on page 7, they can see it plainer than we do. Is it boxes at the *side* of the brood combs? Then Mr. Alley, Mr. Quinby, and others are infringers. Even Mr. Langstroth will have no right in future to put his boxes other than on top. We think both Quinby and Langstroth used such an arrangement before Mr. Hazen took it up.

Many farmers about here ask us of what advantage a Langstroth hive would be over box hives, if they never handled the frames? To answer quickly, and within their comprehension, we told them that, after their bees died out, as they generally do, or were taken up, we would pay them twenty-five cents each for the frames of empty comb, of which a two-story hive would supply twenty. This reason alone, we believe, has always been satisfactory, though we have never yet got one of the combs. One man said he would not take a dollar a piece for his. Another forgot to raise the back end of his hive when he put in the swarm, so the combs were built cross-wise, but he carried the whole upper story to market and got twelve dollars and a half ($12.50) for it—(fifty pounds)—the most honey, or money, he ever got from a swarm in his life.

"About one dozen stings in an hour" was written when we were more of a novice than we are now, if possible, and was then only presuming that the operator was too lazy to use smoke. We sometimes, when tired, sit on a "camp stool" before the hive, and open and examine it as leisurely as we would read a paper, and with the aid of smoke do not get stung at all.

A boy asked us a short time ago how he could prevent a two-story hive of his from swarming. Our reply was to raise three combs of brood above. "But they will sting me!" "Smoke them with rotten wood." (We were just then in a hurry.) Shortly after he "smoked 'em" again, cut out his honey in nice square pieces, put back the frames, and found it far less difficult, we venture to say, than he would find it to arrange Mr. Hazen's guide combs in the boxes. By the way, do your negligent bee-keepers do all that? And could they not just as well put their nice little boxes in a Langstroth hive, after setting half the frames above, in the middle; and then if they *should* take a notion to progress and raise queens, and all that, they have no impediment? And further by the way, our American people are learning to talk queens, and *practice them too*, at a rate that is astonishing.

Hundreds of Langstroth hives are used about here for raising box honey, and have been for years. This season perhaps two dozen Extractors have been made or purchased, and if any one has tried to use them and failed will he or she please to mention it in our next Journal? A lady has just made me a visit, who uses one, *all alone*, and has no trouble at all. Our honey dealers about here pay the same price for nice honey in frames as in boxes. To send them to market, fill an upper story with nice frames and set it for a day or two over a hive, and the bees will fix every frame so that it will carry as tight and clean as you wish.

In regard to the tendency of Mr. Hazen's articles, can Mr. Barnard find one in which he gives any information on the subject, that can be applied to any hive? (His last article in print recommends beginners to throw away their empty combs rather than use it for swarms.) Does he advise anything to be done besides sending him a stamp for particulars? Do not the three replies he has given to the charges we have made against him, all run off into his pile of boxes, and what they have done? In his last he communicates the great discovery that bees will commence work quicker on a piece of comb placed near the brood, than if five inches away! Did he ever hear of such a thing as placing an empty comb *between two brood combs?* Small boxes (one comb) have been filled in that way in forty-eight hours, and no one has ever thought of patenting it.

Why do we not put "A. I. Root, Medina, O.," to the end of our articles? One great reason is that we don't want a host of letters like the following—which I send in the original manuscript.

"Dear Sir:—I see in a piece from you in Adair's " Annals of Bee Culture that you have built a bee " house for wintering bees. Will you be so kind as " to describe it to me in all its parts, and tell me how " you like it? Also, inform me how many swarms " of bees you have, what kind of hive you use, and " whether you artificial swarm them, and your mode " of doing it; and how much upward ventilation you " give them, and where you place it; and when you " begin to extract honey, and how late; and do you " cultivate honey forage for your bees, and what " kinds, and how bees are doing there this season, " and much oblige," &c.

And we here declare that we can give no other answer to such inquirers, than to refer them to the back numbers of the American Bee Journal. There is no use in sending us stamps or money, as we shall return it. Send to the editor, and we presume he will send such numbers as will answer the questions best. The back numbers of the Journal contain all we know, besides much that we have not learned. We would rather pay for them ourselves, than go over the ground that an answer to the above letter would require.

Many have written to inquire why we do not like a side-opening hive? Simply because such a thing is not at all necessary, as every one will decide after having to open many hives frequently. In our opinion it is only those who have had a very limited experience with bees, that think such a thing an advantage. If our hives all had a movable side we should never open it—nor have occasion to do so.

Sometimes we use nine frames in a hive, in queen raising, and sometimes only eight, and it seems to make very little difference to the bees.

Also, frames at fixed and equal distances are very nice in theory, but a great mistake in practice, in our opinion. (We always mean the latter, if we do not say it.)

Many are working and thinking of a hive with the proper number of frames spread out horizontally, so that no upper story will be in the way. Mr. Gallup is, we believe, among the number. A friend has Langstroth hives made in that way, and another made one with Gallup frames. The latter took his to pieces, as he did not like it.* To test the matter, we put eight American hives together in pairs, with the movable sides both taken away. As these were rather tall frames, we have a much more compact hive than Gallup's, and as they were both full of brood when put together, we expected a tall swarm, which we have, but always *on one side*. Half of the combs will be capped over, and as heavy as lead, with little bits of comb built out at the corners, &c., while the other side is deserted, except only so far as it be necessary to take care of the brood. Changing the order of the combs makes no difference, nor mixing them up. They will not be spread out so far, although nothing intervenes, and the combs are continuous from one side to the other.

Some stocks have manifested the same desire to store and seal up honey in the lower part of the Langstroth hive, but raising two, or at most three brood combs above, has always equalized them, so that the honey was stored evenly.

We have just received a pair of spring scales, with a dial like a clock, to mark the weight from two ounces up to sixty pounds. We keep a medium sized stock of bees hung on these, so that their weight can be seen at any time in passing. This serves as a sort of index of the rate the honey is coming in.

Thus, our first test showed the increase of weight from six o'clock in the morning until seven, six ounces; from seven o'clock to eight, six ounces; from eight to nine, thirteen ounces; from nine to ten, fifteen ounces; and after that twelve ounces per hour, until three o'clock P. M.; and then fourteen ounces between three and four; then twelve ounces again between four and five, and five and six; from six to seven, nine ounces; and three ounces only from seven to eight.

For these experiments we are obliged to use an American hive, with only one set of frames, as the Langstroth hives are too heavy for the capacity of our scales. We did not get our hive arranged until six o'clock in the morning, and considerable honey was brought in before that time. Without doubt they gathered ten pounds that day; and we feel sure that our sixty-five stocks averaged as much as six hundred and fifty (650) pounds for one day's work. This is possible only when plenty of room in empty comb is given. The hive mentioned was emptied entirely the day before. The honey gathered was from basswood blossoms, which, in our opinion, exceeds any other plant for both quantity and *quality* of honey.

What would a hundred acre basswood orchard of *cultivated* trees yield? we hope to see it tried, if we are permitted to live long enough.

To resume the scales: twelve ounces per hour is one ounce in every five minutes, and this was readily seen while we were standing before the hive. About nine o'clock we noticed a great many bees falling short of the alighting board, which they could not crawl upon, as the hive was suspended, but had to rest until they could again take wing; but they were so heavily laden that this had often to be repeated. By tacking a piece of cloth to the edge of the hive, so as to drop on the ground, they hummed in as merrily as you please; and the scales then showed fifteen ounces an hour, or one ounce in every four minutes. Now, what do you think about suspended hives, or hives on benches? We took the hint and made an examination, and found many of our hives, where the bees tumbled on the ground and rolled over in their attempts to crawl up the *painted* edge of the entrance to the hive. A three cornered piece of wood sawed rough, made a nice bridge for them. Mr. Langstroth's book suggests the cloth entrance, and we are sure a little aid in that direction will be amply repaid. Give the little fellows every possible facility for unloading easily and speedily, and remember that their little atom of strength is of much importance to them, and that all needless steps or flights should be saved them, as you would save your own.

* P. S. We just now learn that the Langstroth hive thus opened out so as to be only one story high, is not liked.

We wrote you that our three year old queen, that laid so few eggs, had filled her hive quite full of brood early in the spring. This, however, was only of short duration, and her brood, June 1st, did not occupy a circle of more than six inches across, in perhaps four frames. She is pure Italian. Now a question of great moment comes up here. *Will queens raised from her brood have a tendency to be unprolific like herself?* Who can answer? Give us plain facts, from actual experiment; but please don't say "it stands to reason," or theorize. From what experience we have had, we are almost inclined to think that an extra prolific queen was as likely to be expected from that brood as from any other; and we have now a young queen raised from it to test the matter, and will report next month.

The yield of honey from a hive depends *very much indeed* upon the prolificness of the queen. The queen of the colony that gave us three hundred and thirty (330) pounds of honey last year, although now three years old, will very nearly do the same again this season; and if we were going to sell queens, we think we should have prices accordingly from one dollar to ten; the first mentioned queen would be one dollar; the last ten; and others intermediate. None to be sold until her capacity is tested.

If extra prolific queens have a tendency to transmit this trait to their progeny, what a field is here open to us! but, as we have said before, our experiments lead us to doubt.*

* Some writers are of opinion that the good or bad qualities of queens, in this respect, are transmissible to their royal progeny, or inheritable; but this seems to be based rather on reasoning from analogy, than on observed facts. We incline to think that the productiveness of a queen physically well organized and developed, depends mainly on the nursing and nourishment she receives from the workers. When plentifully fed with albumenized chyle, as she can only be in a pretty populous colony, at a favorable period, she will lay eggs superabundantly, as we might term it, for the aggregate weight of the eggs she lays in twenty-four hours, in the height of the busy season, is more than three times that of her own

The queen mentioned last month, which kept a daughter in the hive to assist her, failed after raising another queen under the same circumstances; so that we suppose the bees knew that their queen was failing, or rather, would fail.*

We have been accused of obstinately refusing to examine any other hive but the two-story Langstroth. As we have said before, we cannot see how any other form can answer as well, all things considered. To sum up: Bees would work best in a perfect sphere, were not the combs warmer or more of a protection at their sides than ends; so that an oblong sphere or oval would be most economical. But frames cannot be used in such a hive, nor would they be interchangeable; so that an oblong cube would be next best, were not frames of such size unwieldy. Besides, we wish to have it in our power to contract the size of the hive in winter, yet in such a way that it may be enlarged again for surplus honey, at the proper season, while the bees proceed promptly to occupy the additional room given. This can only be done by bringing a part of the brood into the surplus apartment, and to do this the frames must be all of equal size. Bringing brood into the surplus apartments will not answer the desired end, unless it is *near the main apartment.*

There, we do not believe that any one will say, this month, that they would have cared to have heard *more* from NOVICE.

---

body—a feat which could only be accomplished by the zealous co-operation of the workers, in preparing suitable nutriment for her and administering it with lavish liberality.—[ED.

* On this point, Berlepsch, in the revised edition of his work, says—"There cannot be the least doubt that queens usually become conscious of the approaching end of life, and of their inability to continue laying worker eggs. For, in many instances, I have seen queens laying drone eggs at times when they would not ordinarily have done so—doing this evidently to make provision for the fertilization of the expected young queen. So the workers, likewise, have a foreboding of the termination of the fertility and life of their queen. Finding that she lays drone eggs at what they regard as unseasonable periods, they proceed to build royal cells and rear young queens, to make provision for the emergency anticipated. What I here state are facts, and there is no arguing against *facts*, seem they ever so strange and inexplicable."—[ED.

On the temporary co-existence of two queens in a hive, the Baron of Berlepsch makes the following remarks:

"The old queen, when about to be superseded, is *never* destroyed by the workers, but either dies while the young queen is being hatched, or continues to live till the young one leaves her cell, and is then commonly stung to death by the latter, soon after she becomes fertile. But not unfrequently, also, she continues to live by the side of the young one now fertile, till she dies a natural death—of which Dzierzon and Vogel, each, give instances in the Bienenzeitung. This is certainly the true view, and I have communicated to the Bienenzeitung for 1863, page 269, cases which place it beyond doubt that the workers have little regard for a young queen emerging from her cell while the mother queen is still living and present, becoming attached to her only gradually, and rarely according to her full homage or reverence till after she has become fertile. While, on the other hand, the young queen gradually becomes reconciled to the presence of the old one, because at the outset the workers shielded her from attack. To make the matter more evident, I will cite a single case. On the 15th of May, 1863, I found in a hive a virgin queen and an old one still very prolific. I removed the latter, and very soon the bees acted as though they were queenless, and killed the young one."

[For the American Bee Journal.]

Queenless Colonies saved.

There seems to be a great unanimity among bee-keepers in answering the question—what to do with colonies found queenless in early spring, before drones have appeared. All advise breaking up such colonies, and uniting their bees with other weak stocks. I find every spring several of my colonies queenless; but I have in every case built them up into good colonies by a little painstaking and patient waiting.

As soon as a colony is discovered to be queenless in the spring, give them a frame of brood from some strong colony; or two frames, if you think they can be spared. They will rear a queen, which from the absence of drones, may fail to become fertilized. As soon as you are satisfied that she will become a drone-layer, destroy her, and give the colony another frame of brood, together with the adhering bees—being careful not to transfer the queen, which you can be sure of only by knowing that she is on some other frame. They will proceed at once to rear another queen, which will be more likely than the first to become normally fertile. If, however, this second one should fail, or get lost, try again, by repeating the last process. Meantime your queenless colony is rapidly filling up with worker bees, from the hatching brood inserted; and by the time you obtain a fertile queen, you have a pretty strong colony of workers to come to her assistance. Such colonies will gather honey surprisingly fast, provided the harvest is good, as they leave but little brood to feed. I took all my extracted honey last year—175 pounds—from five or six such colonies, and they were all heavy stocks in the following fall, and this spring were among my best colonies, all having young and prolific queens.

There is, however, another decided advantage in this removal of brood from the strongest colonies, and one I think of more value than the saving of the queenless colonies. It tends to prevent early swarming, and if carried just far enough, may prevent all swarming for the season. In this matter of swarming, I am obliged to differ in opinion from many older bee-masters. Most writers on bee culture regard the earliest swarms as the best. I do not. Early swarms at least in this locality, are not so strong in numbers, and the bee pasturage is not generally so good here, as it is later in the season. Comb-building and consequent breeding do not go on so rapidly, and by the time pasturage becomes abundant, the colony has so diminished in numbers, by natural loss, having not a single addition to the number of outside laborers for at least thirty-seven days from the date of swarming, that they are likely to go into winter quarters without having furnished an ounce of surplus honey; and perhaps even with a hive only partially filled with combs and honey for its own use. Whereas, a swarm coming a month later will be immense in its proportions, and the honey harvest being then at its height, they will accomplish far more in two or three weeks, than very early swarms will in a whole season. At least such has been my experience.

I find that the great bulk of surplus box honey is made by the old colonies, and before swarming. Now, if swarming can be held in check two or three weeks, by removing brood judiciously from the strongest colonies, at such times and to such extent as to leave the hive just as full of bees as it will hold without swarming, then the greatest possible quantity of surplus honey in boxes will be obtained. I do not look for any more *box honey* from a colony, after it has swarmed. It is then best fitted for the use of the honey-extractor, for the rest of the season.

I do not object to stimulating for early breeding in the spring, provided you reduce the full colonies, just before swarming time, enough to prevent swarming; so as to retain all through the height of the honey harvest, very strong stocks for making box honey.

R. Bickford.

Seneca Falls, N. Y., June 23, 1871.

☞ Were it not for the risk incurred of having the queenless colony suddenly attacked and destroyed by robbers, or that fertile workers may make their appearance in such colonies otherwise well conditioned, the process might be unhesitatingly adopted. These risks, however, make constant watchfulness so indispensable that we fear failure would be the result in the hands of the generality of bee-keepers. But where these can be guarded against the plan may be very usefully employed, in combination with another, for securing a very important desideratum in practical bee-culture. The only effectual method yet devised for preventing or controlling natural swarming, is to *reduce the strength of a colony*, so as to check the tendency to division and emigration, though not to such an extent as to superinduce in it a discouraging consciousness of weakness. The judicious and well-timed *removal of brood*, so readily accomplished where movable frames are employed, effects this purpose completely; and the removed brood may either be used—as above suggested—to save and build up queenless colonies; or for artificial multiplication of stock. by starting and gradually strengthening nuclei. Where not needed for the former purpose, a nucleus—or several, if stocks be numerous and populous—may be formed to receive and nurse the abstracted brood, and be built up to full stature, as rapidly as the sources of supply will permit. By this course the bee-keeper, especially if still ardent and inexperienced, may find himself constrained to keep his desire for a rapid increase of colonies in proper subordination, by making it his paramount aim to secure surplus honey from his old stocks; for he will learn to be careful not to remove from them at any time, more brood than the condition of those old stocks and the fertility of their queens will justify. He will consequently be admonished by daily observation, not to start more nuclei or artificial swarms than he can properly supply with brood from time to time, till from the fertility of their own queens they become independent, self-sustaining colonies. Thus good judgment in conducting the first operation conduces to impose and impress on the bee-keeper, though still only a beginner, the proper measure and extent of the second.—[Ed.

[For the American Bee Journal.]

A Trip to Tennessee and back.

On Friday evening, February 10th, by invitation of Dr. Hamlin, I took the cars for Nashville, and arrived next morning in time to meet the Tennessee Apiarian Society at ten o'clock, where I met with many and very warm friends. They appear to be waking up there to the fact that they have one of the best States in the Union for bee-keeping. In fact, Mr. Editor, I should like to try my hand at the business in some of their beautiful valleys. I think I could somewhat astonish the natives in the result. I spent a very pleasant week with Dr. Hamlin, visiting in the vicinity of Nashville. I also met the society again by invitation, on the 16th of March. We opened and examined some thirty or forty stocks of the Doctor's bees, and saw their progress in breeding the queens, &c. The Doctor has two hundred and sixteen stocks of pure Italians. I call them genuine, and I ought to be a good judge. Right here, I will mention that I found the Doctor universally esteemed in his own neighborhood, where he is best known; and from personal acquaintance with him I take him to be a man in every respect strictly conscientious. He is not raising queens and selling from pecuniary necessity, being far above that. I mention this not at his request, but of my own free will and accord, for the benefit of a certain celebrated party, who is circulating private reports detrimental to the Doctor's reputation as a queen-breeder. The Doctor's reputation will live in the estimation of the public, long after said individual has hung himself with his own halter. At least that is the opinion of your humble servant. The Doctor's bees were carrying in meal every pleasant day, while I was there. I shall long remember my visit to Tennessee.

On my way back, I spent a part of three days at Mr. J. S. Hill's, of Mount Healthy, Hamilton County, Ohio. Mr. Hill is a well posted bee-keeper. I was much pleased with his arrangement and management. We examined several of his stocks, and among the rest we found one queenless; and as he was wintering several nuclei with spare queens, he repaired to the cellar for a queen. The first he brought up was dead to all appearance, but we brought her to life and gave her to the queenless stock. While at Dr. Hamlin's we found a nucleus seemingly starved to death. At my suggestion it was carried into a warm room and placed on a table. The bees soon began to show signs of life. I revived the queen and placed her in the queenless nucleus. Now, here are two excellent opportunities to test whether queens that have been chilled or starved nearly to death are good for anything after they have been revived. I may as well tell just here, how to revive a queen that has been chilled or starved. Place her in the palm of the warm hand, and gently breathe the moist breath in upon her; and if there is any vitality remaining in her, you will soon see her legs begin to quiver. Persevere, and as soon as she recovers sufficiently, give her a little food. If placed by the warm stove or a fire, queens will frequently show signs of life, and then die past redemption. But I have digressed from my subject. Mr. Hill's arrangement for clustering natural swarms is excellent; and to my notion he has a honey extractor of his own getting up, that shows ingenuity and looks as though it would work as satisfactorily as any that I have seen, and I have seen several. Any bee-keeper can spend a few hours with Mr. Hill to good advantage. From there my next stopping place was with a brother and a host of cousins in southern Michigan, eight miles south of Hudson. There I found as bee-nighted a set of inhabitants as I have seen in many a day. They have not advanced one step beyond the old brimstone practice. The salt barrel and nail keg are in full blast for hives. I do not know that I can do any better than to give things just as I found them. One had two colonies in the fall. One of them died, and the other was set on a bench, and the woodpecker pecked holes all through the hive. I guess the woodpecker tapped on the hive, and the bees came to see what was the matter. So Mr. Woodpecker fills his craw with bees, and of course sips a little honey. The owner *allowed* that his bees did not do much, or in other words he did not have *good luck* with his bees; and I allowed so to. (A Yankee *guesses*, an Indianian or Tennesseean *reckons*, and a Michigander *allows*, that things are so and so.) At another place they had three stocks in box hives, one in a salt barrel, and a dead one in a nail keg. *They allowed* that bee-keeping did not pay, and I *guessed* they were about right in that notion. At another place still, they had a patent concern for raising the moth miller; but as their father had died, they expected the bees to die too, and when the bees died, as there was nothing to keep the moths warm they died also, and the poor moths' carcasses could be scraped up by the handful. They allowed that they could not have luck with bees, and with their hive and treatment, I was not disposed to dispute their judgment. Another individual had some seven colonies. He was requested to come and see me and have a talk. But he knew a woman up in Iowa that knew more than all the bee-keepers in the world, and consequently it was scarcely worth while to have a talk with Gallup. But before I left I transferred a swarm of bees on a cold day in the above individual's kitchen, to a movable comb hive, and set them to work in good shape. One spectator would not have his bees transferred as they always died. And when I asked him how they were transferred, it was in this wise: the hive was turned bottom up in a large tub, and water poured in the tub. As it rose in the hive the bees were compelled to move or transfer themselves up into another hive placed over the one containing the honey. So much for his transferring. Mine was simply moving the family, furniture, food and all, out of the old house into a new one.

In this vicinity I met an old gray headed gentleman, who volunteered to tell me all about bees, as he had been acquainted with an extraordinary bee-keeper. This bee-keeper took a dozen worker bees, put them in a glass box and fed them; and in an incredible short time they built a king's cell; put one of their number in it, and crowned him king. And Mr. Editor, whether you believe it or not, he said there was one worker less; but that they had made a king out of the other. You can easily see there is a chance yet for us old fogies to learn something. Word was given out that I was going to transfer a swarm for my brother on Saturday. Consequently there was a large crowd out. One said he would like to see me handle a swarm of bees that way in June; another would bet his bees would sting me to death, &c. Among the spectators here I had one of Professor Flander's pupils. He had seen the Professor perform wonders with bees, and had purchased a bottle of bee charm. The result was that he had gone into one of his swarms with his charm, and got most gloriously stung. He now has very little faith in bee charm, yet still thinks he got the worth of his money. In fact I had a terrible time combatting and letting off gas with these *bee*-nighted fellows in Michigan; one of whom knew that moths in Michigan grew from an egg to full size in one night, for he had turned up the hive at night, killed all and brushed off the bottom board, and still next morning there were plenty of them there, full grown! conclusive evidence for him! I introduced three Bee Journals into the neighborhood, so look out for breakers from southern Michigan. They will be able to tell us all about their mode of bee-keeping themselves hereafter. I left one poor fellow with his brain badly affected; but gave directions if his head became too hot with bee on the brain, to pour on cold water, and so keep him cool.

I left Hudson on the 6th of March, and arrived home at four o'clock on the morning of the 8th. Found everything all right, except that my bees had been kept too warm during the warm spell while I was gone, and some of them had got the "dysentery." But the boss is now on hand, and all is well that ends well. Five weeks of constant gas-blowing did not make me lose any flesh. In fact I grew fat on it.

E. GALLUP.

Orchard, Iowa.

Balsam of Honey.

Take fine pale honey	. . . .	4 ounces.
glycerine	. . . .	1 "

Mix by a gentle heat, and when cold add

alcohol	. . . . .	1 ounce.
essence of ambergris		6 drops.
citric acid	. . . .	3 drachms.

This is intended to remove discolorations and freckles, as well as to improve the general appearance of the skin.—*Druggists' Circular.*

[For the American Bee Journal.]

A Cheer from Tennessee.

MR. EDITOR :—I am certain that I like to read the Journal as well as Novice or "any other man," and will now try my hand at writing a few lines for it. (I wish I could write as well as Novice.)

I was much interested in his account of two queens in one hive. But why did he not give us his theory concerning it? He must have some ideas about it. and knows how to put them in writing as well as any one I know of.

I will relate the case of the only hive that ever came under my observation, in which there were two queens together any length of time; and will watch the Journal to see if Novice's case proves to be a parallel one. It was in a stock having a very choice queen from Langstroth,—in '69 or '70. The bees began building queen cells, which were promply cut out, and used. This continued for more than two months, as they kept supplying the place of those taken out. When it was observed that the queen began to fail, the bees were allowed to rear another, which became fertile and performed her motherly office, side by side with the "old lady" for about a month, when the old queen was removed to a nucleus, where she continued laying eggs until she became too feeble to keep her hold on the comb—thus fairly dying in the harness.

I was somewhat interested in Gallup's article on page 12—not enough, however, to send him the "almighty dollar;" for the Langstroth hive is good enough for me. But I am anxious to know what you charge *for that kind of advertisement*, as I may some day have an axe to grind, and would most certainly prefer space in the reading columns to the outside pages! But I am not complaining, for your splendid paper contains many valuable articles that are not advertisements. The one on artificial swarming, on page 23,* is worth any bee-keepers' five years subscription to the Journal. Hurrah for volume seventh!

W. E. L.

Tennessee.

* That article is from the pen of an esteemed correspondent of the Journal, whose contributions have of late been "few and far between." May we not hope that he will let the former spirit revive, and not content himself with merely *thinking*?

[For the American Bee Journal.]

Bee Notes, from Clark County, Indiana.

Having been a close reader of the JOURNAL for the past twelve months, I feel now that I cannot well "keep house" among my bees without it. While I am inclined to think that some at least of the prominent contributors to its columns have more in view the advertisement of their own private wares, than the promotion of the interests of the bee-keeping public; yet I am free to admit that I have gathered many invaluable suggestions from its perusal during one short year. With my renewal for another year, I send a few notes for publication, provided the editor shall deem them worthy.

My first experience with bees was in the spring of 1868. I had heard and read so much of the large things others had done with bees, that I determined to try my "luck," believing that what others had done, I could do. I commenced with a single black stock, taken from a tree in the woods. To this I added by purchase several others, until my outlay for bees, hives, and the Langstroth right, had about reached seventy-five (75) dollars. I had no increase of stocks, and no surplus honey. In the fall, the great epidemic broke into my apiary, as it did into all others in this region; and before the middle of the following winter, I had not a bee left to tell the tale of my folly.

Thus endeth chapter first of my bee experience.

In the spring of 1870, conforming my actions to the old saw that "the best place to find a thing is where it was lost," I invested again in five weak black stocks. These I Italianized, and by artificial swarming, I succeeded during the season in doubling my stocks, but yet got no surplus honey. This was not very encouraging, but was so much better than my first effort that I was willing to "try again."

On the 23d of November I went into winter quarters with ten stocks, none very strong in either bees or stores. They were all in the shallow Langstroth hive. I stored them away in my cellar, first taking off the caps, and slipping four-penny nails under the honey-boards, to give upward ventilation, and then piled them up, one on the other. And right here I wish to acknowledge specially the benefit I have received from one suggestion made in the AMERICAN BEE JOURNAL, in regard to the ventilation of cellars. Although my cellar was dug in a bed of flint gravel, yet everything I put in it in the winter would soon be badly affected with mildew. Some one in the JOURNAL suggested ventilation *from the bottom*. The idea struck me as a reasonable one. I already had a flue built in the wall down to within eighteen inches of the bottom, at which point was an opening for the reception of a stove pipe from the cellar; but I had never had a stove connected with this flue, from above. At the commencement of last winter, I turned the pipe from the stove of my dining-room, which is immediately above the cellar, into this flue. This, of course, created a strong draft in the flue, so much that at times a light piece of paper would be drawn up from the opening in the cellar. In my cellar thus arranged, I stored my bees, in addition to the other articles I usually keep in that place. It is enough to say that, during the entire winter, I never discovered the least appearance of mould on anything in the cellar. Out of ten hives I think there was not half a pint of dead bees; and when I returned them to their summer stands, on the 10th of March, were as dry and clean as when put away, nearly four months before. Hereafter I shall ventilate my cellar from the bottom, whether I store bees in it or not.

Now for my "luck" the present season. The

10th of March, I commenced operations with ten Italian stocks. About the 15th I added to these three black colonies, and toward the latter part of May, two more black stocks. The black queens in these, and their drone brood, were immediately removed, and Italian queens given them. From the ten original stocks, and the five additional, I now have in my apiary *forty-six* full sized strong stocks, and *twelve* half-sized stocks. The small stocks I keep employed raising queens for my own use; but they, each, contain five full sized Langstroth frames, nearly all of which are full of comb honey, and brood, with abundance of bees that seem to feel perfectly at home. I think they will all be strong enough to winter well. In addition to this increase of stocks, I have taken with the extractor considerably over five hundred (500) pounds of liquid honey. I am taking honey nearly every day; and from present appearances will yet get several hundred pounds more, and make I don't know how many more stocks.

In concluding my too tedious communication, I will say that I am satisfied with the profits of this season, but expect to do better in another.

M. C. HESTER.

Charlestown, Ind., June 20, 1871.

☞ We are pleased to receive so gratifying a report from one who was not so discouraged by the disastrous bee cholera of 1868, as to be unwilling to "try again." That there will be seasons of failure in bee culture occasionally, just as there are crop failures and fruit failures, must be looked for as among the probable contingencies of human events; but their actual occurrence should serve rather to stimulate than dishearten.

The heavy losses incurred by many in 1868, were certainly discouraging, and that some were thereby deterred from further prosecuting bee-culture, is by no means surprising; but in most instances, where the business was taken up with renewed zeal and energy, eminent success has crowned the effort. "Years of failure," says the German adage "are years of instruction to the intelligent bee-keeper"—the truth of which saying is well illustrated by such cases as the foregoing.—[ED.

[For the American Bee Journal.]

Letter from West Virginia.

MR. EDITOR:—As it is seldom you receive a communication from this section of the country, I have concluded to send you a short one, if only to let you know that there are a few bee-keepers in our community, who take an interest in, and are trying to keep pace with all the improvements in that most fascinating of all pursuits—apiculture.

As I am but a novice, comparatively, you nor your readers will not expect any new ideas or suggestions from me. There is a common interest and sympathy, which I believe is felt by every lover of bee-culture, which forms, in a certain sense, a bond of union among them, and manifests itself in the desire to learn the success or failure of the others, and also in a generous feeling that prompts those whose knowledge and experience fits them as teachers to instruct their less skilful and less informed brethren. I think no profession, calling, or class can lay claim to more generous impulses. The rivalry which sometimes exists, is for the most part a generous rivalry, or rather emulation, as to who will best succeed, and most advance the cause. I ought possibly to make some exceptions as to this rule; one of which I think may be found in certain parties "who run a machine" in New York.

Having read so many instructive articles from your numerous contributors, I feel as if we were old acquaintances. *Novice*, in the last volume, in "giving in his experience" in regard to the pleasure with which the Bee Journal is received, has given mine. The mails bring me nothing that is received with a more hearty welcome. By the way, if Novice's attachment to that name is not too strongly *rooted*, I think it is time he would resign it to some one else. I would suggest "ADEPT" as a better name for him.

It is only within the last few years that even a few bee-keepers in this part of the country have manifested any interest in advanced bee-culture. It is often quite amusing to hear many of the foolish and superstitious notions that are believed and asserted as facts, even by those who have kept bees nearly all their lives.

This, I think, generally speaking, is a fine country for bees. It abounds in fruit trees of various kinds, besides locusts, poplars, &c., as well as an abundance of white clover, raspberry, and many other honey-producing flowers; and in the fall, the *Aster*, in full supply, comes in, in time to save many late swarms.

But this season, so far, has been the most unfavorable I have known here. The fruit trees bloomed early in April, and some strong stocks swarmed in the latter part of that month and the first few days in May; at which time a cold wet spell of weather set in, lasting for about two weeks, followed by very dry weather up to the present time. Although white clover has bloomed in profusion, it affords no honey, the bees scarcely visiting it. This is our season for storing surplus honey, yet hardly a single stock is working in boxes.

Bees here are always wintered on their summer stands. We do not have the trouble and expense of bee-houses. We, however, find it very difficult to keep Italian bees pure here, on account of the great number of black bees in the country. I hope the time will soon come when the fertilization of the queen can be controlled, and *that* by some simple process that any intelligent apiarian can understand and adopt. The man who will perfect this discovery, will rank with Langstroth and Hruschka, and will "attain unto the first three" among the mighty men in the bee-keeping kingdom.

Some of us find it difficult to procure Italian queens. I sent an order to Mr. Alley, accompanied with the money, nearly a year ago, and I have not yet received my queens. I wrote to him on the subject last fall, and again this spring. In his last letter he promised to send them by the last of May or the first of June; but they have not yet arrived. I am somewhat surprised at this, as he is spoken of in the Journal as a reliable dealer. If he treats many others so, I fear his reputation will suffer. Some people might conclude that others besides the "*heathen Chinee*" are up to "ways that are dark, and tricks that are vain."

I hope with the present volume will commence an increased interest in the Journal, and an increased effort on the part of bee-keepers to augment its list of subscribers; and that the time will soon come when you will find it your interest, as well as that of your readers, to make it a semi-monthly publication. I send the names of three old and one new subscriber.

C. N. Austin, M. D.

Lewisbury, West Va., June 20, 1871.

[For the American Bee Journal.]

Letter from Kansas.

Mr. Editor:—Bee-keeping in Kansas is just in its infancy. Not many have as yet adopted the modern improvements. Many believe in signs, and wonders, and luck. They are too superstitious, and consequently this has been a good field for humbug peddlers. Last fall we organized an association for this county (Douglas), the first one organized in this State. The society holds monthly meetings, and has created quite an interest in the bee line. Such associations are the surest preventives of being humbugged by patent vendors.

Bees do very well here. In fact, we think it a good bee country, considering that we have not many of the best honey plants, such as white clover, alsike clover, &c., which, however, can easily be introduced; and we would advise Mr. W. F. Bason, who "wants to know where there is a good honey district," to come to Kansas and select a good location, where he would have plenty of sumac of the different varieties, and lindens,—a timber range being necessary for the best results. Then buckwheat and clover, or any other honey-producing plant, should be sown, to promote a continuous supply as far as possible.

We have known a hive to throw off six swarms in one season; and all, including the old stock, wintered well on their summer stands, without feeding, besides giving some surplus honey. The fall is our surplus honey season, and we like it much better than when we have to depend on getting our surplus at swarming time. Here we get through with our increase of colonies, and have them in just such condition as we want them to be, when the honey season sets in. A good swarm in August will, in a good season, store fifty pounds surplus in boxes, besides storing in the hive from fifty to seventy-five pounds, thus completely putting the old English adage about swarms out of countenance. If the Extractor will do what is claimed for it, we think a person could take from an August swarm, with the above conditions, from one hundred to one hundred and fifty pounds. We made a forced swarm last year about the 20th of September, and it nearly filled the hive with comb, and stored enough honey to winter on. Yet that was the poorest honey year we have had for some time. If it had been a season like that of two years ago, we would have got at least twenty-five pounds of box honey.

We have been much pleased to see some of your correspondents hitting the various humbug patents and hive venders just about as they deserved. But we were astonished beyond measure to see, in the last number of the Journal, one of the humbug killers set himself up to be killed in turn. Yes, brother Gallup has got a recipe for making bee-hives for the moderate sum of one dollar! This is what we would call a simon pure humbug, selling a description of another man's patent hive. We hope bee-keepers will hold fast to their dollars, at least till friend Gallup *tests* his hive; for he informs us that he has just put bees in them, though he puts forth extravagant claims for it. The standard Langstroth hive is nowhere in comparison (as his language implies). "The advantages are too numerous to even think of," at one time. Now as competition is the life of business, we propose to furnish Gallup's descriptions at the extraordinarily low figure of three cents apiece by the thousand. If Mr. Gallup can't afford them for less than a dollar, we think printing costs more down at the "Orchard" than it does out here. To any one ordering from us, we will throw in the "Twining six secrets" for handling and managing bees, for which the inventor charges ten dollars; by means of which secrets you can increase one swarm to sixty-four in one season, and, in combination with the *Gallup hive*, you could undoubtedly make one hundred, and secure a ton of honey from each hive every year. Novice would be thrown quite in the shade with his 330 pounds, and his dollar honey knife. You see every one is after the *almighty dollar*. Here is another after it, but, as Novice says, "indirectly." G. M. Doolittle, on page 10, discourses on pure Italian queens. The inference from the article is, that he wants to do little and get large pay; thus, "Let the price be kept up at a paying figure." Therefore he makes many statements and assertions which, we doubt, will not stand the test of proof. But hear what he says: "*The queen, besides producing workers with three yellow bands, must duplicate herself;* in other words, *her queen progeny must be exactly like herself.*—One word to those who wish to purchase queens. I would say, get a queen that produces all three-banded workers, uniform in color, and the queens from all duplicates of herself. Then you will get a queen worth having, and anything short of this will be dashed with black blood. Such a queen cannot be raised short of eight or ten dollars."* All of which means that he is the only one that keeps pure queens, and you can get them for ten dollars. On page 241 of volume vi. of the Journal you can read what we take to be a deal better authority than these statements. It is from Mr. C. F. H. Gravenhorst, of Braunschweig, Germany. He says: "They invariably show three yellow bands, sometimes more and sometimes less distinctly impressed. The color of these bands (of which two are broad and one is narrow) varies somewhat according to locality.

* We think Mr. D. does not raise queens for sale.—[Ed.

In Upper Italy, the color of the bands is somewhat light, while in Tessin and the Grisons, it approaches more that of the chestnut. The drones are yellow on the underside of the body, and have two narrow dark yellow (not to say clay-colored) bands on the upper. The queens differ somewhat as regards coloring. Some are yellow to the extreme tip of the abdomen, while others have bands less yellow or brownish, and from the abdominal segment inward their color passes gradually into a darker shade.—Many of these queens produce princesses all uniformly alike of yellow or brownish color; whereas, *the daughters of others* are more or less blackish or dark, not resembling their mothers. But all the queens derived from the districts named, without exception, produce workers having yellow or brownish (orange colored) bands. Such is the archetype of the Italian bee. All deviations therefrom are no longer pure, whether passing in one direction or another." Mr. Doolittle will have to try again. But if it is, as he states, that queens of his kind cannot be raised for less than eight or ten dollars, we must continue to want them. It is the poorest recommendation that could be given to the Italians, that it costs so much to breed one queen. We want no hives or queens that cannot be produced for less money. If the Italians are what is claimed for them; if they breed twice as fast as the blacks, &c., then we can sell stocks for about half what we would have to charge for blacks; and so with queens, But if they are like the Norway oats humbug,—that *on paper* would produce one hundred and fifty bushels to the acre, but in the ground would produce only about half what the black oats do,—then of course the price must be higher, as it costs twice as much to produce them. Now, if we cannot raise Italian bees and queens cheaper than can we can raise the blacks, we will drive every last thief of them out of our apiary; and think a good way to do it would be,—as Mr. Alley recommends in the introduction of queens,—*vomit them to death with tobacco smoke.*

We cannot see why there is so much bother about fertilization in confinement. Any queen that cannot fly out to meet the drones, is of no account; and if she meets a black drone, you have just as good a bee, if not one a little better. It is not yet a settled fact that the Italians are enough better to go to any trouble to keep them pure. If it were not for the trade in Italian queens, we fear their reputation would fall down nearly to zero. The only distinguishing trait we see about them is their disposition to rob and steal. In a neighborhood where there are plenty of black bees, they will store much more honey; they will rob all weakly stocks, and there is where they get it. In towns and cities they will also store more honey. They will get it in sugar barrels, and from candy shops.

Lawrence, July 1871. NOAH CAMERON.

"The bird of evening hour, the humming bee,
And the wild music of the mountain rill,
Seem breathing sorrow, as they murmur by."
W. F. D.

[For the American Bee Journal.]

Our Honey Extractor.

We wrote to Mr. Peabody on the 3d of April ordering the machine; and when we got to the station on the morning of the 14th, on our way to the city, we found it safe and sound, looking none the worse for its long journey from Boston.

We were so anxious to try it that, about a week afterwards, we opened one of our hives and took out the two outside combs, and taking them into a warm room, we uncapped them and put them in the machine. All the family assembled to see the wonderful operation, and we must say that it was not with the greatest confidence that we began to turn, for the honey was stored in the fall, and was very thick. But after a few revolutions we saw that it was "all right;" and in five minutes we had two quarts of extracted honey for ourselves, and two empty combs for the bees.

On the 14th of May we put upper stories on seven of our hives, and on the 24th began extracting honey in earnest. What was our surprise on finding that the first hive we opened had, in the ten days, stored twenty-four pounds of honey, besides building five full-sized Langstroth frames of comb. This exceeded anything in our bee experience; and we could hardly believe our senses when we found that the others had done about as much. And when, on the 29th, we opened our first hive again and got thirty pounds for the five days' work, and the same amount from the second one, we began to ask what can we do with it? At first we had put it into self-sealing fruit jars, which we had used for preserves the year before. Now they are all full, and so are all the other jars in the house. We ordered a gross of quart jars, but while we are waiting for them, what shall we do with the honey? Some one suggests the water-cooler. It will hold three or four gallons, and we immediately fill it. The soup tureen follows, and then the milk pitcher, and we are just drawing on the milk pans, and beginning to think that there may be more pleasant places than a land flowing with milk and honey, when—much to our joy—the jars arrive. But even they prove only a temporary relief; they are soon full; and notwithstanding an order for ten gallons in bulk just filled, we begin to fear that we will be turned out of house and home, to make room for the yield of our *seven experimental* hives.

DANIEL M. WORTHINGTON.

St. Dennis, Md., June 29, 1871.

[For the American Bee Journal.]

From an Iowa Lady.

MR. EDITOR:—While rejoicing over the improved tone and character of the Journal, I still wish it would be more *practical.*

We have plenty of reports of success, also of failures; now let us have the probable reason of each. The beginner scans the pages of the Journal for advice, as to what he or *she* shall do to insure a good yield of honey—that being the legitimate aim of bee-keeping; but there is seldom an article to that effect. Thanks to Mr. Gallup for his excellent paper in the March number, read before the National Convention.

It is very easy to multiply stocks and rear queens, but there is soon a limit to *that* business; *honey* is the real object, and how to get the most of it. Let the experienced ones look back to their own beginning, and they will understand what I (and others) want.

Quite a number of persons of my acquaintance are taking a very lively interest in the business. I send you the name of a young lady who teaches school, but says she is going to try some other means of support; so she has bought six stands of bees, is putting them all in movable frames, is going to transfer the old stocks after swarming, intends to Italianize them, and has subscribed for the Journal. So please help her in her endeavor.

The old theory of having a capped cell before swarming is entirely exploded with me; for this season my bees have very rarely had one, or any preparation for one, when they swarmed. I attribute it to the Italians—they are all of that kind. My black ones never did so. My first swarm came off on the 2d day of May—"Lat. 41°." It cast a swarm on the 18th of June.

MRS. L. HOLLINGSWORTH.

Sandusky, Iowa.

It is only on a thorough mastery of *theory* that successful *practice* can be based—all short of that is mere empiricism. The time is past for trusting to *luck* in bee culture.

The young lady has made choice of what, properly managed, will be a more pleasing and more remunerative pursuit than that which she is about abandoning; yet it requires study, though it will amply repay it. She begins, too, at the right season, and with the right number of colonies. She will not now be likely to be over elated by the flattering, though ofttimes delusive, promises of early spring; and have colonies enough to engage her attention and occupy her leisure, till she can qualify herself and has time to superintend a larger number.

As successful *wintering* is confessedly one of the masterpieces of bee-keeping, *preparing* her colonies for that should be among the things first in order even now; and to that end, it should be borne in mind that plenty of bees is as essential as a large store of honey—the latter being, in some cases, a decided disadvantage. We think many more stocks perish in winter from paucity of numbers than from deficiency of stores.

A swarm from a prime swarm the same season is rarely a desirable acquisition, unless it be in localities well favored with fall pasturage. The parent colony, deprived of its queen, becomes much depopulated before it can have its working force replenished from the eggs of the young queen (if indeed she be not lost or become a drone-breeder). Nearly sixty days will elapse from the swarming before the young bees enter on active outdoor labor, and by that time there is usually little for them to gather. The swarm too—seldom a large one—unless immediately furnished with empty combs and well fed perseveringly, enters on the winter campaign as a feeble nursling, if not as an actual starveling. The proper course, when the thing does occur, is to reunite the two bodies on the second day, after destroying the queen cells; or killing the queen if she is an old one, and giving the colony a fertile one, if practicable.—[ED.

[For the American Bee Journal.]

A few Apiarian Devices.

DEAR BEE JOURNAL:—As Novice has given the Bee-journalers many good hints and devices (not as many, though as I know he might have done), I thought it well to add somewhat to the list.

And, first, I will mention a *frame-holding box.* This is very convenient for holding frames of surplus honey, either when we want to cut out or uncap. The size I use will hold about seven frames. This, when filled, is heavy enough to lift about. The top and front side are each hinged. When in use, the top opens backwards and the front downwards. In the bottom of the box is a tin pan, the size of the bottom and one inch deep. This catches the dripping honey.

I sometimes find another device useful to hold a single frame. Take an inch thick board as long as the frame, and three or four inches broad. Bore an inch hole in the center, through which insert a hard wood pin that is shouldered, and set vertically in a hard wood block. At each end of the board nail an upright, which should be some two inches longer than the height of the frame. Now put this right-angled on the top of the shouldered pin and it is ready to hold the frame, which you can then revolve and examine either side without having to lift it. A tin pan should be made for this also, to catch the dripping.

Every hive should have a glass, through which to see the condition of the colony; and on the inside of the shutter should be tacked a piece of white paper, on which to keep a record of the history of the hive.

A good pocket looking-glass, also, is useful for throwing the light of the sun or of a candle into the hive, to enable you to make a more satisfactory examination. A large spatula is very convenient, to scrape up the loose liquid honey. Have a good sized, flat bottomed, square cornered basket, in which to carry tools when at work. Have a memorandum book, too, in which to note what should be done for any hive or colony—all of which should be numbered with a zinc label. (Here is the receipt for the zinc ink. It will last forever, as I have tried it *twice.* One drachm each of verdigris and sal ammoniac, half a drachm of lampblack, and ten drachms of rain water.)

To get the bees out of removed honey boxes, have a small box set over the honey box hole or holes, through which the bees can pass out, but cannot return. They can go out either under a light tin or brass valve or door, so made as to swing a little above the center, or under a small varnish brush fastened nearly horizontally over the exit hole.

The best smoker I have tried is made of paper and cotton rags. Cut off half of a paper flour sack (a 25 or 50 pounder), spread it out flat, and on it lay two heaping handfuls of *cotton* rags; roll all together tightly, and tie at every two or three inches with good hempen twine. To keep it from burning too much when in use, put a brick or stone over the burning end. We, (that is "we-uns," all of us) are apt to use too much smoke; but then it is a very good thing to fill the bees eyes with, so that they can't see, don't you see, *when they get too saucy*. A small sprinkle of sugar water is a good thing to use, when opening hives.

But I am getting to the end of my sheet, so must dry up. Yet here comes Novice with his railroad! Well, that's a good idea too, especially for all who like him, are raising honey by horse or steam power! With the movable frames, the honey-slinger, artificial combs, and railroad, and Novice for conductor, the old fogy gummers had better "clear the track," you bet.

H. T. COLLINS.

Jacksonville, Ills.

P. S.—The dear little pets have done unusually well hereabouts, up to this time. They have been working with their sleeves rolled up and shirt collars unbuttoned, for many many days past.

Did you ever hear of a man's *naming* all his bees? Some of the boys think mine are all named; and could not that be, if all in one hive had the same name—thus call all those in No. 1. Billy, and all those in No. 2. Polly Ann, &c., &c.? H. T. C.

[For the American Bee Journal.]

"Old Fogies," and "Bee-on-the-Brain."

MR. EDITOR:—Not seeing any correspondence from these quarters in the Journal, I thought I would try my hand. If this is not worth the trouble of printing, throw it away, and there will be no hard thoughts about it.

We had an early spring. Bees swarmed in May, earlier than I knew them for a good many years. My first swarm came out on the 15th of May. (These were natives.) I played blind smart with some of my colonies, but nevertheless do not regret it, for I learned a good lesson therefrom—a lesson for beginners. I set out in the spring fifteen colonies in good condition, and have increased them to thirty-five (natural increase), besides getting some six or seven hundred pounds of surplus honey in boxes. I have procured a honey-slinger, and the way I shall sling honey from the combs will be a caution. I expect to learn another lesson about "slinging," but "a person never gets too old to learn!"

I am now preparing to seed fifteen acres of land with buckwheat exclusively for my bees, from which I expect to realize some profit.

While I write, every now and then I glance at the yellow jackets which Mr. T. G. McGaw sent me. I am so particularly well pleased with them, that I am determined to have no others. I have succeeded in raising two virgin queens from those procured from the above named gentleman. They show "all the marks of their mother." That's what we want. The next trouble is to get them fertilized purely. I am trying the confinement process on a new principle; and if I have success, will give it to the bee-keeping public free of charge.

I am glad to see another lady embarking with us in this delightful pursuit. May many more still be added to the list. I read Sue W.'s article with much pleasure, and agree with her on the extracted honey and unprincipled men. It is an every day occurrence to meet with such men, who will sell to the ignorant public their worthless humbugs, whether in the shape of adulterated or fictitious honey, or patent bee hives, &c.

"*Old Fogies!*"—There are several old stand-by's around here, who profess to know more about the bee than even the veteran Langstroth himself. I had the pleasure of meeting one of these knowing ones the other day, at a neighboring apiary, and we had it up on one side and down the other; but I finally got him where the wool was close. I asked him what he thought of the Italian bees and the movable frame hives? He thought them to be Yankee humbugs. He was blowing his horn about a barrel of honey from twenty-five colonies, and ten pounds of wax from each colony, after taking the honey from them. I asked him what he did with the bees. His reply was that he put them to death with the fumes of brimstone. He was actually afraid to go within forty feet of the bees, unless it was in the dark, and he was fixed up to plunder them in the night; like a thief. (That's a good name for such men.)

"*Bee-on-the-Brain!*"—While there are a few old fogies about, there are many more dreadfully troubled with the bee fever, without much hope of speedy recovery. Some of them have the disease so bad that they have destroyed nearly all their bees, by ill judged transferring and hastily making two swarms from one. The first symptom of the disease shows itself in the shape of "a Journal, a bee-book, and a patent hive;" and the next thing wanted is a dollar for their bees. When you ask them what makes them destroy their bees in this silly style, the answer is—"We work according to the book!" That's what the book says!" Well, that's one way of getting book knowledge! We need a little practical knowledge first, to be got only by watching the operations of some experienced bee-keeper, observing what we see, and treasuring in the memory what we really do learn. By thus working with a man that does understand his business, and by reflecting on his practice, a beginner will become better grounded in the requisite fundamental knowledge, than he ever can be by hastily reading books or essays while he yet does not understand the meaning of most of the terms employed, and has not the least idea whether one process recommended is better than another, or is at all worth adopting. Readers, do not understand me as asserting that no useful information is to be obtained from books or by reading. On the contrary, I maintain that much may be gained thereby, if taken up at the right time and in the right manner; but *beginners* should not "go it blind," nor trust all they read or try everything suggested.

Mr. Editor, I was surprised to find our old friend Gallup setting his hook so late in the season. We have afore now bit, and got bit, several times; but Gallup is a responsible good "old or young" bee-brother, and we are hence not afraid that he will undertake to sell anything that is of no value to the bee-keeper, and I therefore let him pass.

I bought a honey extractor from Mr. J. L. Peabody, of Virden, Illinois. It arrived in due time and was given a fair trial. I must say it works like a charm, throwing out from ninety-five to ninety-eight per cent. of the honey, and leaving the comb uninjured in the slightest degree. I can confidently recommend it to bee-keepers as just the thing, which no kee-keeper who has a single stand of bees, should be without.

I must say something about our monthly visitor.

Mr. Editor, and Bee-keepers generally. We want the old American Bee Journal *semi-monthly*, and how are we to get it? The answer is by paying for it. So here's at you. I will be one of the many that will pay five dollars for one year, semi-monthly. Hoping to hear a general response, I close. T. H. B. WOODY.

Pleasant Valley, Mo., July 7, 1871.

[For the American Bee Journal.]

Amateur No. 2.

After "gobbling up" all there was in the July number of the Journal, we remarked to our better half, that we were foolish enough to try every plan suggested in the Journal for progress in bee-culture. So we rushed to the workshop and made a lot of Novice's Nurseries, and put therein our queen cells that were ready for them. I must say that I "kinder like" the idea. So when they hatch, I will introduce them to the nucleus boxes in my *wire house*, according to the plan of Mr. Langstroth in the same number of the Journal.

I wonder if every bee-man derives as much benefit from reading the American Bee Journal as I do. Here are two ideas—good ones, too—in the July number; and every number has as many that we may put to practice. I think it well to try all that have any show for success. If we fail there is not much lost; if we succeed, there is something more added to our store of useful knowledge.

There is one thing I don't like to see—so much talk about *patent hives*. What good does it do? I don't suppose any man ever got rich selling a patent for a bee-hive. I am sure, if he would spend his time in attending to bees, he would make more money; and if he would give a plain description of his improvement in the Journal, and leave bee-keepers free to use it or not, I am confident that they would be better off. For then many worthless things that are now in use would be rejected.

I am using a hive that I like better than any patented hive I have ever seen, and I propose to give a description of it. I think it must be on the order of Gallup's hive as intimated by him in the July number of the Journal. My hive is two feet long, and thirteen inches wide by fifteen inches deep, inside measure. It is used without a bottom board. If a bottom board is used, cut the board eighteen inches long and thirteen inches wide. Nail two boards across the bottom, so as to form an alighting board, three inches wide in front. The frames are suspended from a rabbet on the sides of the hive, deep enough to admit an air space of three-eighths of an inch between the top bar of the frame and the top board of the hive. The frames are fourteen inches deep, by twelve and a half inches wide, and are held off from the sides of the hive by a three cornered strip tacked on the sides of the hive six inches from the bottom. The top bar is fourteen inches long and an inch and a half wide; projects over side bars three-fourths of an inch, to hang on the rabbets. When suspended in the hive, the top bars form a honey-board. For upward ventilation, or access to boxes above, &c., cut a notch in each top bar about the centre. To hold the frames the proper distance apart below, drive nails with broad heads into the side bars four inches from the bottom. The comb-guide and bottom bar, I put on by sawing kerfs into the ends of the side bars, half an inch deep, and insert thin strips, twelve and a half inches long, half an inch wide and one-eighth inch thick. Fasten with small nails. For the top of the hive, I use a broad board with a one-and-a-half inch clamp on each end, to prevent warping. Now, the most important point is the division board, fourteen inches long, thirteen inches wide, with a clamp on top fourteen inches long and seven-eighths of an inch wide, to suspend on rabbets just as the frames. This board can be shoved up against the frames, if there are only two or three; thus, when the colony is weak, the heat is not lost. A quart of bees in a quart measure is comparatively as good as a bushel of bees in a bushel measure. As the swarm grows larger, add frames to any number desired.

This size hive will hold fifteen frames, but if that is not enough, make the hive longer. If side boxes are preferred, there is plenty of room in this hive. The division board answers the place of a movable side to the hive, and when removed gives every facility for handling frames. I like the broad top bar better than the narrow for many reasons. A double hive is easily made by putting a hive on top, without a bottom board. All the conveniences of the most expensive hive are combined in this; and it can be made in the best style, at a cost of two dollars. I hope I have made the description plain enough for any one to make the hive; if not, you have not spent even one dollar for it.

I will give Gallup one dollar if he will describe his hive in the Journal. Then all bee-raisers will get it once for all. I was sorry that he took the plan for describing his hive. I think the time is not far distant, when patent bee-hive men will have to take to some other calling for a living, for I believe that there is an awakening up on this subject among the people, and they will not much longer countenance such things.

I have not succeeded quite as well as I expected in fertilizing in my wire house. I think because I do not feed regularly enough. I can shake hands with Novice on the fertilizing question, in the common way. Last year I lost over one hundred queens, and did not succeed in a single instance, though I tried all the plans I saw recommended. I think that the wire house I use, or a smaller house—say two feet square—placed over the nucleus boxes, with gauze of such size meshes that the worker could pass, but drones and queens would have to stay in, is the only way to succeed. Many after confining drones and queens together, take the presence of a dead drone with extruded organs, as certain evidence of the fertilization. But this will not do, for I have frequently caught a drone while he was flying, caught him very gently too, yet the very touch caused the extension of the organs and his instant death. I have frequently, also, had them die thus in the cages with the queen, and supposed that flying against the cage caused it.

My Nursery

is made thus: Put two cross bars to your honey frames, drive nails two inches apart, through these cross bars, and also through the top bar, sharpen them well. Make wire cages two inches long and an inch and a half in diameter; fasten at one end with a wooden stopper, and have a wooden stopper in reserve for the other end. Fasten the queen cell on this reserved stopper with a tack, slip it into the cage, so that the cage will fit tightly on the stopper over the cell. Then stick these cages on to the nails in your frame; suspend the whole thing in a hive full of bees, and all will be right. When they hatch you will not have to handle the queen in your fingers. Just slip the cage off the sharp nail, and dispose of your queen as you please.

And, now, hurrah for bee-culture is the cry of

Amateur.

July 8, 1871.

[For the American Bee Journal.]

"The Journal," "Hive Controversy," and "Introducing Queens."

Dear Journal:—Please find with this a little cash, to clear up A. B. J. record for 1871–72. Wish that we could have the Journal fortnightly, by paying double price. Each number is so full of interest, advertisements and all, that when received, Novice-like we go for its contents regardless of every other duty, whether of a business or of a domestic nature. Would gladly take every contributor by the hand, and cordially thank each for his articles. The enthusiasm of Novice, the self-reliance and pluck of Alley, the quaint satire of Quinby, and the crisp and instructive sayings of Gallup, are the seasoning ingredients for a rich treat, made up of the very best materials.

Have read carefully the numerous articles upon the great "Hive Controversy," "Rival Claims," "Honor to whom Honor," &c., &c., and must confess the acrimonious manner in which this subject is being discussed, will not tend to unite the great brotherhood of bee-keepers. The opinion seems to prevail quite extensively, that Mr. Langstroth has not been fairly treated; that some are unwilling to acknowledge him as the originator of the movable frame; and that thousands are availing themselves of his genius, without making a suitable money recompense—all of which may be directly or indirectly true. So far as we have been able to discover, Mr. Langstroth has the credit of being the first to introduce, in a practical form, the movable frames into this country. And when we consider their great utility and advantages, it becomes plainly evident that we owe him a *mountain* of *gratitude* and thanks. He richly deserves it all. But keep your tempers, gentlemen, and do not lose sight of the great fact, that matters of this kind are very rarely settled, so as to subserve the exclusive interest of any one person.

Not wishing to get entangled in this subject at present, we will abruptly leave it and pass on to more congenial topics.

Our bees were wintered in a perfectly dark room in the cellar, under the cook-room, ventilated by means of a tin tube connecting with the cook-stovepipe, as recommended by Mr. Briggs. The hives were prepared by simply removing the caps and supers. The temperature was kept at 32°; the bees remained remarkably quiet during their long confinement of four months; and each stock came out in the spring strong and in a healthy condition. The average consumption of honey did not exceed seven and a half pounds per hive. We have wintered bees in a great variety of ways, but never before got them through so satisfactorily. Good *ventilation* and perfect darkness are indispensable for in-door wintering.

One of the stocks lost its queen last fall, and we did not discover the fact until quite late in the spring. We gave them a nice one, and they very promptly dumped her out of the hive, Tried smoking, caging, feeding, and detaching, but without avail. The little mules obstinately refused to accept a queen upon any terms. We supplied them with a frame of brood in all stages, with young bees adhering, taken from an Italian stock, but it was of no use. Those perverse and stiff-necked old fellows would neither construct a queen cell, nor allow the young bees to do so. The future of that refractory stock looked dismal enough truly; but we were determined to bring them to a realizing sense of their forlorn and lost condition, if it took the last bee, and so went at them in this way: Depriving a stock of blacks of their queen, we put her in a large cage, with muslin sewed over the top, and food enough for a week's campaign; then taking two frames of brood, covered with young bees from a strong stock, we placed them in the centre of the belligerents, and suspended the cage between them. Removing the hive to the cellar, kept them cool and comfortable for three days; when they were brought out about sunset and allowed to fly. We then fed them two spoonfuls of sugar syrup, morning and evening, for several days. On the sixth day we smoked them gently with cotton rags, just enough to confuse and drive them to their stores; and after removing each frame and sprinkling the bees with syrup, we immersed the queen in the syrup, and released her on one of the frames of brood, holding it in our hands until the bees had cleaned her off, that we might promptly check any disposition to smother or sting her. When the bees on this frame had discovered her royalty and evidently accepted her, we replaced the frame in the centre of the hive, filled up with the other frames—feeding as before for several days. A subsequent examination showed that she was accepted, and the stock is now doing finely.

I have introduced a large number of queens and very rarely lose one. I usually deprive the stock of its black queen, and suspend the cage containing the Italian, confined by a piece of cotton or muslin, between two brood-combs, and feed two or three times a day, until the bees release her, by eating through the cotton cloth, which they generally do within forty-eight hours.

We like this plan, as it seldom fails, is easily done, and the hive remains queenless only two or three days. We do not think that any one method will always succeed, as the condition of stocks varies so much. Would recommend liberal feeding, as bees are less disposed to sting the new queen, and more willing to receive her, if kept full of liquid sweets. Am not in favor of the tobacco-stupefying process, although it generally succeeds. Think moderate chloroforming much preferable; but scarcely ever have occasion to resort to such desperate methods.

GEO. S. SILSBY.

Winterport, Me., June 14, 1871.

[For the American Bee Journal.]

Patent Hives.

MR. EDITOR:—The welcome visitor—the May number of the Bee Journal—is received. The first thing we see is some one blowing his horn about his hive. There is Mr. A., speaking of the Bay State Hive as being far superior to any in use. We all know there are as good hives in use as Mr. A. dares to bring before the public. But if he don't watch Novice, he will hit him a rap across the knuckles, as he did Mr. Hazen. It looks as if Mr. A. would like to sell some more territory for his Bay State Hive.* If he does, Mr. Editor, there are advertising columns in the Journal for this purpose. Let the Bay State Hive remain in the Bay State—where it was hatched.

There are too many patent bee-hive men blowing around, and misleading the public with their worthless trash. There ought to be a fair trial given to those hives, and then the one that proved to be the best, should have the credit. How is it that before Mr. Langstroth invented the movable frame hive, these men were all as quiet as mice? But no sooner did he bring the hidden mystery to light, than, presto, every one became an "inventor" (so-called), and the country was flooded with these wonderful things, agreeing only in being infringements of Mr. Langstroth's patent. But, say some, we improved on his patent! Yes, in the way of moth trap, fly holes, etc., which are as big humbugs as ever were brought before the public.

Now let me tell you one thing, and it is this: As soon as a man begins to speak of moth-proof hives and moth traps, set him down as an ignoramus or something worse. It is farcical for them to claim that they *improved* by the application of a moth trap. Who first invented the very best and only real moth trap? Was it not Mr. Langstroth, when he invented the movable frame hive, that gives you control of the bees and all their enemies? What more do you want for this purpose than the movable frames?

As to where you place the surplus honey boxes, that depends on circumstances, and ordinarily is of no more value than a row of pins. *I* want surplus honey boxes on the top of the hive, instead of at its side, back, bottom, or anywhere else.

I close by wishing success to the American Bee Journal, to Mr. Langstroth, and to all deserving bee-keepers.

HALIFAX, 2d.

☞ * Mr. A. has no patent, and of course no territory, to sell.—[ED.

[For the American Bee Journal.]

Improved Thomas Hive.

MR. EDITOR:—As I observe you have readers who use the "Thomas" hive, they may be interested in an alteration I have made, which, *without expense*, has much increased its value. I am not recommending the hive as superior to many others; but only writing for the benefit of those who already have these hives in their apiaries, and do not wish to incur all the inconveniences of a variety of hives in the same yard.

I have always found the slanting bottom of the frames a great objection, as the combs could never be turned end for end. It is quite a simple operation to shake off the bees, and cut down the longer side to the same length as the shorter one. I then saw off the bottom of the hive, so that the bottom of the frames will be only half an inch from the floor, when the hive is used without the bottom piece. The bottom is now to be securely nailed at its sides, holding the bottom board in its original position. The buttons are removed and placed on the side of the hive, so as to hold it in position when it is placed on this movable bottom piece. The entrance hole is now made above the cross bar, instead of under, as formerly, but is closed when the hive is on its movable bottom, for that is now entirely open in front.

When the hives are thus prepared, I put a second hive on the top of the first (of course without its movable bottom), and divide the frames, placing four in each hive, and empty frames between them. My stocks, in ten days, filled the new frames with worker combs. I thus gained the whole strength of the colony, to make this new comb, instead of only a portion of them, as is the case with a swarm; and when filled with brood and mostly capped, I make a new stock with the old queen and a fair proportion of the bees—giving them one of the hives and most of the brood. The old stock is very strong, and works immediately in boxes, or small frames five inches deep, which I find more profitable.

I have found this alteration simple, convenient, and profitable. It leaves the body of the hive very little smaller, and yet more compact for wintering. When emptied, the honey becomes salable in our eastern markets.

The "Thomas Improved" has all the advantages of the double Langstroth used by Novice and others for that purpose.

CHARLES DAWBARN.

Stanwich, Conn., June 29, 1871.

[For the American Bee Journal.]

The Thomas Hive.

The occasion of renewing my subscription to the American Bee Journal, affords me an opportunity of noticing a communication of Mr. G. Cork in the November No., 1870, page 105, through whose consideration I have had the honor of being mentioned in the Journal. Information coming from one who was "formerly an agent," would generally be regarded with suspicion, as being the testimony of a disappointed man, and the eagerness with which he lays hold of a casual remark of a stranger and an inquirer in bee-culture, to turn it against the hive, shows that he must have been hard up for argument. But Mr. C. has a remarkable facility of jumping at conclusions, mixing a little that he does know with much of what he knows nothing. I confess I hardly knew myself as he had disguised me—"formerly an agent," and converting the W in my signature into "Walter." I am still an agent for the sale of the hive, trying, without any misrepresentation, to dispose of it; and, I am happy to say, with steadily increasing success—having sold more this spring than at any time during my connection with it in the spring of 1867. In my neighborhood, I may say it is the only hive used, the number of others being so insignificant. But it is uphill work, trying to sell any improved hive where people have yet to learn that frame hives possess any advantages over boxes of the worst possible shape, large at bottom and tapering upwards.

W. P. TAYLOR.

Fitzroy Harbor, Canada, June 14, 1871.

[For the American Bee Journal.]

Claims to Frames, &c.

MR. EDITOR:—In the May number of the Journal, Mr. Beckwith says, "We don't know what Mr. Langstroth's frame is" * * * * "I suppose the shallow chamber below the honey-board, to be Mr. Langstroth's invention, but beyond that I don't know what it is."

Mr. Langstroth's claims have been so repeatedly published, that it is strange that any inquiring and intelligent bee-keeper should be unacquainted with them. But, as it seems to be so, I would suggest that you copy them again, from the re-issue of his patent, May 26th, 1863, when they were fully re-examined by the Patent Office, and granted. They are as follows, using his own language:

"What I claim as my invention, and desire to secure by letters patent, is—

First. Constructing and arranging the movable comb frames of bee hives in such a manner that, when placed in the hive or case, they have not only their sides and bottoms kept at suitable distances from each other and from the case, substantially in the manner and for the purposes described, but have likewise their tops separated from each other, throughout the whole or a portion of their length, substantially in the manner and for the purposes set forth.

Second. Constructing and arranging movable frames in such a manner that when they are inserted in the hive, the distance between them may be regulated at will, substantially in the manner and for the purposes described.

Third. Constructing movable frames and arranging them in the hive in such a manner that the bees can pass above them into a shallow chamber or air-space, substantially in the manner and for any or all purposes set forth.

Fourth. The shallow chamber, in combination with the top bars of the laterally movable frames or their equivalents, and with their perforated honey-board upon which to place surplus honey receptacles, substantially as and for the purposes set forth.

Fifth. A movable partition or divider substantially as described, when used in combination with movable frames, substantially in the manner and for the purpose described.

Sixth. The use of movable blocks for excluding moths and catching worms, so constructed and arranged as to increase or diminish at will the size of the bee entrance, substantially in the manner and for the purposes set forth."

These are the very words of the patent, and the careful reader will observe that there is not a word said about the size, shape, dimensions, or material of the case, box, or hive, in which the frames are to be placed, nor of the frames themselves. All that is left free to the fancy, taste, or judgment of the person making or using them, or either of them. But the frames themselves, however shaped, with the manner of applying or using them, the shallow chamber or air-space, the movable partition or divider, and the movable blocks for enlarging or diminishing the entrance, are claimed as Mr. Langstroth's invention, and patented as such. Now, as such frames, &c., so constructed and used, were certainly never before introduced in practical bee-culture, either in this or any foreign country, it is hardly conceivable how any doubt as to the validity of the patent could have arisen in the minds of men disposed to act and deal fairly. As Mr. Langstroth himself remarks in his circular—"These claims clearly and fully cover all the styles of frames now in use in the various hives which have been patented in this country, and none of them can be legally used without a license from the owners of the extended patent; the United States courts having decided that no patentee using any of the claims granted to a previous inventor, can legally make, use, or sell such subordinate patent without his express consent. We therefore caution bee-keepers that the use of such hives, unless duly licensed, will render them liable to damages for each and every hive so used."

"While movable comb frames of Huber, Munn, and Debeauvoys, for want of the features invented and patented by Langstroth, have failed to be adopted for practical purposes by European bee-keepers, the Langstroth invention is now endorsed by some of the most eminent foreign apiarians."

This information as to what Mr. Langstroth claims, as granted by the Patent Office, after repeated examination of them, will relieve the mind of Mr. Beckwith and other inquirers, and the result of the suit now brought by Mr. Otis against H. A. King, for infringement of the Langstroth patent, will speedily settle the whole question, and determine the liabilities of parties. Let the *Right* prevail.

H. N. OSBORN.

Concord Depot, Va.

[For the American Bee Journal.]

Two Things Worth Knowing.

The general impression among bee-keepers is, that when a top swarm issues from a hive and then returns, the queen is either lost on the excursion, or did not leave the hive. Last summer I met an exception to this rule. A small Italian swarm issued from a little hive. The little things showed an unwillingness to alight, and made an attempt to leave for the woods. They were met by a shower of cold water, which checked their flight; and after spending about twenty minutes in the air, they returned to their box, all right. The queen rested a little on the front of the hive before she entered. Next day she came out again with her subjects, and took to the woods—which ended her history to me.

Last season I visited one of my hives, to remove from it a frame. As I knew where the frame stood, and was satisfied that I could get it without any trouble, I opened the hive without using any smoke. I drew up my frame, which had a small piece of comb and about two dozen bees. Without thinking that the queen might be on it, I laid it out of my hands, leaning it to the side of the hive, and closed up the box. As I took up the frame, to shake off the bees at the entrance, behold! the queen—the very best Italian queen I had—was on it. At once I reopened the hive, laid the frame with queen and bees on the top of the other frames, and began to tip it a little, so that the queen and bees might descend among their works. But to my very great pain, the queen was no sooner on the top of the frames than she was caught by her own subjects. A battle then ensued. My penknife was unsparingly used, and many of the rebellious and ungrateful subjects fell beheaded at their queen's side. The excitement became intense on both sides, and for protection I now took the queen into my hand, then pulled up the frame, and placed her on its centre. But her legs had hardly touched the comb, when she was caught again, and another battle had to be fought. The penknife proved too sharp for a number of the foes, but they became too numerous even for the knife. I had again to take her up into my hand, and she was yet unhurt. I now besmeared her with honey, and to revenge my injured feelings, I used my fumigator with the greatest freedom; then placed her in the centre of the hive, and left the scene of battle with a wound or two, which I received in the conflict.

But I began to feel anxious about the safety of my queen—one which, at that time, no money could purchase—and in about two hours, I again visited the scene of battle, and to my horror found my queen was held fast, stung, and drawing her last gasp.

Can any of the experienced bee-keepers of the United States inform me, through the Bee Journal, what caused the bees to destroy their mother? Or, wherein did I fail? Or what should I have done in the circumstances? A reply will be thankfully received.

J. ANDERSON.

Tiverton, Bruce, Canada.

☞ Queens are sometimes enclosed by their own workers for their protection, when a stranger queen happens to get into the hive, or when it is suddenly attacked by robbers; but in such cases there are no manifestations of animosity. At times, too, they are so encompassed when returning from the hymeneal excursion, and then always with decided evidence of hostile intent, usually terminating fatally. It is supposed that, on such occasions, the returning queen contracted, while abroad, an odor displeasing to the bees, causing them to reject and destroy her. This, however, is as yet a mere surmise, hypothetically accounting for an occurrence that seems otherwise inexplicable. But rejection and deadly implacability under circumstances like those above stated, constitute a case different from either, and one new to us. Instances, however, have been known where the bees, on the removal of their queen, have almost instantaneously—even before the hive was closed—proceeded to start queen cells, seemingly eager to rear a successor, without delaying to bemoan their loss. Possibly such was the case here. The queen may have been aged and in decline, barely tolerated as yet by the workers, in contemplation of speedily superseding her. Suddenly finding her gone, they may, instead of grieving over their deprivation, have gone to work with alacrity to supply her place, if indeed arrangements to that end had not previously been initiated. If so, would they not be likely to take in dudgeon her unexpected and undesired re-introduction, and treat as a stranger one for whose supposed death they had declined to mourn?

What explanation can others suggest?—[ED.

A gentleman travelling through Grantham, Lincolnshire (England), observed the following lines on a sign-post, on which was placed an inhabited bee-hive:

"Two wonders, Grantham, now are thine,
The highest spire, and *a living sign*."

The wine or fermented liquor of honey is called "*mead*."

[For the American Bee Journal.]

A Warning.

Mr. Editor:—Under the above caption, Mr. J. S. Flory cautions new beginners against the careless practice of reserving black queens for a few days. He had come very near losing a queen that cost him twenty-three dollars, by a black queen getting loose and entering the hive that contained his valuable queen.

I now wish to add another occurrence which has cost me the loss of a valuable queen just received from Rev. A. Salisbury, June 22d. Yesterday evening, about four o'clock, I took out a cage from Davis' Queen Nursery, with a queen five days old, and as she was dark colored I thought I would risk her, by way of experiment. Dr. Davis says, as they know of no other place to go to, they will return to the very spot from which they took wing. Well, I set the cage down five or six feet from the hive that contained Mr. Salisbury's fine queen, and opened the door. The queen took wing at once, marked the place, and was off. After waiting a good while for her return, I gave her up as lost, but left the cage at the same place for her to go in, in case she should return. Late in the evening there were no signs of her return, and I took the cage away. This morning I went to see if there was any sign of her having returned. When, lo! to my great chagrin and surprise, there lay my beautiful Salisbury queen dead at the entrance of her hive. I suspected at once what was the cause. On examining inside, I quickly saw the runaway queen in a cluster of bees. My chagrin was then so great that I mashed her to pieces between my thumb and fingers. If ever I try another queen in that way, I will go at least one hundred yards from any stand. All inferior queens I shall kill at once.

I have failed with all plans of fertilization in confinement; but I am going to succeed next year, if I live (if anybody succeeds). I have in view a plan that will be entirely natural, and yet exclude all impure drones. No *air castle*, this! I cannot get leisure to try it now, so late as it is. I should have to build it first, which would take about two weeks' time.

R. M. Argo.

Lowell, Ky., July 5, 1871.

[For the American Bee Journal.]

A Further Warning.

Mr. Editor:—After writing my communication yesterday at noon, stating how I lost a valuable queen, I acted unwisely before noon, and came near losing another.

Just about sunset, I removed a young queen, not over eight or nine days old, in order to introduce a finer one. Half-a-dozen children were then stopping at my house, to stay over night and start on the train next morning. As they had a curiosity to see a queen, I pulled off one of her wings and mutilated the other, and gave her to them. After playing with her awhile, she got lost in the hall in some way. I looked carefully all around the room, but could not find her. I had no fear of her getting to the apiary, but this morning, as I went to introduce the fine queen, to my great surprise, there was the lost queen in the hive again, wingless or mutilated as stated. Had I not happened to see her at once, I would not have had the least idea of a queen being present. But how she got there after sunset and a distance of thirty-eight yards from the hall door, and passing seventeen stands to her own, and that with one wing off and the other mutilated, is a mystery to me. There was also one gate to pass through, but I suppose she crawled under. When we have a queen that we do not wish to reserve, kill her at once. This shall be my plan hereafter.

Introducing Queens Safely.

In introducing queens, the only plan on which I never failed in a single instance, is this: Put the queen in a cage so constructed as to contain honey in a sponge, protected from the bees without. Leave her in the cage at least six or seven days. Then remove all cells that may have been started, unstop one end of the cage, put a piece of comb in the other, and let the bees gnaw her out at leisure. This is the way I introduce all valuable queens after July 10th, and I have never lost one.

I have tried putting a piece of comb in the cage, and putting the cage in immediately after removing the old queen, but lost every queen in that way, and shall never try it again. From spring until July, I generally use the cage with a piece of old cotton cloth tied over the end, and let the bees gnaw out in twenty-four or forty-eight hours.

In giving directions how to introduce queens, we should say whether the same will do for all seasons. Some directions will do for spring that would fail in every instance in the fall. On page 10 of the Journal for July, friend Nesbit gives a lamentable account of failures in introducing imported queens. But why didn't he tell us the time of year it was? He might have saved all his queens on the plan I give above, which is the same used by Mr. A. Grimm, for fall operation; only Mr. G. does not fix the feed in the cage. I think the feed necessary; but be careful that you do not fix it in so as to besmear the queen with honey. I generally put half a dozen bees in with her to lick the honey off. Bees will not always feed a caged queen, is the reason I think the feed placed in is necessary.

R. M. Argo.

Lowell, Ky., July 6, 1871.

☞ Our mode of introducing queens is as follows: Remove the old queen a day before you propose to offer her successor; leave off the honey board, and place the cage you intend using on the frames, over the place where the bees are most densely crowded. Scent the cage with peppermint, and sprinkle the bees with sweetened peppermint water, or give them a supply of this in a feeding box; then replace the cap or top of the hive. Next day scent the cage afresh, and sprinkle the bees liberally, or feed as before. In the evening, if your new queen has arrived or is available, place her in the cage on the frames, scenting the cage first with sweetened water, and giving the bees another sprinkling or feeding. Next morning, if the bees clustered on the cage show any signs of hostility by hissing or otherwise, carry it ten or twelve steps from the hive, and gently brush them all off. Replace the cage on the frames; scent and sprinkle or feed, as before; and close the top. Repeat this on the second day, and subsequent days, if the bees crowded on the cage give continued signs of discontent; but if otherwise, merely sprinkle or feed, as before; and in the evening, having brushed off the bees, carry the cage to a closed room, lest the queen make her escape; remove the cork or sponge, and tie over a piece of soft tissue paper, besmearing it with honey; replace it on the frames, sprinkle or feed once more, and close the hive. Next morning, if the bees have not liberated the queen, and there are no evidences of animosity on their part, you may safely liberate her yourself, first dipping your fingers in peppermint water. We prefer not putting bees in the cage with the queen, as they sometimes play "tit for tat" with angry outsiders, thus keeping up fight or the show of it, and preventing a speedy acceptance of the queen.

We have introduced many queens safely in this manner, not having failed in a single instance since we adopted it. The advantage is that you have the whole operation entirely *under your eye*, and are enabled to act as may seem expedient. Whether the process will prove equally efficient in the hands of others, remains to be ascertained.—ED.

[For the American Bee Journal.]

Natural, Prolific and Hardy Queens.

MR. JOHN M. PRICE:

DEAR SIR:—I have for years been in the habit of raising my queens on stocks kept in full heart by liberal feeding or otherwise—and have not found any appreciable difference between queens thus raised, and those raised by the bees when preparing to swarm. I had one-half of the queens in my apiary from swarming cells at one time; but they proved no better than others raised under *favorable* circumstances,* from queenless stocks. *While I differ entirely from you on this point, I still think your plan a good one for getting choice queens*†—*perhaps better than any other.*

Yours truly,
L. L. LANGSTROTH,
Per J. T. L.

Oxford, Ohio, April 24, 1871.

* I have been raising queens for my own use since 1865, and have never had one that was equal to natural queens, which I either bought or found in a colony on the eve of swarming. Three out of every five queens raised were lost on their wedding flight. (*Queen raiser's explanation.*) The balance would either be non-prolific, or be short-lived, or be a season maturing, and not able to keep up her swarm until one year old. Mr. Langstroth, and a few others, may be able to hit favorable circumstances once in awhile; but the majority of bee-keepers, under *favorable circumstances*, might do so only once in a lifetime.

† *Choice queens.*—Who wants to raise any other? Especially when they can be raised more easily, cheaper, and with less trouble, than an inferior kind.

Mr. Langstroth, for passable queens raised by the forcing process, finds it necessary to charge from ten to fifteen dollars each. So few can be raised out of the whole number started, that choice queens, by that process, cannot be raised with profit for less.

Mr. Alley says he has paid TWENTY DOLLARS for a queen; and when he hits on a choice one of his own raising, he will not take FIFTY DOLLARS for her. See back numbers of the American Bee Journal.

I put six queen cells into one of Dr. Davis' queen nurseries on the 20th of May, and they all hatched out in due time. The weather was very chilly at nights while they were maturing.

JOHN M. PRICE.

Buffalo Grove, Iowa.

[For the American Bee Journal.]

Queens Piping.

MR. EDITOR:—I wish to tell you what I saw and heard. My hives were very full of bees this spring, when I set them out. The swarming season proper has not yet come with us, though one of my hives has been preparing to swarm for the last four weeks. For five days in succession, I heard the queen piping before the swarm came out. In nine days more they swarmed again, and once more on the thirteenth—making three swarms.

Now, if any of our bee-men ever saw the like I would like to have some account given of it in explanation.

GEORGE W. WHEELER, JR.

Westerlo, N. Y., June 20, 1871.

☞ In the above case, the first was what the Germans call a "*singing first swarm.*" These are produced when an old queen dies, or is superseded, before a swarm has issued, and a number of queen cells are started to provide a successor. Piping will then be heard before the issuing of the first swarm, as there are in the hive several young queens mature and ready to emerge, just as in the case of a natural second swarm. After swarms will issue at the customary time, if at all; and piping will be heard as usual on each occasion. It is an unfrequent occurrence. The first swarm we ever had was one of this class. It came out of an old straw hive, and was followed by another on the tenth day.

Sometimes a first swarm issues unobserved and makes its escape. If another swarm issues subsequently from the same hive, piping will usually be heard before it leaves, and is assumed to proceed from a queen about to leave with a first swarm. This, however, is not a true "singing first swarm," for if further swarming occurs, it will not take place on the ninth or tenth day, but already on the second, third, or fourth—showing that the supposed first swarm was really a second.

Glycerine Balsam.

Take white wax (pure) . . . . 1 ounce.
spermaceti . . . . 2 ounces.
oil of almonds . . . 9 ounces.

Melt together by a moderate heat, in a glazed earthenware vessel, and add
glycerine (best). . . 3 ounces.
balsam of Peru . . . ½ ounce.

This mixture is to be stirred until nearly cold, and then poured into pots. (Instead of Balsam of Péru, 12 or 15 drops of Ottar of Roses may be employed.)—*Druggists' Circular.*

THE AMERICAN BEE JOURNAL.

Washington, August, 1871.

☞ We are in pressing need of No. 7, of the American Bee Journal, of volumes V. and VI. (dated respectively January, 1870, and January, 1871); and will pay twenty-five cents, per copy, for those numbers till our wants are supplied, if sent to the publication office, with the sender's name.

☞ Anonymous communications, especially if referring to personal matters, must be accompanied by the writer's name, to secure attention,—not for publication, but for our information and security.

☞ A new theory respecting the origin, cause, and cure of foulbrood has been broached in the Bienenzeitung, by Mr. G. Fischer. It is in substance that the disease originates when the brood is supplied with an insufficiency of nitrogenous food—that is, when the food, though proper in its kind, is furnished in inadequate quantity; or when, though plentifully supplied, the requisite ingredients are not duly apportioned. To correct this, and counteract the effects of bad nourishment, food containing the proper elements in due proportion, must be furnished in the requisite quantity, at the proper time. Suitable food, so made up, Mr. Fischer thinks is found in the albuminous contents of hens' eggs; and he accordingly resorted to feeding a diseased colony with a mixture of two parts egg with one part solution of sugar-candy, adding a few drops of honey to make it more acceptable to the bees. The brood reared in new comb after such feeding matured in due season, free of disease; as did, also, with two exceptions, that in the cells of old brood comb in the foulbroody hive. The food thus prepared was given at intervals of two days, and according to Mr. F., effected the desired purpose completely—arresting and eradicating the disease, regardless of the old doctrine of contagion.

The process is simple, easy, and cheap; and, if efficient, will prove very valuable. Egg-feeding has, indeed, been objected to by some as injurious; and may be so, if used in excess, but we have never found it so, when employed moderately, at intervals, as a stimulant. If, however, we should have occasion to test it as a cure for foulbrood, we would at the same time use the hyposulphite of soda, suggested by Dr. Abbe, as a disinfectant.

Weight of Bees.

An Illinois correspondent asks—"How many bees does it take to weigh a pound?"

No precise number can be named, as the number will vary with the condition in which the bees are at the time.

In his experiments made in September, 1842, Gundelach found that 2765 workers, taken from a nucleus hive, weighed ten ounces—which is at the rate of 5420 to the pound. A few months later, 1170 bees taken by him from a hive then already several weeks in winter quarters, weighed four ounces, or 4680 to the pound. The difference was ascribed to the fæcal matter already accumulated in the intestines of those last weighed.

October 4th, 1846, he weighed three queens:

The first weighed...........	0.1685	French	grammes.
The second weighed........	0.1960	"	"
The third weighed.........	0.2110	"	"
At the same time, a drone..	0.2352	"	"
And a worker..............	0.1112	"	"

the weight of the latter being at the rate of 4500 to the pound.

Dumas and Milne Edwards give 87.00 millegrammes as the weight of a worker, being about 4000 to the pound; but this is evidently an error.

Schmidt & Kleine say that 366 workers weigh an ounce, and 5376 a pound, but do not appear to have made any experiments themselves; merely accepting Reaumur's statement.

Berlepsch states that 177 bees found dead on the alighting board of a hive, weighed half an ounce. This would give 5664 to the pound.

The usual estimate is that of workers, not gorged with honey nor laden with pollen, 5300 will weigh a pound; and this may be regarded as a fair average. Bees, when preparing to swarm, usually fill themselves with honey, and hence when weighing a swarm, especially if accompanied by many drones, a proper allowance must be made in estimating the number of workers emigrating.

CORRESPONDENCE OF THE BEE JOURNAL.

Braunschweig, Germany, June 4, 1871.—So discouraging a spring as the present, even bee-keepers, who have been in the business fifty or sixty years do not remember to have ever before encountered. On the 19th of February the bees made their first cleansing flight. This was again followed by a cold spell, and from the 26th of the month to the 28th of March we had, with some variations, quite favorable weather. Most bee-keepers had cause to complain of heavy losses, though my colonies passed the winter in very good condition, as, on the whole, I lost only two per cent. of their number. At the middle of March bees carried in pollen and honey, and the colonies were then remarkably vigorous and strong. The hopes of the bee-keepers rose high, but were doomed to speedy disappointment. The 28th of March brought snow and frost, and April gave us only one day (the 19th) on which bees could fly out, the weather having been almost continually rainy and cold. They ventured out occasionally when the sun shone for a few moments; but of a hundred that left scarcely ten returned, being almost invariably caught in showers of rain, snow or sleet. This greatly depopulated the hives, and despite of steady feeding there was a falling off instead of gain. May was an equally unfavorable month, giving us only four sunny days; and to-day (June 4th) the weather, as on the preceding days, is so cold that it is uncomfortable to be outdoors, and we have fire in every chamber. Very large quantities of honey have been fed to the bees, and yet the hives are hardly as populous as they were at the end of March. Those bee-keepers fared worst who make queen raising a business, as it is vain to hope for success therein under such circumstances. Thousands of stocks perished in April; and June beginning so unfavorably will probably still add to the number. We no longer look for natural swarms this season, and dare not think of making artificial colonies. Though I have already fed fifteen pounds of honey to each of my colonies, I cannot yet foresee when this feeding may cease. It is singular that the weather reports in the Bee Journal this spring exhibit conditions of temperature so directly opposite, as regards the state and prospects of bee-culture. How does this happen? This is a question the solution of which must possess a deep interest for all bee-keepers.—C. T. H. GRAVENHORST.

ANNOWAN, ILL., June 16.—Bees commenced swarming the last week in May. They are doing well at this date. I have just one hundred stocks. All but three are in Langstroth hives. My bees are nearly all Italian.—WILLIAM TROYER.

HUBBARD, OHIO, June 17.—The weather is not so favorable for bees as it was last season. Very little swarming yet. Considerable white clover, but weather very dry. It was wet and cold while fruit trees were in blossom.—J. WINFIELD.

MOUNT GILEAD, OHIO, June 20.—I am but a beginner in bee-culture. Four years ago I began with one very feeble stock in a box. Now I have thirty-eight Italians and hybrids, mostly in frame hives. Our bees are now working well on white and alsike clover; the red clover blossom grows too long here for bees to work on. I intend to try some of the new methods recommended in the Journal to procure (pure) "non-flying fertilization." If it can be made practicable, then may bee-keepers truly say the science of profitable bee-culture has advanced another long step. I cannot do without the Bee Journal, and wish it was issued oftener. I read it over and over—so rich, so complete, full of just what *every* bee-keeper ought to know; the ripe experience of the best bee-keepers in the land.—J. GARDNER.

BINGHAMTON, N. Y., June 21.—Bees have done very well in this section in regard to breeding—that is, where they were given a sufficiency of empty combs, and properly handled. Box hives are not generally prosperous; few have swarmed yet; they have so much old honey left over that they have not sufficient brooding space to get up numbers. They will probably, for that reason, do very little in surplus boxes. The weather has been very changeable this month so far. In fact, it rains every second or third day. We find that our Italians, even where they are very strong, build slowly in boxes; in fact, no boxes are finished yet, though they commenced in them nearly two weeks ago. I would like to make an inquiry through the Journal, especially of Mr. Stratton, in regard to side-box hives; but having been confined to the house nearly two weeks, do not feel like writing. We are also very much interested in the foulbrood question, as there is a great deal of that disease in this section, though it has not visited our apiary yet. We wish to get as well posted as possible, so as to be able to do something in the way of prevention, if it should come.—J. P. MOORE.

TOLONO, ILLS., June 22.—Bees are doing very well here now, but the spring has been too dry until within about four weeks past. They are swarming very well in the country.—Dr. H. CHAFFEE.

LISBON, IOWA, June 22.—Bees are storing honey very rapidly, and doing finely, in most of this State; and I expect the report for Iowa for 1871 will be a good one.—W. S. GOODHUE.

WARSAW, MINN., June 24.—Bees are late in swarming; from box hives they leave for the woods. Weak stocks are played out; stocks with plenty of honey are doing well. We are having fine showers, and the prospect for basswood honey is good.—L. B. ALDRICH.

CINCINNATI, OHIO, June 24.—We have a poor honey season near our city this year. Last year I had taken twelve hundred pounds of honey by the 23d of June, against seventy pounds this year. I keep my bees on the roof of my house. Only one of my neighbors, about six miles out, reports a first rate crop. He lives where basswood abounds.—C. F. MUTH.

HAMILTON, IOWA, June 25.—This is the height of the swarming season here, and I have never before heard of so many swarms going to the woods. I had a swarm come out on the 22d inst., and on each of the two following days they came out to leave. But on the first day I cropped the wing of the queen, and they didn't get away. They seem well contented now, and are working for dear life.—J. M. TUCKER.

RICHMOND, VA., June 26.—Bees have not done as well as I anticipated. I think the change in April, from warm weather in the early part of the month, to cool and dry in the latter part, will account for it, for I had one or two swarms before the 8th of April, then no more till the 24th; and I had a swarm on the 24th of June. Out of thirty stocks I have had only ten swarms. My Italian queens, introduced this spring, are laying briskly; and black stocks in which I introduced Italian queens, April 21st, have not over a dozen black workers now.—W. R. POLK.

WEST CHESHIRE, CONN., June 26.—I feel much pleased with my success in bee-keeping this year, thanks to the Bee Journal.—W. H. KIRK.

TIVERTON, CANADA, June 28.—The longer I have the Bee Journal, the better I like it. It is full of interest, and any one who has any taste for bee-keeping, cannot fail to succeed with your valuable monthly publication.—REV. J. ANDERSON.

BROOKLIN, CANADA, June 28.—We are having a good honey season, though the spring was very hard on bees generally. The weather becoming warm in the early part of March, bees were taken out of winter quarters; but it remained too cool for breeding, except where the stock was very strong in numbers. No honey was gathered for two months. The consequence was many stocks became depopulated and finally perished. But since the white clover appeared in blossom it has been one continual harvest, with fine weather.—J. H. THOMAS.

WILLOW BRANCH, IND., June 29.—My bees are doing very well this season in gathering honey. They have filled up the brood chamber with honey, so as to nearly stop breeding. I have ordered one of Peabody's honey extractors, and will try to give them room to breed, as soon as I get it home. White clover is very plenty, with rain enough to keep it sweet.—JONA. SMITH.

MARENGO, ILLS., June 29.—As good a honey season as I have ever known.—C. C. MILLER.

LEXINGTON, ILLS., July 1.—We may send report of honey, bees, &c., at close of the season of 1871, for the Journal, if time permits, the season being very favorable so far.—W. REYNOLDS.

New Waterford, Ohio, July 1.—I have just been taking a trip through Washington, Fayette and Westmoreland counties, Pa.; and on inquiry among bee-keepers, found it was an almost universal thing that there are no swarms, except in one instance. I found a man who said he had several swarms; and as we were walking through his apiary, I happened to look up, and saw a swarm on a little bush, which had come out and settled unobserved. Most folks thought their bees were storing honey pretty rapidly; and one man who keeps about thirty-five stocks, believed he would get about a thousand pounds of box honey this season from twenty-five of them.—C. Blackburn.

Lucknow, Canada, July 1.—This has been but a poor season for bees in this quarter. At one time it was so very hot and dry as to scorch up all the flowers; and lately it has been too cold to be even pleasant. Still we have no reason to complain, as white clover grows here spontaneously, and my bees have done passably well so far.—G. T. Burgess.

Adams, Wis., July 1.—Bees are doing well. Have doubled my stocks this season, and got considerable surplus honey besides.—J. L. Wolfenden.

Council Bluffs, Iowa, July 2.—Bees are doing well here this season so far. Some colonies have filled one set of boxes from the linden bloom, which is the largest crop we ever had in this country.—A. Faul.

Sherman, Texas, July 2.—This is a very good bee country, but there is no energy shown in bee-culture. Bees began to swarm in April. No Italian bees have yet been introduced into this part of the country that I have heard of. The large yellow bee of the South is said to be in this country, but I have never yet seen any.—M. S. Klum.

Millersburg, Ohio, July 3.—Our honey crop in this locality this year so far is very near a failure. Had it not been for the honey dews, our bees would have been almost without natural supplies from the time of the fruit blossoms to the present date. The white clover (our main dependence) yields comparatively nothing, although the bloom was and is equal to any previous season since I became interested in and an observer of the production of honey.—A. B. Frey.

Cadiz, Ohio, July 3.—Our honey season may be called good here thus far, but only about one-fourth of the black bees and perhaps two-thirds of the Italians have swarmed. I have been considerably through the region around Pittsburg, Pa., and find that only about one colony in ten has swarmed, and very little surplus honey will be made. I presume that nine-tenths of the surplus honey made in Eastern Ohio and Western Pennsylvania is derived from white clover. I this season obtained both a Peabody and a Gray & Winder honey extractor. They work beautifully. I let the honey run through a fine wire cloth strainer and through four tubes into four jars at once.

I think we would get more honey per hive, if there were fewer of them in this locality. There are nearly five hundred within a radius of two miles. In our village of 1,400 inhabitants, there are twenty-four bee-keepers. It has been decided by the bee-keepers of this region to have a convention for Eastern Ohio in this place on the first day of November next.—R. Wilkin.

Wenham, Mass., July 3.—Bees have stored no box honey here, and will not this season. There has been plenty of forage, but no honey weather.—H. Alley.

Wilkesbarre, Pa., July 3.—I have something over a hundred stands of bees, all in old Quinby hives but three. They wintered well, but the spring being cold, they soon run out of stores. The first swarm came out on the last day of May, and I have eighteen or twenty since. Bees have not done well here for four or five years past.—T. Hutchins.

Mount Pleasant, Iowa, July 3.—Can anything be done for dysentery in bees? Mine, and those of two of my neighbors, had it very bad this winter and spring. I had thirty-five colonies last fall, and twelve died. Nearly all the rest were very weak till the middle of May, when they began to increase very fast. On the 27th of May I had a fine large swarm of hybrids, which has filled its hive, and nearly filled seven five pound surplus boxes. One of my neighbors had nearly fifty colonies, and lost thirty-four by this disease; another had eighty and lost all but about thirty. They all had plenty of honey.

This has been the best honey season that I ever saw in Iowa, and I have been here since the fall of 1853. The honey is as nice as can be made this side of sundown. It will beat Quinby's honey in tin cells all hollow.—H. M. Noble.

Walworth, Wis., July 3.—I bought seven stocks of bees and transferred them about the 16th of June. The brood has not all hatched yet. They appear to be dead; but as I am new in the business, I don't know whether they died from exposure or injury in transferring, or from foulbrood. Some are full grown and dark-colored; and some are not grown, and white yet. I yesterday cut out all the old comb that I put in the new hive, and will keep it from the bees; but they had access to the old comb that I rejected in transferring, and worked on it a few days. If it is foulbrood, I want to know what to do to get rid of it. Will some one who has experience please advise?

Such a fulfilling of Scripture in the milk and honey business I never saw, as the month of June, 1871, has given us. Our pastures and roadsides are literally covered with white clover blossoms. I have a stock from last season, then a small one, which has four seventeen pound boxes nearly full; and at the present rate they will be full and sealed up in thirty days from the time they were put on, as the cells are being sealed rapidly now on rear ends next the glass, and the bees have yet five days to work on before the thirty expire. —A. W. Davis.

Morristown, N. J., July 3.—I should like to inquire of practical men whether, in view of the high value of labor, in the present state of the New York honey market, the artificial and so-called progressive management of bees is after all, the most profitable? Circumstances alter cases very much; but in my case, and with very little experience, I am inclined to think that, valuing labor at two dollars per day, it is more profitable to store honey in boxes and let bees swarm naturally. Most writers seem to ignore the fact that it takes a great deal of time to perform all these delicate operations; and time is money to most persons, especially in the busy season. I should like to have the opinion of others on this subject.—J. M. N. Kitchen.

Norwalk, Ohio, July 4.—I have about one thousand (1,000) pounds of honey already this year from fifty colonies.—C. H. Hoyt.

Lexington, Ky., July 7.—This has been a very poor season for bees. Out of over two hundred hives I have had only about twenty natural swarms and no surplus in honey.—J. Dillard.

NEW BEDFORD, MASS., July 7.—Bees are doing well at present, and are gathering honey rapidly from white clover. After I get through with my summer's experiments with foulbrood I will give you the results. As I have had no new cases, I am getting short of material.—E. P. ABBE.

ELIZABETHTOWN, PA., July 10.—Bees have done very well here this season having stored large quantities of "surplus" from white clover and locust.—A. EBY.

LIMA, OHIO, July 12.—The spring has been rather unfavorable for bees. It commenced early, and during fruit blossoms (which were abundant) ought to have yielded well. But repeated frosts through April and May destroyed all the saccharine matter the blossoms contained; and even with moderate feeding the bees were not disposed to brood-raising. The consequence was they were in no better (if in as good) condition on the first of June than on the first of April. Up to this time, there has been little natural swarming, especially among the black bees. The weather is now unfavorable, being entirely too wet. —S. SANFORD.

CYNTHIANA, KY., July 12.—Bees have not done well here this year, on account of late frost cutting off all the locust bloom. Very few swarms, and but little or no box honey.—H. NESBIT.

EAST LIVERPOOL, OHIO, July 12.—Bees have not done very well here this summer, either in surplus honey or in swarms. I have only heard of four swarms in this vicinity.—A. J. FISHER.

CINCINNATI OHIO, July 14.—The honey season around Cincinnati is poor, and makes queen-raising very tedious.—A. GRAY.

The Bee-keepers.

MEETING OF THE CENTRAL ILLINOIS ASSOCIATION AT LEXINGTON.

LEXINGTON, Ill., July 13th.—The Central Illinois Bee-keepers' Association met, according to previous appointment, at Lexington, July 13th, in A. B. Davidson's hall. The meeting was called to order by the President, S. C. Ware. D. J. Poor was appointed Secretary *pro tem*. J. L. Peabody, S. B. Ledgerwood, W. G. Anderson, and W. Reynolds, were appointed to present subjects for the afternoon discussion.

Then followed a familiar discussion till the Committee reported the following:

1. The natural and artificial swarming of bees; when and how it should be done.
2. The use of the honey extractor, and the best method of managing bees to obtain the greatest amount of honey.
3. The use of empty combs.
4. Queen raising.
5. The Italian and black bees.
6. Bee pasturage.

The Association then adjourned to meet at half-past 1 o'clock P. M.

At that time the meeting was resumed, and the discussion continued by S. C. Ware, J. L. Peabody, Jacob Hefner, W. G. Anderson, W. Reynolds, J. V. Brooks, and others. The meeting was largely attended and enthusiastic, and a very decided impression made in favor of the Italian bees.

Fourteen new members were secured. The speakers being men of careful observation and extensive experience in bee culture, it was a meeting of great profit to all present.

Adjourned to meet during the week of our county fair.

[For the American Bee Journal.]

A Winter Repository.

Now that winter is over, it seems proper for us to review and note our successes and failures, for future reference.

First.—We find the American Bee Journal what every bee-keeper should have, to be successful, and especially beginners.

Second.—It will not do to undertake, in this northern climate, to winter bees on their summer stands, with a hope of profit, This brings us to the point—What is the best way to construct a repository that will not be as variable in temperature as the wind blows in its changes? We will give our plan, which we think is an improvement in ventilation; and this may lead to further explanation through the columns of the Journal.

Our plan is as follows: We dig into a side hill a space thirteen by fourteen feet and seven feet high, with an ante-room or entry in front, four feet by ten—wherein we claim an improvement. Between this ante-room and the bee-room double doors are placed in a four-inch wall filled in with sawdust. Joists and floor, with sawdust over the whole. Rafters and roof covered with dirt, and the sides banked up with dirt. The ante-room in front is closed by a door set in a four-inch wall filled in with sawdust.

We ventilate by placing an eight-inch square flue horizontally, leading into this ante-room at bottom in front. Within this ante-room is placed an eight-inch square flue vertically, near the bee-room. The upper end is open near the ceiling of the ante-room, and the lower end communicates with a covered trench, which runs lengthwise under the bee-room. This covered trench has inch holes eighteen inches apart, along its length, to distribute the air equally in the bee-room. Two four-inch square flues are placed in the roof, one at each end, for the escape of air. Also, a four-inch flue is placed in the roof of the ante-room. All the flues have valves or slides at their inner open ends, for the purpose of regulating the supply of air.

The mode of ventilating is as follows: Fresh air is admitted through the front flue into the anteroom, which becomes a sort of reservoir for it, equalizing its temperature as it ascends to the ceiling, whence it descends through the vertical flue into the covered trench, is distributed in the bee-room, and passes out at the flues in the roof.

We have wintered twenty colonies in this repository, they remaining quiet as lambs without any further care, with the thermometer standing at 35° above zero, without a variation of more than one or two degrees, whilst outside it has stood all the way from 24° *below* to 50° *above* zero.

Being only a beginner, we have written this to learn, from more experienced bee-keepers, how near we come to being right.

Minnesota. LESAGE.

We delayed inserting this article several months, to have an illustration accompanying it engraved, but failed to get it executed satisfactorily, and think the plan will be sufficiently understood from the description.—ED.

AMERICAN BEE JOURNAL.

EDITED AND PUBLISHED BY SAMUEL WAGNER, WASHINGTON, D. C.

AT TWO DOLLARS PER ANNUM, PAYABLE IN ADVANCE.

VOL. VII. **SEPTEMBER, 1871.** No. 3.

[From the Bienenzietung.]

Drone Production, and Honeydew.

TRANSLATED FOR THE AMERICAN JOURNAL.

The Baron of Berlepsch, when congratulating me on my sixtieth birthday (for which I kindly thank him and his amiable lady) avails himself of the occasion to make some remarks on certain topics which were the subjects of conversation between Dr. Preuss and myself, when that gentleman made me a friendly visit; namely, the production of drones and the formation of honeydew.

1. As regards the first point. In confirmation of the truth that the drones owe their existence exclusively to the queen, the Baron communicates from his Seebach reminiscences the well-ascertained fact that German or black queens, though fertilized by a yellow or Italian drone, and consequently producing mixed workers, some being yellow and some black, nevertheless produces black drones exclusively, whereas yellow or Italian queens occasionally produce black drones also. This observed fact, however (which I have often noticed myself), by no means constrains us to assume that fertilization exerts an influence on the production of drones, and the contradiction of the now generally accepted theory, which it seemingly involves, is by no means difficult to explain.

Of the black or German queen bees existing when the Italian race was introduced, it may confidently be assumed that they were of the pure German race, without the slightest intermixture of Italian blood. But the case is otherwise with the Italian bee, even in its native coun'ry. She is not there invariably found entirely pure, for even in Virgil's day already, the dark colored race subsisted along side of the golden or yellow, and so continues in close juxtaposition to the present day. In the course of time manifold intermixtures have taken place, the prevention of which has become only increasingly difficult, since her transplantation to foreign soil.

A queen may wear a golden yellow garb, yet I cannot regard her as pure Italian, if her mother was not also perfectly pure, and if from among her brood, besides yellow young queens, dark colored ones are also produced. It must therefore not be surprising when queens, proceeding from such brood, though themselves never so bright and yellow, produce dark-colored drones. In this very result, the fractional dash of black blood inherent in such queens manifests itself. Such queens, too, not entirely pure from birth, occasionally produce truly golden yellow drones. But these, also, I regard as suspicious, rejecting them, and giving the preference to drones of less bright yet uniform color, which proceed from queens unquestionably pure. In selecting colonies for breeding, I have regard not merely to the bright color of the workers, but likewise to their industry and placable temperament; two qualities for which my Italians at least are pointedly distinguished from native blacks.

2. My remark to Dr. Preuss that I am not infallible, the Baron contradicts in his congratulatory letter, and remarks: "You are really infallible, for you propounded a theory of which till now not an iota has been disproved. But, in another matter I must controvert your opinion, namely, as regards the formation of honeydew. There is an aphis honeydew, and also a leaf honeydew, as I had an opportunity to satisfy myself only last summer at Tambuchshof." With an opponent who concedes at the outset that honeydew oftimes originates from aphides, controversy may well be waged; but not so with those, who reversing the facts, maintain that the aphides do not produce the honeydew, but that these make their appearance only as a consequence of its production, and as consumers of it. With such we can have no controversy. He who never saw, in the rays of the sun, the spray-like rain of honeydew gently falling from the leafy boughs on which multitudes of aphides are embowered, has in truth as yet observed but little, and may be said to lack altogether the faculty of observation. That which, as the Baron of Berlepsch concedes, in many cases originates from aphides discharging certain unassimilable matters, others insist on regarding as the mere tempting bait or rich repast provided for those and other insects. Meanwhile we know that the aphides are congregated on the underside of the leaf, while the honeydew is always found on the upper surface alone, upon which if the aphides ventured, they would quickly be glued fast, as if by bird-lime.

But if honeydew be, in fact, not produced by aphides alone, but be secreted also by the leaves of trees, there should necessarily be a recognizable qualitative difference between the two products, emanating from sources so dissimilar. Has any one ever detected a difference or even attempted to ascertain whether there is any? I am exceedingly anxious to learn the reasons which constrain so sound a thinker as the Baron to accept or assume a two-fold origin of honeydew. The possible circumstance that when no honeydews occur no aphides are visible, would by no means be conclusive. Aphides notoriously make their appearance suddenly, and as suddenly disappear, so that frequently they are vanished already when their exuviæ or their products are observed. Possibly, too, the saccharine matter of the honeydew may have become dried up before its existence was noticed, then followed a gentle rain or heavy dew, rendering it soluble again and available for the bees; and as these are now first seen visiting it, the superficial observer infers that it was produced quite recently, perhaps only in the previous night. That the honeydew seen on evergreens is the product of a coccus, is a fact not only visible but tangible, though the inexperienced may, in this case also, readily regard the coccus as a diseased secretion of the affected pine branch.

That the saccharine matter found issuing from the vetch, the horsebean, the still closed blossoms of the centaury, and the strongly swollen buds of the pear tree, and on other leaves and twigs recently pierced by bugs or larvæ, is a vegetable exudation, is very well known. Such exudations, forming rich sources of supplies for bees, do not, however, come strictly under the category of honeydews proper. But that the latter should at times be the product of aphides, and again a vegetable exudation or secretion; and that there should yet be no essential difference in its composition cognizable, I cannot possibly believe. If the Baron has irrefragible evidence to sustain his views, I wish he would communicate it, that light may at last be shed on this subject. The notions of those who regard aphides as never the producers, but as always the consumers of honeydew, deserve no refutation. They refute themselves.

DZIERZON.

Carlsmarkt, $^{16}_{5}$, 1871.

[For the American Bee Journal.]

Nomenclature in Bee-culture.

AGRICULTURAL COLLEGE,

Lansing, Mich., July 21, 1871.

EDITOR BEE JOURNAL,

DEAR SIR:—It has often seemed to me, that writers on bee-culture are at times unnecessarily obscure, and often misled by confusion in the use of terms—especially in the use of the words *species, races* and *variety*. These words, seeming to possess in the minds of writers no definite meaning, are generally used in a purely arbitrary sense. I fully believe that we should make real substantial progress, if we would unite in giving these terms a definite meaning.

Now, dropping the Darwinian idea that all life is derived from some simplest form, which is yet far from being proved, we can say that a SPECIES includes all of those animals which have had a common origin, and are capable of an indefinite fertile reproduction through the sexes. Thus cattle are of one species, as we suppose all have come from one stock, and they are ever fertile with each other.

A RACE on the other hand, includes animals bred with care and possessing certain characteristics of form, color and temperament, which they impart to their progeny with more or less certainty, as they have been bred with more or less care. Now, while the characters of species are persistent, the characters of a race from the very manner of their origin are not so fixed. Thus in the cattle species we have several races, as the Devons, the Ayrshire, &c. If the Devons are well bred they will almost invariably show the clear, symmetrical horns, the deep red color, the fine trim form and quick elastic tread. Yet from the principle of atavism or animals resembling a remote ancestry, even the best bred Devon might have short horns, white hair, and a heavy form. This would be improbable, not impossible. Thus, while a species, as cattle, would always be cattle, a race might give increase that would so vary as not to be recognizable; though among thoroughly bred animals marked variations seldom occur.

Now the word VARIETY is frequently used in the same sense of *race*. Yet we think this unfortunate, and would recommend that our apiarists should avoid such use; as it is often employed in another sense, and giving to the same word a double meaning does not tend to clearness. We would restrict the term *variety* to those members of a race which show minor differences, that may be very temporary, or by careful selection in breeding, may become more persistent. Thus we have the red and the white variety of Durhams.

As we come to apply this improved nomenclature to bees, we think all will see and recognize its advantages over the present loose system of expression.

The Apis Mellifica or hive bee is a species, and includes the German, Italian and Egyptian bees, all of which come from an original pair. These all readily cross, and the offspring are always fertile with each other. Their characters as a species are persistent—as all possess males, perfect, and imperfect females in the same colony, and the queen takes no part except to deposit the eggs.

The black, Italian, and Egyptian bees are *races*. Being bred for long years in different localities, and with different surroundings, they have each become possessed of peculiar markings, habits, and temperaments, which, as will be understood from the character of a race, are liable to vary. From the law of atavism already mentioned, any of these races may occasionally show characters of the others, and still be pure breeds.

Now we might cross two of the races, and by careful breeding originate a third race; though this would require long care and patience, which Vogel has shown to be the method by which the Italians were produced. This makes the race none the less valuable; for if, by crossing the Egyptians and black bees, and then by careful selection in breeding from the offspring, we originate a third race, superior to either of the others, and which will keep better only as the result of careful breeding, surely we have improved our art by the introduction of a superior and distinct race. He who should object to Italians on this ground, should rest satisfied with cattle of the lank, ill-formed native breeds.

This truth, that the Italians are the result of crossing the black bees with the Egyptians, does not interfere with their being a distinct race. This they become as soon as they will invariably reproduce their kind; and this truth will make us all the more careful in procuring queens from the best breeders, and will make us take every precaution to insure pure fertilization in our own apiaries.

Again, as we become able to control fertilization, so as to select any males with the care that we do the queens, we may each develop varieties of Italians, as to color, temperament, vigor or industry, or perhaps all; and thus improve even the Italian race.

Mr. Editor, I am experimenting, and will soon write you on the drone question and fertilizing. Bees are doing finely this summer. We expect to have a grand time at the next meeting of our association, which meets at Kalamazoo, at the time of the State fair. I will send notice to the Journal in time.

A. J. Cook.

[For the American Bee Journal.]

Breeding in-and-in.

Some people think that because a good many inmates of an insane asylum are the offspring of blood relations, then all intermarriage of blood relations is most pernicious. Now it may be that a different rule governs in the human family in this respect, from that which obtains in the rest of animated nature, as shown by physiological facts. Or it may result from the fact that the "genus homo" has so deteriorated in domestication, that there is no mortal left without taint of some disease or other. It is certain that nature does not guard much against the mating of kin relations. For instance the buffalo of the plains mates with his own progeny, so long as by his strength he is the superior of the herd, say six or seven years—then mating room perhaps for his immediate descendant. The same is true of the deer of the forest. A flock of quails also consists usually of about equal numbers of males and females. They stay together during winter, and in the spring separate in couples of the same brood. The Jersey cows come from a small island, where this stock has bred in-and-in for centuries; yet for beauty of form and richness of milk, they are the foremost cattle on the globe. Virgil sang of the Italian bees nearly two thousand years ago; and as the area where they are found is very limited, how much must they have bred in-and-in? When a hive swarms the emigrants go to the next hollow tree, perhaps only a few rods from the old one; and as queens and drones fly together many miles apart, who can calculate where intermixing ceases?

I think richness and abundance of food produce fine creatures. The sheep of my native home (Westphalia), living chiefly on heather, are small in size, and produce wool as coarse as dog's hair. In Friesland, adjoining it (which is a fertile country), the sheep are of large size and have the best of wool. Both kinds no doubt came originally from Noah's pair, and the quality of food made all the difference, independent of intermixing.

Queen bees raised when food is abundant are said to be handsomer than those raised when food is scarce. Some writers in the Journal think the queens fly out to prevent breeding in-and-in. More likely nature makes them fly to prevent a weak or wingless queen from mating with a feeble or crippled drone.

I never had any faith in breeding in confinement. I think nature has vetoed it. Putting up a musquito bar around the hive, might enable those to succeed who are anxious about it.

Some bee-keepers think that clipping the queen's wings deteriorates the stock. I do not see why it should. Breeding queens in nuclei, out of season, I should think more likely to have such a tendency.

T. Hulman.

Terre Haute, Ind., August 1, 1871.

[For the American Bee Journal.]

Novice.

Dear Bee Journal:—Honey ceased to be brought in, in this locality, about July 13th; and up to this date (August 9th,) our index hive has not shown an increase of one pound. The bees are flying briskly, and at work, but the honey gathered is not equal to the amount consumed, by about two ounces per day on an average.

Of course many say that their bees are working finely and gathering honey right along, because they *see* them at work; but we have learned to regard this as very poor evidence.

We are watching the dial of the scales anxiously to see when the fall crop commences, as we have faith it will, although we have made our calculation from *sore* past experience, not to be caught short this season, any way. So we have most of our hives with sealed combs of honey in the upper stories, as a reserve force, to assist any stocks that are short.

The advantage of combs of sealed honey for fall feeding has, in our opinion, never been half appreciated; and we are determined for the future to keep a surplus cash capital, or something better than cash even, when stocks are to be strengthened up, of sealed combs of honey the year round. With a stock of these, even a novice may do anything he wishes, at almost any season, with comparative safety.

Our dial shows about two pounds of loss every morning when the bees fly out. Is not that the exact weight of the flying force? We suppose a bee, when going out to work, carries no honey with her, but we really do not like to kill one of the little pets to ascertain—even if there are forty thousand of them. Each little life is what we can easily take away, but that which none but God can give. We think that, with some little help, we can count just how many leave to make a pound—of course counting those that return meanwhile.

We think we mentioned, last season, that we made a series of cages with doors in a frame (eighteen in all), for queen raising. We did not succeed at all then, and are inclined to call it a failure. Our trouble was in thinking it necessary to have honey in the cages, and this, with the cell, occupied so much room that the young queens would get fast and die. *Now* we put nothing in the cage and remove the cell as soon as hatched; and have repeatedly kept queens until they were ten or twelve days old, letting them fly, one at a time, and securing them as soon as fertilized. A queen eight days old will sometimes become fertilized on her first flight, so that this may be accomplished without her going in at all, if she is secured on her return, as soon as she arrives at the entrance.

On one occasion we let three of them fly at once. One came back fertilized; the other two did not return, we think on account of a mishap, as follows: We were using a hive of full blood Italians for nursery, and were raising a great many fine queens with great satisfaction, until some brood hatched from a few eggs laid by one of the queens proved to be hydrid, and the young "mischiefs," as there were no eggs or unsealed brood to give them employment, began looking for something for them to do, for all the world like a litter of young puppies.

We had about a dozen queens of various ages, caged in the hive, and one day were surprised to hear a chorus of queen voices in trouble (are they not *voices?*). An examination revealed these same hybrid scamps reaching through the meshes until they got hold of the queens, then pulling their wings in strips and worrying them to death generally. We failed so far in stopping them that we lost nearly every queen; and the three we let out at one time were of the lot. The young bees gave two of them parting pinches as they took wing, so that we really could not blame them for not coming home. None of the old bees took any part in the persecution, but treated the queens with as much deference and respect as we should expect them to receive.

To test the matter, a new nursery hive was started, by removing the queen from a strong Italian stock. After the cells were put in nursery frame, all the combs were taken away except eight; and the quilt was left off entirely, for convenience. Nearly every cell hatched; the queens are now eight or ten days old, and none of them have been persecuted in the least. As drones are scarce now, these queens become fertilized slowly. We do not think that the circumstance alone of these bees being *hybrid*, was the reason why they worried the queens; but they were hatched after the queens, and young bees must have something to do—*mischief*, if nothing else offers.

Artificial fertilization, we are sorry to hear, makes little or no progress. We thought at first that "AMATEUR" had it at last, and we enjoyed our Fourth of July by making a cheese-cloth "machine," seven feet high and six feet in diameter; put in a lot of drones and two queens seven or eight days old. As the queens circled around and the drones circled after them, we had strong hopes and kept them circling there for several days. But, alas, they circled in vain!

A friend made a house of cloth twelve feet long, but with no better success. We both feared to go to the expense of wire cloth, but determined to do so, should further success be reported. Yet now Amateur feels less certain, and speaks of a smaller wire house—which we have tried repeatedly with variations. Why can't we succeed just once, to give us a little faith? It is true, as we have many times said, that so far as honey is concerned, our present way of letting the queens meet the drones, is good enough, provided we only have an undoubtedly pure queen to rear cells from. But as every bee-keeper wants at least one queen of absolute purity, who is to supply them?

We wonder how many of our readers have enjoyed the luxury of watching their bees at work, instead of dozing and trying to sleep—or still worse, lying awake until seven or eight o'clock, as by far too many bee-keepers and others do—on bright, glorious Sunday mornings. We sometimes feel on rising at five o'clock that we almost have the great, glorious, beautiful world all to ourselves. No one stirring, and nothing to mar the harmony.

We think it was the first Sabbath in June that we arose as usual, repaired to the garden with mouth and eyes wide open, and feeling ourselves "monarch of all we surveyed." Hurrah! something's up! The Italians were hurrying out of their hives on a run, and tumbling over the fence westward, as if they were really going somewhere. There was, so far as we know, nothing in bloom then that should occasion such a stir, and our curiosity was somewhat aroused. We looked over in the direction the bees went, and saw nothing but their busy lines. It was the Sabbath, yet as no one else was up, (sound logic!) it would not be very wrong to follow them. Over fences we went, through the dewy grass, past gurgling streams, but nothing could we see of the bees, except occasionally a swift messenger overhead. A wild cherry tree showed a few at work, a thorn bush a few more. We gave it up, and had turned homeward disappointed, when the hum overhead once more determined us that we *would* find them, and having failed elsewhere, we concluded to try the woods. As the humming increased we felt a thrill of pleasure in thinking we were on the right track, as we approached a low piece of wet, marshy ground.

"Low piece of wet ground, *indeed!*" remarks our better half, over our shoulder—"I should think so, from the condition in which I found your Sunday gaiters, Mr. Novice, and the time them I had in getting ready for you to go to church!"

"But don't you see you shouldn't bother a fellow? Now we don't know where we were last."

"In the mud, Mr. Novice, I can certify to that!"

And now she is gone, we will take up our thread again. Well, the low wet ground was covered with tall shellbark hickories in full bloom; and never did buckwheat field or orchard present a grander jubilee in the way of humming industry.

We got home satisfied, just as our neighbors were "getting up," and were thinking of claiming as an excuse that we were not more sinful than they, had not our minister said in his sermon, a few hours after, that it was none of our business what our neighbors did, and that our chance of heaven would not be one whit better, whatever they did.

We will only add that if a spirit should be cultivated of admiring and enjoying the beauties of the works of our Creator, the advantage of a five o'clock ramble across the fields, in contrast with loafing in bed, would make a vast difference with

NOVICE.

[For the American Bee Journal.]

Unparalleled Yield of Honey!

Unprecedented and Astonishing Success!!

A YOUNG LADY'S REPORT, FOR 1871.

MR. EDITOR:—If your time is not too valuable and space not too scarce, please insert the following short account of the last few months with my bees.

It was on the 29th of May, that my father came home from his northern apiary, and told me that I was to take charge of it the next day (May 30th). It was nothing very unusual to me, because I have done so yearly for the last four years, and therefore I was ready immediately to enter my services.

June and July had always been the most lonesome months of the year for me, and so the former proved to be this year, but the latter was far different from any I overlived, as you will hear hereinafter.

When I first came here I had only forty-eight stocks to take care of, and indeed I must say that it seemed almost impossible for me to stay with so few, as I had been used to have at least over one hundred.

During the month of June, I had thirty-eight young swarms from the forty-eight; but still they were far from being enough to give me a chance to spend all my time in attending to them.

When I came home one evening, to report to father (as I do every Saturday), I complained to him of my few hives, and told him that though they were all very busy, and doing their very best, I could not be satisfied; so he promised to send me more in a day or two. Two days afterward, I received a load with eighteen hives; in about a week another; and some days afterward a third one. Then I thought that there would be more of a chance to be doing something, and so indeed there was.

The stocks which father sent me were mostly young swarms, some of which swarmed twice again, others only once, and most of them only once; so that after the 1st of July I had nineteen more young swarms, and a little honey, as you will soon learn.

June 30th, father was here to examine my hives, when he also made twenty double hives, from which I was to extract honey about every three days; as he thought that during that time they would be filled. July 5th, I extracted my first half-barrel, which was one hundred and eighty-five (185) pounds. When I was through with it, I felt pretty well tired out, and thought it was quite a task for one day; but I had then no idea of what was still to be done. July 8th and 9th, I extracted 1½ barrels, so that I then had two barrels. July 14th, I extracted 1½ barrels, and during the rest of the week 2½ barrels; July 17th, two barrels; July 19th and 20th, one barrel; and four or five days afterward filled the tenth barrel. By this time I had given up the notion of half a barrel being a day's work. You will bear in mind, Mr. Editor, that I was all alone; so that I not only extracted the honey, but also took out the frames, and put them in again.

The room in which I lived all this time was so filled up with barrels and boxes that I feared its breaking down, and was obliged to have some of them removed to another apartment.

This shows what can be done with bees, when there is a good season, and they are properly managed. I am very certain that those twenty double hives, which were mostly young swarms, gave me three times as much honey as they would have given me, had I not extracted the honey. Had there been two strong men, instead of a girl of seventeen years, to take care of more double hives, we might have had a larger number of barrels of honey.

With the honey extracted at home and at our southern apiary (of which my elder sister takes charge), we will have nearly thirty-five (35) barrels of honey, each barrel containing three hundred and seventy (370) pounds. How much box honey we will have, I cannot yet tell; but it will not be a little—perhaps 12,000 or 15,000 pounds. And all this honey was gathered by two hundred and ninety (290) hives—all that my father had left after his spring sales—with their increase, making in all six hundred and fourteen (614) hives. If the month of August should be as favorable for bees as it was last year, we may have another five thousand (5000) pounds of fall honey.

Does not this show that bee-keeping pays? Even if bees did sometimes sting me, so that I got almost discouraged, when the time came again to put on or take off honey boxes, or extract again (which was almost every two days),

I felt very much pleased that I could again fill several barrels. I did not blame my bees for stinging me, and indeed would not have bees which do not sting, else mischievous boys would come and steal the honey.

I have not been absent from my bees a single day for the last few months; but as the honey harvest is over now, I think I shall again get leave to come home.

Of course I can say very little about bee-business, for I only take charge of my apiary during swarming and harvest time; but I am almost convinced that that is the time when the greatest amount of work is required. I have had to work very hard sometimes these last few weeks, but my work has indeed been rewarded.

And now, Mr. Editor, if you should doubt anything stated in my report, I invite you to come out and pay off the visit father and I made you four years ago; and guarantee you will see the largest and nicest amount of extracted and box honey you ever saw in your life.

KATIE GRIMM.

Jefferson, Wis., July 30, 1871.

[For the American Bee Journal.]

A Lady's Comments.

MR. EDITOR:—The August number of the American Bee Journal has made its welcome visit, and its contents read with much interest, as we are anxious to gain all the information we can from experienced bee-keepers—having made bee-culture our business. The more we learn of the habits of the little beauties (the Italians) the more we wish to know.

We have been very successful this season in rearing queens, and having them purely fertilized, and have superseded all our black queens with Italians, which have proved far more prolific than the black queens were.

In early spring we cut out all black and hybrid drone brood, and thus prevented drones from coming out till the black mothers were superseded. We intend to talk Italian bee to our neighbors till we have stocks Italianized for a mile or two around at least.

We have experimented somewhat on non-flying fertilization, and, as others have done before us, "failed." We are a little skeptical on this subject, notwithstanding Mitchell, of Indianapolis, has the secret.* The season, thus far, has been a good one for bees. They are still working, some on white clover and melilot, which latter we deem one of the best plants for honey.

Many thanks to R. M. Argo, of Lowel, Kentucky, for his further warnings on introducing queens safely. We have had trouble to induce our bees to accept strange queens. We finally tried Mrs. Tupper's favorite way of exchanging queens. Taking her for good authority we risked a queen, and following her directions exactly, placed our queen on a frame after the bees had all been shaken off. Placing it with another frame in the new hive, we carried the parent stock some distance away. Waiting an hour or two, we went out to carry more frames to our new queen, and what did we see, but our nice yellow-banded pet curled up on the alighting board dead, and the bees still stinging her!

* Which "secret," as we understand, really belongs to Mr. W. R. King, of Milton, Ky.

Rev. Mr. Anderson, in his communication on page 42 of the Journal for August, after giving an account of his battles with his bees to save a queen attacked by her own colony, asks—"wherein did I fail, or what should I have done under the circumstances?" We think Mr. Anderson should have caged his valuable queen and introduced her into another colony. He does not tell us whether or not he found queen cells in the hive. There might have been a young queen in the hive. We opened a hive a few days since, and found a queen which we pronounced a virgin queen; lifting another frame, we found another queen, the bees caught her, and evidently intended to destroy her. She took wing and flew away. On looking further we found our old queen, which we caught and caged. Being very anxious to save her, as she was one of our best, we introduced her into another colony, but on going to release her we found her dead. Thus there were three queens and three unsealed queen cells in one hive at the same time.

MRS. K. A. D. MORGAN.

Pella, Iowa, Aug. 4, 1871.

[For the American Bee Journal.]

A Few Questions.

MR. EDITOR:—Only to-day has the fact dawned upon our understanding, that if we would longer hold you as our counsellor *something* must be done forthwith. Indeed it was not lack of interest that made us slow to think; but when pleasantly and profitably employed, time flies, and the past year has seemed so short.

We have gained valuable information, while journeying in your company. One thing, though, that we know better every day, does not in the least make us proud; we fully realize how ignorant we still are.

When the Journal comes there is nothing on hand quite as important as searching its pages for something *practical*, that might help us out of a present difficulty.

We are told to remove surplus honey as soon as sealed over. What are we to do when the combs are full for a week, and still it is not sealed?*

* Whenever the combs are filled, or nearly all the cells are full, remove the honey, without delaying for the capping, if the pasturage and the weather continue favorable. Frequent removals under such circumstances, act as a powerful stimulant to incessant labor. If put in glass jars, and the honey should after a time seem to be too thin, it can be thickened without discoloring it, by setting the jars in a vessel of water and exposing them to a boiling temperature for fifteen or twenty minutes. This will also expel any noxious principle or poison it may contain, so that it may be eaten with impunity by those with whose stomachs new honey does not agree.—[ED.

Shall we feed sugar in July and August, if forage is scarce, when the bees have large stores of honey?*

Is lack of honey the cause of perforated cells in brood combs?†

Ten colonies swarmed once each. We followed instructions, and had things our own way in that direction. Just when we supposed all were doing equally well, we found one new swarm greatly reduced in numbers, with uncapped and perforated cells, exposing dead brood. Of course we rushed to the books for light.

The "senior member" declared as his firm belief, that death and destruction was before our bees, in the shape of foul-brood. Indeed, it seemed so sure a case, that the hive was closed for sacrifice. Wiser counsels prevailed, and said hive was carried about half a mile distant, and fed liberally for a few days—which treatment entirely cured *our* foul-brood.

SUE W.

Pacific, Mo.

* Feed sugar syrup whenever forage is scarce or bees cannot fly out from "stress of weather." Feed all young swarms liberally for a week or ten days after hiving, and longer in unfavorable weather. Feed stimulatingly in July and August, however good the forage or ample the stores; but give the queen an opportunity to lay eggs, by extracting the honey from one or more combs, if there be not plenty of empty worker cells in the hive. This will furnish a stock of *young bees* to live over winter and labor in the early spring. Old bees commonly perish in winter, and leave the hive weak in numbers at its close, if young bees be not bred in the fall.—[ED.

† No case of "perforated cells in brood-combs," of sufficient extent to enable us to study it, has ever come under our observation, and we can only guess at the cause. It may possibly arise when the population of a colony, from any cause, becomes suddenly so reduced that the existing brood can no longer be properly attended to and protected.

Young swarms placed in close proximity to strong old stocks, may become depopulated, or rather be prevented from becoming populous, by having its returning bees decoyed to the old stock by the loud humming constantly kept up at its entrance. This, especially, after young bees are hatched, and begin to fly out. We have known a young swarm of Italians thus damaged, and the cause would perhaps have escaped notice, had it not been seen that the old stock, though known to have a fertile black queen, was daily receiving accessions of Italian workers. Placing the hives further apart at once stopped the emigration, and the Italian swarm thenceforward prospered.—[ED.

[For the American Bee Journal.]

More Lady Help Coming.

MR. EDITOR:—Still another lady with "bee on the brain." Truly the sphere of woman's usefulness is enlarging rapidly. It is now three years since I left my western home to visit relatives in Walpole, New Hampshire, and while there I became interested in the "mysteries of bee-keeping," and assisted in the apiary of J. L. Hubbard two seasons. After my return to the west, I concluded to give up my old occupation (that of school teaching) "with its wearisome round of duties," and engage in the more pleasing one of bee-keeping. I purchased five swarms of the common black bees in the old fashioned box hives, and commenced transferring them into the movable frame hive, as soon as the fruit trees were in blossom. Some of the oldest combs I tied in with strong twine, but nearly all of it was held in place by strips of wood on each side. I had good success in transferring, and now have ten swarms of bees. Three of them were artificially made; the others swarmed naturally. The bees are working nicely in boxes, of which the most salable in this vicinity are the square glass ones, that will hold from four to six pounds. The season here has been a fair one, although we have had some rainy weather of late.

I am using a honey extractor manufactured at St. Charles, Illinois, that throws out the honey at a fearful rate; it is quite a wonder to the good people of this village, as it is the first one ever brought here.

ENTHUSIASTIC.

Omro, Wis., July 11, 1871.

[For the American Bee Journal.]

A Report from Illinois.

MR. EDITOR:—I am highly pleased with the Journal, and prize the correspondent's column very highly. It is very pleasing to take up the Journal and get monthly news from our brother bee-keepers, from all parts of our land, learning of their success or failure. This seems to give us new energy at once, for when reading of their success, we are incited to try to rival them, and when we learn of their reverses, it sets us to thinking, lest we fare as bad, or worse.

We well remember, in the spring of 1868, when, of all the stocks put in our cellar the fall previous, we brought out only three weak colonies to their summer stands, how much we were stimulated to greater and greater activity. And we now believe that our success since is partially due to the loss of those colonies then; for we set ourselves to studying with a will, that we might better know our business. We were often asked if we were not going to quit bee-keeping. Our reply generally was that we should yet astonish the natives; at least, we thought we should. The result has been as follows:—from the three surviving colonies above mentioned, and two feeble stocks purchased, we had, in the fall, fourteen stocks and one hundred (100) pounds of box honey.

In the spring of 1870, those fourteen stocks came through in good condition, increased to twenty colonies, and gave me four hundred and forty (440) pounds of surplus honey, mostly in boxes.

The spring of 1871 commenced with twenty colonies, and increased to thirty-one strong stocks; and up to July 10th, the surplus honey yielded was thus:

Box honey........................	377 pounds.
Extracted honey	910 "
Total..........................	1,287 pounds.

Since July 10th, we have not secured any surplus honey, the bees obtaining just enough to keep up breeding quite well. The cause of the present deficiency is owing to the severe drouth, which has prevailed here for nearly six weeks. By actual weight, one of my medium stocks has not gained or lost half a pound in the past four days.

We expect a good autumn, however, from wild flowers, which abound here at that season. We think that in the average of seasons, we could secure as good results, or better than those now reported.

Mr. Editor, we feel glad to think that we did not give up the battle in the spring of 1868. We use movable comb hives, and Italian bees, which in this section prove to be far superior to the blacks. I will close by wishing the Journal and all its readers great success.

F. A. SNELL.

Milledgeville, Ills., Aug. 11, 1871.

[For the American Bee Journal.]

Encouraging Report from Canada.

MR. EDITOR:—Will you be kind enough to send me the August number of the Journal, as my copy has not arrived, and I would not miss it for the yearly subscription, $2.00.

I have been advising my box-hive neighbors to take the Journal, and when they look at the barrels of honey in my cellar, and I tell them that it is the American Bee Journal that gave them to me, they begin to think seriously about subscribing. What is two dollars to pay for the Journal, when we get several extra barrels of honey to replace them?

And now, Mr. Editor, allow me to thank Mr. Adam Grimm, of Jefferson, Wisconsin, for his promptness in shipping me queens. I sent to a queen trader of great repute, last year, for queens, and have not received them yet. Mr. Grimm's came by return of mail, and they are beauties.

This has been a good season for honey, since the white clover came into bloom. But the early part of it was very cold and backward. Bees gathered no honey then, but as most of the hives were well stored with it, breeding went on rapidly; and by the consumption of stores, empty cells were provided for the queen for the deposit of eggs.

I commenced here this spring with six stocks in movable comb hives, and one in a box—seven in all. The box stock never yielded me any surplus until I transferred it, and then only thirty-one pounds in comb, and five by the extractor—thirty-six pounds in all. From my other six stocks, I have taken nine swarms and seventeen hundred and seven (1707) pounds of beautiful honey.

By the way, Mr. Editor, I forgot to say that one of the swarms came from the box, and as I commenced slinging my young stocks as fast as they stored it, the old hive assisted considerably.

I have now sixteen stocks, all in good condition. I sling them every three days. If we should get rain soon, to improve the pasture, I shall get two thousand (2000) pounds. I believe I am in one of the best places in Canada for honey. If Novice was here, he would have to build a tank to hold his honey.

I have not time to give you an account of my apiaries away from home, which I have managed by friends, but will do so at some future time. I have transferred all of the old box hives around here, so bee-keeping is beginning to receive some attention for the last few weeks.

D. A. JONES.

Tecumseth, Ontario, Canada, Aug. 11, 1871.

[For the American Bee Journal.]

The Prindle-Greene Hive.

I do not know whether anybody else ever made one like it or not, or whether it or any part of it is patented or not, nor do I know whether it matters or not. I have no moth-trap, for strong vigorous colonies are the only moth-trap needed, and all moth-trap vendors are either ignoramuses or swindlers. It has no queen nurseries, for all the queen nursery a practical honey raising apiarian needs, is a few small hives large enough to hold two full sized frames, such as he uses in his large hives. In these small or nucleus hives he can raise and keep on hand a few surplus queens for emergencies, hatched from cells made by full *populous* colonies. It has no non-swarming, queen-catching cage, for that is the biggest humbug ever suggested to the bee-keeping public—very little better than clipping the old queen's wings. It can be made a general, though not a universal non-swarmer by a minute's work. It has no outside house or wire to set over it, for that would make it too cumbersome and more costly. It has no permanent bottom board, for if it had we could not pick it up and shake the bees out so easily, after lifting out the frames. In short, it is a plain, simple, common sense hive, divested of all clap-traps, and we do not ask our bee-keeping brethren to "enclose us a dollar." "How are you, dollar?"

It contains ten frames, which are fifteen inches long and thirteen deep. The breeding apartment is "double-cased," with a dead-air space the thickness of a plasterer's lath. The outside case or board runs back beyond the breeding apartment, furnishing surplus honey room for either frames or boxes (in our market boxes are decidedly preferable). The back end is of single inch stuff, and is hinged on, so that we can swing it open, and slip the boxes *into the hive* from behind. This surplus honey apartment has a permanent bottom board, so that we can lift the hive, honey boxes and all up off of the main bottom board. And again, this honey apartment is separated from the breeding apartment by a glass or mostly glass partition. When we wish the bees to go to work in the rear boxes, we lift the partition out, and slip the boxes up to within one-fourth of an inch of the frames of the main hive. The rear ends of the frames hang on a piece of hard wood, which is about an inch square, and is dove-tailed into the sides of the hive, and the glass partition slips *under* this cross piece. Besides the front entrance, there is a small entrance on one or both sides of the hive, which may be opened in the busy season, to let the bees enter right at the mouth of the rear honey boxes. I say *rear* honey boxes, because there are honey boxes on top also. But instead of using a honey board, we simply tack a narrow thin strip across on the under side of the upper honey boxes.

Now this is about all there is of it, without going into tedious detail, which I do not propose to do—even for "a dollar." It may not be so everywhere, but I do know that a double-cased hive is needed in this latitude and climate. Our changeable weather here, and I believe everywhere else, prevents bees in thin hives from attempting to breed, when they ought to be increasing fast, and *are* increasing in "double-cased" hives. It is only little less than nonsense to talk about housing bees in winter, particularly if one has many of them. I believe I have as good a double-walled winter bee house, made for the purpose, as could be made, and after three trials I shall henceforward winter my bees on their summer stands. I have left a few colonies out every winter, and even in their hives they always have come through in better condition than those with extra care in the over-ground cellar. If I am fully settled in any one thing, it is against winter housing. What we want is a good, handy "wintering" hive—one in which bees may breed nearly all winter, and come through strong *early in the spring*, so as to gather the early honey, which is much the best, and which we mostly lose. The posterior honey box room in this hive, when filled with some good non-conducting absorbent, makes an excellent protection against the severe northwest winds of winter and early spring. [Some of our eastern bee-keeping friends will no doubt be surprised that, in this county, September is generally our best honey month. I have had bees work till the 20th of October. All considered, this, I think, is one of the best countries for bees that I have ever seen.]

My friend Hawley Prindle, the principal inventor, joins me in asking a general criticism of our hive, which some of our friends call "The Hive."

J. W. Greene.

Chillicothe, Mo., July 14, 1871.

[For the American Bee Journal.]

Movable Comb Hives.

As I have seen no definite answer to questions about movable comb hives before Mr. Langstroth's patent, I will try to answer them in as few words as possible.

Francis Huber, of Geneva, over seventy-five years ago, used a frame hive, with four sides resting on the bottom board; each comb could be examined on both sides, and returned to its place without injury.

The Germans used movable combs, suspended by a bar at the top. Each comb was removed by cutting the edges from the sides of the hive.

Mr. Langstroth combined the top suspension of the Germans with the four-sided frame of Huber, added a shallow chamber of his own invention, and made a more practical hive than any previously used, in 1852.

The triangular comb-guide has since been introduced by others.

The immovable bottom board, portico, moth-traps, &c., of Mr. Langstroth's first hive, are not now generally used.

Why it is necessary to make an exact imitation to be called a Huber hive, and is not necessary to make an exact imitation to be called a Langstroth hive, is a mystery not yet explained.

H. D. Miner.

Washington Harbor, Wis., July 8, 1871.

☞ The frames of the original Huber hive, as it came from his hands, were in reality what are now called vertical sections; but were hinged together at one side so that though they could be opened like the leaves of a book, they could not be lifted out and returned. A modification of it for that purpose was subsequently attempted by Morlot, Simon, Semlitsch, Hofenfels, and others; none of whom, however, succeeded in producing any valuable result. So far as practical bee-culture is concerned, that which is now conceived to have been a movable *frame*, was and remained a *fixture*.

The modern Greeks, centuries ago, used close-fitting slats or bars for the tops of their hives, to which the combs were attached, and which could be separately lifted out, when all happened to work right. But when that did not so happen, the entire top with its attachments could only be torn out by force, and might also be forced back again. It was half a step in advance, but there it stopped.

It was only when Dzierzon took the thing in hand and constructed a *hive* in which bars could be conveniently used for the support of combs, and these could be taken out, replaced, or interchanged, that bee-keepers were enabled to avail themselves of the advantages which such an arrangement presented. Dzierzon does not claim the invention or even the introduction of bars, but simply that he has made them available in practical bee culture. But he does claim the invention of a *hive* by means of which those bars are made available and useful. The merit of this invention is universally conceded to him. If he had *patented* it, the case might be different. He has never introduced *frames* in his apiary; and where the *piling system* prevails, as it does in Germany, and will probably to a large extent wherever land and lumber are dear, bars are likely to be preferred and retained, at least till they learn to make frames in a simpler and cheaper manner than now.

When Mr. Langstroth took up the subject, he well knew what Huber had done, and saw wherein he had failed—failing, possibly, only because he aimed at nothing more than constructing an observing hive, suitable for his purposes. Mr. L.'s object was other and higher. He aimed at making *frames* movable, interchangeable, and practically serviceable in bee-culture. Dzierzon had effected this for the bar, by devising and constructing a *hive*, enabling him to employ slats or bars in a manner in which they had not been employed before. But of his operations in Germany, Mr. Langstroth was entirely ignorant, and remained so till long after his own devices were perfected, and a patent applied for. Nor could Mr. L. have derived any benefit from the Dzierzon hive, further than as giving him, perhaps, incidental encouragement to persevere in working out his own conceptions. The fundamental ideas of the two men were essentially different. Dzierzon desired to and did construct a *hive* in which the bar or slat could be advantageously used for comb attachment. Mr. Langstroth aimed at and succeeded in constructing a *frame*, and devising a mode of applying it by which it could be rendered of service in *any form of hive* that might be desirable.

Nobody, before Mr. Langstroth, ever succeeded in devising a mode of making and using a movable frame that was of any practical value in bee-culture, or could be introduced even in partial, much less in general, use. *Now*, every boy makes them, and the principle is adopted everywhere, either openly or covertly. What has brought this about?

Neither a bottom board, fixed or movable, nor portico, nor definite form of hive or special shape or size of frame, are embraced in the Langstroth patent. These or any of them may be formed and used as the option of the apiarian may suggest. The triangular blocks for enlarging or contracting the entrance are, however, included in the patent; and for that special purpose they have not yet been superseded by anything better, whether or not they be regarded as of any value as worm decoys.

An exact imitation of the Huber hive is indispensably necessary to entitle it to the *name*, because, as Blackstone might say, its essentiality consists in its entirety. It has a definite form and structure, which, what is called the Langstroth hive, has not. The essential feature of the movable frame—movable horizontally *and* vertically—adapts it for practical service, in any form of hive that is itself of any use; and therefore no precise or exact imitation is required, necessary, or indeed practicable.

The "mystery not yet explained" is, why Mr. Langstroth's claims and merits are perpetually carped at and questioned, while all "imitations," and *infringements* of his patent—even the most palpable and gross—pass the same critical ordeal without cavil or challenge! *That* is the *mystery*, and the *marvel!*—[ED.

[For the American Bee Journal.]

"The American Hive."—"Fertility of Queens."

On page 268 of the June number of the Journal, Novice says—"of all the foolish things about a bee-hive, we believe a movable side is the most so"—having special reference to the American hive.

Although some of his remarks in the article from which the above words are taken, were open to criticism, yet we disclaim any intention of reviewing them for that purpose, or to defend the hive he so mercilessly attacks; our sole object in quoting them being to ask him how the frames can be removed from the American hive without removing the side?

The frames being close fitting at the tops, some fourteen inches in depth, and well glued down by the bees, the idea of lifting them out and replacing, involves a fearful state of things. If the frames were not made close fitting at the top, and did not exceed ten inches in depth, the lifting process would be just the thing.

A few years since, we had several American hives made, with a door in place of the movable side, securing the top of the frames and backs by means of a cleat nailed between them. This worked well, and disturbed the bees much less than the movable side. Still, there are objections to it, which possibly Novice has overcome; therefore, we request him, in behalf of the thousands upon thousands who use this hive, to advise us through the Journal in regard to their use. He certainly has no reason to fear his article will be tamperd with by *our* publisher.

Last March, a gentleman brought us a hive of bees, which he desired to exchange for one that would swarm, saying that this stock had been in the family for twelve years, and never during all that time had cast a swarm; although it was always rich in stores and apparently prosperous. After setting the hive in the bee-house, we found that it was filled with honey, but sadly short in bees. We thereupon stimulated them faithfully until April 16th, when, very much to our disgust, we found that the queen had become too lazy, too old, or too aristocratic to lay eggs freely. Taking her between thumb and finger, we prepared her for burial, and introduced a fine Italian queen in her place, stimulating as before. The change was almost magical, and on June 30th, we found eleven queen cells, and the hive packed from top to bottom with "yellow-jackets." Removing all but three of the cells, and putting them in nucleus hives, we divided the stock into three, giving each of the two new swarms a queen cell, and leaving one in the old hive, which also contained the old queen. Our reason for this was that we suspected the bees had two objects in view when they reared those cells—to swarm, and to supersede the old queen, she being then nearly four years of age. A subsequent examination proved this latter surmise true, as we found the young queen engaged in laying eggs on one comb, and her aged mother performing similar duty upon another. Holding a comb in each hand, and watching the two queens deposit their eggs, we thought, with a curious feeling of partial distrust, of the many obsolete theories that have been promulgated from time to time; and felt that much remains yet to be learned upon points long since regarded as practically settled. A few days after this, the old lady took her final departure.

Our object in writing this is to show the wonderful fertility of this aged queen, down even to the latest moment of her life, having in a period of two months and fourteen days, raised a stock containing not more than one quart of bees to a very populous colony, furnishing bees enough for three good swarms; and also to show the no less wonderful instinct of the queen, or the worker bees, which realized and provided for her final exit, while she was at the height of fertility.

GEO. S. SILSBY.

Winterport, Me., Aug. 5, 1871.

[For the American Bee Journal.]

Plain Box Hives.

I have some experience in bee-keeping, and have used and seen in use, a variety of hives, and have come to the conclusion that there is no better hive for the mass who are not posted in the mysteries of the art (and they are the great majority of bee-keepers in this country), than the simple box hive, of about two thousand cubic inches capacity, for the summer and winter accommodation of the bees, so constructed as to perfectly protect the bees from all wet, and as far as practicable from the extreme heat of the summer sun; and if that is properly done, it will sufficiently protect them from the winter's cold, and prepare them for remaining on the summer's stand the year round. As the form of the hive makes little or no difference to the bees (if not run into any extreme), it may be so constructed as to afford room to apply boxes enough to the sides, or top, or both, as to give the bees an opportunity to work the season through without any change of boxes, or disturbing them at all during the working season. The aggregate capacity of the boxes may be about sixty pounds of honey in the comb, which will be quite as much as a swarm will ordinarily put up in surplus boxes.

I have a number of hives constructed upon the above plan, and stocked with bees, and at the close of the season may be able to give to the public, through the Journal, the result of my experiments. There is no patent behind the curtain, for I have none, and never design to have, even if I succeed in getting up the best hive ever invented.

D. LATHROP.

La Salle, Ills., Aug. 7, 1871.

☞ No form of hive which does not provide for or admit of the ready use of the honey emptying machine, can ever again find favor with progressive bee-keepers.—[ED.

[For the American Bee Journal.]

Gallup's Reminder.

MR. EDITOR:—This is to inform you that we are still on this footstool, and up to our eyes in honey. The season has been an extra good one, and in due time we shall report.

Tell those anxious folks not to borrow too much trouble about Gallup's baiting his hook too late. Let them hold on to their dollars; they may want them to purchase lumber with, to make one of my new hives, when I come to give a full description, as I certainly intend to do in time for next season's operations.

I have too much business on hand to allow me to write for the Journal now; but have any quantity of hash cooking for its readers. As soon as we can find time to put it in shape, they shall have it.

E. GALLUP.

Orchard, Iowa, Aug. 7, 1871.

[For the American Bee Journal.]

Proper Size of Surplus Honey Boxes.

MR. EDITOR:—In common with many others, I like to see the large box question agitated in your columns. Messrs. C. O. Perrine & Co. have set the ball rolling in the right direction. We know that bees will store more honey in large boxes, but the small ones sell more readily and at a higher price, and bee-keepers will stick to them until as good a market is found for large boxes.

This is a question that interests all engaged in the honey trade; and we want every bee-keeper to sit down in some quiet corner of his domicile and write to the Journal his experience upon his methods of obtaining surplus honey.

My own experience leads me to advocate the use of small frames, either in single or double sets, upon the top, or upon the sides of the hive. Small frames have all the advantages of large boxes. When a frame is filled with honey, it can be removed and an empty one inserted. This small frame plan, and the plan of elevating a box nearly full and setting an empty one under it, are the very best ways to keep bees steadily at work.

After reading Mr. Perrine's article in the Journal, and after a personal correspondence with him, I am tempted to ask, and will ask, if there is only one C. O. Perrine & Co. in the United States? This Company certainly show great enterprize in making honey an everyday article for the table all the year round. A few more companies of the same stamp would greatly stimulate the cultivation of the honey bee. The bulk of our honey is stored in the space of two or three months. If this could be delivered at proper times all the year round, honey lovers would buy, regardless of the season.

Our New York city friends tell us that honey, like strawberries and other small fruits, have their season. Now, by looking at the market reports, we find the season for small fruits lasts the entire year; for as soon as the supply from the field is exhausted, we fall back upon the preserved, dried, or canned fruits. The skill of man has been applied to the production of hardy fruits, like the apple, which, with proper care, are preserved in the natural state until new apples are put upon the market in the spring. But, should the apples fail, or the price become too high for ordinary purses, in such case we fall back upon the dried fruit. In handling honey we have an advantage over fruits—we do not have to dry it for preservation; but any day during the year it can be put upon the table, as clear and as fine flavored as when stored by the busy bee in the height of the honey season. Should it assert its freedom from adulteration by becoming candied, behold the transformation which a little heat produces—it becomes as transparent as ever.

Now all that is necessary is to produce the honey in shapes to suit various tastes, and organize companies that will place it before the consumer at proper times, and there is no danger of honey becoming a drug upon the market.

Why, Mr. Editor, I know persons, even in the country, who are very fond of honey, yet rarely get a taste between the two ends of the year. How and when, and in what shape shall we supply these honey lovers? These are questions which we hope to see agitated through the columns of the American Bee Journal. Every bee-keeper is interested in the discussion. Who speaks next?

SCIENTIFIC.

[For the American Bee Journal.]

Honey Extractor and Strainer Combined.

One of the most convenient articles in an apiary, large or small, is a strainer made of tin. It is in two parts—the top, say twenty inches square and ten inches deep; large enough to take in the largest size frame on the four sides. Let the bottom be made of fine perforated tin or zinc, which is made by machinery. The bottom part is made five or six inches deep, and large enough to allow the top to fit in about one inch—a flange being made to prevent the top from slipping in too far.

In the lower part, close to the bottom of one side, a metal faucet may be soldered in, to draw off the strained honey. Legs two inches high, also of tin, at the four corners, are convenient. The cover of the top should have a flange all around, to fit inside, about an inch wide. This is convenient, as when you wish to lift off the strainer you can turn over the cover, place the strainer on it, and it catches the dripping honey.

The writer has found this such a convenience that he could hardly dispense with it. Frames of honey for family use, and bits of comb, can all be kept in such a vessel, accessible at any time, and well protected from bees and flies.

To extract honey from the frames, place them against the sides, with strips between, say an inch from the sides, and suspend the whole concern by four strong cords some eight or ten feet from the ceiling, and twist it up as near as it will go, and then give it a whirl back. My experience is, that after a few turns my combs are clear enough of honey, and it runs through the strainer ready to be drawn off.

Where there are *many* frames, the whole should be suspended by stout galvanized wire, such as clothes-lines are made of, with a swivel at the top to be hooked or screwed to the ceiling. To give a rotary motion, a board must be fastened to the bottom, with a spindle seven or eight inches long, passing into a hole, loosely, about an inch, leaving space between the bottom of the board and the fixture into which the spindle passes, of six or seven inches. Now, just as a boy passes a cord through the spindle of his top and winds it up, so here—only that the cord must be fastened, and the machine turned whirligig fashion.

The strainer is a very great convenience in a family, wherein combs can be kept and cut as wanted. Its use as an extractor, though seemingly complicated in the explanation, is yet very simple, and will be found very easy to one who will make the trial.

D. C. MILLETT.

Holmesburg, Pa., July, 1871.

Although nothing is more simple in theory and practice than the history and care of bees, it yet requires constant and unremitted attention, if we aim at either instruction or profit. Can anything be well done and to advantage without these?

[For the American Bee Journal.]

The Wire Cloth House.

TO AMATEUR.

DEAR SIR:—I have read with much interest your article in the July number of the Bee Journal, touching upon several subjects, among the rest a description of your wire house, in which you empty your frame honey, and have your queens fertilized. To the apiarian, these two items are of much interest at the present time; at least, the latter is one in which many of us are exceedingly anxious to learn *how* to have our queens fertilized by selected drones. I am in hopes others may be as successful as you appear to have been.

By the time this will reach your eye, a more extensive experience in this part of our business will enable you to give us the results of your labors, and I for one, will be much obliged if you will inform us how many queens you have had desirably fertilized in your house, and the number of failures. If you are the lucky chap that has found out THE PLAN, won't there be rejoicing among us? Well, I guess there will; and Novice's new hat will soar up, even if he has to run into the back yard from his wife, to give it a hoist. But I think my queens and drones would spend most of their time in fruitlessly bumping their heads against the wire cloth. Yours,

L. JAMES.

Atlanta, Ills., July 14, 1871.

[For the American Bee Journal.]

Bee Stings.

MR. EDITOR:—In reading the "Bee Journal," I find in nearly every issue a remedy for *bee stings*, but do not remember of seeing spirits of turpentine recommended.

I find it the most efficient remedy I can use. One drop will be found sufficient to deaden the pain of an ordinary sting, and stop the swelling, if applied at once.

If stung around the neck or mouth so much that the poison reaches the stomach, a few drops taken in oil will give immediate relief.

The hands are most exposed (as all bee-keepers *should* own a good bee hat); consequently, a nerve or vein is often stung. In such a case, extract the sting at once, apply the turpentine to the wound, bathe the wrist, the elbow, and the under part of the arm with the same, and in a few moments you will feel no inconvenience.

I have used it for over ten years, and always found it reliable.

OLD FOGY.

Lake City, July 10, 1871.

Though colony after colony of honey bees have dwelt, in uninterrupted succession, in the same apiary, their instinct is not improved, nor their reflective powers enlarged.—MRS. GRIFFITH.

[For the American Bee Journal.]

Alley's Rejoinder.

The Journal for August is at hand, one day ahead of time, as it was received on the 31st of July. I find my name handled rather roughly, and feel that I must make a reply to the statement made by Dr. Austin, on page 33. In the first place, I have not had his money or order on my books for a year. If I remember right, his order came to hand late last fall, and I gave him no encouragement that I could send him a queen. I offered to return his money, but he never called for it. I do not deny that I promised him his queen as many times as he says; but I can say that he was not oftener disappointed than myself. I struck out for two hundred (200) queens in May, but did not get fifty (50), as a cold storm set in and lasted three days. In some, nuclei queens had to be started several times before I got any. Now, I wrote Dr. Austin the reason why I did not send his queen, and the only reply I have seen, I found in the Journal for August. I wonder whether the Doctor thinks that his order was the only one sent in for queens? But he received his queen before his statement appeared in print, and I hope this will do him good. I wish also to give notice to others who have sent me money, and do not now want queens, to send for it; and if I do not send it back in due time, I will agree to have them report me through the Journal. Customers will understand that I cannot raise a thousand queens in a few days. I must have months. Nor can I fill orders in rotation. My business is to raise queens, and accommodate as many customers as possible. One man has ordered a hundred (100) queens. Now, suppose I fill his order at once, and let the smaller ones go. How could I do business in that way? A man who has sent in an order for ten or more queens, finds it most convenient to have a few sent at a time, thus dividing the lot.

I must also suit my own convenience in shipping queens. Queens that must be four or five days in the mail bags, should be sent on Mondays or Tuesdays. When they are not ready to go on those days, those orders must be passed till another Monday comes round, and the queens shipped to parties who can get them in two or three days. And then, when the next Monday comes round, if no queens are ready to ship, or the weather proves unfavorable for fertilizing, they must again wait another week. And so it goes. I wish my customers would understand, that I have been doing the best I could, under the circumstances, to fill their orders seasonably. Most of my customers treat me courteously, and give me all the time I desire to ship queens in. Now and then, it is true, I get a rough letter from a patron; and such correspondents usually wind up with "yours respectfully," but really, I cannot see it.

Well, now, one word about the season. I do not know how other breeders have found it, but this has been the hardest season here for queen breeding that I have experienced. I have two hundred and fifty nucleus hives, and have fed them continually since the last day of April. I trust no one will think that we shall get very rich this year by raising queens. If we can get a living, and get back the money we have paid for bees, sugar, &c., we shall find no fault. I have on my books the names of two hundred and thirty-eight (238) customers ordering queens, and have no fear that Dr. Austin's statement will affect my business in the least, many of my customers returning their thanks for being accommodated so soon, in so unpropitious a season. When a man sends me my advertised price for a queen, and says he needs one to supply a queenless colony, he shall have one if I have one.

My friend Silsby speaks of my "self-reliance and pluck." Well, if a man is foolish enough to put his experience of several years into a bee-hive that he knows must work well, and will write articles to bring it into notice, thus setting himself up as a target for people to shoot at, who think they know more than he does, he must just know whether he has the "pluck" to back up what he says, or else he had better not try his hand at the business.

Halifax 2d got his gun off in a hurry, I think. As his article plainly shows his ignorance of what is going on in the bee-hive, and of what is published in the Journal, let me inform him that Mr. Alley is not at all apprehensive that Novice will hit him a rap across the knuckles, but is confident that if he should at any time do so, it would be done in a gentlemanly way. Halifax thinks that there ought to be a fair trial given to the hives introduced, and that the one which proves to be the best, should have the credit. Have I not made this offer to the Journal within a few months? Why did not Halifax pass along his "top-box" hive? No man took up my challenge, but Mr. Langstroth requested Rev. E. Van Slyke, of West Farms, N. Y., to send for the hive and test it. We shall no doubt hear from him when he gets ready to report. I have not yet heard a word about it, and do not wish to, till he has thoroughly tested the hive. But I have reports from other parties, and as I do not wish to "blow my own horn," I will let them report. The readers of the Journal well know that I have always given Mr. Langstroth credit for all that is due him. I use the Langstroth frame in my hive, and Mr. L. has the credit of the frame.

Halifax seems to have "top-box" on the brain, and wants them on top and nowhere else. Well, who objects to his putting them where he pleases? And should he not be willing to let other people enjoy the same liberty, by placing them on the sides, if they prefer doing so? He charges us with blowing our own horn. Had he read the Journal as carefully as he should, he would know that the last time we described our hive, we were invited to do so by the editor. Let me advise Mr. H., when he writes again, to post himself and then pitch in. Let him examine our advertisements. He will not find that we ever advertised a "moth-trap," or any kind of "trap." We do not sell or use anything of the kind. When he lets us hear from him again, will he let us know wherein the Bay State hive is not as good as it has been represented. Then we shall have something tangible to talk about. We have kept bees for several years, and have written more or less for the American Bee Journal, but have never spent our time in blowing up patent hives. When we can find nothing more interesting to the readers of the Journal, we do not write.

H. ALLEY.

Wenham, Mass., Aug. 2, 1871.

[For the American Bee Journal.]

From New Jersey to New Hampshire.

Since last writing for the Journal I have removed to this place, and being busily occupied, have found but little leisure for writing.

The section of New Jersey where I was located did not suit me, as the coast winds were so troublesome that I could get very little nice honey in the spring and early summer. A large quantity of buckwheat honey may be obtained there, but is not very salable.

The best honey localities we find, on reading the Journal, are not adjacent to the coast. Cool weather in the spring, and dry weather during most of May and June, prevented an early yield of honey, though breeding was carried on pretty well.

The severe drouth of last year, followed by a dry May and June, cut off most of the clover crop, except what was in the hay-fields. Bees commenced storing honey rapidly the latter part of June, and when the hay was cut early in July the storing of surplus honey ceased. In a short time my bees stored an average of perhaps thirty pounds to each good swarm. One colony stored nearly sixty pounds. All of it was removed with a machine.

In the last half of July none but the largest stocks gathered more than enough to supply their daily wants. Then the second crop of clover, golden rod, and other fall blossoms, caused better times.

In feeding bees in the fall I have been best pleased with upright tin feeders, holding about five pounds each. These are supplied with a float, and their inner sides are coated with wax. I like to fill them every day until the bees have enough, placing them in the cap. When necessary to feed in winter, I have used glass fruit cans with good success. By filling them full, tying on a thin strainer cloth, then inverting quickly and setting them on top of the frames or over a hole in the honey board, and covering with the cap. I do not advise waiting till winter, as the later feeding is put off, after the failure of natural supplies, the greater the danger of injury to the bees. A few years ago I made fifty Beebe feeders for spring use, and found them very good for feeding syrup, but have never made use of them for feeding meal and water, as recommended.

Last spring I tried one of Mr. Peck's automatic feeders, and it seemed to be a very good thing to use in moderate weather. I was particularly pleased with some of its features. It has no wood about it to shrink and swell, or sour. It is consequently easily cleansed thoroughly. Then it is absolutely impossible for bees to get drowned or daubed in it, when properly adjusted. I intended to make one on the same principle, but of large size, to try it this season, but have not had time or use for it. I bought a Harrison feeder when they first came round, and used it twice. The first time a little sediment in the feed choked the strainer, and the next time the feed ran through in a much larger stream than was useful or desirable just then.

J. L. HUBBARD.

Walpole, N. H., Aug. 5, 1871.

[For the American Bee Journal.]

Mr. Alley in Business Transactions.

MR. EDITOR:—Please find enclosed the amount due for another year's subscription to the Journal, and accept my heartiest wishes for its increasing prosperity.

I beg leave to avail myself of this opportunity to say that I was both surprised and concerned to find two severe strictures in the August number of the Journal, on Mr. Alley, of Wenham, Mass. Of course I know nothing of the particular points in these two cases, but as I have had several transactions with Mr. Alley, and in every instance have found him fair, upright, and, indeed, must say very *liberal*, I deem it no less a duty than a privilege to give him the benefit of this counter statement.

The hive I bought of Mr. Alley is, in my humble judgment, a model of neatness and excellence in its construction; and whilst I have neither the wish nor the ability to speak of its *comparative* merit, I can only say that I am delighted with it now that the bees have gone fairly to work, and are filling the boxes with honey equal in point of beauty to any I ever saw, the combs being of unusual and extraordinary thickness.

Like others, I have experienced some delay in the receipt of Italian queens ordered from Mr. Alley, but I was persuaded that this delay was unavoidable, and due entirely to the causes so fully and frankly stated in his private letters and in his published statements. And as my patience and confidence has just now been rewarded by the receipt of three beautiful queens, so I hope, "by the same token," that Dr. Austin's longer probation has been crowned by the same happy result; and that we shall hear of a pleasant reconciliation in the next number of the Journal.

We have had a fine honey season in this region in spite of many adverse circumstances, such as the failure of the locust and fruit blossoms, for which we were fully compensated by the abundance and richness of the white clover. From twenty-six stocks I had only eighteen swarms, but even this was far above the general average.

B. J. BARBOUR.

Gordonsville, Va., Aug. 11, 1871.

Honey was one of the first articles of human nourishment.

[For the American Bee Journal.]

Experience of a Tennesseean.

MR. EDITOR:—As it is very seldom that I see anything in your valuable Journal, from this section of the country, and as I have never before dared to intrude upon your columns, I will by your permission, give you the experience of one who has kept bees all his life, upon the old fogy plan. As I have stated, I have had bees in my yard for twenty-five years, in the old box hives, sometimes thirty or forty, sometimes only eight or ten. Sometimes they would swarm, and sometimes they would not.

Last fall there came to my house a vendor of bee-gums, patented by a Mr. Mitchell, of Indiana, who made very earnest efforts to sell me a right for twenty dollars, to manufacture and use the hive. He was truly a very smooth tongued fellow, spoke fluently of his moth-trap, and praised the many advantages of his gum. I examined it and told him I did not like it, and at last got clear of him. But in about ten days he came again, told me that he had sold rights to Mr. A. and Mr. B., and did not wish to leave the neighborhood until he sold me one. I finally bought a right, and he was to come over next day and transfer a swarm for me. True to promise over he came, and put a swarm in, tying the combs in with rag strings. I had the gum set at the proper place, paid him his twenty dollars, and off he went. I watched my bees very closely, and thought they were doing fine. So about the first of March, I thought it was time I was looking at my bees. I protected my face, opened my Buckeye door and made an effort to draw out the bees, honey and all. But, alas! it was "no go." I found everything glued fast with propolis. I pulled and shook until I got the bees most fearfully mad. Then I retired a short distance, called to my aid a hatchet and a large chisel, and by their help I got the bees out. By this time I had received five or six stings, and my ardor on the bee question had considerably abated.

But, Mr. Editor, luckily for me, I had by some means, got hold of one of your Journals, which I read very carefully, for the bee fever was beginning to run high in the country, and I was anxious to learn something about the business. In that Journal I found that two-thirds of your correspondents were in favor of the Langstroth hive. I purchased seven rights; for, mark you, I had eight stands when the Buckeye bee-man came along. He had put one swarm in a Buckeye, which left me with seven in box hives. I had seen in your Journal instructions how to transfer, so I got my better half to assist and at it we went. Instead of tying combs in with rags and strings, I used small strips of thin wood, two on a side. So we got the seven transferred, and I think we made a good job of it.

I also saw in your Journal that the Italian bee was highly spoken of, so I strained a point and bought a queen. I introduced her according to directions, found all right, and in just twenty-eight days, had the pleasure of seeing the yellow fellows sporting in the sun. The first of April found me with eight colonies, seven in Langstroth hives and one in a Buckeye. My colony of Italians being a new thing, my next effort was to get more Italian queens. In order to accomplish this, I transferred my Italian queen to a black stock, destroying the black queen first, of course. In a few days the unqueened stock had started ten queen cells, and in ten days I found all ready to come out. I then went through all my black colonies and destroyed the black queens; and cut out all my queen cells but two to replace them. In a couple of days after inserting a queen cell in each, I examined the queens again, and found three of the cells all right and two destroyed. I was, however, satisfied with my experiment.

To-day, Mr. Editor, I have sixteen strong colonies, all in Langstroth hives, save one; and all Italianized, save four; and I have sold four hundred and sixteen pounds of as nice clover honey as NOVICE ever saw, at thirty cents a pound. I know that Novice, Gallup, Quinby, or any of the larger lights, could have done better; but I think I have had wonderful success.

So far as the Italians are concerned, I like them very much. They are perfect beauties and good workers. But from my very short experience I think the hybrids, as honey-gatherers, a little ahead of the blacks or Italians. But, oh gracious! they are perfect hyenas for fight!

It would afford me great pleasure, Mr. Editor, to see in your valuable Journal some thoughts from our old Tennessee bee-men. There is a Hall, a Davis and a Hamlin, who have grown gray in the service, and would both interest and instruct. Let us hear from you, good friends! Give us your thoughts, and give them freely, upon the various topics involved in bee-culture.

Fearing that I have trespassed, I will close, by wishing you and the American Bee Journal a prosperous 1871, and by subscribing myself,

THE SMALLEST NOVICE.

Tennessee, July, 1871.

[For the American Bee Journal.]

West Tennessee as a Honey Region.

MR. EDITOR:—Seeing the inquiry for a good honey district, in the July number of the Journal, and knowing the general wish for communications from the South, I thought whilst renewing my subscription, I would give you my experience for the past two years.

The year 1869, was a very good one for honey here, and as I saw bees generally doing so well, I purchased two colonies in Walker's movable comb hives, in January, 1870, procured Mr. Langstroth's invaluable book, and with the help of the American Bee Journal, hoped I might be one of those bound for success. That year (1870) was called the poorest one in a long period. A snow storm about the middle of April killed all bloom, and most effectually stopped swarming. I had two swarms previous to that time, which I saved, by giving them a comb of honey, each, from my old stocks.

Up to the first of July, my bees did little more than make a living. Still, I received thirty pounds surplus honey in boxes from the old stocks, and my swarms filled their hives. In 1871, the bees began swarming on the 22d of March. All first and second swarms have filled their hives—two-story Langstroth's, which I have used for this season's increase. I now number twenty hives. Having all new comb, I have used my Hruschka but little. On Monday, June 5th, I extracted the honey from the upper story of one hive, and on the following Monday found it full again, and a considerable quantity capped.

My bees are natives, except one colony of Italians.

A man near here boxed a fugitive swarm about the first of April, and they have increased to five.

If from the above your correspondent thinks this a good honey district, he will find plenty of North Carolinans to welcome him.

10 S. E.

West Tennessee, July 25, 1871.

[For the American Bee Journal.]

Bee Notes from Wayne County, Ohio.

MR. EDITOR :—I am a constant reader of the Bee Journal, and when welcoming its visits, often feel like throwing in my mite with the rest, having bee on the brain at times, like others. I began bee-keeping some years ago (won't say just how many). In 1870, I was the possessor of three stocks—one Italian and two blacks. During that summer my colonies increased to twelve, three Italians and nine hybrid stocks. I wintered them in-doors, without losing a single stock. Last spring I started in good earnest to Italianize them, and increase them by artificial swarming, which I regard as much the better plan, when properly performed. I have now thirty-five stocks, nearly all Italians.

I stimulated in early spring, so that my bees were in good condition when the swarming season began. The present season has not been more than an average one for bees in these parts, owing to the drouth in May and the changeable weather in June. Black bees swarmed but very little this season.

Well, Mr. Editor, and readers of the Journal, I have two Italian stocks to which I paid a little more attention than to the rest, and will give you a statement of my success with them.

One of them gave me eight artificial swarms, (Italians) good and strong enough to survive the coming winter, and each worth fifteen dollars—total from this colony $120. The other gave me three swarms—together worth $45, and seventy pounds of choice box honey, worth, at twenty-five cents per pound $17.50—making a total profit from the second of $62.50, and a grand total from the two of one hundred and eighty-two dollars and fifty cents ($182.50) !

If any of the readers of the Journal have beaten this this season, let us have the record, and oblige E. J. WORST.

New Pittsburgh, Ohio, Aug. 7, 1871.

[For the American Bee Journal.]

Bees in Alleghany County, Maryland.

MR. EDITOR :—As I do not see that anybody is writing for the Journal from this part of the country, I thought I would send you a short letter showing how the bees are getting on here. Mine did pretty well all the fore part of the season, but are not doing anything now, scarcely getting enough to support themselves. My first swarm came off on the 27th of April, and I had to feed it about two weeks, as the weather was so cold here that they could not go out to get anything.

I am using the Buckeye hive. Some say the chambers will stick after the swarm has been in for awhile ; but I say it will not, for I had a swarm in one for about two months, and it has not stuck yet.* But still I do not see why it was patented, unless it was for the *moth-trap ;* and as for that, I advise all bee-keepers to keep it out of their apiaries, as it is more of a hiding place for moths than a trap. I find the best trap is to keep the colonies strong, and then I am not much troubled with moths.

There are plenty of "old fogies," as they are called, in Alleghany county, and they cannot be persuaded to do anything. When I advised one to get a frame hive, he said—"it costs too much," and when I told him he would get his money back again if he would take proper care of his bees—"I will have trouble with them then, and so it will be all the same !" I let him off for I thought there was no use to talk to him.

About one-third of the people in Alleghany county are bee-keepers of their own sort. They have their bees in nail kegs, flour barrels, and various other things imaginable. One man had his hives in grass a foot high. He acknowledged that it was wrong, but had no time to look after them. Three years ago there was hardly a frame hive in this county, and little or no attention was paid to bees ; but now improved bee-keeping is gradually increasing, and after awhile I think Alleghany county may take rank with other counties in this business.

I have one stock of Italians, and intend Italianizing my whole apiary. I am so far the only one here who has any Italians, and it will consequently be a difficult matter for me to keep them pure. Can any person give me a safe plan for fertilizing queens in confinement. There are many plans given, but I do not like to try them, because so many older bee-keepers than I am have failed, and I am but a boy. I would rather take the advice of older ones than try experiments myself.

A BEGINNER.

Cumberland, Md., Aug. 8, 1871.

* Further trial, in a good honey season, will effectually settle that point.—[ED.

If a man intends to keep bees, he must, in the first place, make the hives in the very best manner ; by this we mean, of good materials and of good workmanship. A hive badly joined by an awkward carpenter, is worse than a hollow tree.

[For the American Bee Journal.]

Bee-keeping in the West.

Mr. Editor :—I thought that perhaps a little scribbling from this part of beedom would give you and the readers of the Journal some insight to Iowa bee-keeping. I can say, with not a little pride, that I have paid my *footing* for a short time and became a member of the American Bee Journal family, and should health be spared, intend to continue till death severs me from earthly things.

The year 1870 was a poor honey season with us in Iowa. Our honey was principally honey dew, and though I do not relish the taste of that kind it is still better than none at all. Notwithstanding our poor season bees went into winter quarters last fall in fine condition. We had what might be called an open or mild winter, and bees came through in very good order, healthy and strong in numbers. Spring opened with fine prospects for the apiarian. There was a great profusion of fruit blossoms, and about the 20th of May white clover came in bloom. Since then bees have done nobly in honey gathering, but comparatively little in swarming, The cause of this non-swarming I am as yet unable to tell.

I am highly amused at the remarks of different writers on the Italian bees. I would candidly ask, do those bees deserve the praise that is heaped on them? I answer positively no! I am acquainted with men who have kept bees for years, and have tried the pure Italian bee, and their testimony is that they do not deserve one-half of what is said in their favor. But I do say that the hybrids, as honey gatherers, are better than either the common bee or the full blood Italian. I have one colony, the progeny of a five dollar ($5) queen from an Italian queen breeder, and my word for it a man would think he had run foul of a hornet's nest in opening their hive, which seems like the bursting of a bombshell in a pile of beans; the first thing you know you are the recipient of a volley of harpoons, and looking out for a line of *retreat*. Methinks I hear some one say, "perhaps you have a hybrid queen." Well, perhaps we have, and if so, it don't reflect much credit on the breeder. But I shall give the yellow jackets another trial. The hybrids are somewhat mulish at times, but great "chaps" in storing honey.

A few days since I had a conversation with a professional bee hunter, who said he could tell in a moment what kind of bees were in a tree by seeing the quantity and quality of the honey. "But," said he, "I would as soon get into a hornet's nest as into the presence of Italian bees."

The continuance of the account of bee-keeping in Iowa will be found in some future number of the American Bee Journal. I do not know how it is with other subscribers to the Journal, but I would much like to see it come semi-monthly, and would gladly pay three dollars more for it to accomplish that object. Such are my sentiments. Geo. W. Barclay.

Tipton, Iowa, Aug. 1, 1871.

[For the American Bee Journal.]

Notes from a Beginner.

Mr. Editor :—For some time I have been waiting for a rainy day that I might have leisure to write, for in my short experience there are many items of interest to me, and may be so to others, if you think them worthy of a place in the Journal. First I will speak of

Wintering.

As I told you in my last, I put eleven stocks in my cellar last fall. They came out in tip-top condition, except one, which I judge was queenless when put in, for there was not a pint of bees in the hive, and no queen to be found. My cellar is very dry—three feet above the rock, four feet in the rock, and rock bottom.

Moving Bees.

When I brought out my bees, I had no place to set them, except my door yard. Then I went to work to clear a place in a grove, a little north-west from where the bees stood in the yard, thinking to put all my new swarms there. But I soon found I did not want my old stocks to remain in my door yard; so I wheeled them around towards the grove, and began moving them a little at a time till I could move them ten feet at a time, with no confusion. In about thirty days I had them all in my grove. At first there was a little confusion with two or three hives, a few bees flying about the spot where the hives stood the previous evening, with their hives not more than three feet from them. But they soon became accustomed to it, so that all moved off well.

Feeding in Spring.

I had a swarm rather weak when set out. I commenced feeding it at once—my wife feeding when I was away. As I was gone most of the time in a sugar bush, I did not feed the remainder for some ten days after. The result was, the weak hive gave me my second spring swarm. My first swarm came out on the 23d day of May. I had several swarms before my neighbors had any. I conclude then that there is nothing lost in feeding, but much to be gained.

Swarming.

I made all my swarms by artificial methods, except the first, which left for the woods the next day but one. It had made some comb, and the queen had even commenced laying. I suppose they left, because I neglected to shade their hive, as it was a very warm morning. Then I thought I would do my own swarming. So, as soon as the bees began to hang out, I divided them by one of Langstroth's methods. But something must ever be learned by experience. My first artificial swarm went to the woods, the second day, in my absence of course. But I did not think to give them any brood. To my next I gave two frames with brood and honey; yet, contrary to all the doctors, the next morning they fled. I seized a looking-glass and they lit. I do not know but that they would have lit without the glass. I hived them in the same hive, and carried them to the grove; since which time they have been doing well.

TAMING BEES.

When I first commenced with my bees, they seemed determined to fight it out in their own odd way, by punching me with their tails. They would even come at me in my garden. First one would sing and threaten in angry tones, and then be off again,—only to return with reinforcements. They would hit me first under my eye, and then on my ear, pugilistic fashion. But fortunately I possessed about as much grit as they. By the way, the nose is rather a tender place to be stung. The first time they hit me there, it fairly made me cry. Its effect was like that of a pinch of snuff. I wiped my eyes, blowed my nose, sneezed as well as I knew how, and called for some water. My wife, thinking I wanted a drink, brought it in a tea-cup. I didn't stop to change dishes, but stuck my nose as near to the bottom as it would go. This eased the pain very much. This occurrence almost made me sick of bees, for it was my hardest battle. They are now quite tame. I have divided until out of thirteen (I bought two in the spring), I have now twenty-six. I also bought one young swarm, and got one from the woods; so I have twenty-eight in all. I have made an extractor, and use it too; that is I made it by the help of the blacksmith and tinner; and do not think it infringes anybody's patent.

Besides dividing my bees, I transferred the original stocks from their hives, so that all my bees are now in one kind of hive. All this was done without a bee dress of any kind. I sometimes open my hives without any smoke. Now, Mr. Editor, don't you think that I have tamed them some? I never handled bees before. They are all black bees.

BEE STING—A POISON,

and water, pure water a cure. I am glad to see the columns of the Journal advise the use of water for the cure of bee stings. I add my voice to those of others. I believe water without any adulteration, but of full strength, one of nature's great remedies.

I don't know but this article is already too long for you, so I will close by wishing success to the Journal and enterprising bee-keepers.

H. F. PHELPS.

Pine Island, Minn., July 24, 1871.

[For the American Bee Journal.]

Successful Bee-culture.

MR. EDITOR :—I took my bees out of winter quarters on the 10th of February, numbering forty-two (42) colonies. Of these forty-two, thirty were good strong stocks of Italians. The season opened early, though honey-producing plants were backward. I fed three hundred pounds of sugar to my bees, till they could begin to gather supplies: and took from them by the 4th of July three thousand (3,000) pounds of honey, besides making twenty-five artificial colonies. Feeding seasonably paid well. I have now sixty (60) colonies, in as fine condition as could be desired. Success to the American Bee-Journal.

J. N. WALTER.

Winchester, Iowa, August 7, 1871.

[For the American Bee Journal.]

Wire Clamps vs. Pins.

MR. EDITOR :—I notice Mr. J. J. Whitson gives us, in the Journal for June, an improved wire clamp for fastening transferred combs into frames, which he thinks is a little handier than any other device in use.

I have used strings, splints, wires, and pins, and must say that, everything considered, I prefer small wooden pins driven through gimlet holes in the sides of the frame, into the comb.

These do not have to be removed, and are never in the way. We prefer the wires described by him, to any of the devices heretofore used, except the pins; and still use them when the comb does not fill the frame.

J. T. TILLINGHAST.

Factoryville, Pa., June 20, 1871.

[For the American Bee Journal.]

Another Strange Occurrence.

DEAR BEE JOURNAL :—Something came under my observation the other day, that I am not posted in, and wish to have explained through our Journal.

I divided a colony of bees, moving the old colony to another place, and setting the new hive on the old stool, having placed in it a queen cell. After the queen had hatched several days, I opened the hive to see the young Italian queen. To my surprise I found an old black queen (the old stock divided was pure Italian). I caught her and caged her; and then looked further, and found the young queen.

The question is, how did the black queen come there? I put in only two frames of comb and young brood, and they were fresh from the old stock.

F. M. BAILEY.

Cynthiana, Ky., June 10, 1871.

DESTROYING ANTS.—A French agriculturist reports that, after trying every method known for the destruction of ants infesting some of his fruit trees, he succeeded in effecting his purpose in the most complete manner, by placing a mixture of arsenic and sweetened water, in a saucer, at the foot of the trees. For the larger species, he made use of honey, instead of sugar; and found, in a few days, he could exterminate them completely.

[For the American Bee Journal.]

Notes and Remarks.

MR. EDITOR :—I have been much interested in perusing the July number of the Journal, especially the different articles on queen raising; but was very much disappointed in not finding any results of experiments with non-flying fertilization of queens. I fear all have failed, like myself. This is an experiment that much interests me, as I find much uncertainty in my queens' becoming purely fertilized, owing to black bees being kept near. A man living four miles from me has had queens mate with Italian drones, and no Italians are known to be nearer than mine.

Will "AMATEUR" please inform us, through the Journal, what number of wire-cloth his wire house is covered with; and to what extent he has been successful in having queens fertilized in that house. He says (page 15 of the present volume), "so far as I have tried it, I have not had a single failure;" but does not say that he has had *even one queen* fertilized therein. If it is a success, I am for a wire house.

I know it is contrary to theory, but I have frequently hived a swarm in a hive just painted, and also painted some soon after the bees were put in, and never discovered that it was in the least injurious or objectionable to the bees. I cannot, therefore, agree with the editorial note as to the cause of the mortality of E. J. Worst's bees (page 16, current volume). I think it was war in the hive that killed the bees on the three frames inserted, which were probably nearly equal to the swarm, as he states that it was an afterswarm."

This season has been favorable for increase of stocks, but little surplus honey. The first swarm issued on Good Friday, April 7th.

C. WEEKS.

Clifton, Tenn., July 10, 1871.

☞Nothing stated by Mr. Worst, in his communication, leads us to suppose that there was "war in the hive," in the case of his bees; and if there had been, the cause of such war or animosity would in itself be quite inexplicable. RAMDOHR, who devoted a lifetime to practical bee-culture, and was in the habit of thus strengthening weak afterswarms, says explicitly, when recommending the process, "there need be no fear that these strangers will have a hostile reception. Many years' experience and reiterated experiments have satisfied me that they will be kindly received." If then there was war, what was the cause of a war so unnatural?—[ED.

[For the American Bee Journal.]

Unfertile Queens.

MR. EDITOR :—I have two queens, very large and bright, one born June 15th, the other June 29th, which, up to the present time (August 11th), have not laid an egg; yet all the conditions for fertile and prolific queens are present.

The cells were made in full stocks of fine bright Italians, and removed to nuclei on the ninth or tenth day. The queens issued, small and bright, soon becoming very long and splendid looking, and (in usual time) having every appearance of being fertile. About ten or twelve days after their appearance of fertility, finding no eggs, I began stimulating them, which has been done daily since, although the nuclei are strong with bees, and have an abundance of honey and bee-bread, the bees leaving room in and around the centre of the middle frames, evidently on purpose for the queen to deposit eggs in. I have also supplied them with good empty worker comb at different times.

These queens are from a very prolific family, the mother and sisters being remarkable for their fecundity.

I have heard of similar cases, but not of such long standing. Will some of our experienced queen raisers give their views on the subject, from experience, if possible?

I am keeping these queens to watch the result; but may yet have to resort to dissection and the microscope to solve the problem.

T. B. HAMLIN.

Edgefield Junction, Tenn.

[For the American Bee Journal.]

Two Strange Cases.

Last season I introduced an Italian queen into a colony of black bees for Josiah Turner, Esq. The first of her progeny was beautifully marked, till nearly the whole swarm was Italianized. Then hybrids began to appear, and the Italians to disappear. After some weeks again the hybrids began to disappear and black bees made their appearance, with some few slightly marked ones among them. Now, one would hardly suspect that an Italian had ever been there. The bees have not swarmed. There is no appearance of a change of queen. I believe the same identical queen still remains in the hive. Can any one tell how these changes came about? Did the queen mate with several drones, and if so, at one flight, or on different occasions? I clipped her wings when I introduced her.

Another case. In the early part of May I removed an Italian queen in the apiary of E. O. Maritz, of Raleigh, and introduced her in a hive of black bees, where she remained some four or five weeks. I then removed her some fifteen feet, in a wire cage, into another stock of black bees. After leaving her confined about thirty-six hours, I opened the cage to let her walk out on the comb. But instead of her majesty doing so, she rose and flew (her wings were clipped last season), and in less than a minute's time she was inside of the hive from which she was taken thirty-six hours before. How did she find the way back, if she had not been out of the hive during the four or five weeks she was ensconced there, and marked the place?

There is an increased interest in apiculture, since my advent here with the Langstroth movable comb hive and my reports of northern success. Frequent inquiries are made about Alsike and Italian bees; but last year was not favorable to bee-keeping, and thus far this season has not been as good as the last. There have been very few swarms, and no spare honey. In fact bees need feeding now. The early part of the honey season was wet and cold, and the latter part too dry. I hope it may be made up in the fall.

Most of the drones were destroyed in May already, and queens have nearly stopped laying.

Many persons are going to sow Alsike clover seed for honey and hay. If I had a supply of seed to sell on commission, I could probably dispose of it.

JOEL CURTIS.

Raleigh, N. C.

[For the American Bee Journal.]

The Yellow Bees and the Black.

I have watched, with deep interest, the controversy going on in the Bee Journals of the day, in regard to Italian bees; and have endeavored to read the *pros* and *cons* of Italians *vs.* black bees without prejudice, and have thus far kept silent.

As far as my experience and observation extend, I find that some individual buys a colony of Italians, and his first thought then is—"How shall I handle them so as to reap a small fortune from them in the shortest space of time?" To begin: if he has a few pounds of broken honey the Italians get it; if he has two or three frames of choice empty combs, suitable for brood, the favorite yellow bees are the recipients of it, and his inferior blacks are left to starve it out. The result in each case cannot be doubtful. The feeding the Italians have received stimulated them, they increase rapidly, and the timely addition of two or three frames of nice empty worker comb places them weeks ahead of the neglected blacks, and makes a grand difference in the results of the season.

Twenty-five years ago we thought a box hive, planed, painted, with two boxes on the top, a grand advance in bee-keeping. Then came the sectional hive, with one box on the top of another, and slats between, which was further followed by a host of other *bee traps*. But light broke in on all when the movable frame came into use, and bee-keeping then became a pleasure instead of an annoyance.

From a child I had a passion for bees, and have tried to keep posted on the various improvements in hives and methods of handling them.

When I say that I have the finest apiary in this part of the State, I do not say it to boast, but to show you the result of carefully dividing bees year after year.

In all my colonies there is hardly a hive that has more than five frames over one year old. For five years past I have endeavored to divide my swarms and renew one-half of the combs each year, dividing them up among the new colonies, and cutting out all combs that became thick and discolored, treating my black and yellow bees alike. I believe that I was impartial.

I *never did* and *do not now believe* that the Italians, under the same treatment for a term of years, will do *one whit* better than the blacks.

"And what is the result of your constant division?" says some one. The result is this: I have secured a stock of bees which for size, hardiness and working capacity cannot be excelled by anything that stores honey, whether coming from Italy, Switzerland, Egypt, or any other country. They will reach the honey in any cup that an Italian can; will be found on the wing as early, and retire as late; will send out as many workers to the frame; will store as many pounds or boxes of surplus honey as any others in the same locality.

In fair and impartial experiments my black bees have done the best, two years out of three.

I am willing to admit that if you neglect your blacks; keep them in old almost worthless combs; and divide your Italians; keep *their* combs new and clean; give them the broken honey, &c., they will prove by far the most profitable.

The first colonies of Italians that were imported from Europe were costly, and the increase were quite naturally sold at high prices, and of course the market price for them ranged high. The price was such that those who had Italians divided them constantly, and but very few colonies were allowed to pass over the season without being divided, and one half or more of the combs being removed. The natural result was a large, hardy, energetic race of bees. But had an equal number of black colonies been imported at the same time, and treated exactly alike in every respect, I am safe to say that they would to-day have numbered as many colonies; would have accumulated as great stores, and given their owners as great an amount of surplus honey, and proved themselves quite as profitable.

Such, and such only, I believe to be the true facts in this question—*axe grinders* to the contrary notwithstanding.

Let a man go into the street of every town and argue that one out of three men whose arms are just two feet five inches long, each, could reach two feet seven inches into an iron tube, while the other two could not, and he would be called a lunatic. Yet this is just the position taken by those who advocate that a yellow bee can get honey from red clover, while a black bee cannot. *More anon.*

OLD FOGY.

Lake City, July 24, 1871.

Bee Superstitions in France.

In Brittany, if a person who keeps bees has his hives robbed, he gives them up immediately, because they never can succeed afterwards. This idea arises from an old Breton proverb, which says, being translated, "*No luck after the robber.*" But why the whole weight of the proverb is made to fall on the bee-hives, it might be difficult to determine.

In other parts of France, they tie a small piece of black stuff to the bee-hives, in case of a death in the family; and a piece of red on the occasion of a marriage—without which, it is believed, the bees would never thrive.

THE AMERICAN BEE JOURNAL.

Washington, September, 1871.

☞ We are in pressing need of No. 7, of the American Bee Journal, of Volumes V. and VI. (dated respectively, January, 1870, and January, 1871); and will pay twenty-five cents per copy, for those numbers, till our wants are supplied, if sent to the publication office, with the sender's name.

☞ Several copies of each of the numbers desired, have been sent to us in accordance with the above request, without giving us the senders' names, and hence we know not whom to credit, or thank.

☞ A large number of communications reached us so late in August, that we were unable to use them for this number of the Journal. Luckily there is among them none likely to lose in interest by brief delay in publication.

☞ We need not ask the reader's attention to Miss Grimm's brief and clear report of her success in practical bee-culture, this summer, at one of her father's apiaries, in Wisconsin—*that* will be a thing of course; and after reading it, they will readily join us in congratulating her on an achievement alike gratifying and praiseworthy. The season there may have been unusually fine, but to secure so large an amount of honey as TEN BARRELS from a comparatively small number of stocks, and with so little assistance, argues uncommon skilfulness and unflagging assiduity on the part of the young lady who accomplished the feat—a feat unexampled, we believe, in the annals of bee-culture in this country, or in any other. We have reports from other quarters, quite satisfactory to those who make them, and on the whole very flattering and encouraging; and there are more like them, and perhaps still better, yet to come; but, in view of all the circumstances, we think the bee-keepers of the country will cordially concur in assigning to Miss Grimm the palm of supereminent success in 1871.

☞ Mr. K. P. Kidder, we learn, is still endeavoring to *blackmail* bee-keepers for using or having used the triangular comb guide; doing so under the pretext that the assignment to him of Clark's patent, gives him the right to claim damages. The decision of the U. S. Court in favor of that patent, was fraudulently obtained—as Kidder well knows, having been the prominent agent in that transaction; and neither he nor Clark could sustain their demands by legal process against parties determined to resist them. Under stress of moral pressure, he sued Messrs. Langstroth and Otis *at their request*, as it was *their* desire, and, as we are advised, the desire of the Court, to obtain a re-adjudication of the case. But he (Kidder) *will take special care never to prosecute that suit to an issue*—being perfectly conscious of what that issue must be. Meantime he is trying to put money in his pocket, by victimizing uninformed or timid bee-keepers. He will never bring or prosecute suit against any who will resist his demands, with a determination to contest his right to make them.

☞ From an account given by Dr. Preuss, in the Bienenzeitung, of a conversation he had, last year, with Dzierzon (which was substantially communicated to the Journal, a few months ago, with comments, by Mr. Adam Grimm), it seemed as if Dr. P. desired to create the impression that Dzierzon either did not venture, or felt himself unable, to maintain the correctness of his theory of drone production; if, indeed, he was not himself disposed to doubt or abandon it, at least in part. That this was all wrong, was obvious to us from the whole tenor of the conversation, as reported by Dr. Preuss. Courtesy to a visitor would disincline Dzierzon from engaging in a discussion which must, in view of the Doctor's known position in the premises, almost inevitably have led to controversy. Yet we felt assured that the Doctor's communication would, sooner or later, draw from Dzierzon a distinct disavowal of the imputation that he had changed his views, or had conceived doubt of the tenableness of his own theory, or felt unable to defend or maintain it. We have this now in a recent communication to the Bienenzeitung, which we have translated for this number of the Journal. It will be seen from it that the Dzierzon theory of drone production is still adhered to by its author, fully and in its original form. Let those who have been led to doubt, or who incline to entertain other opinions as to drone production, read the article and reassure themselves that there is no wavering there. For ourselves, we need only state that every clear test to which we could subject the theory, merely resulted in corroborating its truth, and authorizes us to reiterate, what we said on former occasions, that *the drones are the conclusive evidence of the true character and quality of the* QUEENS *from which they spring*—THEIR MOTHERS; that doubt or suspicion created by appearances connected with *them*, must be regarded only as of weight operating retroactively against those queens; and that all queens thus attainted, however large, or bright, or finely marked, are utterly unfit to breed from, and should be unhesitatingly rejected, when purity of race is designed to be secured or perpetuated. *Mark this!* The same principle, too, must be regarded as true, and be adhered to, in scientific attempts to originate and establish an improved breed.

☞ The Seventeenth General Convention of German Bee-keepers meets this year, on the 12th, 13th, and 14th of this month, in the city of Kiel, situated in Holstein, on a bay of the Baltic. The programme, which we have just received, proposes fifteen general topics for discussion. A meeting was to have been held at Kiel last year, but was postponed on account of the war.

☞ The honey plant, of which a specimen was sent to us by Mr. McLay, of Madison (Wis.), is the *Monarda punctata*, or Horsemint, growing, according to Gray, in sandy fields and dry banks, from New York to Virginia, both inclusive. Bees gather honey from it, but what its quality is, or whether the yield is abundant or long continued, we are unable to say, as it has not come under our observation.

☞ Honey gathered by the bees from the blossoms of the CEPHALANTHUS, or Buttonbush, (which grows in moist places, marshy fields, or swamps) is apt *to candy in the cells* a few days after being stored; and probably imparts that bad quality to honey gathered from other sources, if mixed therewith in large proportion.

☞ BEE BOOKS.—Those desiring to procure some scarce works on bee-culture, may have an opportunity (seldom occurring) to do so, by turning to the advertisement of Rev. Mr. Millett, in this number of the Journal.

CORRESPONDENCE OF THE BEE JOURNAL.

CANAJOHARIE, N. Y., July 17, 1871.—I have a little leisure and must tell you what my bees are doing. They wintered finely; every stock was in a strong, healthy condition, when I took them from the cellar. The first natural swarm came out on the 20th of May; but I was after honey more than bees. I put them back and gave them plenty of room in surplus boxes. The result is that I have taken from this stock up to July 12th, about one hundred and ten (110) pounds of box honey, with a good prospect of as much more. Other stocks have done nearly as well; but, as is the way of the world, I am apt to put the best side out. The hum of the bees calls me to action, and I must close.—J. H. NELLIS.

SOUTH FRAMINGHAM, MASS., July 18.—This has been a poor season for bees here. I have not taken any honey from them.—E. EAMES.

BREESPORT, N. Y., July 19.—The season has been unfavorable for bees in these parts. There has been frost each month, and we have had cold drying winds, which kept the bees in their hives.

The night of June 26th, the dew was mingled with honey, but my bees seemed to have little or no regard for it. The night of the 29th brought frost, as usual, and on the 6th of July it was nearly cold enough for another. On the 9th the weather was very hot. Bees are not done swarming yet. The cold in June was detrimental to swarming. Clover is in full bloom, but seems to accumulate small quantities of honey.—J. H. HADSELL.

YOUNGSVILLE, PA., July 18.—Bees are doing *very poorly* here this season.—W. J. DAVIS.

LEXINGTON, ILL., July 17.—Season remarkably good here so far. Will probably send report for Journal at the close, with diagram of bee-house built three years ago. Have waited for time to investigate, both summer and winter—and now am forced to conclude that a bee-house is necessary to judicious and proper management, under any and all circumstances.—W. REYNOLDS.

TYRONE, CANADA, July 19.—Bee-keeping in this section of country is doing very well this year. I have got fifty pounds of honey from one of my hives, and a swarm. I do not allow them to swarm more than once.—J. MCLAUGHLIN.

POLO, ILL., July 19.—I began with five swarms of Italian bees this season, and now have nineteen. Have had "bee on the brain" for several years, and do not expect to get over it. Your Journal is just the thing for such patients.—M. J. HAZELTINE.

CEDAR CREEK FALLS, IOWA, July 19.—Bees here are in good condition. The season is good, and the honey also. Plenty of bees. Late swarming on account of superabundance of forage. Bees carried in pollen in March, and reared brood in abundance. Stocks strong too early for swarms, as the brood combs were filled with honey, and when the swarming season approached, there was no room for brood and swarms were delayed. Those who put on the honey chambers and set the bees to work in boxes, got early swarms and box honey. As I have an axe to grind, I shall say nothing of my hive, or of my success with my own bees at present; but intend to report for Cedar Falls, as to bees and hives, and will give the names of bee-keepers, the amount of honey obtained, and the number of stocks kept.—T. S. ENGLEDOW.

WILLOW BRANCH, IND., July 20.—My bees have done pretty well this season, until within two or three weeks past. The weather got so dry that there was not much to work on. We have plenty of rain now, and I think they will start up again.—J. SMITH.

MIDDLEBURG, VT., July 22.—There are two things I desire very much to see in the Journal, 1st a simple and effectual method of obtaining all perfectly straight worker combs; and 2d, the best way of obtaining honey in small frames, so that when removed from the hive the two sides may be covered with glass, making a small honey box with a single comb, nearly or quite as perfect as if it had been filled by the bees with glass on the two sides. I could send you description of our honey emptying machine, if you wish. It is a perfect success in every respect.—A. C. HOOKER. [Send us the description. ED.]

BROAD RUN, FAUQUIER CO., VA., July 22.—My bees have done remarkably well this spring; but the honey season is now over. They may get some little honey this fall, but not to store in boxes. My hives are crowded with bees, and if I were in the West, where their main dependence is on the fall flowers, I might double my yield of honey.—H. W. WHITE.

LE CLAIRE, IOWA, July 23.—Since the 5th of July to the present time, bees here have not made a living. I use the Gallup hive. They say my bees take all the honey. I say to them to read the Journal, and they would get their share.—T. J. DODDS.

LEWISBURG, WEST VA., July 24.—There will be no honey taken in this section, this season; and very few swarms issued—not more than one in fifty from the black bees. I had from twelve to fifteen, from thirty-five thirty-four Italians and grades. I send you a portion of a plant on which I found the bees working very strong. I wish you to ascertain its name, and report in the Journal. It is a strong growing plant, reaching about two feet in height, branches at the ground into eight or twelve shoots. Grows on thin land. I never saw it till this season.—T. L. Sydenstricker.

The plant mentioned is the *Echium vulgare*, or Viper's bugloss. It is found plentifully in some parts of Maryland and in Shenandoah valley, Virginia. It blooms from June till the frost cuts it down; yields honey abundantly and of good quality; and is said to be the famous Russian bee plant. The books on farming say it is troublesome; but we have never known it to interfere with proper tillage of good land.—Ed.

Chariton, Iowa, July 24.—Bees here are doing better than they have done for the past two years. I have had nineteen swarms from nine stands—three artificial and sixteen natural. They were Italian and hybrids. My black bees have not done near as well, as I have only had one swarm where I ought to have had six or eight. This is to me conclusive evidence that the Italians are the best. Our neighbors are becoming more interested in bee-culture; quite a number come to see my Italians.—J. A. Brown.

Mayville, Wis., July 25.—Is it not strange that I read on almost every page of the American Bee Journal, how much earlier the Italian bees swarm than the black bees; and yet my Italians do not like to swarm at all this season? Blacks, however, cast swarms in the latter part of May. Till now, therefore, not very favorably impressed with the Italians. —A. W. Lueck.

Noblesville, Ind., July 25.—The severe drought in this part of the country has been very hard on bees, especially on the common kind. People in our neighborhood now see the superiority of the Italian bee. My Italians have gathered honey through the dry weather, but the common bees had to fall back on their gathered stores. I have just Italianized my last stand of blacks. I introduced an Italian queen on the morning of the 21st, and on the evening of the 22d—thirty hours after introducing—I went to release her, but found the bees had already let her out. I looked through the hive, but could not find her. As I was about shutting up the hive, I saw her sitting on a weed about six feet from the hive. When I went to pick her off, she took wing and flew away, but in a few minutes I saw her alight on the side of the hive. I picked her off, and she curved herself in every shape, thrusting her sting out as if she wanted to sting my fingers; but my fear of losing her prevented me from giving her a chance. She is a young queen that had just commenced laying in a nucleus. I united two colonies, during the drought, without losing a single bee, by sprinkling them with sweetened water scented with peppermint. My bees are doing well since the middle of July. The bee fever seems to be contagious in this part of the country. I use the Langstroth hive, and think it the best, of course.—J. W. Wampler.

Seneca Falls, N. Y., July 26.—Bees have done only moderately well this season; still it is not wholly over yet. I have had not over half a dozen swarms from forty-two colonies.—R. Bickford.

Chambersburg, Pa., July 27.—Bee culture has not made much progress in this part of Pennsylvania. There are plenty of bees kept, but on the old plan of luck or no luck. Scientific bee culture has yet to take a start here. This, so far, has been a very good honey season here—more so than for several years past. Last year was the poorest I ever knew. White clover was abundant, but did not yield honey; but this year both white and red seem to yield honey freely, and my Italians make good use of the great supply. At gathering honey they are superior to the natives; and, by-the-by, when any man pretends to say that they are no better than the native bee, I think (I suppose I may *think*) that he has yet much to observe and much to learn.—S. F. Reynolds.

Fredonia, N. Y., July 27.—Bees have done well in this section, thus far. The Italians are in my opinion far ahead of the natives. So far as our experience goes, they are more peaceable than the blacks, work earlier and later in the day, in cool weather, and on days when the others will not work. We think they collect at least one-half more than the natives. They swarm earlier; and swarm in seasons when the native bees do not. In short, they are the *model bee*, in our opinion.—H. A. Burch.

Wilfrid, Canada, July 28.—My bees began to swarm early this season, being in latitude 44½°, and wintered on their summer stands (no shed), without any protection but the hives. The first swarm came May 19th. I have increased from twenty-eight stocks to seventy-six; all very strong, with a large quantity of surplus honey.—D. Reekie.

Madison, Wis., July 28.—I made a honey-emptying machine this year, with the outside case stationary, and like it better than having the whole revolved, as I had it in 1869. I see one patented, and patent applied for, on the same principle. I got twelve hundred (1200) pounds of honey from fourteen stocks, besides making twenty young colonies, this summer. The honey was very plenty in June and till about the 10th of July; now there is scarcely any here. I was up about Wisconsin river this week, in a sandy country. I found there a plant that the bees gather lots of honey from. A bee-keeper told me that August was their best honey month, from that plant. I intend to get seed of it this fall for my own use. It grows about a foot high. I enclose the flower. It may grow on any land, if cultivated. Perhaps you can ascertain the name of it. If I could get it introduced here, it would be worth a good deal to me, as my bees can scarce live from this time till fall. There is no buckwheat near me this summer.—J. McLay.

Batavia, Ill., July 29.—Bees have swarmed well, and made considerable box honey. On the whole it has been a fair season. I have Italians and black bees. Of these, the black bees have done best; but the hybrids have outdone both the blacks and the Italians. I find my Italians fractious, and very bad to handle, and prefer the half-breeds to any other bee.—S. Way.

Deering, Me., Aug. 1.—Our honey crop this season, thus far, has been a failure. The white clover yields comparatively nothing. The weather has been so very dry here since the fruit trees blossomed that there was little food for the bees. My bees have not swarmed this season, and very few have swarmed in this county. We have had some wet weather of late, and hope the drought has been broke. I shall not get more than twenty-five (25) pounds of box honey from five colonies, though my hives are full of bees.—Jos. Batchelder.

Hartland Four Corners, Vt., Aug. 1.—We are having the poorest season for bees in this vicinity, thus far, that we had for several years. From twenty-five stocks of black bees, I have not had a single *natural* swarm, and many of them will not give any surplus honey. All of my Italian stocks have given swarms, except one; and from that one I have taken one hundred (100) pounds of surplus honey at this time (Aug. 1). I have already introduced more than twenty-five Italian queens this season, without a single failure. For the past two years I have read every number of all the Bee Journals published in America to my knowledge, and the American Bee Journal is worth more than all the rest.—G. M. D. RUGGLES.

SCHUYLKILL HAVEN, PA., Aug. 2.—I wintered twenty-four colonies of Italians in Langstroth hives, two tiers of frames. The upper box holds one hundred pounds, and the twenty-four hives are full—tops all virgin combs—making twenty-four hundred (2400) pounds of honey in the combs; besides seven swarms, one of which filled top, one hundred pounds. My bees are now gathering rapidly from red clover. People may tell me what they please, in regard to Italians not gathering from red clover; for the last five years my bees have averaged from twenty to thirty pounds per hive, from second crop red clover. I get fifty cents per pound for my honey. So you see it *pays* in this county, right in the heart of the coal region of Pennsylvania. I am now *queening* my black bees, getting the queens from Mr. Alley. They all turn out, well so far. I winter my bees in the cellar, not being willing to risk out door wintering.—J. P. SMITH.

FORT ATKINSON, WIS., Aug. 2.—Our bees have done well, though the drought has cut our honey season short.—C. J. WARD.

NATCHEZ, MISS., Aug. 3.—Our honey crop in this section, this season, has proved a failure. Our spring opened early and gave promise of a good yield, but our hopes have been disappointed. All went well until May, when a rainy spell set in, continuing for about four weeks, preventing most of my black bees (already very backward) from swarming. Comb was started in many boxes, principally by Italians, and all new swarms; but not one box in my entire apiary has been completely filled and sealed. The yield of box honey in my apiary, consisting of fifty-two hives, will not amount to more than one hundred pounds. I have not had time to use the honey extractor this season.—J. R. BLEDSOE.

HUBBARD, OHIO, Aug. 3.—The honey harvest has been better than I expected it would be at the middle of June. We have had plentiful rains since then. The white clover is not quite done blossoming yet. I have taken sixty-one pounds of box honey, four full sized frames of honey and brood, and a good swarm, from one hive; from another, seventy-one pounds of box honey; and from a third, which was very weak in the spring, ten pounds of honey, a good swarm, and six full sized frames and brood. The honey I could sell at thirty cents per pound, so that my bees have paid pretty well. I use the Langstroth hive, with side and top boxes. There have been only few natural swarms here this season.—J. WINFIELD.

NORTH UNION, near CLEVELAND, OHIO, Aug. 7.—I have only ten colonies of bees, but they have gathered honey tolerably well for this locality. But there has been no swarming, except in one instance, and the swarm went off without clustering at all. Last year I lost three swarms the same way, though there is plenty of shrubbery for them to cluster on.—R. HONEY.

MOUNTJOY, PA., Aug. 7.—My bees are doing well this season. I will get the largest yield of honey from one colony that I ever got in one season. My bees are gathering honey fast now. In July the weather was too cool and too wet for honey gathering here. I enclose two dollars, for a new subscriber.—J. F. HERSHEY.

GEBHARTSBURG, PA., Aug. 8.—Bees did well here, this season, so far as breeding is concerned; but as to honey, not so well. A large part of what I got is very bitter, and not good to use. The crop of white clover, which is our chief honey crop, was short, owing to the dry weather, and consequently the supply is small. I generally practice artificial swarming, but this season the bees took the lead, swarms issuing as early as the 10th of May, which is much earlier than we usually have swarms in this latitude. My bees are in fine condition, with still some prospect of buckwheat honey.—W. BAKER.

RANDOLPH, WIS., Aug. 8.—Bees are doing splendidly this season.—E. L. TOWNSEND.

HOLT, MICH., Aug. 10.—Our bees have done well here, this season. Mine have made at the rate of one hundred (100) pounds extracted honey, per hive.—J. L. DAVIS.

HAMILTON, ILL., Aug. 10.—My bees average forty-two pounds of box and extracted honey, per hive. The dryness of the season interfered with the harvest; yet I hope to have some honey from the summer flowers.—CH. DADANT.

PORTLAND, ME., Aug. 16.—Bees in this vicinity have accomplished but little this season. Swarms have been few, and the honey light. I have about twenty-five colonies, which I think are all in good order. I think the JOURNAL grows more and more interesting as it grows older; and I would as soon undertake to keep house without a wife and cook-stove, as to try to keep bees without the *Journal*.—M. G. PALMER.

MONMOUTH, ILL., Aug. 16.—During clover bloom bees here did very well, also during basswood; but since the 1st of July they have gathered nothing. But little buckwheat is sown in this vicinity; still I hope to have a good yield of honey from fall flowers. —T. G. MCGAW.

[For the American Bee Journal.]

Parricides, or Bees Attacking and Killing their Queen.

There is no doubt of the cause, in the case of Rev. Mr. Anderson's loss of a queen, it being produced by poison from a bee—whether from a robber or from one of the inmates of the hive. I could be more explicit and cite incidents, were it not likely to make this article too long.

If there be any doubt, let some one try the experiment, by taking a comb with queen and bees from a hive, place some of the venom on the queen, and she will speedily be killed, while the operator will be likely to get a stab himself.

The more bees that are cut with a knife or otherwise injured, the worse the case will be, even to the killing of some or all the bees in a stock, or the apiary. Robberies and general fights are assisted by the *venom*.

The remedy is to separate the cluster, and drive the bees away from the queen with smoke, placing her in a cage till all is quiet and the odor of the poison dissipated, or disguised with feed, smoke or time. The safest method, and the one we generally use, is to remove the queen as above, and build her up a stock with combs of hatching brood; allowing the parricides to rear another queen.

Deserting stocks or swarms are generally accompanied by robbers in their flight; and on alighting, in their efforts to protect themselves or their queen, poison is given off, and woe be to the unlucky object that gets a "*taint*."

J. M. MARVIN.

St. Charles, Ills., Aug., 1871.

// AMERICAN BEE JOURNAL.

EDITED AND PUBLISHED BY SAMUEL WAGNER, WASHINGTON, D. C.

AT TWO DOLLARS PER ANNUM, PAYABLE IN ADVANCE.

VOL. VII. OCTOBER, 1871. No. 4.

[From the German. Translated for the American Bee Journal.]

Practical Bee-culture.

RAISING LARGE RESERVE QUEENS.

In the "*Honigbiene von Brün*," the Rev. L. Morbitzer, of Raubanien, gives his method of raising reserve queens, in nucleus hives. It is an article prepared with care, showing that its author, besides being a skilful manipulator, is guided in his operations by a clear judgment and sound reason. The importance of having reserve fertile queens constantly at hand for any emergency, is so obvious, that it need not here be enforced, and we proceed at once to the description given of his queen-raising nucleus hives. These are small, being five inches wide, seven inches deep—adapted for four small combs, and ten inches and a quarter high, arranged for two tiers of frames. The dimensions of these nucleus hives may be modified, to correspond with the requirements of the frames in use in any apiary where the system of keeping on hand a supply of reserve queens is adopted.

When and how are these nucleus hives to be used? Mr. Morbitzer advises that queen-raising in nuclei should not be engaged in prematurely in spring, but that it be deferred till drones are hatched and the weather permits them to fly. Beginners are usually too impatient in this matter, unable to brook delay, and thus committing a gross error at the outset:—better wait till the season and circumstances conspire to favor the design. For every ten strong populous colonies in his apiary, he prepares two, three, or four nuclei, but in no case more than four. To this end he removes the queen of a populous stock, usually selecting an old one that should be superseded in the course of the ensuing summer. With the aid of this queen he forms an artificial colony in one of the nucleus hives, placing it in his cellar over night, and setting it next day in some convenient place in his garden, keeping the queen caged temporarily. In the unqueened colony he inserts combs with eggs and brood from such of his colonies as he desires to raise queens from, trimming off the lower edges of the combs, and setting them in the middle of the brood chamber. The colony is then regularly fed every day, with lukewarm honey, that the brood may be properly attended to and become fully developed; and that the embryo queens also be fully developed, the bees must be allowed to fly, to procure the needed supplies of pollen and water.

Eight or ten days later, the additional nucleus colonies are to be formed. With this view small sectional frames containing worker combs had been inserted in the brood chamber of populous stocks, and are now taken out to supply the frames of the small nucleus hives, into which empty combs and combs containing sealed honey are likewise introduced. To procure a supply of *young* workers for these nuclei, the bees clustered on the brood combs of full colonies are brushed off into a transferring hive or any empty box, which is left open. The older bees will speedily return to the colonies from which they were taken, while the young ones will remain and are used to supply the nuclei, which are then placed in a cellar over night, to settle and become reconciled to their changed condition. Next day a sealed queen cell, taken from the unqueened colony, is inserted in each nucleus, and these are replaced in the cellar, where they remain four or five days longer, or until the young queens are hatched. They are then taken out and set apart from other hives in the apiary, if possible on the south or southeast side. When the young queens have been fertilized and disposed of, it is advantageous to replace them with sealed queen cells built for second swarms, instead of using post-constructed cells, for the latter do not produce as vigorous and perfect queens as the former.

In addition to the above, the Rev. Mr. Stahala, of Dolein, has the following remarks, in the same journal, on the process for *rearing large queen bees*: "All experienced beekeepers concur in the conviction that large queens are preferable to small ones. Though occasionally even quite diminutive queens prove to be remarkably prolific, this is nevertheless the exception and does not invalidate the rule. Every breeder should, therefore, constantly endeavor to raise large queens—the larger the better. Such are not only more prolific, but become fertilized earlier, and are less liable to be lost on their excursions."

Mr. Morbitzer cautions breeders against using *post-constructed* queen cells for queen raising. Mr. Stahala, however, dissents from this, and prefers such cells precisely, because from them he obtains the largest queens. "In many cases," says he, "the queen cells built in a hive that has sent out a swarm, are post-constructed—that is, they were started after the swarm had left. Still, among them some very large ones may be found. And according to my experience, queen cells built in or on old combs are invariably smaller than such as are built in new combs. Hence most large cells are found on or near the lower edge of newly built combs; and when it is desired to obtain particularly large and fine cells, I unqueen a colony whose queen for other reasons I may intend to remove, and supply the colony, the day after it has shown consciousness of being queenless, with a frame containing newly built comb stored with eggs laid by a queen from which I wish to breed, the brood and eggs derived from the removed queen, with any royal cells that may have been started, are transferred to other colonies, containing the bees to start queen cells on the new combs given to them."

Mr. Stahala adds—"If from a worker larva a large queen is to be produced, she must not only be reared in a capacious cell, but also be supplied with better and more abundant food, during the entire period she continues in her larval state." This, he says, is best attained by having eggs laid in newly built worker comb. And should it happen that the lower ranges of cells in such combs contain no eggs, they are to be pruned off before inserting the comb. Large queen cells thus obtained are to be transferred to their destined nuclei on the ninth or tenth day, and large and fully developed queens will almost invariably emerge from them. These nuclei, however, must always be so well stocked with bees that the queen cells are kept constantly covered and warm. It is therefore well not to have any unsealed brood in them, as that might induce the bees to fly out in large numbers. It is also well to limit the brooding space as much as possible, so as to confine the heat. Should the season be so advanced that the bees have ceased building comb, insert a frame furnished with mere strips of guide comb in the brood nest of a populous colony, and the bees anxious to close the vacancy will speedily build comb there, if well fed; and the queen will promptly supply the cells with eggs. This may then be transferred to the queen-breeding stock or nucleus, the bees of which may be forced to build queen cells upon it, by removing all other brood combs immediately.

[For the American Bee Journal.]

Novice.

Dear Journal:—This article will be necessarily brief, on account of ill health. Receiving a peremptory order from our physician to be out of doors as much as possible, we construed it as a providential interposition to turn our attention to our basswood orchard project, and have got it so far under way as to have purchased $10\frac{1}{2}$ acres of land for the purpose.

We propose to first thoroughly underdrain it, four feet deep, and then raise the plants from the seed, in hills twelve feet apart. As fast as they get crowded they are to be thinned out. We are collecting all the information we can, as to their cultivation, and would be very thankful for any fact on the subject. If we should not live to see them bloom, some other beekeeper may. Partial paralysis of our right side prevents our hitherto faithful right hand from saying more at present. With kind wishes to all, we remain, as ever, yours, Novice.

[For the American Bee Journal.]

Novice.

Now this is coming a rather sharp dodge to get one of my articles read—I mean heading it *Novice*, for of course every one will at least commence to read it, thinking by the heading that Novice wrote it himself.

But I am satisfied that some of the later subscribers of the Journal would like to know something about Novice, more than they do; and as I had the pleasure of making him a visit last summer, I will say may say about him.

His name is A. I. Root, and not A. J. Root, as it is often printed, and the worst thing about his moral character is that Medina, Ohio, where he lives, is accessible only by stage. He is a jeweller by profession, of about thirty-five years of age I should judge; though as I am not good at guessing, I may be five years wide of the mark; married of course; rather under medium size; trim built; of sandy complexion; very neat in appearance, and I should judge neat about everything he does. One would suppose, from his free and easy manner of writing, that he is a talkative person; but I am inclined to think he is rather reticent, except when his favorite topic—bee-culture—comes up. (Please bear in mind that I only saw him one day, and that I have never seen or heard a word from him, before or since, except what is printed in the Bee Journal.)

The reader of the Bee Journal need not be told that, in everything pertaining to the bee, he is an enthusiast, perhaps over sanguine, yet withal so modest and unassuming in putting forth his ideas, that it is a real pleasure to hear him talk. It is to be hoped that he will make enough failures, or have enough Christian grace given him, to keep him from becoming an egotist.

His apiary presents a very neat appearance. Internally his hives were not made as true as they might have been. In one hive he had a lot of pieces of comb arranged in a frame, laid on a board, and left on the top of a hive, for the bees to fasten together. I have since tried the same thing, only I put paper on the board before putting on the comb, as I find it easier to separate the comb from the paper than from a board.

His hives were placed on separate bottom boards or stands, and a numbered brass check, such as jewellers use on watches, placed on each hive, and a duplicate check on each stand. This was done to number the hives, and to allow the hives when set out in the spring, to occupy the same stands they occupied the previous year. This must be a decided advantage over having the hives numbered in the ordinary way, as one changes often (at least in the spring, with the Langstroth hives) a colony entire from one hive to another, and then, if the number on the hive cannot be changed, it makes trouble with the record.

At the time of my visit he was experimenting in the direction of comb-making. Whether he has made a success of it, or whether the patent of Mr. Wagner covers the whole ground, the Bee Journal does not say. I had much hoped that before this time we could buy comb foundations. When can we have them? If they can be sold as low as has been hinted, I want five hundred of them.

Novice's queen nurseries I have tried, and have failed with them—the bees gnawing them out of the comb. Perhaps I put them in in a blundering way. I have tried his cloth covers or quilts, instead of honey boards, and so far am highly pleased with them. I have used newspapers in them instead of cotton batting, and it answers a very good purpose. I think very few would use wooden honey boards after trying the cloth ones. That one item I consider of more value than a year's subscription to the Journal.

B. LUNDERER.

[For the American Bee Journal.]

A Visit to Mr. Alley.

Having business in Boston during the month of August, I was glad of the opportunity of visiting the apiary of Mr. Alley, in Wenham. I have generally found that the true lover of his bees is an accessible, genial kind of person. I was sure of a welcome from my friend though a stranger, and was not disappointed. A short half mile from the station, the long array of hives scattered through an orchard of pear trees laden with delicious fruit at once pointed out to me the residence of Mr. Alley, and a cordial reception from his wife soon made me feel at home.

Mr. Alley was absent, and waiting his return, I strolled among the hives.

Two hundred hives in full working order is a sight to gladden the heart of an apiarian at any time; but here, where all were Italians, the sight of the golden rings of the bees gleaming in the sun, was a pleasure indeed.

Mr. Alley soon returned with a wagon load of hives well filled with (common) bees; and after a cordial invitation to dinner, enlivened by a most interesting and instructive "bee talk," I had the pleasure of seeing thousands of bees handled in a way which would astonish some of our friends, who are so ready to run at the buzz of one.

As it may interest some of the readers of the Journal, I will give a brief account of the way in which nucleus colonies are made.

Carefully raising the top of a hive, a good whiff of smoke (his fumigator, by the way, is the best I have ever seen) is blown in, and after a short pause, comb after comb is lifted or cut out and the bees brushed off with a light whisk broom into an empty box, the bees clustering together in the most amiable quiet manner. In this instance the bees from eight or ten nucleus hives who had fulfilled their mission, were also brushed in, making one united family. I thought, as I sat by, if discordant human creatures, who oftentimes have so much venom, could thus be shaken up together, and made to be of one mind, what a good thing it would be.

The queen was of course destroyed. And now, with a long-handled dipper, the bees, like so many berries, were measured out into the small hives until all were disposed of; the hives, one by one, set aside, each with its combs, to be ready in three days to receive its comb of Italian eggs.

I saw the mothers of these eggs, and there was no room for doubt as to their beauty and size—the handsomest queens I ever looked upon. If an exception could be made it was the directly imported ones; but only the keen eye of Mr. Alley would find a blemish—if blemish there was.

Of Mr. Alley's hive I can only say that, after seeing one taken apart,—full of bees—the ease with which it was done, and the regularity of the combs, it seemed to deserve all the praise it has received. Certainly the ready access to the main hive, in the full working season, is a great desideratum; and if side working boxes are as successful as supers, or boxes on top, then there is nothing more to be wished for.

For wintering, the hive has important desirable features, viz.: the power of concentration and protection (with the side boxes) from extremes of heat and cold.

After such a bee-lesson, I returned to Boston with a most pleasant recollection of my day's experience.

It seems to be a favorite expression with some of the correspondents of the Journal, that they have "no axe to grind." I certainly have none, and do not care to grind any body else's axe; but I do hope that such a good friend of the Journal, and such a good apiarian, may have (which has not always been the case) a fair trial and ample justice.

D. C. MILLETT.

Holmesburg, Pa.

[For the American Bee Journal.]

Mr. Alley a Fair Dealer.

DEAR JOURNAL:—If I knew half as much about bees, as some who write for your columns *think* they do, I would have written you a letter long since. But, having a wonderful stock of modesty, and not knowing anything strange or interesting to tell, I have kept still. I would not have spoken even now, had it not been that I think Dr. C. N. Austin puts the case rather hard against Mr. Alley. I have had some dealings with Mr. Alley, and have found him a perfect gentleman. I am not sure that there are many other queen raisers quite as honorable. Last summer I sent to him for a couple of queens. He answered that he had so many orders to fill, that he was afraid that it would be too late before he could supply me. I insisted that he should send them on if possible. Well, on the last day of September the queens arrived. It had been very cold for a week, and the poor things were about chilled to death. I did the best I could for them; but by the second morning they were dead. I informed Mr. Alley of the result, and he said at once that he would send me others this summer. He has done so, and I do not think there are any finer queens in this State. They are just regular beauties.

It was no fault of Mr. Alley that the weather was so cold, and the price at which he sells his queens is so low, that a man must be very conscientious in his dealings, who would do as Mr. Alley has done with me.—And, by the way several of your correspondents are afraid of being ruined by Mr. "Alley's cheap labor." Let me tell them that I have an Italian queen for which I paid eight dollars, and I would not give one of the two Mr. Alley sent me, for four like her.

This is the way I introduced my queens. I took three frames of brood out of a populous colony; put them into an empty hive, with the Italian queen caged; filled up the hive with other frames (empty); removed the old colony and put the Italian in its place, and in forty-eight hours released the queen. I find the plan a good one, and do not care whether it is according to the books or not.

With this, find two dollars, which place to my credit, and believe me a constant reader.

John S. McKiernan.

Smith's Mills, Pa., Aug. 19, 1871.

[For the American Bee Journal.]

A Merited Tribute.

Mr. Editor:—I wish to state a few candid facts, although it may savor of having an axe to grind, but I assure you I have none. From pure motives, I wish to state for the benefit of my fellow beekeepers over our broad land, I must say that I have been receiving Italian queens from a good many of our leading breeders, almost ever since they have first been imported into this country; but none of them compare with the two which I received from Mr. Adam Grimm, of Jefferson, Wisconsin. The queens themselves are beautiful, and their worker progeny exceed any I ever saw—every worker being bright and plainly showing the three yellow bands.

Mr. Grimm ought to know the pure stock, as he has been himself to the home of the Italian bee in Italy, where they are found in their purity. Besides, I venture to say that he has more bees on hand than any man on this continent, and all of them are the pure Italian stock.

Elmira, N. Y. H. M. M.

It would almost seem as if the Italian bees were common, or at least well known, in England nearly three hundred years ago, for "rare Ben" Jonson, who flourished in Queen Elizabeth's days, says—

"The *yellow* bees the air with murmurs fill."

[For the American Bee Journal.]

Amateur No. 3.

Dear Journal:—I was so low-spirited when I received the August number of the Journal, that I could not write a line. My bees did not gather much honey from the white clover, and since that time they have done nothing. Even now (Sept. 2), they have not more than two and a half pounds of honey to the hive; and still the weather is so dry that I am afraid they will not make a support for the winter. Yet I live in hopes, and notwithstanding all opposition, I still have the same love for the little pets, and will watch them carefully.

I have just introduced a queen which I received from Italy, and she is doing well. I would here say that a great deal more care is required in introducing queens brought from a distance than those reared in your own apiary. There seems to be something about them when received from the shipping box that the bees do not like; wherefore I always close them in a cage securely, and place them between two frames of honey, near the center of the hive, and let them remain there three or four days without interruption. Then smoke the bees, so that they will fill themselves *full* of honey, and smear the queen with honey, when she will be received all right. Care must be taken to destroy all queen cells, if any are started. I have never lost a queen, when managed in this way; whereas I lost several by putting them in a wire cage stopped with wax, leaving the bees to remove it themselves. Although I have never lost a queen from my own apiary by introducing in this latter way; yet I would say to those receiving queens from a distance, be more careful in introducing them.

I have been reading with interest the discussion going on in various quarters about the famous Dzierzon theory on the purity of drones from mothers impregnated by black drones. I think this question involves a great interest of bee-keepers, and should be carefully sifted. As to myself, I have long believed it false, and do not hesitate to tell my brethren of it. I have had some considerable experience in this matter, and base my opinion on my own experiments, and not on what I read.

If I could be as successful in artificial fertilization as some, I have not a doubt that I could prove beyond question that a queen raised from a pure mother, but mated with a black drone, would not produce pure drones. My neighbors who keep none but black bees have on several occasions had queens fertilized by Italian *drones* and the marks could be traced through the drones as well as the workers. I hope further and more satisfactory experiments will be made on this subject.

In this question, the question of the Italian bee, as a distinct variety, may play a conspicuous part, and will have to be settled first. On this I am quiet for the present, at least. I am satisfied with the superiority of the Italian as it is, whether a distinct variety or not. I believe a cross with the black bees does not injure the quality of the workers, as they will gather as much honey, are quite as watchful, and withal as desirable to the beekeeper.

Hoping that others have had better success than I have had this season, and wishing the Journal prosperity, I remain an

AMATEUR.

Sept. 2, 1871.

☞Of course there can be no objection to experiments made to test the truth of the Dzierzon theory, though a knowledge of what *has* been done would much facilitate the progress and save trouble and useless labor in that direction. Those who make such experiments should take special care, also, that the queens they select to start with are of undoubted purity, if they would hope to reach conclusive results.

The deceptious appearances in apiaries of common bees that have led observers astray, it should be borne in mind, did not present themselves till after the second season subsequent to the introduction of Italian bees in the vicinity of such apiaries—which fact divests the phenomena of their supposed significance. In a few years after that event, very few pure common queens will be found within a radius of five or six miles from an Italian stock, and observations made in such neighborhoods or under such circumstances, are exceedingly fallacious.

Experiments instituted with either common or Italian queens of unquestionable purity, we are well assured, will always result in confirming Dzierzon's theory: and the sooner they are made, and the more frequently repeated, with due and indispensable precautions, the sooner will all doubts be removed from the minds of candid inquirers.—[ED.

[For the American Bee Journal.]

The "Coming Bee."

MR. EDITOR.—It is long since I contributed anything to the Journal, and doubtless a much longer time might have elapsed ere I would have trespassed on your indulgence, but for the fact that I wish to call the attention of beekeepers to the subject which heads this article.

Since the introduction of the Italian bee in our country in 1860, it has been held up to beekeepers throughout the land as what Dzierzon calls it, the "*ne plus ultra of bees.*" This flaming endorsement was doubtless merited at the time of its introduction; but it now has a rival in the field, which, in my opinion, is destined soon to force our striped beauties to a secondary position. The bee I refer to is a *cross* between the Italian and the black bee, favoring the latter in general appearance more than the Italians.

The queens of these bees are not as dark as those of the *pure blacks*, but are *longer* and *larger* than those of either of the pure races, very active, inclined to hide, wonderfully prolific, driving the workers out of the "brood chamber" into the surplus receptacles, whether *boxes* or "store combs;" and not, as is too often the case with the Italians, allowing the workers to fill the brood combs with honey.

The bees of this kind are very docile, easily handled, and readily shaken from the combs. Their wings are large, and their range of flight and acuteness of scent greatly superior to those of the Italians. Their bodies, when young, have a gray and hairy appearance all over. The wings on the abdomen are well defined, very light-colored, but not quite as light as those of the Italians. Although it is difficult at present to describe these bees, yet by one familiar with them, they are easily recognized.

What their looks and appearance will be when they are worked into a distinct breed, it is difficult to conjecture. But a *mixed race* or *cross* between the native and the Italian, is what we want. We want a bee not for *show*, but for honey gathering; and that such is to become the favorite with beekeepers, I am fully persuaded.

The advantages of these bees are, first, their prolificness; second, their disposition *to store honey* in boxes or in any place accessible; fourth, their being less disposed to swarm than the Italians or blacks, and they are more easily managed as *non-swarmers*; fifth, when they do swarm, whether as prime or after-swarms, the swarms are *invariably* large, as might be expected from their prolific queens and disinclination to swarm; sixth, they are easily handled, and very readily drop from the combs when shaken; seventh, their range of flight and acuteness of scent, are greater than those of either the Italians or blacks; eighth, they are more disposed to build *worker* combs than the Italians.

I wish friend Grimm, instead of banishing the black bee out of his neighborhood, had experimented upon crosses a little further than *half-breeds*. It is not my intention to say aught against the Italians, notwithstanding they have their faults, but simply to call the attention of beekeepers to the advantage of carrying the crossing process beyond the cross half-breed. The "coming bee" will, in my opinion, be very closely related to the *common black* bee, but with enough of *Italian blood* in it to form a *distinct* breed.

Let those who have black bees, procure *Italians* as quickly as possible, and they will soon see the advantage of a *mixed race*; and after the first cross there will be no more trouble about handling. I hope that those who have had experience with the kind of bees I have written about, will tell "their experience" to the members of the beekeeping fraternity, for I suppose that others, besides myself, have noted the great advantage of these bees. The few that I have had for the past two years have stored *nearly double* the quantity of honey stored by *my Italians*, and are not nearly so troublesome to handle, for they *run* from *smoke* quicker, and are shaken from the combs very easily.

G. A. WRIGHT.

Orchard, Iowa, Aug. 14, 1871.

☞We suspect that the "coming bee" is still further in the distant future than our correspondent imagines. The second, third, fourth, or even the fifth generation of cross-bred bees, taken as they run or fly, is not likely to have a fixed character, transmissible with certainty in subsequent breeding, if we may trust our own observations; and till such point is reached, it cannot be said that the product possesses any character at all. We have frequently seen the third and fourth generation of cross bred bees, on both sides of the family, and could not perceive that there was yet any "fixity" about them, except that all of them had, invariably, like their remotest ancestry, four wings and six feet. The first cross, however, always proved *true to name*, for *cross* they ever were, through all the moods and tenses. In subsequent crosses this bad trait was perhaps less prominent, but neither was there any indication of a tendency to permanent improvement. Further than the fourth or fifth generation we have no experience to speak of, nor do we think we shall have shortly, as we mean to cut off the whole tribe, "without remainder," next season, by dethroning the queens and substituting pure Italians in their stead—for, as at present advised, we must candidly say those are good enough for us.

But we do not wish to be understood as denying the possibility of originating and establishing a superior breed of bees. Far from it. On the contrary we believe it is practicable and will be done, though not lightly nor speedily. When the principles of scientific breeding shall have been investigated and ascertained in regard to bees, as they have been in regard to other domestic animals, and means devised for carrying on the process with precision and certainty, as a definite branch of business, the way will be open for improvement in this direction, and persons will be found to devote to it the requisite time, attention and skill. Then, and not till then, may the "coming bee" that will *stay*, be looked for with some confidence.

Captain Baldenstein, who introduced the Italian bee in Switzerland long before it attracted the notice of German apiarians, had during eight or ten years, only one stock of the pure race, with a number of hybrid colonies of various degrees of intermixture; but he does not appear to have observed among the latter, at any time, any that were superior or even equal as honey storers to the original, pure Italians. As a genial bee-keeper and close observer, he may be regarded as a trustworthy reporter of what was seen when the first cross-bred bees presented themselves outside of Italian territory. Casual mixture, or loosely managed cross-breeding, has not yet led to any encouraging results. More is to be hoped from systematic methods, when we get into position to adopt and prosecute them; though it will never do to proceed on the Darwinian theory of breeding men from monkies, for that, according to the great dramatist, precisely reverses the natural course, as he told us, hundreds of years ago, that

——" The strain of man's bred out
Into baboon and monkey;"

and we feel pretty sure that if facts be appealed to in demonstration of theory, the poet would distance the philosopher.—[ED.

[For the American Bee Journal.]

An Hour Among the Bees.

MR. EDITOR :—Before I give you an account of a most interesting hour I lately had among my bees, permit me to return my thanks to yourself, Mr. Editor, and Mr. J. M. Marvin, for the proposed solutions of my problem; though I am not yet perfectly satisfied with the explanations given. The event occurred on the 25th of July. The queen was not old, but vigorous. There was neither a young queen nor a queen cell in the hive; the frame, with queen, was not more than a minute out of the hive, nor were there any robbers present.

I could yield to Mr. Marvin's solution, if I could see how any poison could touch the queen before she was first attacked, which was evidently with deadly design. The bees were in no-wise irritated previously. I can easily account for poison getting to the queen after the battle commenced. But I am not sorry for sending my problem to the Bee Journal, as it has been the means of giving an important fact, which but few know, to the public:—I mean, that if a queen be touched with poison from a worker bee, it produces parricides. For this, we must thank J. M. Marvin.

On an afternoon last July, I visited a populous hive to which, a week previous, I gave a fine large queen cell. From my Journal I ascertained that the egg around which the cell was formed, must have been laid at least seventeen days before. On opening the hive, I expected to meet a nice young Italian queen two or three days old, but to my disappointment, the cell was just as I left it, unhatched. Of course I concluded that its occupant was dead. So with my penknife I removed the top of the cell, and behold! a worker issued, or a bee even less in size than a worker. It could run quite smartly among the rest of the bees, though it would have required a day or two more to hatch it. In case the little thing should give me some future trouble, I at once carried it to a queenless miniature hive, and placed it on one of its central combs; but not being fully matured, it was soon dragged out through the entrance as a worthless bee. Since that day I have had some thoughts about the affair, and the conclusion I am inclined to come to is, that the occupant of the cell was too old when set apart for a queen; and were it allowed to hatch in the ordinary way, and live, it would become *a laying worker*. Now, I am sure, Mr. Editor, if my conclusion is erroneous, some of the readers of the Bee Journal will soon expose it.—But as my purpose is to give you an account of an hour among my bees, I must proceed to the other part of it.

Having then taken a spoonful of warm sweets, I opened one of my miniature hives which had an Italian young queen about a week old. I poured the sweets on the top of the frames, closed the hive, and took my seat opposite the entrance, so as to get a good sight of the queen, as she would leave on her hymeneal excursion. The day was calm and bright. The drones were numerously flying through the air; and as the hive was a short distance from the rest, there were but few bees around it, so that every thing was promising a good view of the queen. I had no doubt but she would appear, for I find that to excite the bees with warm sweets will invariably bring out the queen, if she be of the right age and the day favorable. In two minutes after giving the sweets she appeared, large and bright. Having taken a good view of her hive, she was soon out of sight, but soon returned and entered her hive, without much notice being taken of her by the bees at the entrance. In ten minutes she reappears, and now stays away a long time. She is out twenty minutes; yes twenty-five. And now my expectation is at its height. She must soon arrive now, or not at all. Twenty-seven minutes are now past, since she left the box. At last she comes, *pursued by a drone.* He is gaining rapidly on her. She is for entering her hive, but he is before her. Round and round the box they go; but the queen gets again to the entrance. In she goes, with ocular evidence that she had already been fertilized. The drone would also have entered, had it not been that he was met by two or three workers at the entrance, which disputed his right to that hive. But the queen now complained most piteously inside. The hive was opened at once, and I saw the queen held fast on the bottom. Without a moment's delay the fumigator was got, and freely applied to the parricides—for what else can I call them. This compelled them to let go. The queen now ascended the comb, and the hive was closed. But in a moment she came out, flying, and whirling around the box, and after many attempts to enter again, she succeeded, in spite of her vicious subjects. But she was no sooner in, than out she came again, on the wing, for precious life, pursued by the parricides. On entering the third time, she was soon caught, and held fast, till liberated again with smoke. I then caged her, and as I was anxious to test her purity, I introduced her to her own subjects in the evening, as if she had been a strange queen; and in two or three days she had lots of eggs.

Now, Mr. Editor, during this most interesting hour among my bees, I flatter myself with the thought of having learned something. But as I feel my communication already too long, I can only give you the result of some thoughts, without any comment, which are as follows:—

1st. That a very large queen cell may not produce a large queen, nor any queen.

2d. That a queen, on her return, after being fertilized, may be destroyed by her own bees.

3d. That a *laying worker* is produced as described above.

4th. That a queen may pair more than once with a drone. I have not the shadow of a doubt but the queen described in this communication would have done, were it not that she frustrated her pursuer's attempt by entering her hive. What I now feel sorry for is, that I did not close the entrance, so as to see what is seldom seen.

J. ANDERSON.

Tiverton, Canada, Sept. 11, 1871.

[For the American Bee Journal.]

Extracted Honey.

This being the first season that extracted honey has been sold in this part of Maryland, I was very anxious that mine should be put in such shape as to establish a reputation, and secure me a good market in future, when I should have more of it to dispose of.

As soon as I extracted thirty pounds, it was put in a tin can, set in a vessel of boiling water, and kept at boiling heat for twenty minutes. This not only drives off all the moisture, which would have evaporated, if the honey had been left in the hive until sealed, but causes any impurities, such as pieces of wax, &c., which may be in the honey, to rise to the surface, when they can be skimmed off—thus making it perfectly clear; but also expels all noxious substances. It is then poured into self-sealing glass jars, and fastened up while hot.

The first dealer to whom I showed the honey asked me if I would "guarantee it not to candy or ferment." I told him I was very certain it would not do either while sealed up, but was not so certain about it if left open. To test the matter, I left two jars of it open, in a kitchen, all the summer, and the honey is as good now as it was when taken from the hive.

I think heating the honey is very important, and that it fully pays for the trouble, as the combs can be emptied as fast as the honey is stored, without waiting for it to be sealed; thus saving much valuable time to the bees in the height of the season, and much trouble to yourself in not having to uncap the combs. The honey, after being heated, is about the consistency of thick molasses, and beautifully clear.

I have known several instances of persons eating this honey with impunity, who could not taste ordinary new honey without being made sick by it. One of these persons was my assistant in preparing the honey. She had never in her life been able to eat new honey, and now she not only ate of this twice a day, but mixed it with water and drank it, when she was heated and tired, without its having the slightest bad effect upon her.

That it is very popular and sells readily, may be judged from the fact that I have, up to this time, sold over a hundred and thirty-five (135) dollars worth of it, at about twenty cents per pound, from the seven hives on which I used the extractor, as stated in the Journal for August, and usually in the hot weather it is impossible to sell honey at all in this neighborhood. I have not the least fear of overstocking the market with this honey, as it will pay well at fifteen cents per pound, and every one who has used it wants more of it. Besides, it can be used profitably in making most excellent vinegar—which will serve to regulate prices.

DANIEL M. WORTHINGTON.

St. Denis, Md., Sept. 12, 1871.

Until the fifteenth century honey was used instead of sugar.

[For the American Bee Journal.]

Poisonous Honey.

One morning, just before the close of his daily visit to the patients of a hospital of which he was the chief physician, a professor of surgery, accompanied by his pupils, was called to a man who had just been brought to the hospital.

The sick man appeared to be about fifty years old; his blear eyes and repulsive features showed the marks of a vulgar and debauched life. He was suffering from an abscess in the throat. That abscess, large as my fist, and pressing on his windpipe, interrupted breathing, and suffocation was imminent.

"*Messieurs*," said the doctor to his pupils, "if immediate relief were not given to this sufferer, the air would in a few minutes cease to reach the lungs, and he must die. Fortunately it is in our power to save him."

While speaking, the doctor had drawn a dissecting knife from his truss, and directing two *interns* to hold the patient firmly, he made a deep cut in the abscess. Then bending himself over the sufferer, with his fingers he parted the edges of the wound, applied his lips to the opening, and drew out by suction and spat out two mouthfuls of violet colored pus.

When, after this act of self devotion, the doctor received from the hands of an attendant a glass of vinegar and water, to rinse his mouth, the eyes of his pupils were suffused with tears of admiration.

That physician, so devoted to his art and to his patients, was (or *is*, for I hope he is yet living) Doctor Ricord, Professor of Surgery in the University of Paris. His practice, at the time, was worth fifty thousand dollars a year.

"Our business sometimes demands true acts of energy," said the doctor, turning to his pupils. "I trust that in a similar emergency each one of you will remember this example and not suffer his courage to fail. In such case you will feel that the happiness resulting from duty accomplished, is far greater than the act itself. Such an operation involves no danger. The virus of the pus, as well as the venom of animals, has no power to affect the mouth or the organs of nutrition. You may without danger suck the stings of bees and the bites of vipers or rattlesnakes."

I beg all, especially my fair readers, to excuse me for having presented before them a picture apparently so repulsive. I hope for their pardon, in view of the greatness of the admirable act.

This story, narrated to me by a friend of mine, a student of medicine, who witnessed the scene, was recalled to my memory by perusing an article of Mr. Langstroth's, on bee poison, in the American Bee Journal for April last, page 221.

Doubtless Dr. Ricord, less acquainted with bees than Mr. Langstroth, was less competent to speak of the effects of bee poison; and certainly that venom, if put on the tongue, causes headache in some cases, as I have myself experienced. Yet I cannot agree with Mr. Langstroth, when he says that is to the poison contained in the honey that its influence on the stomachs of certain persons is attributable.

Mr. Langstroth says that the bee poison dries on the honey, and a few lines further on, that it is very volatile. A thing volatile does not dry, it evaporates.

But why attribute to the bee poison the cholic experienced by certain persons, after eating honey? I cannot drink milk without suffering from cholic. The *leather soup*, as the coffee milk is named by the *Societé Impériale et Centrale d'Agriculture of France*,* is for me a powerful purgative. Raw fruits, or such as are not perfectly ripe, do not suit me, yet I can eat them, without ill results, if cooked. But by cooking honey loses its delicacy.

I did, however, discover a way to enjoy all these good things without suffering. It is by beginning with a little at first, and eating a little more the next day—being careful not to eat between my meals. After some days, my stomach having become accustomed to them, I can eat them freely, though in moderation. To say that my stomach has become accustomed to them, does not express precisely my understanding of the acquired possibility of eating with impunity what at first was injurious. Everybody knows that soap (itself made of soda) is better than soda for the removal of grease spots from garments. It is because it contains itself some portion of grease. The stomach acts in a similar manner. The gastric juice has to dissolve the food. The first time that such food as honey or milk is presented and put in contact with it, the gastric juice does not possess the elementary constituents necessary to enable it to perform the work. But on the morrow, the blood, constituted in part of the honey or milk, or whatever else, eaten and digested the day before, brings to the stomach and supplies the gastric juice with a portion of the essential elements needed, and the food, now better digested, passes without painful sensations. I have many times experienced this in myself, and observed it in the case of many others also.

Ch. Dadant.

Hamilton, Ills., Aug. 7, 1871.

* See Report of the Department of Agriculture for 1869, page 634.

[For the American Bee Journal.]

Hives and Honey.

I am again seated, pen in hand, with the intention of boring the readers of the Journal with an effusion on the subject of honey bees. So many of the fraternity add a little information to every page of the Journal, just as the bee adds drop after drop to the store of honey in the hive, that it makes others anxious to contribute a little of their experience, though it may be only a mite.

It seems to be the fashion at present to describe hives, and charge a fee for describing, according to one's eminence in apiarian knowledge. Friend Gallup charges one dollar, thus putting himself down at 100 per cent., as at par.

We sometimes think his opinions upon bee-culture much above par; but we will not question his modest decision, and shall hereafter class him as par Gallup.

While reading the many descriptions of hives, one is reminded of the proverb, that "there is but one real good woman in the whole world, and every married man thinks he has that one best, blessed, adorable creature." So it is with hives; every beekeeper has the very best hive. Many want side storers, and a *few* don't. Some want side openers, and others would banish them to Tophet. Now I use a *three side* opener, and like it. It contains two sets of frames, one above the other. The upper set I can remove without opening the sides. By opening the sides, I can remove the lower frames, without disturbing the upper ones. The rear opens, and is devised to contain twelve four pound boxes, or a series of small frames. The sides can be removed, and cases containing either large or small frames or boxes can be applied. The hive has a removable cap, and an adjustable bottom-board. These are the general features. Should I give a full architectural description and charge for it according to my eminence, I would fix the price at about five cents—for I feel myself away down below par Gallup, almost at the foot of the ladder. The name of this hive is "*The Star-spangled, Universal, Trio-side-opening, Apis Mellifica Casket.*"

My experience during the past honey season, confirms me in the use of *small* frames. They may not be so convenient to ship to a distance as boxes, but for local sales they can't be beat. I find that if you appear before a customer with a box for which he will have to pay from three to five dollars, he will often look at the amount several times and finally put the money in his pocket, refusing to buy. Whereas, if you present a neat frame for about fifty cents, he will buy every few days, and spend three times three three dollars, for honey in this shape. It is much like selling candy. If the retail dealer was obliged to sell it by the box of several pounds' weight, his sales would be few, while the sale of stick by stick is rapid and profitable. We must study to popularize honey in the comb, for extracted honey will always be looked upon with suspicion, for *it will be adulterated*. It is almost impossible to get pure extracted honey in any of our cities. While there are honorable dealers, there are also those so dishonorable as to palm off a poor quality of doctored molasses for honey; and a small quantity of adulterated honey gives a bad name to a large amount of pure honey. If extracted honey is to become an everyday article of use, its price must be put down cheaper than any article by which it is adulterated. We will then, and not until then have the pure honey on sale in our largest cities.

Extracted honey would be profitable at a very low price, for it is great gain to keep the breeding chamber emptied of honey. Extracted honey also bids fair to have a powerful rival in the new rising industry of *grape sugar*. Honey as we all know comes under this head, and grape sugar can be made from shavings, rags, sawdust, and any kind of cellulose; but the cheapest material is corn and grain. From the pure starch obtained from any kind of cellulose, a syrup can be made that resembles honey so closely that few can detect the difference; and when this industry becomes thoroughly established, it will take the lead, and extracted honey will have to fall into line upon some uniform price *per gallon*. But, Mr. Editor, I have already written too much, and will close. SCIENTIFIC.

Hartford, N. Y., Sept. 7, 1871.

[For the American Bee Journal.]

Patents, and Patenting Inventions.

So much has been and is being said against patented inventions, especially "Patent Bee Hives," that it would almost seem to be the only side of the question that would bear discussion.

After waiting a long time to see something in the Journal from some patentee, in defence of their motives and rights, we have thought that something might be said in their favor.

It has been written in the Bee Journal, and elsewhere, that patent hives are a curse to bee-keeping. Let us see if this is true. In this case we must not be partial; we must include all. Now, shall we go back to the old box hive, and say it is the best? But some will say "the Langstroth is good." So it is, but it is patented, and therefore should come under the rule that "patent hives are a curse to beekeeping."

To Mr. Langstroth we are indebted for the principle of the movable comb, as introduced in this country; and to him we should give the honor and pecuniarily respect his claims. With these considerations, improvements should be allowed. Mr. Langstroth drew his ideas from those before him, and others should have the same right. How would it have been with other inventions, had no improvements been allowed? Savery with his steam engine, Fitch with his steamboat, Howe with his sewing machine, Morse with the telegraph, and so on through the list?

It is a law of the universe that there is no stand-still. We are either improving or going back to rise again; and perfection may be considered as the plant that is matured, as then decay is its destiny. If the proverb is allowed, that "necessity is the mother of invention," then we must allow that without necessity there would be no invention. Suppose some inventions are counterfeit, and do more harm than good, should we say that all are worthless? The best test of a genuine thing are the numerous attempts to counterfeit it. An article of no value is not worth counterfeiting.

But says some one, if you have anything of importance, you should give it to the world, or you are not a public benefactor. A public benefactor is an exception, not the rule. Besides an invention given to the world, of whatever importance in itself, would not be introduced without more labor, time, and money spent in introducing them when a person is pecuniarily interested in its introduction; and this selfish world would not accept anything so unnatural to its views. "Necessity is the mother of invention." That would not imply that an inventor should help the world before he helps himself.

Where is there a man who is continually crying—"down with patent rights! They are humbugs," &c., who is willing to advertise something of value to the world for nothing? On the contrary, where has there been a discovery of great value, but has had the greatest number of opposers?

If these men that are crying humbug would consume half as much time in instructing the illiterate beekeeper in the science of bee-keeping, there would be less complaint of being deceived, and we should move on. But these fault-finders do not write or talk to show the way. They have other reasons. Some of their talk is like the gas that arises from fermentation in consequence of having been soured. Hence the effervescence; or some cry "sour grapes!" Some have an unusual protuberance of the cranium in this direction, and do not think of anything else to say.

A correspondent writing under the caption of "My Patent Bee Hive," in the Journal for May, says—"what intelligent beekeeper can read the heading of this article without feelings of indignation and disgust? Of disgust, when he thinks of the legion of foolish and worse than useless devices, &c. Of indignation, when he remembers, how those devices are combined with valuable qualities," &c. Further on, he says—"Inventions grow." That would not imply that they grow by jumping from one great invention to another, leaving out all the minor ones. If we reason by analogy, little by little is the law of nature, and with inventions it holds good.

Every invention, however small and seemingly worthless, helps to build up and bring out greater ones. They may seem worthless, but some part may serve as an index finger to point to something of real value. Therefore inventions will continue to be made so long as the end justifies the means. Ideas are not new, although we call them so. It is their combinations that makes them new to us.

The attentive readers of our American Bee Journal are not likely to be humbugged by patent-right men, especially if its contributors write to instruct rather than to find fault. We do not remember ever reading any of Mr. Langstroth's writings wherein his text was "down with humbug," &c. But for fear to be thought ours is, we will stop.

Enclosed find two dollars for the Journal, for we use it in our business, and expect to do so while we are a being (Bee-ing).

SESEAYE.

Pollen, in botany, is the farina or fertilizing powder communicated by the anthers of flowers to the pistils.

Wax dolls never indulge in laughter. They belong to the *cereous* family.

[For the American Bee Journal.]

Patent Hive Deceivers, &c.

MR. EDITOR:—As I have not noticed anything in the Journal from Southwestern Missouri, I will write you a few lines.

My occupation calls me from home occasionally, and in the last few days, only a few miles from here, I was much surprised to find many of my acquaintances paying for a movable comb bee hive and right, when they were really getting nothing deeded to them except a moth trap and a bee-feeding box underneath the hive—which I consider not worth a hill of beans. I asked a friend, who had just bought one of these gull-traps and right, to show me his hive; which he was quite ready to do. "Here," said he, "is the Improved Movable Hive. I can take out the combs; divide the bees and swarm them, as I please; raise queens; shake out the moth-worm, &c. Down underneath here is the moth-trap, to catch the miller; put some water in there, and he will get drowned. Back here, too, is the drawer to set in food and water, all so good and nice. But I think I will only use the upper part, and not bother myself making the lower apartment. The movable frames are what I wanted."

I said, will you show me your deed? He soon produced it, and, sure eneugh, it was just as I expected to find. I told him I saw that the patent vendor had only deeded to him the right to make and use the moth trap and bee feeder; but had not given him the right to make and use the only valuable thing there was about the hive. Said he—"Then, it seems, I have got only what I do not care for, and am liable to pay some one else for the frames." It is even so, said I; your deed gives you no right to use the frames—they belong to the original patentee or his assignee. The price this man paid for a farm right was ten (10) dollars; for hive and right, fifteen (15) dollars. I could hear of the patent vendor selling ten or a dozen rights and hives in that neighborhood, amounting to from one hundred and fifty (150) to one hundred and eighty (180) dollars; all sacrificed by these people for not being posted. Had each of them taken the American Bee Journal, it is not likely that any one of them would have paid ten dollars for a moth trap and bee-feeder.

Readers, let us try to circulate the Journal among beekeepers generally. Some of you may say that two dollars a year is too much for the paper. But, remember, it is devoted exclusively to your interest, and not sustained by money obtained by selling devices that are of no use, or pretending to convey rights not embraced in the patent. Instead of helping to deceive and defraud you, it is striving to keep you from being imposed upon and robbed. No man can keep bees with success and profit without the Journal; and the man who cannot afford to pay two dollars a year for a paper that monthly brings him valuable information from all parts of the country, had better not spend his time with bees.

I consider the July number of the present volume worth a year's subscription to any beekeeper. The new volume has started as an advance on the old ones, and we feel assured that if supported as it ought to be, it will continue to improve from month to month, and from year to year. Beekeepers want a paper that they can, in all respects, rely upon; that has no interest in misleading any; and is ready to stand up fearlessly for the right on all occasions. Such a paper we have in the AMERICAN BEE JOURNAL. Let us all join in giving it an adequate and cheering support. Sustain it well, and we shall save money by being kept from the clutches of harpies. There are many also just beginning to feel an interest in bee-culture, since it has been shown to be a profitable business when managed with ordinary care and intelligence. All these should have the Journal to pioneer them on their way, and give them the rich experience of practical men who have been long and successfully engaged in this fascinating pursuit.

Let me add a few words more, of local interest. Beekeeping here is progressing of late. Formerly it was managed on the old-fogy principles. We have not much natural pasturage here for bees, and the country is still so new that artificial pasturage is not yet plenty; but bees are doing tolerably well at present, everything considered.

E. LISTON.

Virgil City, Mo., Aug. 29, 1871.

[For the American Bee Journal.]

Bee Season's Operations.

MR. EDITOR:—The past was a remarkably early season. I set out my bees on the 10th of February, calculating that I should have to return them, as I still expected cold weather. In this I was disappointed, as the bees continued flying daily, as if it were summer. This caused them to use up their stores very fast, and I judged that, at the rate of consumption going on, they would soon run out of stores. I resorted to feeding, and gave them a considerable quantity of syrup to save them from perishing—purchasing for this purpose three hundred pounds of sugar. Some old beekeepers around remarked on this, that beekeeping did not pay; enjoying a laugh at me for feeding my bees. I let them laugh, as I felt confident there was a good time coming for me and my bees. Well, swarming time came on, and the old fellows kept looking for swarms, but were doomed to disappointment; while I was getting honey by the ton, and making plenty of artificial swarms. Then, as an old negro said—"they begun to laugh out of de odder side of their moufs!"

We shall be more careful hereafter, and always keep honey enough in reserve to give each colony ten pounds if necessary. They will be sure to pay it back richly. No honey worth mentioning could be obtained by the bees till the 10th of May. Though the trees bloomed in profusion the bees were kept from visiting them by constant high winds from the south. After the 10th, they gathered sufficient for their own use; though the hives were not near as populous at the end of May as they had been at the beginning of April. Still, by a little attention properly directed, they were kept in good condition for summer's operations. We pitched the honey out Novice fashion, when the season fully opened. Any person who would secure the most honey from his pure Italians, will use the honey extractor. This we find to be of vital importance with the Italians; but in an apiary of five or six hundred stocks, several extractors would be needed, with suitable assistants to operate them, otherwise even Novice would be kept on the run.

I notice in the August Journal an article from the pen of N. Cameron, of Kansas, pitching into some of our old bee-writers pretty strong for a man from the wild country, and charging the veteran Gallup with seeking to impose some device on the public. If Gallup does not deserve a place in the Journal and allowed to have his say, I think no one does. All novices in beekeeping that have been reading Gallup's articles, should hold him up as their teacher. It is plain enough to me why Gallup made the statement he did, since I have studied the matter over. I have come to the conclusion that he adopted that plan merely as an excuse for not writing awhile. Readers have become so attached to his writing that they expect him to lose too much time from his farm. He is right in the course he takes, for like some of our queen breeders, he ought to look out a little for his own interest.

J. N. WALTER.

Winchester, Iowa.

[For the American Bee Journal.]

Comments on the Past Season.

MR. EDITOR:—Here we are again with our bees in September, and we shall have to confess that ours have not done as well as we expected they would in the spring. Still, we are not going to complain, when we look at some of our neighbors, whose bees have not done as well as our own.

The month of March was very warm here, and in the latter part of it the bees brought in a considerable quantity of pollen. But April was cold and wet, and the colonies rather lost than gained in population; and when the weather became warm my hives were crammed with brood. By the way, spring feeding is a "big thing." It tells for the next three months, and in fact for the whole season. We did not have much fruit bloom here, and as we had got up our bees to the swarming pitch, some colonies nearly ran ashore for honey, having so many young bees to feed. But we carried them through safe till clover came into bloom, and then got out our machine and took out two hundred and thirty (230) pounds of nice honey, when a drouth came on and stopped our work in that line.

Our bees were ready to swarm early, and were through with that before our neighbors had any drones flying. I did not let them swarm as much as some do, for I was fearful of a bad season; and in this I think I hit the nail on the head. At the present time I have twenty-four colonies in good shape for wintering. Buckwheat has yielded a good lot of honey; the hives are well filled; and in some cases the bees are filling boxes; so that I can safely say I shall get three hundred pounds of honey in all—which is better than I have done before. But if the season had been as good as the previous one, I could, with the facilities I now have, just as easily have got one thousand pounds.

The last was a very bad winter here for bees. Some beekeepers lost as high as sixty colonies. I lost only two, one of which was queenless, and the other failed from carelessness. In the fall my hives were crammed full of honey, with hardly any empty comb. As I had no extractor then, I had to take out three or four combs from each hive, and mass the bees on a few combs, and that is what saved them. Beekeepers who did not use this precaution have told me that their bees died, leaving their hives full of honey—an occurrence which they could not understand or explain.

I am sorry to say that I have had one case of foul-brood in my apiary; though I think it is cured now. I extracted all the honey and removed the queen, letting all the brood hatch that would. I then filled the cells with a solution of hyposulphite of soda; let it stand in over night; then emptied it, and took the combs over to the Thread Factory and immersed them a few hours in a solution of chloride of lime; then rinsed them, threw out the water, and gave them back to the bees in a clean hive. They have raised a number of sets of brood since, and I think are all right now. For one, I am willing to give Dr. Abbe all praise for the remedy, and thank him besides; for it is a great discovery if it holds foul-brood in check. I think, as a class, beekeepers are not always willing to give each other due credit for advances or improvements made in bee-culture; but are rather too apt to go on the principle of "it's big I and little *u*."

Some correspondents appear to think that Gallup is rather rough, because he wants a dollar for the description of his hive. I do not. If he has made a valuable improvement on his hive, he should have his pay as well as any one else. A man may work a lifetime for the public and get no thanks for it. If the grumblers will look over the Journal for the last five years, and read Gallup's articles, they will find things worth much more than a dollar if practised, made known by him with no reward except the pleasure enjoyed from helping onward the inexperienced who were groping their way in the dark. When the hash on which he is now at work is cooked, it is likely we shall want some of it on our plate.

I have read the September number of the Journal, and am much pleased with it. We learn something new from the Journal every month, and expect to do so while we live to read it. Cannot something be done, Mr. Editor, to have it come semi-monthly? Can't you manage to take a vote and see if the beekeepers won't go in for it and pay four dollars a year instead of two? It is well worth the money, being the best paper in the country on bees. This all will admit, and the beekeepers ought to see to it that it can be published more frequently, for the advantage and benefit would be on their side.

I am glad to learn that there are beekeepers in other sections of the country, who are doing better in the business this year, than we are here in the New England States. Seasons and the weather vary, and our turn too will probably come round in due course. Novice had better look well after his laurels, or Miss Katie will take them. G. H. Bassett.

North Bennington, Vt., Sept. 8, 1871.

[For the American Bee Journal.]

Why the Bees Did Not Swarm!

Mr. Editor:—I see from the correspondence of the Journal, that in nearly all the States there was very little swarming among the bees this season.

I think I can give the reason or probable cause of this. The natural instinct of the queens induces them to commence laying about the time New Year comes, or most generally from the first to the tenth or fifteenth of January. They will usually lay a small circle of eggs in two or three of the middle combs; in February they enlarge the circles, and still further enlarge them in March, adding some more combs to those already containing brood. They proceed thus progressively, till in April and May they have their combs mostly filled up, and when the last or fifth large circle is ready to hatch, the colony is ready for swarming, in a natural season.

This season the weather having been warm in February and March, the bees had their three larger batches ready for swarming about the last of April and first of May. Most of the Italians swarmed about that time, or during the latter part of May and beginning of June. The queens then rested from their labors, and honey being plenty, the workers filled up nearly all the brood combs with honey, and very few afterswarms came off. But the season advanced too fast for the black bees, whose natural swarming time is from the latter part of May to the middle of June, the brood cells were rapidly filled with honey, leaving no empty ones for the accommodation of the queen, and hence very few swarms came from the black colonies.

I opened strong hives to get bees to make nuclei, on the 19th of April. They had their queen cells run out, with larvæ in them, and we had swarms in April this season. I made artificial swarms on the 10th of April to start queen cells, and they did well. One of the old colonies that I removed to a new stand, after having taken out one-third of its combs and bees, and all the old workers returning to the old stand, still made me sixty pounds of surplus honey; and I sold the hive after the honey season was over for fifteen dollars.

I do not let many swarms come off naturally. I make artificial swarms by controlling my colonies and directing their labors to honey gathering, instead of encouraging their swarming propensities. When I see any of my colonies that are likely to swarm, I open their hive and take out two frames containing hatching brood, with all the adhering bees, leaving the queen in the old hive. I set these combs in a new hive, and go to two or three other colonies and take two combs from each of them, setting them in the new hive, with the frames first removed. Do this in the evening, or, if you separate in the morning, always set them in a dark cellar till late in the evening, and then let them out. When you go to unite the frames always blow smoke on them for a short time, and the bees will unite with distressing each other.

I can take out a frame or two of brood once in awhile, and thereby control the swarming in almost all cases, and have my bees store honey during the whole of the honey season. And by taking out the frames from the center of the hive, the bees are not stopped from storing honey, but are rather incited to labor the harder.

When you let a hive swarm naturally you nearly destroy the honey storing of the colony for that season. But by controlling swarming you will never stop the storing of honey, checking it very little indeed, while you add one-fourth or one-third to the number of your stock, and have all good strong colonies in the fall. By taking their old brood combs from the old hives at that season of the year, the colony will in almost all cases build new worker combs; and by getting the new in the center of the hives, your old stocks will be much healthier and more vigorous. Always notice if you have a last year's swarm equally strong with an old colony in the spring, that the former will generally be first to swarm.

I see by the Journal that the ladies are taking some interest in the cultivation of bees. When you see the ladies take hold of a business like this, they generally do it in the right way and succeed well.

I have got up a new hive, and am almost afraid to say anything about it in the Journal, for I see in the August number that friend Gallup, having slipped in a few words concerning his hive in the previous number, gets a rap on the knuckles on every side. Now, if he had got it patented, made a great blow about it, got out a boasting advertisement and a flaming show bill, and charged five or ten dollars for a right and a description, it would all have gone off rapidly, like hot buckwheat cakes in the fall, spread with plenty of butter and honey.

ALFRED CHAPMAN.

New Cumberland, West Va., Aug. 21, 1871.

[For the American Bee Journal.]

Facts on Queen Raising.

MR. EDITOR:—I see in the July number of the Journal Mr. J. L. McLean, of Richmond, Ohio, undertakes to philosphize away the longevity and fertility of artificial queens, on the ground that the length of life in "a being is in the ratio of the time intervening between birth and puberty."

We understand from the article the birth of the bee to be fixed at the period of the hatching of the egg and not when it emerges from the cell.

I will here pause, and inquire whether or not Mr. McL. is not laboring under a mistake, when he takes the position, that the period intervening between birth and puberty is shorter in the case of an artificial queen, than in that of a natural one?

1. The birth of the bee is fixed at the hatching of the egg.

3. All larvæ, whether in worker or royal cells, are fed on the same kind of food during the first five days.

3. On condition that the royal cell is built the third day after birth, so that the queen emerges from the cell in ten or eleven days from the time the cell is started, is the period between birth and puberty of the queen shortened? I think not. She only lived and was fed in a worker cell as she would have lived and been fed in a royal cell for the first three days; but the length of time from birth to puberty is the same.

The dimensions of the cell do not always determine the size of the queen reared therein; but is indicative of the amount of food placed in the cell.

When queens are reared under the impulse of natural swarming, the largest cells are filled one half inch in the bottom with food, and the cell lengthened out to give the queen the proper amount of room; and after the cell is vacated a large proportion of the food is left behind unconsumed. But the food consumed and not that which is left, has to do with the life of the queen.

Do artificial queens get a sufficient amount of food? Under most circumstances they do. This is demonstrated in the size, color, health, and their early fertility. When manipulation is correct, such queens are as large, as bright colored, go upon their bridal trip as early, and commence depositing eggs as soon after copulation as natural queens. Does the circumstance of the mother depositing the egg in the royal cell and its hatching there, give the embryo queen an advantage over the one worker deposited and hatched in a worker cell, on condition that it is nursed for a queen from birth? *I think not.* No food is put in the worker or royal cell until the egg hatches, and then the same kind is given for five days, though not always, I think, the same in quantity. Hence the importance of having the larva fed in view of a queen from *birth*, but not from the depositing of the egg—as this always, both in a worker and royal cell, remains without food till birth. A. SALISBURY.

Camargo, Ill.

☞ It is yet an unsettled point whether the queen ever deposits an egg in a royal cell. We put the question to Mr. Dzierzon some years ago, and his reply was that though he had opened and inspected thousands of hives in the breeding season, and watched queens when laying in worker and in drone cells, he had never seen one laying in a royal cell. He called the attention of beekeepers to the matter, in the Bienenzeitung, and asked whether any one had seen the queen in the act of laying in such cells; but no one has ever answered affirmatively. Has any American beekeeper seen it?—Our own *impression* is that she does so, but only when the mouth of the cell has been properly prepared for the purpose by the workers.—[ED.

[For the American Bee Journal.]

Queen Cells and their Contents.

MR. EDITOR:—To-day I had a large swarm of bees come off from one of my hives. They were clustering on the fence, when I discovered them. The honey season being over, I determined to open the hive they came from, destroy the young queens in their cells, and return the swarm to the parent hive. On opening the hive, it was very full of brood, mostly sealed over. The first two queen cells I cut out contained each a dead larva. The third cell had its cap nearly cut round by the young queen, ready to emerge. I removed the cap, and placed the young queen in a cage for future use, if needed. The fourth cell contained a dead *worker bee* dwarfed in size, as you will find on examination. The fifth cell—the most singular, contained a *worker bee* and *a queen*, both dead. These had evidently been dead several days, for on attempting to remove the queen (as I thought,) I pulled the head off the worker. By opening the cell carefully and removing them together, you will find their legs entwined together as they died. The sixth cell contained a *live well developed worker bee*, with her head to the base of the cell. I killed her and returned her to the cell, as you will find her. The seventh cell contained a live queen pupæ, well developed.

The cells as you will see, are of usual size and position, and in outward appearance were like ordinary queen cells. I have never heard of two bees being hatched in one cell, and what is more striking, the one a worker and the other a queen. Can you account for it?

The cells evidently had never been disturbed or opened from the time the bees had sealed them up, until I opened them with a pair of slender point tweezers that I carry in my pocket to remove stings, &c. The cocoon or silk covering inside was perfect, until I opened them.

Last spring the parent stock was a three-quarter blood black bee. They swarmed on the 19th of May. On the 20th I removed the queen cells and introduced an unimpregnated Italian queen (taken from a full hive after it was sealed, and hatched in a nucleus). She was laying on the 27th of May and the hive has done well ever since. Her progeny has a slight dash of black blood.

I have packed the cells in a tin box, and think they will go safely by mail. Cell marked No. 1 contains the dead worker; No. 2, the queen and worker; No. 3, the workers alive when opened. They were a curiosity to me, and as such I forward them to you—hoping they will arrive safely. A. L. BROWN.

London, Ohio, July 29, 1871.

☞ We received the box in good condition, and found the contents of the cells as described. We have often read of workers found in queen cells, but never before of a worker *and* a queen.—[ED.

No person ever got stung by hornets who kept away from where they were. It is so with bad habits.

[For the American Bee Journal.]

"Natural Hardy Queens."

The American people is held by all other nations, as an intelligent people, endowed with sound, practical ideas. Indeed, all classes of citizens in the United States are favored with a sound, clear mind, unbefogged with foolish notions—except one class of society. I mean the *beekeepers!* Since the late promulgation of the modern theory of improved bee-culture, the minds of all those who had "bee on the brain," have been thoroughly disturbed. The unreasonable theory advanced is that by the method of artificial queen raising, bees can be multiplied *ad libitum* if not *ad infinitum*, without at all consulting those insects as to their own proper disposition or wishes. All the feeble-minded of the fraternity of beekeepers—that is the great majority of those who own bees and like to attend to them, have accepted that theory as indisputably true; and all, unconscious of the fallacy of such a system, claim, in spite of common sense and contradicting evidence, that queens thus artificially raised are as good as, or even better than those produced by natural swarming; and continue to incur the risk of their own ruin and the ruin of the race of bees, "by *acting against reason, nature and common sense.*"

Among the feeble-minded fellows I can cite one who, after getting forty-six colonies by that bad method, imagined that his cistern was full of honey gathered by his bees, and that by turning a crank he had filled, one after another, all the pots in his kitchen, and then the boilers of his neighbors, and afterward, some thousands of glass jars with water, labelled—"WHITE CLOVER HONEY, from A. I. Root, Medina, Ohio." Astounding hallucination!

Another of the same set, who inhabits Wenham (I do not give his name, because I fear to turn his innoxious mania into furious folly), has imagined to raise queens for sale. So much deranged is he on this point, that he never perceived that of every five queens which he tries to raise, three fly away on their wedding trip and are lost, and the remaining two are either drone laying, or lay eggs which do not hatch, or at least are a year in maturing. And what is the more wonderful, that the man not only seems content with his business, but that all his customers—equally purblind—are content also and in the perverted craniums imagine that the queens they receive, though nearly or quite dead, are thoroughly prolific, filling their hives with brood and honey which exist only in their owner's imagination.

Such, during the six or eight years past, has been the mental state of the American beekeepers at large. Fortunately Providence, who always has eyes open in order to produce the saviour of the nation just at the right moment (Ex. Napoleon III. for France), has prepared in the West, a man whose mission it is to recall the beekeepers from vain imaginings to common sense. The predestined man is Mr. John M. Price. His first attempt at prophesying having been without results, he retired under his tent. But the *feu sacre* has anew taken possession of him, and we can hope that this time his crusade against a lunacy so wonderful, will be crowned with success.

Plaisanterie apart. Mr. Price, are you then riveted to your theory? Unfortunately, after giving us the means of refutation in your own contradictory writings, you furnish, in the American Bee Journal for August, a new weapon against your arguments.

In a preceding article on the same subject, I have proved that, by your bad method of dividing your colonies to the utmost, *making ten from one,* you can obtain only poor and unprolific queens. Now you say that some queens artificially raised, are one year old before reaching maturity. Then, as some of your queens become good after awhile, may it not be that the progeny of the one I sent you was such?

I too have had queens which matured late; but never when they were put in good strong colonies. I can give you a good instance of delayed maturity. One of my neighbors, Mr. McC. sold me last winter a second swarm of 1869. The queen of that swarm was so poor a layer, that her progeny did not fill her hive in all 1870, and in February 1871, the colony was near starving. I transferred the combs in March, adding a comb of honey and one of brood, and at the end of May I killed that queen with regret (she was black), for she had become wonderfully prolific. Thus the queen had been nearly two years *in becoming mature* as you would say; or before being placed in circumstances indispensable for the development of her fecundity, as I understand the matter,

Believe my experience; quit your system of spoiling your colonies by such dividing as you have narrated in the American Bee Journal of 1868, 1869 and 1870; use exclusively strong colonies to raise queen cells; keep the bees with honey liberally given, if the weather is unfavorable for gathering. Then you will no more complain of the small number of cells started; nor of the poor quality of the queens raised; if you put those young queens in populous and well supplied colonies.

I hope that, after one season of such trials, you will acknowledge with me that the swarming fever has no more value for raising good queens, than a fifth wheel would have for your wagon.

CH. DADANT.

Hamilton, Ill., Aug. 9, 1871.

[For the American Bee Journal.]

Crippled Bees. Queen Killing. Honey Plant.

MR. EDITOR:—I have also something to tell my brothers in bee-culture, though as I am afraid they all know so much more of such matters than I do, I feel a little hesitation in writing, since possibly no one will learn much from so poor a hand.

What I wish to state is that one day I noticed some of my bees dragging others out of their hive, though I felt confident they were neither robbers nor young unfledged bees. Why this was done, I could not tell. They did not sting their victims, as they would sting robbers, but merely dragged them to the edge of the alighting board, and gave them a kick as it were, by way of hint to leave the premises.

On close examination, however, I found there was something wrong with the bees thus treated. I killed a few of them, and found their feet and legs enveloped in filmy fibres about the thickness of a hair and from an eighth to a quarter of an inch long, and in some of them their lower mandible was affected in like manner. They could not crawl up any perpendicular object, nor help to gather honey or pollen, and as in the bee household loafers are not tolerated, spunging on the labors of others, they were summarily ejected like drones out of season—the motto of the industrious insect seeming to be—"*root hog, or die!*" Ever ready for self-defence, they still have no compassion for the wounded or crippled, though unwilling to commit murder in cold blood and turning them out to wander away and get lost. I cannot account for this occurrence. It is not the effect of moth web. I am acquainted with that. Nor is it anything hanging to their legs, but appears to be some kind of growth, at least so it seems to me. Perhaps it is nothing new to your readers, but it is to me. Who can explain it?

In the August number, Mr. J. Anderson gives an account of a nice queen being destroyed by her own children, because she was out of the hive a few minutes. That circumstance comes so near one I witnessed myself that I will give an account of it, letting it pass for what it is worth. Last year, in September or October, I sent to Adam Grimm for two queens. Both arrived safe, and I introduced them according to the printed directions accompanying them. They were accepted by the bees, and this spring the hives were well filled with yellow jackets. One day I wished to look at them, so I got some rotten wood or rags (I forget which), and smoked them a little. I then raised one of the combs outside out of the hive, where I saw a bunch of bees about the size of a walnut, on the bottom board. The thought struck me immediately that they had assailed my queen. I took my knife and easily parted them, and behold two scoundrels crawled away with their stings fast in the body of my nice queen. I felt bad, I assure you, all that day, and did not sleep much the following night, thinking of the mishap, and wondering how it came about. Did I strip her off the comb when I raised it up, that she fell in their midst, or how came it that they attacked and killed their mother? I set her on another frame after she was stung, but she was instantly attacked again. I closed up the hive and let them have their own way. Next day, at noon, I caught the rioters dragging her out. In nine days there were fourteen queen cells in the hive, ready to hatch.

I have one thing more which may be of interest to the bee keeping fraternity, who appear to be on the look-out for some plant that will bloom after the white clover fails and last till buckwheat comes in. I think I have found such a plant. Further experiments will show its value. I am almost afraid to tell Novice, lest he should get drowned in honey; but then again, it would be so sweet a death that perhaps he would not care much, as we must all once die. Well, what do you think it is? Open your eyes, ears, and mouths, and listen! It is what we here call tame peppermint. One of my near neighbors has a small patch of it, about six feet by twelve, in his yard. I pass the place three times a day in going to my meals, and observed the plant in bloom long ago. They tell me it blooms until frost. The bees are there busily engaged every time I pass, if the weather allows them to be out. I have an idea that the honey gathered from this plant must have a very pleasant taste and aromatic flavor. This patch was raised by setting out a few stalks for tea, and in two years' time it has spread to what it is. I think it prefers a moist soil, but not too wet. Let those who have fence corners and waste spots try it.

Bees did not swarm much here in June, though some did tolerably well in that way; but August swarms I see and hear of almost every day. Your patience is no doubt running low, so I will close this my first epistle, signing myself

A MILLER by profession,
but not a MOTH MILLER.

Duncan's Mills, Aug. 10, 1871.

[For the American Bee Journal.]

About Fertilizing Queen Bees.

MR. EDITOR:—The September number of the Journal has made its appearance, and its contents well digested. Like others we are not satisfied until we have read all it contains. The more we read and the more we learn from it about the little pets, the more we wish to know.

We have been very successful this season with our bees. We have raised several queens, and experienced considerable trouble in getting them properly fertilized. With some we had success, but with others not. Some were fertilized in confinement, and some in the open air. We failed to a great extent with our new fertilizing cage. It would not work as well as expected. Like others before us, we "failed," and have come to the conclusion that this mode of procuring fertilization will never work as was desired, though Mr. N. C. Mitchell claims that he has brought it to a focus. I think nature has provided a way, by which the bee may propogate its species, and that the only way with success.

IN AND IN BREEDING.

In last month's Journal, Mr. T. Hulman gives us his views on in and in breeding. I must beg leave to differ with him to a certain extent. He refers us to the buffalo and other herds, and speaks of the Jersey cow as coming from a small island, where the stock has been bred in and in for centuries, and still they exist distinct and pure.

But we do not call this in and in breeding, if we understand the matter right. But if we take a Jersey cow and a pure male from the same herd, and raise calves from these two, and when they arrive at maturity, we breed to the same male as before, and so on, and do not change, what will be the result? Why the stock will finally run out; in other words, the stock will degenerate until there will not be a trace left of them. Although the Jersey cattle come from a small island, they were not allowed to breed in this manner, but are bred carefully not sister to brother, but to distant relatives. So with the Italian bee. If you take a queen and drones from her, and allow her offspring (queen) to mate and be fertilized by her drone progeny, my candid belief is that they will naturally degenerate and finally cease to exist as Italians—that is, if you keep on breeding in this manner for three or four generations.

But some one will say, they are all Italians, and how can you keep them from breeding in and in when they have free access to the open air? The answer is, the queens meet drones from another mother and of a different family; and by so doing keep up the race to the standard mark of its required qualities. As I have bred queens and had them fertilized by drones of the same mother, I found after breeding them in this way for several generations, they would gradually lose their good qualities, and finally become dwarfed to a certain extent.

Why do queen breeders, if you buy more than one queen from them, state to you that "this one is not akin to the rest I have sent you?" Mr. T. speaks of the human family as not being injured by intermarriage (that is the way I understand him). Now I do not believe in relations marrying at all; it does to some extent injure their offspring. But this does not come up to the point, as I view in and in breeding. Suppose he takes the case of a brother and sister marrying. Undoubtedly he will find the case plain enough that their race (or offspring) are deficient in more or less of the required elements of the human family. I would guarantee that if this were the case, the human race would so deteriorate or degenerate that there would not be a sound or perfect man or woman on the globe.

In breeding queens, or anything else of the kind, I always select from some other family, the males from which I wish to breed; and by so doing I keep up the required qualities of whatever stock I am breeding or raising. I will admit that queens reared in a swarming hive, are somewhat larger; but as to their being any better or longer lived, I am unable to determine.

I do not write this, Mr. Editor, thinking that the gentleman is wrong in his views, but he gave his belief, and I give mine—a privilege which each has a perfect right to enjoy.

Beekeeping is waking up in these parts. I intend to talk nothing but Italians hereafter to those engaged in it. The Italian queens prove to be more prolific than the black queens are.

Tell Mr. Gallup that we intend to hold on to the almighty dollars, whether to buy lumber to make one of his hives, or not.

We are expecting to enjoy a splendid time at the next meeting of our association at Manchester, and will report the proceedings of the meeting at an early date, for publication.

In concluding my tedious communication, I will say that I am satisfied with this year's profits, but expect to do better in another.

T. H. B. WOODY.

Pleasant Valley, Mo., Sept. 11, 1871.

[For the American Bee Journal.]

The Test of Purity Again.

I am much pleased with a part of G. M. Doolittle's article on purity of Italian queens. I have experience to corroborate his. More than two years ago I put a few of the facts to the beekeeping world, through the American Bee Journal, but I presume they were not then considered worthy of attention. I had a *most beautiful* Italian queen (which was superseded only a month since) that produced all extra nice three-banded workers of deep color. Yet half of her drones were bluish-black, and many of her queens as black as a crow. And what was not less strange is, that her worker grand-children mostly became glossy black in their old age. I think Mr. D. has suggested the proper test at last. Why not be governed in breeding bees by the same rules as in other stock? That is, breed on and on in the same line till the sixteenth or twentieth generation, and till "like produces like." The fact is, workers are simply imperfect bees, and their qualities—be they better or worse—cannot be taken as a test. Now, gentlemen bee-breeders, let us have a pedigree. Tell us, and *prove* to us, how far back your queen bees have produced their like.

Nor does it matter whether the Italian bee "is itself a hybrid" or not. The best of our improved cattle, hogs, and other stock, were originally crossed. If it is a *fact* that the Italian bee *is* superior, we want the breed "established;" and this can be done only by breeding forward long enough or tracing back far enough. The unimportant matter that bees originally came from Italy, or that they are of the "latest importation" is not enough for a good stock man.

But I am not satisfied that Mr. D. has settled the matter of queens mating with two drones. A friend of mine whose word is current with me in everything else, and who does a good deal of experimenting with bees, assures me he has repeatedly had a queen mate with two drones on two different days, and that "it" killed both drones. If other female animals "mate" with a plurality of males, why may not queen bees also? The authors and writers are not the only ones who are at work on the bee question. After three years' experience, I am still of the opinion that *much* of the *great difference* between black bees, Italians, and hybrids, is imaginary. For the sake of truth, science, and common sense, let us have less exaggeration.

J. W. GREENE.

Chillicothe, Mo., July 18, 1871.

From Christmas to Candlemas, a careful bee-master should consider any worker bee in a healthy hive worth a three-pence.—HŒFFLER.

[For the American Bee Journal.]

Two Queens in a Hive—Another Singular Occurrence.

MR. EDITOR:—I am really only a beginner in bee-culture, though I have had some bees for sixteen years, and purchased a Langstroth book and hive from Mr. Otis, at the St. Louis Fair in 1860, and have taken five volumes of your Journal. Still, in all this time, I paid very little attention to my bees until the fall of 1869, when I got some Italian queens about the first of October. In the year 1870 the bees did not do well in this neighborhood, so that I might say I commenced last spring. I was absent from home on the 3d and 4th of June, and when I came back my son said that seven swarms of bees had issued while I was away, and that one of them was the largest he had ever seen. They had all been hived in box hives, as I had but few section hives, and my son did not know how to manage them. On the 6th of June the big swarm came out again and settled on a bunch of lilac bushes, right at the ground, and I had quite a job getting them off. But I succeeded at last, put them in one of Adair's section hives, and they went to work with a will. On the fourth day after, I put on two honey boxes of nine sections each, and some of the bees went to work in each of them the same night. In less than two weeks they had the brood chamber about full, and three combs and some small pieces in each box; when the honey failed from the prevalent drouth, and they did little more than live, up to July 25th, when I concluded to take the queen and put her in a box hive that had become queenless. I was expecting to receive some Italian queens in a few days, and intended to give one to this hive. I carried the chamber to the cellar, hunted out the queen, cut off one wing, caged her, stuck her down through the top of the box hive, and left her there twenty-four hours, when I pulled out the stopper to let her pass out of the cage whenever she pleased.

I did not get the Italian queens until the 5th of August, making eleven days; so I expected to find plenty of sealed queen-cells in the hive from which the queen was removed. I carried it to the cellar (as honey was still scarce, and robbers very plenty), and commenced at the front to look for the cells, clearing the combs of bees as I did so. I found one cell near the center of the third section, which had evidently been torn open. That was all I found till I came to the center of the chamber, when I took off the back, and there was a queen right on the face of the first comb. I caught and crushed her, supposing she was a young one just hatched—as eleven and five made the sixteen days, if the bees had taken a larva five days old to raise one. But, to my surprise, when I came to brush the bees off the comb, I found the cells contained young larvæ and plenty of eggs not yet hatched. Not another queen cell could be found in the chamber, so that I concluded the old queen had played the same game as did Mr. Argo's runaway. Next evening I thought I would drive the bees out of the old box hive and see if there was any queen there;

but they would not move, either with rapping on the hive, nor with smoke blown in at the entrance. They would come up to the top of the comb, and run around the edges of the hive very briskly, but would not go up into the box; so I concluded I would next day transfer them to a section hive from which a small swarm had deserted, and then give them a queen from another hive. I smoked them a very little, to put in an Italian queen, and carried them to the cellar; but still they would not drive. Then I pried off one side of the hive and cut out the combs (smoking the bees back out of my way), and when I came to the third sheet, behold there was a circle of capped worker cells, larvæ of all sizes, and eggs! Now I did not know what to think, but transferred what comb there was that was worth anything, put the chamber in the case, and shook the bees out on a sheet in front, and *there was the queen with only one wing*, sure enough. Now, gentlemen, there must have been two queens in that hive for a number of days, with no sign of quarrelling.

And now, Mr. Editor, I think I have spun my yarn pretty long for the first time, and suppose I had better stop.

C. T. Smith.

Trenton, Ill., Aug. 14, 1871.

[For the American Bee Journal.]

Retrospective Inquiries.

Mr. Editor:—In renewing my subscription, allow me to say that I could not well do without the Journal. Though young in the fascinating study of apiculture, I have learned to know that the more knowledge we have of the *nature* and habits of the bee the greater will be our success. My experience has not been *all honey*, but my failures have all been good lessons. With this view of the matter, drawbacks should only stimulate us to try and do better next time. Some of my friends think me crazy on this subject, but a man (or a woman either) must be enthusiastic to succeed well in any undertaking.

As the Journal is a vehicle for thought and experience, I will, with your leave, put a few questions to some of your correspondents.

I will then first address myself to Querist. On page 55, vol. 5, Mr. Seay takes the ground that "the first and highest law of nature in insects is self-preservation in caring for offspring. The honey bee seems to be endowed with this instinct for the purpose of preserving brood in the hive." On page 83 of the same volume, you, Mr. Querist, call in question the foregoing statement, by asking—"If the preservation of offspring is the strongest instinct that governs the honey bee, then why does she remove unsealed larvæ from the cells, to make room for a rich honey harvest?" On page 76, vol. 6, Mr. Seay makes some very strong points on his side of the question, which have not yet been met by you or any one else. Now, are we to conclude, from your long silence, that you have given up the point? If not, please give us some *facts* supporting your view of the subject. For, if the honey bee differs from all other insects in this respect (as she no doubt does in others), then the fact ought to be established, so that it will add to our knowledge of the wonderful little insect.

J. M. Price.—There appears to be some difference between you and Mr. Langstroth, regarding queen raising. No doubt your experience in this direction has caused you to come to the conclusion that the *best* queens can *only* be raised by a colony having the swarming impulse. But Mr. Langstroth, in accordance with his observations, says: "I have for years been in the habit of raising my queens in stocks kept in full heart by liberal feeding or otherwise, and have not found any appreciable difference between those thus raised and those raised by bees when preparing to swarm." Now, as the line must be drawn somewhere, do you consider *all queens artificial*, except those raised by a colony under the swarming impulse? Please give us a reason, if you can, *why* queens are better when raised in this condition than in any other. Is it in the nature of the *egg*, *quantity* or *quality* of food given to the larvæ, or what?

Novice, take my ☞. I would like one good hearty shake of yours. I thank you for all the information you have given me. That article in the August number is worth more than "*a dollar*." Your experience is always welcome. I have, this summer, been much exercised on the subject of *straight* and *worker* comb. I have not succeeded as well as I would like, for the bees would be a little stubborn. Now, as I want to be "master of the situation," and you are an *old novice*, please give us your *best* method, so as to obtain the *best* result.

Everybody (Gallup excepted).—Last fall my bees did not stop breeding till late, and used up the most of their bee-bread. This spring being wet and cold, they could not work much on rye-flour, and by the time they could gather pollen some of the stocks were very weak. Now, as good coffee-sugar is a good substitute for honey, I would like to know whether bee-bread has ever been analyzed and a substance found, single or combined, that would be a good substitute for bee-bread, to be fed when required. All information will be thankfully received by

Querist No. 2.

[For the American Bee Journal.]

Bee Notes from Southern Indiana.

SEVERE DROUTH.

We have just passed through the severest drouth that has been experienced in this section for many years. For about two months it did not rain enough to lay the dust. The ground had not been thoroughly wet since May. Almost every honey-producing flower, with all other vegetation, was literally "dried up." The red clover and the white had ceased to bloom, and almost to live. The corn tassels were bleached and wilted. The buckwheat—our main dependence for honey at this season of the year—had not moisture enough to grow stalks or leaves, much less blossoms. In short, the bee-pasturage was almost entirely cut off.

RAIN.

But this long drouth was brought to a close last night by a copious "water fall." It rained for more than twelve hours, almost without intermission. The parched and thirsty ground is now thoroughly moistened, and in a few days we may look for a revival of vegetable life. I have about eight acres of buckwheat, which I think will soon furnish good pasturage for my seventy stocks. I did expect to get considerable surplus honey during the buckwheat season, but now shall let my bees have all they can make from this time till frost. They have been, during all this dry weather, and are still, breeding profusely. This has made a heavy drain on their stores. The honey in a few of the stocks had got so low that I began to feed them. But I think they will be able to take care of themselves in a few days. If they fail in this, however, they shall not suffer; they have done too much for me this season, to be driven into winter quarters with scanty stores.

BEE FEED.

I have been feeding with a very simple and cheap food. I bought a few gallons of sorghum molasses at forty cents a gallon. In this I put water and honey in the proportion of one quart of water and one pint of honey to one gallon of molasses. This mixture I boiled until it was of the consistency of thin molasses. When cooled, I poured it into cards of empty comb, about one quart to the hive. It was wonderful how soon, after these cards were returned to the hives, the bees would lick up this syrup and deposit it in other and more convenient parts of the hives.

TWO QUEENS IN ONE COLONY.

I have recently had an interesting case of two queens in one hive. In looking over one of my stocks, to which I had last spring given a young queen, I accidentally discovered two fertile queens, each quietly passing over the combs as if unconscious of the presence of the other. The younger had been there several weeks, as her brood was then hatching. Of this I was certain, as the brood of the older was pure Italian, while that of the younger was badly marked.

I removed the older queen to another hive, that had been without a queen for some time. At the same time I gave the hive to which I removed this queen, a card of unsealed brood. The queen immediately began to deposit eggs in the combs. The workers, although they had acknowledged her as their sovereign, commenced the construction of queen cells. These cells were sealed over, and one of them hatched out, in the presence of the old queen, she not attempting to disturb them. The young queen, as soon as she had emerged from the cell, destroyed the other cells, but did not do or say aught to the old queen, nor the old one to her. I tried very hard to get up a fight between them, driving them together and catching one and putting on the other; but they did not seem to recognize one another as of the royal blood. In due time the young queen became fertile. She continued laying in the presence of the old one, frequently on the same card with her, for two weeks or more, until I removed the old queen. In attempting to introduce this old queen to another hive, I lost her, else her biography might perhaps be rendered still more interesting by other remarkable incidents.

What could there have been about this queen that kept her from interfering with other queens, and that restrained them from disturbing her? There was nothing peculiar in her appearance, except that her body was rather short. She was quite prolific, and her progeny were well marked. The workers, however, seemed to apprehend that she was an extraordinary *bee*-ing, for she was always, or at least whenever I saw her, surrounded by a crowd of admiring and apparently amazed subjects, their heads turned toward her, and ever and anon gently touching her body with their antennæ, as if to say: "What *are* you, any how?"

FREAK OF HOSTILITY.

I have also had another peculiar queen case. While examining one of my full stocks, I found a number of queen cells started. Supposing that the bees were proposing to swarm, and to prevent the queen from getting away, I took her up in my fingers and clipped her wings. When I returned her to the top of the frames the workers gathered upon her, just as they would on a strange queen, and in a few moments had her closely confined in a dense cluster. It was with difficulty that I could release her. I removed her to another hive. Why the bees should reject her, I could not conceive. She was a young queen, not over two months old, and was tolerably prolific. At the time she was depositing drone eggs.

FERTILIZATION OF QUEENS.

For the past month I have had much difficulty in getting my young queens fertilized; and this while I have a good many young drones. The dry, hot weather has seemed to prevent the queens and drones from desiring to mate. I have one queen now over a month old, that has just begun to lay. I did not experience this trouble early in the season.

INTRODUCING QUEENS.

I have recently given the plan suggested in a late number of the American Bee Journal, of hatching queens in cages, a pretty thorough test. I put about twenty sealed cells in as many wire cages, two inches long and one and a half inches in diameter. These I suspended in a strong stock that was, at the time, destitute of a queen. The young queens hatched very well, but unless I removed them within a few hours afterwards, they invariably died. The workers refused to feed them while thus caged. I then tried putting in the cages pieces of sponge saturated in honey, from which I thought the young queens could feed themselves. But this was attended with the same result as before—the queens died. Out of the twenty I did not save more than five or six.

I have also tried Mr. Langstroth's plan of introducing young queens, just hatched, into full stocks. In almost every instance the workers deliberately dragged them out, as if of too little importance to be allowed hive room. From some of these stocks I had removed the old queens just before attempting to introduce the young ones. Others had been queenless for several days. I have seldom had any success in my efforts to introduce unfertile queens.

A FERTILE WORKER.

My neighbor apiarist, Mr. P. D. Boyer, has had quite a siege with a "fertile worker," in one of his hives. This stock had been destitute of a queen for some time, when he gave them some sealed queen cells. In a little while afterwards he found these cells torn out and an abundance of eggs scattered through the combs, in both worker and drone cells. Supposing that another queen had by some means got into the hive, he made a thorough search, several times repeated, for her, but searched in vain. He then, suspecting the presence of a fertile worker, looked time and again for her, but he could see no difference in the appearance of the workers. Eggs continued to be scattered profusely through the combs, sometimes as many as five in one cell. The bees built what looked like queen cells over the brood of this *layer*, but they failed to hatch. After several efforts he succeeded in getting them to receive a fertile queen, and then all went on right. The brood from this *animal*, whatever it was, hatched out *drones*. Those that were in drone cells looked just like other drones. *Quære.* Have such drones the power to fertilize queens?

M. C. Hester.

Charlestown, Ind., Aug. 25, 1871.

[For the American Bee Journal.]

Another Beginner in Iowa.

Mr. Editor:—In reading your valuable paper, I see now and then a word from a beginner, and being in that plight of misery myself, I thought I would let your readers know that there is still another new hand, trying to gain a livelihood by the way of stings and honey.

I am yet a young man, just starting in life, a resident of Jefferson, in Greene county. My attention was first called to the "little busy bee" by W. H. Furman, Esq., of Cedar Rapids, who is well-known throughout the State, as a first-class apiarian and breeder of Italian queens. He attracted my attention to that branch of industry, while exhibiting at our County Fair, last fall, and of him I purchased, my first stand of bees, in the "Langstroth Hive," also Langstroth's work on "*the Hive and Honey Bee*," and then subscribed for your valuable Bee Journal—neither of which I would now do without.

Last spring I bought four more stands, all Italians; thus making my start with five colonies. I concluded to commence right, by placing myself under the instruction of a practical bee-man; and am spending the season in the apiary of Mr. Furman, at Cedar Rapids. I have found that, for a novice, there is something to learn. My success thus far has been a doubling of my stock, two hundred and three (203) pounds of honey from the lower part of the hive, taken by the use of the slinger, and ninety (90) pounds of box honey. Reports from home say that the bees are still storing honey rapidly from some source.

Why do not some of the writers tell us more that would be of practical benefit, with less of "I," or "my hive," &c.? For instance, their method of preventing robbing, which I find to be one of the greatest difficulties at this time. A little advice in this line, I think, would be gratefully received by beginners generally.*

Edwin A. King.

Cedar Rapids, Iowa, Aug. 21, 1871.

* ☞ The former volumes of the Bee Journal contain many articles and suggestions on preventing and checking robbery by the bees.

[For the American Bee Journal.]

Introducing Italian Queen Bees.

I have had good success by the following method:

Take for a bottom a board six inches square; for ends two one inch strips; for sides, glass five by six inches; top two and a quarter by six inches, inside the space inclosed by the glass. Cut most of it out. One large hole covered with wire cloth; a smaller hole covered with a pasteboard card made to slide, the end projecting outside for handle. Put a frame with comb inside, with queen. Set the box over the bees; withdraw the slide a little, and let three or four bees up. After awhile let up a few more, and repeat the operation till the box is full of bees. In two days more, withdraw the slide and the queen will go down. The honey boards I use favor this method. They are made of plasterer's laths dressed to a quarter of an inch; the ends halved, and fastened with 2½ oz. tacks. The middle piece that runs lengthwise, is one inch thick and two inches wide, nailed on the top, which makes six holes.

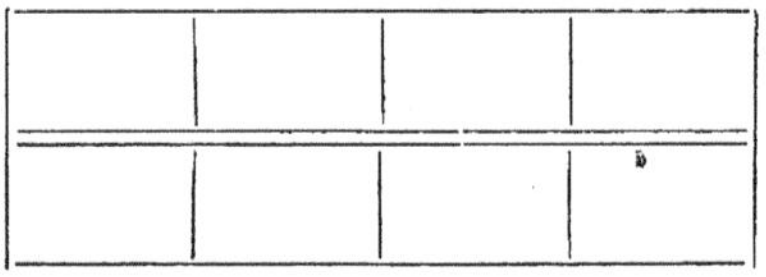

Under the long middle piece tack straps of tin to project three-fourths of an inch into the square spaces; make a separate corner for each hole, to remove when the boxes are put on.

J. Winfield.

Hubbard, Ohio, Aug. 3, 1871.

Bees.—The Paris (Ky.) *Mercury* says: Farmers tell us that this is a prolific year for humble-bees—they have never seen as many "in their born days." In numerous instances farmers have stopped plowing in consequence, the bees being troublesome to the plowman as well as to his team.

THE AMERICAN BEE JOURNAL.

Washington, October, 1871.

We learn with sincere regret that our friend and correspondent, Novice, was prevented by physical disability from furnishing us with his customary monthly contribution—sending us only a brief note instead. We trust that relaxation and exercise will soon restore to him health and vigor.

Mr. Langstroth, also, as we are informed, is again prostrated by the return of the malady from which he has so often, long, and grievously suffered. May he, too, speedily recover and be permanently restored to the enjoyment of health.

The London "*Journal of Horticulture*," of August 3d, announces the death of Mr. T. W. Woodbury, known to most of our readers as "The Devonshire Beekeeper." He died on the 26th of July, and by his death England lost one of its most intelligent and thoroughly trained beemasters.

The Marquis of Balsamo-Crivelli, distinguished as one of the most enthusiastic and spirited bee-keepers of Italy, died at Milan, on the 8th of April, after a short but painful illness, aged 71 years. He was indefatigable and highly successful in his exertions for the revival of bee-culture in his native country, enlisting the active co-operation of a large number of patriotic citizens in founding the "*Central Association for the encouragement of Bee-culture in Italy*," and was a regular contributor to the Italian Bee Journal.

The "*Bienenzeitung*" also notices the death of the Rev. Joseph Stern, a veteran German beekeeper, and a writer on bee-culture. He died at Weissenkirchen on the Danube, in Lower Austria, in the 74th year of his age. His numerous contributions to the "Bienenzeitung," in the course of the past twenty-five years, were the result of long experience and close observation in the management of his apiary; and we always turned to them eagerly, sure to find his remarks and reflections as instructive as they were attractive.

Our last number contained a communication from Dr. Hamlin, of Edgefield Junction, Tennessee, respecting queen bees laying non-hatching eggs; and in this number we have another on the same subject from Mr. Jerrard of Levant, Me.

It was, till within a few years, the accepted doctrine that queen bees lay no addle eggs, or eggs that do not hatch. But recent observations have shown that this is an error. In September, 1870, a queen bee, whose eggs were thus defective, was sent to Professor Von Siebold, of Munich, with a request that he would dissect and examine her, and report the result. He found her spermatheca well filled, and the spermatozoa therein still living, or in motion—exhibiting all the usual appearances under the microscope. The ovaries contained egg-germs and eggs in all stages of development, with corpuscular evidence that she was a laying queen, in all respects normally well formed. But, from anything perceptible, no opinion could be formed why her eggs did not hatch. If there had been any obstruction in the neck of the spermatheca, preventing the fertilization of the eggs, these should nevertheless have hatched, producing drones, and causing the queen to be or become a drone-breeder. But as this was not the case, the non-hatching may have resulted from the omission by the workers of some important part of their duty, if it be true that proper treatment of the eggs by the brood-nurses is essentially requisite for their development. Or rather, as the Professor seems incline to assume, the cause may ultimately be traced to some defect in the physical organization of the queen, preventing the due development of the egg-germs or eggs in her ovaries. But for a satisfactory solution of this question, Prof. Siebold thinks we may yet have to wait long, as the means of making such profound examinations of the processes of egg formation and development, at present available, are wholly inadequate to the purpose.

☞ In reply to an inquiry from Canada, we say that those eggs of a queen bee, which are impregnated when passing the mouth of the spermatheca, on their way down the oviduct, produce workers (*undeveloped females*) or queens (fully developed females); and those eggs which pass down the oviduct without receiving impregnation from the spermatheca, produce drones or males. Usually, fertilized queens commence depositing by laying worker eggs; the subsequent laying of drone eggs being governed by season or circumstance. Occasionally, indeed, young queens do, for a short time, lay drone eggs when beginning to oviposite, and later commence and continue laying worker eggs. But this is a very rare occurrence, which Prof. Von Siebold accounts for satisfactorily. When a queen once begins to lay worker eggs, there is no subsequent regular alternation in the deposit of worker and drone eggs. She will lay either kind, as the season or the wants of the colony prompt her to do, or till her supply of spermatozoa is exhausted. Then she becomes a drone egg layer exclusively, and continues such till her career is ended.

☞ One of our correspondents, this month, appears to doubt whether the so-called "Taylor frame," which once for a season, like the Cardiff giant, served for a gull-trap, was not invented and used in England, before that of Mr. Langstroth was patented in this country. We will give the reader the facts in the case, though that which never had an existence can hardly be said to have a history. Properly speaking, what is designated as the *Taylor frame*, never existed anywhere, save in the fertile brain of Martin Metcalfe, who figured so prominently in opposition to the extension of the Langstroth patent, on which occasion he tried inconsistently to palm it on the credulity of beekeepers as an *old* thing, while claiming to be himself the inventor of movable frames. We presume our correspondent got his idea of the alleged invention, and his impression of its priority, from a certain pamphlet published by Metcalfe, while he was yet flourishing in his own placard and biography, like another notorious infringer, as "a distinguished apiarian." On page 28 of that pamphlet, an effort is disingenuously made by its maladroit compiler, to create the impression that the frame he figured and presented to notice, and which was so obviously an imitation of one of the forms of the Langstroth original, was described and figured in Taylor's book, published in England, in 1838—thus making it antedate the Langstroth patent. But the truth is *no such frame*, NOR FRAME OF ANY KIND, *is mentioned, described, or figured in that edition of Taylor's book, nor in any one of the four subsequent editions thereof.* It first came into view IN THE EDITION OF 1860—*nearly eight years after Mr. Langstroth's patent was obtained!* And it is not even then claimed by Taylor, as *his* frame. He says, explicitly, that it is a modification by some one else, as an improvement on the Bevan *bar* hive; but from the tenor of his statement, it is manifest that he had seen and copied from Mr. Langstroth's book (second edition, 1857); for, in a note on page 205, he quotes *verbatim* from it, and refers to Mr. L. as "an American author." It will thus be seen that the insinuations and reckless assertions made by Metcalfe, respecting the alleged Taylor frame, and the impression fraudulently sought to be made by him, that it was described and figured in 1838, or anterior to the date of the Langstroth patent, are wholly unwarranted—having no foundation in truth.

A correspondent of the *Prairie Farmer*, who appears to be a good and successful practical beekeeper, fails, we think, in some instances, in accuracy of observation. Thus he says:—"In one case I put a queen cell in a clean comb, and the next morning she was on the combs, and the next morning she had filled a frame six inches square nearly full of eggs, which hatched out worker brood." We are too well aware of the frequency of abnormal occurrences among bees, to accept everything that "the books tell us," as undeviatingly correct under all circumstances, or at all seasons; but in the above statement there are physiological difficulties involved which make it evident that the writer must have been deceived. Conceding that the young queen may have left her hive in quest of drones on the day she was hatched, (which is an extreme improbability, though still possible), and that she was then fertilized, the fact that time is required for the formation and development of the egg-germs in the ovarian tubes, and for their passage thence through the oviduct, renders it further exceedingly improbable, not to say actually impossible, that hatchable worker eggs could have been laid by her so early in life as on the day after she was hatched. Prof. Leuckart, of Giessen, found that in a royal pupæ, nearly ready to emerge from the cell, many of which he has dissected, no egg-germs were ever present: and Dr. Dönhoff, who dissected a young queen forty-eight hours after fertilization, found egg-germs only in the ovisacs of the ovarian tubes. It seems thus exceedingly unlikely, or rather physically impossible, that a queen could lay hatchable eggs within twenty-four hours after leaving her cell. We admit, freely, that bees sometimes indulge in unaccountable freaks; but they are never such as involve a palpable disregard of natural laws, or grossly violate the process of physical development; and hence, we infer that, in this instance of alleged precociousness, there must have been unconsciously an error of observation.

CORRESPONDENCE OF THE BEE JOURNAL.

CORNERSVILLE, TENN., Aug. 17.—I have kept bees all my life, and do not know how I did so long without the Journal. I like it better the longer I take it. My bees did very well till the first of June; since then, till now, they have done nothing, though I hope they will yet fill up sufficient to winter. The linden bloom failed here this year. There was bloom on hardly one tree in ten or fifteen. I have had only five natural swarms this year, out of seventy box hives. I intended to transfer to Langstroth hives, but when I saw that the linden bloom would do no good, I concluded to wait until next spring.—J. F. LOVE.

PELEE ISLAND, CANADA, Aug. 12, 1871.—I see from the correspondence of the Journal that the yield of honey in different localities, varies very much the same season; as also does the yield in the same locality in different seasons. Although our stocks may be managed upon the most approved system, it seems that the yield of honey is as much dependent upon the different atmospheric changes of the season, as a crop of wheat or grapes, which are very uncertain in most localities. My bees wintered well on their summer stands; found blossoms and pollen as soon as it was warm enough for them to fly; bred rapidly and made early preparations for swarming; but unfavorable weather caused them to destroy queen cells and postpone it till the last of May and the first of June. A drouth of six weeks cut short their supplies, and they did not gather any until the first of July, when the basswood came in blossom; and continued until the 10th. In the meantime we had rain and white clover blossomed most profusely, but not a bee noticed it, and they remained idle for ten or twelve days. When the clover was nearly dried up, they commenced working pretty freely upon what was left, but were hardly able to supply their daily consumption. Now (Aug. 12), they begin to gather pretty freely from some weeds in woods and marshes, a dark colored honey. All the white honey has been taken from them to give room for this.—T. SMITH.

OTISCO VALLEY, N. Y., Aug. 21.—This has been a very good season here for bees. A large increase in colonies, and a full average yield of honey. From forty-eight colonies wintered, I have increased my stock to eighty-two. All are in splendid condition to go into winter quarters. I have also taken twenty-eight hundred pounds of very nice box honey. This I consider very good for a novice in bee-culture.—H. ROOT.

CAMPBELL'S CROSS, CANADA, Aug. 22, 1871.—The more I read the American Bee Journal the better I like it. With such close observing men as Novice, Gallup, and others whose writings I might mention, beekeeping is being brought from, I might say a business of uncertainty and loss, to one of profit and pleasure. We call this one of the poor seasons in this part of Canada. Owing to the dryness of the weather, the flowers soon failed, and the consequence is there is not much box honey. Later in the season we had some honey dews that have made the hives in good condition for wintering. With the use of the honey machine and the aid of the Italian bees, I have secured a large quantity of pure honey during the short honey season, that I would otherwise not have had.—H. LIPSETT.

DANVERS, MASS., Aug. 25.—Bees have not done much in this section, as far as surplus honey is concerned. They came out in good condition in the spring. My seventeen colonies swarmed some twelve or fifteen times, and we have got about one hundred or one hundred and twenty-five pounds of honey. I read of big stories in the Journal, but would rather read of more small stories. Those who succeed best are those most apt to tell of their success, and those who do not succeed do not like to tell their stories among the big stories, for fear of being laughed at. My bees are in good condition, only one colony wanting feeding out of seventeen. I doubled up my swarms and put them back. I sold three of them, and one left for the woods.—E. E. PORTER.

ELM GROVE, WEST VA., Aug. 25.—Having taken a great interest in the reports contained in the Journal from various parts of the country, of the season, I would say that the yield of honey has been very good in this section. Bees commenced to gather pollen from the elms about the middle of March. The fruit trees were full of bloom, and bloomed very early, but did not yield much honey. The white clover was in bloom by the 20th of May, but the weather being a little dry, there was not at any time a heavy bloom. There was more rain the latter part of June, which prolonged the season till the middle of July, thus giving the bees a long period in which to store honey. There did not appear to be an excess of honey at any time, but a good regular supply throughout the season. The weather was bright, and not excessively hot, so that the bees could work all the time. We have all the forage necessary for a good honey supply. A few of my hives yielded ninety pounds of surplus box honey, and also some extracted. First swarms issued on the 9th of May, but they were easily prevented from swarming by a little attention. There is a fine prospect of fall pasturage, and it is just the beginning of the fall season here at this time.—J. BAIRD.

LAWRENCE, KANSAS, Aug. 26.—The prospects are good for a yield of honey this season. August has been a good month for honey, and if we have a few showers the season will last till frost, which generally comes about the middle of October.—N. CAMERON.

FENN'S MILLS, MICH., Aug. 28.—I wintered my bees in clamps, *a la* Mr. Schultz in Langstroth's book, with the exception that I gave them more ventilation and did not cover the outside with straw. Found but few dead bees when I took them out, but the combs and doors were somewhat soiled, and some of the combs a little mouldy. Very little honey consumed. The weather was very warm in March, but cold in April and the fore part of May. One swarm came out and left the 28th of May; filled their hives properly, but did not go to work in boxes by the second week in June, and lay still till into July. Then they commenced swarming, without stopping to fill the boxes, except a few of the most backward ones, which did well in boxes and did not swarm. Such populous swarms I never saw before. They have all filled their hives, and some of the first filled several boxes each. I want to see those plates, etc., of comb frames invented previous to the Langstroth patent, so as to be able to distinguish between his and other frames; for it is still a question in my mind if he has invented the Taylor frame, published by Munn about the time Langsroth obtained his patent.—H. HUDSON.

RIPON, WIS., Sept. 3.—In this section of our State the summer has been a strange one. The honey season commenced in June, and for three weeks I could not have wished my bees to do better in honey-making. July 1st the change came; swarming stopped, and bees remained idle up to date. Large prime swarms, coming from June 29th to July 7th, have not made five pounds of honey in the body of the hives, and will have to be fed largely or taken up. The old stocks are very heavy, and in fine condition for winter; and in three weeks' work in June, sixty-six of them filled one hundred and thirty (130) six, eight, and fourteen pound boxes. A long continued drouth is the cause of our losing July and August. We expect nothing from September, for we are as dry as a powder mill, and no prospect of any change.—R. DART.

CONSTANTIA, N. Y., Sept. 4.—My bees have not done well this summer. I got only five new swarms from twenty good strong stocks, and but very little surplus honey. I think the season has been a poor one for bees in this county (Oswego).—W. SHELDON.

POCAHONTAS, MO., Sept. 4.—I enclose two dollars for the seventh volume of the American Bee Journal. I am a farmer, but have made more clear money from the sale of honey this summer than from my wheat crop. Much of my success I owe to the editor and contributors of the Journal.—J. C. WALLACE.

PALMETTO, TENN., Sept. 7.—Bees have done no good in this part of the country this year.—J. F. MONTGOMERY.

GUELPH, CANADA, Sept. 7.—Enclosed please find two dollars, subscription for one year from January 1st, 1871. Send me all the back numbers, and keep me on your list as a constant subscriber.—P. H. GIBBS.

[For the American Bee Journal.]

Introducing Queens.

I promised to report the first case of failure in introducing a queen without caging, where a queenless colony had started queen cells.

Well, I have failed. I have had two queens introduced in that way, killed. All went well enough until the latter part of July, when the drouth cut off the supply of honey. Then, when I made an artificial swarm by removing the hive and setting a hive containing brood but no bees, in its place for the returning bees to occupy; after these old bees had started queen cells, I gave them a queen, and they killed her. I think if there had been a yield of honey at the time, or if the bees had been younger, I should have succeeded; but I have been headed off so many times by the bees, and in so many ways, that I begin to despair of being sure of anything in bee-culture.

July 11th, I set hive No. 19, containing brood but no bees, in place of No. 20. Three days later, I gave them, without caging, a fertile queen. On the next day I found her imprisoned—one party of the bees fighting for her, and another against her. I then took an *empty* hive, No. 33, put in the queen, leaving room at the entrance for positively only one bee at a time to pass, and set No. 33 in place of No. 19. The result was a dead queen. I then gave No. 33 a frame of brood to start queen cells; and after they had them started, I gave them a crippled queen that I did not care to save, to see what they would do with her. She was promptly imprisoned, and I left her to her fate. A few days later, on going to cut out the queen cells, I found them destroyed and the crippled queen laying eggs.

On the whole, I am inclined to think that I can succeed better in this way than in any other, with the same amount of trouble.

August 1st, I received a queen from Adam Grimm, and desiring to run no risk, I took a plan that I think is *sure*. But "there is many a slip" &c. I bored a two inch auger hole in the bottom of a Langstroth hive; tacked a piece of wire cloth over the hole on the inside of the hive and another piece over it on the outside; took from a second story of another hive a couple of frames containing no brood except such as were ready to gnaw their way out of the cells; put this brood in the empty hive with the hole in the bottom, being sure that not a single bee remained on the comb; then put in my queen with her half dozen attendants, closed up the hive bee-tight and placed it over a full colony, with no intervening honey-board, so that the heat could ascend through the wire cloth to the hatching bees. If this works well, I think I shall try the same plan for making an artificial swarm.

C. C. MILLER.

Marengo, Ills., Aug. 4, 1870.

[For the American Bee Journal.]

A Fertile Queen whose Eggs do not Hatch.

I have a very fine looking Italian queen in one of my hives, that has been laying for a month or more, yet none of her eggs have hatched. She was reared in a full swarm, under the swarming impulse, and is remarkably large and handsome. That she mated with a drone I am sure, having observed the visible signs of connection on her return from her bridal tour.

Is this common? I have reared several hundred queens during the last three years, but never had a case of the kind before to my knowledge.

G. W. P. JERRARD.

Levant, Me., Aug. 10, 1871.

☞ The above was marked for insertion last month, to accompany Dr. Hamlin's communication respecting two similar cases, but was accidentally misplaced.

[For the American Bee Journal.]

Introducing Queens.

MR. EDITOR:—I give below my mode of introducing queens the present season, which if you think worthy of a place in the Journal, please insert.

In introducing queens this season I have proceeded as follows: Removed the old queen, several hours after which I smoked the bees in the hive from which the queen was removed, and also the one from which the queen to be introduced is to be taken, quite thoroughly with tobacco smoke, till some few became giddy. I then took out the frame on which the queen is and held it to the entrance of the hive desired, brushed off a few of the workers, which set up a lively humming; then brushed the queen from the comb and saw her well in the hive. As soon as she was upon the comb, I gave them more smoke.

I found this process very simple, and have thus far succeeded in every instance. At the time honey was very abundant, or about June 13th. Others who have tried this plan under more unfavorable circumstances, would do me a favor by reporting result. I am a little fearful that if the yield of honey was light, this plan might not succeed. Let others give us their experience. I, for one, want more light on the subject.

F. A. SNELL.

Milledgeville, Ills., Aug. 12, 1871.

[For the American Bee Journal.]

A Wax Extractor.

MR. EDITOR:—I have invented a wax extractor, which I will describe without charge, as follows:

Get a piece of fine wire cloth, three feet square. Bend it in the form of a square box. The bottom is made of board, with a hole in it large enough through which to insert the comb, and fitted with a movable wooden cover. Take a large kettle, fill it with water, and put in your wire cloth box containing the combs, loading it with a stone or stones, heavy enough to keep it under water. Boil one hour. Then let it stand till it gets cold. The wax rises to the surface of the water, and can be taken off when cold.

If it is desired to have the wax in one mass or a nice cake, put it in a skillet, remelt it, pour it in a vessel, and let it get cold, and you will have as nice wax as anybody wants.

In the summer this should be done after dark, or you will be annoyed by crowds of bees from the apiary. I boil mine after dark, and let it stand till morning. Then I put it in a small skillet, remelt it, and pour it into cups, leaving it stand till cold.

I hope I have given a sufficiently clear description.

C. E. WIDENER.

New Cumberland, Md., Sept. 2, 1871.

AMERICAN BEE JOURNAL.

EDITED AND PUBLISHED BY SAMUEL WAGNER, WASHINGTON, D. C.

AT TWO DOLLARS PER ANNUM, PAYABLE IN ADVANCE.

VOL. VII. | NOVEMBER, 1871. | No. 5.

[For the American Bee Journal.]

Weight of Honey Bees.

TRANSLATED FOR THE AMERICAN BEE JOURNAL FROM THE "BIENENZEITUNG."

According to the investigations of the Baron of Berlepsch, 5,600 outlying worker bees weigh a pound. These are for the larger part honey gatherers resting from their labors, and with their honey sacs nearly empty.

According to my own weighings, one pound of bees brushed from the combs in the evening contains 4,300 bees, consisting in part: 1st. of honey gatherers; and 2d, of young bees engaged in nursing the brood, whose stomachs contain the partially digested constituents of the food (pollen and honey) administered to the larvæ.

Again, a pound of bees driven out of a hive early in the morning in the working season, contains 4,050 bees, and comprises both honey gatherers and young bees, the honey gatherers constituting much the larger portion. These have gorged themselves with as much honey as they could appropriate in the hurry of departure.

Further, a pound of swarming bees, regardless whether prime or second swarm, contains 3,600 bees. These, as is well known, consist altogether of older workers and young bees sufficiently mature to fly, with an intermixture of drones, taking with them a sufficient supply of food or honey, to serve them three or four days, though it is fair to assume that, in the hurry and confusion incident to emigration, some of them come away with stomachs empty, or nearly so.

And, finally, at the close of the breeding season (or about October 10th), a pound of bees killed with sulphur fumes, contains only 3,000, having, in preparation for wintering, more or less honey stowed away in their stomachs, and some fæces in their intestines.

The average of these figures is 4,110 bees to the pound. As regards swarming bees, I remember to have read, many years ago, in some small treatise on bees, as follows: "There are not, as is commonly stated, 175 swarming bees to the half ounce, but only 123." On trial, I found there were not more than 120 such bees in half an ounce. The Baron of Berlepsch is correct, when regretting that he neglected to test the weight of swarming bees, he expressed the conviction that of them 4,000, at most, would weigh a pound. The numbers I have given above were ascertained with the utmost care and precision, and I now present them in tabular form:

Description.	1 lb.	2 lbs.	3 lbs.	4 lbs.	5 lbs.	6 lbs.
1. Outlying Bees,	5,600	11,200	16,808	22,400	28,000	33,600
2. Bees Brushed Off	4,300	8,600	12,900	17,200	21,500	25,800
3 Bees Driv'n Out	4,050	8,100	12,150	16,200	20,250	24,300
4. Swarming Bees,	3,600	7,200	10,800	14,400	18,000	21,600
5. Bees in Autumn	3,000	6,000	9,000	12,000	15,000	

A swarm weighing seven pounds will contain 24,200 bees; and one weighing eight pounds, 28,800.

Now, if 13¾ ounces of expelled bees contain as many individuals as 15 ounces of swarming bees, then a driven swarm weighing five pounds will have appropriated and carried off 6¼ ounces less honey than a natural swarm of the same weight.

Again, if 15 ounces of swarming bees contain as many individuals as 18 ounces of bees in autumnal repose, then a swarm weighing four pounds have twelve ounces less honey in their stomachs than the same weight of bees in repose, &c. The number of bees in swarms weighing seven and eight pounds is purposely stated, as I have myself had swarms weighing seven and eight pounds severally. Such gigantic swarms always produce astonishing results in favorable seasons.

The numbers and weights given in the above table are designed to furnish the readers with a guide or norm, according to which they may institute comparative experiments—the results of which should be communicated for publication.

Let me add a few queries:

How much more honey will a heavy swarm secure than a lighter one, weighing a specified amount less? How strong must an artificial swarm, consisting of No. 1, No. 2, or No. 3 class bees be, that it shall be able to secure the requisite winter supply of stores, without extraneous assistance? Is there any perceptible difference—and if so, how much between the product of a natural and an artificial swarm having an equal number of bees, whose internal and external relations are precisely similar? and if the latter should come short of the former in productiveness, what should be the weight of an artificial swarm, in a subsequent experiment, to enable it to keep pace with the other?

E. POHLMANN.

Sayn, near Coblenz, April 20, 1871.

An Ill-treated Queen.

TRANSLATED FOR THE AMERICAN BEE JOURNAL.

I divided a colony, making an artificial swarm, and using the old queen for that purpose. Eight days afterwards I examined the parent stock, to see how many queen cells had been built. I found twelve, of which I removed ten, leaving two, that a queen might certainly be reared. Eight days later, in the evening, I heard a young queen teeting in this hive, and on opening it, found a fine large yellow queen on one of the combs; when, almost at the same instant, another young queen, handsomer still, than the first, issued from the second cell, on another comb, and was evidently preparing to fly. I caught her,—beauty of color and shape inducing me to preserve her. I formed a small nucleus, using three combs with sealed brood and the adhering bees, starting thus what should soon be a pretty strong colony. I kept it in my cellar four days, and then set it on its destined stand. The bees immediately began to fly, and I soon saw the queen issue and take wing. In about five minutes she returned, evidently not fertilized, and entered the hive. In a few moments the bees became agitated. I opened the hive, and was astonished to see a dense cluster of bees, about as large as my fist, lying on the bottom. Surmising that the queen was imprisoned therein, I blew smoke on it freely, but without effect. I then separated the cluster by means of two small sticks (and some force was required to do so). I found the queen among them, but still uninjured, and having caged her, placed the cage among the bees, which instantly covered it, enraged and furious. I so left matters till next morning, when harmony and peace being re-stored, I released the queen, and she passed among the bees without renewed annoyance. On the first and second days after this, I saw no change, but on the third day the bees showed as much agitation as on the former occasion. On opening the hive, I found another cluster on the bottom, from which I again released the queen, finding her this time very weak and with one wing and a hind leg injured. She appeared as though fertilized, and I inferred that she had been attacked on her return from her bridal trip. I put her in a cage, and left her among the bees till morning, when, finding all peaceable, I liberated her, and she was kindly received. On the fourth day I was not a little surprised to find her laying. Some of the cells contained eggs, and others larvæ, though none of the latter were yet sealed. The young bees, when mature, were very pretty. I wintered her as a reserve queen, and gave her to a queenless colony next spring, but found her dead in front of her hive in May following. Her successor, reared from her brood, was a handsome queen.

Possibly the bees of this nucleus, having been taken from another hive, may not have missed the young queen while she was absent, and on her return mistook her for a stranger and an intruder.

VOGEL.

Introducing Queen Bees.

We translate from the German the following instructions for solving this prime puzzle in bee-culture —giving both the process and the reasons for each operation. The writer says that, in hundreds of cases, he has never known it to fail, when the directions were strictly adhered to. If it is *sure*, it need not be an objection that it is *slow;* as it involves less waste of time than the loss of a valuable queen.—[ED.

If your bees are in a common box or straw hive, drive them out in the usual manner into an empty box or hive, then shake them out on a sheet, seek for and remove the queen, and return the bees to the empty hive or box. Let them remain in it undisturbed, till by their restlessness they show that they have become aware of their queenless condition. Then fumigate them with tobacco, sprinkle them with sugar water, and introduce your new queen among them, gently and uncaged, having previously besmeared her with honey taken from the hive from which they were driven. She will be readily and gladly accepted. Let the bees and queen remain together thus confined in the unfurnished hive twenty-four hours. Then shake them out on a sheet and run them into a movable comb hive, into which the combs have been transferred from their original hive; set them on their stand, and matters will proceed peaceably and prosperously.

If your bees are in a movable comb hive, then after catching and removing the queen, take out the combs in rotation and shake the bees down on a sheet, carefully brushing all of them from the combs, and set these in an empty hive. Now run the bees into an empty hive or box, and let them remain in it till they show signs of queenlessness. Then fumigate them with tobacco, sprinkle them with sugar water, and introduce among them your new queen, uncaged, but besmeared with honey, as directed in the former case. Let them remain thus confined twenty-four hours, and then run them into a hive in which their original frames and combs have been inserted. They will be content to feed themselves after their forced and prolonged abstinence, and so rejoiced in the possession of a fertile queen as to refrain from doing her bodily injury.

In this process the following are the points essential to success:

1. The bees to which a queen is to be introduced, must be altogether removed from their old hive into an empty one or a box, that nothing —not even the odor of their late dwelling—may remind them of their former queen.

2. The hive or box into which they are transferred, must contain neither brood nor combs, so that the bees may be completely non-plussed, and made more thoroughly aware than otherwise of their destitute and helpless condition. They will thus be completely dispirited, little disposed to make hostile demonstrations, and ready to receive and cherish a fertile queen when properly presented.

3. The introduction of a new queen should not be unduly delayed, but made as soon as the

bees strongly manifest grief or distress for the loss they have sustained—that is, about one hour after the old queen was taken away.

4. The bees must be well fumigated with tobacco and sprinkled with sugar water; and the queen besmeared with honey taken from the old hive, if such is to be had.

5. The queen must not be rudely thrust among the bees; for all hasty or violent movements cause momentary irritation, placing her in jeopardy. She must be gently presented, unconfined, and allowed to mingle with the masses without a struggle.

6. The operation should be undertaken in the evening, a little before dusk, as bees are more peaceably disposed then than earlier in the day.

7. The bees, with the introduced and now accepted queen, must remain together, confined in the unfurnished hive, till the evening of the following day. Then hunger, and the desire for better accommodations, will have effectually subdued the rebellious temper of every individual, and rendered the new home and the new queen quite desirable objects to them.

[For the American Bee Journal.]

Novice.

Dear Bee Journal:—We are very thankful to be able to write to you again. After six weeks of outdoor life, and an almost exclusive diet of beesteak, we feel so much improved, that we began to conclude our "mission" is not finished by considerable.

Mr. "B. Lunderer," thinks we are not a talkative person. (By the way, we really wish we deserved the high compliments he paid us,) and we wish to say to him and many others, that Novice certainly has the will, though not the *power*, to talk and to answer all the letters written to him. Our present ill health is very much owing to the mental strain necessary to treat every one civilly and give inquirers the attention they should have; until a day in the woods, where we were secure from seeing any one, was a positive luxury.

In regard to our basswood forest, in one of our rambles we discovered a forest of fifteen acres, which the owner had sufficient good sense to fence up from all stock of every kind, for six or seven years, so that young timber of every description had grown up unmolested. We were overjoyed to find there thousands of young basswoods, from one inch to fifteen feet high; and we are going to commence transplanting right away, removing a shovelful or more of the wild wood mould with each tree.

The piece of woodland mentioned looks like a mine of wealth to us, and we hope it may prove such to its enterprising owner.

Mr. "B. L." before mentioned, hopes we may have reverses, &c., enough to keep us from becoming egotistical. Bless your heart, "B. L." and a host of others, we only think we shall have to tell the whole truth, however humiliating.

We wrote you two months ago, Mr. Editor, that we had sold about two tons of honey, and besides had nearly all the upper stories of our hives filled with combs of sealed honey, for making all short stocks good for the winter. Well, we know our index scales had shown a regular decrease in weight, weekly and almost daily, since the middle of July; but still we somehow hoped that other stocks had done better, until about the first of October, when we found that the index stock had about consumed the thirty pounds left in the hive when we stopped extracting—the drouth this fall, and other adverse causes, having totally spoiled our usual fall pasturge.

Of course prompt meaures *should have been taken at once*, to see that none were in danger of starving, but we put it off until about a week ago. (We should like to charge what follows to "ill health," or some*thing*, or some*body* else; but the plain truth is we were careless and put it off—something that will never do in bee-keeping), when we found that No. 1, was starved dead—with the very best queen too, in all our apiary. She might have been saved, but was *neglected* and FORGOTTEN until dead. This roused us up. We went to work and hitched our index scales to every hive, and found we should have to feed over a thousand pounds to put all in good order.

We *thought* we fed promptly all that were in danger, but when we came to No. 12, we found it "silent in death." Thus was another of our best stocks gone, and the one that was emptied last of all in July. We tried reviving as before, but it was too late. The queen (a fine one, and probably next to No. 1) was still alive, and a dozen or two of bees that gathered or stole enough to keep alive. These we put in a cage over another hive "*ad interim.*" Next day she had got out of the cage, and was killed of course. "Clearly an accident!" many would console themselves with saying. *But there was no accident about it! A beekeeper has no business to cage queens so carelessly that they can crawl out*, nor to perform any operation with bees in such a miserable "slip shod" way. We feel sick whenever we think of it.

Some stocks had no honey; so we must give them twenty-five pounds, and say ten additional to enable them to secrete wax to seal it, raise brood, &c. With the old Novice feeder or any feeder we ever saw, it would take a month's time and no end of vexation and stickiness, to get it done. The idea was intolerable, with sixty-three hives to supply. Of course our thirty-two story Langstroths were better off, but they all needed feeding some—that is, after we equalized the sealed honey.

We had one barrel of honey left, for which we then had received an offer at twenty cents per pound, coffee sugar syrup can be made for a little more than ten cents.

Now right here we protest that if anybody else concludes to do as we did, and fails, do not blame us nor say we recommended it. From many previous experiments, we concluded to sell the honey and feed coffee sugars, twenty pounds to a gallon of water and four teaspoonfuls of cream tartar, to prevent crystallization.

Our index scales had shown that a colony of

bees can gather ten to fifteen pounds of honey in a day; and if so, what should hinder them taking twenty or twenty-five pounds in a day and night, from a suitable feeder? And we did make a stock take twenty pounds in nine hours, without more than five minutes' work of our time. It was done in this way. We got a tea-kettle; removed spout and handle; soldered perforated tin over where the cover goes; put on a screw top, like those on oil cans, near the perforated tin, to fill it by. Now set it on the scales and fill with as many pounds of syrup as you wish. Fix the screw cap and ears that held the handle, so as to form three legs. When this is inverted over the frames, your work is done. Invert it first over a pan, until it ceases to run a stream, and you will have no leaking.

Hoping this may save others as much time as it has saved us, we are yours and all beekeepers,

NOVICE.

P. S. All letters giving us facts, are thankfully received. Please make all inquiries through the Journal.

[For the American Bee Journal.]

About Queen-Raising.

I have raised and shipped, by mail and express, eight hundred and twenty-five (825) queen bees during the season just past. Of this number, less than twenty-five (not 25 per cent.) died or proved worthless when they reached their destination. One of the latter was found to be a drone-laying queen, and one a queen that laid eggs which would not hatch. This one was returned to me safely from Ohio, by mail. She was handsome, and had the appearance of a good laying queen. A very few have been reported as hybrids—less than ten. I think that twenty-five queens would cover the loss by mail, including those that proved to be impure. Purchasers acknowledging the receipt of queens, would invariably write that they were in good condition (many of them adding: "they were as lively as crickets when received").

A few of my customers lost some of their queens in introducing, but most of them were well satisfied with the queens sent to them. Somewhat over two hundred of the queens sent from my apiary went into the State of Illinois,—a fact speaking well for my stock in that State. For several seasons I have supplied the best and most prominent beekeepers in the country with queens, and through their influence have received more orders than I have been able to supply. I have received orders for more than fifteen hundred (1500) queens since January, 1871; and when I started last spring, I had on my book orders for more than four hundred queens. In August I had in operation two hundred and eighty nucleus hives, besides the full stocks on which I was raising queens; but to supply the demand for queens is more than I could do.

Beekeepers who visit my apiary express the opinion that I must lose a good many queens when they fly out to meet the drones; but such is not the case. I have been very fortunate in that respect, and have lost comparatively few. I set my hives very irregularly, and ninety-five out of every hundred queens that fly out, find their own home when they return. The number not returning is very small.

I find it much easier to raise queens than to raise drones after the honey harvest is over; and it was only this season that I discovered a sure way to get drone eggs deposited—and this I can effect even from a young queen, as well as from an old one. All who have visited my "queen nursery" in queen raising time, well know my process for getting large, healthy, and prolific queens in nucleus hives. My method is this: The nucleus is filled full of bees, which are confined from twelve to eighteen hours. Then they are allowed to fly out. As soon as I can prepare the brood (eggs just hatching) they are furnished with material to raise queens; furnished with feed, and a good supply of this kept up till the queen cells are sealed over. When the time arrives for the cells to hatch (from ten to fourteen days after the nucleus is started), those that cannot be separated without injury, are put in a small hive that has glass sides, so that both sides of the comb can be seen. Here they are kept, and as fast as they hatch put in cages, with a few workers, and then introduced to such nuclei as are in condition to receive them kindly.

I confess that I find the operation of introducing young virgin queens over to nucleus hives, a very difficult job. In many cases, where the queen is not hugged to death, her wings are so injured that she cannot fly. Of course such queens must be destroyed. Where cells can be transferred, it is always advisable to do so. I have removed a laying queen from a nucleus hive, at the same time inserting a queen cell ready to hatch, and in the course of an hour had the young queen safely introduced. But this is not a safe way; the hive should be kept queenless at least twelve hours.

During an experience of twelve years in raising queens, I never knew one to make her marriage flight until she was five days old; and I have watched them very closely too. In the months of June, July and August, they will be fertilized when five days old, if the fifth day is warm and pleasant; and in forty-eight hours later, eggs can be found in the cells, if the hive contains plenty of workers and food. One day, in last June, I knew of forty-five queens being fertilized in the course of two hours.

For breeding, I use the largest, purest, and most prolific queens I have, and keep them in nucleus hives during the breeding season. I do not allow drones to be raised from the same queen used for breeding queens, and intend to cross my stock as much as possible. All the queens I raised in May last cost me five dollars each; and I do not think that queens can be raised profitably in May. A full stock of bees that will make five nuclei in May, would make ten fully as large in June. Then, too, they will require less feeding at the later period, as forage is then generally abundant in this part of the country, the weather warmer, and four times as many queen cells will be constructed. Fifty nucleus hives, started the first week in August, constructed over four hundred queen cells; if started in May the same number of bees would make only about one hundred and fifty cells.

I have read all that has been said in the Journal about rearing queens. Now, I will challenge the most scientific beekeeper and queen bee-raiser to produce from ten to one hundred queens better than I will raise in nucleus hives, five inches deep, eight inches from side to side, and five inches from front to rear. The queens shall be selected at random, from two hundred and fifty nucleus hives, between 1st of June and 1st of September. Any man has the privilege to call within the time named, and select the queens from any hive he pleases; and if he finds better queens than he can find in my hives, he will not be asked to pay for those he has from me. I have always had better success in raising queens in nucleus hives than in full full stocks; and, as a general thing, I can get more queen cells constructed by putting one quart of bees in a nucleus hive, than I can get in a full stock.

During the month of June, when the honey harvest was at its height, I removed the queens from two of the fullest colonies I had. The result was, sixty odd cells were built, about twenty producing good large queens; from the rest came the smallest queens I ever saw. The large queens were started from eggs just hatching; whereas, the small queens were reared from larvæ, just about ready to be sealed up when the queens were removed. And as the larvæ, from which the smaller queens were reared, were several days older than those from which the large queens were raised, of course the small queens hatched first; and if the cells had not been removed from the hives before the first queens hatched, those hives would have had very small (ten days) queens. This has always been my experience in raising queens in full colonies. Queens raised in nucleus hives, after the plan I have given in this article, will be found large and prolific. H. Alley.

Wenham, Mass., Oct., 1871.

Michigan Beekeepers' Convention.

Agricultural College,
Lansing, Sept. 29, 1871.

EDITOR AMERICAN BEE JOURNAL.

Dear Sir:—The annual meeting of the Michigan Beekeepers' Association, which took place at Kalamazoo, was well attended, the papers read very able, and the discussions very lively and interesting.

One gentleman present, Mr. Bingham, of Allegan, contended that the black bee was superior to the Italian. The only point of superiority named was greater readiness to store in boxes. This opinion was assailed by nearly all present.

Mr. Bingham uses a hive with frames only five inches in depth. With this, and black bees, he has taken sixty pounds of box honey from each of his colonies. Said honey was reported to be the best sold in the Chicago market this season.

Favorable reports of the honey season come from all quarters.

Foul brood was reported in Wayne, Oakland, Monroe, and Lenawee counties.

Valuable papers were read, all of which I will send you, in hope you may find room for them in the Journal.

A. J. Cook, *Secretary.*

REPORT OF PROCEEDINGS:

Kalamazoo, September 19, 1871.

The annual meeting of the Beekeepers' Association of Michigan was held in Corporation Hall this evening. President A. F. Moon, of Paw Paw, was in the chair, and A. J. Cook, of the State Agricultural College, was secretary. But a very few members were in attendance.

The topics of foul brood and diseases of bees were discussed. No one knew of any remedy for foul brood, but it was the opinion of the speakers that it was caused by the want of proper ventilation in the hives.

Adjourned till to-morrow morning, at 8 o'clock.

SECOND DAY.

Kalamazoo, Sept. 20, 1871.

The meeting was called to order by president A. F. Moon, of Paw Paw. J. H. Porter was appointed secretary. Dr. Bohrer, of Indiana, was appointed president *pro tem.*

Mr. J. H. Everard, of Kalamazoo, proposed as a subject for discussion, "What is the best method of extracting surplus honey?" Mr. Everard related his experience and what he had seen at Allegan in hives used by Mr. Bingham. Mr. Bingham took from one hive nine boxes, containing six pounds each. Mr. Marvin asked, "What is the shape of the hive and the management?" Dr. Bohrer stated that if the boxes be too small, enough bees cannot be clustered to keep up animal heat; therefore in cold climates two sets of frames will be preferable to small hives.

Professor Cook, of Lansing, suggested that the subject would be dsicussed to-morrow when it would be in order. On the subject of artificial fertilization, Mr. Everard said that in his experience artificial fertilization had proved a failure. Professor Cook related his experience in the trial made in the green-house of the Agricultural College under the most favorable circumstances. Failure was the result. Mr. Knapp had tried Mitchell's plan pretty thoroughly and practiced the plan. After visiting Mr. Mitchell and getting all the information, he did not succeed in a single instance. He tried thirty queens and lost them all. Mr. Balch stated that he had one queen with a defective wing, which was fertilized and was prolific. In other cases he failed. Mr. Moon stated that he received a letter from Royal Oak stating that a wingless queen was fertilized and became very prolific. He thought the old way was the best. He said that by feeding early in the spring and getting them out before black drones were matured he was successful in raising working bees. Mr. Balch stated that by hiving bees very late he had succeeded very well, and thought it better than early in the spring.

Mr. Marvin expressed his faith in green-house fertilization, and thought if everything was dry, so that their wings be kept dry, it would be better. Professor Cook replied that in the experiments he had made every precaution had been taken—that the drones seemed frightened, and that among all animals it was hard to bring about copulation under fright.

Mr. Marvin thought bees might be educated so that drones would not be frightened. Mr. Clements thought that drones kept in confinement would not be so frightened. Mr. C. Balch had failed in all his efforts at bee fertilization. Mr. Moon said that twelve or fourteen years ago he had tried a plan which cost more than it was worth. Dr. Bohrer stated that there was a time when he hoped it would be a success, but that he thought in many places it was not necessary. In his locality there were very few black bees, and, therefore, he was not troubled with them. Bees might be confined to the hives by cutting notches in a piece of tin. Bees cannot be educated beyond the laws controlling their natures. He is never troubled with moths in his Italian bees; he frequently finds them among black bees; he thinks that many may have been deceived—that the bee was fertilized after entering the hive. Mr. Bingham, of Allegan, said he would like to know the superiority of the Italian bees over black ones. He thought there was a good deal of humbug about the claims set up for Italian bees. He had found them no better than black bees.

Then the question of artificial fertilization was on motion laid on the table, and the question of the relative merits of Italian bees was taken up and discussed by the meeting. Dr. Bohrer gave his experience with Italian bees. They are more docile, allow themselves to be handled with more ease; less trouble to make money from honey.

Professor Cook thought there was another point, as to their stinging. They worked on red clover; he observed them so working. They were not known to rob others, but made more honey than black bees around them.

Mr. Porter said he knew that black bees were worse at robbing, and were defeated in their attempt on the Italians at the Agricultural College. Mr. Bingham said the difference might be accounted for in the difference in handling. Italians were more addicted to swarming, even when they had no royal cell. The black bees do not swarm without royal cells. Italians fall short of what is claimed for them.

Mr. Moon said he had had black bees swarm, and put them back seven times without a sign of a royal cell. The Italian bee has proved very valuable. He would rather have one Italian than two black swarms. His greatest argument was that they would cling to their cards, when the blacks by puffing in a little smoke would rush out of the hive, and that it was almost impracticable to practice artificial swarming.

Mr. Everard never knew a single swarm to be injured by worms, no matter how much reduced.

Mr. Moon was glad that the subject had been agitated. He was of the opinion that what has been said about Italian bees was exaggerated. Mr. Marvin asked Mr. Bingham if he had any experience in "slinging" honey with black bees? Italian bees could not be made to work in boxes. In Germany they do not pretend to use boxes, but confine themselves to frames. He does not believe that worms ever destroy bees until they have been so reduced that they were as good as dead.

The discussion was continued for some time, when on motion the subject was laid on the table.

The question was next considered as to the propriety of offering premiums for the best hives and honey. A little discussion took place in regard to what a hive should be, and what should be done to save farmers from being swindled. Mr. Bohrer thought the best way was to instruct the farmers beginning in agriculture. When men are properly educated they will be able to judge what a hive should be.

It was suggested that a hive should be cheap, simple and durable. Simplicity was strongly recommended.

A motion was made and carried that a committee be appointed to say what a good hive should be, and report the same to the convention this evening. Messrs. Rood, Bohrer, and A. C. Balch were appointed such committee.

The convention then adjourned till 7 o'clock this evening.

EVENING SESSION.

The continued illness of President Moon compelled him to go home. Hon. H. Huff, of Jonesville, was appointed chairman *pro tem.*

The meeting was addressed by Mr. Rood, on the subject of "Foul brood." His paper on the subject was quite lengthy. He gave a full description of this fatal disease among bees, and how to distinguish it, and gave some sage advice in regard to handling other colonies or permitting other bees from using the honey of the affected colony. It is contagious as small-pox is to man, and as fatal as cholera. The speaker could assign no cause for the disease, nor any effectual remedy. After the paper had been read, a very general discussion ensued, but the result was to leave it with no more light than when the meeting opened, as regards the cause, or of any cause for it.

Mr. M. M. Baldridge, of St. Charles, Ill., then read a paper on the Honey Extractor, its management, and the treatment of extracted honey. A very long discussion followed the reading of this essay, during which Mr. D. S. Heffron, of Chicago, made some very interesting remarks in regard to the treatment of honey after extracting it, and of preparing it for market. When the discussion closed, the committee to whom was referred the matter of hives, &c., made their report through Dr. Bohrer. It is as follows:

We, the committee to whom was referred the matter concerning the requisites of a good bee-hive, have had the same under consideration and submit the following:

1st—For out-door wintering we recommend a hive not exceeding twelve inches in depth nor less than ten inches inside of the breeding chamber, for use in northern latitudes.

2d—For in-door wintering a hive may be made as shallow as five inches in the breeding apartment.

3d—We believe the breeding chamber should not contain less than 2,000 cubic inches actual breeding space, nor more than 2,500, the same to be so constructed as to admit of upward ventilation at pleasure, and the entrance to be contracted so as to admit of no more than one or two bees to pass or repass at the same time during the winter, believing that every heavy current of air being allowed to pass through at this season of the year will serve as a cause of disease.

4th—We believe that a hive to be cheap in cost to the beekeeper, and, at the same time, adapted to procuring honey, either in the comb or by the use of the melextractor, should be so constructed as to admit of boxes of shallow frames, or of frames equal in size with those of the breeding chamber. This we regard as a hive well adapted to general as well as special purposes.

5th—We would not under any circumstances, recommend or encourage the use of any but movable comb hives, feeling well convinced that no other method will enable the beekeeper to make the profession successful and profitable.

E. Rood,
G. Bohrer,
A. C. Balch.

After some discussion, in which the hive question was pretty thoroughly *ventilated*, the resolutions were passed with only one dissenting voice.

The meeting then adjourned till to-morrow morning. There was quite a large attendance this evening, and great interest was manifested in the discussions.

THURSDAY MORNING.

Kalamazoo, Sept. 22, 1871.

Mr. McKee, of Laingsburg, occupied the chair this morning. The following officers were elected :

President—Ezra Rood, of Wayne.

Vice President—Mr. McKee, of Ingham.

Secretary—A. J. Cook, of the State Agricultural College.

Treasurer—Arad C. Balch, of Kalamazoo.

Dr. Bohrer, of Indianapolis, was made an honorary member. The subject of hives was again taken up. Mr. Bingham defended side opening hives. Dr. Bohrer and Mr. Rood opposed them. Dr. Bohrer preferred the Langstroth hive.

Mr. Baldridge used an extra hive and changed his bees in the spring. This system, he said, worked well with him.

Dr. Bohrer thought the Convention ought not to act on the subject. Practical beekeepers understood what they wanted.

Mr. E. Gallup read a very carefully prepared and interesting essay on "Artificial and Natural Queen Raising," for which the society voted him their thanks.

Mr. Marvin read a paper prepared for the meeting upon "The Production of Honey and the Forage for a Great Yield of Honey." It was well received, and the author was by the meeting thanked for the same.

The association then adjourned, to meet again this evening.

EVENING SESSION.

The feature of the evening session was the paper read by Dr. Bohrer on the subject of "Drones and Queen Bees." The views set forth in the paper were endorsed by members, especially by Professor Cook, of Lansing, who is well known as an accomplished entomologist, and by Mr. Heffron, another close observer of insect life.

The secretary was instructed to notify delinquent members to pay their dues forthwith.

The subject of foul brood was brought up again. Mr. Edward Mason believed foul brood was caused by the death of the larva, caused by chilling when the hives were exposed. This view was vigorously combatted by Mr. Rood, Dr. Bohrer and many others.

Secretary Cook announced that there would be a session to-morrow morning, when some important questions would be introduced for discussion.

The Convention then adjourned.

[For the American Bee Journal.]

A Trip to Michigan.

Mr. Editor :—Sometime previous to a regular meeting of the Michigan State Beekeepers' Association, held at Kalamazoo, during the 19th, 20th, and 21st of the present month, I received an invitation to be present with them and participate in the discussion of the different subjects that might be brought before them during their several sessions. But what has, by some means or other, got to be termed *the drone question* (which phrase is understood to have reference to the influence exerted upon the drone off-spring of the queen bee, through the medium of her fertilization, as well as the ability of a drone from a virgin queen to impregnate a queen), was more particularly assigned to me than any other. As my views, however, on that subject will be likely among other parts of the proceedings, to appear in print, I will not here repeat any portion of the argument which I used in support of the Dzierzon theory. I say in defence of the Dzierzon theory, because I heartily endorse it, and because such a subject would naturally embrace his theory, or rather bring us to consider the correcting of his views. But I will confine myself to a description of what I saw and heard during my trip. My route lay by way of Fort Wayne, Indiana, at which point a change of cars was necessary. From this point I could reach Kalamazoo by taking either of two different routes—one being direct and the other leading thither by way of Jackson. But as the latter route is the longest by at least sixty miles, I sough to avoid it if possible ; yet from neglect on my part to look at my railroad guide, or, still worse, the neglect of the ticket agent to give me what he knew to be reliable and truthful information, when I asked it of him, I soon found myself on the way to Jackson. As it was now too late to retrace my steps, I concluded to make the best of a bad thing, and accordingly spent time in looking at the character of the soil and the improvements growing out of industry and general enterprise among the people who inhabit the country through which the road runs, I found much of the soil to be of such quality as to be well adapted to the production of nearly or quite all the crops peculiar to our Northern States ; and as the country in southern and central Michigan is somewhat dotted with small lakes and soil which was once covered by them, it must most unquestionably produce a large amount of honey-yielding plants, of a kind and quality requiring little or no special cultivation. In addition to this, these lakes are surrounded by a soil fertile in the production of the different kinds of grain and roots commonly cultivated by the farmer.

These lands are also mostly well adapted to the cultivation of special honey-yielding crops, such as buckwheat and the different varieties of clover. In fact, the face of the country is such as to effectually guard the bee keeper against excessive drought, as the land immediately surrounding the lakes is low and well calculated to furnish forage for bees during dry weather; and when there is an excess of rain, the uplands will produce the various honey-yielding plants already mentioned. Thus the people of such portions of Michigan as above described, have the natural resources furnished them to make the occupation of bee-keeping highly remunerative.

On reaching Jackson, I found it to be one of the most enterprising inland cities I ever visited. The State prison, located at this point, which I visited, and found its various buildings and shops to be large and well adapted to the preservation of the health of the inmates—the number of which, as well as I remember the statement of the conductor, is at present six hundred and fifty-two convicts. While passing through the shops, where men were engaged at labor, and at learning a trade, in the different mechanical departments, the thought struck me quite forcibly that it would be a very easy matter so to arrange the prison grounds as to admit of a small apiary being kept within their limits. This might not only prove to be a source of profit and income to the State or the capital invested, but would furnish such convicts as are not physically able to engage profitably in other manual pursuits, an opportunity of becoming acquainted with a branch of industry highly remunerative, and at the same time well adapted to weakly constitutions.

On my way from Jackson to Kalamazoo, I found the country to be very similar in character to that already described. On reaching the latter city, I was delighted with its appearance and the enterprising character of its inhabitants. I registered my name at the Kalamazoo House, as I had been requested to do by Prof. Cook, until such time as he was able to meet me ; and as he was not in the city on my arrival there, I spent the afternoon on the State Fair Grounds. The fair being then open, made it quite an interesting place to visit. But during my stay in Kalamazoo, I was displeased with only one feature of its regulations—which is the custom of permitting the hackmen and omnibus drivers, while halting in front of the hotels, waiting for passengers, to indulge in one continued and unearthly cry of—"Here's your hack for the Fair Grounds," or for the railroad, as the case chanced to be. This is not only very impolite, but very disgusting to such as are in possession of perfect hearing. Police regulations should compel those men to address travellers in an ordinary tone, not above that used in common conversation.

On my return from the Fair Grounds, I met Prof. Cook, and found him to be what I hoped to find, an agreeable and intelligent gentleman, besides being tolerably grod-looking; but as that is a matter of not very much importance to any one except his wife, I shall not say much about. Mr. Porter, one of the Michigan Agricultural College students, was in company with Prof. Cook. With him I was made acquainted and found him likewise to be a gentleman of intelligence, and of good looks also. I deem it a matter of some importance to the unmarried female portion of the bee-keeping fraternity to make mention of this latter fact, as Mr. P. has not yet, I believe, committed matrimony. He is well posted in the habits of the honey bee, and long may he live.

At eight o'clock in the evening I went, in company with the above named gentlemen, to Corporation Hall, where a number of beekeepers had assembled, among whom was Mr. Marvin, of Illinois, who is a beekeeper of as good sound sense and wit, as any with whom I have met. The meeting was called to order by President Moon, and several subjects of interest were discussed during the evening. In the afternoon of the next day, I had the pleasure of again meeting with my much esteemed friend, Mr. E. Rood, of Wayne, Michigan, who always adds materially to the interest of beekeepers' associations, by his solid argument and wit. Mr. M. M. Baldridge, of Illinois, was also present. From him I learned a new method of disposing of drones while in the egg state. The plan is rather novel and somewhat funny, yet I think will prove effectual. They are disposed of by pouring cold water into the cells containing the eggs, by which they will be chilled to such an extent as to prevent their hatching.

I met a number of other gentlemen, whose names I cannot now recall; but taking the members of the Michigan Beekeepers' Association all in all, they are certainly a good body of men. Too much praise cannot be given to Prof. Cook for the efforts he is making, and the success he is meeting with, in the advancement of apiarian science at the Agricultural College of Michigan, where bee-keeping is taught the students, among other branches of industry. By this means an intelligent and scientific class of beekeepers will soon be scattered throughout the different parts of the State ; and should the efforts of both the College and the State Association be kept up, as now set in motion, the State of Michigan will always hold her position of prominence in bee-keeping interests.

Alexandria, Ind., Sept. 26, 1871. G. BOHRER.

[For the American Bee Journal.]

The Production of Honey.

A Paper read before the Michigan Beekeepers' Association, September 21, 1871.

By J. M. Marvin, of St. Charles, Ills.

To produce honey in large quantity, a great deal depends on the beekeeper. He or she should have natural or acquired ability, to have any large amount of success, just the same as in other branches of business. The stock of bees should be of the best character, and kept up to the highest standard of excellence. Good success must be had in producing large quantities of surplus honey, stored by light-colored, good tempered bees. Nothing short of this will satisfy the American bee-keeping public at present.

In small and large apiaries a swarm or a stock, or more, will show superior working qualities, by sending out sometimes double the number of workers to the fields, that other hives of equal numbers do. What is the cause? Or how can we improve the working qualities of such stock at large? Italian stock at their first introduction, and our native stock in newly started apiaries, are generally better workers at first, or until they are bred in and in too long, without a change of stock. Some close observer may say a swarm or stock, or more, may get possession of a limited field, and hold possession by beating others off! We should say, thereby showing their superiority.

The superiority of the Italian bees may be seen while working on the flowers. We have seen five of these bees on a single thistle head, and more on a squash flower. Not so many of the more wild black. These are off on the first approach of a neighboring black bee; to say nothing of the well-bred yellow bees, which stick to the source of feed until their bodies are as large as some queens.

It is now quite easy to improve any valuable quality in bees, as we have control over the hives, combs, and bees, and can rear males or females from any particular mother, at pleasure.

The atmosphere has an effect on honey producing, which we can control in some measure by planting honey producing trees and shrubs for shelter, as well as honey, when enough do not grow naturally for the stock. The atmosphere is more apt to be good for the production of honey over an uneven surface of country. More or less honey producing trees, shrubs and plants are left standing on such uneven land, as it is hard to cultivate, and more or less water is near or on the surface of such land to modify the effects of the atmosphere. A variety of soil, also, is generally found in the uneven sections of country, and is favorable to the growth of the different species of trees, shrubs and plants. Some seasons the same varieties of plants will yield more honey on light sandy soils; in other seasons the low, moist, rich land will give the only yield of honey from the same variety of plants. Fruit trees, shrubs and plants are generally planted on a variety of soils, and usually yield enough for the stock. If not, more should be planted.

Alsike clover sometimes smothers itself out on some soils and seasons, by its excessively large growth; but it yields honey every time, on any soil, and in all seasons, as far as heard from. Buckwheat is variable in its yield, but pays me well in honey alone. Polanisia purpurea yields no honey with me, in two years' trial on three varieties of soil. Mr. Fairbrother, of Jackson county, Iowa, writes me he has thirty years' experience with it, and likes it well, although it is variable in its yield. He also writes that he grows raspberries, buckwheat, and other plants for honey; and has had twelve years' experience with melilot or sweet clover, and now has ten acres of it. I conclude that the ten acres are enough for their stock, as the partner wrote me several years ago that they should increase the acreage until they had forty, unless a less quantity proved sufficient. It is the best honey plant with me.

There is no doubt that borage and catnip will pay to cultivate where labor is cheaper and stock more numerous, as these plants need more thorough culture than others, at least in this section.

To get large amounts of surplus honey, a regular business should be made of keeping good strong stocks of bees, at the time or times of a yield of honey in the flowers. It will pay to feed a stock of bees, at the right time, the right amount of feed, to rear bees with, not to have the feed stored in combs for sale. Reducing the stock in the fall to a good working number, and using the combs, honey and bee-bread in the spring, as capital to work with, is a paying business to employ the time of the keeper. There is probably no man living at the present time, knows the full value to a stock or stocks of bees of judiciously used feed. I make the assertion that the same value of feed fed to a stock or stocks of bees, pays better than any other stock feeding on the farm. Any one doubting this, will please give me the name, kind of stock, value of feed, time, and place, and oblige the writer.

In the management of extracted honey, it should be kept in a dry, well ventilated room, until it thickens or granulates. After that it can be kept in a cellar. If kept in barrels the hoops should be often tightened, as the barrels shrink more with honey in than when empty. If the honey is put in crocks or jars, it should be kept from hard freezing. We have lost several jars, both large and small, by frost cracking. There is no apparent injury to the honey from freezing. It puzzles some beekeepers to keep some varieties of honey until it is cured or consumed. There are exceptional cases, when the bees need the help of the keeper with the extractor, to secure the honey in the hive for the use of the bees. (It may be the extractor and clearifier in the hive, combs and honey, may check if not cure disease in bees and brood.) A barrel of some varieties of honey, of forty-two gallons, will shrink to forty or less in thickening or granulating; and will expand to forty-four gallons, or more than a barrel, in heating to a liquid state again. Honey in the combs should not freeze hard enough to break the sealing, as it lets in the air and cold, and the honey granulates more readily—which is not generally desired in comb honey, however it may be wished for in the liquid honey.

To detect sugar in honey, expose it to air and cold, or give it time to granulate. The honey or fruit sugar being similar, grains unevenly round, and more or less soft, varying in different samples in solidity and shape, from cane sugar grains—these being more the form of a prism, and hard.

[For the American Bee Journal.]

The Iowa State Fair—Bees and Bee Hives.

Dear Journal:—I started from home on the 13th instant, for Cedar Rapids, the seat of the Iowa State Fair this year. My main purpose in going was to be present at the Beekeepers' Convention. I can say I was well paid for going, not only in seeing some of the finest stock in the United States, but making the acquaintance of persons engaged in my favorite occupation, namely, bee-keeping. After looking around at the different departments, I went into one of the halls, and on a table or counter I saw as fine a lot of honey, both extracted and in the comb, as was ever exhibited at any fair. This honey was from the apiary of our friend, W. H. Furman, of Cedar Rapids. His box honey could not be surpassed anywhere, and his extracted honey was very fine. Friend Furman had several observing hives on exhibition, each containing a fine Italian queen. I would say that my prejudice against the yellow-banded chaps has somewhat subsided.

Here we met Mr. Furman in person, and Mr. Editor, if you ever get west of the Father of Waters, you will be well repaid for your time in visiting Mr. Furman; you can depend upon that. The next bee man we met was a Mr. King (if we mistake not the name). He, like ourselves, is just making a start. We are confident he will be successful. It cannot be otherwise. A man that carries such an honest-looking face, and is so courteous in his manners, will make any hive of bees hum with joy when he is present. Not only in the presence of bees will his presence be felt, but wherever he may go. The next beekeeper we met was Mr. C. H. White. In him we found a bee man in every sense of the word. We have no fears that he will not be successful in his favorite occupation, for he takes the Journal. Our next movement was to the bee hives. Here we met Mr. R. R. Murphy, well known to the many readers of the Journal. We were glad to make his acquaintance, and hope it may continue for life. Friend Murphy had two of his honey extractors on exhibition, and also a Langstroth hive. The workmanship was good on both hive and extractors. May success crown his labors abundantly. The next acquaintance we formed was that of your correspondent, Mr. J. E. Benjamin. We could plainly see that his native element, in which he likes to be, is the apiary. In the hands of such men as friend B. a hive of bees will prosper anywhere. May he ever be successful in his enterprise. We found Mr. Frank Krause a go-ahead bee man—one who understands the principles of bee-keeping. We hope our acquaintance with him may continue. Men like him are always successful. Paul Lattner, Esq., and Mr. W. S. Goodhue are bee men "all over." Bee-keeping was the favorite topic on which they dwelt. There are many others whom we would like to introduce to you, Mr. Editor, and to the readers of the Journal, but lack of space forbids us to lengthen out "our piece."

All the bee men we met were men of intelligence; none of the old fogies of the box hive; but modern beekeepers in every sense of the term—men, who, by their presence and their support will make the "Central Iowa Beekeepers' Association" a *success*.

The bee hives on exhibition, according to what each exhibitor had to say, was truly a grand collection of hives. A person had choice of a hive from the new fangled moth trap device—that will catch every moth that comes in sight, to the plain, simple, readily understood, and easily managed Langstroth. We don't want any of those hives that will catch and kill, or scare the life out of every poor moth that comes along. Yet not only do some of these, it is claimed, perform this important feat, but all you have to do is to put a swarm into one of these splendid palaces, shut up every entrance but the moth trap, and set it in a white clover patch or a buckwheat field, and begin to take off the surplus honey as fast as the combs are capped over—and your triumph as a beekeeper is secured. It will astonish the uninitiated to see the large amount of surplus honey that may be garnered by simply letting the "busy bee" look out through the moth trap of some of these fanciful contrivances.

Another thing we cannot refrain from noticing. We find friend Langstroth has almost ruined bee-keeping by inventing that hive of his. He forgot to put in a few strips of tin here, and a few carpet tacks there; and missed it much in not giving his frames the proper twist and size. They are a little too short at one end, and a little too long at another, and the bees will sometimes stick them fast with propolis—why didn't he think of it and stick on a piece of candy for them to nibble at instead, to "sweeten their imagination," and teach them to quit using bee-glue? Then, too, his frames are too close together, or perhaps a little too far apart; and you have to take off the top and remove that plaguey honey board to get a sight of them. Why didn't he invent a hive that opens automatically, and manage to have the well-filled honey combs lifted out by a spring, without disturbing the poor little tired bees? Alas, having failed to do this, he has left to others the necessity of setting their ingenuity at work to concoct some all-embracing contrivance, with a moth-trap appended, constraining the poor bee after laboring hard in the field and returning home toil-worn and travel-stained, to crawl over, and under, and through the mysterious labyrinths of a "trap" before it can reach the inside of the hive proper.

Then again, Mr. Langstroth (like the anticipating ancients, who stole and used all our happy thoughts) has *infringed* on sundry new inventions—his patent being dated 1852, and theirs in 1870! Alas, my patent right friends, after Mr. Langstroth set the "egg" on its end, anybody can do it. Why is this? Why are you forever bellowing against the Langstroth hive? Some of you are as old as Mr. Langstroth; why didn't you invent hives with the movable comb principle and introduce them, and reap honor in an honest way?

G. W. BARCLAY.

Tipton, Iowa, Sept., 1871.

[For the American Bee Journal.]

At the Iowa State Fair.

MR. EDITOR :—We propose relating what we saw and heard, about bees and bee hives, at the Iowa State Fair.

Upon entering the fair grounds we were not long in finding the apiary department, which was well represented by Mr. W. H. Furman, of Cedar Rapids, with a great display of honey in boxes and extracted honey in glass jars, which attracted a great deal of attention.

The hive department was represented by different parties, of which we will speak as taken down on our memorandum.

The first hive we examined was a bee hive (patented of course), by T. F. Engledow. This gentleman was very enthusiastic, and explained his hive in a manner that would make the uninitiated believe it was a perfect palace. Well, we will commence with the frame of this hive—a Langstroth frame, with some modifications, hung by means of metal straps forming hooks, which hang on iron rods. The frame has a centre stay of pine wood, about three-quarter inch stuff. I asked him if he had that in for the bees to keep warm, as it takes up the very best part of the frame, and divides it into two, separating the brood circle, instead of having the brood circle in the centre of the frame. Any beekeeper can see the disadvantage of having heavy strips of wood passing through the frame. Between the frames and the bottom of the hive is a space of three or four inches. I said to him the bees would build comb between the frames and the bottom. The answer was that they had not done so. I wish you could see the entrance of his hive; you would laugh at the absurdity.

The next hive we examined was Jasper Hazen's non-swarmer. In my opinion it is a poor thing for a beekeeper who has many bees to attend to. The frames fitting tight to the sides of the hive, we asked the man attending it, how he got the frames out when they were stuck with propolis. He said he could take them out very easy, but I could not see it.

Then followed the Common Sense Bee hive of D. R. Reed, of Kansas. For my part, I could not see where the common sense comes in. If *brass* and blowing will make it such, the proprietor is capable of doing it. Oh, beekeepers, this is the hive that has a moth trap, in which can be put some secret bait which attract and destroy the moth and not kill the bees. It also has a device to shut the bees in the hive in winter, so that they cannot fly out and get chilled. The frames hang on the rabbet with screws in the frames, and the least jar puts them all in motion. The honey box arrangement, too, is worthy of special examination, and admiration! In my judgment this Common Sense Bee hive is a humbug, and as great a swindle on the credulous beekeeper as was ever put before the American people. The proprietor is doing all he can to introduce it. He has advertised it in large letters on his horse blankets, and makes all the noise he can about it, when he can get a crowd to listen to him.

The next hive was that of Mr. W. R. King. It has a moth trap and the frames are all tight-fitting at the top.

Then followed a model of a bee house, invented by a man named Glass. It would have done you good to hear him give a description of the structure. He said any kind of bee hive could be put in it, and they would do better than out of it He showed us the entrance for the bees. It is made of tin. He said the moths would fly around the entrance and could not get in, and would continue flying around so long that they would die of exhaustion. He said he had seen them do so, and knew it was a fact. He also had three blocks clamped together to represent a beehive, and a small wooden lever to lift them off the shelf, to put under another box for the bees to work in. He said he always had three on at a time, and took off the top one, and that he never had any experience with movable frame hives. He stated also that the drones laid eggs, for he had seen them do it, and he had kept bees for twenty years. I asked him if he took the *American Bee Journal*, or any other bee paper? he said, No. I felt very sorry for the old man, for I thought he would never get to know what progress had been made in bee-keeping. When will all this humbugging stop, and these sharks with pretended or useless patents cease to gull the people?

Mr. Furman had a stand of Italian bees on the fair ground, and showing the people how to handle them and the frames. Mr. D. R. Reed had the old dodge bees in his hat, while talking to a large crowd. Both were ordered to take their bees off the grounds, as the officers said it was against the regulations to have bees flying there. We all looked "down in the mouth," and had to forego seeing bees handled that day, feeling very indignant at the officers. But Mr. Furman went to the secretary for redress. It seems there was a misunderstanding about the matter, and the next day Mr. F. exhibited the bees again, and extracted honey from the comb with the honey extractor, on the fair grounds, as before, with satisfaction to us all.

We also had a meeting of beekeepers, and took the preliminary step to organize a Beekeepers' Association, for Central Iowa. The secretary was instructed to send you a copy of the proceedings.

Bees have done well in our section, this season.

JAMES RIGG.

Iowa Falls, September 21, 1871.

Chautauqua County, New York.

THE BEEKEEPERS IN COUNCIL.

Second Annual Convention.

ALL BEES AND NO WASPS.

The 2d Annual Convention of the Chautauqua County Beekeepers' Association, J. C. Cranston, President, was held at the Chautauqua House, Mayville, Tuesday, Sept. 12th,—the same place of meeting occupied by the "Wasp" Convention last year. By reason of the large number held as witnesses or jurors at the Court House a goodly number who had intended to be present were deprived of the privilege. Consequently Geo. W. Norton's expected essay on "Wasps," and Dr. Horton's lively description of the manner in which bees inevitably "go" for himself and horses, and how he has been the victim of two or three runaways, and nearly lost a span of valuable horses because of bee stings, and how he hated bees and their honey, and how the bees returned the compliment—were lost to the Convention. Still the session was one of profit and interest. Some ten towns were represented, and the time mainly occupied by an informal debate in which each related their experiences, and during which much valuable information was elicited.

O. E. Thayer, of Carroll, reported 16 stocks of blacks bees. By reason of the drouth the honey was harvested early and he realized less than last year. He also lost by a neglect in the spring to put on the surplus boxes in the proper season. His honey readily brought him 30 cts. a pound. He was now Italianizing his entire stock.

J. B. Knowlton, of Clymer, had 16 stocks in the spring, which had increased to 40. A part were Italians. He should continue Italianizing. Owing to the weak condition of his stock he had but little surplus honey. The Italian bee stored more than the blacks. He used the Quinby movable comb hive.

M. Cook, of Ellicott, had 10 swarms black bees in the spring in the old-fashioned box hive. Eight of them had yielded 10 new swarms: two had flown away. He got two swarms by alternation in 18 days. His object had been to increase his stock more than to gain surplus honey. He had 25 new swarms in another place with an average weight, Aug. 1st (honey and bees), of 43½ lbs., the smallest weighing 22½ lbs. He required 20 lbs. on the average to carry a swarm through the winter. Steady cold weather was better than variable, and out-doors better for wintering than the cellar. He had tried it in a dry cellar, but the comb dampened and mildewed. He lost half his bees in trying it. In steady cold weather bees become torpid and will not eat. He ventilates at the top of the hive, and feeds his bees at the top. He transfers after swarming as early as possible—3 days to 10. He would not wait 21 days. If transferred in April old comb would generally have to be put in and the more of that the worse you are off. New comb would do. You also destroy more or less brood by transferring in the spring.

N. M. Carpenter, of Ellery, has been in the bee business 12 or 14 years. For several years he pursued it indifferently, but finding it pleasant and profitable he gave it more attention. He considered it more profitable—two to one—than any other branch of farming. He commenced with the Quinby hive and rarely lost a swarm, and his bees had uniformly paid him 100 per cent. This year he had put in 28 swarms in a hive of his own construction and was still better paid. The more care he gave his bees the more profit. Last year his bees turned him an average income of $26 a hive. This year he started with 32 swarms — six Italians — used movable frames, and had realized over 1000 lbs. surplus honey, and 81 new swarms, which he had put in 40 hives, and which would bring him $15 a swarm. His bees swarmed too much and robbed badly. He got a first swarm from every hive. If a non-swarming hive could be invented, which would enable them to control the movements of the bees, the profits would be much greater. He could not yet decide upon the comparative merits of the Italians and blacks. The former would not work on red clover or on the same flower with the black, but they would work when the black would not, and were more active and vigorous. He would differ with Mr. Cook upon the amount of honey necessary to winter stocks.—he had got through on 5 lbs., and then again it had taken more than 20. He handled his bees a great deal and was familiar with their condition. He had noticed 8 or 10 stocks placed in a row, ventilated alike, which appeared alike in all respects in the fall but in the spring some had their honey entirely consumed and others but a little—some weak and others strong. He wished to ask the occasion of this difference.

J. M. Beebe suggested that the stocks might have been robbed. Robber bees act very often like young bees just commencing to fly, and will rob when supposed to be flying. Mr. Carpenter had tested the matter and did not believe that to be the reason.

W. R. Cook, of Harmony, said bees had not done as well in his section as last year, because of the drouth—better the fore part of the season than later. He wintered 43 swarms black bees in good condition—lost none— had increased to 75 swarms. His object had been the obtaining of surplus honey. Not all of his stocks had swarmed. He should have in all about 1,700 pounds of surplus. He used the Kidder hive. Mr. Ford, P. M. at Steadmanville, started in new in the spring with five swarms which had yielded nine new swarms, and sufficient honey to winter. No surplus honey except in the Kidder hives. Mr. Newhouse also started with five swarms and had gained seven and 200 pounds of surplus. He had studied bee-keeping since he was 18 years old. He could tell whether a swarm had lost its queen by observation, without examining. He could generally prevent an increase of stocks by giving plenty of box room.

Mr. Carpenter could not prevent at all in that way.

Leroy Whitford, of Harmony, used artificial swarming and liked the system. He was troubled with too much swarming. One swarm a season was enough. He had 13 swarms in the spring and 27 now. Had made but 270 pounds of surplus. Two of his stocks were Italians. He had noticed that they were more reluctant to begin working in boxes than the blacks, but that they would work when common bees would not. On the whole he could give them the preference.

Wm. D. Onthank, of Portland, had five swarms of black bees in the spring after losing seven by too much swarming the season before—three swarms to a hive. This year the five swarms produced four, and 130 lbs. of surplus. The first swarm came out July 1st, which is late. He prevented swarming by promptly taking off the full boxes and putting in an empty one. He wintered out doors in preference to the cellar, but would protect them from the wind.

Mr. Whitford gave his bees all the box room he could—did no good.

B. W. Cook had a six-year-old swarm he had treated in the way mentioned by Mr. Onthank, and it did not swarm. He sold it and it swarmed *four times*. That was all he would say.

Mr. Knowlton stated that he had kept a strong heavy swarm four years without swarming. He put a large cap on the hive, and it swarmed *five times*.

Peter Miller, of Sheridan, had obtained from 36 stocks 38 new ones and 1500 lbs. of surplus.

Jos. Cook, of Sheridan, had obtained from 23 swarms black bees, 12 new ones and 600 lbs. of surplus.

J. C. Cranston, of Sheridan, stated that his bees were, or had been, of the common variety, but that now half of them were Italians. How they came so was to him a great puzzle.

J. M. Beebe answered that his black queen had unquestionably mated with Italian drones in the neighborhood.

Mr. Cranston further said he had obtained 200 lbs. of surplus from four swarms.

Oliver Waterman, of Stockton, commenced in the spring with 12 swarms, all in Langstroth's hives. He commenced feeding a part as soon as the weather would admit. His first young swarms, from bees he had fed, came June 5th, and from bees he had not fed, June 10th. He took off, July 11th, 17 three-pound boxes from bees he had fed, and 9 boxes from bees he had not fed. June 22d he had three young swarms come out. He put one in the Beebe hive and the other two in Langstroth's. July 10th his Beebe hive swarmed; also took off 27 lbs. box honey. He put that young swarm into a Beebe hive when it also swarmed July 29th, when he took off 27 lbs. box honey. The mother swarm gave 36 lbs. box honey. Total from the mother swarm: three swarms of bees and 90 lbs. honey. One of the Langstroth hives gave him one young swarm and 27 lbs. surplus, July 19th, and the other yielded neither swarms nor surplus. From his 12 year old swarms he had received 17 young swarms and 400 lbs. of surplus. Two of his old swarms, apparently strong and healthy, had neither swarmed nor made honey. He did not understand it.

J. M. Beebe, of Casadaga, had obtained from 15 old swarms of Italian bees, 15 young swarms and 1000 lbs. of box honey. His first swarm issued May 12th, and a second issue May 22d. The old swarm stocked up again and threw out another first swarm July 2d, and a second swarm July 15th. The first young swarm also threw out a swarm July 10th, making six stocks and 100 lbs. of honey from one swarm.

J. G. Harris, of Westfield, had 51 stocks of black bees which had swarmed but little—only eight new. His neighbor, Mr. Rolph, had 47 Italian stocks in the spring and 80 now. He could not see the most honey in the Italians. From a less number of stocks he had realized more honey than Mr. Rolph. He had his doubts about Italians gathering more honey from flowers than the blacks. He once asked M. S. Snow his figures on the amount of honey from his best Italian swarms, and found that his blacks had in one case made two pounds more, and in another four pounds.

Mr. Carpenter stated that he had a stock of black bees in an old-fashioned Quinby hive that had netted him $40.

Mr. Beebe explained that the Italian was superior to the black, because so much more prolific. By placing guide combs in his boxes he has no trouble about their not working. He never had a black swarm earlier than June 10th. He would like the opinions of the rest on the best marketable size of honey boxes. He uses 3 and 4 lb. boxes and can get 3 cts. a lb. more than for 6 lb. boxes.

Mr. Carpenter is satisfied bees will make one-third more honey in larger boxes.

Mr. Beebe did not deny that more honey might be produced, but could they get as much for it? He should next year put out 1½ lb. boxes. If consumers were willing to buy glass, nails and wood for honey, he was willing to sell and make the small boxes.

Mr. Harris said bees would make more honey in 20 or 25 lb. boxes than smaller ones. He thought 6 lb. boxes were marketable and small enough.

Mr. Whitford used a double tier box—bees lost less time than with single boxes.

Lyvenus Ellis, of Pomfret, had 18 swarms in the spring from which he obtained 14 new swarms and 1400 pounds of surplus. He has no Italians.

P. G. Tambling, of Pomfret, has been a bee-keeper for 30 years and has had 70 old swarms at one time. Some 26 years ago he was robbed of all his bees. Two years afterwards a swarm came back to him, from which he calculates he has had over 200 swarms. The last swarm lived through and was one of the three that he found alive in the spring of 1870. That year they doubled. This year he had 13 swarms which have produced him 250 pounds of box honey. The largest yield from a young swarm was 40 pounds. In his experience, the more care that was given to the bees the greater the profit. Hives are of importance, and some are better than others, but the one essential thing is care.

B. G. Watkinson, of North Harmony, commenced April 19th with 11 hives of bees; nine out of the eleven were taken 20 miles in a spring wagon and express 180 miles by rail, then re-shipped into a lumber wagon and taken 12 miles, making in all 212 miles, and when set upon their summer stands he found them in good order. May 11th drones flew for first time. Swarming commenced June 19th. He put the new swarms in the American hives. Surplus honey about 250 pounds, and 12 young swarms. No surplus from the young swarms, and but 40 boxes partly full from the old stock. Received an Italian queen of Gray & Winder, of Cincinnati, Ohio, July 10th, and placed her in a hive of black bees, and now the bees are half Italians.

J. O. Wood, of Chautauqua, has obtained from 18 swarms of black bees in the Beebe hive 16 new swarms and 500 pounds of surplus. From one hive he obtained 80 pounds.

H. P. Woodcock obtained 96 lbs. of surplus honey and three new swarms from two stocks.

Dr. H. B. Arnold, of Pomfret, considered the great want of beekeepers at the present time to be a hive in which bees can be worked exclusively to honey. The Common Sense hive with the proper management would prevent swarming.

Mr. Knowlton asked if Italians were more apt to rob than the blacks. Beebe and Carpenter said yes, but Mr. Knowlton had not so found it.

W. H. S. Grout, of Poland, commenced in the spring with 25 swarms—six hybrids—from which he had taken with an extractor 1700 lbs. of surplus, besides 59 lbs. of box honey. One swarm of hybrids produced two new swarms and 125 lbs. of surplus. From another he got 129 lbs. and one swarm, and from a third 91½ lbs. and one swarm. The hybrids are more profitable than the blacks.

G. D. Hurd, of Corry, favored artificial swarming and large honey boxes.

Essays were read by the President and H. A. Burch, of Sheridan. By request of the Association we shall publish Mr. Burch's address in our next issue.

J. M. Beebe having offered an Italian queen bee, worth $3, to the one who had secured the most honey from a young swarm kept in the Beebe hive, the Secretary opened and read the various letters presented, as follows:

Wm. Smith, of Casadaga, reported 81 lbs. from a single young swarm. He commenced with 11 swarms which had produced him 14 new swarms and 120 lbs. of surplus honey, besides $107 worth of honey which he had sold.

Fayette Munger, of Pomfret, reported 72 lbs.

H. P. Woodcock, of Casadaga, 72 lbs.

Geo. Landers, of Charlotte Center, 72 lbs.

Jos. Cook, of Sheridan, 51 lbs., besides filling the hive.

J. O. Wood, of Chautauqua, 50 lbs. His bees swarmed late.

Wm. Smith was awarded the prize.

The chair announced that Hon. M. P. Bemus had authorized him to state that if the Convention re-adjourned to Mayville, Bemus Hall would be at their service. The hall they now occupied they could also have free.

On motion it was resolved to hold the next spring meeting of the Association at the American House in Jamestown, on the 2d Tuesday of April, at 10 A. M., and the annual meeting at Mayville, on the 1st Tuesday of September.

The officers for the ensuing year were elected as follows:

President—J. M. Beebe, of Casadaga.

Vice Presidents—M. H. Town, Arkwright; J. H. Davis, Busti; O. E. Thayer, Carroll; Henry Harrington, Cherry Creek; Lewis Simmons, Charlotte; J. B. Knowlton, Clymer; J. O. Wood, Chautauqua; Jos. Rhodes, Dunkirk; Merritt Cook, Ellicott; N. M. Carpenter, Ellington; L. Weeks, Ellery; L. Goulding, French Creek; E. Perrin, Gerry; C. E. Randall, Hanover; W. K. Cook, Harmony; Ira Whittaker, Kiantone; H. Q. Ames, Mina; Dr. H. B. Arnold, Pomfret; Wm. D. Onthank, Portland; W. H. S. Grout; Dr. S. Collins, Ripley; H. P. Woodcock, Stockton; Otis Skinner, Sherman; Jos. Cook, Sheridan, J. Vincent, Villenova; J. G. Harris, Westfield.

Secretary—D. E. Benton, Fredonia.

Executive Committee—W. K. Cook, Panama; Ira Porter, Pomfret; Jas. Cook, Sheridan; J. G. Harris, Westfield; Leroy Whitford, Harmony.

On motion, the thanks of the Association were tendered to Horace Fox, of the Chautauqua House, for the free use of his commodious hall.

The Association then adjourned.

From the above report it is apparent that beekeeping properly conducted is entirely profitable, and that the common stock is being rapidly Italianized, and are deservedly growing in favor, notwithstanding their robbing habits. It is also apparent that these semi-yearly discussions are of practical benefit to beekeepers. A portion of the members brought specimens of honey produced, making a larger honey exhibition than is usual at our fairs. There were also on exhibition four kinds of hive—American, Beebe, Common Sense and Kidder.

[For the American Bee Journal.]

Report from Albany county, New York.

The season of 1870 was not a very favorable one for bees in this locality. We prepared for winter eleven colonies—Italians and hybrids; and wintered them on their summer stands, in single inch hives, with cotton batting over them. All came out right in the spring of 1871, excepting that about half of them were weak, in consequence of being weak when put up the previous fall. We fed them rye meal as soon as they would work in it, and also fed them sugar syrup, and equalized the brood. Some of them had too much honey, which we extracted, and thus gave the queens room for laying, which they rapidly improved. We would not do without the invaluable honey extractor, if used for this object alone.

We increased the eleven colonies to twenty-five. Two of the increase were natural swarms, the rest were artificial. All have honey enough to winter well—some of them too much. We have taken three hundred and sixty-two (362) pounds of extracted honey, and sixty (60) pounds in small frames. Nearly all of it is light colored, as there was but little buckwheat honey gathered this season in this section.

We found one colony badly diseased in the spring, so that we received no profit from it, excepting the honey the old combs contained when it was transferred to an empty hive. We took no increase from two others, and obtained only the sixty pounds of honey from them. All the increase and nearly all the extracted honey, therefore, was taken from eight colonies. This does not compare with some reports that we read in the Journal, but we are very well satisfied with it.

Our extractor is a wooden one, well coated inside with beeswax, which was spread on and heated in with a hot sad iron, the square edges of which, fitting into the corners nicely, spread the coating well. The beeswax prevents the wood from absorbing honey, and keeps it sweet and nice.

We run the extractor with the gearing of an apple-parer, which works satisfactorily, since we use stays to keep the wire cloth up to its place.

We think the ladies are pretty well represented in the September number of the Journal, and that Miss Katie Grimm has done remarkably well, both as to the amount of honey obtained and amount of work done, by one so young, and of the weaker sex.

We hope that friend Gallup will send on that "hash" soon, as we are getting awful hungry.

W. D. Wright.

Knowersville, N. Y., Sept. 16, 1871.

[For the American Bee Journal.]

Apiarist, or Apiarian ?

Mr. Editor :—Mr. Choate once reproved an opposing lawyer for "overworking an adjective ;" but I am sorry to find the large majority of writers on our science slight a highly respectable *noun* and "push it from its place," by saying apiarian when they speak of a beekeeper. Now, all the dictionaries (Worcester, Webster, &c.) tell us that *apiarian* is an adjective, and means "belonging or relating to bees ;" whilst *apiarist* means "a keeper of bees." If, contrary to Washington's solemn warning, we will "quit our own to stand on foreign ground" even in our language—if honest, plain *beekeeper* is not fine enough for us, if we will be pedantic, let us at least be proper, and not run the risk of being styled malaprops.

Criticus.

☞ Though not at all inclined ourselves, to "push a respectable noun from its place," we cannot concur in the opinion of our esteemed correspondent that *apiarist* is the proper or preferable word, or that *apiarian* is now or still an adjective only. These words may be so set down in the dictionaries at present ; but dictionaries are primarily mere lists, inventories, or registers of the words which a language comprises ; and words must necessarily get into use before they can get into dictionaries. They must first come into reputable, if not general use ; and that, after all, settles their meaning and their legitimacy, of which facts the dictionaries can simply make record, when the word-hunters, like scientific explorers of other fields, have succeeded in finding, classifying, and arranging them in their portfolios.

In this particular case, Johnson has neither of the words ; as in his time the language was probably still too poor to count such terms among its hoarded treasures. They came into common use long after he had finished his lexicographical "drudgery." So far as we can now call to mind, Kirby is still the only English author, who uses the word apiarist ; at least he is as yet the only one cited in the dictionaries as a voucher for it. Now, Kirby is or rather was, in his day, very good authority in matters entomological—such as the structure or habitat of a bug or a butterfly ; but, even with his Bridgewater treatise to back him, he can hardly be ranked as a classic in English literature—especially when made sole sponsor for the word, against the many belle-letter scholars, who use *apiarian* instead, and have succeeded in giving it standing and currency. By and by the dictionary-makers too will find out that there is another and equivalent term in good use, and will then give us that also *as a noun*, as they did aforetime with regard to *sectarian*, presenting it to us in both capacities, though as nouns we had already the twins, *sectary* and *sectarist*. Nor does the mere *ending* of the word necessarily make it an adjective, or we should have to interchange *veterinarian* and *veterinary*, calling the latter *a noun*, and classing it with equally awkward itinerary.

Bee-father we regard as a better word than either of those under notice, being good old English too, or sound significant Saxon. But, for the ladies' sake (who are fast coming to be denizens of bee-land, and will soon embellish it with "floral embroidery"), we presume it will have to be set aside—and *beemaster* likewise, retaining homely *beekeeper* only, as quite fine enough for us ; though it is a term much too comprehensive—embracing many to whom neither the insect, nor the science, nor the fraternity will ever be greatly beholden.

But apart from this, and to better purpose, we desire to say that there are other words besides, now in use in bee-culture, for which the dictionaries have not yet made room ; and as the science advances, we shall doubtless be constrained to introduce many more, doomed to wait for registry and formal adoption till the word-mongers happen to light on them in their explorations. Of late the term *apiarism*, seemingly in substitution for bee-culture, is beginning to be used by English writers ; though its precise meaning appears to be not yet settled. From the German, too, we have the word *apistics*, which, like *statistics*, *linguistics*, and others from the same source, may be reluctantly admitted, but is yet likely to be sooner or later accepted, as the general term for the science which in this utilitarian age, is destined to take and hold no insignificant rank among those contributing to the wealth of nations.—The German beekeepers are favored with an ampler terminology, or are more easily helped. Their language, besides being more copious, is more plastic and accommodating. They no sooner find, or feel, or fancy the need of a word, than straightways they coin one for the occasion, and it goes into use at once. The English are more choice and chary, and will long submit to great inconvenience, ere they venture to take the bold step of manufacturing a new word; and when at last the word comes it is received coyly and looked at mistrustingly, like a strange bee in a hive—and ten chances to one, it is finally, like her, rejected and cast out. As bee men, we should be less exclusive, and set the example of readily adopting any well-formed and expresive word that avoids circumlocution and saves time. We are building up a science, and why should we not have the right or enjoy the privilege of concocting or correcting its nomenclature? Surely, there is nothing unreasonable, presumptuous, or arrogant in that.—[Ed.

[For the American Bee Journal.]

Natural, Prolific and Hardy Queens.

ANSWER TO MR. CHAS. DADANT, IN AMERICAN BEE JOURNAL FOR OCTOBER, 1871.

In answer to Mr. Dadant, I will say that I am not (and he knows it) the discoverer of the fact that artificial queens are, on an average, worthless in comparison with natural queens, and in my articles I have given honor to whom honor is due. I have only corroborated the statements of such experienced and successful beekeepers as Bidwell Bros, of St. Paul, Minnesota, Adam Grimm, of Jefferson, Wisconsin, E. Gallup, of Orchard, Iowa, and of other correspondents of the Journal.

I bought a queen from Mr. Dadant, which he guaranteed should be pure, prolific, and purely mated, and by his letters promised to make all right, if she proved otherwise. Inside of two weeks after receiving her, I informed him that she was unprolific. He answered my letter and again promised to make all right. In about a month or five weeks, I informed him again that she was worthless, for I had to keep up her swarm. Then he asked me not to destroy her, but keep her over the winter, and if she did not prove prolific in the spring, that he would replace her. (*Showing that he also knew that artificial queens were sometimes a year in maturing so as to partially keep up their swarm.*) In the spring I informed him that she was still worthless, and she gradually became more unprolific, and her queens more *non-egg-hatching*, until she died, in the beginning of July. He, I suppose, thought it would be smart or sharp to repudiate a voluntary bargain on his own part, and informed me that, as I had made such a fuss about the queen, he would not send me another. I think the queen averaged a little worse than any I have raised, that lived long enough to lay an egg.

In one of his articles Mr. Dadant says that I have given the probable cause of her unprolificness—the *chilling* she received in transit here. Of that I know nothing. I only gave the facts. But as he guaranteed her safe arrival, the chilling did not release him from the guarantee, or his promise to replace her, if not as guaranteed.

And right here let me say that I have never raised artificial queens in such small swarms as bee authors recommend, or bee breeders have heretofore (until this discussion commenced) used. For the last three years, when raising either natural or artificial queens, I have used only my largest and most vigorous stocks. As Novice says with a pint of bees he would take his chances with any one, Mr. D. quotes Novice's success. Novice, one year ago had, with artificial queens, been so successful that he had to send to Mr. Grimm (who is a strong defender of the natural queen theory, and I believe averages most of the time five hundred swarming hives), for twenty-five queens, to replace those that died of old age. Turn to Novice's articles and figure out, if you can, how, under any circumstances, he could have any queens over seventeen months old—except the thirteen he had left over after his heavy and unfortunate loss of bees. (He had thirteen queens at that time, provided none has died within those seventeen months.) I have six black natural queens now living that are four years and six months old.

Four years ago this subject was brought to my mind by articles in different papers, and my heavy loss of bees from the worthlessness of artificial queens. (Artificial swarming I have nothing to say against at present.) I have proved the truth of my position to my entire satisfaction, and am therefore RIVETED to the theory. What does Mr. Morbitzer say in the article in the October number of the Journal, translated from the German? He says it is advantageous to replace them with queen cells built for second swarms, instead of using post-constructed cells, FOR THE LATTER DO NOT PRODUCE AS VIGOROUS AND PERFECT QUEENS AS THE FORMER. So you see, Mr. Dadant, it is not only in America that OBSERVANT BEEKEEPERS have discovered the fact that ARTIFICIAL QUEENS ARE NOT AS GOOD AS NATURAL QUEENS; but in other countries also, thousands of miles away, with vast oceans between, and by persons speaking another language, has the *fact* that *artificial queens will not on the average be as large as long-lived, or as prolific as natural queens*, has been observed and published.

When reading the American Bee Journal, one day, on the subject of non-swarming, I noticed that the different correspondents advised the beekeeper to examine his swarms and destroy the queen cells weekly, as the only sure method to prevent swarming. After thinking the subject over, I concluded that that trait in the bees could be utilized to advantage, to procure natural queen cells; and that, by taking advantage of it, natural queens could be had in sufficient number to Italianize an apiary in any one season. (Now the great and only justified point advanced by the artificial queen advocates is, that it is the only way to get cells and queens, from a selected queen, in sufficient number to Italianize or for sale.) And for that purpose it would be better to save them, and instead of trying to repress the swarming to endeavor to stimulate it. I have for two seasons done so, and have freely given the result of my experiments and my method of doing so, and even the novice who has read this discussion, can see and will remember that the opponents of natural queens have not said, and cannot say, one word against it. They have only done their best to make beekeepers believe that an unnatural mode is as good as the way that the Creator of all has given to the insect to reproduce or propogate itself.

The result of my experiments with natural as against artificial queens is, that I prefer to raise and keep one natural queen with any two of the best artificial queens that I have as yet been able to raise; and I have raised artificial queens in as large colonies, as I have used for natural ones at same time of year. And if the artificial queen sent to me by Mr. Dadant is a good sample of what he can raise by artificial process, I would not give one natural for all that he has ever raised, all that he has at present, and all that he will raise in future—though he says in his article, believe my experience, and do so and so. If he has given me a specimen of his experience with the same truthfulness as he has given me a sample of fairness in his dealings, I want none of it.

JOHN M. PRICE.

Buffalo Falls, Iowa, Oct. 10, 1871.

[For the American Bee Journal.]

What Harm?

DEAR JOURNAL:—There seems to be a disposition on the part of some writers to frown down the custom of describing new hives and other devices in the columns of the Journal, which, if successful, would detract very much from the general interest and value of this periodical.

Bee-keeping is yet comparatively in its infancy; movable frames are just beginning to be adopted; the melextractor and other devices are practically on trial; and where one beekeeper adopts these, hundreds are still looking on and awaiting results. In consequence of this progressive state of bee-culture, numbers of thoughtful practical men are devising *real* or fancied improvements; and hence it becomes of paramount importance that the Journal's readers have descriptions of such improvements, that they may avail themselves of such as their judgment approves. The simple fact of this or that thing being patented, should not prejudice an impartial mind against it. It may be very valuable, or altogether worthless; but if the inventor did not believe his discovery to be a valuable one, he certainly would not incur the trouble and expense of securing letters patent, and the far greater trouble and expense of introducing it to the public. This, however, is of no sort of consequence to any person, save the one immediately interested, for no intelligent beekeeper will be imposed upon, while much that is valuable may be gained by reading descriptions of the vast number of patented and non-patented bee devices that are found worthy of adoption by our best apiarians.

It is quite probable that the time has gone by when any patented bee devices will really pay the patentee; therefore it would seem that few should feel encouraged to secure letters patent. Yet the facts prove the reverse to be true, and while such persons are disposed to incur the risk, others should not complain, for no one is obliged to purchase; and no one need be humbugged while *bee books*, and *bee journals*, and bee intelligence are everywhere available.

When such beekeepers as Quinby, Gallup, Hazen, Thomas, Alley, and many others, construct, *test*, and recommend hives, it is quite safe to place confidence in them; and when they kindly write a description for the Journal, let us not greet it with contemptuous allusions to that which is none of our business.

The fact that a perfect hive has not yet been invented—a fact that is clearly proven by the great variety in form of hives used by the best apiarians in the country, should deter all who have the true interest of beekeeping in view from discouraging the efforts of first-class men in this direction, but rather gladly welcome the largest freedom to all who furnish such descriptive articles. We therefore repeat our text—"*What harm*" can these articles do? May they not, on the contrary, possess positive value? We believe the latter to be the sentiment of nineteen out of twenty of the Journal's readers.

How much better for all concerned, if those writers who are unfortunately afflicted with an hereditary or acquired habit of fault-finding, would ventilate it by pointing out wherein hives are faulty, rather than indiscriminately pitch into every one who has the temerity to write of an improvement that has cost much study and experiment. We do not wish to be understood as being an endorser of patented or unpatented humbugs of any kind, for we well know that unscrupulous men have taken advantage of the general ignorance of beekeepers, and imposed upon them all sorts of worthless *bee traps*. But that time has passed—intelligence assumes the place of darkness, the underlying principles of bee economy are getting to be well understood; and therefore our voice is for improvements—especially when made by our leading apiarians. Let all such write freely for our excellent Journal, thereby enhancing its value and usefulness.

GEO. S. SELSBY.

Wintersport, Me., Oct. 4, 1871.

[For the American Bee Journal.]

Comments on Divers Topics.

MR. EDITOR:—It has been some time since I troubled you with an article for your valuable Journal; not because I have lost interest in the subject, but because I have been too busy to write, even to my friends and regular correspondents. Still, I have not failed to swallow everything new that I discovered in the Journal; though some of it I have to throw up again. For instance, the different plans of non-flying fertilization. Like Amateur, I have "grasped at every plan that had the least shadow of success, and some that had none;" but the result has been the same in every case—*a failure*. I succeeded last evening, however, in actually forcing a queen to be fertilized, to all appearance successfully. I will report the result at some future time.

The subject of queen raising seems to figure quite conspicuously among breeders; yet hardly any two of them agree as to the best and easiest mode of securing hardy and prolific queens by forcing. Mr. John M. Price states that he has "been raising such (forced) queens for the last six years," and that three out of five have been lost on their wedding trip, while the remainder would be "non-prolific," or otherwise imperfect. Very persevering, indeed, must he be to follow up a practice for six years, that has given him nothing but imperfection. Now, I hold that it makes no difference whether our queens are started by bees under the swarming impulse or not, so long as they are fed for such by full stocks from the time the egg hatches, other circumstances being equal—that is, in regard to abundant forage or liberal feeding.

On page 12 of the current volume, Mr. J. L. McLean states the reason why forced queens are often less hardy and less prolific than those raised by colonies under the swarming impulse; and gives a very good and successful plan to secure them started from the egg, or of securing to the young queen at least fourteen days in which to mature. I practice a plan somewhat similar, but my method secures to them one day more at least. I proceed as follows: first, I deprive a vigorous colony of their queen, and leave them queenless at least six days. On the evening of the sixth day, I insert an empty worker comb in the centre of the hive containing my queen mother, placing the comb on which I find the queen by the side of the empty one, with the queen between them. She will seldom fail to fill the empty comb pretty thoroughly with eggs by the next morning. On the morning of the seventh day, I take out all the combs from my queenless hive, and destroy every queen cell the bees have started. I now insert the comb containing the eggs from my selected queen, in the centre of my queenless hive, and as the bees therein have no other brood from which they can raise queens, they are obliged to start them from these eggs. This plan has a decided advantage over that given by Mr. McLean, in that the bees having been queenless for some time, will at once start a large number of queen cells, and are not likely to delay and start others two or three days later, as they are apt to do when just deprived of their queen. To make this still more secure, I examine the hive about noon of the third day, and make a note of the cells that have then been started. I examine again a day or two later, and if I find any new cells started I destroy them; but it is very seldom that they start any after the third day, and they seldom do much towards constructing the queen cell till the egg hatches.

About the same results may be obtained by giving to a full colony, thus queenless and broodless, a comb containing brood without regard to the age of the brood; but it is essential that the comb contain eggs or larvæ just hatched. Then, by examining each day, and making a note of or marking the cells that are started each day, and destroying all that are capped over in less than five days from the time they were started, you will secure full five days for the feeding of the queen larvæ—which is all they can receive under any circumstances, as they remain sealed eight days, and are three days in the egg, in which period of course they receive no food.

I am sorry my friend Gallup gets pitched into so hard from every quarter.. I was at his place this summer, and really think he has got something nice in the way of a bee hive, if it is properly managed. But here let me make a suggestion, accompanied by figures, for the benefit of those who are urging their queens to more than ordinary labor. It will be admitted by all who have been observing, that, under ordinary circumstances, a queen bee is capable of laying on an average, about two thousand (2000) eggs daily. This she will continue to do for, say, five months in the year, or a total of three hundred thousand (300,000) eggs per year. The average life of a queen will not exceed three or four years, say three years; in which time she will have deposited nine hundred thousand (900,000) eggs. All these, or nearly all, have to be fertilized from the contents of the spermatheca of the queen. Now if we urge our queens to double the amount of labor (which we can easily do), will we not have to renew them proportionally so much oftener, or every eighteen months?

Before I close I must suggest an improvement in one kind of beehive, for the benefit of those who are using it, and that is the Buckeye. I never yet have seen one of the original form that was even manageable—say nothing of being convenient. The change I would suggest is this: First, tear off the moth nursery, and burn it, to destroy all the eggs and larvæ of the moth; then turn the hive down on its back, and nail up the ends; nail strips on the inside upper edges of the sides, to form rabbets for frames; cut the frames down to the bottom of the surplus sections, and nail thin strips on, projecting at ends, to hang on rabbets; put on loose honey-board for surplus boxes, or an open box for surplus frames; a cover, to keep surplus chambers dark; and cut a hole at bottom of one side, for a fly hole. One man made this change in a lot of these hives, and could then manage them very well; would prefer new lumber, however. Of course, after making this change, it would be covered by the Langstroth patent.

So far, this has been a splendid honey season in this locality. I think I shall be able to give a report, this fall, that will be satisfactory to all, and I am sure it will be satisfactory to your humble servant and well wisher.

J. E. Benjamin.

Rockford, Iowa, Aug. 10, 1871.

Mr. Robert Johnson, of Kossuth, Des Moines county, Iowa, reports that he has colonies of bees that gave him one hundred and fifty pounds of honey each, during the past year.

[For the American Bee Journal.]

Transferring Bees.

I have transferred bees at almost all seasons, but have not usually been pleased with the results when done later than the first of July. I much prefer to transfer in April or May, making two swarms of one, if the strength of the colony will permit—thus we have artificial swarming and transferring combined. But the object of this writing is to give my method of securing the combs in the frames. I used to use wooden or wire clamps, and at first wax, but finally adopted the following plan, which may not be new to many, but it was new to me, and also original; and has given the very best satisfaction, being neat and convenient, and doing away with the necessity of several after jobs, such as removing clamps, &c., which follow most methods.

I simply prepare my frame with a triangular comb guide on the top, as I would for the bees to build on, also nail in a bottom, and if the frame be a deep one, or the comb new and tender, I put in a middle support with comb-guide on the under side, just like the top bar. I now cut a piece of comb just long enough to go from the top of the frame to the middle support, or to the bottom, as the case may be. I then cut along the centre of the top of the comb, and into this cut bed the comb-guide in the top of the frame, and bring the sides down around the guide so that it may fit closely. Now bring the frame to an upright position, by lifting the transferring board with it to support the comb until up, when it will stand any reasonable amount of shaking, without falling out.

Levant, Maine. G. W. P. JERRARD.

[For the American Bee Journal.]

Honey Resources from Strange Quarters.

BY REV. E. L. BRIGGS, *Ottumwa, Iowa.*

DEAR JOURNAL :—As anything strange or new in the line of bee-culture always attracts my attention, and wakes up my one idealism on this subject wonderfully, I write to say that a discovery which I made last week raised this propensity almost to fever-heat. While visiting about five miles in the country, my host showed me his five colonies of bees, with a manifestation of pride and interest somewhat unusual. "This Langstroth hive," he said, "has filled six boxes once, and about eight days ago, I put on another set of boxes, and five of them are full again." There they were, sure enough! White, clear, beautiful, all full to the last cell. "Pretty well, for black bees!" was my mental exclamation; and with something like a sigh, I thought of my large, beautiful, yellow Italians, which had not done as well as that.

But the secret came out while walking over his farm, about an hour afterward. "There," said he, "are a couple of Jack oak trees, around which the bees fairly swarm every morning and evening; and I can't see what they can get off a Jack oak."

Turning our steps to the trees indicated, I saw the bees at work as he had said. This variety of oak is forming its germs or bloom, if it can be called such, for its next year's crop of acorns. These have already the shape of the cup or husk in which the ripe acorn is embedded before it falls out. In this cup the pistillate portion is formed, from which honey is constantly oozing, and if not disturbed forms large drops, which fall upon the leaves below. I picked off several leaves on which it had fallen, and from which, in turn, it dripped off upon others, where it stood in large quantities. No wonder the little pets were revelling in flowery nectar in rich abundance!

But I was to meet another wonder, "You see that little oak tree down in the field? Well, the bees have been swarming around that all summer, and I have seen them gathering something off the ground, where it stood in a pool." Of course, I went to that tree. "There," said he, pointing to some dark patches on the ground, "is where the bees work every morning." Casting my eye up the body of the tree, I saw it was wet with some substance, drops of which were suspended from points on the rough bark.

The woodpecker's had picked hundreds of small holes in the bark, from about the size of a small lead pencil to the size of a lady's thimble. And from under the bark was flowing out a substance of about the consistency of honey, perfectly transparent, and differing in no way from common honey except that I thought I could detect in this a slight oaky taste; while that from the Jack oak bloom was as free from any disagreeable taste as pure white clover honey. This tree was of the variety called Spanish oak by the people here.

Here were two sources of honey from which the bees could gather any amount that they could find room to store. Mr. Novice, we will believe anything that you can write concerning the amount of honey a colony can gather, provided you ply your honey extractor diligently. Yes, we will believe Mrs. Tupper's seventy-two four pound boxes from one colony report; provided she will inform us that there are plenty of Spanish oaks and corps of woodpeckers to work them, and a forest of Jack oak in bloom near her apiary.

Bees have generally filled all the surplus room they had this year, in Southern Iowa.

The melextractor is certainly an invention in the right direction. Intelligent bee-culture is a resource of pleasure and profit but little understood as yet, by most of us. The multitudes, too, engaged in promoting it are benefactors of the race, who have sent and are sending bread to the hungry, and "butter and honey" also. Let the workmen be multiplied to gather the sweets, and may all eat of the good of the land.

My beautiful Italians still maintain their good character. The three light colonies which I brought here from Mount Pleasant apiary, are now a snug family of twelve—all heavy and strong in numbers.

I have been experimenting with a hive of my own construction, in which I think I have found the secret of inducing bees to build in surplus boxes and frames at once. So far it has met all my expectations, and I grant those expectations were high. The public will have the benefit of this hive shortly. Sept. 12, 1871.

[For the American Bee Journal.]

Still they Come!

MORE QUESTIONS FOR "NOVICE."

DEAR NOVICE:—Will you please answer the following questions through the Journal.

What method of artificial swarming did you adopt in 1869, when you increased eleven stocks to forty-six?

How do you shade your stocks in summer from the rays of the sun?

Do you paint your hives? And if so, what color, and how do you mix the paint?

Does the Peabody extractor work as well as you expected?

Are the queens you purchased from Mr. Grimm last fall as good as the queens you raised from the original one you purchased of Mr. Langstroth?

Some of the above inquiries may have been answered by some of your articles in the Journal; but if answered again in full you will greatly oblige many readers of the Journal, as well as a young BEGINNER.

[For the American Bee Journal.]

Linden and Buckwheat.

I agree entirely with NOVICE as to the value of the linden tree as a honey producing plant, and before perusing his article in the August number of the Journal, I had devised a plan to secure the planting of linden trees around my farm.

I have resolved to sow linden seeds and plant linden sprouts, in order to start on an acre of ground a nursery of linden trees. These lindens will be planted in rows four feet apart, and twelve or fourteen inches in the row, making ten or eleven thousand to the acre, and will be cultivated the same as an acre of corn.

As soon as some of the young trees will be strong enough to resist cattle, I will offer them *for nothing* to the farmers owning land adjoining my tract, to be planted as avenue trees around these farms. Every section of land has four sides, three hundred and twenty rods in length, and with trees planted on the boundaries, two rods apart, there will be six hundred and forty trees to each section. My section, and the eight around, nine in all, will furnish room for 5,760 trees—none of which will be any further than one and a half miles from my apiary. These trees will begin to yield honey in less than from ten to fifteen years, and for ages the harvest will go on *crescendo*, for the linden is a very long-lived tree.*

Besides, all my neighboring farms will have a better appearance than the naked prairie presents, and travellers will, in summer, be grateful to him who has kindly prepared so umbrageous a road. In France, nearly all the trees in the avenues and squares in and around the cities are lindens. In my former home, the city of Langres, some thousand of lindens, five or six hundred years old, were the delight of the inhabitants. But, alas! in consequence of the war, nearly all of them have been cut down, and the poor bees—innocent victims of human folly—will starve amid the devastation.

Do you not think, Mr. Editor, that it would be well for the Beekeepers' Conventions to petition the Legislatures for an act requiring every roadside to be planted with linden trees? Such a measure, aside from the delightful shade it would provide, would add millions of dollars every year to the wealth of the nation.

When I first came here, all the farmers around me were persuaded that buckwheat was an injurious crop, and of course none was raised. Yet, as I wanted some for my bees, I sowed one or two acres and got some bushels of seed. Next year I offered portions of that seed to all my neighbors gratuitously. Three or four of them accepted it, and I have made the same offer every year since—always with some success. The result is that now there are more than twenty acres of buckwheat around my apiary, although I have this year given away only five or six bushels of seed. I got this result at a very trifling cost, for half a bushel of seed is enough for an acre.

As there are here also, in the woods and meadows, plenty of Spanish needles, golden rods, and asters, to intervene with and follow the buckwheat, and as the Italian bees do not work on buckwheat when they can find anything better, my summer crop is nearly as good as my spring honey, and I sell it yearly without difference of price. CH. DADANT.

Hamilton, Ills., Aug. 10, 1871.

[For the American Bee Journal.]

Bee-culture in College.

MR. EDITOR:—In a recent lecture Mr. Quinby said—"It is time that all our agricultural colleges had a professor of apiarian science." I would state that we have in College a class of twenty-five who get the theory and practice of bee-keeping this term.

All who take any course, get not only the science of bee-culture, but have practice in all the operations of the apiary. The students handle the bees with as much ease as veterans, and take great interest in the Hruschka, the queen nursery, and all the various experiments.

Last year we had black bees which were very cross. Many of the students were afraid of them, and with excellent reason. Now we have none but Italians, which are very gentle, so that over one hundred and forty students go in and out among them with entire freedom.

We noticed early in the season that the Italians worked largely on the red clover.

Agricultural College, A. J. COOK.
Lansing, Mich., July 21, 1871.

---

* We have doubt whether the honey crop from the *European* linden is certain yearly, or whether the tree furnishes a permanent resource, except in soils and a climate peculiarly adapted to its growth. In the Capitol grounds and in the public avenues of Washington, we have known this species to fail in yielding honey twice in seven years, and some of the trees die annually, apparently in consequence of the drouth usually prevalent here after July 1st. The *American* linden blooms later, yields honey in seasons when the other fails to do so, and appears to be a hardier tree, in *this* vicinity.—[ED.

THE AMERICAN BEE JOURNAL.

Washington, November, 1871.

☞ We occasionally receive complaints from subscribers that the Journal fails to reach them, or does not come to them as early as it does to other subscribers at the same or neighboring post offices. We can only say that we do not think the fault lies with us. We are as careful as we well can be in addressing and mailing the Journal, and are ever anxious that it should reach its readers promptly. That it should reach all by due course of mail is certain, as with a single exception since the publication commenced, all the papers have, in each successive month, been placed in the post office here on the same day and at the same hour, and we are assured that they are regularly despatched by the first following mail. So far as is in our power we are always willing to supply missing numbers when informed of failure.

☞ For quickly furnishing a colony with the requisite supply of honey or sugar syrup, we think the large size BEEBE FEEDER is very convenient and serviceable; though if the main body were made of glass it would, in many respects, be an improvement.

THE following letter from our friend and correspondent, Mr. Gravenhorst, reached us after unusual delay. The discovery of fossil honey combs is an interesting fact, particularly at this time, when the twice exploded "development theory" is again pressed on the attention and acceptance of inquirers. Whatever seeming evidence in behalf of that theory may be drawn from other sources, it is very certain that the natural history and physiology of the honey bee furnish nothing of the kind; but quite the reverse. Apart from this, however, the fossil honey combs now found show conclusively that bees were wax-secreting, comb building, honey gathering, and honey-storing bees—just such as they now are, as far back in the distant bygone ages as human investigation can probably reach. We need not trouble ourselves about the precise period at which the process of fossilization commenced. We shall leave it to Lyall and the geologists to settle, according to their principles, the date of the stratum in which those fossil combs were found; and then taking the changes effected in the bee in the intervening period till now, to—0, as the facts prove, we shall, let Darwin and the transmutationists take up the "wondrous tale," and figuring out on those data the problem of supposed pre-existent changes and metamorphoses, tell us how much of the antecedent eternity was requisite to develop the fancied primordial germ of incipient existence into a perfect bee, such as we find it to have been already at so remote an era of the backward abysm of time when petrifaction began:

BRAUNSCHWEIG, GERMANY, *August* 24, 1871.

The August number of the Bee Journal interested me highly, in several respects. The article from Prof. Menzel, on "*The Age of the Honey Bee*," I read with much gratification, especially as I am in a position to make it somewhat more complete. Menzel says: "The only specimen of the honey bee, in a fossil state, hitherto found, occurs in the insect-bearing stratum of the quarries of Œningen." (See Bee Journal, Vol. VII., No. 2, August 1871.) When Menzel wrote this he was of course not aware that other and stronger evidence of the existence of the bee—the *Apis mellifica*—in the antediluvian period, is now at hand. Quite recently, when visiting the Archducal Museum of Natural Science here, I found therein three specimens of petrified honey combs discovered when a large bone—three feet long and a foot thick, evidently part of the skeleton of a mammoth—was exhumed, in the vicinity of Braunschweig. These fossil combs have cells of precisely the same diameter and depth as those now built by our common or German bee, and are as attractive and beautiful in appearance as though newly constructed. Chance led me to the discovery, and Prof. Menzel will doubtless be greatly delighted, when I communicate the fact to him. I will shortly send to the Bienenzeitung a more full account of this interesting discovery, and shall be pleased if you will insert the article in the Bee Journal.

As regards the essay in the July number of the Journal, "*On the Introduction of Young Queens to Colonies that are Queenless*," I must say that the Rev. Mr. Langstroth has herein again very correctly observed and experimented. My experiences coincide altogether with his; and the process, properly applied, is of great value in bee-culture.

Our honey prospects have improved greatly since the beginning of July. On the 5th of that month I fed my bees for the last time. Then a change in the weather took place, and forage became abundant. From the 7th of the month till now, with occasional brief intermissions, honey flowed plentifully. Chief of all, the heath district now warrants high expectations. On the 9th of this month I removed thither, though twenty miles distant, nearly one hundred of my stocks; and thus, if God please, we may perhaps still be able, at the close of the season, to speak of a good honey year.

C. J. H. GRAVENHORST.

☞ We have repeatedly advised beekeepers to disregard Kidder's claims to *royalty* for the use of the triangular comb guides, yet still inquiries come respecting the legality, or *illegality* rather, of his or his agents' demands. We can only restate the fact that he has no valid patent, and no right to make any claim.

On this subject we find the following remarks, by the editor, in the "*Western Farmer*," published at Madison, Wisconsin, where the fraudulently procured decision, on which Kidder and his agents rely, was obtained.

"Mr. Kidder owns a patent issued to Mr. Clark, which he claims covers a device used in the Langstroth Hive. Mr. Langstroth claims that this patent is invalid, and also that it does not, even if valid, affect the device used in his hive. In the United States Circuit Court, at Madison, Wis., in January, might add in extenuation of this blunder, that the 1870, a decision in Mr. Kidder's favor was obtained in a trial against a Mr. Trask, who was using the Langstroth Hive. We stated at the time, and now repeat, that the case was not fully tried; that the defendant was in collusion with the plaintiff; that there was, practically, no defence; and that this decision should not have the slightest weight with any one. Mr. Langstroth and his agents have publicly guaranteed to save all users of their hive from any loss in consequence of any decision of the courts against them. We understand that they will consider it a favor if Mr. Kidder will commence a prosecution against any one—if they are informed of the fact. We have heard of many threats of prosecution by him and his agents, but no case, except the one referred to above, where such prosecution has been carried to a trial. We do not know whether the Clark patent is valid or not. We do not know whether persons using the Langstroth Hive should pay Mr. Kidder or not. But we do know that the decision relied on by them, as a means of frightening people into making such payments, proves nothing, and should not be regarded. The experience of the past seems to show, also, that the man who refused to make any payment when demanded is not further troubled—at least not by prosecution."

A Test of the Dzierzon Theory.

The Baron of Berlepsch, in the late revised edition of his work on "*Bees and Bee-culture*," speaks of the evidence of the correctness of the Dzierzon Theory as to the production of drones, as follows:

"If the male or drone egg does not require impregnation, all Italian queen bees, of pure race, must certainly produce pure Italian males or drones; and all queen bees of the common or black race, must as constantly produce black males or drones—even though such queen bees were fertilized by males or drones of the opposite race. And such, too, is found to be the fact. I will not, however, refer to the Italian queen bees for proof of this, because here we may easily be deceived, by regarding as a pure Italian, one in which there is, from birth already an admixture of black blood. But the pure black or common queen bees, fertilized by an Italian drone always furnish unmistakable and conclusive evidence of the truth of this statement. Of more than thirty such queens which I have had opportunity to observe, there was not among all the *drones* produced by them, a single one to be found that bore any resemblance to an Italian drone. All of them were obviously of the pure black or common race; whilst the *workers* proceeding from the eggs of those queens showed diversities of marking and coloring. To which of the races a drone belongs is distinctly shown by the central or lower side of his abdomen. If that be *yellowish* in color, the drone is either a pure Italian or a hybrid; if it be *whitish*, he is a pure black or common. The dorsal or upper side of the abdomen is deceptive, as some pure common drones show brownish rings."

Cure for Bee Sting.

On this topic, of such poignant interest to many, whether beekeepers or not, Mr. S. Way, of Batavia, Ills., writes to us, as follows:

To cure a bee sting, let the patient drink half a tumbler of whisky as soon as stung. This will keep the poison from going to the lungs. A wet sheet or pack is good after the whisky. I have used this and the pack for years in my family with perfect success.

We fear that if this remedy be popularly accepted as a specific, some inveterate topers might find it agreeable to get into a habit of being stung.

We have the following remedy also from Mr. F. J. Dougall, of Stouffsville, Canada.

"I find the best thing for the sting of a bee is alcohol. Bathe the part stung with it immediately. It will kill the pain and stop the swelling. It has proved itself to be the best thing I ever tried. It was by accident I found it would give relief."

Another correspondent recommends the immediate application of pure spirits of turpentine.

CORRESPONDENCE OF THE BEE JOURNAL.

CHARLESTON, ILLS., Sept. 14, 1871.—We have to report again another very unfavorable season for bee-keeping in this locality. Since the 1st of July the drouth has prevailed to such an extent that few colonies have stored any surplus honey, and many will require feeding to carry them through the winter. Thus we have had two poor seasons together for bee-culture, in this section of country, and this will, of course, discourage many in the pursuit of bee-keeping.—J. DAVIS.

HENDERSON, ILLS., Sept. 15.—Bees are doing very well here this season. They are storing honey so fast that there will not be room to keep up enough brood, and we will have few bees, per hive, to pass the winter.—A. MCDILL.

CEDAR CREEK, N. J., Sept. 15.—I think it has been too wet in this vicinity for bees to do very well. Towards the last of July my bees were almost destitute of honey, and commenced to drag out the young. I fed them with candy, which seemed to put a stop to it. They have been busy at buckwheat lately, which is their only hope, except feeding.—E. KIMPTON.

CINCINNATI, OHIO, Sept. 22.—The honey season has been very poor in this vicinity, on account of late frosts last spring, and the white clover being burnt out by the drouth last season; still our bees have given us a net income of fully one hundred per cent. on the investment this season. The white clover is unusually luxuriant at this time, giving a fine prospect for honey next season.—M. NEVINS.

LYNCHBURG, OHIO, Sept. 22.—My stock of bees is small—only nineteen colonies, all in the Langstroth hives; but have not made honey enough to pay for the Journal. Bees in this section have not done anything.—J. STEVENS.

EXCELSIOR, MINN., Sept. 25.—Enclosed find two dollars for current volume of the Journal—should have sent it sooner, but waited until I went to the city, where I could obtain a money order; and waited also to include report for the season.

You may as well consider me a life subscriber, as the Journal is simply *indispensable*; a single number frequently being worth more than the Journal ever cost me.

This has been a good season for bees; better than usual. The linden season was very fine. All our surplus honey is linden honey, and I never saw any finer. I do not think anything in the honey line can surpass it—combs white as snow, and extracted honey the color of the clearest, finest amber. But there has only been a slight secretion of honey since the linden season. I rather overdid the extracting business during the linden season, retarding brood production, and giving the bees a backset generally. I linden season ended very abruptly, as the result of a great hail-storm and sudden change of temperature, occurring three or four days sooner than I expected the season to close. I had to break up one stock, and feed 120 pounds of honey to thirty-seven others. This result suggests that some experience and prudence are requisite in this business, as well as in bee management in general.—J. W. MURRAY.

RED OAK JUNCTION, IOWA, Sept. 27.—You may count on me as a regular subscriber, as long as bees continue to gather honey and I live. I bought two stocks of Italians last May. Within a week one stock disappeared, leaving the hive empty. I commenced feeding the remaining stock, and when they improved I divided them. I now have six strong stocks in Champion hives. They are full of honey and I have taken enough to last my family all winter. I bought five acres of ground adjoining the corporation limits of Red Oak. I intend to set it out in fruit trees, and stock it with a hundred or more stocks of bees, to give me employment outside of the confinement of the store. How many can one man take care of?—E. D. GREGORY.

AUBURN, N. Y., Oct. 3.—This season is my first at bee-keeping. Commencing with two Italian and nine native colonies, the latter in box hives, which I transferred to Langstroth hives. May 18th, they filled four frames in the Langstroth hives. Five swarms were obtained artificially, and six by natural swarming. My old stocks had six frames to fill before surplus was stored. Now for the results, which are minutely correct, except that no time is charged to their account, for personal services.

385 lbs. box honey at 30 cts. per lb.	$115 50
100 lbs. unfinished boxes, at 25 cts.	25 00
36 lbs. saved when transferring, 20 cts.	7 20
14 lbs. wax, 28 cts	3 92
11 new swarms, 4 Italians and 7 natives	100 00
	$251 62

CONTRA.

2 Italian colonies bought	$20 00
9 native colonies bought	45 00
20 Langstroth hives, $3	60 00
Right to use the same	10 00
	$135 00
Credit for net profit	$116 62

This may not be as good a showing as many veterans in the business are able to give, but it is eminently satisfactory to a tyro in bee-culture, and fires my ambition to make greater efforts in the future as the study of the little beauties is a constant source of pleasure to me.—CHAS. D. HIBBARD.

HOME, MINN., Oct. 9.—Set me down as a subscriber for—I was going to say ever—as long as I live. I am but a beginner, having started, a year ago, with thirteen stocks; increased them last year to thirty-five, and obtained nine hundred (900) pounds of surplus honey, without the extractor. This season I increased them to seventy-five stocks, and got thirty-eight hundred (3800) pounds of surplus honey, with the extractor. I owe a large part of my success to the Journal.—F. H. HARKINS.

FRANKLINTON, N. Y., Oct. 9.—This has not been a very good season for bees in this section. Only about two weeks of buckwheat bloom is all that my bees worked on, in boxes, to amount to anything. I shall get some 1800 pounds of honey. I am building a bee cellar, house, and shop all together. I shall winter eighty or ninety colonies, and shall always take the Journal while I keep bees.—B. FRANKLIN.

GNADENHUETTEN, OHIO, Oct. 9.—We have had a good season for honey in this neighborhood, but from some cause the bees did not swarm. We made an attempt to extract honey with a honey extractor, and got along very well with it; but did not find ready sale among the people for the honey. They all prefer the box honey, even at a higher price.—S. LUETHI.

GALESBURG, MICH., Oct. 9.—Bees did well here in in the fore part of the season. The latter part was rather dry, but I managed to have all my stocks strong. I have now thirty colonies in movable comb hives, and they average forty pounds to the hive. I have taken six hundred (600) pounds of surplus honey this season.—H. B. CLARK.

CINCINNATI, OHIO, Oct. 9.—The honey season has long since closed, with very poor results; so far as surplus honey is concerned, in this section of country. Had the beekeepers used the melextractor earlier in the season, the result would have been quite different. But we waited for box honey, and got none. The hives are brim full of honey, too much for the safe wintering of stocks. My stocks at my home apiary, are full to the bottom; I shall empty out some of the centre combs.—A. GRAY.

[For the American Bee Journal.]

Non-Hatching Eggs.

MR. EDITOR :—In the last number of the Journal I find a communication from G. W. P. Jerrard, of Levant, Me., in regard to non-hatching eggs of the queen bee. I have had a similar case. As Mr. Jerrard wishes to know if this is common, I can answer for myself only. In August last I gave a young Italian queen to a stock of black bees. She commenced to lay shortly after, but rather sparingly ; and I soon discovered that, from some cause, her eggs were not hatching. Supposing that the workers had objections to her (as I had a queen just destroyed by the same stock), I commenced to stimulate them, by feeding, until the queen was laying profusely ; without, however, producing any better result. She even deposited four and five eggs in the same cell at last, for want of room.

The queen was nice, large, and lively ; and of course I was disappointed in her. I further took some of her eggs and introduced them in another colony ; but they would not hatch there. Eggs from another colony, which I introduced in her hive, readily hatched—the workers starting queen cells immediately from them, seeming to have a true knowledge of the situation.

Dr. Hamlin's queen refused to lay—otherwise perhaps her eggs would have hatched.

Any information or suggestions throwing light on this subject, will be gladly received.

EDGAR MCNITT.

Centre Village, Ohio, Oct. 7, 1871.

I don kno ov enny bissiness on the breast of the earth that will make a man so lazy and useless, without actual killing him, az hunting wild bees in the wilderness.—*J. Billings.*

[For the American Bee Journal.]

Improved Bee Hives.

The object of improving bee hives is, or ought to be, to combine simplicity and cheapness of construction with facility in the management of the bees; and the hive which does this to the greatest degree, is the best hive. A hive which costs five dollars, is too expensive for the majority of beekeepers: it takes too much of the profits. And one which costs but a single dollar, if so made that it is not easily manipulated, or if it be not conducive to the storing of surplus honey, or not effective in the rapid building up of colonies, is too cheap for any beekeeper. As all who keep bees for profit, need to rear some queens for their own use, their hives should be so constructed as to be convenient for that purpose; and they should be so made as to conform to the instincts and needs of the bees in storing and consuming their winter's food.

With these necessary adaptations in view, let us reason as *how* to make a good hive. It is presumed at the start, of course, that the hive shall have movable comb-frames, as they are indispensable to success.

First, then, as to *capacity*. It is believed by the most successful apiarians that a capacity of about two thousand cubic inches is sufficient for the needs of a strong colony, both for breeding purposes and for storing the winter supplies. But small colonies, as second and third swarms, do not, at the start, need so much room, and will build combs more rapidly in a space adapted to their size. Hence, means for regulating the capacity of the hive should be provided; and for this purpose nothing is better than a close-fitting division board. To use a division board successfully, the hive must be *narrow* one way, with the frame running the narrow way, and the entrance at the end of the hive, or side of the frames. The swarm or colony may then have four, six, eight, or ten frames, as it needs. The hive must also be *tall*, to secure the storing of winter supplies in the proper place, viz., *above* the brood and the cluster. In the common form of the Langstroth hive, the division board cannot be used successfully, neither can the bees store their winter supplies where needed.

We can readily see, then, that to combine the proper capacity for the main hive with the necessary shape — narrowness and tallness—we shall have a hive with dimensions somewhat as follows: say, twelve inches from side to side, fifteen inches tall, and fifteen inches from front to rear. This will give abundant space for brood and winter store.

But the principal object in keeping bees, is to secure surplus honey, and provision must be made for this.

Those who wish to obtain their surplus stores in boxes, may place them on the sides of a hive of the dimensions indicated above. Such a hive will accommodate boxes to the aggregate capacity of one hundred pounds or more. An outside casing may cover the whole.

But, to secure the largest quantity of honey, we must use the Extractor; or, if not, we may obtain it in frames suspended in the rear of the main hive, much more readily and rapidly than by the use of boxes; and in either case, whether we use the Extractor, or take the honey in the comb, by frames, we need only to lengthen the hive, so as to hold two or three more frames than are needed for winter purposes.

With a hive thus constructed, we shall need no *cap* other than a plain board, with cleats on the under side to prevent warping or being misplaced. Neither shall we need a honey-board, which is an expensive and troublesome arrangement. Of course, then, we need no air space above the frames, and no rabbets to hang them on—simply hanging them on the edges of the box which composes the hive, making the tops of the frames close-fitting to each other throughout their whole extent.

As to a bottom, we need only a plain board, detached, with strong cleats on the under side.

The writer of this has used the Langstroth hive many years, also the American and other patents, and has constantly studied to improve them. The result thus far is, that he has a hive that can be made here for two dollars, which, as he thinks, has many advantages over a host of patents, with few disadvantages, and no unnecessary fixings. It can be adapted to the needs of a large or a small colony; will hold and winter two strong colonies at the same time; or can be used for three, or four good queen-raising colonies.

The inside dimensions of this hive are: twelve and three-fourths inches from side to side, nineteen and one-fourth inches from front to rear, and fifteen and three-fourths inches deep. It contains thirteen frames and a division board. Entrances at each end; top of frames closed; cross-bars through the middle; top and bottom detached.

This hive is not patented, and the only feature in which it resembles the Langstroth hive is in having movable frames. If any of the readers of this desire to try the hive, and cannot make one from the description, I will cheerfully give full directions; but all correspondents must enclose stamps or money sufficient to pay me for my time, stationery and postage.

W. C. Condit.

Marysville, East Tennessee.

Bees and Honey.—Great and increasing attention to bees and the production of honey, is one of the "signs of the times" at the North and West, but *our* people do not seem to have awakened yet to the importance of the subject. The cash value of the honey made in the United States, every year, amounts to several millions of dollars, and the cost of producing it is a mere trifle. If the people of the South and Southwest would devote a little time and attention to this matter, they would be agreeably surprised at the great results from light labor and care. With the Italian bees, new and improved hives, &c., the business is reduced to perfect simplicity, and the profits are unfailing and sure. We earnestly advise our readers to give bee-keeping a reasonable and proper share of attention at once.—*New Orleans Home Journal.*

AMERICAN BEE JOURNAL.

EDITED AND PUBLISHED BY SAMUEL WAGNER, WASHINGTON, D. C.

AT TWO DOLLARS PER ANNUM, PAYABLE IN ADVANCE.

Vol. VII. DECEMBER, 1871. No. 6.

[For the American Bee Journal.]

Novice.

Dear Journal:—Owing to the protracted drouth, we have not got our ten acre farm in condition for planting the basswood orchard, and may not now until spring, as we have decided to thoroughly underdrain, subsoil, and manure it.

We are going to set the trees twelve feet apart, and thin out when too crowded. We shall raise hoed crops on the land for the first two or three years, to ensure thorough cultivation. As many prominent horticulturists are taking quite an interest in the project, we are going to try and guard against failure, if possible.

Our opinion is, that Mr. Price is totally wrong in the position which he so persistently adheres to; and if he has himself turned over our former articles, he should know that we purchased from Mr. Grimm, the twenty-five queens, almost solely to replace those whose progeny were too nearly black bees. See vol. vi, page 78. And, further, several of our dark, artificial hybrids that we discarded, were so much more prolific than the pure ones from Mr. Grimm, that we have sincerely regretted killing them; and shall, in future, save extra prolific queens, even if only one-banded.

Mr. Grimm raises queens in small nucleus boxes, we think. Will he tell us where he gets his queen cells? and will he also tell us whether he agrees with Mr. Price's position? We should agree with Mr. Quinby exactly, who has given his views at length, and his practical experience in the matter has been considerable. Both natural and artificial queens are, like Mr. Price's, sometimes poor, especially when raised out of the swarming season, and when an abundant supply of food is not coming in, or some of the other requisites are wanting. Some of our very best queens have been raised with less than a pint of bees; but we find it more difficult, with so few, to secure all other requisite conditions.

The questions on page 116, are all answered, we think, some of them at great length too, in back numbers of the Journal; but we will briefly go over them here, and sum up.

1st. Twenty of the forty-six queens were raised after the loss of our only pure queen, by cutting the brood combs, or those having eggs and unsealed larvæ, into pieces about one by two inches. These were put in hives containing empty combs, and set in place of each of our weak eleven remaining stocks. Extra cells were cut out and put in nuclei made from the old stocks, still further reduced for the purpose. All this was done in the swarming season, and the twenty queens raised were all good prolific ones, although the returning bees, in some cases, gathered around the small piece of brood comb, were not over a teacupful.

Of course we had no known pure queen after this to get brood from, and were obliged to use brood from some of the twenty—intending to replace them, if too dark. Many of these were only one-fourth Italian; and slicing off the drones' heads last year, gave us more hybrids again, as many of the original eleven queens were then replaced.

The twenty-five queens from Mr. Grimm were ordered to replace the poorest, and to have pure stock to rear from next spring.

2d. Our hives are shaded by grape-vines, trained on the plan of "*Fuller's Grape Culturist.*"

3d. We always paint our hives white, and hire a painter to do it.

4th. About the Peabody Extractor. Our assistant says she thinks it turns a trifle harder than our old home made one, the case of which does not revolve; but it is simpler, neater, more convenient, and much more durable. After a good deal of study on the matter, we think, all things considered, that we should prefer the Peabody to any we have seen.

Remember, you asked a delicate question, as we have advertised them; but we have tried to make the answer honest.

Three of the Grimm queens ceased laying gradually, when less than a year old—something we have seldom, if ever, seen in our own, or those from Mr. Langstroth; and we are going to purchase a queen of Mr. Langstroth, to raise our queens from, next season, Providence permitting.

Hoping to meet all our friends at the Convention in Cleveland, we are, as ever,

Novice.

Indigo, bound dry on the wound, is a sure cure for rattlesnake bites, scorpion and bee-stings, &c., says a Mormon who has tried it.

[For the American Bee Journal.]

Essay on Queen Raising.

By Elisha Gallup.

Read before the Michigan Beekeepers' Association, September 29, 1871.

In natural queen raising, the cell is built and the egg deposited therein, and not the cell built around the egg, as some assert.

The first requisites in natural queen raising, or natural swarming, are: warm weather, abundance of forage, and a large stock of bees. We find that queens raised under such circumstances, are almost invariably large and prolific, and if we examine the cells, we find that the larva is supplied with an abundance of food—floating in it, in fact. And there is a mass of this food still left, when the young queen leaves the cell at maturity; a mass not unfrequently as large as a common marrowfat pea. Nearly the reverse of all this is true, in raising forced or artificial queens. These are mostly raised in small nuclei, containing comparatively few nursing bees, or bees capable of preparing the necessary food; for it requires *young* bees to prepare this food. The consequence is, the larva is supplied with an insufficient quantity of food; and if we examine we shall find that not more of it is furnished than is actually consumed—there is none left in the cell when the queen leaves. You will probably say that if she is fed just enough, she must be just as perfect as one that receives a superabundance. But we must bear in mind that the nymph or chrysalis is continually drawing in moisture through the pores of her abdomen from the mass of food, up to the time of her maturity, when we find the mess dried up; whereas before maturity it is still moist. The queen raised under all these favorable circumstances will almost invariably be large, prolific, and long-lived. We have, in fact, had them at the age of four years as prolific, to all appearance, as they were the first season. A queen so raised will be full sixteen days coming to maturity, from the time the egg is deposited in the cell. Queens raised in small nuclei, with insufficient food, or in insufficient quantity, &c., are imperfect and not long lived.

We have never been able to discover any difference between artificial and natural queens, when they were properly raised. To explain this so as to be understood, we will give the right conditions and the wrong conditions. We deprive a small and a strong stock of their queens, in the height of the breeding season. They have large quantities of eggs, larvæ in all stages, nursing bees, &c. They are also gathering forage in abundance, and consequently the nursing bees are preparing large quantities of food for the larvæ. Under these favorable circumstances they almost invariably commence from the larvæ just hatched, feed abundance of food, and there is an abundance of warmth. Consequently we have just as good queens, prolific, long-lived, &c., as any natural queens can be. Remember, I am not here writing theory, for I have been a close observer on this very subject, during the past eighteen years. On the other hand we have a strong stock of bees that have lost their queen, and before we discover the loss, the brood is all hatched out. They have now no larvæ to nurse, and are consequently preparing no food for any. We give them a card of brood from which to raise queens, and they will almost invariably select larvæ from three to five days old to rear queens from. But suppose they should select one just hatched, it will be fed on an insufficient quantity of food, and is consequently imperfect. The warmth in such a colony, through the inactivity of the bees, is not near as great as it is in one where all branches of industry, such as nursing, gathering, &c., are carried on at the same time. Queens raised from larvæ which hatch in eight days, die of old age in from ten to twelve weeks; those hatched in ten days are worthless in eighteen months; and those hatched in small nuclei, with insufficient food and warmth, although they may be twenty-four days in hatching, are worthless too.

To sum up. The conclusion is—Raise your queens in strong stocks, which have abundance of eggs, larvæ, nursing bees, &c.; and if they are not gathering forage abundantly at the time, supply them regularly and artificially, and they will be all right. After the cells are sealed, we can transfer them to nuclei or queen cages. But nucleus hives should be kept strong in bees, and receive abundance of food, in order to keep up the proper temperature. Recollect that I have never said that all artificial queens are worthless. But a large proportion are, as they are usually raised. Mr. Langstroth, Mrs. Tupper, and some few others, take particular pains to state that they raise all their queens in full colonies. We will venture the assertion from our own experience, that a large proportion of the queens sent out by Tom, Dick, and Harry, have either been superseded or are worthless, at the end of eighteen months.

The next question is, how to raise pure Italian queens; and here we shall in all probability tread on somebody's corns. There are all manner of dodges got up by queen breeders, to account for their impure queens. Some assert that the pure Italians are a cross themselves. Some assert that three-striped workers are a test of purity. Some say that we can test their purity by taking them to a glass window. Some allege that the queens must be all light colored, &c., &c. We were among the latter class two years ago; but our views have been somewhat changed since then. Our Durham cattle were not started from pure Durhams. Now if our Italian bees were started from black hornets, and have been bred up to their present standard, until they have become a fixed breed, and have thus continued to be a fixed type, breed, or race for hundreds of years in their native country, Italy, why can they not be bred in this country just as well as in Europe, and just as pure? These are questions for our consideration. What are the characteristics of the imported Italians—that is, those imported directly from Italy? The queens are almost invariably dark colored; some of them almost black; or of a dark rich golden or leather color. The workers are three-striped, rather darkish in color, considerably so when compared with our Americanized Italians. Their abdomens are long, tapering, and they carry them well up on a level. The queens are extra prolific, almost invariably. The drones are, as a rule, smaller and very dark colored; in fact seem almost coal black and glossy a little way off. But if we examine them closely, we see their color tinged with a dark orange hue; and scarcely any hair on their abdomen visible to the naked eye. Our Americanized Italian queens on the other hand, are a light yellow, and not very prolific. The workers are a light yellow, and if they come up to the standard, very light colored. The abdomen is not so long and taper as that of the pure Italian brought from Italy; and when they are fanning in front of their hives, there appears to be a sort of joint in the abdomen. When we come to the Americanized drone, we have an extra large hairy fellow. Some of them very bright yellow, and of different shades of color, &c., &c.

Now, we will start with a pure imported Italian queen. We raise queens from her, and they are fertilized with black drones. Yet some of them produce all three-striped workers. We select such to breed from, and we have the Americanized Italian. Now we keep selecting the lightest colored and largest drones, &c. (This is about the way it is done.)

Again, we start with a black or common queen. She mates with an Italian drone; and then we breed from this queen up to the fourth generation, and all her successors mate with Italian drones, and we again have the Americanized Italian to perfection.

All this is done by accepting three-striped workers, and selecting the lightest colored queens, and rejecting the dark colored ones. We have at present in our yard two queens that are admired by visitors as models of purity. Yet we know that their grandmothers were raised from an impure mother, and fertilized by a black drone. Still the workers from those two queens are perfect Americanized Italians; and nine out of every ten visitors select these two stocks as perfectly pure. The fact is, the American bee-keeping public will not, as a rule, accept a really pure queen to breed from. I could relate some curious facts about some of our American queen breeders, but will not at present do so. For the past two seasons I have rejected extra light colored queens, and all queens that produce extra light colored, large, hairy drones, as breeders; and it is the first time in nine years that I have met with any satisfactory results I am now satisfied with the same colored queens, drones, and workers, as we get direct from Italy. I am also satisfied that the Italians can be raised here, as well as in Italy. Why do they not deteriorate, or turn back to the blacks, in that country, if they are not now a fixed race?

It is rather curious, and sometimes laughable, to read the statements of our queen breeders. Some assert that only a very small portion of queens raised are fit to breed from; and yet they do not give any reason why it is so. Now, it certainly seems to me that if the queen is an imported one, and all her successors mate with pure drones, all ought to be fit to breed from, so far as race is concerned. But if the position I have taken is correct—that is, that our queen breeders will not breed from pure queens, but rather from Americanized ones, as our friend Dadant calls them, or mules, as our friend Gardner denominates them, then there is nothing strange in the alleged fact that a large proportion of the queens raised show the black blood, and that quite *distinctly*. The cross has been so recent that there is no fixed type or character to the breed. But we must not attribute all this to the breeder; for in hundreds of cases the customer is not satisfied with a pure Italian queen. None other than an Americanized one will suit their taste or fancy. I know of several cases where pure queens have been returned or rejected, and the parties have come to me with their complaint; and I have recommended the complainant to apply to another breeder, who raises mules, and they were perfectly satisfied.

[For the American Bee Journal.]

Rearing Queens.

For the last four years I have been more less extensively engaged in rearing Italian queens; and during that time have experimented somewhat with different methods—always aiming at rearing fine large queens cheaply, and have finally hit upon the following arrangement, which is entirely satisfactory to me; and I can see no way that queens can be reared and fertilized at less cost.

I make small frame hives or nuclei of two stories high, the upper story projecting out over the lower, so as exclude the rain. The bottom is nailed on to the lower story, while the upper has neither bottom nor top, being covered by a plain board laid on, with a weight upon it to keep it in place. Four small frames containing combs are suspended in the usual way in the lower story, with an entrance on one side, and a feed trough on the opposite. Across the top of the frames are laid four strips about one-fourth of an inch square, and on these strips are placed six cages two inches cubic, the four sides being of wood (thin), the bottom wire cloth, and the top glass, laid on with listing between, to prevent the escape of heat. A one-inch thick piece of sponge one and a half inches long, is secured in one corner, hanging downward.

When it is time to commence operations, I remove the queens from strong stocks, to get queen cells. When these are eight days old, I get common bees from a distance, and give to each nucleus hive a little more than a quart of bees. Two days latter I remove my queen cells and give each nucleus in the lower story a sealed cell nearly ready to hatch. I then fill the sponges in the cages with honey, and into one corner of each cage I attach a sealed queen cell by means of melted wax; and then put in a lot of bees—fifty or more, probably—to take care of the cell and the young queen when she hatches.

All being finished, the cages are set closely together on the strips over the frames, wire cloth side down—the six cages just covering the top of the lower story, thus preventing the escape of animal heat from below, and it all passes up through the wire cloth into the cages, to help keep up a proper temperature for the young queens. By lifting off the cover from the upper story, and looking down through the glass tops of the cages, we are able to see at a glance which of the queens have hatched each day, and record the same on the under side of the cover.

When the queen in the lower story has hatched and become fertile, she is removed, and the oldest one in the cages is let down, and when this one is fertilized she is taken out, and the next oldest let down, and so on.

By opening these hives about three o'clock in the afternoon, on pleasant days, we can usually find the visible signs of connection on the queen, and remove her at once.

G. W. P. Jerrard.

Levant, Me., Nov., 1871.

[For the American Bee Journal.]

Foulbrood.

Dear Journal :—I am almost afraid of wearing out my welcome by appealing so often to you, especially on the same subject; but you know it is natural to be garrulous on that topic in which one is most interested.

Last year I was almost discouraged by the rapid and destructive spread of foulbrood in my little apiary; but this year it has been a pleasure, rather than a sorrow, to watch and control it.

Only a few of those treated last year with sulphite of soda or chloride of soda and lime, as conducted then, with honey and pollen remaining in the combs, proved to be permanently cured, when brood was raised in the spring, although all trace of the disease had been removed in the fall, and the combs continued through the winter to be *apparently* healthy.

All colonies (with the exception of one which contracted the disease in the fall) that were treated in the early summer, according to Quinby, remain free from disease to this day. In fact one of these has been my best, giving me two early swarms, which, with the original hive, have yielded one hundred and one pounds of box honey, and ninety-five pounds of extracted, leaving in each hive about thirty-five pounds for winter.

The season being somewhat earlier than usual, the hives were removed to their summer stands, from the best of all bee houses, the "Novice," early in March, and all those which were diseased the fall previous were placed a few rods away from the others, in a lot surrounded on three sides by a very high board fence, with a barn and the out-buildings connected forming the fourth, and separating it from the apiary. This was the hospital yard, and the seclusion proved sufficient protection, as there has been no case of contagion this year in the apiary, which now numbers eighteen colonies.

Is it not a fact that bees, unless greatly demoralized, have little inclination to rob out of their own enclosure?

This summer's experiments have been to test cures in two ways. One by pruning, the other by emptying the comb with the "Peabody," and disinfecting them before restoring them to the bees again. The bees themselves, of course, were shut up and made to consume all the diseased honey which they carried with them.

First pruning. Early in March I removed the bees from two infected hives to healthy ones which were well supplied with stores ; but from having lost their queens were nearly tenantless. Now after one of these had become well filled with brood, a part of the frames were removed to strengthen a weak colony, making three hives which were occupied more or less with brood from the transferred stocks. All these were found diseased in April. How did this happen, when the bees had been confined without food for nearly two days before they were given to healthy combs? Probably forty-eight hours in their sluggish state, in the cool weather of March, is not time enough for the consumption of the diseased supply. One hive was so badly diseased that pruning was useless. The other two were so slightly affected that I determined to prune, removing the first row of healthy cells around those diseased, and to this day they are perfectly healthy. One of them was prevented from swarming by cutting out queen cells, and the other threw off a large swarm during the summer.

The others, with two more as badly diseased, were treated as follows : All the honey was extracted, the combs washed in clean water, and then immersed for a few hours in a solution of chloride of lime, after all the cells which had contained disease had been washed out with either sulphite of soda or chloride of soda, then washed out again with clean water, immersing them and emptying with my "Peabody." In this way two were perfectly cured, and remain so. In the third, the disease slowly reappeared, and after it had made a good headway, the queen was removed and given to a healthy colony. (I have frequently done it with impunity), the brood allowed to hatch, while a new queen was raised, and as soon as she began to lay, the colony was shaken into an empty hive on the old stand, and confined for a day and a half. Meanwhile all the putrid larvæ was removed from the combs by the atomizer and water, and all the honey removed by the extractor. The combs, after being washed in clean water, were immersed for a night in a solution of caustic acid, washed again in water, and given to the swarm. The disease reappeared in less than three weeks in two out of the six combs. On the supposition that this occurred only in cells not thoroughly disinfected, and that the contagion had not been spread through the hive, I concluded to prune. All the disease was carefully removed, and now six weeks afterwards, there has been no new invasion, and to all appearance it is healthy.

I consider my apiary pure, and the hospital without a case, and if next spring it continues so, I shall try various experiments to recreate the disease.

I still have two hives testing the time cure. One with honey and disease undisturbed, the other with combs emptied of their contents and washed with clean water. They will be furnished with colonies next spring, and placed on the sick list in the hospital.

Although the experiments have not been as complete and varied as I could have wished, owing to the almost complete occupation of my time by other duties, I have, however, done enough to satisfy myself that the following memoranda, which I have noted in my apiary book, are correct.

1st. If foulbrood is discovered very early, and there are only a few cells affected, prune, and spray with a solution of sulphite of soda. Prune for a week or two, as often as fresh disease is discovered, but if it reappears in the next crop of brood in any quantity over four or six cells, condemn the colony to be treated, if sufficiently early in the season, according to Quinby, as a new swarm.

2d. If early in the season, and the disease is not too far advanced to prune, or pruning is ineffectual, treat according to Quinby, for although the combs can be cleansed and disinfected, so as to be safely used again, the trouble of doing it, and the danger of doing it carelessly, is so great that the advantage is in favor of treating it as a new swarm and feeding back the purified honey, to stimulate the making of new combs.

3d. If discovered in the fall or too late in the season for treatment No. 1, or No. 2, empty all the diseased cells with the atomizer and a solution of sulphite of soda (two ounces to a tumbler of water), return the combs and honey undisturbed, and if there is any evidence of disease in the spring, treat as circumstances require, either by No. 1 or No. 2.

E. P. Abbe.

New Bedford, Oct. 15, 1871.

☞ Treating foulbrood colonies as new swarms is by no means a reliable method, especially when the disease has assumed a malignant type. It has been practiced by the Germans many years before movable comb hives were introduced, sometimes successfully, but more generally unsuccessfully, even in early stages of the disease. Dzierzon tested it very thoroughly when the malady devastated his apiary, but found it entirely unserviceable.

[For the American Bee Journal.]

Queen Progeny of a Failing Queen.

Novice desires to know if queens raised from queens that are failing in prolificness, would be prolific or not? and requests *facts*. I comply with his desire by making the following statement:

In August, 1870, I had a queen that failed to lay, and was superseded. When she began to fail I took out one frame of brood and eggs and placed it in an empty hive, with one frame of honey; put in enough of young bees and old to cover the frames well; fed sweetened water, and got four queen cells. I took three out and put them in a queen nursery, which through carelessness were lost. The one left in hatched and in due time the queen mated with an Italian drone. I gave them one full frame of brood, and one half full of comb and honey. They filled up to eight frames, and came out all right through the winter, except some mouldy combs. I gave them two frames of honey, and in a month another. By the last of April every frame was full of brood and uncapped honey. I put on an upper story containing two combs of drone cells. At the end of May, she had filled top and bottom. I took out five frames of brood, looked well over them for queen cells, but saw none. In —— days after this she came off with an enormous swarm. I took out a frame of brood and gave it to them. In two weeks they filled up the six centre frames full of brood and eggs. The third week I raised them to the upper story, which they also filled. What troubled me most, she was so prolific it was all brood and no honey. I took them out of the two-story hive, and put them in one two feet wide, putting on at the same time four 15 lb. boxes. I took from them also four frames of brood to strengthen up others. The following is the amount of honey and brood taken from them:

4 frames full of brood.		
12 " " honey, ...	96 lbs.	
4 boxes " "	60	
	156	
Old hive.		
8 frames of brood.		
4 " honey, ...	32 lbs.	
Machine honey, taken at seven times, say an average of 30 lbs.,	210	
		242
Total, ...		398 lbs.

Doubting Thomas may question the above. I cannot help that. *Natural* queen raisers may do the same. I have a dozen queens, raised this year, just as good.

I forgot to state that the old hive is a two-story, which is now full, top and bottom. It could easily spare fifty pounds of comb honey.

F. Crathorn.

Bethlehem, Iowa, Oct. 12, 1871.

☞ Please send us the full report for 1871.

[For the American Bee Journal.]

Foulbrood.

Mr. Editor:—In July, 1870, I had five strong stocks, from two in the spring. The last of August found me with most of the brood dead. The combs were made into beeswax. In September, the three hives nearest, six or eight feet distant, showed a few cells of dead brood, say five to twenty in a comb. The last of May, 1871, two of these, with from one-half to nine-tenths of the brood dead, were driven out, the hives closed, and put up chamber. The fourth, with say one-eighth of the brood dead, was driven out June 29th, and the hive put up chamber. The fifth swarmed June 24th, and the swarm went to the woods. The old stock showed some signs of foulbrood in August. In September, after repeatedly sending by porter to Green Bay and Buffalo for hyposulphite of soda, without success, I wrote to a druggist at Green Bay, and found they had always kept it, at thirty-five cents a pound. Having sent to Dr. Abbe in the spring for an atomizer, which cost five dollars and somewhat less than a dollar postage, say six dollars, I tried it (the hyposulphite) on part of the brood combs; but as it was cool weather, and the bees had quit raising brood for the season, they were rather slow in cleaning out the dead brood: and as there was plenty of honey sealed over in the presence of the disease, and I did not wish to extend my experience in 1871, they were brimstoned September 23d; and so closed the record of the five stocks of 1870, but not quite of my bees.

The swarm of June 24th came out in the afternoon, lit and waited till 4 o'clock P. M., and my wife notified me as they were off for the woods, southeast, through bushes 15 to 30 feet high. I followed by the noise, and losing that, kept my course by the sun. After eighty rods came within hearing, and found them entering a pine tree thirty inches in diameter, the hole being about twenty-five feet from the ground, and an inch in diameter. It followed a knot slanting downward six inches, to the top of the hollow; and about four feet below was another hole made by ants—giving a fair chance for upward ventilation. Before dark that day the tree was down and sawed three times off, and next morning before breakfast the swarm was on the old stand, with a good comb of brood from the old stock, which has been removed to a new place.

The three stocks put in empty hive in May and June were transferred to one hive on the 1st of August, and filled it on basswood blossoms, gathering as fast as a new swarm. The hive, with frames, was baked over the stove, being raised an inch or more on blocks, to prevent the bottom of the hive from burning. It was heated till the resin started on the outside (process not patented).

These two stocks have showed no signs of foulbrood. They were carefully examined September 25th. The brood had all left the cells, and they were well filled with bees. They weighed forty-three pounds each, net; and allowing ten pounds for bees, combs, &c., had thirty-three pounds of honey, each.

My record for two years gives, for 1870, with two hives in the spring and twenty combs, three hundred pounds of honey, worth ninety dollars. For 1871, forty pounds of extracted honey, and twenty pounds of honey in the comb, worth twenty dollars. Thus making for the two years, one hundred and ten (110) dollars, less the empty combs. Thirty-six empty combs were made into beeswax, for fear of keeping foulbrood. A few healthy combs would be worth more than a dollar each, in an ordinary season. There were six days in June, and nine days in August on basswood blossoms, that a stock made more than one pound surplus per day, requiring fifteen days to lay in a year's supply for 1871.

Henry D. Miner.

Washington Harbor, Wis., Sept. 28, 1871.

[For the American Bee Journal.]

How Foulbrood Spreads.

It may be spread by young bees entering the wrong hive on their first flight, before they are old enough to gather honey. As young queens sometimes enter the wrong hive, on returning from their wedding flight, so may young workers.

A hive of mine was lost by foulbrood in August, 1870, and in September the three nearest hives, six or eight feet distant, had foulbrood. There were no signs of robbing. It might have been carried in by the bad air from the diseased hive.

That young bees are not destroyed by other bees in the breeding season, I infer, because I have taken combs from several hives into a shop to extract honey, shaking off the bees into a large pan. The old bees flew out through the window to their homes; the young bees, remaining in the pan, were taken out, emptied before my hive, and always peaceably received. Drones may also enter other hives, without molestation.

The last of June, 1871, a stock with one-fourth of the brood dead, was driven into an empty hive. The old hive, with wire cloth fastened over the entrance, was put up chamber, and a swarm of young bees hatched out, without any old bees to brood them. To save these, I concluded to put them in an empty box for three or four days, and then give them to another hive. I put a piece of comb with eggs in the box, so they could raise a queen; took them over half a mile through the woods one day, to where I was hoeing potatoes; shook and brushed them off before the box, fastened the old hive tight and took it home. The next morning they flew lively, but towards noon became more quiet. I raised the box and saw two or three bees on the comb—all that remained of one or two quarts of young bees, that had never been an inch from their hive before. They had found friends to pilot them to a better home.

H. D. Miner.

Washington Harbor, Wis., Oct. 25, 1871.

[For the American Bee Journal.]

Kentucky and Tennessee Beekeepers.

Mr. Editor:—As we have just returned home from Tennessee, having been on a tour of *inspection* among the beekeepers of Kentucky and Tennessee, we thought it likely that a few lines regarding our visit to some of the largest and best conducted apiaries in the United States, might be of interest to the readers of the American Bee Journal. We left home August 3d, for Lowell, Garrard county, Kentucky, the home of R. M. Argo, known to all beekeepers throughout the United States, and to some of those in Europe. We found him at home, awaiting our arrival. After spending a pleasant night, resting our weary bones, we were the next morning shown through the apiary by friend Argo and his son. Just here, let us say to the boys, that Willie Argo is one of America's best beekeepers, and will, one day make his mark among the apiculturists of this country. He is only twelve years old, and to see him among the bees, helping his father, would make many a *professed* beekeeper ashamed of himself. We were shown many, yes, very many fine colonies. and in fine condition, considering the dry weather and early frost in Garrard county. We were shown several fine imported queens. Fine queens were boxed and shipped each day we were there, and orders continued to come in from every quarter of the United States and from Canada. Let us here state what I evidently believe to be true, that R. M. Argo is one of the most reliable and *conscientious* men we ever met or dealt with. Never, no, never would he send out a queen without first seeing her progeny, that he might know that she was purely fertilized. If such were ever the case, it could only be through some mistake, to which we are all liable sometimes. And I may here say, that some of our largest queen raisers are making entirely too *many mistakes* of this kind; and we fear some of them do so willingly. Yes, we believe there are not a few who do not care, so they get your money. We are sorry that this is so; but when numbers of our Kentucky apiarians tell us that they have each tried Mr. ———, and Mr. ———, and that three out of five of the queens received were hybrids, or produced hybrids, we are justified in making the statement we have. And we will further state, that no man who has from three to eight hundred colonies of bees to look after, can do them justice, and rear *pure* queens for sale.* One hundred and fifty to two hundred colonies are all that *one man* can manage *successfully*, and rear queens *safely;* and he will then have to employ help during the swarming season. But we will return again to our subject. After spending several days with friend Argo and family, very pleasantly and profitably, we took the train for Richmond, (Ky.,) to attend the fair, commencing August 8th. We there met and made the acquaintance of some of Madison county's best beekeepers. Among them were W. C. Peyton, Dr. W. H. Hogan, W. M. Thomas, and T. J. Gordon, all live apiarians, seeking to attain the topmost round in the ladder of apiarian science. After spending several days, looking at some of the finest stock, and talking bee until everything around began to buzz, we took the stage for Lexington, twenty-five miles distant, and had a glorious hot and dusty ride. On arriving, we took Paddy's trotters, and made for Mr. M. T. Scott's, partner of Dr. John Dillard, in apiculture. Mr. Scott lives about three-fourths of a mile from the city. We were received very pleasantly, indeed, by Mr. S., took a look through his apiary, and found everything in apple pie order, the apiary consisting of about two hundred colonies. Owing to the death of a neighbor's child, Mr. Scott was not able to show us many of his fine queens. This is one of the apiaries that Kentucky can brag on; and two more congenial, well posted apiarians cannot be found. Be it remembered, that Dr. Dillard is President of the Apiarian Society. He is not only a big man in size, but he is a giant in intellect, both in physic and apiculture. We shall have more to say about him hereafter. Through the kindness of Mr. Scott, we got a good saddle horse and away we went, out to Mr. Burbank's. Mr. B. lives about two miles from the city. We arrived there well soaked with rain; and a great blessing was the rain to that country at that time, though we did get wet. We were received cordially, and by a good fire I soon felt all right again. After talking with Mr. B. until a late hour, we retired, and slept off some of the jolts we had received in a miserable stage coach. Next morning, Mr. B. showed us through his large and well arranged apiary of two hundred, or more colonies. It is, indeed, beautiful to behold, situated as it is, in such lovely grounds, well shaded, to protect both the colonies and the operator from the extreme heat of the sun. Among other improvements shown us by Mr. B. was his improved hive, which has some excellent points, especially the arrangement for ventilation. After taking a thorough look, and learning all we could, Mr. B. took us to the city in his rockaway. There we met with Dr. Dillard, of whom we have already spoken. The Doctor is, indeed, one of Kentucky's big sons, weighing *only* two hundred and sixty pounds, and he has a soul as large as his body. Should any of my readers ever be so lucky as to meet the Doctor, they will find all we have said to be true, and more too. We went out with him to his brother's (where he was boarding), and remained over Sabbath. On Monday, we returned to the city, and it being court day, we there met a large number of Fayette county's best beekeepers, and with Mr. Burbank, we talked bee, beehive, and melextractor all the day, for Mr. B. had one of Grey & Winder's extractors on exhibition in the court house yard.

At four P. M. we took the train for Cynthiana, Harrison county, the home of Mr. Henry Nesbit. Arriving there, we found that friend Nesbit lived some two miles in the country. We took a carryall and went out, arriving in time for tea (something we always aim to do, so as not to miss our grub), and we indeed fared sumptuously, for if any Kentucky lady knows how to fix up things to eat, it is Miss Nesbit, for we must tell you, that friend Henry is a widower; and though such is the case, you will see no bachelor doings around him.

We had long wished to visit the apiary of America's bee-king, and were determined to do so this trip. He is, indeed, entitled to the name, and any one that visits his apiary will say as we have said—"behold the ingenuity of man!" His arrangements are perfect in all their parts. The tasteful arrangement of his hives; the way they are painted and shaded; his arrangements for raising queens; his winter quarters for his colonies—all, yes, everything is as near perfection as well could be. He showed us through very many colonies, and we saw some as fine queens as man

* We cannot concur in these views. A beekeeper, possessing the requisite qualifications, and who has made the necessary arrangements for business, can manage a thousand colonies of bees for queen raising and connected purposes, just as efficiently, though certainly not as easily, as a hundred. Of course, such a man will supply himself at the proper time with the necessary help and other appliances.—[ED.

ever looked upon. Quite a number were late importations from sunny Italy, imported direct by himself.

After remaining several days with friend Nesbit, he took us over into Bourbon county, to see the apiary of Dr. J. J. Adair, near Shawhan Station, on the Lexington and Covington railroad. We found the Doctor a very sociable man, indeed, and full of bee talk. He has an apiary of about one hundred and seventy-five colonies; and here we found the greatest variety of hives we ever saw collected together in one apiary. We soon found that the Doctor's attention was too much engaged with his farm and fine stock to give his bees the necessary attention. He was about the first man in Kentucky that bought an Italian queen. After being there a short time, we found ourselves out of order from over-eating, and had to call on the Doctor for a narcotic, which he administered, greatly to our relief; but we found we should be unable to return with friend Nesbit, so bidding him farewell, we remained with Dr. A. over night, and next morning took the train for Lexington, and thence to Eminence, Henry county, to attend the fair commencing there on the 22d of August.

There we met Dr. C. Bright, and Dr. L. E. Brown, both of whom are well posted beekeepers. Dr. Bright takes a great interest in apiculture, his mind being entirely engrossed with physic and bees. He has a splendid apiary of pure Italians, his stock being principally derived from Mr. Langstroth and Mr. Burbank. He informed us that it is impossible for him to supply the demand for Italian colonies. Dr. Brown has short horn cattle, Berkshire hogs, Southdown and Cotswold sheep, as well as Italian bees on the brain, and if he does not let some of them lose their short horns or their yellow bands, it will be curious to us. He says his bees are doing well, and told us that from one colony of Italians, which he bought last spring was a year, he now has twenty-eight colonies, and hundreds of pounds of surplus honey. We say, go it, Doctor.

After spending several days looking at the fine stock of which Henry county can boast, we took the omnibus for Shelbyville, where the fair commenced on the 28th. There we met many and dear friends, for it was in this (Shelby) county that we were born and raised. It was here that we first took lessons in beeculture, in 1853. It was in that year that we hung (not our harps upon the willows, but) sticks in our box hive, for the bees to build to. This was several years before we ever saw or heard of a movable comb hive. We found that some of our old acquaintances and friends were beekeepers, and several of them on a large scale. Among them, we found Mr. Shelby Vannetta, Mr. Isaac Payne, and Mr. Jos. Allen. In fact, there has been a general waking up there, and you will find but few with their bees in the old box hives. Mr. S. Glass and Capt. Stuart are two of the largest apiculturists in that county. Their colonies are numbered by the hundred. After spending a very pleasant week, indeed, and talking bee and bee hive to our satisfaction, we hastened on to Franklin, Simpson county, the fair commencing there September 5th. Franklin is a beautiful town of three thousand inhabitants, on the Louisville and Nashville railroad, 135 miles south of Louisville, and 50 miles north of Nashville. Here we found some live beekeepers. Among them, Mr. T. Proctor, Mr. John Brevard, Mr. J. N. Steele, and many others, too numerous to mention. And whom, besides, do you think we should meet here, but Dr. T. B. Hamlin, of Edgefield Junction, Tennessee. The Doctor had his hive on exhibition—the Langstroth. Remember, the Doctor owns the State of Tennessee in that hive, and Simpson county being a border county, we of course met numbers of Tennessee beekeepers at this fair. The Doctor and ourself talked bee and bee hive for a whole day, and when the committee on bee hives came around, you ought to have seen us in our shirt sleeves, spreading ourselves. But the Doctor could not be prevailed on to stay more than one day. We will here state that we examined the apiaries of the gentlemen before mentioned, and found all in fair condition, considering the early frost and the dry weather. We partook freely of the hospitalities of our hosts, Messrs. Proctor, Brevard, and Steele; you may say what you will, about good things, but Kentucky would beat them all. Our appetizer is all right yet. Among the Tennessee beekeepers whom we met, was a Mr. McDonald, from Sumner county. His whole soul is in this great work. After spending a week here, we went back to Louisville, to the fair commencing on the 12th of September. Here we met with many who are interested in bee-culture, some of them on a large scale. Although it was a rainy, bad week, we talked bee well and freely, and think were well paid. Here we met an old acquaintance from Indianapolis, Mr. Wilkerson, with the Wilkerson bee hive, an invention of his own, lately patented. We could not prevail on him to stay more than one day.

From Louisville we went down the Nashville road again, stopping at Bowling Green, in Warren county. This is a flourishing town, of four thousand inhabitants. Here we talked bee early and late, for we found but few whom we could call apiarians. Mr. S. S. Potter, and Mr. A. Simmons, are the largest beekeepers in this county, and are very much interested in bee-culture. We are much indebted to them for courtesies shown to us. As we now had one week between the Bowling Green fair and the Nashville, we spent most of the time at Franklin, Kentucky, interviewing the beekeepers of that section as to the locality being a good one to establish a large apiary, and for the manufacturing of bee hives. We were fully impressed that Franklin is a good location for both purposes, and are now of the opinion, that we will locate there. Should we do so, we will notify the beekeeping public, and still hope to have our old customers, as well as new ones, call on us for both hives and fine stocks, as well as *pure queens* from imported ones.

After spending several days at Franklin, we hastened on to Edgefield Junction, Tennessee, the home of Dr. T. B. Hamlin, the bee-king of the South, and President of the Apiarian Society. The Doctor, *indeed*, remembered us, for we had met at Franklin only two weeks before, besides having met at Indianapolis in December, 1870. We found the Doctor as busy as a bee among his bees. In fact, until late at night, was he feeding his nuclei. Among the new acquaintances formed, was that of Mrs. Hamlin, a most estimable lady, indeed; Mr. Barber and lady. Mr. Barber, the son-in-law of Dr. H., is a Kentuckian; also, Mr. Barnum, partner of Dr. H. in a large nursery, called the Cumberland Nursery; also, Mr. W. E. Ladd, formerly of Newport, (Ky.), but now assisting the Doctor in his apiary. We were sorry, indeed, that Mrs. Ladd was absent in Kentucky on a visit, as we should have liked to make her acquaintance. We also met Mr. Oscar Hamlin, the Doctor's son, and Mr. Shaw, who is employed in the manufacture of hives on a large scale, for the Doctor and Mr. Ladd.

After eating a hearty supper, we talked with Doctor H. and Mr. Ladd about bees for several hours, then retired, resting well; and were up early, and out among the bees. This was, indeed, a busy time with the Doctor and Mr. Ladd. as well as Mr. Barnum, for bees, as well as bee hives and fruit trees, had to be prepared for the fair the coming week.

We will here state that the Tennessee Agricultural Board does something, which very few, if any of our Agricultural Boards do, that is, they give the Apiarian Department some notice, offering premiums on best colony of Italian bees; also on best colony of black bees, on bee hives, on melextractors, on finest ten pounds of comb honey, on finest ten pounds of extracted honey, extracted by melextractor; also premium for the best general display of honey. The Apiarian Department was placed in charge of the Tennessee Apiarian Society, with Dr. T. B. Hamlin and Mr. J. A. Fisher as superintendents.

We remained with the Doctor until the following week, giving our aid to get all ready for the fair. We had a look into fifty or more of the Doctor's fine colonies, and were shown very many fine queens, many of which were imported. The Doctor has three hundred colonies of fine pure Italians, and his arrangements for rearing queens are excellent. He can be called the bee-king of the South. We found Mr. Ladd an apiculturist, indeed, well posted in every department, and ready at all times to demonstrate what he knows. He has but few equals within the sphere of our acquaintance. All things being in readiness, we started for the fair. On arriving, we found the Apiarian Department well represented in bees, bee hives, and honey; but there was only one extractor on exhibition. The Adair hive was represented by Dr. Davis; the Logan hive, by Mr. ———; the Tennessee improved, by Mr. J. C. Owen; the Langstroth, by Dr. T. B. Hamlin, W. E. Ladd, Mr. Barnum, and others; and the Triumph, by your humble servant, W. R. King. Dr. Hamlin had two full colonies of Italians, besides several nuclei, on exhibition. He took the premium on the best colony of Italian bees; also on best general display of honey (no competition). Dr. Davis took the premium on best colony of black bees, in Adair hive, there being one other, in old box hive. Mr. J. A. Fisher took premium on extracted honey. It was fine, indeed. Mr. Stuart, on best comb honey. Dr. Hamlin, President of the Tennessee Apiarian Society, and superintendent of this Department, took the premium on *his hive*, the Langstroth. As I was a stranger, and a long way from home, I kept quiet, and looked on, listening to outsiders; and it was the general talk that the Tennessee Apiarian Society did not intend that the Langstroth hive should be beat, for their President owns the State of Tennessee for that hive. Besides, they had adopted it as a Society, and they mean to hold on to it, no matter what better hive may be shown them. We say this was the general talk outside of the Tennessee Apiarian Society. We were advised, before we went to Nashville, not to enter our hive for exhibition; that there would be no show for us. But we were not to be bluffed off in this manner, for we have attended, in person, this fall and last, fourteen fairs with our hive, and it has also been exhibited at over twenty other fairs, by other parties, and it was never beaten before; consequently, we were not afraid to exhibit anywhere where we would find unbiassed, competent men to act as committee men. We will soon prepare a description of our hive for the American Bee Journal, to be illustrated by cuts, so as to let it come fully before the beekeeping public.

Fearing that we are wearying you, Mr. Editor, we will close by promising to send you shortly an article on non-flying fertilization, according to our plan, which has proved successful the past season, in every instance except one. We will also tell you something about N. C. Mitchell's method of fertilizing queen bees in confinement, and *where he got his plan.*

W. R. King.

Milton, Ky., Oct. 24, 1871.

[For the American Bee Journal.]

Does the Queen Bee Lay Eggs in the Queen Cell?

On page 85, of the October No. of the Journal, the editor asks the above question of American beekeepers. As I came so near seeing that important action on one occasion, I will relate what I have already told my friend Gallup, at the time of the Indianapolis Convention.

Two years ago, in the latter part of May, I examined every one of my colonies, for the purpose of clipping the wings of the queens that had not already been so treated on some former occasion. I had carefully examined every comb, but could not find the queen of the second hive I opened. I therefore renewed the search. On taking out the second frame, I noticed a queen cell of nearly full size, built on the front edge of the comb, and there also I observed the queen withdrawing her body from that very cell.

As I could not look into the cell without difficulty, I opened it and found on its bottom an egg, fastened in the same manner as we find them in worker and drone cells. Whether this cell contained an egg before the queen inserted her abdomen into it, or not, I did not know, but could not imagine for what purpose she inserted her body, if it was not with the design of depositing an egg therein.

In former days, I watched hives with queen cells very closely, when the cells were sufficiently advanced for the reception of an egg, but I never before noticed a queen near a queen cell—usually finding the first eggs on my examinations in the morning. These eggs I found fastened on the bottom of the cells, the same as in other cells, and I was then satisfied that only the queen herself could do it. A. GRIMM.

Jefferson, October, 1871.

☞ It is known that, under certain conditions. numerous queen cells are sometimes started in colonies, and again deserted and abandoned, in their rudimental state, by the workers—having been advanced only so far as to have received, at most, a form resembling somewhat that of a miniature acorn cup. It is also known, that such queen cells as are designed by the workers to be used, from first to last, for queen production, undergo various modifications in the course of construction, and even after they have been capped over. Mr. Grimm's observations, given above, render it almost absolutely certain that the queen does deposit the egg in the royal cell—a point about which there has heretofore been much doubt and controversy; but which, in view of his statement, can hardly be regarded as debatable any longer.

But it now becomes desirable to ascertain the precise form of the royal cell—particularly the diameter of its mouth, at the time the queen makes the deposit. We conceive the size and form of these cells must, at that time, so greatly to resemble those of the common worker cells, as to induce or *tempt*—if we might not rather say, *mislead*, the queen to use them as egg depositories. For it does appear altogether unlikely that a queen, even when perambulating the comb in quest of empty cells, would be led or misled to lay an egg in a wide-mouthed cell, placed so differently from any which she had been accustomed to see, and so little resembling them. It hence seems probable that among the various changes and modifications which these cells are known to undergo, from their foundation to their *ultimate*—not their first *apparent*—completion, there is one which deceives the queen, or misleads her to take it to be a common worker cell, though somewhat oddly placed. And, further, that this modification is of such nature as to enable the queen, when ovipositing in such cell, to impregnate the egg, which it would seem impossible for her to effect in a wide-mouthed cell, such as the royal cell is usually conceived to be. We cannot suppose, either, that a queen, consciously and voluntarily, lays an egg in the royal cell, for the purpose of initiating the production of a rival or a natural enemy, to which she is known to bear instinctive implacable hatred, and for the destruction of which from—or even prior to—its birth, her strenuous efforts are exerted and directed.

At all events, there remains a mystery here, to the elucidation of which close observation and patient watching, if not "happy accident," may lead. That a queen can distinguish at least between cells of different size, is evident from her careful avoidance of drone cells at certain periods; and as it is not supposable that she designedly selects or elects a cell for the purpose of depositing therein an egg, destined to produce her deadly natural foe, is it not more probable that she is deceived into doing so, by strategy on the part of the workers? and that the same strategy secures, at the same time, another primary object of the arrangement and operation—the impregnation of the egg deposited? We may, ere long, have occasion to recur to this subject, and discuss it more fully in its various aspects and bearings.—[ED.

[For the American Bee Journal.]

Improvement of Bees.

Can bees be improved? This question is not without its importance to the beekeepers of this country. But so little has been done in the way of effort in that direction, that we are left without the light of any very extended experience to guide us. Yet there are facts within our reach which will aid us in coming to a correct conclusion in regard to it.

There is a marked difference in bees. The difference in the bees of the northern and southern portions of the United States—the black bees of the north and the gray bees of the south—is well known. In this region we have both, with various shades of mixture. A close observer of our native bees cannot fail to notice differences in size, color, temper, disposition to gather honey, and disposition to rob. The same is true, even in greater measure, of the Italian bees. They not only differ widely from the black and the gray bees of this country, but they differ among themselves. They differ in size, in shape, and in color, and marking. They differ also in disposition. While they are, generally, more tractable than the natives, some are more irritable than others. These and other differences seem not to arise from admixture of foreign blood, but from a tendency to vary from the primitive type. And this tendency I believe to be greater in the Italian than in the native bees.

Another important fact is, some queens are far more prolific than others. And if we judge by analogy, we will be compelled to believe that superior fecundity is transmissible. It is so in the case of all our domestic animals, and among all other organized beings, as far as we have had opportunity of accurate observation.

It is a fact worthy of consideration, that the queen impresses her own character upon her progeny more strongly than the drone does. The progeny of a pure Italian queen, which has mated with a black drone, show much more of the qualities of the Italian than of the black race; while the progeny of a black queen and an Italian drone, resemble the black bees more than the Italian.

From the above-named facts, it seems reasonable that by careful selection, bees, as well as any other kind of stock, may be greatly improved.

And if we had no race of bees superior to our native blacks, which we certainly have in the Italian race, it would pay to give attention to their improvement. For this purpose we must select our very best stock to breed from, rejecting all that show inferior qualities. In a few years, by this process, our native bees could, undoubtedly, be made far superior to what they now are. But it is wise to begin with the best. The Italian bees are, in nearly all respects, superior to the natives, and inferior to them in nothing; and with the greater tendency to vary from the ancestral type, they present the most promising field for efforts at improvement. In order to make improvement, the beekeeper must familiarize himself with the special qualities of the several stocks in his apiary, and constantly select the best from which to raise queens. If we could choose the fathers of our bees, as well as their mothers, improvement might be more rapid; but, I have come to the conclusion that fertilization in confinement is impracticable. It may be accomplished now and then; but the failures will be so many, that it will not pay to attempt it. Most of the reported cases have been, in my judgment, failures. Queens and workers are so nearly of the same thickness, that no reliance can be placed on so arranging the place of entrance and exit, that the workers can pass and the queen cannot. Let a wing of the young queen be clipped, and then if she becomes fertile, we will know that she did not fly abroad and meet a drone in the air.

As far as my observation has extended, there seems to be no hope of improving our bees, by crossing the Italian and native races. The progeny of a pure Italian and a black drone are nearly as good as pure Italians; but any further cross is altogether undesirable, unless it be a further infusion of Italian blood. I have quite as many bees of mixed blood as I want. I have destroyed all queens that will not produce pure Italian drones, and will be careful not to have any more of that kind. M. MAHIN.

New Castle, Ind., Oct. 31, 1871.

[For the American Bee Journal.]

A Bee Orchard.

MR. EDITOR:—I am sorry indeed to see our friend Novice suffering from paralysis. Nobody's contributions would be more sorrowfully missed. May his sickness be of short duration.

The following would be my plan in planting a linden orchard. I would buy the quantity of trees needed from a seller who takes them from the woods when about an inch in diameter, with good roots; and set them about twenty-five feet apart. If I could not do this, I would contract for the quantity wanted with a nursery man, to be sprouted from slips or cuttings, in a hot house during winter, to be set out in the spring.

Linden is a soft wood, and will readily grow from slips. This will save a great amount of care and labor, indispensable when raised from seed. I have planted trees (linden) taken from the woods, which lived and did well, when dogwood and rock maple died. I have also a European linden tree, which though a handsome shaped tree, does not grow near as fast as its American sister (*Tilia Americana*). When in Germany a few years ago I saw a linden tree, two hundred years old, as large as an American sycamore. How I wished that I had a few dozen of them in the new fatherland.

Setting the lindens at twenty-five feet a part, I would set the German willows (Saalweide) at twelve feet. They also grow from cuttings, in wet ground. I think I saw some in Mr. Langstroth's yard. I also have two of them. Englishmen call them palm trees. They are very ornamental, and furnish the earliest pollen in the spring. Dzierzon recommends them highly.

Lastly I would fence in the whole with the Japanese quince. They are strong, and can be early trained to turn stock. With their scarlet blossoms they present a most beautiful appearance in the spring, and also furnish early food for the bees. Nurserymen would supply them at reasonably cheap rates, or contract by the quantity. They are to be grown from slips also, in hot beds.

Linden trees prefer low good ground. I would drain, subsoil, plough deep, dig the holes four feet cubic, and fill with rich ground, but no fresh manure.

One nurseryman of our town offered to sprout quince for me last year, when I intended to buy some, but did not get ready.

I repeat my best wishes for Novice.

P. HULLMAN.

Terre Haute, Ind., 1871.

[For the American Bee Journal.]

The Melextractor.

MR. EDITOR:—I receive many inquiries as to my opinion of the benefits to be derived from the use of the melextractor. The questions are something like the following: When is it proper to commence its use? Is it best to operate in or outside of an enclosure? How are we to get the bees off the combs, when we wish to extract the honey from them? Will the unsealed brood be thrown out with the honey? And whose extractor is best?

As to the benefits to be derived from its use, I will state that had I not used it during the past season, my honey yield would have been almost an entire failure. My bees seemed determined to store honey nowhere except in the breeding chamber. So much was that the case, that in several instances they almost crowded their queens out of space in which to lay eggs, before I could reach them with the extractor. Yet in very few instances was there any disposition manifested to enter the surplus boxes, whether situated on the top of the hive, or at the side. This was the case even where I had furnished them boxes with combs, as an inducement for them to enter them. My apiary was mostly used for queen-breeding, so that I had no fair means of determining the amount of honey I might have procured, and I devoted my bees entirely to honey gathering. I had near twenty stocks which I used mostly, though not exclusively, for this latter purpose, and extracted from their combs a fraction over two forty-four gallon barrels of linden and white clover honey. Had the honey yield been propitious from the latter, I feel confident that my yield would have been doubled. I give the extractor credit for at least three-fourths of the honey I obtained during the past season.

From the foregoing considerations, namely, that I found my bees unduly slow, and in nearly every instance almost wholly unwilling to work in boxes, I recommend the use of the melextractor to the beekeepers of the country, as the best means of securing the largest yield of honey possible. True, it will be a little more difficult to sell it, until the beekeeper establishes for himself and his honey an honorable reputation. In some instances this is already accomplished, and such honey sells rapidly and at fair prices, so far as facts have come to my knowledge.

I commenced extracting honey on the 10th of June, and left off near the 12th of July. From this it will be seen and understood that it is proper to begin to extract honey as soon as the combs begin to get heavy, and to leave off whenever there are indications that the honey yield is closing up. I did not wait for the bees to cap the honey over in the combs before extracting it, as with us the season was dry, and the honey, as a natural consequence, was not thinned down to the consistence that would render it liable to sour. Had this been the case, I should probably have been more tardy about extracting it.

At first I operated in my cellar, where I was not exposed to bees, and the temperature was quite cool and pleasant, after I had got quite warm in opening hives. But as I could not take the combs from more than one hive at a time, I found myself exposed to such a succession of sudden changes from hot to cold and the reverse, in going to and from the cellar, as was about to make me sick. I therefore moved my quarters to a room above ground, where I operated with closed doors. I find that to operate in the open air causes more or less bees to follow up the machine and prove a great source of annoyance, besides many of them get drowned in the honey.

I got the adhering bees off the combs partly by gently shaking the comb either directly over the breeding chamber, or at the entrance of the hive. The remainder I brushed off with a small hard broom, made by tying six or more tops of broom corn together with a piece of wrapping twine. I was of course careful to see that the queen got safely back inside of her hive in each case. I found it necessary to run the extractor with care, in cases where I was extracting honey from combs containing unsealed brood, as many larvæ were thrown out when the machine was run at a high speed. Persons using the extractor will, in a short time, learn about what speed to give the machine.

I used Gray & Winder's extractor, and found it to be a most excellent machine. It is geared, which requires much less labor in getting up the necessary speed. It does its work well, and is, I think, decidedly the easiest to clean of any machine I have yet seen. It is also constructed in such a manner as to entirely prevent any of the lubricating grease from getting into the honey. The honey, on being extracted from the combs, runs out of the machine into a vessel underneath the can, as soon as the speed is stopped and the extractor brought to a stand still.

I make it a custom to run the honey through a common meal sieve before putting it into permanent receptacles. By this means very small particles of comb or cocoons are separated from the honey, and it is left in a perfectly pure state.

In conclusion, I would say in regard to extractors, that I feel a delicacy in recommending any particular machine in an article like this. Yet I feel in duty bound to say that unless an extractor is geared it must require much more labor to bring its speed up to the proper point for throwing out thick honey than one having two wheels and a crank attached. I have not seen all the geared machines. There may be several good ones, but in my opinion, one that is made so as entirely to prevent the honey from coming in contact with wood is preferable to one that does not possess this quality. I have already stated that I put my honey into large barrels, but I do not like the plan in case I wish to sell in quantities to suit the grocers in our cities, as they will not in many cases purchase as much as a barrel at one time. I would therefore recommend it to be put into ten gallon casks, and it will sell readily in most cases. Some, however, prefer putting it into two or four pound jars, with a handsome label attached, giving an account of the kind of honey the jar contains. This, I believe, is the manner in which Novice puts up honey for market.

I hope to be pardoned for making this article so long.

G. Bohrer.

Alexandria, Ind.

[For the American Bee Journal.]

A Colony of Bees without Brood, On September 22d.

A half bred Italian colony was deprived of its queen, and supplied with a queen cell from pure stock. When the time came round that young workers should have hatched, that colony was examined, and neither any brood nor any hatched workers were found. Only five eggs were found at the bottom of cells in the middle worker comb. I concluded that I had one of those queens whose eggs do not hatch, and immediately removed her to a nucleus, for preservation and experiment—knowing that the bees in the colony thus unqueened would hatch those eggs, if they were hatchable.

A week later the colony was again examined, and to my surprise, a queen cell was found built over each of those cells with the eggs, and several of them were already sealed. It was evident that the bees had stopped breeding at the beginning of the month of September, on account probably of the very dry weather.

I have still to mention that the queen referred to had supplied fully one-half of the cells of a comb on the fourth of September; and it was therefore not her fault that the bees had raised no brood. I subsequently re-introduced her to her colony.

In this locality, bees do not usually stop breeding before the end of September, and the queens continue to lay a few eggs even through the month of October. From these the workers will raise queens, if deprived of their queen intentionally or accidentally; and in a number of cases I lost valuable queens, which had been introduced and accepted, simply because I neglected to destroy those queen cells.

A. GRIMM.

Jefferson, October, 1871.

[For the American Bee Journal.]

Non-Hatching Eggs.

MR. EDITOR :—Many cases are now reported of queen bees laying eggs that do not hatch. About a dozen such have come under my own observation or actual knowledge. Then, too, other nearly analogous phenomena have been noticed—namely, of non-laying queens. I can report one such case myself. About the middle of August, I came to one of my hives, intending to remove the surplus honey, for extraction by machine; but to my surprise found no brood of any grade, nor any eggs. That hive had given me a natural swarm, but was still well populated, though it soon proved to be queenless. I put in a fertile queen, caged between the combs. Forty-eight hours afterwards I found the queen dead. I then inserted a queen cell, and next day found that cut out and destroyed. The hive was then left in this condition several weeks, when I made a close inspection. The hive was no longer so well populated, but I found a nice yellow queen, bred from hybrid brood, and bearing all the signs of being a prolific queen. Nevertheless I saw not a single egg in the cells. I killed that queen at once and tried to introduce another, but again without success.

A few days after this, I opened a strong nucleus, to examine the expected just hatching young bees, as the queen had been marked in due time as impregnated. But no brood in any stage, nor eggs, could I see. The queen was a splendid looking one, and the workers treated her with the usual tokens of respect. What could have been the matter with her, that she laid no eggs at all? A similar case came under the observation of Mr. Adam Grimm.

The honey season here was cut short by drouth, and little honey was stored after the basswood bloom was over. A few hives filled small boxes with thistle honey. We had no buckwheat blossoms, nor any other fall pasturage, such as we had last year.

I am tired of the box honey business as my hundred colonies and their eighty-four swarms yielded me only two thousand (2000) pounds of box honey; and had it not been for honey-slinger aiding me to take four thousand (4000) pounds more of extracted honey from the main hives, I should have had a small harvest. But the bodies of the hives were so filled with honey, that I had to take from fifteen to twenty-five pounds from every hive—still leaving from twenty to twenty-five pounds of honey, per hive, for the bees to winter on.

If the next season prove to be as favorable as the last two were, I shall put the honey-slinger in operation earlier, and thereby double or treble my profits.

W. WOLF.

Jefferson, Wis., Oct. 5, 1871.

[For the American Bee Journal.]

How to utilize Wax.

Beeswax is quoted pretty regularly in the price currents, as worth thirty-five to forty cents per pound. This means in large cakes of pure wax weighing several pounds a piece.

This price would hardly pay a man for the trouble of getting it out, if he had anything else to do. A ton of iron may be worth thirty or forty dollars; but converted into steel, and made up into needles, it would be worth probably $200,000.

On a small scale, beeswax may be similarly increased in value and made worth much more than forty cents per pound, simply by converting it into small cakes of a size such as every woman wants in her work basket. Looking about the house the other evening for a mould of suitable size, I found a dozen small glass salt cellars, having a cavity about an inch in diameter and three-quarters of an inch deep, which I immediately made use of—casting nearly two hundred small cakes of wax, weighing about sixty to the pound. They would no doubt retail readily at five cents a piece, or three dollars per pound—an advance of *six hundred per cent.*

They can be cast and cooled rapidly, and the moulds used over and over again, care being taken to grease them properly before each casting.

How can a winter's evening be spent more profitably than in making up a few hundred such cakes of beeswax?

R. BICKFORD.

Seneca Falls, N. Y., Nov. 1, 1871.

☞ We have known beeswax to be thus "utilized" more than twenty years ago, and for the same purpose exactly, though to much greater profit, and by means too of precisely the identical salt cellar moulds. The only difference that we are aware of, consisted in the employment of bleached wax, costing then about eighty cents per pound, and the insertion of a splendid suspensory riband in each cake. Though these cakes were then cast either plain white or of various colors, we presume it was the riband "improvement" that added so largely to the commercial value of the much admired little work basket appendage, as made it find a ready market at ten or twelve cents, each; or at the rate of six or eight dollars per pound.

Thus it appears that if friend Bickford, or any one else, had obtained a patent for this invention. Mr. A. B. C., or Mr. O. P. Q., might come forward, contesting his claim to the originality of the "new manufacture," and show that he could at most have only the merit of being the mere *re-intro·ucer* of the convenient little ante-frizzler. Alas, there is positively nothing new under the sun, nowadays. We knew an old lady—a most excellent good-natured and kind-hearted lady, we remember she was—who having no gloves, always used her apron to protect her hands from the roughness of the brush-handle. Yet not long since a shrewd Yankee, with an eye to business, contrived a neat though somewhat fantastic pinafore for the same purpose; and sought to get a patent for it as "a new and useful invention!" What new thing comes next? Nobody, in these latter days *inv-nts* anything—that's a settled if not conceded point. They merely *introduce* new "notions;" and *queer* notions some of them are found to be on inspection.

But—*rev'nons à nos moutons*—we have no doubt that the suggested use of wax, the by-product of the honey bee, could still be made with advantage and profit—supplying to the busy seamstresses of every neighborhood relief from a daily felt want. in a neat and acceptable shape, to the manufacture of which they would gladly extend a liberal patronage.—[Ed.

[For the American Bee Journal.]

Remarks on Various Topics.

Mr. Editor:—It is about time for me to renew my subscription for the seventh volume of the Journal; and while writing I will give you some facts pertaining to beeculture—the honey season in this locality; the raising of queens, and how I introduce them to queenless colonies, and how I obtain queen cells.

TO OBTAIN GOOD QUEEN CELLS.

I unqueen a strong colony. In this way I get cells more natural, and the best cells are always at the bottom or lower edge of the comb, or in some aperture. These cells are always longer and more fully developed than those on the face of the comb. Now here, friend Price has gone down on artificially raised queens like a thousand of brick; yet I have fifty (50) colonies of bees, all of which have artificially raised queens, and some of these are three years old. In selecting my cells for breeding purposes, I use only the largest and best ones. There will be some found not much larger than drone cells. All such I throw away. Perhaps it is here that friend Price has made his mistake, causing him to condemn artificially raised queens. Possibly, too, that revolvable hive which he uses addles his queens. When I first commenced breeding Italian queens I used all the cells I could get, but soon found that to be wrong, as I would always get a lot of small short-lived queens. After discovering my mistake, I used only the larg st and most natural shaped cells, and the queens I now raise are long-lived and handsome.

A SINGULAR CIRCUMSTANCE.

I have to relate an occurrence in my apiary, this season, that is rare, namely: A colony that builds queen cells, and the old queen still remaining in the hive. I opened this hive in April and found sealed queen cells, and the queen in the hive without a wing. I began to suspect the bees were about to supersede her, though there was plenty of brood in all stages, from eggs to hatching bees. She is a queen I have been breeding from these three seasons. I paid ten dollars for her, when I bought her from Mr. Langstroth. I removed the queen cells, and introduced them in nuclei. In a few days, opening the hive again, I found more queen cells. and removed them also. The bees kept on building queen cells, and I kept on removing them as fast as they were sealed up. They have queen cells to-day, and the old queen remains in the hive up to this time. During this period I missed removing one cell, which hatched, and the young queen was killed and dragged out of the hive. This is the first case of this kind I have had; others, perhaps, have had the like,—Mr. Langstroth, possibly.

INTRODUCING QUEENS.

There have been a great many different opinions with regard to introducing queens. Queens may be safely introduced at certain times, in almost any way. Near swarming time, or when bees are gathering honey rapidly, queens will be more readily received.

I have introduced queens in different ways, and under different circumstances. When I first began to raise Italian queens, and introduced them to black colonies, I was led to suspect that the bees had to remain without a queen six hours, and first become conscious of the loss of their queen, before another could be safely introduced. But I have since found that to be unnecessary.

In making artificial swarms, before closing up the hive, after removing the old queen, I have introduced the new queen in the old hive, sometimes by sprinkling with sugar water scented with peppermint; others by caging for forty-eight hours; and found them all well received. Others I have left in the cage three days and liberated them among the bees, after daubing them with honey. These were also well received.

I find it best to make your swarms, and let the old hive remain till about sun-down the same day you make your swarm, or say six hours. By that time the most of the old workers will leave the old hive and return to the new hive on the old stand. I then introduce the queen, first sprinkling the bees with sugar water scented with peppermint. I find they are almost invariably well received, and the old hive remains without a queen only a short time.

I have introduced queens just hatched, and found it could be done without any trouble. When I have introduced a queen several days old, the bees would at once confine and destroy her. I have had the bees to confine queens after they have been liberated two days and commenced laying. It appears that the bees get alarmed by the opening of the hive and clinch the queen and would kill her if not liberated. I find it is best to let a hive remain undisturbed ten days after liberating the new queen; though this is not always necessary.

These are facts that have come under my own notice. Facts are what we want—no theory. Every man should write just what he knows to be facts, and nothing more. We want no guess work, that would be likely to lead new beginners astray. Now for

THE HONEY SEASON.

In the spring the most of the colonies were not very well supplied with honey, owing to the poor honey season the previous year. And then the spring itself was unfavorable. By the time the linden trees blossomed the honey in the hives was nearly all exhausted; but the blossoms coming two weeks earlier than common, just saved our bees from starvation. The lindens gave us the best yield of honey this season that they have for many years, and this caused the bees to swarm very liberally; and about that time I began to expect a great honey yield this season. But after that honey harvest was past, bees gathered very little honey till the present time, owing to the dry hot weather. Now we are having frequent showers, and the bees have commenced storing honey quite briskly. I look yet for a liberal yield of honey, provided the weather keeps warm, with frequent showers. I must not forget to tell you about one of my colonies, how it gathered honey at the time of the linden blossoms. In ten days it filled a Langstroth hive, ten frames, and two twenty (20) pound boxes.

The honey season has closed with a fair yield—the best we have had for several years.

MR. PHELPS' APIARY.

I visited Mr. Phelps' apiary a few days ago. He lives about twelve miles west of me, on Skunk river. He started last spring with some forty colonies; and the result of his operations is that he has increased his number to upwards of eighty stocks. He told me that he had sold eighteen hundred (1800) pounds of honey, and has now on hand, in his beehouse, two tons of honey in the comb in frames, besides several barrels of extracted honey.

My bees are in fine condition to go into winter quarters. J. W. SEAY.

Monroe, Iowa, Oct. 29, 1871.

[For the American Bee Journal.]

Some Interesting Items.

RENEWAL OF SUBSCRIPTION.

MR. EDITOR:—Enclosed please receive two dollars, for volume seventh of the American Bee Journal. I would have sent it long since, but wished to give you at the same time my experience in wintering bees and introducing queens.

WINTERING BEES.

I have tried wintering in the cellar for three winters, and my cellar is a dry one; but, invariably the combs became mouldy, and the bees filthy from cellar confinement; while those wintered on their summer stands, were without exception found to be in good trim in the spring.

I never try to winter any colony not supplied with as much as thirty-five (35) pounds of honey, clear of the hive that contains them. This is easily ascertained by knowing the general weight of the hives before putting a swarm in.

My plan for wintering on their summer stands is simple. I use the Langstroth hives—setting them on several pieces of scantling, two by four inches, placing the front piece flat and the rear piece edgewise, and putting the hives on them, facing the south or southeast. I then drive two pieces (say a lath cut in the centre) on the west side, near the corners of the hive, and on the east and rear the same way, leaving the front open. Next pack in oat straw (or any other straw, or hay) tight between those stakes and the hive, after having first removed the slats from the honey board, and covering the honey board with carpet or any other cloth, to protect the bees against cold and give them upward ventilation. A strong swarm protected in this way, would stand a "Siberian winter."

INTRODUCING QUEENS.

My plan for introducing queens has never failed when fully carried out. In the first place, I remove the queen I wish to supersede, having the queen that I wish to introduce ready in a wire cage, with some half dozen workers of the colony from which she was taken. Then insert the cage between the frames, having the paper plug of the cage so tight that the bees cannot dig her out. Use rotten wood smoke freely, from first to last. Just before closing the hive sprinkle the whole swarm with a solution of sugar in water, with plenty of grated nutmeg to give it scent. Let the hive remain forty-eight hours without further disturbance; at the end of which time give them another thorough smoking, so as to subdue them well. Then open the hive, blow in smoke from the top, sprinkle well with sweetened nutmeg water, making sure that the queen has been wetted with the solution. Now remove the plug from the cage, cover up again, and let the queen come out at pleasure. In five or six days, or sometimes on the third day after liberating the queen, examine the hive for any appearance of queen cells, and destroy them if any are found.

I do not claim this plan as original with me, but I do claim it to be always successful.

THE YIELD OF HONEY.

The honey season closed here about the first of July, and the bees did nothing since till some time in September, when there was a revival of pasturage on which the bees worked about two weeks. The honey then gathered was obtained mostly from heartsease,* the yield from which was abundant here.

*Probably the *Viola striata*, or pale violet, which is common in some sections westward, and blooms from April to October, yielding more honey than any other variety.—[ED.

In all, my colonies have made about seventy-five (75) pounds surplus, each, this season. The drought was too severe and protracted for much honey gathering.

THE ITALIANS, AND THE BEE JOURNAL.

I am fully satisfied of the superiority of the pure Italian bees, over the common black bees. Also, satisfied of the successful career of the American Bee Journal. More anon.

H. W. WIXOM.

Mendota, Illinois, Oct. 9, 1871.

[For the American Bee Journal.]

Large Surplus Honey Boxes, or Small?

MR. EDITOR:—I have been a reader of your valuable Journal for several years, but never attempted to contribute anything to its columns. As writing for the public is out of my line of business, I considered myself excused from that duty. Yet, after reading "SCIENTIFIC'S" article, on page 59 of the December number, I thought I would comply with his wish, and give my experience with large boxes and small. I may have to do a little axe-grinding, Mr. Editor, before I get through, but will bear on as lightly as possible.

My first experience was with large boxes, holding from twenty to forty pounds each, placed on the frames without honey boards. By this method I could get a satisfactory yield of surplus honey, but I found it would not bear transportation as well or sell as readily as in smaller boxes.

Next I tried six-pound boxes, and from that down to three pounds, with one comb. The three pound boxes I found would sell in the New York market five cents per pound higher than four to six pound boxes. But, after using the three pound boxes two years, I learned that bees would not work to as good advantage in them as in the larger boxes. Then I decided to use the large boxes again, thinking I should get enough more honey to balance the difference in price; but when it came to selling time again, I had more trouble than ever to dispose of the large boxes.

This convinced me that we must combine the advantages of both large boxes and small, if possible. This I tried to do, by using the small frames, which secured the advantage of the large boxes in full, but that of the small ones only in part, for the frames will not handle or ship as well as the small boxes, because the combs in the frames will vary in thickness, so that they will not pack promiscuously without marring the combs.

Not satisfied with this method, I experimented still further, and at last hit upon a plan of arranging small boxes, so that they secure the advantages of both sizes so near to perfection that after three years' trial, I am satisfied to use them altogether. Bees will store as much honey in them proportionally as in large boxes, and the combs are all built of the same thickness and perfectly straight, one in each box, so that they can be packed promiscuously in any sized package for shipping, and the combs cannot touch each other. If desired, each comb can be encased in glass, making a nice two pound box that will sell for five to seven cents per pound more than five or six pound boxes would. Last year I sold in this shape eleven hundred and sixty (1160) pounds, in the Oswego market, at seven cents per pound above the market for other styles.

These boxes are arranged in rows, in a shallow case secured by keys, so that the whole set can be handled as one box. The outside boxes are closed by glass. A tin partition is placed between each box, leaving a half inch open space on each side for communication. Finished combs can be easily removed, and empty boxes put in their place at any time.

This article is getting longer than I intended, so that I will leave further description of the improved boxes till I get cuts. They were patented November 22d, 1870.

One word to Novice. We have the basswood orchard fever here also, and would like to hear more on the subject in the Journal. Mr. A. Battles, of Girard, Penna., advertises tulip and linwood trees at two dollars per thousand. That is cheaper than we can raise them here from the seed.

GEO. T. WHEELER.

Mexico, N. Y.

[For the American Bee Journal.]

To Prevent Bees Robbing.

DEAR JOURNAL:—I have read of and tried the use of gum camphor and kerosene oil, to prevent bees robbing, and find they have good qualities for the purpose. I have also read of a piece of glass being stood before the entrance of the hive being robbed, for the robber bees to strike their heads against it, in their hasty flight. But the only *complete* and *easy* remedy I know of, consists in making a little ante-room in front of the hive being robbed, through which the bees must pass before they enter the main hive. This has proved effectual; for while the bees belonging to the hive have no fears in passing the ante-room, the robber bees by no means like the idea of being caught in such a trap. Like any other robber, they want a fine easy chance of retreat. To be cornered up, with only a small aperture to escape by, is contrary to their common sense; and so they seem to be about as much afraid of entering this *ante-room*, as a bear is of putting his foot in a trap. If, however, the strange bees have got so full possession of a hive, that they come with a rush, like soldiers storming a fort, it may be necessary to first break the jam by other means. This can be done by covering the hive with a sheet, and tucking it under the bottom board. The bees can then come out of the hive, crawl around, get the air, and go back when they please. They cannot, however, fly away; and robber bees coming can see nothing but a sheet—an undesirable object for them to hang round. The force of the attack will probably be broken in two days, when the sheet may be removed, and the ante-room applied in the morning. The bees in a hive robbed being usually small in numbers, it may be well, on the first morning after the sheet has been removed, to close the ante-room entirely, so that there can be no entrance from without, until the bees from the hive have filled said room. Then it may be opened a little, and all will be right. To make the ante-room, take two blocks, from one to two inches thick, and about five inches square, and place a corner of each against the hive on each side of the entrance; bring the other two corners nearly together, then cover them on top, and the work is done. The bottom board should extend beyond these blocks, so as to give the bees an alighting board. The shape of the blocks will be a guide to them, to enter at the right place. As the danger of fighting decreases, these blocks may be put further apart, till removed altogether.

The above mode of preventing robbing is given by Mr. C. Dadant, in the April number of the Bee Journal, vol. V., page 204, and I consider it of importance enough to be worth republishing. Besides, a correspondent in the last Journal asks for such information. I tried the above with three hives, that were being robbed last spring, in an apiary of twenty-nine hives, and it worked to my satisfaction. Last fall, in preparing for winter, while there was no honey to be gathered, and bees consequently most inclined to rob. I have given to a hive a quart of sugar syrup in the morning, while the weather was warm, and no harm followed; and this fall, while there was no honey to be gathered, my bees *threatened* to fight, but something in the form of the above house, only with a side opening, effectually prevented harm, as robber bees do not like to be cornered.

Mr. Editor, I wish through the Journal to request correspondents of the same, *not to war on each other*, for we are *brethren*. Whatever is brought to light as an improvement in agriculture, be it patented or otherwise, let us content ourselves with showing what *we know*, for or against it. We are not all *best* suited with any one thing. Any one who thinks he knows something to advance beekeeping, should be encouraged to make it public. We probably have as yet heard from comparatively few of those that take our Journal.

Some have advised having the Journal published semi-monthly, at double price; but I would advise that if all the matter truly important that is written is not published, the Journal be sufficiently enlarged to publish the same, with price to cover expenses.

By the by, where is Mr. J. H. Thomas, of Ontario, whose articles we once so frequently and profitably read? I should be happy, now, as formerly, to hear from him.

The honey season here this year has been so bad that we do not like to talk about it. "*We* have nothing to say." ALONZO BARNARD.

Bangor, Me., Oct. 11, 1871.

It is really disgraceful for such a country as ours to import wax or honey. We ought ourselves to export thousands of tons of each every year.

[For the American Bee Journal.]

Precision Wanted.

MR. EDITOR:—On page 6 of the July number of the Journal, Novice tells us how to make his queen nursery and how to apply, and then adds —"You can thus cage all the queen cells in a hive, without cutting a comb, and when removed your comb is uninjured." I was surprised when I put this and the following together—"and if on the edge of the comb all the better."

I always supposed that Novice gave practical facts and teachings. Well, his teaching might be true, if the cells were but *sparsely situated* on the *edge* of the comb. Yet since they are often huddled together in groups of half a dozen or more, he would have to use the *dissecting knife*, and *remove* or *mutilate* some of them before his cages are applied, unless indeed he cages two or three of them together. Then, again, he did not tell us what to do if a cell is found on each side of the same comb, so that they would be enclosed in the cage when in place. Perhaps the queens will not get to each other through the comb. Let Novice explain himself.

I am sorry that I caused my friend Argo to lose a queen, by not being a little more explicit about how far to remove the nursery away from the hive, when he went to let his queens loose. Little did I think that he would not remember the teachings of the books, and remove them far enough, so that they would not make a mistake about their locality and return to the wrong home, as his queen did. That point should always be guarded against, as some queens may not be as particular as others, to mark their precise location, and hence may vary a few feet, if deceived by a similar mark in two objects; or, as in his case, on finding her home vacated, seek the nearest hive, though dissimilar in appearance, since they are inclined to social and family relations.

Of course we should remember Mr. Argo's warning, for there seem to be exceptions to general rules, and there may be one in reference to his queen returning to the locality from which she had been removed. Still the general rule holds good, if the hives, nuclei, or cages are removed far enough from each other.

JEWELL DAVIS.

Charleston, Ills.

[For the American Bee Journal.]

Observations and Reflections.

MR. EDITOR:—I am much interested in reading your Journal. Of some things mentioned in it by beekeepers I have had experience, and know them to be true. Of others I will not say I know them to be true, neither will I say they are false, for I have no means of testing them to a certainty.

I have the impression from some source that those who have made the honey bee a study, state the queen in her bridal flight mates with only one drone, and never after that mates again. How this is known I am at a loss to learn. If the queen mates on the wing, or otherwise, out of the hive and away from observation, may she not mate with more than one drone? In my experience in raising queens, I could watch their departure from the hive; keep the time of their absence from home; and take notice of their appearance on their return. When returning with the genital organs protruding, filled with a whitish substance, I considered them fertilized, and would watch their movements with care afterwards, taking notice when they commenced laying, &c. Thus I have tested this matter of queen mating until I am satisfied that the same queen leaves the hive on two successive days, and returns with the same evidence of copulation, and after that ceases flying. In other cases I have caught them on their return to the hive with marks of having mated, and clipped their wings; and then, on the following day, at the hour when the drones were on the wing, I saw them come forth also and attempt to fly; and I would pick them up and place them in the hive again, though in some cases I lost them. In one case I had a fine Italian queen, which flew on twelve days in succession, before she came back with marks of having mated. (I had but few drones at the time, and there were then no bees kept within thirty miles of me.) She flew on one or two days after that, but returned without giving evidence of having mated again. She produced a finely colored progeny, but was a very slow breeder and her workers were not very energetic.

From these observations I have come to the conclusion that a queen may mate with more than one drone, though not necessarily always Should she be sufficiently fertilized by one drone, she would not fly a second time. Should she mate with drones of different blood, her workers would show it, and if not sufficiently fertilized, she might show it in her slow breeding.

I do not give this my experience and observation in this matter to upset other theories; but to state them as facts coming under my own observation in bee-culture. And I am anxious to know how any one can state to a certainty that a queen mates with only one drone. I have written more on this subject than I intended, but if it will add my practical knowledge to bee-culture it is well enough.

A. J. SMITH.

Ukiah, California, Sept. 17, 1871.

[For the American Bee Journal.]

Report and Suggestion.

The past season has been rather a poor one, for honey, in this vicinity, owing to a cold wet spring and a dry summer. Forty-two colonies, wintered without loss, in large Langstroth hives, on their summer stands, with honey-boards replaced by cotton batting comforters, gave me only eight swarms (two of which flew away in my absence) and about nine hundred and fifty 950) pounds of surplus honey—two hundred and twenty-five pounds of which was taken by the extractor.

The new swarms were each supplied with one or more frames of sealed honey, taken from the old colonies; and now the forty-eight stocks are in good condition for wintering.—With my present plan for wintering, I have no more fear of losing a colony in winter, than I have of losing one in summer. I have not lost a colony the three past winters.

To prevent robbing, keep the entrance to all weak colonies open only half an inch, till they get strong. Strengthen them up as rapidly as possible, with maturing brood from other colonies. I have had colonies queenless from March till June or July, without their being attacked by robbers, when the entrances were thus closed.

To cure robbing after it has vigorously begun, tack a piece of wire cloth over the front of the portico, and leave it until the bees have nearly done flying at night. Then remove it, allowing the robbers to leave, and the outside members of the robbed colony to re-enter. Replace the wire cloth, if there is fear of the robbing being continued the next day. Give the robbed colony a frame of brood and adhering bees, if it has no queen. If it has a queen, cage her for three days, and give brood and bees, as before.

R. BICKFORD.

Seneca Falls, N. Y., Nov. 1, 1871.

[For the American Bee Journal.]

Report from New Boston, Illinois.

We have sixty Thomas hives; from which we had taken three thousand (3,000) pounds of honey, making an average of fifty (50) pounds to the hive.

Our best hive yielded 175 lbs. Our four best averaged 133½ lbs.; and our fourteen best averaged 94 lbs.

Our honey slinger, made of oak, does its work perfectly, and has not soured, as feared by some, while using it two seasons.

In shipping honey we have concluded that the only safe way is to accompany it and *know to whom* you sell. Nearly a year ago we expressed 590 lbs. to A. F. Moon, Paw Paw, Michigan. It was received somewhat damaged, and sold for us on commission, but we have not yet received the first cent from him.

Paying dear for a lesson, we sent to C. O. Perrine a trial keg of honey, after receiving his price, viz.: from 16 to 18 cents for slung honey, for which we received a trifle over ten cents per pound—saying that it was one-third water. The same honey, drawn from the same barrel, is being used by us and neighbors, and called thick white honey.

J. P. Fortune, of Bloomfield, Iowa, writes us: "I sent one barrel to C. O. Perrine, which has been lost, or at least it never reached its destination."

Yours, for a sweet living,

PALMER BROS.

New Boston, Ills., Oct. 4, 1871.

[For the American Bee Journal.]

Report from Le Roy, Illinois.

Mr. Editor:—I thought it might not be uninteresting to your numerous readers, whilst sending you two dollars to pay for the Journal (which you have been good enough to send me in advance of payment, if I would also send a few notes and observations on the past season.

Bluebirds made their first appearance here on the 4th of March, and robins on the 6th. On the 8th, I set twelve stocks of bees out of the cellar. On the 14th, one stock was robbed. On the 16th, bees gathered pollen from witch hazel. On the 7th of April, bees gathered the first honey from the yellow willow. On the 9th, came the first cherry bloom. On the 10th, bees carried in rye-flour, and the first wren was seen. On the 14th, transferred two stocks, one of which had no queen, but a fertile worker. I gave it a queen from another stock, and they have done well.

The early spring opened finely for bees, until they raised so large a quantity of brood, that, had it not been for very high cold winds during all the time of the blooming of the fruit trees, they certainly would have done well; but their large quantity of brood proved their misfortune. Many of the negligent beekeepers' bees starved out and ran off; and I may class myself with the number; for one of my stocks, finding that they could carry all the honey they had, took it and departed, leaving considerable brood. Thereby hangs a tale. On the third day, my runaway bees returned, bringing with them another swarm. After killing the black queen of this accompanying swarm. I put all of them into the hive which the deserters had left, fed them, and took care of them till they could take care of themselves; and they have since done very well. Here, methinks, I hear some one ask, how I knew that it was my runaway swarm? I knew it, because I have the only Italian bees within ten or fifteen miles of this place; and they had a beautiful Italian queen, whose progeny was hybrid.

Many of the starved out bees came to my house. They seemed to be aware that I knew their wants, and would take care of them. Some would settle, as in regular swarming; and when such had a good-looking queen and a large number of bees, I would take care of them; giving them some empty comb, and feeding them. They have done well in every case. Others that came and would not settle, gave me a good deal of trouble, and injured my bees very much. They would force themselves into every hive in my apiary, seeming to think, as it was certain death to remain out. it could but be death to enter. This kept up such a terrible disturbance and war among my bees, that I could scarcely go among them. I placed cotton balls, saturated with kerosene and camphor gum, at the mouth or entrance of my hives, but all did no good; and when they took to stinging me, I abandoned them to their fate.

About May 10th, bees began to gather considerable honey, and again raised brood. The white clover came in bloom about the 20th, and by the first of June, they were ready and had made preparations to swarm; but owing to the bad weather, very few swarms issued. Owing to the excessive drouth, the white clover blossoms, and all other sources of honey, were cut off about the 25th of June; and robbing became the order of the day among bees. As in the spring, the colonies having a large quantity of brood and large stocks of bees. which all had to live off the then accumulated stores, they became pretty destitute by the time the buckwheat came in, and so weak in numbers when it did come, that we got very little or no surplus honey. Yet our stocks generally are in good condition to go into winter quarters.

I have transferred bees in every week since the middle of April (except in the month of July) to the third week in October. I have lost none, and all have done well.

I have used several kinds of movable frame hives, but I like one of my own improving (on which there is no patent) better than any that I have yet seen or used. There is no patent on it, except on the frames, and for those I give Mr. Langstroth credit. It is a plain, side-opening box, with movable bottom and top, so that I can use one, two, three, or more, for one swarm of bees, if I wish to do so. But as this article has already become too long, I will close. I don't know when the time commenced with my Journal, but please do not let it end.

A. T. Bishop.

Le Roy, Illinois, Nov. 9, 1871.

[For the American Bee Journal.]

A Moan from Maine.

Dear Journal:—I always dislike sending a bad report from Maine, not only on account of its discouraging influence on bee-culture, but for the fact that it is not pleasant to recount one's own misfortunes. Yet, justice requires a faithful record; therefore I send you a brief retrospective view of "bee-ism" in Maine for 1871.

Thanks to the fall pasturage of 1870, the bees wintered well, and came through to the warm days in April in fine condition. Then the season promised most auspiciously; but the cold and dreary days of May more than counterbalanced those favorable conditions. and down went our sprits correspondingly. Still we could not believe that we were to have four poor seasons in succession, and accordingly braced up our courage and commenced stimulating, that our hives might be full of workers for the time of the fruit blossoms. Never have we witnessed a more profuse display of these blossoms; but they came and vanished like a beautiful vision, and the yield of honey was very light. Therefore we were obliged to continue stimulating till the white clover blossomed, which was unusually late, and of short duration; the drought most effectually dried it up, after yielding moderately for about ten days. Since July 10th, we have not been able to discover that our bees have gathered a particle of honey; consequently stocks are sadly reduced in bees and stores.

But few hives have honey enough to winter them, while hundreds are now actually starving. We have seen many hives that contained from twenty to forty pounds, each, of honey in May, with from one to five pounds only in October. Nothing but liberal and persistent feeding can save such stocks; and how few comparatively will do this? Hence we predict for the beekeepers of Penobscot valley, and some other sections of our State, a greater loss of bees this year, than they have experienced for twenty-five years, with possibly the exception of 1865. It is true that strong stocks in favored localities, have filled their hives and stored some surplus; but these cases are the exceptions; and the frequent ominous words of our better half—"The sugar barrel is nearly empty! Oh, those bees do use it at a fearful rate!" continually reminds us of the almost unparalleled scarcity of honey throughout the entire season of 1871, and how ruthlessly the bright fantastic air castles of visionary beekeepers have been dispersed, and instead of revelling in liquid sweets, as Gallup says, "to our eyes," we have the cold satisfaction of purchasing barrel after barrel of sugar, to save the little pets from starvation.

By uniting our weak stocks and feeding up to the required standard, we have our bees now in fair condition for winter, and shall look forward to next year's operations with increased interest and hopefulness.

Many beekeepers complain that in the process of uniting, their bees invariably fight until large numbers are killed. To all such we would recommend the following plan: Smoke both stocks and remove one queen, and if the bees are flying freely gradually move the hives towards each other, say a foot or so each day, until they are side by side, which will generally require two or three days. Select a cool day, and after smoking them thoroughly, remove the frames with the adhering bees from both hives, and replace them alternately in the hive designed for them—selecting the full frames, and being careful to secure a good supply of pollen or bee-bread. Set the hive in the centre of the space that was occupied by the *two* hives, and feed with honey or sugar syrup for a few days. The smoke and nursing up creates so much confusion among the bees that they are quite willing to accept the situation without resorting to a fight.

Geo. S. Silsby.

Wintersport, Me., Oct. 25, 1871.

[For the American Bee Journal.]

First Report, from a Beginner.

The September No. of the Journal, replete as its predecessors have ever been with much that is requisite to guide the apiarian bark, has been received, and contents as usual carefully perused. I am sincere in asserting that each and every number is worth, to me at least, the price of a year's subscription.

Impaired health, for want of proper exercise, compelling me to abandon the tripod, quill and scissors, I have decided to engage in apiculture. As other duties required my attention the present season, I have deferred engaging, to any extent, in the business, until next spring, when I desire to start with a reasonable number; but as I have managed six stocks the present season, I must report success.

Last April I took from my father's apiary of fifteen stands kept in box hives (which averaged him for many years from six to eight pounds of box honey to the hive, and a few swarms each season,) six stands and transferred them into movable comb hives. One of the six, a second swarm that barely came through the winter, I put in a double story hive, each story of which contains about 2100 cubic inches, and each holding ten frames. By close economy I got six frames of comb containing some brood and two or three pounds of honey. These with four empty ones were placed below and the remainder above. The four were speedily filled, but as the bees manifested no desire to begin operations above, I raised two frames from the brood chamber and placed them above, filling their places with empty ones. They were at once filled, and by the 10th of August the remaining eight were also filled. These frames weigh about ten pounds each, making a hundred pounds of honey and comb, besides the four empty frames filled below. This result was attained without spring stimulation, or anything of the kind. What the result would have b en had this stock been populous and stimulated in early spring, we can only conjecture.

The other five stocks, one half more populous than the one just mentioned, yielded about thirty pounds in boxes to the hive, besides filling three empty frames below. My neighbor who "trusts to luck," has had neither surplus honey nor swarms, and considers this the poorest year in twenty for bees.

Hoping that my success may encourage the efforts of our *enlightened* beekeeping brethren throughout the land, and that the shadows of Novice and a host of others whose lights shine from under a beehive instead of a "bushel," may never grow less, I respectfully subscribe myself

Rusticus.

Canaanville, Ohio, Oct. 11, 1871.

Effects of a Bee Sting.

At Highgate, (Vt.) the other day, Mrs. Kingsley Steinhauer was set upon by a swarm of bees and nearly stung to death; she lay some time as if dead, and then her whole flesh became purple, as though mortified. She is now recovering,—*Boston Journal*, Sept. 4, 1871.

Mr. Goff disturbed a swarm of bumble-bees while burying out West, and came near having a burying of his own. The bees stung his neck, and his throat swelled so that the whole family had to take turns feeding him soup with a squirt-gun.

THE AMERICAN BEE JOURNAL.

Washington, December, 1871.

☞ We need copies of the first number of the current volume of the Journal (July, 1871), and will pay twenty cents each for them, till our want is supplied, to such subscribers as do not file their papers and will send them to us.

☞ We regret to learn that on account of the editor's ill health, the publication of the next volume of the "ANNALS OF BEE-CULTURE" will be delayed till the spring of 1872. Heretofore this work was issued in the fall, which is not thought to be as suitable a time as that now proposed, and the occasion will be availed of to make the desired change.

☞ Two years ago we suggested the addition of glycerine to sugar syrup as a bee feed, to prevent candying. We found it satisfactory on trial, and several correspondents used it with advantage. Adding half an ounce or one ounce of glycerine to a pint of the syrup while yet warm makes a suitable mixture, though a larger proportion of the former may be employed where it can be procured cheap enough to make it an object. Pure inodorous glycerine is itself an excellent occasional bee feed, but is commonly too high in price for economical use; nor should we advise it to be used exclusively, if that were not an objection. We have never tried cream of tartar to prevent candying, and incline to doubt its availability for that purpose.

It is commonly supposed that only since the introduction of movable comb hives has it been ascertained that young bees in vigorous colonies, remain within their hives eight or ten days after being hatched, engaged in nursing, comb building, &c. But this is an erroneous impression. Lucas, in his "*Introduction to Practical Bee-culture*," written in 1818, and published at Prague in 1820, states it distinctly as a fact then well known, and confirmed by observation, that "young bees do not show themselves outside of their hives till the ninth day after their birth, when, if the day is fair, they join in the general jubilation of the colony, and thenceforward participate in the out-door labors of the workers." Lucas probably used an observing hive, though he nowhere expressly states that he did.

In a late number of the Bienenzeitung a correspondent denies the correctness of the general opinion that queen bees will, under no circumstances, employ their stings, except against their peers or rival queens. He states that when properly excited they will sting like other bees, though the same causes or treatment will not produce in them the requisite excitement. They will bear much teasing and pretty rough handling, without showing symptoms of irritation; and to induce them to sting some special manipulations, not easily described, seem to be necessary—such as threaten to endanger life. The correspondent, Mr. Tittel, of Freidorf, says he received his first sting from a queen bee on the 31st of May, 1869; was stung by another on the 14th of June; and by a third on June 18th. On the 23d of June, 1870, he was stung successively by six queens; on the forenoon of the 28th, twice by the same queen, and in the afternoon repeatedly by another. And in thei nterval between that date and the 8th of October following, he managed to get himself stung by queens more than twenty times.—The stinging, he states, produced very little pain and scarcely any swelling. The sting was never retained in the wound; and in no instance did it penetrate deeper than one-third its length.

A Mr. Gindley had previously reported in the Bienenzeitung for 1866, that he had been stung by a queen bee. Though he felt a slight pain, no swelling was produced.

The Rev. Mr. Kleine, of Hanover, made numerous efforts to cause a queen to sting him; but was successful only once.

☞ The following communication reached us so late that we have little room left for remarks. The bees accompanying it were crushed in the mail to a shapeless mass, and no offensive odor was perceptible. As in this case the bees died in their hive, the disease, whatever it is, seems to differ materially from that prevalent in several of the Western States in 1868. In every instance then, we think, the bees deserted their hives, usually leaving considerable stores of honey. The honey of the hive in question should be examined, as it may possibly contain some noxious principle fatal to the bees that gathered it.—Honey gathered from fir trees has been known to be very destructive to bees, some large apiaries having been ruined by it.

What is it?

About a week since I noticed an unusual stir about the entrance of one of my strong hybrid stocks. At first glance I suspected robbery, but more minute observation showed there were no robbers about, as the ejected bees were evidently of the same family. For the past three days, bees have been compelled to remain in-doors, as the mercury is too low to permit flying. This morning I visited the hive again and found a fearful quantity of dead bees on the bottom board and about the entrance. I cannot detect any symptoms of dysentery. "*What is it?*"

We have had a dry season this year, and several late honey-dews. My impression is that this honey-dew has something to do with it.—Let us have the opinion of some of our experienced apiarians. The hive—a two-story Langstroth—contains a hundred pounds of honey. I have forty-nine colonies besides this one, in my home apiary, which as yet present no symptoms of disease.

W. D. MANSFIELD.

Canaanville, Ohio, Nov. 17, 1871.

CORRESPONDENCE OF THE BEE JOURNAL.

MOUNT FLORENCE, KANSAS, Oct. 16, 1871.—I cannot do without your invaluable Journal. You can count me on your list as a constant subscriber.—F. GRUBBE.

LEWISBURG, PA., Oct. 27.—I think the past season hereabout has been pretty good for surplus honey, but not at all so for the multiplication of swarms.

If any of your correspondents give information as to the storing of extracted honey in wooden casks, showing what material is best, I wish you would publish it. I should suppose that most woods would impart their flavor.—G. R. BLISS.

OTTAWA, ILLS., Oct. 28.—As I have kept bees for fifteen years, I thought, as a matter of course. I knew something extra about them; but happening to visit one of my neighbors, who keeps bees, I was somewhat surprised to see how much better his were doing than mine. On inquiring of him how he managed them, he said, in the first place, he took the AMERICAN BEE JOURNAL, and learned all he could from that, and then his own experience and common sense filled up the balance. I *borrowed* the Journal, and bought some works on bees, and soon found, that if I had never had bees, I should have been better prepared to enter on the business than now. I found I knew nothing really and scientifically about them. It was too late to get my swarms into movable frame hives, which I find are the great desideratum. I have twenty seven colonies, fifteen of which made about three hundred (300) pounds of honey, off of buckwheat blossoms. I shall sow four acres of Alsike clover next spring, and sow buckwheat twice, about the middle of June and July. I have bought twenty-five more colonies, some of them weak. I shall unite the weak ones, as an experiment, and give the result. I enclose two dollars, a year's subscription for the Journal.—L. SOULE.

RIDGEFIELD, CONN., Oct. 28.—Bees have done well here the past season, mine having averaged over fifty pounds of surplus honey, per stock. Italians again showing their superiority as honey-gatherers. I have lots of bee matters to talk about, but will defer it until I get more time.—S. W. STEVENS.

HERMAN, ME.—Bees have not done anything in this section for the past two years. Last year I had ten stocks, and did not get one swarm. This year I had fifteen, and got two swarms, and have to feed a part of my bees to winter.—J. ALLEN.

GIRARD, PA., Oct. 30.—I notice that Adam Grimm seems to practice natural swarming. Will he please tell us if he considers that preferable to artificial? An opinion from one so successful as he has been with bees, cannot but be of great benefit. My bees have done well for the last two years, having doubled with each year. I have now seventy-five colonies; am using the Beebe hive altogether, as I consider it the best movable frame hive I have tried.—A. BATTLES.

PEORIA, ILLS., Nov. 1.—We have a very fair season for bees in this part of Illinois, though the amount of surplus honey is not so great as during some seasons, owing to the fact that the bees came through the winter in great poverty, and consequently spent all the early part of the season in providing for and rearing their young.—W. T. GREEN.

CHINQUACENSEY, CANADA, Nov. 6.—Bees have done very well this year. They gathered nearly all their surplus honey from the basswood blossoms, but have gathered none since.—J. PICKERING.

HOPKINSVILLE, KY., Nov. 6.—This has been a very good honey season; and if I could spare the time, I could make it profitable to keep bees. I have about seventy stocks on hand, and they are in good condition to winter. I would like to engage a reliable young man for another year, to take charge of my apiary. Can such be had? I will give a portion of the proceeds, or an interest in the whole stock. This is a fine location for an apiary. The Evansville, H. & Nashville railroad passing through our place. I want some one who *is willing to work.*—G. B. LONG.

OQUAWKA, ILLS., Nov. 8.—Bees that have had care, have done well here. One stock of Italians gave me 165½ lbs. cap honey, and have 40 lbs. more in their hive now than they had in the spring. Old fogy's bees have done very poorly—no swarms, no honey, but plenty of moth. He don't take the "Journal."—C. W. GREEN.

AURORA, ILLS., Nov. 12.—I have forty-two colonies of bees, some pure Italians, some hybrids, and some native blacks, all in good condition for wintering. The first part of the season here was excellent, but after July our bees could do very little. I have different works on bee-keeping, but find your valuable Journal comes as handy as a little pet.—J. DIVEKEY.

MONMOUTH, ILLS., Nov, 13.—The season here, taking it through, has been a good one for honey. Most stocks in this section have too much honey and too few bees for wintering well. But very few bee-keepers in this county have yet begun to use the movable comb hive. On the 9th of this month, I saw bees carrying pollen, which I suppose was gathered from sweet clover. We have had several nights of freezing weather.—T. G. McGAW.

[For the American Bee Journal.]

A Report from Ontario, Canada.

MR. EDITOR:—Will you allow me to inflict upon you some bee news from these parts. I commenced bee-keeping four years ago, having at that time been afflicted with a very bad (or good) attack of "bee on the brain," I thought that I would begin with one hive and the Bee Journal; but owing to natural stupidity, or something else, my visions of immediate wealth took a backward stride; yet I gained in knowledge what I lost in money. By the way, Mr. Editor, let me here remark that some people appear to acquire knowledge at a remarkably rapid rate. For instance, I have a neighbor (and I see by the Journal that other localities are troubled in the same way) who has had bees for one season, and could put Gallup or Novice, or any of the greater lights to the blush in five minutes, by his superior knowledge and experience.

These last two years I have done very well, as I have increased my stock from four hives to twenty-three. I thought to control swarming by getting ahead of some of my colonies this year. Accordingly on the 24th of May I made two artificial swarms. But this seemed to be only an incentive to redoubled exertion on the part of the little rascals, as one of the swarms cast three swarms and gave me forty-two pounds of surplus; and the old hive cast one very heavy swarm, and gave me twenty-three pounds of surplus.

The other hive which I divided, did very near

as well—whereas the rest of my hives did not do so well, leaving aside the artificial swarms.

This, Mr. Editor, I think was doing pretty well for this part of the country, considering the operator and the season. This has been a very poor season, during the first and last part; but I believe I owe part of my success to stimulative feeding in the spring. The last half of June and the first half of July was the only good time for bees here this season. I intend to go in for honey next season, if all goes well this winter. So tell Novice to be very careful, or this frozen region will be after him with a sharp stick.

Please, Mr. Editor, if it is not presuming, I should like to be classed among your *life* members for *our* Journal; for as long as I can raise the needful I must have the Journal, as I do not see how any one can keep bees without it. By the way, Mr. Editor, please let me know if I can get the first two volumes, and what they will cost.

As you must be getting bored almost to death, I had better stop. But first I should like to shake hands all around, and HURRAH for the old stand-by, the AMERICAN BEE JOURNAL. Yours, bee-nightedly,

GEO. T. BURGESS.

Lucknow, Ontario.

[For the American Bee Journal.]

Bees in 1871.

My field is two miles east of Albany city, in North Greenbush, though Albany is my post-office. My field for honey is but an ordinary one, and the season less favorable than the last, or an increase in the number of swarms required a larger field. My neighbor, not one hundred rods distant, with one colony and one new swarm, had no surplus. Another bee man three miles off, with eleven colonies, had less than one hundred pounds of surplus from them all. His bees did the best of any I have heard of in the old swarming hives in this vicinity.

I have, with my new swarm, thirty colonies; but the unfavorable season and limited field have so shortened my surplus that I got but about half a ton from the thirty colonies. The colony that gave me two hundred (200) pounds last season, gave me but one hundred and forty-three (143) pounds this season. This was rather a disappointment to me, as I had hoped an improvement upon last season. I had last season expressed, in some communication, the hope of being able to do better than two hundred pounds to one colony, and our agricultural society had offered a premium of twenty dollars for the largest amount of honey from one swarm. This season friend Quinby had the hive that gave two hundred (200) pounds, and mine gave but one hundred and forty-three (143) pounds. Still there were some alleviating circumstances.

1. I flatter myself that St. Johnsville gives a much better field for surplus honey than my bees have access to.

2. That though Mr. Quinby took the highest premium, he had to use my patent to accomplish it. Duty to others may require me to say so much.

My most successful colony is one of ten that I purchased in 1867, for Italian bees, of a neighbor some three or four miles from my residence. Some were more strongly marked than others, and probably all of them were hybrids. In the five seasons it has cast no swarm, and I regard it as the best colony I have ever had or ever seen. Is there any convenient way to secure new stocks from that colony, unmixed with other strains? If the stock yard, the breed of horses, the stye, the flock, and all the different beasts or fowls of the farmer may be improved indefinitely, why may not the apiarian's stock be benefited by following the same course? and what would be the easiest and safest course to adopt to try experiments to this end? An answer from the editor of the American Bee Journal, or of distinguished apiarians who are familiar with every rope in the beekeepers' craft, would be very gratifying to one who is too far advanced in life to make many experiments in the business, and too young in the apiculturists' business to know much of their management.

The colony is in a hive of my latest patent—"Hazen's Eureka Hive," with bars instead of frames.

I know not but the thought is a visionary one, and the object unattainable; but if our business may be greatly advanced and its profits increased largely by the introduction of queens from a distant country, may we not improve our stock by securing our new stocks by our best old stocks? The colony has had its breeding apartment in use five seasons, and the comb is of course somewhat darkened and old. Would it answer to confine the colony another season to the breeding apartment and thus secure an early swarm, and then remove the brood combs to as many nucleus hives as there were queen cells in the hive, giving one cell to each, and then remove the whole to a distance from other bees, to secure, at the issue of the queens, the service of the drones for the queens, to secure the purity of all the stocks, or will this be unnecessary?

I have been interested and instructed in the pursuit of my business by your Journal, and through it have formed something of acquaintance with numbers of able men in the business, of whom I shall have pleasing remembrance what little time memory holds its seat.

With best wishes for your success, and the success of your useful Journal.

I am yours respectfully,

JASPER HAZEN.

Albany, N. Y.

[For the American Bee Journal.]

Letter from Kansas.

DEAR READER:—It is not often that we will occupy space in the Journal. Occasionally we like to have our say. Suppose that we do hit some of our "old bee writers," what of it? They have been hitting others; and to have a little conceit knocked out of them, once in awhile, may do good. We would judge that some of them fancy all beekeepers in the country are looking up to them as teachers; when the fact is they have told us long ago nearly all they know about beekeeping, and their articles now are chiefly speculation and theory, putting forth ofttimes some new fangled notion not even tested by themselves. And they thus keep a little lot of beginners fooling away their time, experimenting on those tricks that are vain.

As to Kansas: the harvest is past, the summer is ended, and the bees are all right. The season has been a very good one, also up to the 8th of June the bees nearly starved. From that time till the first of August there was just about enough honey to keep them breeding well and make the necessary increase.

The honey harvest closed this year about the 15th of September, although in some years it continues a month longer. As this was our first experiment with the Extractor, of course we are away behind those that have had more experience. Even Katie Grimm has beat us so bad that we are almost ashamed to tell how little we were able to do. Three hundred and thirty (330) pounds was our best day's work—which was on the 9th of September. But by referring to the Journal, we see that on the 15th of July, Miss Katie extracted 2½ barrels, or nine hundred and twenty-five (925) pounds. Our surplus amounted to one hundred (100) pounds to each stock, counting the increase.

We have never told you what kind of hive we are using, nor what a cheap honey extractor we have got. We are afraid to do so, lest some of you would want to give us a dollar for a description. Our hive suits us very well, and we are going to let every body else use just such hives as please them best.

Our main difficulty heretofore was in getting the combs straight in the frames. This season, however, we hit on a comb guide that works to a charm ("Oh, how pleased was I!"). But as there has been very little said on the subject of comb guides since we have been a reader of the Journal, we are not certain that we have not hit on somebody's patent, and have after all nothing but what beekeepers have been using for years. However, if there is any one that is in trouble about getting straight combs, we will describe our guide in a future number of the Journal.* Any one can make it, and it cost but a trifle. As far as tested, it don't fail once in a hundred times. Besides, we have our bees make use of our surplus wax in comb building. How is that, Mr. Walter, for a "wild country?" Don't you think the Orchard beeman would like to know how to do that? By the way, your apology for him was rather lame. It would have been better if you had said he wanted to see whether any reader of the Journal was foolish enough to send him a dollar. We think it doubtful whether there was. There was one, however, that sent us five cents, and we don't think he would have done it, except for the Twining "six secrets," to use in connection with the Gallup hive. Here is his letter in the original Ms., only with the name and date cut off. The orthography is a little amusing, and somewhat peculiar.

"Mr. Noah Cameron, Dear Sir, you will find enclosed 5 cents, for whitch pleese send me Gallup's discriptions for makeing Beehives and the twinning Six Secretes for handling and manageing Bees.
and except my kindest thanks for the Same.
Yours truly,
——— ———"

We will guarantee that he has not taken the Journal long, or he would not have invested even five cents for the "secrets."

Small Queens.—What little experience we have had with such, is that they are of little account. Some will do first-rate for the first season; but most of them will fail to be good layers in the second, and some fail entirely. We deem it one of the most important things in beekeeping, to keep all your stocks supplied with good, vigorous, prolific queens. It makes more difference than it does what kind of a hive you use. And how to raise good queens is a subject pregnant with interest. Its importance cannot be overestimated. In our humble opinion it entirely eclipses the hive question.

There has been a deal said about natural and artificial queens; yet nothing conclusive has been established. There are many poor queens among both kinds. We are of the opinion that depends upon the attention that they get in the larvæ state. All small queens should be rejected. They are evidently not fully developed. They have had a scant supply of the royal food. There are also many poor queens among those that are of good size. Why this is so, we are unable to say. It may be the fault of bad breeding. All our queens should be under our eye, to see that they are physically perfect before they are allowed to take charge of a colony. It is a good point when your queen can fly immediately on her exit from the cell.

We had a hive this season in the same fix that one or two correspondents have previously mentioned. The brood was dying and there was scarcely any of it capped over. The conclusion we arrived at was that the bees had swarmed at a time when the hive was full of eggs and young larvæ: and that they had left too few bees for the work they had to do.

As this letter is long enough already, we will only add that at a meeting of the Kansas Beekeepers' Association there were three delegates elected to the National Convention to be held at Cleveland, in December. They are Dr. L. J. Dallas, William Barnes, and your correspondent.

N. Cameron.

Lawrence, Kansas.

In a favorable season, the first fifteen days of the new-establishment of a swarm in a hive are employed in the most active labor. There is sometimes as much work done in that short time, as in all the rest of the season that is left for working.

*By all means let us have the description soon. Numbers are anxious to get a "sure thing" in time to arrange for next season's operations.—[Ed.

// AMERICAN BEE JOURNAL.

EDITED AND PUBLISHED BY SAMUEL WAGNER, WASHINGTON, D. C.

AT TWO DOLLARS PER ANNUM, PAYABLE IN ADVANCE.

VOL. VII. JANUARY, 1872. No. 7.

Non-hatching Bee Eggs.

Translated for the American Bee Journal, from the "Bienenzeitung."

Since I first stated, in my essay on alternation of generation, in "*Parthenogenesis in Insects*" (1858, page 62), the fact, based on an observation made by Mr. Hucke, that there are queen bees whose eggs, though regularly brooded, fail to hatch, the number of such instances noticed by others has become so multiplied that the Baron of Berlepsch — who once, in confident conviction to the contrary, boldly offered to give twenty of his finest Dzierzon hives stocked with Italian bees, for one such queen—has felt himself constrained to devote a special paragraph to these "addle eggs," in the new edition of his celebrated work on Bees and Bee-culture (1865, page 86).

In accordance with previous observers, Berlepsch infers, from the absence of brood, that the eggs are in reality addle. He assumes that they remain entirely without any advance towards development, though brooded; and looks for the cause of this in the defective constitution of the mother, in consequence of which she has lost, either wholly or partially, the ability to produce eggs having the germ of vitality. Of the same opinion is Professor Von Siebold, as is shown in a communication from him in a late number of the Bienenzeitung (1871, page 171), wherein he speaks of the addle condition of bee eggs, though he was unable to detect anything abnormal either in the queen sent to him, or in her eggs.

I confess that I coincided in this view respecting the nature of the eggs in the instance referred to, till the autumn of 1868, when I had opportunities in rapid succession to investigate three cases of so-called *addleness*, and then found reason to change my opinion.

The first of these cases occurred in the apiary of Mr. Dörr, in Mettenheim. On the 23d of September, I received from him the following communication respecting it:—"For two months past I have been watching the oviposition of a queen bred this year, continually finding eggs in the cells, but never any larvæ, sealed or unsealed. Three weeks ago I examined the hive, and found, as I had found four weeks before eggs, and eggs only. Inferring thence that a change of queen had taken place, I regarded these eggs as the first batch laid by the new queen. Since then, three weeks more have elapsed to-day, yet I found no trace whatever of brood; but, as before, eggs only. Under these circumstances the population of the hive having become much reduced, the area of oviposition is no longer large, yet I find in each cell in this area several eggs, and in some instances as many as five.* But I can readily see that always one of these eggs has been recently laid, because the larger number have already, by drying up, become shrivelled or shrunken—some being, as it were, mere shells. I would particularly request attention to the fact that oviposition appears to have proceeded regularly, for there always was one freshly laid egg in every such cell.—On the whole, I cannot account for the facts thus observed except on the assumption that this queen lays addle eggs only."

Mr. Dörr's kind offer to send me the queen and eggs for examination, was of course thankfully accepted; and I very soon received both, with an additional note from him, in which he stated that the queen was hatched on the 12th of July, when drones were plenty; and that she had been laying since the beginning of August, though no being, endowed with vitality, had ever issued from any of her eggs.

I found the queen, both externally and internally, perfectly normal and well-shaped. The ovaries and oviducts were richly stored with eggs in various stages of advancing maturity—those organs being still well developed for so late a period in the season. As in the case also, mentioned by Prof. Siebold, fertilization had taken place, and the spermatheca contained a dense mass of still mobile spematozoids. Their dissection furnished nothing that threw any light on the subject; but the matter assumed a different aspect when I subjected the eggs themselves to investigation.

Even the first egg placed under the microscope, though still fresh and of the usual appearance, satisfied me that the assumption that these eggs were addle, was altogether unfounded. Instead of an amorphous yolk, *it contained a perfectly formed embryo*, with the usual external and in-

* In several of the cells of the comb sent to me, I found even seven or eight eggs.—*Note, by Prof. Leuckart.*

ternal appendages (even the amnion); so that, without further knowledge of the circumstances, the egg had to be regarded as normally endowed with life. And all the rest of the eggs were just like the first one examined, so far as their shrivelled state allowed me to form a judgment—most of them, however, being so shrunken that the embryo, as such, could not be exhibited.

The "addleness" of these eggs was consequently merely apparent. Their failure to hatch did not result from lack of inherent power of development, but from the simple fact that the embryo, formed entirely as all such embryos are, had not power to emerge from the egg. Neither the egg shell nor the amniotic sac showed any abnormal thickening, and the embryo itself was entirely normal. There was consequently no physical or mechanical obstacle to prevent hatching; and there remains hence only the assumption that the seeming addleness of the eggs resulted from the premature death of the embryonal germ.

What I have here stated respecting the Dörr case holds good also as regards two others, which were presented to me almost simultaneously for investigation. Here also the apparently addle eggs contained normally developed embryos. One of these cases, however, was of special interest, because by it was furnished the experimental proof that the embryos do not hatch, even when the eggs containing them are placed in other hives. This fact was communicated to me by Mr. E. Böttger, teacher, of Weissenberg, in Saxony, in a note, as follows:—"Last summer I had two cases presented to me, in which young queens laid eggs incapable of producing living larvæ. The first of these queens was found in a colony belonging to Mr. Schmidt, of Zwörsty. She was killed and cast out by the bees two months later. The second occurred in a colony belonging to Mr. Fanghühnel, of Hartingsdorff. She laid a vast number of eggs, in perfectly regular order, in thirteen different colonies in which we successively introduced her, and all of which proved to be lifeless. Eggs from other hives, and even drone eggs, were regularly hatched when inserted in any of the hives containing this queen. By repeatedly inserting brood combs containing eggs from other queens the population was kept up in the colonies with this defective queen."

As this case shows evidently, the cause of the premature death of the embryo germs must be sought for in the eggs, or rather in the mother which produces those eggs. But whether it will ever happen that the cause shall be discovered, is extremely doubtful. We know of analogous cases in human subjects, though not even plausible explanations of the occurrence have yet been furnished; and queen bees producing so-called addle eggs may be classed in the same category. Eggs truly addle—that is, eggs containing no embryonal germ susceptible of development, have not yet been found among those laid by queen bees.

LEUCKART.

[For the American Bee Journal.]

Rearing Artificial Queens, and their Value.

When I commenced Italianizing my bees, I laid down certain rules under which I would proceed the following spring. One of these was, to raise drones and queens so early in the season that the young queens would have no chance to mate with black drones. To get drones early, I wintered in nuclei and full hives, twelve virgin queens. All of these were got through the winter safely, but I lost seven of them the first few days after wintering out. From the five which were saved I succeeded in raising, at the lowest estimate, three thousand drones, that were flying as early as the 20th of April. I had succeeded also in raising more than a dozen queens hatched between the 10th and 15th of April. Every day that was warm enough for bees to fly, the queens as well as the drones appeared to be just as lively and active in their excursions, as in summer weather; and I, of course, expected that the queens would speedily become fertile. But I was doomed to disappointment. None of those queens became fertile until the 7th of May, when three of them commenced laying drone eggs, and soon appeared to be regularly fertile. At that time, however, drones had made their appearance from common stocks also.

Most of the queens that I reared so early, were small, did not prove to be very prolific, and were superseded the same season by the workers. When the queen cells in which they were hatched were built, no young workers had yet been hatched, to my knowledge; and bees could not yet gather pollen in the fields. I tried once or twice more to raise early queens, but always with poor success. I am now fully satisfied that, to raise prolific and large queens, a colony must have a large number of young workers, and must be supplied with plenty of honey and *fresh* pollen newly gathered in the fields. The colony must also be closely watched; all queen cells sealed before the third day after making the colony queenless, and all cells built after the seventh day, should be destroyed. If sealed too early, the young queens hatched from them will nearly always be small; if too late, such queens proved to be very unprolific with me, and were sometimes superseded very shortly after becoming fertile.

In my location it is early enough to commence breeding queens between the first and the fifth of May. During the months of May, June, July and August, good queens can be artificially raised, if the proper stocks are selected, well treated, and properly watched. No stock should be compelled to raise two sets of queen cells in succession. I always found the second lot inferior to the first; and as bees nurse a smaller number of royal grubs better than a larger one, they should not be allowed to build more than eight or ten cells. Queens reared at a time when little or no pollen is gathered, are usually smaller and less prolific than those reared with plenty of pasturage. Therefore, queens reared in the month of September are not near so valuable as queens reared in the preceding month. Queens artificially reared are, in most instances, as good as natural ones; but not all of them. I will not deny that I think more highly of natural queens than of artificial ones; but we cannot always get them, when we want them, and many a stock would be lost if we depended exclusively on a supply of natural queens. Those queens, too, greatly vary in prolificness and longevity; and I must concede that I have, and have had, many an artificial queen that I preferred to natural ones.

* * * * * * * *

I had written the foregoing article about ten days before the arrival of the last (December) number of the Journal, thinking it would be in time yet after receiving that number, I retained it; and I am now really glad that I did so, as this gives me a chance to comply with the request of Novice and say how I get my queen cells. But to satisfy Novice and other readers of the Journal that I have been breeding my queens in the same way for a number of years, I send you, Mr. Editor, one of my circulars for 1868, with the request to insert here what I said in it about queen raising:

RAISING QUEENS.

When I first commenced raising queens, I raised them on pieces of brood comb with eggs and little worms, which I had inserted into a little hive (nucleus) with three small frames 6 inches wide and 5 deep that were filled with comb and honey and a small lot of worker bees. This I found was a poor way. I now deprive a good colony of bees of their queen, let them build queen cells, and on the 9th and 10th day I cut out all of them but one and divide and insert into as many nuclei as I have queen cells, and then I either take bees enough from the hive I cut out the queen cells to start the nuclei, or take mostly young bees from another colony and keep them shut up until the young queen hatches, and then open them in the evening a little while before sun down, when scarcely ever any bees will return to the parent hive. In this part of the country it is useless to commence raising queens before the 1st of May. Scarcely ever any queens will get fertile before the middle of May. If they are fertile they may be introduced into large colonies.

To this I have to add that, during swarming time, I stock all my nuclei with queen cells built in hives that swarmed naturally; and that, in nearly every instance, I take the tested queens sent off, from full colonies that have natural queens. The twenty-five queens sent to Novice September 15th and 22d, 1870, were artificial *untested* queens that had just commenced laying and were not more than fourteen days old. They were, consequently bred at the end of August or beginning of September, or at a time when the best breeding season was over, and they could mate only with old drones artificially produced. If only three out of those twenty-five queens ceased laying before they became one year old, Novice had better luck with them than I expected. He might have had the very best of artificial or natural queens, and not fared better. It is my opinion that Novice and many other beekeepers should not delay ordering queens to a time when the best queens cannot be raised. Whether he will do better by ordering queens of Mr. Langstroth or not, if he should order twenty-five *untested* queens so late as September 12th, I am unable to say; and I will not even report my own experience for fear that I might prejudice anybody against Mr. Langstroth.

If several of Novice's dark hybrid queens were more prolific than the pure ones obtained from me in the extra good season of 1870, it is not yet proved that they would have been the same in the poorer season of 1871. But I will concede that they were, and if so, he only experienced what numerous other correspondents of the Journal reported. I cannot think that Novice wrote his remarks about the twenty-five queens obtained from me, in a fault-finding spirit, as I have received a number of letters this summer, stating that the writers ordered queens from me, because Mr. Root recommended me to them. Only for fear that some of the readers might get a wrong impression have I written this explanation. I will only add that among the forty-three queens imported direct from Italy by myself, and successfully introduced in my own stock, were a small number that were very little prolific; and that all of them, save one, died in their second or third year, and that one only lived until this summer—having been only a very moderate layer for the first two summers.

A. GRIMM.

Jefferson, Wis., 1871.

[For the American Bee Journal.]

Queen Mothers and Improvement of Stock.

DEAR JOURNAL:—Much is said among bee-keepers about queen fertilization in confinement, about providing pasturage, and about the relative merits of Italian and black bees, &c.;—all looking, we take it, to the increase of the honey crop, while comparatively little is said upon the topic which heads this article.

The fertilization of queens by selected drones, seems at best to make *very slow progress*; while some are ready to pronounce it a miserable failure. However desirable it might be, if practicable, we consider the wise selection of queen mothers, as of far greater importance. Any tyro can constrain bees to rear queens, but not *every* "Novice" can tell whether such queens possess real value, or not. Possibly every apiarian of experience has observed that there is a vast difference in the yield of different colonies in the same apiary, under the same conditions of management, pasturage, age of queens, form of hive, and strength of colony. Another fact, too plain to escape the notice of the observing beemaster, that, in wintering, some colonies consume twice the amount of stores that other colonies of the same working force do, whether wintered in special depositories or on their summer stands. Hence we conclude there is a difference in different colonies of the same variety of the hive bee. There are desirable or objectionable qualities observable in every colony. It should be the aim of the breeders to breed for the desirable and to breed *out* the objectionable features of his stocks. When this is done the "coming bee" will be one of large producing qualities, beautiful in appearance, amiable in disposition, not a large eater, nor yet an enormous breeder. The large eaters are not the large producers, neither do I find the slightest relation between irritability and industry; often the crossest colony being the poorest workers. This is equally true, whether among blacks or Italians. In my earlier experience in breeding the Italian bee, I supposed that the queen that was large, yellow, and very prolific, possessed all the requisite qualities for a suitable queen mother, provided of course that she was considered pure Italian and her royal daughters were duplicates of herself. But I found by selecting queens of great fertility, I could produce a race of bees that would increase almost beyond limit, giving more of their labor to the rearing of brood, than the amassing of stores, and very much disposed to swarm, issuing in times of scarcity of honey, being *crowded* out by superabundance of numbers. I account for this from the fact that it is the prevailing instinct of the bee to rear brood and amass stores. With some the former, while with others the latter trait prevails. Under box, log, or straw hive management of the black bee for ages past, the inclination to run to excessive brooding was no doubt kept in check by occasional poor honey seasons, when such colonies would perish of starvation. By our present system of management, with movable comb-hives, and breeding rather for increase of stocks than surplus honey, we do not get the most productive bees. When urging the matter of improvement of bees, I am met with this *clincher*—"bees are *bees*, creatures governed by instinct, and that instinct unchanged from what it was thousands of years ago." But, my dear sir, does your horse, your cow, your pigs, or your poultry, possess a faculty, higher than instinct? Yet who will say no improvement has been effected in those domestic animals, in the past twenty-five years." What dairyman would think of stocking his farm with those long-legged, slim-bodied kine that could trot a mile inside of three minutes? Or what pork-raiser would think of fattening a drove of those four-legged land sharks with protruding tusks, such as our fathers made bacon and sausage of thirty or forty years ago? (Unless he possessed the feeding apparatus figured so minutely in the April number of the AMERICAN BEE JOURNAL last spring!) No farm stock at present is more susceptible of improvement, or would yield more readily to the skilful hand, than the honey bee. So fully am I convinced of the vast field of improvement open to the apiarian of the present day, in the wise selection of queen mothers, that I will venture the opinion that the yield of honey might be at least doubled from the same number of colonies, and that too without increase of bee pasturage.

In any apiary of a hundred colonies, some stocks will be found much superior to others. Let us step into such an apiary and select a few queen mothers. They must be from stocks that have come through the previous winter with abundant stores, showing the workers not to be enormous eaters. The queens must not be less than one year old; still better if they be two or three years old, showing longevity, and no attempt ever made by the progeny of either to supersede her. I do not fancy the superseding breed, unless it be at a time when there is a manifest reason for such a procedure—as, for instance, the queen is approaching the sunset of a well-spent life. The workers must be beauties; less matter about the queen herself, on that point. "Handsome is that handsome does." The workers must be industrious; not loitering at home, when honey awaits them in field or forest; yet sufficiently cautious not to sally forth in unpropitious weather, to return no more. They must be amiable in disposition, when out of the hive, not volunteering an attack on the apiarian, his family, or visitors, when passing near the hive. They must be reasonably good wax-workers, and yet not disposed to run too much to fat. I have observed both of these extremes, at times too when such results could not be attributed to the *age* of the workers.

Beekeepers have been wont to ascribe the difference in the product of different colonies to the nature of the combs, some having too much drone comb; others, to the hive, it "had no moth trap." "Use *my* hive, and your swarms will be all productive!" I do not ignore the fact that there is often too much drone comb; nor that some hives are *better* than others. Yet these reasons do not give a satisfactory solution of the question. I present the subject of the improvement of our bees by the judicious selection of queen mothers, in view of the almost total failure of fertilization in confinement; and if we breed only from such queen mothers as I have indicated, a few years will rid us of all objectionable drones. It is a matter too of practical importance—just important to the extent that it does matter whether we get fifty dollars or fifty cents, each, as the profit of our colonies. In the laudable effort of our best apiarians to supplant the black bee by a superior kind throughout all this sunlit land of ours, it is not strange that breeding for superior excellence in that superior variety, should for a time be lost sight of, or receive inadequate attention, so long as the supposed standard of purity was maintained.

I believe a majority of breeders of queens have not only done the best they could under the circumstances, but have done *nobly*. They have planted largely, but the pruning time is at hand. Let unprofitable queens be gently prepared for decent burial, as soon as better ones are ready to take their places. Let our motto bee *improvement*, onward and still onward; if we would reap the best results in the fascinating pursuit of bee-culture.

In conclusion, Mr. Editor, allow me to express the hope that friend Gallup may be able to see the "*reason* why" not all queens of equal purity are suitable queen mothers; and that to maintain the Italian as a "fixed race" is not alone sufficient for our purpose.

W. J. DAVIS.

Youngsville, Pa., Dec. 1871.

[For the American Bee Journal.]

Light Wanted.

Mr. Editor.—I wish, by your permission, to put another question through the Journal, for solution. It is this—Can a pure Italian queen, whose progeny for the first few weeks all show the *three yellow bands distinct*—thus being purely tested, sent off, and introduced into another colony—afterwards produce workers, half black bees, and the rest having only one and two bands? Or, in plainer words, can a pure queen, tested pure, afterwards produce hybrids? If any of your readers know of such cases, will they please communicate them to the Journal?

On July 11th, I shipped *three tested* queens, to a gentleman out west. July 13th, he writes "queens arrived safe, caged and put in the hives to remain forty-eight hours." The next letter was to this effect—one queen died in the cage; the other two are at liberty.

August 14th, he writes—"one of them shows fine workers in their daily play; but the other does not yet give very pretty workers, being too dark colored." Again, August 18th, he writes—"I have just opened the hive in which the queen is, that produces the dark colored workers, and find she is giving about three-fourths black bees, and the other fourth one and two banded hybrids. It is now one month and six days since I set her at liberty in the hive"

Now upon the receipt of the letter of the 14th, I know that there had not appeared a hybrid bee in either of the stands, for I had been daily among the hives, But, to be sure of no mistake, I went to my books to see if I was not right in the number of the hives, 36, 64, 68, from which I had taken the queens. I then opened each hive, examined carefully, and could not find a two banded bee in either of them, much less a black bee. I then, August 22d, wrote to him that he must be mistaken in having the same queen he got of me.

He answered on the 26th, "I know she was not killed in the first fifteen days after she was put into the stock, as she was there to be seen, and no queen cells were made in that time. Hence she could not be superseded by a black queen. If she has since then been superseded, it has been by a queen raised from her own brood and mated with a black drone. Now in the first fifteen days of her existence in the hive, I opened it as many as three times, and found the facts as stated above." Again, August 28th, he writes, "Since writing you on Saturday, I have again examined that stock of bees, and begin to find an occasional three-banded bee. If she left good stock with you, it will certainly appear here, if she was perfectly fertilized."

On the receipt of this last letter, I again carefully examined the three hives mentioned above, with the same result as before—not an impure marked worker in either of them. I felt satisfied I had sent him *purely* tested queens; but as he was not satisfied, as was clear from his letters, I sent him another queen, September 12th.

Now, to this day, there has not appeared a hybrid bee in either of the above stands. Hence one of two things must be true. Either the queen got of me was superseded, or if she was not, she produced hybrid workers after being removed from her stand here—a case I do not recollect ever hearing of. Some may try to explain this case, by saying the queen met another drone, after being removed. I do not believe a queen is ever impregnated but *once and for life.*

The above case is a strange one to me, for if true that a queen, after producing purely marked workers for the first few weeks, can afterwards produce hybrids, then how can any breeder be certain that the queen he is sending off is pure? I was as certain of the purity of these queens when I shipped them, as I ever was of any queen; and after I had shipped them off, had I discovered within three weeks a single black bee with a two banded bee in either of the stands I took the queens from, I would have been satisfied that I had sent a bad queen. But as no such sign was discovered and has not been even to the present time, I can give no other explanation; but leave this for your readers, who may know of such cases, to explain.

R. M. Argo.

Lowell, Ky., Nov. 22, 1871.

[For the American Bee Journal.]

Cross-Bred Bees.

In the October number of the American Bee Journal, there is an article under the caption of "*The Coming Bee,*" upon which I wish to offer a few thoughts. I do so the more freely, because the writer requests any one who may have had experience with the kind of bees he describes, to report. I do not know what special qualities he may have found in bees less than half Italian; but my observation of that kind of bees, has given me a very poor opinion of them.

I have a number of colonies, the progeny of pure Italian queens fertilized by black drones. These I have found to be but little more inclined to sting than pure Italians. One of them, in fact, is as good natured as any bee I ever saw. They rarely if ever attack any one, when the hive is not disturbed; and I have extracted the honey from their combs, and have opened the hive many times for other purposes, without their manifesting anger. Other colonies of half-bloods are a little more belligerent than this one, but none of them are as much so as black bees generally are. I am aware that half-bloods have a bad reputation for ill nature, but as far as my observation extends they do not deserve it.

I *had* a colony whose mother I thought was pure, and they were terribly cross. It was nearly impossible to smoke them into submission. They would obstinately refuse to fill themselves with honey, and as soon as the hive was opened, they were ready for battle. But on close inspection of the progeny of the mother of this queen, there was found to be in them a dash of black blood. So these very cross bees were less than half Italian. I have had other colonies less than half Italian, and have found them to be invariably more belligerent than the first cross; and I have failed to perceive in them any superior qualities which the pure Italians do not possess in larger measure.

I have some curiosity to know how Mr. Wright has ascertained that his mongrel race are greatly superior to the pure Italians in their range of flight and acuteness of scent! I have several colonies now, a majority of which are somewhat less than half Italian. They have received pure Italian queens this fall, and within a few days the pure Italians in those hives have been bringing in loads of pollen, procured somewhere, I know not where nor from what, while only now and then does one of the mongrels bring in anything; and yet the latter outnumber the former perhaps five to one. This fact (and it has been ascertained by careful observation), would seem to place the pure Italians ahead in acuteness of scent or range of flight, or in something equally important. If Mr. Wright, by some lucky accident, has hit upon a cross which possesses superior qualities, which qualities can be perpetuated, I shall be glad to know and acknowledge it; and will be glad to procure a queen of him. But I apprehend that he will find that he has been hasty in his conclusions. It may be well for him to continue his experiment in that direction, and report results of more extended observation.

M. MAHIN.

New Castle, Ind., Nov. 2, 1871.

[For the American Bee Journal.]

Introducing Queens.

Since I commenced to raise queens I have tested many methods for introducing them to full colonies. Last season I introduced a good many queens successfully in every case, in a simple and easy way; and I have no doubt others can do it equally well. My new method is this: Remove the queen from the hive to be re-queened (and it matters not what kind of hive the bees are in—whether with frames, or without frames). Three days later, fumigate all the bees with tobacco smoke, or wet them down with sweetened water, scented with essence of peppermint. Then introduce the queen at once, and she will be kindly received. Remember, the time for leaving the hive queenless is *three days*, and *not* longer, while the hive contains brood. As soon as the queen is introduced the bees will cease to work upon the queen cells, and none of them will be capped over. In a few hours after the queen is introduced, eggs can be found in the cells.

I introduced a few queens last season, without first removing the queen from the hive to be re-queened. I cannot recommend it as a safe way in all cases; but perhaps by giving this method a trial, a way for introducing queens safely, without first removing the queens, may be discovered. The theory is this: most beekeepers know that when a queen has been caged or removed from her colony three or four days, that she is then not more than half as large as she is when in a full stock, laying two thousand eggs a day. Well, we should say that she is in good fighting trim, or much more so than a queen that *is* in a full stock, and laying her two thousand eggs per day, with her abdomen full of eggs, &c. Now, if we can introduce a strange queen (one that has not been in a full colony for three or four days) by cheating the bees, so that they will not know one queen from another, as I do when I introduce with tobacco smoke, we shall have two queens in one hive, and if they happen to meet in "mortal combat" in the course of a few hours after the queen is introduced, it will be seen at once that the strange queen has the advantage over her antagonist (the old queen), as her condition is much the best for fighting, she not being burdened with thousands of eggs.

I was successful in three cases. In the fourth case the bees kept the two queens for ten days, and the one introduced was missing one day when I looked to see how they were getting along together. The queens introduced had their wings clipped, and thus I could distinguish one from the other. I hope some of your readers will more fully test this plan next season. My plan for introducing with tobacco smoke was given in the Journal for July last.

It seems Alley is not the only man who makes a "smoke house" of his beehives and "vomits his bees to death" (See *Amer. Bee Journal* for November, page 98). I wondered why it was that your correspondents so misconstrued what I said about giving bees tobacco smoke. One of them recommended giving bees chloroform instead of tobacco smoke. Well, I am of the opinion that not many readers of the Journal took much stock in the chloroform concern. I have used tobacco smoke for twelve years in handling bees, and never saw any ill effects resulting from it yet.

I still have another way of introducing queens. It is not original with me. I got it from Mr. George S. Wheeler, of New Ipswich, N. H. Mr. W. removes the queen, and then crushes her, and daubs the queen to be introduced with the dead body of the one removed. He says he has been successful in every case. I tried it on one queen, and did not succeed. I found the bees going through the hugging process, and so removed the queen, and introduced her successfully three days later.

Many beekeepers have an idea that queens can be introduced only during warm weather. This is not the case. I introduced them late in October, and have introduced one since November came in.

H. ALLEY.

Wenham, Nov. 8, 1871.

[For the American Bee Journal.]

Eggs laid in Queen Cells by the Queens.

MR. EDITOR:—I see on page 139, December number of the Journal, a circumstance related by Mr. Grimm, of his seeing a queen withdrawing her abdomen from a queen cell and finding an egg in it; and also some editorial remarks in regard to the shape of the cell, &c

Now, I will relate to you and the readers of the Journal what came under my personal observation lately: Some time about the 10th of June I and my assistant, Mr. Meldrem, were looking over a hive of Italian bees, to see what condition they were in, as I wished to raise young queens from the mother of the colony, a very beautiful queen. We came to the comb she was on, and there were a number of queen cells on it. They had smooth, thin walls, and were in the condition they usually were when I found eggs in them. I told my assistant, who was then rather new at the business, that, judging from their appearance, the queen would lay in them in a day or so. Each one of them (six in number) was carefully inspected, and there was no egg to be seen in any. We watched the queen depositing eggs in worker cells, close by the queen cells. She laid quite a number, and then I turned the comb, so as to view the workers on the other side as to their markings, while my assistant still kept watching the queen. Presently he said, "Hold still, the queen has inserted her abdomen in a queen cell, and is laying in it." I did not turn the comb, for fear of disturbing her. Soon he said she had come out, and he pointed to the cell she had left. She was then close to the side of it, and there was an egg in it. I know my assistant to be a man of truth, and furthermore know there was no egg in any of the cells five minutes before. The cell she had laid in was about the usual length of queen cells after they are sealed over, and the diameter of the mouth was larger than that of a drone cell. I could see no difference between that and the other five without eggs. I thought at the time, where does the compression theory come in? I kept watch of the cell, and it was sealed over in due time after the larva had hatched, and the young queen is now in my yard, a very prolific one. The old one I let a friend have, after a good deal of persuasion, as he had accommodated me many times. Now, the compression theory may be correct, yet I have seen queens so often laying in worker and in drone cells not over one-eighth of an inch in depth, that I am inclined to doubt it. I cannot see either why a queen should be misled to lay in a queen cell, as swarming is the way ordained by the Creator of all things for bees to "multiply and replenish the earth." As the old queen leaves with the first swarm, it seems necessary that some way should be left for the remaining bees to secure another royal mother. Neither does it necessitate that the young queen should be a "rival or natural enemy," for in all cases that have come under my notice when, from scarcity of forage or other causes, swarming was postponed, the workers tore open the cells and destroyed the young queens. Only in cases of supersedure are the young queens allowed to hatch, and then frequently the young and the old queen remain peaceably in the hive, and even on the same comb, until death by old age takes away the mother. G. M. DOOLITTLE.

Borodino, N. Y., Dec. 5, 1871.

☞ According to the foregoing, and the previous communication of Mr. Grimm, given in our last number, we may assume that queens do, at least occasionally, lay eggs in royal cells. But then comes up the question, if those eggs are suffered to remain there till hatched and the larvæ be then nursed to maturity, what will the product be—queens, or drones? Is it certain, also, that eggs laid in such cells by queens, or the larvæ springing therefrom, will be suffered to remain there and mature, after the workers discover their true character? Leaving out of view altogether, for the present, the queen's ability or inability to impregnate the egg deposited by her in a queen cell, may we not inquire whether she has the physical ability to place and attach an egg properly in such a cell? And may not instinct impel the workers to discard and throw out of them all eggs not found properly placed and attached, replacing them by others of their own choice and selection? Let the bearing on some of these points, of the facts stated in the ensuing article by Mr. Hewitt, be duly considered, before hasty conclusions are drawn *pro* or *con*. In the case there related, the workers were the agents, both in inserting the eggs in and in removing them from the queen cells, as circumstances existing at the time required or prompted them to do. And as, in each of those instances, they evidently proceeded in accordance with what, humanly speaking, we might call the dictates of sound judgment, may we not ascribe to them, in other instances also, impulses prompting them intuitively or instinctively to the course which the law of their existence demands and prescribes?

Furthermore, queens undoubtedly lay eggs in very shallow cells. But has it occurred to the observer to inquire what, if allowed to remain there and the larvæ hatched therefrom be nursed to maturity, such eggs will produce? When laid in rudimental, shallow cells, are they not usually discarded and thrown out by the workers, if this do not happen at a time when they are naturally predisposed to tolerate and cherish drone brood? And if the eggs so laid chance to be retained, and are properly brooded and the larvæ nursed to maturity, will the product be workers or drones? We know of only a single occurrence in point; but the issue there may indicate what is ordinarily to be looked for as the result of such contingencies. A few years ago a bee-keeping friend set a top box having glass ends on the hive of one of his most populous colonies, whose queen was remarkably prolific. Within the box were fastened strips of new worker comb, to allure and guide the bees, which at once took possession and went to work, sedulously building worker cells and storing honey in them nearly as rapidly as they were built—many of them being then less than half finished. When these combs were extended nearly to the bottom of the box, the queen happened to find her way into this upper story, and laid eggs in such of the rudimental shallow cells near the apex of each comb as still contained no honey. Then finding no further call or room for her services in that quarter, she withdrew and recommenced oviposition in the main hive below. Observing the eggs in the shallow cells our friend's curiosity was excited, and he closely watched the ulterior proceedings and awaited the issue. The workers did not remove or cast out those eggs (this was in the month of June), but brooded them till hatched and nursed the larvæ, extending and slightly widening the side walls of the cells, in due time sealing them with *convex* caps; and finally there issued from them several dozen of *small drones*—such as are usually bred in *humped* worker cells—as the result of that demonstration. Hence, reasoning from analogy, while conceding that queens do not unfrequently lay eggs in royal cells, may we not claim—till direct, conclusive evidence to the contrary is furnished—that those eggs are either discarded and cast out and replaced by others, under the auspices of the workers; or if, in rare cases, hatched and nursed, produce *drones*—usually *still-born*, or prematurely perishing in the cell. —ED.

[For the American Bee Journal.]

Eggs in Queen Cells.

MR. EDITOR:—Having read in the December number of the American Bee Journal an article from the pen of Adam Grimm, and your comments on the same, in regard to the depositing of the egg in the queen cell, I have concluded to relate a case that came under my notice in the summer of 1860. One day during the swarming season several swarms came off in quick succession. One alighted on the body of a dead plum tree, and being hurried, I was somewhat rough with them, and suppose I injured the queen, but I got it into the hive and carried it to a stand. Immediately afterward another swarm was hived, and placed near the one spoken of, after which but little notice was taken of them till the eleventh day. On that morning I found that the bees after building some combs in the first hive had nearly all deserted it, and found the queen lying dead on the ground in front. The deserters had joined the other swarm, and after filling the hive with comb and brood the bees had passed through a crevice in the honey board and were building in the upper chamber, from which I immediately removed them and put on boxes. In the afternoon of the same day this colony swarmed. Nearly all the bees left with the swarm, and flew directly to a tree in the woods. After returning from following the runaways, I opened the hive, and on the edge of one of the combs I found a cluster of four queen cells. I examined them carefully. There was no egg in either of them. The next morning I opened the hive again, and there was an egg in each of the four cells. About the middle of the day, as there were so few bees in the hive, I added to it a very small swarm having a queen. I looked again in the evening, and the four cells were again empty. This is conclusive evidence to me that, in this case, the eggs were placed in the cells after the queen left the hive, although they (the cells) were built while she was in it. Now, if in some cases the workers transfer the eggs to the queen cells, is it not more than probable that they do it in all cases, whether the queen is present or not?

Previous to this occurrence I had read Langstroth's work, in which your theory in regard to the impregnation of the egg is given, but was not able to account for the sex of the queen, if the egg in the queen cell is deposited there by the queen mother. Since then I have no hesitation in endorsing your theory in regard to pressure producing impregnation.

I have owned and handled bees for more than twenty years; have used the movable comb hive since 1858, and have been a reader of the Journal for the last six months.

MILTON HEWITT.

Perryopolis, Ohio, Dec. 12, 1871.

☞ The foregoing communication may serve to throw light on an interesting problem in bee-culture. The facts stated have not, we believe, been remarked before by any observer, and attention being now drawn to the matter, we trust it will next season be made a subject of careful investigation. The insertion and subsequent removal of the eggs is of itself a curious circumstance, and is probably significant. Future observations may enable us to trace its bearing on the production of queens. Observers, however, should constantly bear in mind that the object of inquiry is not to sustain or confute theory, but to elicit and establish truth.—[ED.

[For the American Bee Journal.]

Italian Bees Not Working in Boxes!

In the second line of the second column, page 102 of the Journal for November, 1871, we find the above remark, reported as made by Mr. Marvin, of St. Charles, a prominent apiarian who keeps Italian bees, and, so far as I know, keeps them exclusively. Similar remarks we find on page 109.

As box honey is most convenient for transportation to market, and fetches nearly double the price that extracted honey does, this would really be a grave charge, if it had any foundation. When I stopped selling in the spring, this year, I had only two hundred and ninety (290) colonies of bees left. Eighteen of these were queenless or had drone layer queens, and five of them became so weak that I united them with other weak stocks. A number of strong stocks were weakened in May and June, by taking bees from them to start over one hundred nuclei. These two hundred and sixty-seven (267) colonies increased to six hundred and forty-four (644), and gave nine thousand nine hundred and forty-six (9,946) pounds of box honey. At the end of July we had estimated it as amounting to twelve thousand (12,000) pounds; but, owing to the great drouth, the bees replenished their stores in the main chamber from the contents of the boxes. This yield would no doubt have been increased by four thousand (4,000) pounds more, if we had not used the extractor, and five hundred (500) pounds besides from hives that had been weakened in starting the nuclei—increasing the average yield to fifty-four (54) pounds per hive. I do not think that this looks like failing to work in boxes.

I had stocks that gave two sets full of box honey, equal to sixty-six (66) pounds, and a swarm besides. The best stock I had gave two swarms artificially made, and, with these swarms, one hundred and forty-six (146) pounds of box honey. I used fifteen frames full of comb to secure that result.

Doubtless those beekeepers who report a failure of Italian bees to work in boxes, have not the genuine Italian bees, such as we get direct from Italy. They have tried only the shining, beautiful, gentle Italian bee that does not sting, and is valued so highly by queen breeders, as it proves most satisfactory to purchasers, who consider it purest because of its beauty. I have repeatedly reported my experience with these bees in the Journal. I found the same fault with them, and will concede that they are not worth keeping, if kept to secure box honey. There seems to be one great fault with them. They cannot or will not produce wax as the black bees, the hybrids, or the *unrefined* Italian bees from Italy. They are usually very weak in the spring, and recover too late to do much. The same observation has been made by other beekeepers. During last summer I received orders for queen bees from two customers that had got queens from me two years ago. Both write that the workers reared from these queens were much crosser and not as fine looking as their other Italian bees, but proved to be very productive. "Send me another queen," says one, "of the same brood. I do not care how cross the bees may be. I want bees for business, and not for show."

I have been experimenting this summer with the *coming bee*, as a correspondent of the Journal names it, and will send a report respecting it in a short time.

A. Grimm.

Jefferson, Wis., Nov. 1871.

[For the American Bee Journal.]

The Honey Extractor, Side Boxes, &c.

Mr. Editor:—I see in your valuable Journal that some prefer the use of the honey extractor, to the entire exclusion of boxes. Others prefer boxes entirely, and will not allow even a place for the Extractor. Now, I take the ground that both are advantageous. I have one of J. L. Peabody's machines, which works to perfection. The machine is easily cleaned, and will last a lifetime.

I am frequently asked what proportion of the honey I can get from the comb. I would say, without fear of contradiction, that I can take ninety-five per cent. of old or ninety-eight per cent. of new honey from the combs, without injuring them in the least, and that with less labor than would be required to take the same amount in boxes. The honey when taken as it is gathered seems quite thin, and looks as though it might sour; but it gradually becomes thick until it has the same consistence as other honey, and as cool weather advances it becomes candied. At least such is my experience. As to obtaining more honey with the Extractor than can be secured in boxes, I will give an instance to prove that such is the case. Quite late in the season (about the time basswood commenced to bloom) I made two artificial swarms, as near alike as possible: one black, the other Italian. On the black swarm I placed boxes, and used the Extractor with the Italians. Now for the result. I took from the black swarms (they filling their hive with comb and honey sufficient to winter) twenty-four pounds of box honey. The Italians have comb and honey the same as the others, and I have taken one hundred and twenty-four pounds of honey, making a difference of one hundred pounds in favor of the Extractor. Now, if we allow one half for the superiority of the Italians over the common bee, we still have fifty pounds, or twice the amount stored in boxes, in favor of the honey extractor. I admit that with us the extracted honey is not so salable as box honey, and therefore I prefer to produce both. H. Alley and some others recommend using boxes on the sides of the hive, and say these are a success; but with us, this season, they have proved otherwise. From the 25th of June to the 25th of July, the weather was quite cool, and within that time we had most of our surplus honey stored. The nights were very cool, and every morning the boxes placed at the sides of the hive would be found almost or entirely deserted, while those on the top would be well filled with bees. The consequence was that I obtained double the quantity of honey from the top boxes that I did from those placed on the sides. There was no difference in the size of the swarms that I could perceive. Had the weather been very warm, I presume the difference would not have been so great. Boxes holding about six pounds are those in general use here; yet they do not sell for as high a price as smaller ones holding two or three pounds, with but a single comb in each box; there is an objection to these small boxes, because the bees cannot keep up the requisite warmth in them, or work to so good advantage, unless they are constructed on the plan of those of Mr. Geo. T. Wheeler, of Mexico, N. Y. He has the boxes so arranged as to secure the required amount of animal heat, and still have each comb built true and even in each small box when separated. The glass, if any is used, is put on after the box is filled. There is also another advantage about these boxes, that is, the bees always finish the combs in the center of a large box first. All that you have to do is, to open the case of boxes, and so soon as any are full take them out and place empty ones in their stead. This stimulates the bees to greater activity, and overcomes the difficulty so often experienced of getting bees to work in a second set of boxes.

I am highly pleased with the American Bee Journal, and do not see how any beekeeper can do without it, even if not keeping more than two or three stocks of bees. Would it could come twice as often. Wishing you and the Journal much success, I remain yours,

G. M. Doolittle.

Borodino, N. Y., Nov., 1871.

[For the American Bee Journal.]

Comb Honey, or Extracted?

MR. EDITOR:—As we are on our way home from the convention at Cleveland, and have to undergo the painful ordeal of "laying over" to-day at Louisville, Ky., we thought we could not spend the time more pleasantly in any way than in writing to the Journal. We attended the convention mainly to satisfy ourself by consultation with honey raisers from different sections of the country as to the comparative profitableness of raising box or extracted honey. Or, rather, we wanted to learn more particularly whether we could in the future stand a reasonable chance of selling, at a fair price, all the extracted honey we could raise—say at one-half the price that comb honey commands.

If the convention had satisfied us fully on this point, we, for one, should have imbibed our full share of the motto: "Be happy," that was displayed so conspicuously on the wall in the rear of our venerable and pleasant looking president.

We went to the convention strongly prejudiced in favor of running our apiary for extracted honey alone, as we have it arranged now for that kind of management; and as we commenced this year with only eight double hives and seventeen single ones, and increased the stock to thirty-six two-story and sixteen single ones, and obtained nearly two tons of extracted honey, we felt certain that in another year, we could increase the stock to one hundred colonies, and obtain ten thousand (10,000) pounds of honey. This, even at ten cents per pound, would pay handsomely. But where could we find a market for all this in bulk? And as there are hundreds of beekeepers who could, and perhaps will do the same thing, is there not danger of the business being overdone?

We all know that the fruit business has been overdone, and the days for fancy prices are gone. That business certainly offered no more inducements than the production of extracted honey does now, even at ten cents per pound. The fraud of adulteration could be lived down, if there were any reasonable prospect that the demand for extracted honey would nearly keep pace with the production. Another trouble is, that the low grades of West India honey must always come in competition with it.

It is generally admitted that we must build up a market for extracted honey; and as it is a maxim among fruit men, that "he that introduces a new fruit, must be its own buyer," we are a little afraid this might apply also to extracted honey. Above all things in the world, we dislike to have anything to sell which nobody wants to buy. We find that there is already a good market for comb honey almost anywhere, and in many cities, there is not half a supply. On our way to the convention and back, we talked with grocery men in Nashville, Louisville, Indianapolis, Cincinnati, &c., and find that they are all anxious for consignments of box honey, saying that they can get from twenty-five to thirty-five cents per pound for it. It sells very readily, and they say they never had so large a supply but they could sell it all in a few days. But none of them wants to sell extracted honey. The complaint is that it goes slow; that their customers are afraid of it; that there has been so much adulteration, that most buyers of honey, who are not judges, prefer to buy and pay more for comb honey, for fear of being imposed upon. That many of their customers, when wanting a simple sweet, will generally buy molasses or syrup, because it is cheaper; while the wealthy classes, who wish it principally for show on the table, want nice white comb honey. These are about the facts which we have been able to gather from grocery men, and we hope that others, who have had more experience, will tell us if they are correct.

On the other hand, we have an exalted opinion of the speed and power of railroads; but especially is our impression lively as to their *smashing* ability; and in the distant future, we can see visions of smashed-up honey combs, which my little pets and myself have labored so hard all the year to fix up so nicely. And, saddest of all, to receive from our grocery man the discouraging intelligence that "your honey arrived very much broken, and leaking badly; and if we can sell it at all, we shall have to sell it very low."

If we could only sell extracted honey, how simple and nice it would be only to have a good honey extractor and a lot of good iron-bound whisky barrels, and we could ship to the end of the world, and the railroad men might tumble it about to their hearts' content, without damage to it or me.

How shall we send our honey to market? When shall we send it? Where shall we send it? To whom shall we send it? Upon this subject, we feel that our ideas are rather "tangled" up, and, like the drone question, it is as clear as mud to us. Brother and *sister* beekeepers, we want your advice on the *honey* question. The drone question we leave for Dr. Bohrer, and feel that he will be found ready and equal to the occasion, if not *superior* to it.

S. W. COLE.

Andrew Chapel, Tenn.

[For the American Bee Journal.]

How to make Super Hives.

The way commonly recommended by beekeepers, to get up super hives from which to extract honey during a plentiful yield, is as follows: Put a box of the same size as the lower or main box, without bottom or honey-board, after removing the latter from the hive that is calculated to be doubled, on the top of this, and removing a part of the combs from what is now the lower chamber, into the upper story—filling up both sections with empty frames, and putting a honey-board and cover on top of the upper section. By following this advice in former days, I found that it did not work according to my anticipations. It appeared to me as if the large amount of empty room all at once given, discouraged the bees, or so cooled-off their brood-nest, that they were unable to build much comb, or leave the hive for the collection of honey. The bees built only a small quantity of comb, and at the end of the season had stored less honey than hives which I had only supplied with boxes. I have since adopted different methods of making double hives. One of these is the following: At the time when the honey harvest commences, or about two weeks previous, I select such stocks as I intend to use as double hives. I do not choose the strongest hives with very prolific queens, but such as are only of medium strength, because otherwise the colony might insist upon swarming, and thus spoil the game. For each of the hives selected, I have one of the super hives ready, into which I place all the brood and store-combs but one, of a colony that has already swarmed naturally—after brushing off every bee from those combs into the mother hive, which remains on its old stand, and into which the young swarm returns voluntarily, because the queen either would not fly, or is returned by the apiarian. By doing so, the super hive is at once filled with as many frames as I find it desirable to have in it; the colony gets a large access of workers from the daily hatching brood, and the cells are filled with honey as fast as the brood leaves, if the harvest is good. Only in a few hives the queens will continue to breed in these super hives, by refilling the middle combs with eggs. In little more than a week, the brood from the former queen will be sealed, and the combs can be emptied of honey without fear of throwing out the larva, or breaking the combs, as brood combs and old combs are much stronger than new ones. Of course, the apiarian does not increase his stock any by this method; but he will not fail to get a large amount of extracted honey from the super hive, and in good season, a good yield of box honey from his swarm, that received all the bees of the stock it came from, and one frame with brood besides.

A second method is the following: About a week before the honey harvest commences, I will unite as many hives as have swarmed *only once*, on the same day on which they swarmed, making one of two, treating one as the main hive, and using all the combs of the other to fill up the super hive, with all the bees of both stocks that remained in them after the swarms left. The new or double hive they created, I set on a new stand, giving the young swarms the stands of the old stocks. In this way I get an increase of one stock from two. The young swarms will be strong, supplying box honey in a good season; and the double hive thus formed will in a few days have no unsealed brood in any of the comb, and could all be emptied of honey, if found desirable. But I advise bee-keepers to clear out the super hive only every three days, if full or nearly so. I have not had any double hive that was formed in this manner, give a second swarm, or that had not a large amount of honey stored. In the double hive, there will be a young queen in the fall. If desirable, such a double hive can be separated a little before the end of the honey season, and the queenless part supplied with a fertile queen, if increase of colonies is wanted; otherwise, the combs of the upper story may be emptied and kept for future use, immediately after the main honey season is over, and the bees will store what little honey they still gather, in one hive, which is more desirable than to have it stored in two.

A third way to make double hives, is this: Put on a super hive, and furnish it with empty combs, if you have them. The colony will occupy those combs immediately, if strong enough. I use no honey-board between the hives, and put one or two combs or frames less in the upper story than in the lower, to keep the bees from sealing over the honey as quick as they would do if they had the full number of combs. I have had them lengthen the cells, so that some of the combs contained twice as much honey as they would otherwise do.

I have extracted honey from the main hive repeatedly, but find it much more difficult to remove the bees. There is usually brood in nearly every cell, and this is injured or thrown out, if not very carefully handled. After two years' trial, I recommend getting up double hives for the extractor.

And now, Mr. Editor, I hope that the foregoing will be plain enough to be understood by beginners in the bee business. I am well aware that I write nothing that is new to experienced beekeepers, and would not even have thought to write for beginners, if I had not received many letters of inquiry, that I got tired of answering and explaining separately.

ADAM GRIMM.

Jefferson, Wis., Nov. 25, 1871.

[For the American Bee Journal.]

Bee Hives.

MR. EDITOR :—The above caption is now one of the "vexed question" ranking with that of the "purity of Italian queens." After all that has been written about the hive by the most prominent bee-*men*, I hate to add anything; but as the Journal is open to all, to give their views and experience, I will candidly give mine for what it is worth. Of all the hives I have seen and tried, none have suited me better than the regular Langstroth. But even that does not come up to my view of what a good and useful hive ought to be. In the April number of the Journal, current year, page 240, J. L. Hubbard describes just *the hive we want.* I will give his words :

"We want a hive which can be completely closed and fastened, so that it can be set in a wagon, or sent off by express, safely, whenever it is deemed desirable. It should not take over five minutes to fasten it securely, leaving sufficient ventilation. It should be of such a shape that it will pack to good advantage, for convenience of winter storage and transportation. The frames should remain firm. In hives where the frames are not fixed they will swing easily after being used in the machine. I specify these needs, because it is so often necessary to remove bees, and with many kinds of hives packing is inconvenient, taking up much time; and also because the subject of moving bees from one location to another, to gather different crops of honey is attracting attention. This branch of business would undoubtedly be carried on quite extensively, if hives were as easily moved as so many boxes of beans. I have never yet practiced this; but want to get my hives in such a shape that I can do it, as I believe in it. Will not those who have done so, give us some ideas of the subject?"

I exactly agree with Mr. Hubbard, in the above description of *the hive we* want, and shall adopt the Triumph Bee Hive by W. R. King, as I think it comes nearer the above description than any I ever saw or heard of, except Adair's sectional hive, which I find too inconvenient to handle. The Triumph has close fitting frames, or *fixed;* can be closed up and fastened in less than five minutes, and has sufficient ventilation for transportation in the hottest weather. It is the best ventilated hive I have ever seen. It is also well adapted for wintering on the summer stand. The close fitting frames literally making one hive in another, which is warm in winter and cool in summer. Also, by means of a partition board, it can be enlarged or contracted at will, and in a few minutes, to suit the size of the swarm; and in the honey-gathering season it can be enlarged, so as for the bees to make all surplus in frames in the body of the hive and on top; and it is well adapted for the extractor. If the apiarian would rather have his honey stored in caps, he can be accommodated with this hive. It is also self-cleansing by means of a moth-trap drawer in the bottom; but that is of minor importance. It can be made without the moth-trap; but I think that by means of the moth-trap drawer, it is the best self-cleaner and ventilator I ever saw. Also the frame of this hive is just the size I want, being 9x12 inside, and is a great advantage to those rearing queens, as three or four of such frames will make a pretty strong queen-raising nucleus, which can be kept strong by exchanging frames with full hives, and so save the trouble of feeding and reinforcing with bees. The frames are so adopted as to secure straight combs. These are only my views, as I have tried only one of them this season, and it has given satisfaction, convincing me of the superior advantages of this hive over many others, I will not say over all others, for I want to try a thing, and in fact always do try a thing, before I give my experience, or what I know of it from experience. I have not given all the advantages of this hive yet; but the length to which I am spinning this out, warns me to stop for the present.

R. M. ARGO.

Lowell, Ky., Nov. 27, 1871.

[For the American Bee Journal.]

Cursory Remarks and Observations.

DEAR EDITOR:—I intend again trying to drop you and the readers of our beloved Journal a few of my thoughts, experiences, &c., in order to give you a better chance to select such articles as may seem best calculated to promote the worthy cause of bee-culture. I think many others of your subscribers who have hitherto contributed nothing in this way would confer a favor on the bee family and often aid the inexperienced if they would take notes of what is daily transpiring in their apiaries, and send them to the editor to give him a larger supply of materials from which to select. Nor should any feel disappointed if his contribution does not appear, but rather be glad that there was in the editor's possession some article better suited for publication, or just then better adapted to the passing season.

The first thing I do when I receive the Journal is to put a few stitches in the back, rip open the edges of the leaves, take a hurried glance over the pages, and if the mill is not running empty, pick out what interests me most. I often have to let it drop, and run to some work, but that evening it gets pretty thoroughly finished, even if it takes till twelve o'clock to finish it. In two days after receiving it I would be ready for the next number.

Well, I see in the August number that Novice has a bran new scale, to test matters closely. I received one also about the same time, but, brother Novice, I would not trade even with you, as you say yours only weighs sixty pounds, and you cannot weigh a Langstroth hive on it. My scale cost fifteen dollars. It is a Fairbank's and Greenleaf double beam platform counter scale, with brass hopper, and will weigh two hundred and eighty-four (284) pounds, and as low as half an ounce. I like it very much, and think it is the very thing for bee keepers. They should each have one. I had a hive of hybrids in a Langstroth on the scale from the 16th of August, with the following result: August 16th, gain ½ lb., 17th, ¾ lb., 18th, 1 lb., 19th, 1½ lbs., 20th, 2½ lbs., 21st, 1¾ lbs., 22d, 2½ lbs., 23d, 2¼ lbs., 24th, 3¼ lbs., 25th, 2 lbs., 26th, 3 lbs., 27th, 4½ lbs., 28th, none, rainy and cold, 29th, lost 1 lb., 30th, gained 1 lb., 31st, 4 lbs., Sept. 1st, 5 lbs., 2d, 5 lbs. The hive was then removed and another put on of black bees, not quite as good results. I did not try my best hive, which would have shown much better results. When I weighed them this fall, I only found out which was my best hive. The above can be considered the product of fall pasturage. Novice's, I judge, was spring honey, as his article had to be in Washington by the 10th of August. My hive was always weighed in the evening. In the morning it always lost from two to three pounds. I cannot see how Novice's gained from six to thirteen ounces so early as from six to seven, seven to eight, and eight to nine o'clock in the morning. Mine only commenced gaining from twelve to six in the afternoon. On September 23d, they were still gathering at the rate of one and a half to two pounds per day. Soon after that frost stopped their operations. My best hive goes into winter quarters with one hundred and seventy-six (176) pounds, hive and all. Take fifty pounds off for hive, leave one hundred and twenty-six (126) pounds. Take off again thirty-five pounds for bees, combs, and winter stores, would leave ninety-one pounds of surplus, that I could yet extract if I had an extractor. Do you think, brother editor, that thirty-five pounds is enough to allow for bees, combs, and honey for winter, if they are wintered out of doors?*

My present stock consists of twenty-five colonies in Gallup-Langstroth hives. I place them with their backs together, stuffing hay between them and around the hive, with the exception of the front. The north and west sides are boarded up and covered, leaving the east and south side open. Last winter I had them in my cellar, which is very dry, with not quite as good results as I should have liked to see. How the present plan will do, I may let you know, if we live next spring—as wintering bees is one of our greatest difficulties; that is wintering them successfully.

I suppose my subscription will soon run out, but send the Journal right along, and your money will soon follow.

I have some lumber ready for Gallup hives, as quick as we get that "hash," if it pleases me.

My article is getting long, so I will close, wishing success to you and the Journal, and subscribing myself as before.

A MILLER, *by profession,*
but not a MOTH MILLER.

[For the American Bee Journal.]

Useful Suggestions.

MR. EDITOR:—Many of our experienced apiarians, who write very interesting articles for the Journal, are not explicit enough in describing the smaller details of any process or article described.

First.—For instance all of our eminent beekeepers agree that feeding in the spring promotes early breeding and a consequent great yield of honey, if nature does her part. Various styles of feeders are described, and recipes for making stimulation bee-feed, and just when and how to introduce it to the bees. But in no instance, as I have thus far seen, do they tell us *how much* to feed at a time. If a beginner is to buy sugar for spring feeding by what method can he estimate the amount required? Is there no definite rule to guide us as to how much to feed to a good strong colony daily? Those who advocate and practice feeding should be able to tell us somewhere near how many pounds or ounces per day, will put the queen in the best possible humor for depositing eggs rapidly and right end up with care.

Secondly.—The honey emptying machine has been described many times in the Journal, and directions published telling us how to get up home-made machines. But the writers all forget to tell us what kind of wire cloth to use to support the comb in the machine. In the construction of my machine, I first used fine woven wire, but it was liable to clog and required greater speed to extract the honey. I now use coarse wire cloth, with better success; yet think of dispeusing with wire cloth altogether another season, and use long strips of tin, one inch wide, doubled lengthwise and placed about one inch apart. I operate the extractor in our cellar, which is a very convenient and capital place. The honey runs directly into a strainer, and from thence into jars or barrels. My strainer will hold twenty-five pounds, tapers down to a point, and is provided with a stop-cock at the lower extremity. Jars placed on the scales under the strainer, can be filled to a nicety, and not a single drop of the precious sweets wasted. I find it pays, in the long run, to have everything in the apiary fixed and convenient.

Thirdly.—Movable comb hives are indispensable to successful bee management; but among all the *pros* and *cons*, descriptions and controversies, the length and breadth of the frame is discussed continually, still I have seen no word about the thickness of the frame. Perhaps thickness was settled before I caught the bee fever, about two years ago. But examination of hives at present shows a diversity of construction upon this point, for frames raging from ⅞ inch to 1⅛ inches in thickness, are used. In the American, Bay State, and others, ⅞ inch is the standard. Mr. Quinby uses an inch frame, with half an inch space. Others use 1⅛ inch frames, with ⅜ inch space. And here I would ask Mr. Quinby what is the use of so much space between the frames? Are not the bees inclined to fill out the space, and build more drone comb, than in a thinner frame? My little experience leads me to discard thick frames, for my bees seem determined to build drone comb in all thick frames, while ⅞ inch frames give better results. And I can see but a trifle difference between Mr. Quinby's inch frames and half-inch space, and a 1⅛ inch frame with ⅜ inch space.

A large number of beekeepers will soon be constructing their hives, and a little light from those who have experimented and given the subject years of thought, would no doubt interest a large number of your readers. We want the *thick* and *thin* subject agitated, as well as length and breadth.

SCIENTIFIC.

[For the American Bee Journal.]

The Onward Movement.

MR. EDITOR:—I send you to-day two dollars for the seventh volume of the Journal, for a young man who has never kept bees, but who is going to begin; and he will succeed, for he commences with the Journal, as his *first step.*

It has been my experience that those who have kept bees *for years,* in the old way, and ought to have gained at least a *desire* for improvement, are slow to adopt new ideas; while the new beginner is all alive to its importance, and will commence with movable combs and Italian bees, and comprehend their value, while

* The quantity of stores required depends much on the mode of wintering adopted, the kind of hive used, and the character and deviation of the winter. Mr. Bickford's method is inexpensive, easily managed, and if carefully executed with a stock having a due proportion of young bees and a healthy fertile queen, is invariably successful.—[ED.

old fogies are plodding along with their brimstone boxes, and complaints of poor seasons and poorer luck.

In this section of country the season of greatest harvest varies very much from year to year. This year it was in August, from Clethra (pepper bush) and red clover; last year it was in September and October, from the Michaelmas aster and the golden rod; and the year before it was during July, from white clover.

Those who keep their stocks always strong, do well; while the rest go hit or miss. For instance, this year, from my eight or nine colonies, I have gathered over four hundred pounds of honey, and increased to eighteen colonies. Others in this neighborhood have not had a pound of surplus honey from a greater number of stocks; and it is not at all strange that young beginners ask my advice, instead of going to those who keep bees in hives and with the ways handed down from their great grandfathers.

In reading over quite a number of books which have been published for the last hundred years on bees, I was astonished to find so much in them which harmonizes with modern ideas, and so much also which has been claimed as new inventions and recent discoveries—movable frames, guide combs, artificial swarming, stimulative feeding in the spring, uniting weak colonies in the fall, the use of puff ball and tobacco smoke, side surplus boxes, ventilation or air chamber over the combs in the main hive, and under the surplus boxes, the treatment of foulbrood a hundred years ago by *pruning* and extra feeding. All these, and many more points of interest, are plainly discussed; and there is only one solution to the mystery that so few knew of or appreciated them, and that is—"*Our Journal*" wasn't born. Yours, very truly,

E. P. ABBE.

New Bedford, Mass., Nov. 20, 1871.

☞ There are folks who wish in their hearts that the AMERICAN BEE JOURNAL had *never been born*, since they can no longer venture to palm off old things as their own *discoveries*, without fear of detection and exposure.—[ED.

[For the American Bee Journal.]

Start of a New Correspondent.

MR. EDITOR:—I am a new beginner in apiculture, and wish to ask one or two questions. *First.*—How is it that we hear so many bee men talking about *swarming time*, and letting bees swarm when in movable comb hives? I take it that one of the great advantages of the movable comb hive is that colonies may be divided up at the owner's will, and not have any "swarming time."

Second.—What is the best plan to work on when transferring from an old box hive to a new movable comb hive? I hear some say that they have taken the old hive, and turned it bottom side up, and set the new hive over it, rapping smartly on the old hive, when the bees would all leave, and take to the new hive. I have tried it in the month of August, when there were a great many young bees, and could not in any instance drive more than half of them, as the young bees would not leave the combs. But the last ones I transferred I got out with very little trouble, in the following manner: I took the old box hive and carried it away a few rods from its stand, turned it bottom side up on a suitable bench or a box. Then, with a cold chisel, cut the nails so that I could take off one side of the hive. By the time I have pounded enough to cut the nails I will have the bees in a much more tractable state, and the young bees will crawl over on the outside of the hive, and cluster and stay until I get ready to shake them into the new hive. After cutting out the honey, I shake the young bees into the new hive, and the old ones will have flown to the old stand, where a decoy hive or box should have been placed to receive them. These I also shake in front of the entrance of the new hive. The brood combs I transfer to frames, fasten them with wooden pegs, and insert in the hive immediately. Now, I am a new hand, and may have asked questions which have been answered many a time in the Journal; but I have not seen it, of course.

I started with two colonies, which I bought last spring—one in a box hive, and the other in a small tobacco keg. The small one I had to feed to bring it through. The keg colony gave me a natural swarm, June 20th. The other did not swarm at all; but about the first of August I made an artificial swarm from it, by taking four or five quarts of the bees that were clustered outside of the hive and putting them in a new movable comb hive, with one or two frames of brood comb, and setting the new hive in place of the old one, and setting the latter away in a new location. In sixteen days I found that the bees in the new hive had a new queen out (there were no queen cells in the brood combs inserted), and in less than one week she was laying eggs. The frames of brood were taken from a young swarm which I bought for three dollars—furnishing the hive myself. Soon after this I made two swarms of the young swarm from the keg, and also transferred both old colonies to new movable comb hives. On the 21st day of August I transferred two swarms, and gave them three frames half full of brood combs from their old hives, but no honey; and in three weeks they had three hives full—sixty pounds each. The bees and brood combs were given me if I would take the honey out.

I have now eight stands, all in movable comb hives, and intend to do something more next year. I have done almost all kinds of handling with them, except introducing queens, and shall try that next year. I never saw but one swarm of Italian bees, and they were so cross that I could not see them until they were out of sight, for they drove me out of the yard several times. They were said to be pure Italians, but I doubted it and thought they were hybrids, for they acted like yellow jackets.

One thing more, and I will bring this communication to a close. For one of my neighbors I drove bees enough from a colony to make a new swarm, and placed them on the old stand. They had not been there three minutes before another swarm (which had been transferred two weeks previous and were working well) were coming into this hive, and all went to work as peaceably and quiet as any single swarm. The swarm that left its own hive had several pounds of honey and plenty of brood in all stages. It made a good thing for the new swarm, for it gave them a queen at the start to go to work with. Who can account for this occurrence?

I consider the Journal an invaluable aid to bee-keepers, and could not think of being without it now. You may count me in as a regular subscriber, and I shall probably not inflict so long a communication on you very often.

J. W. CRAMER.

Oneida, Ills., Dec., 1871.

[For the American Bee Journal.]

Lessons of the Past Season.

MR. EDITOR :—As an inducement to others to report their summer's work through the Journal, I have concluded to send you a statement which approximates very nearly what I have done for my bees, and what they have done for me. "Old fossils," as a matter of course, will pursue "the even tenor of their way" despite all "book larnen" and reports, but to the wide awake, live apiculturist, the experiences of others form a "bed rock" upon which to rest secure from defeat and disaster.

I used the honey-slinger only a little, by way of experiment, and that near the close of the season.

I commenced last spring with ten hives of bees, which have increased to twenty.

Box honey procured	510 lbs.
Extracted	40 "
	550 lbs.

I have sold 248 pounds of it at an average of 27 cts. per pound, making $66.96. The remainder, for the sake of carrying out this calculation, we will estimate at 25 cts. per pound, making for it $75.50.

Total value of honey		$142 46
Value of colonies		200 00
Aggregate worth of honey and colonies		$342 46
From which deduct,		
Cost of ten new hives	$25	
" " honey boxes	10	
" " 10 old colonies	100–	135 00
Net balance		$207 46

Being about 153 per cent. on the investment.

Seven of the colonies furnished no box honey. The average yield of the remaining thirteen colonies was 39¼ lbs. each. Greatest yield from any one of the thirteen was 98 lbs., least yield from any one of the thirteen was 18 lbs. I might have taken more honey, even in boxes, but as bee-keeping is a collateral business with me, I failed to give my apiary sufficient attention during the honey harvest. The colonies are all in good condition for winter.

PRINCIPAL HONEY HARVEST.

I commenced taking honey the last week in August. Swartweed or "heart's ease," as it is called here, furnishes the best honey and the most of it. The last run was upon the golden rod, and the "thousand and one" other yellow blossoms that deck the prairies late in the fall. The last combs built are of a yellowish cast. All those from the "heart's ease" are light colored, and very rich and attractive in appearance,

The President of our State Association, Dr. L. J. Dallas, of Baldwin, has about four thousand (4000) pounds of it bottled up and for sale ; so that if any one is curious to know just how nice this "*Extract of Kansas Swartweed*" tastes, he will know where to get it. I do not design this as an advertisement for the Doctor, as he will have no trouble in selling it at a fair price, without such notoriety.

GENERAL REMARKS.

I am using some hives of my own "getting up ;" some of the Hoosier ; some of the Adair ; and some of the Quinby box hives.

I have one stand of Italians, and four hybrids ; the others are large, light colored blacks. The hybrids have done better than the pure blacks, and as well as the pure Italians, but I think that the pure blood Italians, everything else being equal, are better adapted than the blacks or any cross with them, to the climate, as well as to the great variety of the pasturage found upon the plains of Kansas.

M. A. O'NEIL.

Black Jack, Nov., 1871.

[For the American Bee Journal.]

A Bee Feeder.

DEAR JOURNAL :—We are an ardent advocate of stimulating bees in early spring, and through August and September, let the hive contain ever so much honey. Novice's idea of "cash capital" in the form of capped honey in frames, is good—nothing better for strengthening weak stocks ; yet we do not always have as much as we need, and if we had, we want to give it more in the form of natural supplies to induce breeding.

We have been using a feeder this fall which, for cheapness and utility, we deem the *ne plus ultra* of feeders ; and with your permission, Mr. Editor, will try to give a description sufficiently plain that those "who run may read."

We make a frame say six inches square of slats one inch or more wide ; cover this one side with thin muslin, drawing the edges of the cloth up all around the frame on the outside, and tacking them to the top. Then we make another frame of slats half an inch wide and six inches square. This is nailed on the bottom, leaving the muslin between the frames. The feeder may be placed over any sized hole in the honey board, where the bees can readily pass under it, without obstruction or having to climb several inches. By removing the honey board, it can be set on the frames; but it will then be necessary to lay something over the top. If "liquid sweets" run through faster than is desirable, melted wax may be spread over a portion of the bottom, or thicker muslin may be used.

RUSTIEUS.

Ohio.

[For the American Bee Journal.]

The West St. Louis County (Mo.) Beekeepers' Convention.

The first quarterly meeting of the "West St. Louis County Beekeepers' Association," was held at Manchester (Mo.), on Saturday, October 14th, 1871.

In the absence of the President, the Vice-President, J. C. Holocher, was called to the chair. The minutes of the last meeting were read and approved. The next order of business was the reading and adoption of the constitution, which, after considerable debate, was, with some modification, adopted.

On motion of A. Herzog, a committee of three was appointed to prepare subjects for discussion—namely: T. D. Woody, G. Kropp, and W. H. H. Woody.

Pending the action of the above named committee, the Vice President addressed the Convention in regard to the object of the same, briefly touching upon several very important points pertaining to apiculture.

The committee reported the following topics for discussion:

1. Natural *vs.* artificial swarming.
2. When is the best time for placing surplus honey boxes on hives?
3. What is the most profitable size for honey boxes?
4. Bee pasturage.
5. Wintering bees indoors or out.

These topics were then taken up in order, for discussion.

1. Increase of Stocks—Natural *vs.* Artificial.

Mr. Kropp said he had no success whatever in the increase of stocks artificially. He had tried it, but the bottom had fallen out. He favored increase by natural swarming, and considered such swarms superior to any artificially produced.

Mr. W. Woody said that artificial increase of stocks was best for one reason; you could increase them to the amount desired with less trouble, and have them in better condition for wintering, than if natural swarming be relied on.

2. Best Time for Applying Surplus Honey Boxes.

Mr. T. H. B. Woody thought the best time for putting on surplus honey receptacles was (if pasturage was favorable) as soon as convenient—the sooner the better; for a few days lost can never be regained. He would suggest, that as soon as the bees showed signs of gathering honey from the fields, was the time when boxes should be placed on hives; and as soon as filled and capped over, they should be taken off, and other boxes substituted in their stead.

Mr. Kropp said he practised the same method, but found that after the removal of the field boxes, the bees did not like to resume work in the empty boxes given to them. For one, he should like to know if there was no way to compel them to work in the empty boxes given them.

Mr. J. C. Holocher said he did not know of any way by which bees could be made to work immediately in boxes, without inserting a small piece of comb in the box. This, he believed, would answer the purpose admirably.

3. Most Profitable Size of Honey Boxes.

Mr. Herzog thought that boxes with glass sides, that would hold about four-and-a-half or five pounds, are the most profitable size.

Mr. J. C. Holocher thought that boxes containing about eight small frames—each frame weighing from one to two pounds—are the proper size for market. They will sell more readily, and have a better appearance.

Mr. Dosenbach had had no experience in selling or raising honey, for he had just commenced beekeeping last spring. The season was not favorable for storing surplus, but he thought the small frames the best.

Mr. T. H. B. Woody did not want box honey at all. He believed in the use of the melextractors, for you could get a larger yield, besides returning the empty combs to the bees, which was of great advantage to them.

Mr. Kropp thought boxes would do for him, for a person was liable to "sling too much from his bees," if he uses the extractor.

The hour being late, and some of the members wanting to leave for home, the remaining two topics were laid over until next meeting.

Having no further business for the convention, Mr. Whiting, of Pacific, (Mo.,) was called on for an address on apiculture, to which he responded substantially as follows:

Ladies and Gentlemen: I must confess that I am unprepared for this occasion. Being called on so unexpectedly, you must not expect me to begin at one end of bee-culture and go to the other; but I will briefly touch one or two minor points. *Who should keep bees?* I reply, one and all. All persons who own a rod of land should keep bees; and if you do not have the rod of land, keep them, any how (Laughter). If you reside in the city, it affords you an opportunity to keep bees. If you live on the mountain tops, or in the vale; if you are a mechanic, or a farmer, or a lawyer; whether you are rich, or walk in poverty's vale, you can keep bees; and they will return you a handsome reward for your care and trouble. Allow me, therefore, to say to one and all, "*keep bees;*" and to keep them successfully, it is of no difference whether you own a foot of land or not. You have a free pasturage for your bees. "*Keep the bees,*" and they will get the honey for you (cheers). Now, kind friends, I must bid you adieu, and close my short address. But I will say, go on with this work, and read on, and put it to the test. This is the only way to keep clear of all humbugs. Remember that bees need attention in the proper way, and at the proper time; and if you attend to this rightly, you will undoubtedly reap your share of success. With this I close, thanking you for your kind attention and hospitality during my visit.

At the close of this address, the association returned their sincere thanks to Mr. Whiting for the interest he had taken in the association, and in beekeeping generally.

On motion, it was resolved, to hold the next meeting at Ballwin, on the first Saturday in January, 1872, commencing at 10 o'clock, A. M.

On motion of Mr. Dosenbach, the association then adjourned.

J. C. HOLOCHER, *Vice President.*

ENUE DOSENBACH, *Secretary.*

[For the American Bee Journal.]

Notes from Northern Iowa.

DEAR JOURNAL:—Perhaps a few notes from Northern Iowa will be as interesting to the readers of the Journal, as notes from other States are to me. I see the accounts from some parts report a total failure of the honey season, while in others it was tolerably good. We have had an extra good season here, both for surplus honey and for increasing stocks. My bees stored honey from the 15th of April to the 15th of September (five months), without any cessation. I had twenty stocks in the spring, which I have increased to fifty, and have taken sixteen hundred (1600) pounds of surplus honey. I did not get an extractor till after the basswood season was over, or I would have taken one hundred pounds from each stock. I had eight colonies in the spring that gave me eight hundred (800) pounds of honey and ten new swarms. My new swarms are mostly artificial.

The plan I adopted was to drive out a swarm and set it in the place of the parent stock, and remove the parent stock to the place of a strong colony, removing the strong colony to a new place. I do not know which is the best plan to make swarms, but all plans worked well this year. After I had doubled my colonies by artificial swarming, they swarmed ten times more, just to show me that I wasn't boss.

My bees were all black, that gathered the honey; but through the kindness of friend Gallup, I obtained nine nice Italian queens, which are all comfortably situated in their new homes. I also sent to Adam Grimm for a queen, which came by return mail, and has proved to be all right.

I am a new beginner in the improved style of beekeeping. Last spring I said to my neighbors that I intended to double my stocks and take a thousand (1000) pounds of surplus honey. They said I had "bee on the brain," and that I would meet with obstacles enough before fall to cool my fevered brow. But by the help of the American Bee Journal, and many valuable lessons from Gallup, I have succeeded far beyond my expectations.

Mr. Editor, I think that "bee on the brain" is essential to success. If a person has other business on the brain, his bees will go neglected. I take solid comfort in my daily walks among my little busy workmen, while attending to their many wants. My wife, who takes pleasure in assisting in the swarming season, often takes charge of them in my absence. But when it came to extracting, what then? Why, there was honey in every dish; honey all over the house; our hands and clothes were all daubed with honey; and, to put in the variations, the bees were so loving they lit on wife's face—eyes she had, but they saw not, neither did they want to see the bees again until a short time ago, when returning from town with a bundle of goods (bought with *honey*, you know), she gave them one look, which said: you little scamps, I forgive you.

I hope to meet lots of warm-hearted beekeepers at the Cleveland convention, where I expect to have a good time.

J. W. LINDLEY.

Mitchell, Iowa, Nov. 14, 1871.

[For the American Bee Journal.]

Report from Bethlehem, Iowa.

MR. EDITOR:—In compliance with your request, I send report for 1871. I will be as brief as possible.

In the spring, I found I had twenty-six stocks, in good order, one queenless, one crippled, and one black colony. The latter I had run against an artificial Italian, as reported in the November number of the Journal. It was so weak that it could not stand the cold, and gave up the ghost. The queenless one I doubled up, and killed the crippled one, giving the combs to others. Examined and equalized the colonies, gave each a due share of bees, as near as I could, and about fifteen pounds of honey.

I also bought four swarms in gums and box hives. Two of these had cast swarms before I got them home. All new swarms were fed until their hives were built full of comb, when the weather rendered it necessary.

The result of the season's operations, was an increase to forty-nine (49) strong stocks, and two weak ones.

2,550 pounds of extracted honey.
1,502 " of box and frame honey.
500 " in old combs.

I cannot say much of the manner in which my bees have been put to into winter quarters, on account of the very serious accident I met with, which prevented me from overhauling them before putting them away. I had put in empty frames for them to fill. They usually lengthen out the cells, when put in late in the seson, instead of starting new comb.

FRED. CRATHORNE.

Bethlehem, Iowa, Dec. 11, 1871.

[For the American Bee Journal.]

Inquiries and Remarks.

MR. EDITOR:—I wish to ask several questions through the Journal, and will try to answer some in the first place.

I received two splendid queens from friend Benedict, on the 9th of August, and introduced them to black colonies in the afternoon; the first one according to his directions, by placing her on the comb near the centre of the chamber (only I dipped her in sugar syrup scented with peppermint; with which I also thoroughly sprinkled the bees, shaking them up well before turning them out of the box, instead of diluted honey, as directed.) This was done at about three o'clock, and the next day at about noon, I went to the hive and saw a dense crowd of bees in one of the entrances. I scraped them out, and there they had the queen hugged up in their centre. I released her and put her in a cage, which I inserted between two brood combs. She did not appear to be hurt, but the next morning she was dead. Why did they drag her out, after so many hours?

With the other one I followed D. L. Adair's plan, by scenting all alike and dropping her in among the bees. She was well received, and has done well. On the evening of the sixth day I brushed all the bees that had killed their queen from the combs in the chamber and removed the chamber from the case that had the Italian queen and put the other in its place. I brushed the queen and bees all off in front, and gave the chamber to the queenless colony. On the eighth day I opened it and found two queen cells capped, and three more started on the face of a piece of drone comb. I caged the two that were capped with Novice's cages, according to his directions, and when I opened the hive to see how the young queens were getting alnong, I found the cages cut loose, so that they dropped out when the sections were parted, and both queen cells destroyed. Two of these cells on the drone comb were capped over, but neither of them ever hatched out. I tried the cages on two more cells in another hive, and they were also cut out; but one of the queens was all right, and is doing well. Now I would like to know why it is so, if Novice's bees do not cut them out?

Next, I would ask Mr. C. E. Widener why a piece of wire cloth, two feet by four, would not be as good, or better than a piece three feet square, to make his wax extractor? It would make a box of one foot square and two feet high, which could be put in a much smaller kettle, than a box nine inches square and three feet long.

Then, again, I would like to know what is to become of the brood and eggs that are in the combs when introducing queens by the German process, on page 98, November number.*

Some one has asked how to keep the worms out of the hives? I would answer, simply by keeping your stocks strong, especially if there is any Italian blood about them. I had a box hive of black bees that got weak, and one morning I saw robbers pitching into it. I closed the entrance and carried it to the cellar, letting out the robbers when I got inside the door. Next day, about ten o'clock, I removed a stock of hybrids (which I suppose has a black queen that mated with an Italian drone, as I know of no chance for an Italian queen to have got in there), to the place from which I had removed the weak stock, and set the weak stock in the place of the hybrids, never dreaming that it was infested with worms. Next morning I saw that some cocoons had been carried out of it, and on turning it up I found a good handful of shatterings that the bees had made in cutting out the worms and cocoons, besides about twenty cocoons and a great number of worms of all sizes. I cleaned out the shatterings every morning, and in four days all cutting out ceased, and I did not find another worm in the hive all summer. This fall I transferred it to a frame hive, and did not find a single worm in the combs, though they were badly cut up near the top of the hive.

Trenton, Ills., Nov. 6, 1871. C. T. SMITH.

* See note on page 167.—[ED.

[For the American Bee Journal.]

The Season of 1871, in the Oil Region.

MR. EDITOR:—It is a long time since I have contributed anything to the Journal and as I have seen nothing in it from any of the beekeepers in the oil region, I concluded to write a few lines.

We are on a level here now with many of our friend beekeepers throughout this broad land, for we have had a very poor season here for both honey and increase. Very few swarms issued this summer, in this section. I had only ten swarms from seventy-six stocks. My first swarm (a hybrid) came off May 19th, and this new swarm swarmed June 27th. My first swarms of black came off June 30th.

The spring of 1871 opened exceedingly promising, both to the farmer and the beekeeper; but the drouth in May materially checked the prosperity of the latter. Our stocks were not as populous on the 1st of June as they were on the 1st of May. I saw drones flying in my yard in April, which I never saw before since I have kept bees—now seven years.

Now as concerns the honey slinger, I do not think its use would be altogether economical for this section, as our only dependence is white clover and buckwheat. Now suppose we had abstracted the clover honey, and depended on buckwheat for winter stores, would we not have been far below the level of many beekeepers who have a continuation of forage throughout the season?

Old stocks generally are in good condition for wintering, but the swarms are not. We have had a very changeable season, with frosts in every month except August, since October, 1870, and of course shall have for the next six months. Drouth was the cause of the total failure of buckwheat honey.

I met many of my neighbors at the election, and after inquiring after the welfare of my family and bees, some wanted to buy bees, and some wished to engage hives. Mr. G. said that he had bought the right of the American hive for this township from Mr. King. I told him that essrs. L. & H. own the township, having bought it three or four years ago. *Well, I don't care* said he, *I have paid Mr. King for it, and am going to have it.* Now said I, Mr. G. I reckon you are pretty badly sold, and drawing from my pocket the October number, volume seven, of the American Bee Journal, read him Mr. E. Liston's article on page 82, and also some other articles in the same number, and then asked him how is that for high? This is the paper you want to pioneer you through. It will knock all this humbuggery higher than a kite. Suppose you bought the right, what do you get? Oh, the side opening, &c., &c., said he. Now, replied I, look out for breakers, and look before you leap. The word American is a great word, and this American is a great nation; but the American hive is no *g-r-e-a-t t-h-i-n-g-s.* M. WILSON.

Meredith, Pa., Oct. 16, 1871.

[For the American Bee Journal.]

A Word of Explanation.

Our correspondence extends from Maine to Oregon, and from Canada to Texas, *all free of charge*, and before publishing the article charging the dollar, we had as high as thirty-six letters in one week, on the hive question, leaving out of view our correspondence on other subjects pertaining to bees and bee keeping. We did not wish to give a description of our hive to every one, until we had fully tested it ourselves, for after what Mr. Alley and Mr. Green said of us we actually did not know how much of a *fool* we might be. Another thing—it is not to be supposed that every *green-horn* can manage a large hive until after he has learned to use a standard hive.

Our article referred to above was intended as a burlesque on those chaps that have a hive that beats all other hives in existence, &c., and the dollar that has caused such a *fuss* was intended to stop the costly correspondence, which we are foolish enough to think that no person living would or could stand. And it has done it pretty effectually.

We had our reasons for getting up such a hive as we have, and any person who has attentively read our articles ought to know that when the proper time came we should certainly give them the description *free of charge.* It would be for our personal benefit and a great relief to do as Novice does—that is, refuse to answer correspondents entirely. But when we come to consider how many thousands there are that wish for information, and yet feel a delicacy about asking for that information publicly we cannot refuse. Therefore after working hard all day we devote hours of the night, when others are sound asleep, to answering the inquiries of correspondents, and yet for all this, see the *kicks, cuffs* and *abuse* we receive through the Journal from certain gentry of the long-eared persuasion. Please excuse us, Mr. Editor, for giving them just one little touch of our pen. The worst we wish them is that they might be placed in our position for one year. We would also state here that a Mr. Jones, of some place in Canada, sent us a dollar, but neglected to give us the name of his post-office. Will he please take notice?

THAT HIVE OF GALLUP'S.

Our standard hive is twelve inches from front to rear, twelve inches high, and eighteen inches wide, inside measure, containing twelve frames, and having a cap eight inches high. Our nucleus hive is in the same form, containing twelve frames, with four apartments, each apartment containing three frames (standard frames). We will say it extends east and west, or is an oblong square. The entrance to one apartment faces the east, one south, one west, and one north, with a honey board over each apartment, so that each can be opened without disturbing the bees in the others. In one of these nucleus hives we raised the past season twenty-eight queens; had twenty standard frames filled with nice worker combs, extracted sixty pounds of surplus honey, and are now wintering four spare queens in it, with abundance of honey to winter on. Now you can readily see that in the fall we can readily put all those combs and bees together in a standard hive by removing three of the queens, and have a good standard colony. We can exchange combs, brood, &c., with any standard colony, for strengthening up, supplying with honey, or for any other desirable purpose. Four and a half inches is the right space for three combs, but we make it five inches. This gives ample room for handling, without endangering the queen. By working four nuclei in one hive they are of a mutual warmth, one to the other, and there is no more danger of losing a queen than there is where we have each separate.

Then we have what we call an *emergency hive.* If we run short of hives we can put one of these together in about twenty minutes, and by having a supply of frames on hand we are all right. This is simply an open box without top or bottom, containing twelve frames. We saw off a rough board for a bottom and one for a top, and put a swarm in. This hive can be completed at our leisure, so there is nothing lost.

Our next hive, in outward appearance, looks so much like a Langstroth hive, with Langstroth entrance blocks, that we really think he has somewhat infringed on our rights, and we take this opportunity of telling him so.* We call this hive our "Youreka, Back Action, Extraction, Reversible, Revolvable, Non-Swarming, Movable Comb, Twin Bee Hive." (Please to take notice that hereafter we shall charge a dollar extra for simply writing the name in full of this wonderful hive.)

This hive is simply a case made Langstroth style, with a centre board with passages for bees, and containing one set of our frames directly in

*Keep a sharp lookout, or the "Great [Humbug] American Apiarian" will *sneak* out a patent on these blocks, and prosecute both Mr. L. and yourself as *infringers!*—[ED.

the rear of the other portion, and entrances at both ends just alike. We made six of these containing thirteen frames in each apartment, or twenty-six frames to the hive. We made one containing sixteen frames in each aparrment, or thirty-two frames to the hive, and this gave us the most satisfaction. We made a cap eight inches high for appearance sake, and for wintering purposes, and thus we can set boxes over one set of combs and use the extractor on the other. We make the roof in the Bay State form, independent of the cap, so that it sets on over the chamber or cap, sugar box fashion. In summer if we do not use the cap we can lay it away, and the roof protects the main hive.

In future we shall make the caps high enough to hold a set of standard frames for some of our queens occupy the entire twenty-six frames, over four thousand (4000) cubic inches, with brood, and we are bound to furnish them with room according to their strength, even if they do lay themselves to death, though we have no fears on that head. Now we shall have our fifty-two frame hive, a thirty-two frame hive, a twenty-six frame hive, a twelve frame hive, and nucleus hives, all containing the same size frame, and any frame in the yard will fit in any hive in the yard, and in any place in any hive, and they are all reversible.

This article will be too long to permit us to give the management, but, friends, we will now come down to dead earnest. No joking now! A large colony of bees will store surplus honey, while a small one scarcely makes a living. Any colony, especially the Italians, will store more surplus honey in the same apartment with the queen than they will otherwise. Nearly every person familiar with the Italians has noticed this trait in their character—that is, their reluctance to take possession of surplus boxes, in comparison with the black bees. This was very forcibly illustrated by Mr. Langstroth at the Cincinnati Convention. When we give the queen room according to her strength, she will breed beyond all our previous calculations—that is, a good, prolific queen. A hive to suit our notions must be so constructed that we can enlarge or contract the brooding and storing capacity at will; or, in other words, one in which we can manage the smallest or the largest swarm to best advantage.

As this article is getting long, and we must soon close. Our first swarm came out on the 14th of May. We hived it in one end of our thirty-two frame hive, making use of the division board the same as we do in our standard hive. As soon as the bees commenced building drone comb we removed the division board and filled up with worker combs. When these were all occupied with brood we filled the other end of the hive also with worker comb, moving some of the sealed brood into that apartment, and replacing with empty worker comb in front. The queen soon began to spread herself most gloriously into all parts of the hive, and when the basswood began to bloom, we had a bursting swarm in that hive, you had better believe. The last of June we commenced using the extractor, first taking all the honey from one end of the hive, and the next time all from the other. We extracted from that hive every third day, and we now know that we ought to have taken it out every other day, for it was all of it half sealed every time, which you will readily see involves a loss of time, a waste of honey, especially when they are gathering rapidly. At one time I did not overhaul it for five days. Consequently they filled up the combs, built queen cells, and on the 4th of July out came a rousing swarm (celebrating the 4th, I guess). I have them in a box, extracted all the honey from the parent hive, cut out the queen cells, and returned the swarm. They went to work with a will. In overhauling the hive I endeavored to keep the brood about equally apportioned in each apartment. The queen passed into all parts of the hive freely, and the workers poured out and in, at both ends of the hive. The regular entrances were left open to their full capacity, besides an inch hole in the centre of each end, yet during a large part of the time both porticoes were clustered full of bees at night, when they quit work.

In thirty days I obtained from the hive fifty (50) gallons of excellent thick honey (a gallon will weigh twelve pounds). An average of twenty pounds per day for thirty days in succession is not bad for one swarm of bees. I took five and a half gallons from that hive the first week in September, have at least six gallons more in the hive, over and above what will be required for wintering the swarm.

Mr. Editor, please to tell Novice that I am not going to tear down that hive yet. My better half suggests that I put on a steeple, and call it a church instead of a bee hive! What a congregation, and what excellent sermonizers.

And now, Mr. Editor, if any more of them 'ere donkeys wish to bray at Gallup, don't hold them back a particle, just let 'em bray!

Orchard, Iowa, Dec., 1871. E. GALLUP.

[For the American Bee Journal.]

A Puzzle.

Some time in August, last summer, I killed the virgin queen of a nucleus hive, because the bees had crippled one of her hind legs so much that I feared she was unable to become fertilized. Next day I opened this nucleus for the purpose of inserting a new queen cell, and found the bees perfectly quiet and content. On examination I found among them an apparently fertile queen, whose wings were clipped. As there was no other nucleus within ten feet of this one, where did this queen with clipped wings come from? There was standing at that distance, directly behind this one a nucleus which had swarmed off; and as at that season of the year, I nearly always clip the wings of the young queens as soon as they become fertile, the queen of this decamping swarm could probably not accompany the workers, may she not have fallen to the ground and afterwards travelled ten feet ahead, and then been *boosted* up by the workers of the other queenless nucleus? Or how did such a queen get in there? A. GRIMM.

Jefferson, Wis., Dec. 1871,

THE AMERICAN BEE JOURNAL.

Washington, January, 1872.

1872.

While politicians are cogitating and agitating the question of a *new departure* or of *no departure*, seemingly with little prospect of reaching a satisfactory solution, beekeepers may, we think, look forward with confidence to an extraordinary and unprecedented advance in their business in the year on which we are just entering. They are on the verge of a new era—old modes and practices, old-fashioned hives, and hives as hitherto constructed, are destined to be superseded; and that which a few years ago was a mere by-play in the commerce of the country, is about to assume a prominence and an importance hardly conceived of even by the sanguine a year ago. But those who would reap benefit from this progress in improvement, must keep themselves advised of each onward movement as it is made.

☞ Very many articles intended for this number of the Journal, reached us too late to be available. The holidays compel us to be early on the ground, or lag lamentably in the rear.

☞ We have received a copy of "VICK'S ILLUSTRATED CATALOGUE AND FLORAL GUIDE;" for 1872, published by James Vick, Rochester, N. Y.,—a decided improvement on those previously issued.

☞ The instrument called *rafraichisseur* by the French, and used by them for perfuming gloves, handkerchiefs, &c., which we mentioned two years ago, as employed by Major Von Hruschka in introducing queen bees, is simply the instrument long known in this country as *the atomizer*. It is made in various styles, and sold at prices varying accordingly. It can be readily obtained from or through any druggist. Very good ones are sold here, in Washington, at fifty cents each, and they are quite as efficient for the purpose designed, in bee-culture, as those much higher in price.

☞ We do not share the apprehensions of several of our correspondents, as regards the overstocking of districts with bees, or over-production of honey. In a new business, such as beekeeping for commercial purposes is, occasional difficulties will undoubtedly present themselves, but are sure to be of only temporary force. It will be some years yet before the ordinary sources of forage in any district will prove inadequate to supply the colonies kept there, if these be properly managed; and then artificial pasturage can be furnished to an almost unlimited extent. Amid a large and rapidly increasing population, also, the demand for honey is a certain and growing one, and likely to keep pace fully with the supply. Of course, we do not suppose that "fancy prices" can or will be kept up, nor is it desirable that they should be; but the business will, on the whole, always be remunerative, especially as new uses for the article will, from time to time, come in to sustain the markets. With care and attention almost every beekeeper can open and secure for himself, in his own neighborhood, a good and steady market for the product of his bees; and then, even "extracted honey," which now causes so much uneasiness in some minds, will command a good price, and be readily sold. This home market, within his immediate reach, the beekeeper who aims at a steady and *paying* business, should strive to establish and cherish. Suddenly rushing large quantities of honey to a market unprepared to receive it, and there ordering forced sales, will, as in the case of any other article of merchandise, produce depression of price and loss. This should be avoided, and may readily be guarded against, as honey is by no means a perishable commodity that must be promptly disposed of, like the small fruits of our gardens and orchards, but can be easily and safely kept stored (especially in barrels), and brought out as called for by the requirements of the market. Dealers, too, will soon become aware of this fact, and supply themselves with honey, as with other merchandise, to provide for the exigencies of trade.

German Beekeepers' Convention.

The Seventeenth Annual Meeting of German Beekeepers was held in the city of Kiel, in Holstein, on the 10th of September, and the three following days. Professor Hensen, of Kiel, was President, and Dr. Möbius, also of Kiel, first assistant or Vice President. The second assistant, Mr. Schmid, of Eichstadt, who is the only permanent officer, and is delegated by the Bavarian Government, was prevented by illness from being present, and Dr. Ziwansky, of Prague, was unanimously chosen to supply his place. There were about four hundred beekeepers in attendance. The President announced that donations for distribution as premiums on articles sent for exhibition, were received, as follows: from—

The Prussian Royal Agricultural Department	$300
The City of Kiel	300
The Agricultural Union of Holstein	50
Various Agricultural Societies	61
Aggregate,	$711

which would be allotted by the Committee on Premiums.

Mr. Mölling, as representative of the city of Kiel, made an address of welcome, and stated that the inhabitants of that city and of the entire province, were rejoiced to learn that this useful body had selected Kiel as the place for the annual meeting in 1871, and were well aware that the selection had been made with the express design of promoting bee-culture in that quarter, where, though bees were kept, improved modes of management were scarcely introduced.

Then followed discussion of the various topics announced by the Executive Committee, consisting of the President and the assistants—the chief of which were Living Bees, Bee Hives, Implements of Bee-culture, Honey, &c.--the debate, in each case, being opened by the person propounding the topic, if he happened to be in attendance.

Salzburg, in Bavaria, was chosen as the place of meeting in 1872, and Count Lamberg was appointed President of that meeting, and Professor Dr. Königsberger, First Assistant. The city of Halle was named as a desirable place for the meeting of 1873.

The proceedings and debates have not yet been published, but will appear in the December numbers of the Bienenzeitung.

Beekeepers' Convention.

In conformity with the previous understanding the beekeepers convened at Cleveland, Ohio, on the 6th instant, united in one body under the name of the North American Beekeepers' Society, adopted a constitution, and elected the following officers :

President.—M. Quinby, St. Johnsville, New York.

Vice Presidents.—A. Benedict, Bennington, Ohio; J. E. Hetherington, Cherry Valley, New York; E. J. Peck, Linden, New Jersey; Seth Hoagland, Mercer, Pennsylvania; D. L. Adair, Hawesville, Kentucky; Dr. T. B. Hamlin, Edgefield Junction, Tennessee; Dr. G. Bohrer, Alexandria, Indiana; E. Rood, Wayne, Michigan; M. M. Baldridge, St. Charles, Illinois; R. C. Otis, Kenosha, Wisconsin; J. W. Hosmer, Janesville, Minnesota; Mrs. E. S. Tupper, Brighton, Iowa; A. S. Stillman, Louisiana, Missouri; Dr. L. J. Dallas, Topeka, Kansas; W. D. Roberts, Peru City, Utah; Rev. W. F. Clarke, Guelph, Canada.

Secretary.—H. A. King, New York.

Recording Secretary.—A. J. Cook, Lansing, Michigan.

Corresponding Secretary.—A. I. Root, Medina, Ohio.

Treasurer.—N. C. Mitchell, Indianapolis, Indiana.

When we receive them, we shall select from the proceedings of the society, such items as may appear to be of interest to our readers.

We are by no means partial to the plan adopted, of organizing a national *society*, as we do not believe that it will best conduce to the advancement of the object which should be chiefly aimed at—the promotion of bee-culture in the United States, or in North America. The meetings of bodies thus organized, will usually have a slim attendance, exert a very restricted influence, and ultimately fall under the control of a clique. We like the German plan much better, and the experience of many years shows it to be admirably adapted to rouse interest and spread information, both theoretical and practical, over a wide extent of country. Attempts may, even there, be made to *run* the meetings in the interest of designing parties, but they are quickly detected, exposed, and thwarted, by those who have no "axes to grind."

Mr. H. A. King, in desperation, has attempted to show that Mr. Langstroth did not invent the kind of movable comb frame which he has patented, and which has been so eminently successful in making bee-culture a pleasant and profitable pursuit. He hopes to effect this by presenting a list of parties who, it is claimed, also *thought* of this thing, tried to produce it, *and* FAILED. This is a very novel mode of ratiocination, indeed, and ought to entitle Mr. K. to a fourth or fifth patent, quite as good and valid as any he now has, or ever *pretended* to have. Invention, within the meaning of the patent law, we have always understood, was the "conception of some new and useful thing, and the embodiment of that conception in a *practicable* form;" and "he who first *perfects a device* and makes it *capable of useful operation*, is entiled to a patent, and is the *real inventor*, though others may have had analagous ideas, and experimented to bring them into use."

Now, how stands the case with these alleged prior American inventors? Admitting the accounts given by them to be true, it is notorious that their frames, and all their attempts to make and use them, were *decided failures*—so regarded even by themselves. They and their miscarriages quickly sank into oblivion, being dead and buried, till Mr. King, like a body-snatcher, comes and resurrects them from their graves, to string up their bones *in terrorem* in the limbo of some museum of misbegotten and abortive conceptions. Certainly their contrivances, whatever they were, *were not practicable* movable frames, like those of Mr. Langstroth, or there could be no controversy about them now. Nobody (except it be some sanctimonious skin-dresser) ever quarrels about the carcass of a skunk, but all rejoice when it is decently interred, and are glad to let it rest undisturbed. There never was a living principle in any of their inventions, or they would not have died and "made no sign." There was in their frames (admitting they ever made any) some inherent fatal defect or vice, involving failure as a necessity; for, despite of all their skill and efforts, the fact is patent and undeniable, that *each and all*, in order due, *did* FAIL. This uniform and universal disappointment, and the consequent abandonment of experiment after experiment, are the demonstrative and conclusive proofs of failure. *Success* is here the only infallible evidence of SUCCESS, and it utterly refuses to testify in behalf of any for whom claims are now set up; while it proclaims, trumpet-tongued, the *practical* efficiency and high merit of the Langstroth frames. No sophistry can set this aside, nor will King's plausible effort to deck Falsehood in the garb of Truth, avail him aught in the end.

We have here referred only cursorily to the case of the American pretenders. That of the foreign claimants, we shall consider and dispose of when the Court has given King his *quietus*.

Mr. H. A. King sent us what purported to be a copy of the Baron of Berlepsch's Declaration. We declined to publish it:

1. Because, though obviously procured to be used in court, it is not in a shape to constitute legal testimony.

2. Because, even if all right in manner and form, publication before it is submitted to the court, is improper.

3. Because we did not know how much garbling it may have undergone in King's hands. We do know that he shamefully garbled Mr. Langstroth's letters to suit his own base purpose; and the presumption is, that he would not hesitate to garble the Baron's paper likewise, for a similar purpose. We did not feel disposed to be caught in such a trap.

4. Because we are not willing to be made instrumental, by him or any one else, in efforts to forestall public judgment, or mislead public opinion.

We say so much from respect to the beekeepers of the country, and not from any regard for Mr. K.

Mr. H. A. King says: "Many believe that Mr. Langstroth first heard of the German frames through letters to Mr. Wagner, prior to 1852." This is an insinuated untruth, about equivalent to an asserted falsehood. Before the spring of 1852, we never heard of Mr. Langstroth; and we never knowingly saw him, nor had we any conversation or correspondence with him till after the 1st of August, 1852. We always understood that Mr. Langstroth applied for his patent in December, 1851, up to which time, and for many months thereafter, there were no *practical* frames in use in Germany, as we are prepared to show.

[For the American Bee Journal.]

Introducing Queens.

Mr. EDITOR:—The German method of introducing queens, translated by you and published on page 98 of the November Journal, whereby all the bees are taken from the hive and kept in a box for twenty-four hours, seems to be all right, save in one important particular.

Would it not be *ruinous* to expose the brood for that length of time, without a bee in the combs?

There is no doubt that bees will accept a strange queen, very readily, when removed from their own hive; but the difficulty with me in thus introducing them has been indicated above.

I have found that if the bees are returned to their hive with the new queen, before they become thoroughly hungry and fully realize their hopeless condition, they are very apt to destroy her.

Should you be able to suggest a remedy, please favor your readers with it through the Journal.

GEO. S. SILSBY.

Wintersport, Me., Nov. 6, 1871.

☞ The difficulty suggested, it strikes us is only apparent, in the case of common box or straw hives. It is not necessary, we apprehend, that *all* the bees, literally speaking, should be driven out; and from such hives this is hardly practicable. A sufficient number will always remain to take care of the brood; and, on transferring, these should have charge of the combs containing the unsealed larvæ, which alone require nursing and attention in ordinary temperature. Where movable comb hives are operated on, the combs containing unsealed brood may be placed temporarily in a nucleus hive, after the mass of bees has been shaken off by a sudden jerk or shock. A sufficiency of young bees will usually remain adhering to such combs, to protect and nurse the larvæ. If operating in cool weather, brood just hatched may need some further protection, such as placing the hive or nucleus in a warm room. But the sealed brood can safely endure exposure to a greater degree of cold than is usually supposed; and it is yet unascertained how much cold and deprivation larvæ, just hatched, can endure without injury. Of course, the less of either to which they are exposed, the better.—[ED.

[For the American Bee Journal.]

Overstocking.

MR. EDITOR:—I think this subject is deserving much more attention than it receives. In ten seasons and the following winters, since I commenced my experiments in beekeeping, two winters have passed very fatal to the interests of beekeepers in this immediate vicinity. In 1863 or 1863 two-thirds of the bees in this vicinity starved to death in the winter. I had been taught no danger of overstocking, and half or more of mine perished in the winter following. The harvest of 1866 again proved destructive to the bees in this neighborhood, from starvation. In 1869 the bees had increased, so as to reach a large number for our field, and two-thirds of the bees within a few miles in any direction, starved—perhaps three-fourths of them. To give an idea of results, I must refer to others, as after the first of the three starving winters, I fed my bees in October, and again early in the spring, to carry them through to the flowers. But one neighbor, who placed in winter quarters over thirty colonies, had four colonies to commence the next season with. They increased so rapidly that, in the fall of 1869, he had over thirty colonies. In the spring of 1870 all had starved to death but two. In the whole vicinity three-fourths had died off. One friend, five miles from me, who lived in a very favorable field, supplied abnudantly with white clover, went as high as one hundred colonies, but in the spring of 1870, all were starved but five.

The results in my own experiments, have been thus. In 1867, after so many perished, my best hive gave me one hundred and seventy-four (174) pounds; and my four best gave five hundred (500) pounds. In 1868, my best hive gave one hundred and forty-two (142) pounds; others decreasing in proportion. In 1869 I placed my bees in three fields, some two miles apart, and secured perhaps as average of fifteen pounds—the best might have given as much as forty pounds. Then followed the desolating winter of 1870. Three-fourths of the bees cleared out, dead. Bees with a fair field averaged about fifty pounds. My best hive gave me two hundred (200) pounds. This season, the bees in the vicinity having been increased by swarms, fell off, say twenty-five per cent., from last year in surplus. My best hive, that gave me two hundred pounds last year, fell off to one hundred and forty pounds. From past results I must expect less favorable returns next season.

With such results in succeeding seasons, ought I yield to the arguments so strongly urged that there is no danger of overstocking? If there is no danger of overstocking, why do beekeepers with a few hundred colonies, divide them into several apiaries and place them in different fields?

Rev. Mr. Langstroth writes—"Probably there is *not a square mile* in this whole country, which is overstocked with bees, unless it is so unsuitable to beekeeping as to make it unprofitable to keep bees at all." I think it probable that there are few square miles of ground occupied by farmers where one colony might not be kept on each hundred acres. With a non-swarmer, with box room for one hundred pounds of honey, that amount of honey, or even the half of it, would be very pleasant to the family. I think the family should wish to try it. If two, or three, or five colonies could find an ample field on that area, so much the better. No doubt the country affords fields where a hundred colonies would do well. If I had two hundred, I should rather have two fields for them.

I remember, seventy years ago, one hundred colonies in my father's yard. At the same time his brother had about the same number in his yard, three miles from my father's. *Now* their sons, in the same fields, have not been able to exceed about one-tenth of that number. I suppose our country affords every variety of fields, from one hundred colonies capacity down to one single one. If you put a hundred colonies, where but fifty can be sustained, or fifty stocks where but ten can be supplied, or ten where only five can be supplied, you overstock your field, and a large part of your bees will be likely to perish. Either our country has not such a variety of fields, or there is danger of overstocking.

JASPER HAZEN.

Albany, N. Y.

☞We incline to think that the unfavorable results reported above sprang rather from mismanagement or ill-adapted management, than from overstocking. It remains yet to be ascertained what one colony *seasonably made populous* and *duly so kept*, can be made to produce in any location in one season. But the beekeepers of this country are now in a fair way of finding it out; and when that is known, it will not be very difficult to ascertain how many more *such colonies* can be kept in the same location, without interfering with each other's productiveness in the aggregate.—[ED.

[For the American Bee Journal.]

The Diseased Stocks.

DEAR JOURNAL:—Since the date of my hurried note of Nov. 17th, my bees have continued to die. Up to date some fourteen stocks present sad evidence of disease, while more dead bees are found on the bottom board of nearly every hive in my apiary than should be thus early in the winter. The mortality is greater among the Italians and hybrids than among the black bees. The bees fall to the bottom board in a stupefied condition, very few seeming able or willing to leave the hive of their own accord. Some, however, remain on the top of the frames, and others between the combs. I have resuscitated quite a number of deceased bees after they were subjected to three or four days of freezing weather, away from their hives. I examined the stock first alluded to, inspecting each comb in turn and as nearly as possible left out all the diseased bees. For a few days I thought the proper remedy had been applied; but it was not so, for they are now dying as before. I detected nothing wrong with the honey, but still that does not argue that the "wrong" was not there.

I concur on the editor's suggestion that the honey may contain a noxious property, but where did the bees gather it? It was not from the *fir* tribe; as there is scarcely a fir tree within foraging distance. Hence we must look elsewhere. If a portion of the honey does contain the "fatal principle," how are we to detect it, as we are not sufficiently versed in chemistry to analyze it? I shall take away the stores from the stock just affected, and give them sugar syrup, adding a small proportion of glycerine.

W. D. MANSFIELD.

Canaansville, Ohio, Dec. 11, 1871.

☞With the above communication we received a small box containing a number of dead bees from the diseased stocks. They do not look like bees that have died of old age, and there is nothing in their appearance which indicates that they perished from any slowly operating cause; nor have they the peculiar offensive smell that attends or proceeds from foulbrood. Under the circumstances we think, with Mr. M., that change of diet is probably the most efficient means available for arresting the malady.—[ED.

THE *Pittsburgh Legal Journal* says:—

"Though a law paper [or one devoted to any other speciality] may be started, it cannot be kept up without money, and though a subscription is a great compliment, the payment of the cash triples the obligation."

// AMERICAN BEE JOURNAL.

EDITED AND PUBLISHED BY SAMUEL WAGNER, WASHINGTON, D. C.

AT TWO DOLLARS PER ANNUM, PAYABLE IN ADVANCE.

VOL. VII. FEBRUARY, 1872. No. 8.

EDITOR OF AMERICAN BEE JOURNAL:

Please insert the article on movable frames from December No. of Mr. King's paper, so that my comments upon it may be better understood by your readers.

MOVABLE FRAMES.

Is Mr. Langstroth the Inventor?

"If Mr. Langstroth is not the inventor, who is?"
SAMUEL WAGNER.

It is not in a spirit of unkindness that we enter upon the discussion of this question. Messrs. Langstroth, Wagner, Otis & Co., have been doing all they could to injure us and our business, but we do not want to retaliate. Other motives prompt us. The state of public feeling; the earnest solicitations of numerous apiarians; vindication of ourselves, and duty to the beekeepers of America. These are some of the motives which prompt us to publish these facts, and we think that our visit to Europe, and the particular attention we have given this whole year to the history of movable frame hives, give us ability to do it understandingly.

For centuries, the Grecians used bars in their hives, similar to the narrow top-bars now used in movable-comb hives, but Francois Huber, of Geneva, Switzerland, was probably the *first inventor* of the present style of movable frames. This was about three-quarters of a century ago.

Many different editions of Huber's excellent book on the honey bee have been printed in several cities of Europe, all containing plates with engravings of his hive.

Huber first made an observation hive containing a single comb, with glass on each side. As it was difficult to winter bees in such a hive, he set several side by side, removing all the glass except the panes on the outside. The bars of these frames were too wide for a single comb after removing the glass, which led him to construct a hive with *frames*, having bars about 1¼ inches wide, securing them together by hinges. This was the regular Huber hive, but one plate in his book shows narrow bars resting in rabbets in a case or hive with long screws like side bars for elevating the comb, naturally suggesting what is called the "bars and frames" in England, and "movable frames" in this country and Germany.

For nearly half a century, beekeepers advanced no farther than the use of the Grecian bars, with honey board and supers above, usually bell glasses in Europe, because they are cheaper there than wooden boxes with glass sides. Bevan and others placed one hive upon another. It is a common remark in England that his book, "Bevan on the Honey Bee," has furnished matter for most of the later works on the subject, both in England and America. Rev. C. Cotton, an able English writer, and author of "My Bee Book," says, "A Reverend American author obtained his frontispiece"—the queen surrounded by workers—"from his book, but spoiled the engraving by mistaking what he intended as the appearance of the queen in the act of laying, for a representation of the queen with her sting protruding"—a very unnatural occurrence. We confess we thought croakers about similarity of names of papers came near copying book titles, when we took up a book published in Dublin, "Richardson on the Hive and Honey Bee." These works contain nearly the same matter that is found in all the late works, and one of them "The Beekeeper's Manual," not only describes and illustrates the use of honey boards and supers or bell glasses, but also the use of the *shallow chamber*, about which so much has been said of late.

W. Augustus Munn, of Dover, England, was probably the first to invent narrow frames to be used within a case or hive. He made his first hive with frames in 1834. By 1843, he had taken out a patent in Paris, France (for the hive had been in too general use in England), and a friend using the hives had described the same with an engraving in *The Gardener's Chronicle*, a journal of large circulation, published in London (bound volume for 1843, page 317). This hive really embraced all the practical features of the movable frames of to-day. The same was also described in a pamphlet by Major Munn, in 1844, and in the second edition, 1851, he describes the same with triangular frames to lift out at the top. His descriptions, though brief, show that he was familiar with supers, and that with his oblong frames he used a honey board, the shallow chamber, and surplus honey boxes above; to all of which Major Munn has made solemn oath, perfectly invalidating the pretended claims of Mr. Langstroth.

The Russian, Prokopovitsch, perhaps, should be mentioned here, for he supplied the market at St. Petersburg with thousands of pounds of honey *in frames*, but his frames were not used in the breeding apartment, and therefore do not invalidate Mr. Langstroth's claims, though his hive was described in a pamphlet in 1841.

We shall next mention movable frames used in France. M. De Beauvoys is the author of a series of excellent works on bee-culture. In the second edition, published in 1847, and the third in Paris, 1851, he describes movable frames containing all the features of the most perfect frames now used in this country, and we shall show by the description of the storifying system, using boxes for surplus honey above the breeding hive, that Mr. L.'s attempt to evade this testimony is simply ridiculous, though it might do before a purchasable patent office examiner.

We wrote to Europe for these works, but all in vain. When we reached London, we found that Mr. L. had purchased copies of Mr. Munn's work, but *we* could find none, though our friends assured us that they would find a copy somewhere by the time we returned from the continent. When we visited Paris we found but one person of whom we had heard that we might possibly obtain a copy of M. Debeauvoy's work. We were glad to find the books in his possession, for the author had been dead some years. But our polite Frenchman, M. Hamet, declined to part with the books. We could not persuade him even to *loan* us the 1851 edition, though we offered abundant security for its safe return. Mr. Hamet however expressed an earnest desire that we should secure the works, and gave us the address of a publisher where we might possibly obtain them. We were successful and secured a double set of these valuable books.

When we returned to London, Major Munn nor a half dozen other friends had succeeded in finding a single copy of his work of 1851. We authorized the offer of a reward, first of one pound, to be increased to five pounds, rather than fail. Two weeks after we reached New York, and only a few days after our satchel had been stolen with one set of our French books and other valuable European documents, Major Munn's 1851 pamphlet came safely by mail.

The name of Augustus Baron von Berlepsch, formerly of Seebach, Germany, now of Munich, Bavaria, should be next mentioned among European inventors. We have the hive which he presented March 16th, 1852, to the Editor of the *Bienenzeitung* (the German bee journal, published at Eichstadt), a description of which was published in the May number for 1852. The hive is stamped with the seal of Dr. Buchner, Royal Notary Public of Munich. The document containing his oath was lost in the stolen satchel, but we have just received a duplicate similarly stamped, from which we have taken the following facts (we sent a copy of the document to Mr. Wagner, and also to Mr. Mitchell. Mr. Wagner returned the copy, refusing to publish it): The Baron of Berlepsch says, that in the winter of 1842-43, he first heard of Dzierzon's hive with movable bars, and obtained a sample which he perceived to be an invention of the first rank, but still in its infancy, and that the bars should be replaced with frames. He made frames for a hive in which he put a swarm *early in June*, 1843, but was troubled to keep the frames the proper distance from each other. He remedied this partially in 1844, and in 1845 he left *space between the frames and the walls of the hives* to prevent the bees from gluing the side bars to the walls. In 1846, he and his partner, Jacob Shultze, obtained fifty glass jars or bell glasses, and thirty of them were filled in *May*, 1846. We saw samples of these frames, and they were *exactly* like the narrow frames with tops, so improperly called "Langstroth" frames, in this country. They were used with all the features—air spaces, shallow chamber, perforated top, and surplus or bell glasses above—from 1846 to 1850, when they were improved by side projections, and described in the German Bee Journal, as before stated, in May, 1852. The Baron von Berlepsch says, "Mr. Langstroth's claims *are ridiculous.*" He heard of them in 1856, through an intelligent American beekeeper, Mr. Phineas MacMahon, from Philadelphia, who was not a little surprised to see eighty movable comb bee hives full of bees, and was told by the Baron that the frames in them had not been changed since 1851. "Now I know," said he, "that Mr. Langstroth is not the inventor, but I wonder how he heard of the frames." The Baron replied that he supposed Mr. L. got it of Paul Reinhard Backhaus, *to whom he sent hives in* 1851. Lina Baroness of Berlepsch writes that she has received a letter from a son of Mr. Backhaus, stating that his father returned to Germany in 1857, and that he had much to say about Mr. Langstroth. He returned to Dubuque, Iowa, in 1860, and soon after died. *We are on the track of these hives*, and will produce them, if they can yet be found. We will now only briefly notice the use of

MOVABLE FRAME HIVES IN AMERICA.

There are many others who used movable frame hives in America prior to Mr. Langstroth, though many believe that Mr. L. first heard of the German frames through letters to Mr. Wagner, prior to 1852.

The first printed description of a movable frame hive published in America, was given in *The Scientific American*, March 6th, 1847, page 187. The inventor, Jacob Shaw, Jr., then residing in Hinckly, Medina county, Ohio, now lives in Shelby, Ohio, and *has the same old hive in his possession.* We have seen the hive, and it meets *all of Mr. L.'s claims.* This is but one among many others used by beekeepers in America prior to 1852.

We can only mention the *names* of others now. A. F. Moon, Edward Townly, Dr. Metcalf, Andrew Harbison, and W. A. Flanders, making Mr. L. only the *seventh son*, and it seems that he too, like all other seventh sons, has been called Doctor. We really pity Mr. L., and would gladly have permitted him to enjoy the honors claimed as his own, but the great mass of beekeepers are losing all sympathy for him since he united with his former foe, Mr. Otis, and thus made it our duty to search out the facts and make them public, Though it has cost us three or four thousand dollars, we shall not be the loser in the end, as we shall be able to bring out some improvements in bee-culture that will reward us, as well as advance the cause of bee-culture in America.

We lately returned from St. Paul, and have just learned that Mr. Otis has permitted Mr. Hosmer's case to be dismissed, and says he shall give it all up, if Mr. King has got the evidence spoken of some months since in the JOURNAL. We have now informed Mr. Otis of the facts in our possession, and hope he will be content to retire to private life, and cease to perambulate through the country, *vainly trying* to collect blackmail from the honest apiarians of America.

H. A. K.

H. A. King on Movable Frame Hives.

Expecting that the U. S. Court will soon pass judgment upon many of the matters referred to by Mr. King, I should not at this time have noticed his article, but for the damage it might inflict upon owners of territorial rights in my patent; so many persons taking for granted that what is not answered, must be unanswerable.

I object decidedly to the heading which Mr. King has given to his article: "Movable Frames. Is Mr. Langstroth the inventor?" because it conveys the impression that I claim *absolutely* the invention of movable frames, when I have repeatedly, in Mr. Wagner's Journal and elsewhere, stated that movable frames were used in Europe before my invention.

It is true, that when I applied for a patent, I knew nothing of any movable frames except those of Huber; but even after becoming acquainted with the frames of Munn and Debeauvoys, I was satisfied that mine, as described in the original patent, need not be confounded with theirs. Finding, however, that these foreign inventions were continually alleged to be substantially the same as mine, I applied for a reissue of my patent, and submitted to the office copies of Munn, Debeauvoys, and such other works in my possession, but not in their library, as had any bearing on movable frames. In this reissue "an improved construction and arrangement of the frames of bee hives" is claimed, and the difference between this improved construction and that of Huber, Munn, and Debeauvoys, is clearly shown. Mr. King cannot be ignorant of my true position; for in his attorney's answer to the suit of Mr. Otis against him for infringing upon the Langstroth patent, he nowhere assumes that I have claimed the absolute invention of movable frames, but only attempts to show that I am not the inventor of the style claimed in the patent.

This misstatement of the very point at issue, has been dwelt upon at more length, because it so aptly ministers to the prejudices of those who have represented me as the mere introducer of a foreign invention, and yet "claiming everything," and because it is evident from his "declaration," that the Baron von Berlepsch really believes it, and deemed it important "to prove in the case of Otis v. King, that long before Mr. Langstroth applied for his patent, there were used in Germany, and the rest of Europe, hives with frames!"

Mr. King's statement, that Huber was probably the first inventor of the present style of movable frames, is incorrect, the *present style* of frames being that which inserts them in a case; whereas, the Huber frames, when put together, formed a complete hive without any case.

The reference to Cotton's frontispiece, is uncalled for, as I have in my work acknowledged my indebtedness to Mr. Cotton for this beautiful engraving. Those who have read my treatise, well know the care which has been taken to give to Bevan and others, full credit for what has been borrowed from them.

Does Mr. King accomplish anything with intelligent men, by insinuating the similarity between the title of my work and that of Richardson's except to exhibit an intense eagerness for fault-finding?

That Taylor's Beekeeper's Manual illustrates the use of honey boards and supers, is true; but Mr. King has not found in it the shallow chamber claimed in my patent. The readers of the Journal must bear with me, when I place my denial side by side with his affirmation, and remember that he has made this necessary by attempting to forestall the verdict of the proper tribunal.

It is admitted that Major Munn patented his bar and frame hive in France, in 1843; that it was very briefly described with an engraving in the London Gardener's Chronicle, for 1843, and very minutely described and illustrated by Mr. Munn in the first edition of his work, in 1844. Mr. S. S. Fisher, late commissioner of patents, and counsel for Mr. Otis, after careful examination, can find nothing in this hive which invalidates a single claim in my patent. It is not what Mr. Munn did, but what he described in some printed publication issued prior to my application for a patent, that will satisfy the requirements of the patent laws. Of this, Mr. King must be well aware, as his "answer" to the suit, *amended* since his return from Europe, makes no reference to the Major's oath.

Munn's triangular frames of 1851, were intended to remedy the defects of his oblong frames of 1844, the failure of which is acknowledged in the second edition of his work. Mr. Fisher can see nothing in these triangular frames in the least damaging to the claims of my patent, and I believe that the Huber hive is more serviceable, both for practical and scientific purposes, than either of Mr. Munn's.

We come now to the inventions of M. Debeauvoys. His frames of 1847, were made *close fitting, both to the sides and top of the case containing them.* Could any of our practical beekeepers be persuaded to use them, even if furnished free of cost? His frames of 1851, had their tops close fitting to each other, with no plan of any kind for securing the surplus honey outside of the frames of the main bee-chamber, and even to secure the surplus there, he used a complicated arrangement of double frames, connected by rings and movable pins and staples. Although in 1853, he materially simplified the construction of his hive, he does not in the last edition of his work, in 1863, even so much as *suggest any arrangement for supers or boxes.* Mr. Hamet, the editor of the French Bee Journal, says in his work on bee-culture (1859), that the removal of frames from this Debeauvoys hive, is often more difficult than from the Huber hive, and that the hive has never been accepted by practical men in the great beekeeping districts in France. The construction of both his hives was described in my reissue, and Mr. Fisher can see nothing in them that invalidates my claims.

Has Mr. King weighed carefully the language he has used in extolling the inventions of Munn and De Beauvoys? "This hive" (Munn's) "really embraces all practical features of the movable frames of to-day." "He" (Debeauvoys) "describes movable frames containing all the features of the most perfect frames now used in this country." After asserting that these old foreign inventions had "ALL *practical features*," and "ALL *the features of the* MOST PERFECT frames *now used in this country*," ought he not to make a bonfire of his patent papers, and then call on all other patentees of movable frame hives to do the same, that they may no longer be engaged in the disreputable business of selling patents which have no new features of any practical value?

Passing over Mr. King's account of his long and tedious search for books (all of which, and more besides, Mr. Fisher would cheerfully, as a matter of courtesy, have loaned to his counsel), we come to the deposition of the Baron von Berlepsch. In the Bienenzeitung, for May, 1852, there is no illustration given of this hive, and the "description" of it to which Mr. King refers, is in such vague and general terms, that for aught that appears, the Baron might only have used Huber frames inserted in a case. Even if the Berlepsch frames had been illustrated and fully described, they could not have invalidated my patent, which was applied for more than four months before this article was published in Germany! Mr. King, in his "amended answer," makes no reference to the Baron's hive, or to his "declaration;* and as this answer, filed *after* his return from Europe, as regards foreign inventions is substantially the same with his *first* answer, it may be presumed that after putting himself into personal communication with the editors of the European bee journals, and with the most eminent apiarians abroad, he has found nothing to allege against the validity of my patent, which had not been previously known and weighed by Mr. Fisher and myself.

We come lastly to the claims of parties in this country to a prior invention of the frames described in my patent. The claims of Mr. Shaw were for the first time brought to my notice by the amended answer of Mr. King. From Mr. Shaw's deposition, which has recently been taken, it appears that he used a metal case with double metallic water-tight

*There are some things in this document, which deserve special notice, and I cannot but hope, as Mr. King has given it to the public before offering it in evidence in the suit, that Mr. Wagner will publish it with suitable comments, either in this or the March No. of his Journal.

walls, into which he could pour a hot fluid to allow the safe removal of the frames, if the bees fastened them to the case, and that the cover of this case was a metallic reservoir filled with a fluid for drowning the bee-moth; that he only made a single hive; that he never could obtain a drop of honey from it in boxes or supers; that the first two colonies which he put in it, after remaining in it for a longer or shorter time, ran away from it; that the last swarm died in it, and that becoming discouraged, he laid it aside. Does Mr. King seriously imagine that an abandoned device, which conferred no benefit whatever either on Mr. Shaw or on the public, will aid him before the courts in overthrowing the claims of my patent?

The testimony of Messrs. Moon, Townley, Metcalf, Harbison, and Flanders, was presented when I applied for the extension of my patent. The examiner, in his report to the commissioner of patents, commenting upon a part of the testimony, says: "Such testimony on the part of the opposition, and this is representative of the whole, becomes an argument, and a very strong one, in favor of this applicant;" and the commissioner, by extending the patent, sustained this report.

In this review of Mr. King's article, I have by no means attempted such a vindication of the claims of my patent as will be presented to the court, but only such comments as Mr. King himself has made necessary that the public may not be unduly influenced before the case can come to trial.

In the beginning of his communication, Mr. King says that I have aided Mr. Otis and others "in doing all they could to injure him and his business;" and in the November No. of his paper, he says that I have been doing all that I could "to aid such men as Otis in their malicious designs against most of the enterprising beekeepers of the United States." Now, Mr. Otis is the sole owner of the larger part of the territory in my patent, but he has not, since 1867, been connected in business with me. He is attempting to get a decision from the U. S. Court, by which he can protect his rights under the patent, against those whom he regards as infringing upon them. If I should in any way discountenance or obstruct him in his appeal to the law, or if I even failed to give him all the aid in my power, would it not be a gross breach of good faith on my part, not only to him, but to other parties who have purchased an interest in my patent? Are not the beekeeping public sick of this seemingly interminable controversy about the validity of my patent? and do they not desire to have it legitimately settled as soon as possible? Had my means permitted, I should long ago have asked the courts to decide the question.

There are some other personal matters in Mr. King's article, which, before they are noticed, make it proper to quote here from my address to the beekeeper's of the United States, published in the April No. of this Journal.

"In the contest which must soon come before the courts of law, I hope that every legitimate weapon which can be used to break down my patent, will be brought forward; and I now hereby invite all the beekeepers of the United States, and all anywhere else, who may see this appeal, to send to Mr. King, against whom suit has been brought, for infringing on my patent, any information contained in books or printed publications in any language, prior to the issue* of my patent (October 5th, 1852), which seems to have any adverse bearing on my case, and to bring forward any knowledge they may possess of any invention made in this country, but not described in print, by which the claims of my patent may be either weakened, limited or invalidated."

*I ought to have said prior to my *application* for a patent in January, 1852.

Does Mr. King, when suggesting that I might have bribed the patent office examiner, or that I might have conspired with Mr. Wagner to patent a foreign invention as my own, suppose that the beekeepers of this country will consider him as using the "legitimate weapons" of an honorable warfare? or that they will ever give credit to such unworthy insinuations?

L. L. LANGSTROTH.

Oxford, Ohio, Jan. 11, 1872.

Baron von Berlepsch and Movable Frames.

MR. EDITOR:—Mr. King, having procured a "Declaration" from Baron von Berlepsch ostensibly to be used in a law-suit, and having published the declaration before offering it in evidence, I desire to give the substance of it to the readers of your Journal, with such other matters as will enable them to judge of its true value.

The Baron says: "In the winter of 1842-3, I first heard of Dzierzon's invention of a bee-hive with movable combs and the next spring I hastened to obtain one of those hives.

When it arrived, I recognized at a glance that this was an apiarian inventi n of the first rank, but that it was, as it were, in its infancy, and that the bars had to be replaced by frames if this invention was to have any lasting practical value." He then states that he made a hive with frames instead of bars, and put bees into it in June, 1843. He then details the successive steps by which he learned to keep the frames separated at suitable distances from each other, and from the walls of the case. He says that "in 1845, the hive had been improved to such a degree that the frames could be easily removed and replaced," but that for want of "wings or ears on their four corners, many mistakes occurred, as often the combs would be too close or too far apart." He next relates how in 1846 he and his partner had thirty-six glass jars filled with honey, by using them as supers over his hives, and says: "with these imperfect hives I raised bees until 1850, without being able to make any improvement on the frames. In order to keep them apart at proper distances, we pressed at that time little pieces of wax between the ends of two frames."

The Baron next describes the improvements which he made in arranging the three tiers or stories of frames in his hive, and how in 1850 his partner suggested that by putting "projections of half an inch on two ends of the upper part of the frames, they could be held always in the same position and the bees would have the proper room between the combs." This necessitated the replacing of the frames without being able to turn them, but he says: "Now I had discovered what was wanting. In the winter of 1850-51, I had frames made whose upper parts had on all four ends a projection of one-fourth of an inch. Now there was no obstacle to replace the frames at your pleasure; in short, the practical frame such as it still exists to-day, was invented. Practical experience in the summer of 1851, confirmed the invention again, and in the spring of 1852, I sent to the Editor of the Bienenzeitung an improved hive, which was transmitted by him this year to Mr. H. A. King." * * *

"In view of the above, it really appears ridiculous to me that the American Langstroth claims to have invented the frames himself, and attaches such great value to the building of honey in vessels of glass and other materials by means of the bung-hole. This invention might be claimed with more right by the

Russian Propokovitsch, for he had frames in his hive a long time previous to myself; they were in fact very imperfect, but still they were frames." * * * * * * "But the claims of Langstroth to be the inventor of the frames, are nothing new to me, for in the summer of 1859, I received a visit from a most intelligent American beekeeper, Phineas MacMahon, from Philadelphia, who expressed no little surprise when I showed him about eighty full frame hives, and told him that the frames had not been changed since 1851. The American then declared that now he had proof that Langstroth was not the inventor, only he wished to know how he could have heard of it, as I had as far as he knew, never published an illustration of the same."

I replied that I supposed this had been done by Paul Reinhard Backhaus, to whom I had sent some hives to America in 1851. Mr. King writes to me, "Langstroth's principal claims are the air space above the frames and the board above it with holes for passage of bees into supers (bell glasses or boxes"). That is, Langstroth's principal claims are based on the vacant space over the frames, and the cover with the bung-hole for the passage of bees into the bell glass. I can hardly comprehend how Langstroth can attach the slightest importance to such things which exist as a matter of course, for the merest beginner must comprehend that there must be at least so much space between the frames and the top that the bees can reach the bung-hole, and through that, the super. This vacant space must be at least one-fourth of an inch in height. * * * * The vacant space in Langstroth's hive, as it is described in his "Practical Treatise" of 1859, is, however, much too high. This hive moreover is so bad that even the most inexperienced beginner in Germany would condemn it. I myself do this most distinctly, and declare this hive decidedly impracticable. The above shows conclusively that I used hives with movable frames and employed glass supers long before Langstroth's patent. * * * Langstroth does not seem to be familiar with bee-literature, otherwise he would know that beekeepers have had vessels of glass or other material, built full of honey by means of the bung-hole, for centuries past, a long time before the moveable frame was invented." The Baron after describing the hive sent to Mr. King, so that it may be properly identified, concludes his declaration thus: "But this sort of a hive has gone out of date a long time since and in all Germany as well as in the rest of Europe, those shapes have been introduced a long time since, which I have described in my work on bees, 2d edition. It has no longer any practical value in bee-culture, but as a specimen of that first invention it will prove in case of Otis *v.* King, that long before Mr. Langstroth applied for his patent, there were used in Germany and the rest of Europe, hives with frames. Many witnesses can be brought who can swear to it that I have raised bees in frame hives at Seebach Castle ever since 1843, and made the improvement of these hives my special study."

Having thus given the substance of the Baron's declaration, I shall before commenting upon it, give also the substances of his communications to the Beinenzeitung prior to the publication in 1855, of the first edition of his work on bees.

THE BERLEPSCH FRAMES.

In a communication published in the Supplement to the Bienenzeitung, No. 9, May 1st, 1852, the Baron says he sends to the Editor a sample of a hive invented by him and called "*Stehender Rahmenlüfter*" (upright frame ventilator) which he regards as "the most perfect hive then known." It is said he, "partly a glass hive, a perfect ventilator and perfect Dzierzon." In internal arrangement, he said "it is unequalled, and the inner space may be enlarged or diminished at pleasure, and every comb taken out." It is "less squat and clumsy than the Dzierzon hive, has not the cold but the warm arrangement of combs; each comb may be removed without cutting; and building them fast to the sides or bottom by the bees, is rendered absolutely impossible." Nevertheless he thought this hive would never come into general use, or exert any influence on bee-culture regarded as a branch of industry; because with all its simplicity in the view of an intelligent beekeeper, it is "too complicated and too costly for the ordinary peasant." Finally he requests the editor, if conceding the hive is what he (Berlepsch) claims it to be, "to *describe* and *illustrate* it in the Bienenzeitung; otherwise to consign it to his *lumber garret.*"

In a note to this article, the editor speaks of the "*Rahmenlüfter*" as ingeniously devised, adopting and combining what is valuable in previous inventions, and presenting some advantageous peculiarities of its own, and as being "well calculated to be used with satisfaction by an expert, possessing the necessary pecuniary means." At the same time, he concurs with the Baron's opinion that the hive is "too complicated and dear," and hence not likely to come into use extensively, though it may be employed by amateur beekeepers and investigators." No *description* or *illustration* of it is given, however, and its peculiar construction could only be guessed at.

In the Extra Supplement to the Bienenzeitung, No. 21, Nov. 1st, 1852, is contained the first subsequent reference to the *Rahmenlüfter*; by the Baron, or any one else. It is a letter addressed to Dzierzon, censuring him for having written and published a book imperfectly explaining his system, and inadequately describing his hive. "I blame you for this," says he, "that for four years—from 1848 to 1851, inclusive—I have had in use, under the name of Dzierzon, hives entirely different from yours, and basing my judgment on those *monsters*, have spoken disparagingly of your hives and your methods, to the numerous beekeepers visiting me at Seebach, thus exposing myself to deserved derision. * * * * * * * * * I was constrained to let my carpenter work according to those nearly unintelligible intimations. Very soon I had fifty handsome single hives made (costing me more than $200), and I began eagerly to *Dzierzonise*, but with the poorest results. Already, in 1849, doubts arose in my mind as to the correct construction of those hives, because I could seldom get out a comb without breaking it, and sometimes the whole internal structure would topple down, forcing me to conclude that your whole device was based on a sandy foundation, and the use of my so-called Dzierzons was abandoned, and the remainder were managed on the swarming system.

But your fame was constantly spreading farther, and being fully convinced of the correctness of your theory, I travelled *incognito* to Brieg, in the fall of 1851, and thence afoot to Bankwitz, carrying a small valise, finally wending my way to Carlsmarkt. There I presented myself to you as a traveling overseer from Meissen, in search of a situation, who was unwilling to miss the opportunity when passing through Silesia, to see the most celebrated apiarian of his day, and examine his apiary. As regards bee-culture, I demeaned myself as an ignoramus, allowing you to exhibit and explain everything. *At a glance I saw that my hives bore scarcely any resemblance to yours, and were of course, unserviceable.* I was ready to jump out of my skin, not only because of the heavy pecuniary loss I had incurred, but for the more heavy loss of four years time, and the manifest derision to which I had exposed myself. * * * * * * * * As for the rest, one might like the Galitzean forester, be ready to flog one's self for stupidity in not having long since hit upon your invention. How near did Huber come to it? how near Propokovitsch? how near, I myself? Only think, in 1843, induced by the description and illustration of the Propokovitsch hive, I constructed one in which each comb hung in a frame and could be taken out. I also cemented guide combs to the frames, and all worked exceedingly well, except that in no conceivable manner could I fasten the separate frames properly in the hive or case, made in all respects like yours with a door behind. It was, and ever continued to be, a mere juggle, like Jähne's hoop hive. Had I inserted the frames *crosswise* instead of *lengthwise*, I should have had your hive earlier than you had it yourself, and should not have had occasion to solicit Mr. Schmidt, as I now do most earnestly, to dispatch the model *Rahmenlüfter* to his lumber garret."

On this occasion, and in the letter from which I have been quoting, the Baron presents to the notice of Dzierzon and invites his criticism of his twenty-eight hive Bee Pavilion, of which he gives an extended and minute description, together with an engraved illustration.

This article was written and dated October 12th, 1852 (just one week after my patent issued), and the Baron's description of his Pavilion, does not contain a word about *frames*, nor does the illustration show any; though the latter does show *bars*, and bars with guide combs attached. We hear nothing more about frames in a Berlepsch or a Dzierzon hive, till in the Extra Supplement to the Bienenzeitung issued March, 1853. The Baron then writes to Dzierzon (Feb. 16th, 1853), "There are *now* no longer any *bars* in the (Pavilion) hives, but *frames* exclusively, so that the combs are suspended on all four sides between wood, and cannot possibly break down. These frames which I have had in my *Rahmenlüfter* since 1843, are by far more convenient than *bars*. With them it is never necessary to cut loose the combs from the sides of the hives (which is always a smeary job), but one can draw out the entire frame with the comb built in it. It is true these frames make the hive much dearer, for they must be made by an expert carpenter, so that thay may neither warp nor part, and therefore for economical reasons, I omitted them at first in this new hive." Still the Baron did not formally advocate or defend their use till March 8th, 1855, when he appended some notes in their behalf to a communication which appeared in the Bienenzeitung of March 15th, 1855.

I shall now contrast some of the statements made by the Baron in his "declaration," with others contained in the above letters.

In his second letter the Baron speaks of having exposed himself to "deserved derision" by condemning a hive, the plan of which he never understood, while in his declaration he seems to speak as though in 1843 he was so well acquainted with it that he recognized at a glance the importance of the invention, and sought to improve it by substituting frames for bars. In his letter he says: "In no conceivable manner could I fasten the separate frames properly in the hive or case made in all respects like yours, with a door behind. It was and ever continued to be a mere juggle," &c.,* while in the declaration, he says that in the winter of 1850-51, "there was no obstacle to replace the frames at your pleasure; that in short the practical frame as it still exists to-day was invented—that practical experience in the summer of 1851 confirmed the invention, and that in 1859 he showed an American about eighty full hives and told him that the frames had not been changed since 1851." Some of the statements in the declaration, as to the practical success of his frames in 1850-51, seem the more difficult of explanation, when compared with others made by the Baron in the Bienenzeitung for February 1853, in which he says in substance: "After I had satisfied myself by the experiments of 1851 that normally the queen is the mother not only of the workers, but of the drones also, I became exceedingly anxious to see her supply drone cells with eggs. I wished to obtain ocular demonstration of the fact. To this end, in the fall of 1854, having meantime examined properly constructed Dzierzon hives at his apiary, I made one like them, only that it had a glass door in the roar, with a wooden cover over it. It was made of such width as to suit the combs of some of my old hives; and about the middle of October, I selected sixteen combs containing a sufficient winter supply of honey, but consisting of worker-cells exclusively. There was not a single drone-cell in any of these combs. I inserted and arranged them in two tiers, one above the other, and introduced into the hive a strong colony with a young queen. In the spring of 1852, I fed them lavishly with slightly diluted honey, two weeks before the rape came into blossom; and on the evening of the 12th of May, the bees began to hang out in clusters. On the 16th I observed that on all the combs the cells not stored with honey were filled with brood. I now took out the first comb of the lower tier facing the glass door, and inserted one containing chiefly drone cells, there being only about 250 worker cells in a portion of it."

The Baron next details with all the glowing enthusiasm of a genuine naturalist, his first sight of a normal queen laying eggs successively in drone and worker cells on the same comb. Now if his frames in the summer of 1851 were a practical success, where was the necessity of his constructing a Dzierzon hive, and transferring bees and combs into it, for an observation which could as well if not better have been made in his own hive? If however, his frames were inserted lengthwise instead of crosswise, we can easily see why he adopted in the fall of 1851, the crosswise arrangement, in order that he might see the queen on the outside comb through the glass door at the back of his new hive.

I deeply regret that Mr. King, by the wide circulation which he has given to the Baron's declaration, has compelled me in strict self-defence to seem to censure a man whose name I have never mentioned without respect. It is hardly necessary for me to say that American beekeepers have such a just appreciation of the great services which the Baron von Berlepsch has rendered to apiarian pursuits, that they will not judge him harshly, even if they cannot satisfactorily harmonize some of his statements.

I do not at all complain that the Baron has pronounced my claim to have invented frames, to be "ridiculous," when he supposes that I call myself the absolute inventor of frames of every kind, and the first to have removed surplus honey in glass or other supers! Believing that I have made such insufferable pretensions, he might very naturally suspect that I was base enough to patent his invention as my own.* Can any one who has read the Declaration, be at any loss to conjecture by whom he was so grossly misled as to the true nature and extent of my claims? Mr. King might doubtless not only have informed the Baron what I actually claim, but have given him

* Let any one attempt to adjust, Propokovitsch fashion, *lengthwise* instead of *crosswise*, in a hive opening at the back, three tiers of frames, one above the other, and he will quickly understand the Baron's "juggle."

* I never heard of the Baron of Berlepsch until informed by Mr. Wagner, in August, 1852, of his article in the May number of the Bienenzeitung; nor of P. R. Backhaus, until the "declaration" was given to the public.

besides, the date of my application for a patent, Jan. 6th, 1852, four months before the Berlepsch hive was brought to the notice of the public. If he had done this, does any one believe that he would have brought the Declaration over the ocean?

The Baron's condemnation of my hives as "decidedly impracticable" may at first surprise those who have secured tons of honey from them; but it will not weigh much with them after they have learned from his own account, how entirely he failed, until he actually saw it, to get any proper conception of the Dzierzon hive.*

If the Baron and myself could have a personal interview, I believe that all misconceptions on both sides might be easily removed. I think that he would be amused to learn that it was the sight, on the table of a friend, thirty-four years ago, of a large bell-glass super, filled with beautiful honey combs, that induced me to purchase my first stock of bees. If we should discuss "bee literature," he would be surprised to learn that in 1790, the Abbé Della Rocca (Vol. 3. Pl. 3) gave an illustration of movable bars *with wings* similar to his own, for keeping the bars at proper distances. If we should venture upon the still broader field of *unpublished experiments*, Mr. King could speedily make us much more ashamed of our "stupidity than the Galitzean forester," by presenting to us an inventor who before the era of Propokovitsch, and while still a youth in his teens, did by one surprising bound of genius, attain results which cost us so many toilsome years of observation and experiment. And if we needed anything more to make us humble, there might be "summoned from the vasty deep," such a crowd of republican aspirants to Huber's throne, that like the despairing Macbeth, we should be ready to cry out

"What! will the line stretch out until the crack of doom?
Another yet? *a seventh?* I'll see no more!"

The Baron and my readers will excuse me for attempting by a touch of pleasantry, to relieve this very dry discussion.

L. L. LANGSTROTH.

Oxford, O., Jan 12, 1872.

---

*It is not unusual for men of great ability to get very imperfect conceptions from drawings, while others quite inferior in intellect, can learn as much from a drawing as from a full-sized model.

[For the American Bee Journal.]

Overstocking with Bees.

And how to secure a large income from Beekeeping.

In one of his writings on bee-culture, the Baron of Ehrenfels states, that he owned a thousand hives of bees, all of which were so located, that he could visit them in an hour's ride; and that he moved them during the buckwheat bloom to the rich district of the Marchfeld. He seems to have written under the impression that a good location could not be overstocked with bees. He started his several apiaries with one hundred and fifty colonies, each in the spring; and keeping for each apiary one overseer or beemaster.

Lucas, another prominent beekeeper and writer on bees, in his treatise published in 1820, concedes that a location might become overstocked, if the bees of many different apiaries should be moved to a single locality, as there might then be more bees than flowers on which they could work. At the same time he is of the opinion, that the honey secreted by a flower could be and ought to be collected as fast as it is secreted. If it was not thus collected, it would evaporate and be lost. Hence it was all the same whether a blossom was visited once or oftener during the day, and it would yield the same amount of honey at every collection; while none would be left after a change of weather, or if not collected at the time it was secreted. Is this indeed so? I cannot say that I made a close observation on any other than basswood and buckwheat blossoms. Basswood secretes its honey in five little leaflets, that constitute the envelope of the bud before blooming. These little leaflets contain, in good weather and in a good season, a drop of honey as large as and sometimes larger than a large pin's head; and a bee can gather a good load of honey from a dozen of these flowers. This honey is not washed out by a moderate shower of rain, or by dew during night time. If not gathered it is found there for a number of days, and in warm dry weather becomes as thick as the thickest honey in a hive. In some instances the leaflets containing that honey, wilt, dry up, and remain adherent in the seed bud for quite a while, and bees will visit them sometimes for more than a week after blooming. Last summer dried up honey was found in them for about ten days after they had dropped off, and bees were seen in large numbers every forenoon, collecting from them bass honey, that had become liquified during the previous night. About noon they would cease gathering, and stopped flying. I hold that this honey is of greater thickness than honey just secreted, and bees will be able to lay up in store for their owner, a larger amount if they have a chance to gather it in a locality close at hand. There can be no doubt that the area in which the bees of an apiary collect their honey, must be enlarged in proportion to the number of stocks kept; and they will be able to collect all the honey secreted every day, if there are enough bees to do so, and the honey will then have no time to evaporate or thicken. Quinby states somewhere in his "mysteries of beekeeping explained," that the pasturage for bees ought to be within half a mile of the apiary, to be of much value to them. I am willing to extend that distance to a mile; but the question is not the distance to which bees fly and gather, but how many stocks could and ought to be kept in one location, with the greatest profit to the beekeeper. Since it is evident that honey does thicken and is not lost if not gathered immediately, it must be evident, also, that the smaller the number of stocks kept in the vicinity of the pasturage, the smaller must be the ability of the bees to visit every flower, or to visit them repeatedly during the day, and the thicker must be the honey gathered. Of course the state of the atmosphere has a certain influence, as well on the secretion of honey, as on the thickening of it. Rain washes the honey out of most kinds of flowers; and we find bees lying idle after a shower, while white clover is in blossom, whereas they continue to gather honey during a moderate rain in basswood blossom time. To come to an answer of my question, it is not necessary to investigate the influence of the weather on the secretion of honey in flowers. This is a matter we cannot change. We have to take the season as it is—whether it be a good one, or a poor one. The location of my home apiary is doubtless a poor one, so far as gathering white clover honey is concerned; but honey in basswood blossoms is as abundant here as anywhere; and I have satisfied myself that I can secure a fair amount of surplus honey, if I aim at that, instead of working for an increase of stock or pure queen bees. Five years ago was a good season for basswood honey. My bees—at that time numbering three hundred and ninety-three colonies in my home apiary, after swarming—worked fully as lively as they did this season. The weather was as good during the time of basswood blossoms, as it was this season, and basswood flowers were as abundant also. After gathering for a week, a number of stocks were examined, and while the combs were nearly all filled with honey, the bees had just commenced sealing it. This season, when I commenced with only one hundred and thirty-seven colonies in the spring, and had during basswood blossoms only about two hundred stocks at my home apiary, the stocks I examined on the third day after they commenced gathering from basswood blossoms, had sealed quite a quantity of honey. All stocks that were supplied with boxes gave a fair amount of honey; and a number of double hives that I had erected, could be emptied every three or four days, having commenced to seal their honey. Five years ago, only a small number of stocks had made box honey, most of the hives had just commenced, when basswood blossoms were over; and on examination a week or two afterwards, I found that nearly every stock had more empty combs in the brood chamber than they needed. No doubt the thin honey had shrunk much in thickening, and the consequence was the bees had to empty some of the combs, to prepare others for sealing over. In my northern apiary, where I had only about one hundred and fifty hives that season, the brood chamber of the hives was full, and I got a satisfactory amount of box honey. Being fully convinced then that I had too many stocks in my home apiary, I concluded to start my southern apiary, with one hundred stocks taken from the former.

Last year, when I had more than two hundred hives at home, after swarming, my average yield of honey was only about nineteen pounds per hive. This year, by using empty combs enough to fill twenty double hives, and some boxes partly filled with combs, I got two thousand and fifty (2,050) pounds of box honey, and a little over four thousand (4,000) pounds of extracted honey—or an average of about forty-four pounds per hive; and I had taken from those one hundred and thirty-seven hives I started with, fifty-six divided colonies and swarms to my northern apiary, thirty-three to a location four miles east, and twenty-nine three miles south. These one hundred and eighteen colonies gathered and stored a little over twenty-three hundred (2300) pounds of honey in the comb in boxes, and gave seventeen maiden swarms saved, besides several that went off and were lost. This amount, added to that gathered at home, would increase the average yield of the original one hundred and thirty-seven stocks at home, to nearly sixty-one pounds, by an increase of one hundred and ninety-eight new colonies.

The thirty-three colonies moved east from my home apiary, were a very weak and poor lot of stocks that had either been queenless last spring, or *artificial stocks* with only three or four combs. They gave eight swarms and a little over eight hundred (800) pounds of box honey. I am fully satisfied, that most of them would have been unable to store a winter's supply if kept at home. But where I had put them, they had nearly the whole field to themselves, as only twelve colonies besides were kept by other parties, in their range of flight.

I have often watched bees gathering honey from flowers in locations where bees were plenty. They went over them very fast, and often were followed in half a minute by others that did not even stop for an experiment of collecting honey from the same flowers. Such bees necessarily lose much time in their search for flowers that contain honey, even if it be conceded that honey is secreted continuously during the blooming of the flowers; and then too, such honey will not have had time to thicken, and the bees will in addition, lose much time in waiting for the thickening of such honey after it has been gathered.

I well know that bees fly two, three, or four miles, in a time of scarcity, but I have noticed that the stocks gain little if any at such a time. Five years ago my Italian bees were found in great numbers in a field of white clover, three and a half miles from home. At that time they gathered just enough to sustain themselves; while about a dozen colonies kept only one-fourth of a mile from the same field were working actively in boxes. In former days I sometimes stated that during basswood time, a thousand colonies could be kept in one location, and all would do well. I have somewhat changed my mind on that point. The bees of those thousand colonies, if in good condition, would perhaps gather honey enough to winter on; but they would lay up very little honey for their owner. They would gather the honey, in their range of flight, as fast as it was secreted, and many bees would visit blossoms that had already been rifled only a moment before. The honey gathered would be a very thin article, subject to large shrinkage, after collection; and instead of still finding luxury ten days after basswood blossoms are over, every drop would be gathered when it ceased to flow. I am fully satisfied that a beekeeper would not get as much surplus honey from a thousand colonies kept in one location, as he would from one hundred. And then, outside of the basswood season, they would not be able to collect enough to feed their brood and sustain themselves. They would continually lurk around among their neighbors, for the sake of espying a chance to steal a little, and a continual feud would be going on.

Bees, too, seem to know that there are too many of them, if a large number is kept in one location. When I had less than a hundred colonies in one location, I obtained in ordinary good seasons a swarm from nearly every hive. When I had a hundred or more, the swarming propensity decreased. Of three hundred and four (304) colonies, wintered out and kept in one location, I received only about fifty natural swarms, although I had not sought to prevent swarming. This season I had in my southern apiary, from one hundred and five colonies only sixty-eight swarms; and those colonies and swarms, with ten artificial swarms, gave four thousand (4,000) pounds box honey, and twenty-eight hundred (2800) pounds of extracted honey. After my spring's sale, I had in my northern apiary, only forty-three colonies (not forty-eight, as my daughter reported by mistake), and with the exception of a dozen colonies of second quality only—four of them queenless in the spring. They produced fifteen hundred (1500) pounds of box and thirty-seven hundred (3700) pounds of extracted honey, and increased to eighty-six good colonies. Their average yield of honey was nearly one hundred and twenty-one (121) pounds per hive, while that of the stocks in my southern apiary, nearly all of which were in prime condition in the spring, was only about sixty-four (64) pounds per hive—being little more than half as much. I have not overlooked the fact that they gave about three pounds more of box honey per hive; but their average weight per hive, when wintered in this fall, was nearly five pounds less than that of the stocks in my northern apiary. It seems therefore that a hundred colonies, in one location, are a larger number of stocks than should be commenced with in the spring.

There is no question with me any longer, that the smaller the number of stocks kept in one location, the greater will be the yield of honey from a single colony. But the question is not, how can a beekeeper secure the largest yield of honey from a small number of stocks, but how can he secure the largest income by keeping bees? In answer to this question I will say, by keeping and managing well a large number of stocks scattered in different apiaries, none of which should contain more than one hundred colonies in the spring. If he could arrange so as not to start with more than fifty in one location in the spring, it would probably be all the better. If placed three miles apart there will be no danger of *overstocking*, in ordinary seasons. A boy or girl twelve or fifteen years old can watch such an apiary in swarming time, and outside of it an active apiarian could superintend a dozen such apiaries. Of course he can only do this if the bees are worked for box honey, and everything is prepared and in readiness when wanted. But if the bees are kept to secure extracted honey, a competent person must take charge of each apiary during the honey season. If double hives are prepared before the beginning of the honey season, a good keeper might work about sixty hives, if he had his stocks in a condition that they would not trouble him much with swarming, while busied with extracting honey.

A. GRIMM.

Jefferson, Wis., Nov. 29, 1871.

[For the American Bee Journal.]

Non-Flying Fertilization.

MR. EDITOR:—To undeceive those who have been misled, and to guide those aright who are in search of the true track, we subjoin a minute and accurate description of our arrangements and method to secure the fertilization of queen bees in confinement.

1. We build the fertilizing room, which is in dimensions six feet by eight, and eight feet high to the square. This room is studded, as though we were going to weatherboard it. We put in a frame, two feet by three, at one corner for a door. We make a tight floor, and beside plank up the sides and ends two feet high, commencing at the bottom. We now get eighteen yards of common brown cotton cloth (not too open), cut it in two pieces of nine yards each, sewing the two together lengthwise. These two widths of the cloth will cover the remaining open space not planked up, with the exception of the top and door. It is best to stretch the cloth on the inner side, putting in a tack now and then, until it is tightly stretched all around. It will take two persons to accomplish this in order to have it done right. After getting it stretched tight, lay a strip of wood or a lath over the cloth on each studding and nail it down. This will prevent the wind from tearing the cloth loose. Also tack the cloth to the edge of the plank all around, placing a strip over the edges as over the studding. Having done this much, we finish the roof by getting us a pole or studding ten feet long, which we set upright in the centre of our room, nailing it fast to the floor, and bracing it by nailing to it four braces, four or five feet from the floor, nailing the foot of each brace to the floor. We now get sixteen yards of common dark calico, have it cut into six bias pieces and sew them up, when they will be in tent shape. We leave an opening at the top for our pole, having a gum strap fastened in said opening, that it may fit *tightly* around the pole, coming down on a pin which we have put through, two or three inches from the top. We now tack the bottom edges of the calico to the inside of our frame, covering or overlapping the tip edge of the cotton cloth. We now have a house whose roof is made of calico in tent shape. We next make a tight fitting door of plank, leaving an opening near the top, twelve or fifteen inches square. This opening we cover with a piece of No. 12 or No. 16 wire cloth. In the far end from the door, and near the top of the room, we arrange a shelf upon which we place old honey combs, the cells of the upper side of which we fill with sweetened water and honey. We are now through with the fertilizing room; but have just reached that part of the programme *which is to be strictly followed, or*

you will fail in every instance. Although it may seem that all is yet to be done is merely to set in the room a colony or nucleus with an unfertile queen with plenty of drones and the work will be done, I tell you this is not so, for you may make the finest greenhouse in the world, and fill it with all the honey-producing plants, even though you have enough to produce honey sufficient for ten or twelve strong colonies, and yet you will fail to have queens fertilized therein. And why? *From the simple fact that the drone is intimidated by the presence of the fiery workers!* If you so arrange it that the drones and queen can fly in and out, while the workers cannot, you have it right. I know some of you have already said it cannot be done. Well, we shall see.

2. In the first place, we never raise our queens in little boxes, six or eight inches square. We form our nucleus in our hives, four to a hive, with three full sized brood frames to each, by using division boards—letting the bees out from one in front, from another at the back, and one out at each end. Thus they do not conflict with each other; and should you on any occasion let them fly in the air for fertilization, the young queen will seldom get into the wrong place when she returns. We raise our queen cells in the full colony, discarding every cell that is not capped over by the ninth day, and especially all the small ones. We insert our queen cells in our nucleus, and on the top of the board that covers this nucleus, we paste a piece of paper, on which we note the time when it will hatch. We now make some *fertilizing boxes* (so called). These are all made so that they will receive two brood frames each. Let the frames hang upon a small strip tacked on the inside. Have your boxes wide enough that you can easily get your finger and thumb between, to handle the frames readily. Make the bottom of these boxes of No. 10 or No. 12 wire cloth. When the frames are hung in the boxes they should not touch the wire bottom. Nail a strip three-eighths of an inch square on top of the wire cloth, all around the bottom of the box. This is to hold the wire cloth up off the brood frames, upon which we shall presently place it. We now have several queens which have just hatched. We go to a strong colony, open it, and pick out two combs *that have plenty of maturing workers with their heads sticking out of the cells.* They are making their first appearance. We shake (not brush) *all* the bees off; if there is *only one left*, we pick him off. *Be sure not to leave a single worker on these two combs.* We now place these two combs in our wire-bottomed box. (We forgot to say that we have a three-quarter inch hole in one end of this box, near the bottom, with a button over it). We then go to a hive that has plenty of fine drones. We open it and select (not an old drone that has been flying in and out of the hive for weeks, but) those that have light-colored heads. They are young drones, which have never yet seen the outer world; and when you turn them loose in the house we have built, they will not know but that is the dimensions of the world in which they are to play their part and die. But if you take an old fellow, he is like a spoiled child. When you attempt to curb him he will *laugh* and attempt to get out. We put these young drones in our wire-bottom box, through the three-quarter inch hole, for it will not do to take off the cap of the box, as the young bees just hatched would crawl out. We next go to our nucleus hive and put in the young queen. Then we place these boxes over the brood frames of a *strong* colony, and let them remain there five or six days. At the end of that time, we take off the boxes with the young unfertile queens, drones, and young workers, and set them on the floor of the fertilizing house which we built at the beginning.

3. Let us now see what we have in these boxes. *First*, a young unfertile queen, six or seven days old, anxious to meet the drone. She passes in and out, three or four times a day. *Second*, we have twenty or more drones, that have never flown in the open air. They are not conscious of a larger, brighter world abroad. They fly around and around and are satisfied—even glad to know that they have such a world as this, free from the fiery old workers. Here they have it all to themselves. *Third*, we have a fine lot of young workers, *only six or seven days old*, too young by ten or fifteen days to leave the combs, even for play. Do you now think we let the queen and drones fly without the workers?

As soon as a queen begins to lay, we remove the box, making up a colony from the frames that were in them, and giving it the queen. If not, we place these boxes out under a shed, setting them on an old blanket or other woollen cloth, until such time as we wish to use them.

When we want more queens fertilized, we proceed as above. We never leave any of those boxes in the fertilizing house till the workers begin to fly out. Herein is *the whole secret of fertilizing in confinement:* KEEP OUT THE WORKERS. We know that when the queen meets the drone on the wing naturally, the workers are far beyond, at a distance, sipping nectar from the flowers. During the month of June, when we have thousands of drones, if you wish to know where the *drone yard* is, take the course that your bees are flying from the apiary, and by the time you have traveled six or eight hundred yards, you will come to a place where the whole atmosphere seems filled with bees. No man ever heard more buzzing. Some would think that a large colony of bees was passing overhead. No, they are the drones from your apiary. Here are tens of thousands of them. When your young queen leaves the apiary, she takes the same course, led by the hum of both workers and drones. On and on she goes, and before she is aware of it, she has reached the desired haven. But do you find any workers flying around in this locality? None, not one. They are all far beyond, in the fields.

Now, brother beekeepers, I fear I have wearied you; but it takes considerable space to explain this non-flying fertilization, so as to make it fully comprehended. Although I have been very particular to describe it in detail, I doubt not some will fail to understand it, for I know that it is next to impossible for half a dozen men to read an article, and all understand it alike. If there are any questions to be asked, please ask them through the Journal, between this time and the first of April, as I shall be too busy after that date to furnish answers. When any man tells you he has had queens fertilized *in the hive*, and *four at* a time, just tell him from me that he says—what's not true.

No man ever yet contracted the entrance to his hive and let out the workers, and kept the *unfertile queen from coming out*, and thus had her fertilized in the hive. If he did, all I have to say is that he either has larger young queens than I have, or his workers are smaller than mine. It can't be done! I have had many queens fertilized, last season, by the foregoing method, carrying out every manœuvre just as I have presented them; and my old fertilizing room now stands in Mr. Moffett's yard, in Trimble county, Kentucky, where I had my apiary the past summer. But whether I will build one here at Franklin, Ky., is not yet decided. I think I thall not have use for one, as I find but few colonies of black bees near me, and these I will Italianize early in the spring.

W. R. KING.

Franklin, Ky.

[For the American Bee Journal.]

Novice.

Mr. EDITOR and BEE JOURNAL FRIENDS in general: We are most happy to announce that our late indisposition has so nearly disappeared, that we are enjoying perhaps as good health as we ever did before. We are in fact feeling so jubilant over restored health—"that greatest earthly blessing"—that we can hardly refrain from persecuting even our friends of the Journal with some account of the way in which it was brought about.

For eighteen weeks our sole diet was lean meat, principally beefsteak; and for fourteen weeks we did not taste even so much as a crumb of bread, nor any vegetables of any kind. Of course brisk out-door exercise was absolutely necessary to digest such a diet, and when unable to walk or work, riding was kept up forenoon and afternoon, almost constantly.

After about twelve weeks, not only a pound of pure beef at a meal, but even four pounds per day, were eaten with pleasure; and when our physician informed us that we could safely take vegetable food once more, we did not care half as much about it, as we did the first month. We were told that the safest vegetable food to be taken at first was "cracked" wheat, or wheat ground in a coffee mill and boiled in simply pure water, with a little salt, of course. Our physician advised using a little butter; but we took the liberty of adding a little honey (remember that we had tasted none—not even a drop of anything sweet—for nearly five months), as we had a few jars of clover honey, put up in June, 1870, that was so thick it could be cut with a knife.

We find ourselves so well satisfied with the above diet that we now eat scarcely anything else, except that and beef, and only hope that our readers will find it half as delicious, on trial, as we do, as we can finish almost any quantity with impunity for breakfast or dinner. We are allowed only beef for supper even now. We cannot speak as favorably of any fruits or vegetables. When we add that our weight increased seven pounds and a half in *seven* days, on the above regimen, we hope no one will accuse us of having a "passion" for steel-yards and spring scales.

Is it possible that any one can have faith enough in what we have just narrated, to be benefited thereby? That much abused "good old Dame Nature" will cure us of all ills as willingly as she mends a broken bone, if she only has *opportunity* and *materials*, is a fact which we fear is but very imperfectly realized.

On page 137 of the December number of the Journal, Jewel Davis asks for more precision in regard to our queen nursing. We certainly should have said—"You can thus cage all the cells in a hive, that would be available in the patented queen nursery, or by any other means." We hope owning a patent has not made him unskilful with unpatented devices.

On page 162, C. T. Smith, we fear, did not make his cages carefully, nor put them in place securely. When we described the device, we had given it a pretty fair trial, and had kept a number of queens caged thus until old enough to let their sister queens get fertilized and commence laying. Then they were removed and used, and the next in age released, and so on.

We always push the wire points past each other, which were then waxed together, so that they could not well fall out, and we cannot remember that we had any trouble in that way. After the yield of honey ceased, they "quarrelled" some, as we have before mentioned. If those who succeeded, and those who did not, could *all* reply *this minute*, we should like to hear the result.

We certainly did not intend to speak of the queens we got from Mr. Grimm, in a fault-finding spirit. We were much pleased with them, considering the season in which they were reared (which we were informed of before buying), and the price we paid. We really were not aware until reminded, how our brief statement of our decision to send to Mr. Langstroth for a queen, seemed to reflect on those we purchased from Mr. Grimm.

Mr. Hazen's fear, on page 167, of overstocking a locality with a dozen hives, or less, sounds strangely as if he had read our Journal with insufficient care. When we had a dozen hives or less, our yield was nothing near, per hive, what it is now every year with over sixty. And

WHAT WE CANNOT DISCOVER

is a single instance, where large apiaries are yielding less, per hive, than small ones. We will try and not think this article too was written solely with a view of eliciting inquiries in regard to his patent hive, that the large results mentioned refer to.

HURRAH FOR GALLUP!

Old hats and new, give them a full vigorous swing and "three cheers," and HURRAH again! Why, old fellow, what makes you so modest? Do you really mean to say that you have taken SIX HUNDRED (600) POUNDS of honey from one hive in one season, and been so quiet about it? Why we are going to make such a fuss, that you can hear us from "Maine to Mexico," when we *beat it, next summer.*

You don't tell us half enough about it. You gave them combs, you say; but really, now, *did you give them no brood* or young bees, as Mr. Hazen does? We have no fears that we can produce a *ton*, if that course be allowed.

We would like to state it thus—How many pounds of surplus honey can the progeny of one queen produce in a season?

One matter we almost forgot. Mr. Hazen speaks of bees starving on account of overstocking. Bless his heart, has no one ever told him that we now give our bees their winter supplies, as a farmer provides for his cattle and sheep; only we simply take about as much trouble to do it as would require to stack up the quantity of hay that an animal would need over winter, and turn them in the lot to keep themselves. Does he consider *feeding* "violence" too? After the several hundred pounds his bees have given him, does he let them starve? Does the "society for the prevention of cruelty to animals" not include insects among the objects of their care? If they do, oh, my! what a task they will have!

Mr. Editor, do we find too much fault? Somehow we fear our pen runs too much that way; and for that reason, in fact, we decided not to say a single word about the *Cleveland convention*, just to check any such lurking disposition. There was much *there* that we were pleased with, and many persons whom we were glad to meet, and things that we would not have missed under scarcely any consideration; but now look here, old pen, you'll just get yourself flopped away on the shelf, if you don't shut up. It's no business of yours if Mr. King did forget to tell us how he "loved Mr. Langstroth," as at the Cincinnati convention; nor why he changed his mind about being secretary, after publishing to the world in his paper, flatly that he wouldn't *no how*.* Of course he knew nothing derogatory to Mr. Langstroth's fair name, until he found that that gentleman could neither be *bought* nor *driven*; *nor did he then*, until he went to Europe with the *fixed determination* to "hunt up something!"

Once more, old pen, is it our business to start up. If the mass of beekeepers are satisfied to pass it all without notice or comment, why should we? If King's conventions are painful to us, we won't go to any more—that is, if we could only tell when he was going to preside."

We are sorry to see Mrs. Tupper's remarks on artificial swarming reported so different from what she did say—especially the latter part, which we fear would be rather exhaustive even to *Iowa bees* the past season. We presume the reporters did not notice it before it got into print.

And now, brother beekeepers all, hurrah for the rows of—not jars, but—barrels of honey this time. "Our better half" suggests *clean white barrels*. Whiskey barrels don't look well.

Barrels of honey for 1872; one from each hive, and from Gallup's hive TWO!

NOVICE, AS OF OLD.

* "*Nolo episcopari*," is the cry of every hypocritical scheemer. [Ed.

[For the American Bee Journal.]

Notification.

MR. EDITOR:—Allow us, through the Journal, to inform its readers and save them the trouble of writing to us, that we are out of the Italian bee business and have neither queens nor colonies for sale. Six years' experience has satisfied us that we can make a more profitable use of our bees than to use them to breed queens at present prices. Hence we have withdrawn from the business, with the intention of never resuming it, except perhaps to accommodate a few personal friends with queens, when we have them to spare.

In this connection, we wish to say a few words in relation to our experience in buying queens, and to give

CREDIT WHERE CREDIT IS DUE.

We have bought quite a number of Italian queens; we have bought them both in the United States and in Europe; we have bought them of several different parties, and paid for them prices varying from seven francs to fifteen dollars, each. While, as a general rule, we have been fairly and honorably dealt with, and good queens have been sent to us—some of them valuable ones; justice to Mr. Langstroth requires that we should give him the credit of sending us the best and most valuable queen we have ever received, judging her by her prolificness and the uniform high color of her queen, drone, and worker progeny. We have bred queens from her to the fifth generation, with the same uniform high color of the workers from each succeeding generation of queens. We consider this a test of purity that is perfectly reliable, no matter how highly colored the queens, drones, and workers are.

WANTED!

In the summer of 1870 we had two queens not more than two-thirds of whose eggs would hatch workers; the remaining one-third would produce drones, though deposited in worker comb. We are in want of such a queen next year; and if any reader of the Journal who has one during the season of 1872, will send her to us by mail, we will reciprocate the favor in any way he may suggest. It is immaterial to us whether the queen is pure Italian, black, or mixed.

J. H. TOWNLEY.

Parma, Mich, Dec. 20, 1871.

☞ A queen that has been very prolific, will usually, when superannuation approaches, deposit eggs in worker cells, a portion of which, gradually increasing in number, will produce drones. She is almost certain to do this largely, if the period of superannuation happens to be in May or June:—The supply of spermatazoa in the spermatheca of such a queen being nearly exhausted, many of her eggs, though laid in worker cells, pass without impregnation. That such queens are unconscious of impotence in this regard, while they may have a foreboding of their impending fate, is evident from their continned oviposition in worker cells exclusively.—[Ed.

[For the American Bee Journal.]

Transferring Bees.

There are, all through our country, great numbers of bees still in box hives, and some even in the old-fashioned hollow log, which, by the way, is just as good, or a little better. Many of our people have not yet discovered that to make beekeeping pay, the bees must be in movable comb hives. But they are waking up, not only to the importance of bee-culture, but to the necessity of having their bees under complete control.

Those who are not informed on the subject, regard it as a very formidable undertaking to transfer a colony of bees, stores and all, from an old hive to a new one; but those who have experience in it, find it unattended with difficulty. To be able to do it in the easiest manner, however, is quite an accomplishment in the bee-keepers' art; and knowledge and skill have not yet made such advancement that improvement may not be made by the interchange of experiment and observation. And, with your permission, Mr. Editor, I will give some of the results of my little experience.

After trying nearly everything recommended for holding combs in place until the bees fasten them in frames. I have fallen back upon slender strips of wood held in place by wire. The strips should be made of tough straight-grained wood, and should be a little more than an eighth of an inch square. They should be long enough to reach a little above and a little below the frames, and have a notch in each end to receive the wires. Tough wire should be used, stiff enough to hold the sticks somewhat firmly, and yet not too stiff to be easily wrapped around the ends of the sticks. The wires should be cut about three inches long; half of the sticks should be counted out and a wire attached to each end of each stick, by two or three turns of the wire around it, in the notch, and then they are ready for use.

I use a transfer board, having blocks nailed on it to hold the frames in place while the comb is being filled in. It has also grooves to receive the sticks, which are to be fastened on the lower side of the frame as it lies on the transfer board. My frames being only twelve inches wide, I use two pairs of sticks to each frame. When every thing is ready, I lay down two of the sticks having the wires on them, in the grooves of the transfer board, and lay the frame over them. The frame is prevented from getting out of place by the small block, nailed to the board. Having cut out a piece of comb of suitable size, I lay it on the frame, or, if not too wide, put the upper edge within the frame, pressing it against the under side of the top bar, and with a sharp knife trim the projecting edges of the comb, so that it can be forced down into the frame. This is much better than to lay the comb on the board and after having marked and trimmed it, spring the frame over it. It is quicker and more easily done, and there is less danger of injuring the comb. When the comb is in place, I lay two sticks having no wires attached, immediately over the two that are under the comb, wrap the ends of the wires around them, and raising up one end of the transfer board to bring the frame to a perpendicular position, put it into the hive.

Unless a hive is very populous, and the weather warm, I do not take the trouble to drive the bees out before transferring the combs. I smoke them pretty well before removing them from the old stand, giving them time to fill themselves with honey. I then carry the hive to a convenient place, set it down bottom upward, drive the bees down with smoke, and with a cold chisel cut the nails, and take off one side of the hive, so as to expose the combs to the best advantage. The tools needed, besides hatchet and cold chisel, are a long-bladed carving knife and a three-eighth inch iron rod having at one end a steel blade bent at a right angle, and about one inch and a half long from the angle to the point; and at the other end a handle such as is used for small chisels. This tool is about twenty inches long. It is used for cutting off combs which cannot be conveniently reached with a knife.

Four or five heads of broom corn tied securely and firmly together, are better than anything else I have tried, for brushing bees from the combs.

After placing the first comb in the new hive, I brush all the bees on combs subsequently cut out into it, that they may cluster on any brood it may contain. When all the combs are in the new hive, I shake the remaining bees down in front of it, let them go in, and then place it on the old stand. It is well always to place an empty hive, or a box of some kind, containing a piece of comb from the hive, on the old stand to receive and retain the returning bees, until the work is done. It is better that the comb contain unsealed brood.

I have transferred bees in March and in November, and in nearly every month between, and have never had them do otherwise than well. I have had less trouble with robbers in March and in October and November, than in May and June. It is not a good plan to transfer many colonies on the same day, unless it can be done in a house that will exclude robbers, as all the bees in the neighborhood will, after awhile, be attracted by the exposed honey.

M. Mahin.

New Castle, Ind., Dec. 23, 1871.

[For the American Bee Journal.]

Notes of a Beginner.

MR. EDITOR, and beekeepers generally, *greeting*:—The honey season is past, and ere this we have all counted our profits, if not in dollars and cents altogether, then in bees and honey; and many a sweet morsel we shall enjoy during the winter. Some of us, too, are doubtless able to supply others with a portion, provided they pay for it. I say *us*, for I number myself now as a beekeeper, or at least as beginning to be. Though I have to acknowledge some failures, during the past season, yet, taking it altogether, as I had never handled a bee before, I am quite well satisfied with the summer's operations—which sum up as follows:

Commenced with 13 stocks, in almost all kind of hives, at a cost of $8 each,	$104 00
27 hives, at $2 each, ...	54 00
2 queens, at $2.50 each, ...	5 00
Total, ...	$163 00

An increase of 13 stocks, $8 each, . .	$104 00
Increase in value, by Italianizing, . .	55.00
600 lbs. of honey, at 20 cents per lb., .	120 00
1 swarm from the woods, ...	8 00
Total, ...	$287 00

The balance, $124, may go to pay for time.

I do not give these figures because they show very great profit, but to give facts. I do believe that while a few will reach such figures as Novice and Grimm, the majority of beekeepers will only attain to a less amount. But, of course, in order to progress, each must strive to be one of the successful few.

NOVICE'S QUEEN NURSERY.

Immediately on receipt of the Journal, I made several, perhaps a dozen of these nurseries; but succeeded in saving only two queens by them. I guess I must have bungled somewhat; but Novice did not tell us how he had succeeded. Will he please tell us whether he has been successful with them? Novice says, after removing the wire cages, the combs would be uninjured. Now, in my operations the bees would in every case gnaw the comb on the inside of the cages, and the old ones on the outside; so that sometimes a piece of comb would fall out on removing the cage.

INTRODUCTION OF QUEENS.

I have been almost uniformly successful in introducing my queens this summer, by simply removing the black queen and immediately caging the Italian queen, and putting her between the combs at the top. In about twenty-four hours I would release her without any further ceremony, except that two or three times I used smoke or sweetened water. I also mixed up my bees, by changing frames, bees and all; and had no fighting but twice. Late this fall, however, I used chip smoke to unite my nuclei.

LANGSTROTH'S METHOD.

I would here say, that upon two occasions I found a young queen, just hatched, perhaps not over five hours old. I at once sought for and destroyed a black queen, and immediately without any ceremony, put her on a frame, holding it in my hand. She was well received, and has now a fair stock of bees as her progeny. They are hybrids. The other was introduced to a nucleus, from which I had taken the queen just a short time before. She was received without any molestation, and in due time given to a full stock.

THE HONEY EXTRACTOR.

I do not know but I overdid the thing by the use of my extractor. I did not get it finished as soon as I wished, so that some of my stocks were full of honey, and waiting for me. I think my figures would have been larger if I could have used the extractor earlier. I emptied most of the stocks twice. The second time about the middle of July. At this time most of my bees seemed to resent this kind of treatment, not by stinging, but by a sulky behavior. They seemed to stop working with their usual energy; yet they continued to work some till the last of July and August, but not to give me any surplus. Not suspecting that all would not be as well as could be, I did not examine them till some time in October. I then found no brood or eggs, and they were not as well stocked with bees as I should like them to be. But, still, all seemed to have honey in plenty. Now I suspect I ought to have fed them some in July; and this I acknowledge is my fault, for Mr. Langstroth gave me directions in full, in Hive and Honey Bee, but I did not follow it out to the letter.

A BEGINNER.

☞ The writer's name became detached from his communication, and lost. Will he favor us with it?

[For the American Bee Journal.]

Satisfactory Results.

MR. EDITOR:—Once upon a time I promised the readers of our Journal that I would make a report of the season's operations (1871); but after looking over the reports of some in former numbers of the Journal, my faith in my ability to make the best report for the season was somewhat "dampened." For instance, when I read Katie Grimm's report, I thought "How wonderful is man" and the honey slinger, and yet how much more wonderful is a woman with such energy and strength! Indeed, my three hundred pounds of honey for one day's work, sunk into utter insignificance in comparison, and yet I am very well satisfied with the results of the season in my own case. Now for the figures.

The spring of 1871 found me in possession of twenty stocks of bees, about one-half of which were blacks, and the remainder Italians and hybrids. Five of the number came out of winter quarters so weak that I received no profit from them in swarms or honey. These colonies I built up without any aid from other stocks; and four out of the five commenced with only two combs each, in the spring. From each of the five I have taken two queens, forcing them to supply themselves with others from sealed queen cells; and they are all now in prime condition for wintering, with their hives full of combs and bees.

Wishing to get all my stocks Italianized this season, from the other fifteen colonies I formed twelve nuclei for raising queens to supply my new swarms and Italianize my natives. This I succeeded in doing, without trouble; have sold about forty dollars' worth of queens to my neighbors, at reasonable figures; and am wintering ten queens in their nucleus hives, seven of which are purely fertilized.

My honey account for the season, stand as follows:

Pure white basswood honey, extracted,	700 lbs.
Mixed and dark, " "	200 "
In small frames and boxes, ...	600 "
In large frames, in upper story, . . .	200 "
Making in all, ...	1700 lbs.

The fifteen colonies have given me, besides, an increase of twenty swarms, all of which are in winter quarters in good condition.

In extracting I only operated on my old colonies, and such of the new ones as had been supplied with empty combs, except where I extracted from new combs for queen raising. And, by the way, I get much finer queens from new combs than I can get from old.

My honey I have sold at from twenty-three to twenty-eight cents per pound—averaging fully twenty-five cents.

The profit for the season would foot up as follows:

For honey sold (1200 lbs. at 25 cents per lb.), ...	$300 00
Honey still on hand (500 lbs. at 25 cents),	125 00
Queens sold, ...	40 00
Twenty new swarms, worth $10 each, exclusive of hives, ...	200 00
Making a total of	$665 00

Or, an average of $44.33 per colony.

The colonies from which I extracted most freely, gave me the most box honey this fall, and are in much the best condition for winter, being better supplied with bees hatched late in the season. From this summer's experience with the extractor, I have come to the conclusion that, in a season like the past, all the honey we can get with the extractor is more than clear gain.

J. E. BENJAMIN.

Rockford, Iowa, Dec. 15, 1871.

[For the American Bee Journal.]

Timber for Honey Casks.

A correspondent of the Journal asks for information on this subject. I put my honey in ten gallon oaken casks, and do not perceive that they impart any taste foreign to the honey.

MR. GALLUP—WHERE IS HE?

Let's hear a word. There are some of us (who did not send the dollar, of course,) who are waiting patiently for the promised description of his bee-hive. I am particularly interested, for I adopted the form given by him in the Journal some time since.

I bought up some stocks this fall, so that I have now in my cellar thirty-eight stocks in good condition, according to my poor judgment, and I am waiting anxiously for the end of a long winter, when the little workers will show how they have borne confinement. Till then, adieu.

H. H. PHELPS.

Pine Island, Minn.

[For the American Bee Journal.]

Report of Progress.

DEAR JOURNAL:—We always welcome your appearance on our tables, for well do we know that we shall gain some useful knowledge from your pages. How sorry we felt for Novice, when reading his article in the November number, and found that even he can get into trouble. Taking warning from his sad experience, we appointed ourself an investigating committee of one, and entered on duty at once. As we had used our extractor rather late in the season, we examined those hives first that we had taken from last, and found they had filled the empty combs about half full. These we had placed in the centre of the hive, as we returned them from the extractor. (*Was that right?*)

The past season was a good one for bees in this locality. They worked busily on buckwheat and smart weed until it was killed by the frost.

We commenced the season with twenty-six (26) stocks, and increased our number to forty-eight (48), and reared about seventy-five (75) queens. Our yield of surplus honey was not great, yet we found our stocks all in good condition for winter, except a few late swarms, which we supplied with full frames kept in reserve. Now, thought we, all are in good condition for winter, and dismissed the matter from our mind, giving our attention to visiting friends. But on moving our stocks to the cellar, we found that one weak one which we had supplied with honey had been robbed, and the bees were dead. We also found another stock dead, with abundance of honey. The bees were clustered just below the honey, some had crept into the cells, while others were clustered over them. Can any one tell us what killed those bees?

All our bees are Italians except some few hybrids. We have sold queens, bees and honey to an amount of one hundred and forty dollars, and have considerable honey on hand still. We sell all our honey at twenty-five cents per pound.

Flattering ourself that we had been rather successful in queen rearing, we determined to procure imported queens, and to be certain that they were imported, we concluded to play importer for once. Some time in August we ordered a package of eight queens from Edward Uhle. We waited with patience till the 12th of October, when they arrived by express. There was no time lost in bringing them home, and with no small degree of anxiety did we proceed to examine box after box. To our surprise and joy we found every queen alive. We expressed one to a friend, and now came our trouble. Seven valuable queens to be introduced, and so very late in the season!

Yet the trial must be made. We caged the queens, destroyed those of the stocks, and immediately hung the cages containing the strangers into the several hives, left them thus four days, then raised the cages and tied over the top of each a bit of newspaper smeared with honey, replaced them, and left the bees to liberate the queens at will. On examining them ten days after we found each queen lively and perfectly at home among her American subjects.

If we are successful in wintering them, we shall be able to furnish pure Italian queens to all who may favor us with their orders next season. Having been successful in importing we shall continue to make new importations from time to time, in order to keep our stock good.

MRS. K. A. D. MORGAN.

Pella, Iowa, Jan. 3, 1872.

[For the American Bee Journal.]

Report of a Season's Work.

MR. EDITOR:—Not having very much to do at present, I thought I would give the readers of your valuable Journal some account of my last season's operations.

On the first of May I found all my stocks in the weakest possible condition. There were forty-eight colonies in all, having lost twelve during the winter and spring from having forced queens. I raised several queens the previous season, and by the first of June every one was dead. Hence I consider forced queens of but little account, as I bought several such, and never had one to live a year from the time I got her.

Thus on the first of May I had forty-eight stands. They were so weak that I only got seventeen swarms from the whole. The first swarm came out on the ninth of June, and the remainder afterwards, up to the tenth of July. The first swarm gave me one hundred and twenty pounds of honey, and my bees, old and young, sixty-five stands, averaged me nearly eighty pounds of honey each. About one-half of this was extracted, for which I got fifteen cents per pound. For box honey I obtained twenty cents per pound. From the 1st to the 15th of August I took all the honey from each and every hive. After that they had nothing to work on but buckwheat. Some twenty-five stands made from eighty to eighty-five pounds of honey each. That is they filled their hives, which required from forty-five to fifty pounds, and filled besides some twenty-five boxes with from thirty-five to forty pounds each—all from buckwheat. The rest filled their boxes full and put from ten to thirty pounds in their boxes. Every hive I have on the place has rather too much honey, as they are not wintering well, and this is the greatest trouble I have in wintering bees. I have seen it stated by some that their bees did not get enough honey to winter on. Now such a thing I have never known here. My pasture is all artificial now, but I have sold my farm and bought another in the grove, some six miles to the south. Here I am going to put out a large pasture, such as alsike clover, mellilot clover, and buckwheat. There are plenty of thorn bushes, wild plums, crab apples, elm, maple, and hickory trees, and not less than one hundred acres of basswood or linden trees within a mile of this location. If there is any honey in linden I expect to get some. I think I have the most favorable situation for bees that could be found in a long travel.

R. MILLER.

Malugin Grove, Ills.

[For the American Bee Journal.]

A Few Inquiries.

MR. EDITOR:—As the time has come around for my subscription I wish to ask a few questions.

1st. At what time does the "basswood" blossom in Central Illinois? I live on the prairie several miles from timber, and never saw basswood in bloom. I am thinking of planting a grove in the spring, and should be pleased to hear from parties having basswood trees for sale.

2d. At what age does the basswood tree begin to yield honey? Our honey supplies in this locality consist mainly of white clover, buckwheat and Spanish needles. In wet seasons bees have abundant pasturage, but in dry ones they "go for the grapes" and any other fruit that suits their taste. There are hundreds of pounds of grapes destroyed by bees in this neighborhood in the past two seasons.

Our town site is one mile square, and there were about four hundred colonies of bees located on that area last season, but owing to the drouth and the great number of bees, I fear a portion of them will fail to take wing in the spring of 1872.

I would also like to ask Mr. R. M. Argo if he kills more bees when manipulating his close fitting frames than he does when using frames that hang half an inch apart.

I close by proposing three cheers for Gallup and the American Bee Journal.

S. W. LOUD.

Virden, Ills., Jan. 8, 1872.

☞ We doubt whether the *bees* injured the grapes as charged. We have never yet been able to find one attacking a sound ripe grape, peach, or other fruit, though we have often seen them appropriating the juices of such as had been injured by wasps, or other insects, or birds —thus making themselves useful by gathering up and saving what would otherwise have been lost. Let grape growers and fruit culturists use their own eyes carefully in watching birds and insects, and they may be undeceived. The recently introduced European sparrow, however valuable it may possibly prove to be, as a caterpillar exterminator, is almost certain to do more damage to vineyards in one season than bees have done since the day that Noah became a vigneron.—[ED.

[For the American Bee Journal.]

Introducing Queens; or the Grand Modus Operandi.

MR. EDITOR:—Having tried many of the plans given in the Journal for introducing queens, I found there would still be some failures occasionally. Now here is a way that has proved sure every time: Make a box of the same dimensions as the hive, six or seven inches deep; nail on a board for a bottom; on the upper edge tack on cloth to prevent the escape of smoke; bore a hole through one of the sides to blow smoke through. When operating, set the hive on this box; then load your fumigator with puff-ball, and proceed as Mr. Quinby directs, and drop the bees. Look out for the queen, if she was not destroyed before you smoked the bees. The better way is to kill the black queen before smoking them, as then they do not need to be smoked so much. Have ready another box, about three inches deep, with bottom, and inch holes through its sides, covered with wire cloth, to let in fresh air. Put the bees in this box and set the hive over them. When the bees revive, and begin to climb up, put in your Italian queen, and keep the bees confined till next morning. They should also have upward ventilation.

Can some one tell me, through the Journal, how to keep my bees from swarming? I would rather have honey than swarms.

The past season was not as good as last year. My bees made one-third less honey this year than last. PETER LIVINGSTON.

New Salem, N. Y., Dec. 28, 1871.

[For the American Bee Journal.]

Report from Pratt's Hollow, Madison Co., N. Y.

MR. EDITOR:—The commencement of our season here was poor, but by the 20th of June the bees began to get honey pretty freely, and so continued until the first of August, as our season ends early with the basswood bloom.

I hived one large swarm on the 16th of July, and in fifteen days they filled a common box hive and six 5 lb. boxes. I think I never saw bees get honey faster than they did this year from the basswood blossoms.

I began the season with twenty-five colonies. They increased to forty-five, mostly by natural swarming. I took from them—young swarms and all—nine thousand eight hundred (9,800) pounds of box honey, including weight of boxes, and sold it in that form at an average of twenty cents per pound.

I doubled a good many of my young swarms. I think that those I thus doubled averaged me sixty pounds of box honey per hive, while those that I hived singly did not average over fifteen pounds to the hive. Will it not pay to double young swarms, where they can be bought in the fall for five dollars each? I can buy plenty of black bees in this county, in box hives for that price.

I think the golden willows are a great help to bees in the spring. I was at my father's in Oneida county, about the first of May. There are a great many of those willows there, and I think his bees came in as loaded from them as they did here from the basswoods. This year the bees got such a start from the willows, that they commenced swarming as soon as the apple trees came in blossom, or say the 18th and 20th of May.

My best colony, this year, of black bees in a box hive, gave me one hundred and fifty (150) pounds of box honey. A good many of the boxes had a considerable amount of dry comb in them. I think I can get one-third more honey in that way than by single capping. My best half-blood colony gave me one hundred and twenty-five (125) pounds of box honey, with only the natural start combs in the boxes.

I had a few Italians and half-bloods. They commenced swarming about one week earlier than the blacks.

My bees were mostly in box hives. I could have got more from them if they had all been in shallow Langstroth hives. I am making a hundred Langstroth and a hundred Quinby hives for the coming season.

Probably twenty of my swarms went to the woods. One large swarm that I had trebled, started work in the hive, and continued about forty-eight hours, then left for the woods without alighting. I expected a hundred pounds of honey from it, if it had stayed.

G. T. FEARON.

Dec. 29, 1871.

[For the American Bee Journal.]

Queens, and Corresponding Hives.

On page 114 of the November number of the Journal, Mr. Benjamin says he feels sorry for friend Gallup. Now, save your sorrow, friend B., for we can stand any amount of such *pitching in.* But the amount of correspondence that I had before I sent that article charging the dollar, no live man could possibly stand. Those same chaps that have done the pitching in, would like to have Gallup devote his entire time to correspondents, and then kick him for not doing more. Still, this is not what we started for in this article. It is about that queen's laying herself to death in our Youreka, Back Action, Extractor, Reversible, Revolvable, Movable Comb, Twin Bee Hive. It is a well known fact, that some queens will lead out a swarm, fill a standard hive, lead out another swarm, and fill that hive, still lead out a third, and fill that hive also. And with us, such prolific queens are almost invariably long-lived. We have had them retain their full prolificness the fourth season, and do as well as a majority of queens still in their fifth season. But, suppose your figures are correct, and on my principle a queen will produce the workers to gather eight hundred (800) pounds of honey in one season; or, on the old plan, it takes her three years to produce the same result; we say, let her spread herself. There may be something more here yet, that you have not thought of. We once removed a large swarm of bees (from a house) that had been there a number of years, and they had a queen as large again as a common one. Again, we removed a swarm from a large bass-wood log, and found the old queen a tremendous large one (not as large as an ox, but large for a queen). We also found extra large queen cells, and made three extra large swarms from the old log. Queens and queen cells were extra large, that were raised in our large colonies last season. The bees seem to expend large amounts of wax on the cells, and place an extra large amount of food in them. D. L. Adair, in his "Outlines of Bee-Culture," says, on page 13: "*It is found in practice, that the queen is more prolific in a hive where she is not crowded for room to deposit eggs, and the whole population is more industrious.*" And on page 17, he says: "*Queens raised in full sized chambers, are larger, more prolific, and live longer,*" &c. In practice, certainly, we agree with Mr. Adair. If this is correct, then, in an extra large colony, we can raise extra large queens to meet the emergency. So far, so good. Right here, we will say, that Mr. Adair's section hive is used in just as many forms, with the same size frames or sections, as we used in our hive. We obtained some valuable suggestions from him and his hive at the conventions last winter. After using the extractor, we formed an opinion of what we wanted for a hive, and we went to the conventions chock full of our ideas, and Mr. Adair was the only individual we found there that had formed the same opinions; or if others had, they kept them to themselves. We do not intend to use large hives exclusively, but in connection with our standard hives.

E. GALLUP.

Orchard, Iowa, Dec., 1871.

[For the American Bee Journal.]

Virgin Queens becoming Drone Layers.

One year ago last summer, I had at one time secured so many hatched queens and maturing queen cells, from stocks that had swarmed naturally, that I had a queen in each of my one hundred and three (103) nuclei then running, and quite a number of queens left which I preserved in nuclei that had no fertile queen. In a number of instances those extra queens were neglected or killed by the workers, as soon as the queen at liberty became fertile. A small number, however, was saved in such of these nuclei as had lost the queens at liberty, during their wedding flight. Much occupied, then, by other pressing work, I did not liberate those queens until they were fourteen days old. They were readily accepted by the workers, and I noticed some of them making their wedding flight the same day they were liberated. Three days afterwards I examined the nuclei containing those queens, and found five of them fertile and laying. This was on the seventeenth day after they were hatched. A few days later I had occasion to fill a large number of orders for untested queens, and shipped those five among others. Think of my surprise when I found the progeny of all those five queens was drone brood in worker combs! Of course I had to send other queens immediately; but this turning drone layer at so early an age, was contrary to all my former experience. A queen that had hatched on April 4th, at the time when I wintered out my bees, did not commence laying until the forty-third day of her age, and laid worker eggs exclusively in worker cells for three months and a half, when she commenced intermingling some drone eggs among worker brood, and was then superseded. Three other queens hatched on April 15th, and at liberty in their hives, commenced laying drone eggs exclusively on the 23d day of their age. At one time in the month of September I had forty-five queens, none of which were impregnated, on account of cold, rainy weather prevailing, over three weeks old. The weather had changed, becoming fine and warm, and all these queens, except a few that were lost or killed, were impregnated in the course of two days, and became regularly fertile.

If the above reported experience of young queens becoming drone layers when caged fourteen days in warm weather, should be confirmed by further observation and corroborated by the experience of other queen breeders, it would seem to be established that virgin queens could not be kept long in cages or queen nurseries without detriment, even if they should not be neglected or killed by the bees in whose hives they are placed for preservation. I find, however, that worker bees that have a prolific, fertile queen in their hives, will try their best to destroy virgin queens kept in queen nurseries or cages—probably apprehensive that their own queen was in danger.

A. GRIMM.

Jefferson Wis., 1871.

[For the American Bee Journal.]

In Peace Prepare for War.

As there is not much to be done now that our pets are snugly stored away in their winter quarters, perhaps dreaming of better days, probably now is the most favorable time to mature our plans for the coming season.

We have read carefully the Journal for 1870 and 1871, and have been expecting so see somebody recommending for the management of bees, a plan like our own, or one very similar; but as we have not seen anything quite like it, we will give it for whatever it may be worth.

Mr. Editor, this is no new fangled thing. We have practiced it for the past ten years, with the best results. Like many readers of the Journal I am located where forage consists almost entirely of white and alsike clover; and those situated like myself will be the ones that will be benefited by my plan. Every beekeeper knows that, in such locations, the time for gathering honey is very short—at longest not more than sixty days. Now, if you expect much surplus, you must have very populous stocks to gather it. Then comes the question, what do we consider strong stocks? Well, we consider a hive that did not swarm, a good stock, generally giving us a good surplus; and yet even such sometimes fail to come up to our standard. But we will now try and give you our plan for making working swarms. Let me here remark that my experience has been with black bees and natural swarming. The past season I introduced about twenty Italian and hybrid queens.

And now, Mr. Editor, for example, I have on hand fifty-four stocks, provided all come out right in the spring. Suppose these all send out a swarm each, fifty-four in number—what shall I do with so many swarms? I have only twenty empty hives, and am determined not to make any more, because it is *honey* that I am after, and if I should double my stock, I should not get honey enough to grease a pan-cake.

I will now try to explain how I manage. A few days before swarming commences, I locate all my empty hives in my yard, just where I want them to stand through the season. I have all swarms in a basket hive as they issue, and carry them to the hives designed for them. Do not forget to mark day and date on every hive both old and young. We will now take it for granted that you have already hived eight new swarms. Well, if any of them have been hived three, four or five days, it makes no particular difference, though we prefer four days. Now introduce another big swarm in each. But a neighbor tells us we could not put two of his swarms in one of our hives. Moonshine! We never had two swarms in our life, but we could make room for them, and keep them at work too, when anything sweet was to be found abroad. But we are off the track again. Well, we said put in another big swarm. But we want a fair fixing—half a dozen platforms, four feet long and three feet wide, made of inch boards. Nail two strips on the top, one at each side to project two inches, to clamp on the bottom board of the hive to be doubled up. A board, of course, is nailed at the other end, which makes it level with the hive that is to receive the swarm. Now, when you have nailed a lath on each side of your platform, to keep the bees from falling on the ground when they begin to scatter; one thing more, and we are ready for action. Raise the front of the hive that is to receive the swarm one inch. Of course, you have during the day taken off the honey board and covered the top with neat and handsome glass boxes. Our hive accommodates forty-five pounds in six boxes; or if the extractor is to be used, put on the upper story. All being in readiness, bring along your swarm in an old box hive, for as a matter of course you did not have them in a frame hive, because it would be quite a job to shake them out of the frames. Now, with one jerk drop the bees on your platform, one foot in front of the hive to run them in. They will scatter all around for a minute or two, but do not disturb them till they begin to travel for the hive; then keep them moving till all are in. The next morning set the hive level, but still raised on all sides, three-eighths of an inch from the bottom board.

The reason why you want several boards or platforms, is, that you can be doubling up six or eight swarms at the same time, and you will do it in half an hour. One thing must not be forgotten—this operation must be done after sundown, and when it is nearly dark. The swarms will then unite without the loss of a single bee. Now double up all your new swarms as fast as possible, for every day counts. At the same time keep making new ones, till you have used up all your hives. We take it for granted that you have now made fifteen new swarms all doubled up thirty single ones; and providing all your stocks send out a swarm, you have twenty-four to come yet. Well, we will try to find a place for them, where they can be made useful. We will now return a swarm back to every one that has swarmed. And here the question is often asked—what do you do with the extra queen? Well, if I had any use for a queen, I should preserve her; or if I had a choice of the two, I should keep the best. But in this case I have no use for queens, so she may pass in with the swarm, and next morning you can have a funeral. But we are going astray again. We said we should send back a swarm to every old stock that had sent one out. But, if it can be avoided, do not return a swarm to the hive it came out from. We have returned hundreds of second swarms back to their own hive; but in this case, an old queen still under the swarming impulse, will sometimes lead the swarm out again. Now for further operations. You have to-day four swarms, of course in box hives, and let them stand just where you hived them till nearly dark; but during the afternoon you prepared four old stocks to receive them. I mean by this, that you have destroyed all queen cells to be found in said hives. If so, put on your surplus boxes or upper stories; bring on your platforms and douce the bees thereon. Shake all four swarms out on their platforms, and by the time you get back to the first one, the bees are making for the hive. With a little brush of some kind keep them moving till all are gone in. If, when you have returned a swarm to each old stock, the swarming still continues, make one or two more new swarms, till all are disposed of.

Now you have what we term a lot of strong swarms, not here and there one in the yard storing, as in most cases where swarming is allowed and every swarm hived separately; but every one storing surplus. How is that for high?

It may be, if the season is a good one, that some of your first hived double swarms may send out a swarm in about four weeks. If they do, our plan is to catch the queen, return the bees and let them raise a young queen. This has never failed with us. Give them plenty of room to store surplus honey, and you will not be troubled much with swarms.

A brother beekeeper suggested to us last season that Italians and hybrids will not bear handling and doubling like the black bees. We shall give them a fair trial the coming season, and should such prove to be the case, we do not want them, as we are not prepared yet to believe that a single swarm of Italians will store as much honey as two swarms of blacks.

It may be that some beekeepers will object to this method of ours, in returning the swarms to all the hives that had sent out a swarm, destroying all the young queens, and returning all the old ones. Now, Mr. Editor, we honestly confess that we were a little skeptical on this point ourselves, for the first two or three seasons; but time has proven to us that it made not a particle of difference. Our stocks are to-day just as good as they ever were, and we think even better. Our loss in queens has not amounted to more than one in twenty-five the year round.

And now, Mr. Editor, light your pipe* take the American Bee Journal, and sit down in the shade, where you can watch these stocks, as the bees fly out in all directions from the hive. It will make you smile; and you may just bet your old boots.† that if there is any honey to be found, you will get your share. We have never had a season so poor since we adopted the plan, but a little double swarm would fill the hive with combs and store honey enough to last till spring. But we have known plenty of singly hived swarms starve before the first of December.

The past season a brother beekeeper condemned our plan on the ground that such a quantity of bees put in one hive, will invariably build too much drone comb. But it must be remembered that the swarm was hived four days before it was doubled; and if the weather was good the greater part of the combs are then already built or well started. But we have not been able to discover any difference. Some stocks build more of such combs than others. But do not be alarmed; the working force of your hives will be ample so long as the flowers last, and they will go into winter quarters with all the bees you need. In fact, we have sometimes thought the hives contained too many bees to winter well.

Our esteemed brother Ezra Rood, of Wayne, Michigan, paid us a visit last season, in swarming time, expressly to investigate our plan. We demonstrated to him our best Grecian style, and he went home as he said to put it in practice. As we have not heard from him since, we do not know how he likes it. Brother Townley of Parma, has practiced this plan, more or less; but as he has been extensively engaged in raising queens, we think he has not fully carried it out.

We also visited brother Temple, of Ridgway, Michigan. He has a large apiary, and after talking with him, we explained to him our method. He promised to try it, and at the following State Fair, held in Jackson, he told us, if he had known this before, he could have sold hundreds of dollars' worth more honey; and he is another convert.

But, Mr. Editor, we have spun a pretty long yarn and will try to close. We should feel more at home holding the plow-handle than writing articles for the Journal, because many of its readers have forgotten more than we have ever thought of.

About hives we have nothing to say. We use a well made box, with frames. Cost about seventy-five cents. Two coats of paint, and the nail holes puttied up. We are a jackknife carpenter, and do our own work. We think very loud sometimes that if men would study bees more and fixings less, they would get more honey.

We have forgotten to mention one thing that has been useful to us. In swarming time it often happens that two swarms go together, and they prove more or less troublesome till one of the queens is killed. We have often had them swarm out two or three times, before finally concluding to stay. But we manage them in this way now. As soon as such swarms are hived, set the hive in a shady place on the ground, of course with a board under the hive. Raise the hive all around on blocks one inch thick. Now take any kind of thin cloth, having no holes or rents in it. Spread it over the top of the hive and reaching down to the ground. Pull the bottom of the cloth out tent-like, and lay stones or bricks on the loose ends, or anything that will keep all tight. Be sure that no place is left where a bee can get out, and they will remain perfectly quiet. By next morning one of the queens will have been destroyed; then put the hive on its stand, and all will be right.

If we have an unruly swarm we tent them out till sundown; then unite it with some other; and the trouble is at an end.

Long live the American Bee Journal, and may it see many happy new years.

J. BUTLER.

Jackson, Mich., Dec. 28, 1871.

* *Fumigator*, if you please. We do not now smoke. [ED.

† Not worth a dime! [ED.

[For the American Bee Journal.]

To Prevent Combs from Breaking.

The following is the way I prevent the comb from breaking while using the honey extractor, in cold weather, in fall or winter. It works with perfect satisfaction to me.

I use a zinc can with a tight cover and a hole near the bottom to let the honey out of. It is through this hole that I admit the steam. First I shave the caps off of two combs, put them in the can, and put on the cover, then having a common tea kettle boiling on the stove, I raise up the can so that the steam will enter at the aforementioned hole, turn the comb gently for three or four minutes, and then you may turn as fast as required without the least danger of breaking the combs. This is much better, and far less trouble than letting the combs stand in a warm room two or three hours.

J. PICKERING.

Brampton, Ontario, Canada.

THE AMERICAN BEE JOURNAL.

Washington, February, 1872.

☞ Ill health during part of the past month, prevented us from giving the Journal the usual attention, though we flatter ourselves that we have managed, notwithstanding, to make up a very readable paper.

☞ On the 14th ult., a subscriber mailed to us at Byron, Mich., a letter enclosing two dollars, but omitted to give us his name. Whom shall we credit? Another subscriber, writing from Ipswich, Mass., on the 8th ult., enclosed two dollars, but likewise failed to give his name. In his case, we ventured to *guess*. If wrong, will the writer please correct us?

☞ Mr. G. W. Childs has sent us a copy of the PUBLIC LEDGER ALMANAC for 1872, containing a large amount of statistical and other information, in a condensed and compact form. The almanac is not for sale anywhere, but ninety thousand copies of it were printed by Mr. Childs, to be presented to subscribers to (Philadelphia) Public Ledger.

☞ Mr. A. Gray, of the firm of Gray & Winder, Cincinnati, Ohio, intends going to Europe in the spring, to procure a supply of pure Italian queen bees for his own apiary. He will also take a limited amount of orders from others desiring such queens, to be sent to them by express from Cincinnati on his return. Terms $15 per queen. Orders accompanied by the cash, either in registered letters or post office money orders, should be addressed to him prior to March 15th next. Mr. Gray is an experienced bee-breeder, and will no doubt, make careful selections.

☞ To Mr. Langstroth's exposure of H. A. King's operations, and his dispassionate and dignified notice of the Baron of Berlepsch's Declaration, we need not invite attention—the interest felt in the subject will command it, of course.

☞ We purpose next month to insert the Baron of Berlepsch's Declaration, into the making of which he was unwarily entrapped by the wily misrepresentations of H. A. King. We reserve, till then, any remarks we may have to make with reference to it.

☞ A slight error occurred in the January number, in our reference to Mr. Langstroth, which, though of not much importance, we desire to correct. Instead of "Before the spring of 1853 we never heard of Mr. Langstroth," read "Before the autumn of 1851." We then first heard of him from the late Rev. Dr. Berg; but we never saw him or had any conversation or correspondence with him till after the 1st of August, 1852, as we stated last month.

☞ The preposterous absurdity of claims made now to having invented movable frame hives twenty-five or thirty years ago, must be evident to every candid man, who reflects for a moment on the prerequisites which the intelligent use of such frames involves; and who is aware of what was the highest advance which practical bee-culture had reached in this country, when Mr. Langstroth made his invention and published his book. We have no hesitation in saying (and doubt not that all thinking beekeepers, old enough to know the facts as they then existed, will agree with us), that when Mr. L. invented his frames, and before he published his book, there were not three men in the country (unless instructed by him) who could have used a movable comb hive intelligently and successfully, if one had been presented to them ready stocked. Beekeepers had to be *educated* to use the frames—that is, they had to learn how to manipulate with them, before they could manage them with any prospect of success. Many, very many intelligent beekeepers, long accustomed to manage bees in common hives, tried to use them, and failed, because they relied on mere practical skill, without having previously qualified themselves, in some degree, by studying the science and theory. Hundreds, subsequently very skilful and successful operators, well remember the day when first they *ventured* to undertake the *job* of opening a hive and removing a comb crowded with bees; and many laughable stories have we heard from the lips of such, when detailing their unlucky experience and frequent discomfitures.

And now, men, who still occupy only *back seats* and the *lower forms* in the schools of apiculture, come forward and claim that they, *even they*, invented these frames a full quarter of a century ago! Why, they might as well claim to have invented car-buffers and couplings, railway switches, and track-laying machines, a lustrum or two before George Stevenson dreamed of the first locomotive that ever run by steam! Such people should reflect for a moment how preposterous their pretensions are, ere they commit themselves so egregiously.

CORRESPONDENCE OF THE BEE JOURNAL.

LOS ANGELOS, CAL., Dec. 25, 1871.—Bees have been able to fly and work up to this time, with the exception of about five days, it being rainy. But they found little honey since the last of August, as the weather was very dry. Vegetation is, however, starting finely now, and bees will soon have plenty of honey. There are a number of beekeepers here that have one hundred or more colonies; but the AMERICAN BEE JOURNAL and improved bee hives are not known to them.—J. BECKLEY.

LUCAS, MO., Jan. 6, 1872.—Bees laid up a good supply, and to spare, of liquid sweets this season. I had only eleven stands or colonies; and they averaged *two hundred and forty per cent.* profit the past season, above expenses. "How is this for high?"

Many of my farmer neighbors complain because the money-lender asks twenty per cent. for the use of his money, and say they can't make that at farming. Bees are the fellows for me. They board themselves and work for nothing.—DR. D. L. LEWIS.

SOUTH ROYALTON, VT., Jan. 6.—We did not have an average yield of box honey, in this section, the past season, and next to *no* swarming. A large portion of the box honey was of poor quality, dark, and bitter, the product of "aphides" or plant lice, and the so-called honey dew. In some towns, however, bees did well, storing a fine quality and a fair amount. Four-fifths of the beekeepers are using the Langstroth hive, *pure and simple;* and the remainder are fast coming into the ranks.—D. C. HUNT.

WINCHESTER, VA., Jan. 8.—Our bees started in the spring as finely as we ever saw them; and with the abundance of fruit bloom we had, I looked for many swarms. But out of eighty colonies of black bees and eight colonies of Italians, I had only two swarms of blacks and two of Italians. They worked finely on white clover, alsike clover, and blue thistle, until the 15th of July. After that time, I do not think they made any honey, as I put one stand on a pair of scales, the 20th of May, and they never increased an ounce in weight after the 15th of July. The largest amount of honey stored in one day was three and a quarter (3¼) pounds on the 5th of June. The largest amount of honey got from one stock of black bees was seventy-one (71) pounds; and the largest amount from an Italian stock was one hundred and six (106) pounds, in twelve pound boxes with glass sides. I use the Langstroth movable comb hive; and like it better than any I have ever tried. I have never had my colonies heavier in honey than they are this winter. Some of my friends recommend me to take some of the honey from them, but I think I shall let them alone.—B. F. MONTGOMERY.

VERMONTVILLE, MICH., Jan. 9.—My success has been indifferent, thus far; and my bees, I find, approximate closely to the cost of Horace Greeley's turnips. I have sixteen colonies in my apiary, all in Langstroth hives; one colony of pure Italians, the remainer blacks. I hope, however, to be able to give you a better report hereafter.—H. J. MARTIN.

BLAIRSTOWN, IOWA, Jan. 15.—I have kept bees for only two years. I commenced with three stands in box hives, on shares, and put eleven in movable frame hives, in my cellar this fall. I use the Langstroth hive, only *deeper* than the usual form. Mine are 14 inches wide, 15½ deep, and 11¼ high. I like this form better for this windy prairie.—H. D. MOELLER.

[For the American Bee Journal.]

Tennessee Apiarian Society and Outside Talk.

MR. EDITOR:—In the December number of the Journal, Mr. W. R. King, of Milton, Ky., in speaking of the Apiarian Exhibition at the Tennessee Agricultural and Mechanical Association Fair, recently held at this place, in which he had entered his "Triumph" hive, says:

"As I was a stranger, and a long way from home, I kept quiet and looked on, listening to outsiders, and it was the general talk that the Tennessee Apiarian Society did not intend that the Langstroth hive should be beat, for their President owns the State of Tennessee for that hive; besides, they had adopted it, as a society, and they mean to hold on to it, no matter what better hive may be shown them."

Now, as this does very great injustice to the Tennessee Apiarian Society, I desire, as a member of this Society and as one of the superintendents of the Apiarian Department, to totally deny that any such feeling existed in the Society. My relation to the Society is such that such a question could hardly be discussed where I would not hear it, as I probably see more of the members between times of meetings than any other member, and I can assure Mr. King that I have never heard one word spoken, as *outsiders* inform him. The only thing that gives the least plausibility to any partiality for the Langstroth hive, is the fact that, some three or four years ago, the Society adopted a resolution *recommending* the the use of the Langstroth hive. At that time the right to this State was owned by Mr. Otis, and not by Dr. Hamlin, the President of the Society. He only purchased the right of the State about one year ago. There have been additions to the Society since then, and no one has any right to infer what hive would be endorsed by a vote of the Society now. And right here a few facts in regard to the status of some of the members of our Society will go far to refute the *outside* talk referred to by Mr. King. The Vice President of our Society prefers the Adair hive; another member of the Society uses the Adair hive, and owns the patent right for this county; another uses what he calls the "Tennessee Improved" hive, which was in competition with other hives at the Fair; and still another has an invention of his own (a side-opening and side-surplus box hive), which he uses exclusively, and will introduce it soon. Two others use both the "Buckeye" and the "Langstroth" hives; and two others use the "Alley" and "Langstroth" hives. To any one acquainted with the number of active members of our Society, this will be conclusive evidence that they are not so wedded to the Langstroth hive as to turn out in a body to prevent any other hive from taking a premium.

Now I have not the least doubt that Mr. King heard just such talk as he states, for I have heard the spirit of it myself, but I doubt if it was very *general*, or if a single person, not interested in other hives spoke of it.

There is a certain hive in use in this part of the country, called the "Buckeye." Two or three years ago, at the Fair held at the same place, the Langstroth hive, entered by Dr. Hamlin, took the premium over the Buckeye. The Buckeye parties chose to believe that this premium was awarded to the *man* and not to the *hive*, Dr. Hamlin being the most prominent apiarian in the State, and they have declined to enter their hive for premium since. I do not allude to this to open any discussion as to the fairness or unfairness of the award, as it was before my bee days; but only to account for this present *outside* talk Mr. King heard so much of. I have several good friends interested in the "Buckeye" hive, and after I was appointed one of the superintendents of the Apiarian Department, knowing their feelings about it, I tried to induce them to exhibit their hive, honey, &c., for two purposes—to make a large exhibition in my department, and to prove to them that they should have fair play. I thought the result of my assurance was that they would exhibit; but on Fair day I found that they still declined to do so, and were still of opinion that no one but Dr. Hamlin could take a premium; and it is not at all improbable that Mr. King heard outside talk as he states, but is the Tennessee Apiarian Society, or Dr. Hamlin, responsible for such unfounded prejudice, or for the Doctor purchasing a hive on which he can take premiums? Why do not these persecuted friends join our Society and outvote and outtalk the Langstroth members, if they choose. They have been repeatedly invited and urged to do so, but they seem to seek martyrdom.

Now the awards of premiums at this Fair prove that everything is not cut and dried for the Doctor's benefit, as intimated, but that he stands on his own merits, like the rest of us, for of the three premiums taken by Dr. H., two were without competition, and of the three entries by the Doctor, when there was competition, he only took one premium, and that was on his Langstroth hive.

This was my first experience at any fair, either as a manager or exhibitor; but knowing the squabbles that so often arise over awards of premiums, I determined and prided myself on my efforts, to have everything done most fairly. It was the duty of the superintendents of each department of the Fair to appoint committees in their respective departments, and as my co-superintendent, Dr. H., was an exhibitor in every item in the bee line, and I only in one, namely, "extracted honey," he turned the entire matter of committees over to me, without any suggestion as to the make-up of them, more than to express the hope that it would be done in a manner to give every one a fair chance, as he wanted nothing more; and I, when it came to premiums on "honey," delegated Mr. King to make up the committee and superintend the awards, which he did on a day when I was not on the grounds at all.

In making up the committee on hives, the name of every one, with that of the hive he used, was laid before the exhibitors for their approval, and all agreed that the committee was satisfactory. Some of them were entirely unknown to me until that moment. Each exhibitor then explained the merits of his own hive, except Dr. Hamlin, who, being one of the superintendents, thought best to allow his employee, Mr. Ladd, to set forth the merits of his hive. I did not see Mr. Barnum on the ground.

Of the committee of five two were members of the Tennessee Apiarian Society; and one of these two, notwithstanding he uses the Langstroth hive, voted for King's "Triumph," hive. It is proper to state that Mr. King's hive is not in use here, and his exhibition at the Fair was our first sight of it.

As to the charge that the Tennessee Apiarian Society will hold on to the Langstroth hive, no matter what better hive may be shown them, I will merely say that we are too smart for that. The only earthly interest we have in any hive is in the one from which we can get the *greatest yield of honey;* and if it is demonstrated that that can be accomplished by lodging our bees in a pumpkin, we will all use pumpkins.

I have necessarily made this communication rather long, but my apology is to place the Tennessee Apiarian Society in its proper light, to do justice to the officers of the Fair, and to assure Mr. King that it was not a cut and dried affair on the hive question, notwithstanding outside talk. And I herewith leave my statement to the judgment of beekeepers interested in the honor of their co-laborers, if Mr. King did not have fair play.

J. W. FISHER.

Nashville, Tenn., Dec. 13, 1871.

[For the American Bee Journal.]

Report from Hartford, Wisconsin.

CROWFOOT BRO.'S APIARY.

In May, 1869, we had two hundred and one colonies of bees, mostly Italians. It was such a bad season that we lost by actual starvation forty-nine colonies in the summer, and put up only one hundred and fifty-two in the fall. In the spring of 1870 we took out only thirty-two, and of these we lost eight before the 1st of June. We let them increase to eighty-two that summer, and got about seven hundred pounds of honey in boxes. By June, 1871, they had decreased to seventy colonies, and in the summer of that year we had thirty natural and fourteen artificial swarms, and obtained by weight fifteen thousand (15,000) pounds of extracted honey, and a little over one thousand (1,000) pounds of box honey. Some of our colonies have now over one hundred pounds of bees, bee bread, honey and combs per hive. We think there will be about four thousand pounds of honey in the hives in the spring, which we can take out, but this is only guess work. If it should prove to be correct it will make in all a little over twenty thousand (20,000) pounds of honey from seventy colonies, besides the increase in swarms. You are at liberty to publish this, but we have no time to answer letters of inquiry. We have stated facts, and that must do.

CROWFOOT BRO.'S.

Hartford, Wis., Nov. 30, 1871.

[For the American Bee Journal.]

Winter Reared Queens.

Away back somewhere in the Journal, some one asked what Dr. Gallup's opinion is about queens hatching in winter and becoming fertilized in spring. We have had such cases ourselves, and have already given our ideas of them in the American Bee Journal, but will now give them again, along with some other information. Our idea is that queens hatched in midwinter remain to a certain extent comparatively dormant; or, in other words, their age does not advance. The editor says on page 9 of No. 1, vol. 1, to this effect: *in autumn and winter bees may be said not to grow older, though advancing months in age.* Last fall I received an Egyptian queen from Mr. A. Gray, and being anxious to see her progeny, I commenced stimulating and got three cards filled with brood. When that brood hatched out, or soon after, the Italian bees were all used up or dead with old age and labor. Whereas if they had been left to themselves they would have lived until their places had been supplied with young bees in the spring. In two cases I have changed black bees all to Italians in September and October, simply by stimulating to rear brood then, and it is a well known fact that if left to themselves at that season there would have been any quantity of blacks remaining the following May, and but very few Italians in the fall.

By the way, we were to test the working qualities of these Egyptians. So far I prefer the Italians, but their fighting qualities are excellent. E. GALLUP.

Orchard, Iowa.

[For the American Bee Journal.]

The Proposed Improved Hive.

MR. EDITOR:—On page 120 of the American Bee Journal for November last, Mr. Condit gives us an article on "Improved Bee Hives," in which he says that a hive which costs five dollars is too expensive for a majority of beekeepers; and one which costs but a single dollar, if so made that it is not easily manipulated, &c., is too cheap for any beekeeper.

Thus far I agree with Mr. C. He then says 2,000 cubic inches is believed by the most successful apiarians to be capacity sufficient for a large colony, for breeding purposes and storing winter supplies. He goes on to describe his cheap hive of *thirteen* frames, the dimensions of which are 19¼ inches from front to rear, 15¾ inches deep, and 12¾ inches from side to side, which makes a hive of over 3700 cubic inches.

Why does he want to go so far astray from *the most successful* apiarians, making his cheap hive almost double the proper capacity?

Now I beg the privilege of differing with Mr. C. about this shaped hive being easily manipulated. Any beekeeper who has ever handled frames knows that it is difficult to lift out a frame from a full stock when the frames are fifteen inches or more deep. But when the frames are *close fitting* at the top, and 15¾ inches by 19¼, it is indeed a formidable undertaking to remove them.

I am not partial to a side-opening hive; but with such sized frames as Mr. C. describes, and close-fitting at that, I think we should want a "side-opener."

I have used the movable frames for fifteen years, and find the Langstroth hive, with frame *ten* inches deep, just the thing for this section. And if I were in Tennessee, or still further South, I would prefer them still more shallow. My experience is that the bees winter in them fully as well, if not better, than in deeper hives.

When we remember that Mr. C. writes from Tennessee, where the bees can fly out, more or less, every week in the year, I cannot see why he objects to the Langstroth or other shallow hive, unless he has an *axe* to grind (even if it be only a twenty-five cent one).

I am confident that the Langstroth hive, with its large amount of surplus honey room, is just the thing for the South; and it does not cost "*five* dollars" either.

Let us take another peep into Mr. C.'s hive, and see if there are not other objections to it, with all its "cheapness." In the first place, it is too large (3700 cubic inches); but we will admit he can control the size with his division board. So, too, can we with the Langstroth hive, the Triumph hive, or almost any of the patent frame hives, or non-patented ones either. They all use the division board to contract the size of hive, to suit smaller swarms, or for queen raising.

Mr. C. says his bees work out at *each end* of his hive, or crosswise of the frames. Now, when we stand by the hive to open it or take out the frames, the most convenient place to stand is at the side of the frames. This, in this case, would be the front of his hive, which would be a great annoyance to the working bees when returning heavily laden from the fields.

He says, to secure the largest amount of honey we must use the Extractor. Well, his frames are *close fitting*, consequently are *one and a half* inches wide, and the combs are usually about seven-eighths of an inch thick. So that when he puts them in the Extractor, the wide frame will hold the comb off from the supporting wire; when the machine is put in motion the comb will break out, and he will have a "sweet" job to fasten them in again.

Then, he has a *cross bar in the center* of his frames, which is objectionable, as that is the place where we want *brood* and not wood; and to leave out his cross bar, his frame is too large and *deep* to handle or extract, and as the combs are usually not fastened at bottom, they would break down.

How does Mr. C. propose to ventilate his mammoth hive? When full of bees, in warm weather, there would be heat enough in it to almost roast a sirloin of beef. His frames are close fitting at top, so that no heated air can escape; and there is no cooling dead air space between the top of the frames and the top lid. I should hate to be one of his bees, to be roasted alive.

Mr. C. winds up by saying he will give a full and complete written description of his hive; but all correspondents must send stamp and money enough to pay for stationery, &c. We suppose he means about *twenty-five cents* for DESCRIPTION. Cheap enough! Seventy-five per cent. below *Gallup.*

We have no "axe" to grind, but write simply to show that Mr. C. is mistaken in a good hive for Kentucky, Tennessee, and more Southern States.

With the best of feeling towards Mr. Condit and all other beekeepers, I am,

Very respectfully,

H. NESBIT.

Cynthiana, Ky., Dec. 10, 1871.

AMERICAN BEE JOURNAL.

EDITED AND PUBLISHED BY SAMUEL WAGNER, WASHINGTON, D. C.

AT TWO DOLLARS PER ANNUM, PAYABLE IN ADVANCE.

VOL. VII. **MARCH, 1872.** No. 9.

Mitchell & Co. Reviewed.

EDITOR AMERICAN BEE JOURNAL:—Please insert the following extracts from Nos. 15 and 16, October 15th to November 1st, 1871, of N. C. Mitchell's bee paper,* that your readers may have both sides. L. L. LANGSTROTH.

"A Word to Our Subscribers.

"You will remember that we gave notice in the last number of the Journal, that we would publish in this number the claims and disclaims of Mr. Langstroth; and just as we go to press, we received from Rev. H. A. King of the *Beekeepers'* Journal, the statements of Baron von Berlepsch, who is an eminent beekeeper of Europe, and as it will look well in print, and being just the thing to read in connection with Langstroth's claims, we propose to publish it.

The reader will notice that Mr. Langstroth claimed everything; but finding that the commissioner of patents would not allow the claims as presented, his attorney cunningly devised another plan. His motive is apparent enough, his efforts being given to mystify the claims in such a manner as to deceive the beekeepers in general, and determining to be obtuse as possible. He proceeds to draw up the disclaims of Mr. Langstroth, and in fact makes such a perfeet job of it, that one must sift it thoroughly or he will not be able to see through both his claims and disclaims. To properly understand it, one must need be an attorney, and a pretty clear-headed one in the bargain, or he would never see his way through the fog of legal lore which envelopes the whole proceedings.

We *were* of the opinion that Mr. Langstroth had two claims that would hold good, neither of which would we give a fig for, and recent developments have confirmed us in the impression that should the case ever be tried in any court having jurisdiction in the United States, that said court will cancel the celebrated Langstroth patent; and we have serious doubts as to its ever being brought up for a test. Mr. Otis is the man *Friday* in Mr. Langstroth's life, and the very course of Mr. Langstroth's man *Friday* permits us in taking this view of the subject.

In the year 1863, this man Otis commenced suit against a number of men. We will mention the names of some: A. F. Moon, Vanslyke and Austin and others, all using different hives. This man *Friday* kept these cases before the court until even his stupidity comprehended that a compromise with the parties was out of the question, and accordingly withdrew them, and we are told that Otis paid the cost in every case.

But it seems at last, that Otis did get judgment against Charles Austin, and the decision of the court Mr. Otis had copied into Mr. Langstroth's *circular*, and paraded all over the United States, as a warning to all users and manufacturers of movable comb hives, and told them that their turn would come next. Nevertheless, movable comb hives flourished, improvements were made, and progression has kept steadily onward.

Now let us look into this case, and see what there is in it. There is only one judgment that the Langstroth party can show any one; and were we to assert that said judgment was obtained by default, you would say is it possible? and yet 'tis not only possible but true.

* I have been unwilling to call N. C. Mitchell's bee paper the "National Bee Journal," or Mr. King's "The Bee Journal and National Agriculturist," for reasons that I think will be deemed sufficient by all fair-minded men. In 1861, Mr. Samuel Wagner published the first periodical devoted to bee-culture ever issued in this country; its title was the "American Bee Journal." In consequence of the business disturbances created by our lamentable civil war, this publication was suspended one year from its first issue. In 1866, Rev. E. Vanslyke advertised that he would publish a monthly periodical, devoted to the interests of bee-culture, under the title of "American Bee Journal." On being informed by Mr. Wagner that this was the title of the periodical published by him in 1861, and the publication of which he intended soon to resume, and that therefore, while he conceded the right of any one to publish a periodical on bee-culture, he must object to his using this title. Mr. Vanslyke very honorably changed the name of his paper to that of "Bee Gazette." The editors of our prominent agricultural papers know that articles from the "American Bee Journal" have been credited to Mr. King and Mitchell's periodicals, and Mr. Wagner has been repeatedly informed that parties have subscribed for them, supposing they were subscribing for the "American Bee Journal." I do not hesitate, therefore, to stigmatize the conduct of Messrs. King and Mitchell in assuming titles so well calculated to deceive, as grossly unfair, and I believe that the public will sustain the charge.

The suit was commenced in 1863 and closed in 1866. Time and again Mr. Austin appeared ready for trial, and yet it was deferred, and at last he determined to waste no more time, being aware that should they take judgment by default, he could at any time open the case.

So, in his absence the case came up; a judgment was found against him. That was just to their hand, and we are told they even paid the expenses incurred by the suit, not even calling upon Mr. Austin to settle one cent of it (very clever that). We don't see why they did not want the benefits derived from the judgment, and why they made no use of it save to herald it all over the country. We don't say it was a put up job, but it smells of it and tastes of it.

Otis is a cunning man, and he would be glad if Austin would permit him to take judgment; and as Otis has left Austin go scott free, what else does it look like? *Who will name the bantling?* Are we not right in charging that if Otis can prevent it, we will never have another decision upon the Langstroth patent! They dare not risk it. Their only desire is to scare somebody into paying them for what does not rightly belong to them.

If Mr. Langstroth's claims were to hold good, not one movable comb hive in twenty could be held as infringers upon the Langstroth patent; and as we have been compelled to come out in defence of the beekeepers, we must perforce make it lively for Mr. Langstroth's man Friday, and shall also give in our *future* numbers, the cuts and drawings of movable comb hives used *before Mr. Langstroth obtained a patent*. and that will enable all beekeepers to read Mr. Langstroth's claims understandingly. Both him and his man *Friday* have no one to blame but themselves in bringing this discussion before the public; if it is notoriety they seek, we propose to give them enough of it.

It will be remembered, that during the early spring months of this year, that Mr. Langstroth and his *right-bower* were swinging round the circle. Chicago was favored with their presence, where they sent out red hot shot broadcast through the medium of the *Prairie Farmer*, threatening direful things to all beekeepers using the movable comb hives. That article was copied (as was intended by them) into many of the agricultural journals of the United States—a *cheap way of advertising*—and at that time we put forth our mightiest effort to keep from opening our battery upon them; but after due reflection, concluded to wait further developments. From thence the pair proceeded to Wisconsin, and were there skinned to the tail by Kidder. Mr. Langstroth struck a *bee line from there* to more congenial climes, and his man Friday went at his old tricks, viz.: skinning everybody that he could find that was green enough to hold still. The instrument used for skinning was threats of bringing suits against said persons, and dwelling upon the enormous amount of costs they would be put to if suit was commenced against them.

Of course it took; for if there is anything our farmers dislike, it is a suit at law; and rather than have any trouble, they would shell out beautifully. Others that would not come down with the needful, were told to look out for the United States marshal, and are still looking out for him, vainly, it must be confessed.

Many of them have written to us for our opinion, and have asked us to publish the Langstroth patent. For a long time we hesitated, Mr. L. being an old and honored beekeeper, and for whom we have ever entertained the best feelings; and in all candor, we must say that we dislike very much to say anything that will wound the feelings of Mr. Langstroth, having ever held him to be a good and worthy man; but human nature can't stand everything; and so long as he keeps that man *Friday* in the field, harping upon infringements, he must look out for breakers, for we shall defend the right and the people against fraud to the last.

Had Mr. Langstroth and his *right bower* been satisfied with their just claims, and kept about their business, they might this day have been in the same condition as the Yankee (*that got rich by minding his own business*).

We pity Mr. Langstroth for having selected such an instrument as Otis to represent him, and then persist in following him to the last ditch; and they will soon be floundering in the same ditch together, and no one will be to blame but yourselves. You dug the ditch, and the Good Book says: "they that dig a pit fall therein." Well; you will not be the first that have learned that fact when too late.

We also read in the Good Book of a certain Haman, that had a gallows prepared on which to hang a so-called infringer by the name of Mordecai, and *was himself hung thereon!* Mr. Otis, how do you like the picture?

In justice to Mr. Moon, let me here state that I have written this article without first consulting him, and he is not in the least responsible for it."

N. C. MITCHELL.

Personal.

"We are sorry to be compelled, in the present number, to depart from our usual course, in not allowing anything to enter our columns that could in any way be considered personal; and also that we have to attack so good a man as the subject of this personal, the Rev. L. L. Langstroth, patentee of the Langstroth bee hive.

Mr. Langstroth, let us say that we do not wish to injure you in the least, but we feel bound to say to you, *as a friend that you must haul down that black standard of extermination;* that cry of wholesale prosecution must stop; the beekeepers demand it; they claim the right to make improvements, and if need be, invent bee hives, and experiment in any way they may see proper.

As the case now stands, we must perforce take sides with either Mr. Langstroth or the people; one or the other must go to the wall.

There is, in our opinion, but one way left open for Mr. Langstroth, by which he can hope to escape honorably, and that way is, take the Langstroth hive as it now stands and is used throughout the United States by hundreds and thousands that are ready and willing to pay for them. No one has ever demanded of them any pay for the right to manufacture and use them. If Mr. Langstroth will take his hive as it is, we would not have any objection to him getting a renewal of his patent. As it now stands, Mr. Langstroth has received scarcely anything for his invention, and is not likely to. As it now is, he may be considered unfortunate in having selected such a man as Otis to represent him. That man, Mr. Langstroth must get rid of, or his good name will suffer. We are of the mind that he has influenced Mr. Langstroth to make war upon beekeepers in general, and Mr. Langstroth is now called upon to decide between the beekeeping fraternity and Mr. Otis.

If he continues to back up Mr. Otis, and to endorse his procedures of enforcing war upon the so-called infringers, then we intend to enter the field, and will use every honorable means to force both Mr. Langstroth and Otis to the wall, and in doing so, we believe that we are acting in the defence of right and justice."

N. C. MITCHELL.

In publishing what he calls "the claims and disclaims of the Langstroth hive," Mr. Mitchell ought to have adhered strictly to the *original* instead of entirely suppressing the Italics in passages where those Italics were manifestly intended to direct the attention of the reader more particularly to the vital points. This manifest breach of good faith will prepare the reader for his subsequent misrepresentations

"The reader will notice that Mr. Langstroth claimed everything." Those who read my careful disclaimer of the Huber, Munn, and Debeauvoy hives, *republished by Mr. Mitchell himself*, will be at no loss to see that I did *not* claim everything. When Mr. M. asserts that "finding the commissioner of patents would not allow the claims as presented, his attorney cunningly devised another plan," he was either ignorant of the facts in the case, or he had referred to the files of the patent office to obtain the proper information. If he wrote these comments upon the way in which my re-issue was obtained, in utter ignorance of the facts, he must be a very reckless man ; and if he wrote them after having informed himself of the facts, he must have strange notions of truth and honor. It is more charitable to presume that the habit of making wild and extravagant assertions* based only on a vivid imagination has "so grown by what it has fed on;" that he has actually lost the power of correct discrimination and sober statement.

Let me state some *facts*. 1st. *I had no attorney*, but managed my own case before the examiners whose duty it is, and not that of the commissioner, to pass upon applications for the re-issue of a patent. 2d. There was only a *single claim* objected to by the examiners, Professor Charles Page, now dead, and Addison M. Smith, Esq. Professor Page called my attention to the fact that he had seen—I think he said in his father's apiary—a shallow chamber over bars or slats nailed fast, so as to have no lateral motion, and that one of my claims was broad enough to cover this device. I give the claim as it stood in the original and the one in the re-issue, which I substituted for it.

CLAIM IN RE-ISSUE.

The shallow chamber in combination with the top bars of the latterally movable frames, or their equivalents, and with the perforated honey-boards upon which to place surplus honey receptaeles, substantially as and for the purposes set forth.

ORIGINAL CLAIM.

The use of the shallow chamber or air space placed over any hive having bars or slats in combination with a perforated cover or honey-board on which to place surplus receptacles of any kind substantially in the manner and for the purposes set forth.

May 26, 1863.

Within the last few months, I have seen, in a French work published in 1842, the same kind of shallow chamber over the fixed bars or slats, mentioned by Professor Page. It is both figured and described, and if Mr. King thinks that it will help him advantageously to amend his answers to the suit of Mr. Otis, it will be cheerfully furnished to his counsel.

There are some grains of truth in the statements of Mr. Mitchell. My disclaims are *not* as clear to the general reader as they would have been if the patent office had allowed me to retain the whole of my original specification as it now appears on their files. In this specification I carefully described the features of the Huber, Munn, and Debeauvoy hives, and showed in what respects they differ from my invention. It was objected to as unnecessarily minute, furnishing information highly interesting to inventors of bee hives, but which the office ought not to allow on account of the expense of copying it.

If Mr. Mitchell thinks that the court has only to pass upon the Langstroth patent to *cancel* it, why should he so bitterly complain of Mr. Otis, who is striving to give them an opportunity of deciding upon it? Why should he assault him with such vulgar abuse? Will not the public infer that if the bringing of Otis' suit against King to an issue would kill my patent, that both Mr. Mitchell and Mr. King would be glad to have the issue met.

In due time the beekeepers of the country will have ample proof who are the parties who are afraid to have the matter tested, and why they have sought by *indecent* accusations to forestall public opinion, so as to cripple Mr. Otis' pecuniary resources by putting it out of his power to collect money due him for territory sold. They have missed their aim ; the money will not be lacking, and the suit will be pushed to trial. I pass over with a brief notice Mr. Mitchell's long account of suits. Unfortunately these suits were not *in equity*, the testimony was

* See, for example, in his circulars and papers the repeated assertions that he could in a *single season* multiply his colonies *one hundred fold*, and that he had control of a patent for making artificial comb which would revolutionize beekeeping, when no patent had been issued for such an invention, and the plan though ingenious proved a failure.

taken by the defendants *ex parte*, without their being obliged to give Mr. Otis notice, so that he could be present and cross-examine their witnesses. Mr. Gifford, of New York, advised him to withdraw them for this reason. The judgment against Austin was for using the Kidder hive. It was obtained by default, because Mr. Kidder did not see fit to contest it. Mr. Austin used but *a single hive*. The object of the suit was to test the validity of the Langstroth patent, and show that the Kidder hive had infringed upon it, and Mr. Otis had no need to call upon Austin for any special damages.

When I personally informed Mr. King, about a year ago, that I regarded all his patents as infringing upon mine, he very pleasantly told me "that he would make a big fight," to which I replied, that we were glad to find at last a party who had so much at stake that he must defend himself, and test the validity of the patent to the satisfaction of the public.

Since that conversation, several propositions have been made by Mr. King to compromise the matter, in one of which he says that he has evidence, which if properly attended to, will, he is confident, invalidate my patent; but it will cost a large sum of money, and he is unwilling to engage in a controversy, and for the sake of peace would prefer paying this money to obtain a license under the Langstroth patent. For the sake of peace, he was willing to get a license under a patent which he could prove to be invalid, and thus join in calling upon beekeepers to pay for using what was public property! Surely, Mr. King's ideas of right and wrong need amending as much as his various patents, nearly every patented feature of which he has after trial discarded. (See April No. of American Bee Journal.)

Mr. Mitchell says: "If Mr. Langstroth's claims hold good, not one movable comb in twenty will be held as infringers upon the Langstroth patent." Now, we feel confident that the very reverse of this will be judicially pronounced true, and that not one movable frame hive in twenty will escape being enjoined as infringing upon the Langstroth patent. As to our great surprise, Mr. Mitchell has so handsomely endorsed us as a clear-headed attorney, he will surely review his opinion upon this matter, and thus make a proper use of our astuteness. We will charge him no fee for our "legal lore."

Let us look a little into that "threatening article" in the Prairie Farmer, from Mr. Otis and myself. I will first give the article:

"CAUTION TO BEEKEEPERS.

All persons using the Triangular Comb Guide, or "bevelled edge," in Langstroth hives, are cautioned against paying K. P. Kidder, or agents, for such use. *At our request*, he has sued us, and we believe the courts will soon decide that the said guide is public property, and that we are not infringing his rights in the Clark patent.

L. L. LANGSTROTH,
Oxford, Ohio.
R. C. OTIS,
Chicago, April 20, 1871. Kenosha, Wisconsin."

This was written after Mr. K. P. Kidder had served notice upon us that a suit would be brought against us for infringing upon his rights under the Clark patent on the triangular comb guide. Does the advertisement "threaten direful things to all beekeepers using the movable comb hives." It is true, that it was inserted as an advertisement in some of the leading agricultural journals of the United States, but the bills we paid for thus attempting to protect the public* would never have suggested to us the idea of *cheap* advertising.

We have little doubt that Mr. Mitchell did "at that time put forth his mightiest effort to keep from opening his batteries upon us." Neither Mr. King nor himself have ever made even a moderate effort to open their smallest batteries upon their *friend Kidder*. *He is an enemy to the Langstroth patent*, and must have every opportunity of levying unchecked his detestable black mail upon the *Langstroth* public. Messrs. King and Mitchell know well that he is defrauding the public, and that by their silence they are lending him aid and comfort.

Can those who have read Mr. Mitchell's abuse of "the old and honored beekeeper for whom he has ever entertained the best of feelings," can they, even by the largest stretch of charity, help believing that he enters upon his work with a hearty determination to strike hard and wound deep, and that his professed "tender mercies" are as "cruel" as he dared to make them?

Only a short year ago, he and Mr. King professed at the Cincinnati convention to be my warmest friends; and Mr. King, in particular, could hardly say enough in my praise, asserting that "He (Mr. Langstroth) first made high bee-culture possible by his genius and industry," and expressing his regret that his book contained some reflections upon Mr. Langstroth, which were published in misapprehension of the facts, &c. Had I sold myself to these men at that convention, and joined hands with them in maligning Mr. Otis because he asked the highest tribunal of justice in the land, the United States Court, to listen to his case, and decide whether or not the patent of which he owned the largest part was valid, and if valid; to speak with the strong voice of law to all infringers upon it, and give them to understand that there was such a thing as a legal patent on a bee hive, and that its owners had some rights which the courts would compel all parties to respect—had I then and there acted with such atrocious bad faith towards not only Mr. Otis, but towards every other party who have purchased a territorial interest in my patent, that the only way of explaining my conduct would have been the conviction that I had sold myself for filthy lucre, or had become weak and imbecile from disease; yes, had I there become the associate of Messrs. King and Mitchell, and like some others, their tool and dupe, I might have been allowed to pass my hat

* As we cannot do justice to Mr. Kidder in this article, we propose in a future number of the American Bee Journal, to give the Clark patent and Mr. Kidder's course as owner of it, a thorough examination.

around for *a little charity* to be doled out by the men who had enriched themselves by preying upon my invention.

Let not the honest and true men, who in all good faith purposed to raise a Langstroth testimonial, imagine that I mean in the least to reflect upon them, or that I shall ever forget their generous appreciation and cordial reception; and let those whose sinister motives, though veiled under the most plausible and hypocritical pretences, needed for their detection only the simplest sentiments of truth and honor, *venture if they dare* to unveil further the plots and intrigues of the Cincinnati convention of February, 1871.

Both Mr. King and Mr. Mitchell have repeatedly taken occasion to say that they "PITY" Mr. Langstroth. Beekeepers of America! I trust you will never see your old friend and servant fall so low as to become really an object of pity to such men as Messrs. King and Mitchell.

What have I ever done or said, as Mr. Mitchell intimates, inconsistent with progress and improvement in bee-culture? unless it be that kind of progress which has its beginning, middle and end in appropriating the work of other men's brains. If such easy virtue in the matter of dealing in patents is to carry the day, what need of learned judges to interpret our patent laws. A new highway will have been opened to the highest success. To travel safely on it, only patent some contemptible *gim-crack;* some frivolous if not noxious conceit; attach it to the valuable patent of a *bonâ fide* inventor; enrol yourself among the bands of humbugs and infringers; sign articles of agreement that on the principle of "honor among thieves," you will in no ways interfere with each other's piratical proceedings, but prey only upon the innocent public. Misrepresent, slander, and if needs be blackguard every man who has rights and dares to stand up in their defence, and if some men are to be credited, you are in a fair way to become one of the "great American apiarians," and world-renowned inventors, who stand in the very front ranks of progress and improvement. I will venture the prediction, that in due time the public will put their seal of honest condemnation upon all such preposterous pretentions.

"Raro antecedentem scelestum
Deseruit pede poena claudo."

Hor.

Justice outstripped, seems often halting in her pace,
Yet seldom is she beaten by a bad man in the race.

L. L. LANGSTROTH.

Washington, D. C., Feb. 16, 1871.

The *Mahonia aquifolium*, a species of barberry growing wild in Western North America, and introduced in European gardens as a beautiful flowering plant, is spoken of in German bee journals as a valuable, handy, early blooming honey plant. It is a bushy shrub, three or four feet high, said to blossom profusely in advance of peach, cherry and plum trees, and is frequented by bees in crowds. How is it in these respects in this country?

The Debeauvoys Hive.

The following communication comes to us alike unexpectedly and unsolicited, and yet comes quite opportunely. In the article concocted by H. A. King, which was given in the last number of the Journal, that veracious and fair-dealing dealer in worthless patents refers to the book of Mr. Debeauvoys and says the author therein "describes movable frames *containing all the features of the most perfect frames* now used in this country." If, before writing these words, King even saw and examined the Debeauvoys hive, or read a correct description of it and its frames, he must have known that he deliberately penned a gross misrepresentation, for the purpose of deceiving and misleading his readers. The Debeauvoys frames lack the essential features of the most perfect frames now used in this country, and for that very reason proved to be a failure in practice, so decided and irremediable that, after full trial they were rejected and abandoned. Perhaps, after reading Mr. Dadant's description of the hive and his account of its fate in France, King may begin to suspect that his efforts at deception have not been quite as successful, in this instance, as he hoped they would. He is doomed to yet other equally overwhelming and mortifying disappointments.

Honor to whom Honor is due.

In the patent hive contest which arose between Mr. Langstroth and Mr. H. King, I have no more wish to give my opinion than I have the desire of supporting either side. However, I think it is my duty to tell what the Debeauvoys hive was when the first two editions of Debeauvoys book were published. I had those two editions (1844–1847) in my possession, and manufactured hives with their directions, for my own use.

The frames of the Debeauvoys hive were as broad as the interior of the hive, *i. e.*, close-fitting at the sides, and supported in the hive by two strips of wood nailed inside of the hive and at the distance of ⅜ of an inch from the bottom.

The hive had its roof slanting and nailed. The bottom was movable. The two sides were movable doors, through which the frames could be taken out. These doors, being of the same size as the frames, could be pushed in the hive to contract the space. They were held in place with hooks. The frames were kept apart by nails driven in them at each side.

The hive worked well when new and empty; but after the bees had glued the frames, it was difficult to remove them, without breaking the combs.

It would have been entirely impossible to remove them at all, without separating the ends of the hive from the frames with a chisel.

This hive, which had gained 2,500 proselytes in France, was very soon abandoned by all; and the disciples of Debeauvoys returned to the old-fashioned straw hive. (*Vide L'Apiculteur*, Paris, Fevrier 1869.)

The inventions of Debeauvoys were disastrous for French bee-culture The tenacity with which the majority of French beekeepers hold fast to day to the old system, is due to the defects of the movable frame hives that they tried at first, "Chien échaudé craint l'eau froide."*

The Berlepsch hive is not much better than the Debeauvoys hive, if we are to believe what M. M. Bastian and Mona say of it.

Mr. Bastian writes in his book, "*Les Abeilles*," Paris, 1868, page 148, "The Berlepsch hive costs "from 15 to 20 francs; besides it has to be built of "very exact dimensions, for the slightest varying "prevents the frames from fitting in it."

* "A scalded dog dreads even cold water."

On the other hand, Mr. Mona writes in the Italian Bee Journal, "*L'Apicoltore* (Milan, July, 1871), "page 205, whatever have been the defects of my "hive and methods, four years ago, I am not responsi- "ble, if they were not superior to the level of bee- "culture in Europe. This vertical hive (Berlepsch "fashion) with 24 frames *arcipropolisabili*, placed on "top of the other, with diaphragms and small comb "covers, with insufficient ventilation, and other "*delizie*, was soon replaced by another system, that "was altogether easier, cheaper, better, and more "productive."

In the "*Journal des Fermes*," Paris, August 16th, 1869, page 324, Mr. Mona writes—"An American "beekeeper, Mr. A. Grimm, visited me in Septem- "ber, 1867. He advised me to adopt the American "form of hive (Langstroth's), which he himself "used on a large scale. He asked for some boards, "some nails, and a few tools, and after a short time "he presented to me a pattern of his hive. I found "the length of the frames disproportionate, but I "soon recognized the advantage of the movable cover, "and after a few weeks of hesitation, I resolved to "make a hundred hives of the same kind, with "shorter frames. I used them for the last two years, "and I acknowledge that they are very useful for me, "the handling of the frames being very speedy."

The reader will notice that the date of the construction of these hives is in accordance with the four years of which Mr. Mona speaks in *L'Apicoltore*.

It appears from the above that while the disciples of Debeauvoys in France abandoned his hive, and the disciples of Berlepsch and Berlepsch himself groped to improve their own hive, L. Langstroth gave to the American beekeepers an easily constructed and easily managed hive, which, from the beginning until now, rendered the best services to bee-culture.

I do not know whether these facts can have any influence on the law suit now pending, but I owed to Mr. L. Langstroth, I owed to truth, I owed to the history of bee-culture, the publication of the above facts.

I send one copy of this to each of three American bee journals. They will publish it, if they think proper.

CH. DADANT.

Hamilton, Ills., January, 1872.

[For the American Bee Journal.]

Novice.

DEAR BEE JOURNAL:—We really believe we have got at something. Just listen! It may not be new to some of our bee friends, but it is new to us. You remember how we fed our bees in October last, on coffee-sugar syrup, and sold our honey for twenty cents per pound.

Perhaps we did not tell you, but it is a fact, that three-fourths or more of twenty-five pounds we made them weigh was the sugar syrup, and we decided to risk the experiment, being sure that all other conditions were complied with.

Well, to-day (Feb. 12th) being very bright and warm, we put out one stock, just to hear bees buzz once more, and to see them fly.

Our "better-half" had just finished hanging out her morning's washing, when we announced our determination, and the white linen (or cotton) was flapping largely in the breeze.

"Now, Novice! *Please* don't put the bees out to-day. My white clothes (they are *white*, Mr. Editor, if we do say it), will be all spoiled with their nasty work, and I shall have to wash them all over again."

We argued that we would only set out a few hives at the further side of the apiary.

"But they will fly all over, you know they will, as they always spot the snow for acres around; and you will get your coat spoiled too."

"We will take it off," we suggested, suiting the action to the word.

"But your shirt will be worse yet."

We were near to the bee-house by this time, and (Mr. Editor she *isn't* difficult; she knew where the old coat hung, and so did we, but old coats are too much bother. (Ours are all old enough, we thought.) We would be careful. We are *always careful*, unless something interests us very much, and then we sometimes forget. No. 61 was on its summer stand in a trice, and out came the yellow pets just as tame and just as we used to handle them in October. Out they pour as we raise their quilt, and in our haste to see who should see the queen first, our white shirt sleeves (*Monday* morning, you know), were forgotten, until we made the pleasant discovery that there were no spots on the snow, nor anywhere else; and there isn't a spot yet, though they have flown freely. We have read in the Journal of some such occurrence, but have always had a little doubt about their first flight in the spring not showing some discolored spots on the clean snow; but now we have it verified sure.

They have wintered unusually well, and we really begin to think sugar-syrup *safe* for wintering, if for nothing more.

Still further. A neighbor just came in, who borrowed our "tea-kettles" after we had finished feeding, and fed sugar-syrup to *a part of his bees that needed it*—all wintered in the open air in a row. Before we had time to ask, he mentioned that those stocks fed had not discolored the snow at all; while the old box hives, heavy with honey, had stained the ground and their hives as well, badly.

If the "tea-kettles" were a patent-right article, what a testimonial in their favor this would be!

This forenoon a gentleman called to get our opinion as to the cause of his bees dying in a house made like ours, and brought one of the combs for us to examine, We at once pronounced it "that bee disease" of the spring of 1868; and on looking carefully, we found the honey thin, with occasional small bubbles, and a taste that was not just right. He said his bees had worked quite late in the fall, and in some of the boxes the honey had soured.

Now, is the cause of that "bee disease" not apparent? It certainly is to us, and before we lose again all but eleven out of thirty-eight colonies, we will give them clear comb and coffee-sugar syrup. If any one else has had a like experience, please give it to us in the Journal.

If bees will always winter safely on sugar syrup, why not remove *all* the honey in the fall, and feed them up with sugar and the tea-kettle feeders? (Twenty-five pounds in nine hours you know.) Then we can really "cover the arithmetical patent-right formula" of doubling *surely* and *safely* every year for twenty years. Honey paying for labor and hives, so that Mr. Apiarian can then retire from active duties and live on his little independence.

If Mr. Quinby and Mr. Langstroth, both, would give us their experience on wintering on sugar alone (coffee or crushed sugar), we should be more obliged to them than we can tell.

Mr. Editor, our weight is now 137½ lbs., (usual weight for the past ten years 125 lbs.), and we suspect that our success in wintering on sugar (the *bees* we mean; *we* shall eat the honey), will add at least 10 lbs. more.

One thing more. We fear that we have not made ourselves clearly understood, judging from something that Mr. Gallup says in regard to answering letters; for nothing gives us greater pleasure than to answer letters like the following (names omitted):

"Wis., Jan. 27, 1872.

"*Dear Sir*:—While in Medina last summer, I was "very much interested in your apiary. The thought "suggested itself to me of raising bees also, and I "have now made arrangements by which I can have "as many bees as cash and time will allow.

"If you would give me any advice as to beginning, "and tell me what book or books to read, I would be "much obliged.

"*Yours, respectfully.*"

We believe we have never failed, in a single instance, to answer such inquiries as fully as we knew how. But when some one demands of us the results in detail of our experiments for the last five years, we cannot help referring him to the back numbers of the American Bee Journal. And when we have done so, so briefly as to perhaps seem unfeeling or rude, we most sincerely beg pardon, and will try and not think that we would like to keep bees on "Robinson Crusoe's Island."

Then, old Bee Journal, good-bye until next month. As ever,

NOVICE.

[For the American Bee Journal.]

On Wintering Bees.

BY REV. E. L. BRIGGS.

The best mode of carrying our bees through the winter is doubtless the most important question now being asked by the apiarian.

It is not the receptacle in which they are kept, so much as it is the condition of the colonies when they are put into winter quarters, which determines their prosperity to the greatest extent, according to my experiments. If frost or dampness has already accumulated among the combs, by severe cold weather, and they are in this condition when the hives are set in the cellar, of course this dampness will produce mouldy combs; and this in turn will produce dysentery among the bees and cause the combs to be polluted by their untimely discharges.

Bees should be put into their winter receptacles long before severe freezing weather occurs; and always when the combs are free from dampness. In the latitude of 40° to 42°, not later than from the 1st to the 15th of November. In such cases, if kept in a temperature of from 32° to 45° F., they will remain almost dormant for the next three months, and very often, for five months together. But just as soon, after, they begin to manifest the least uneasiness, as it is safe for them, they should be set out upon their summer stands, and allowed to take a fly for a day or two; and then return to the cellar again, to remain until spring weather permits them to begin to gather pollen. I think from five to eight pounds of honey will carry a colony through from the 1st of November to the 1st of April, under such circumstances. But from this until the blossoming of white clover, they will consume, in rearing brood and from being constantly active, perhaps as much as, or more than they did during the five months of winter confinement.

It is very important that the bees should be set out to take their winter fly, in just the right kind of weather, or great loss will accrue from their being chilled and never regaining their hives again. I have seen the ground almost covered for rods around, when set out in cloudy or windy weather. It should be a clear sunshiny day; perfectly calm, if possible; and the thermometer up to at least 50°. Then each colony should be set upon the stand just where it is to be placed when put out again in April, or great loss will accrue from them returning to their old entrance and never finding their way home again. Several such days occur almost every winter about the middle of February. This is the time to set them out. But better not set them out at all, than to set them out on a cool, raw, windy day; for to reduce their numbers greatly now, is almost fatal to their next summer's prosperity.

After a day's joyous recreation, they will remain quiet in their winter repository, when returned, though breeding will go on in the hive a little more rapidly than in the former part of the winter.

I have in a former article, given the best mode of ventilating a cellar, which I have ever seen described. But even a poorly ventilated cellar will do, if these precautions are observed.

When the combs are perfectly dry, and before hard freezing weather has commenced, set your bees in a dry dark cellar. Leave the fly holes open as in summer; open a small hole or crevice, such as a half-inch bit would make, near the top of each hive, for upward ventilation; leave them as quiet as possible until the middle of February: set them out on a calm fair day, until they have taken their flurry. Then return them to the cellar as before; let them remain until bees begin to gather pollen; then return them to the stand they occupied before, and let them remain for the spring and summer.

Unless diseased from some outward cause, bees will suffer next to no loss under such treatment, and the combs will come out as bright as in the fall, and not more than half of the honey will be consumed that would be, if left on their summer stands.

When the next number of the Journal comes to hand, it will be the time for setting out the bees.

Concerning my method of spring management, I shall speak in another paper.

E. L. BRIGGS.

Knoxville, Iowa.

[For the American Bee Journal.]

The Twin Hive as a Non-Swarmer.

Just before swarming time I remove three large colonies, combs, bees and all, into three of the twin hives, setting them on the same stands. I then fill up the other end of the hives with comb, removing some of the brood into the vacant part and placing that end of the hive in front. This brings the working force into the vacant end at once. Now by managing so as to have the apartment that the queen was in always supplied with empty comb, there was no disposition to swarm. Now, read attentively Mr. Beckford's article, and also the editor's note on page 30, of the August number of the American Bee Journal, in regard to abstracting brood to prevent swarming, and you have the idea exactly; only, instead of removing this brood to other hives or colonies, we keep it in its own colony. Consequently we have gained the desired end, and still have kept all our working force at home, thus keeping our stock always strong; and strong stocks are the ones to gather honey every time.

We went into this experiment on purpose to test the hive as a non-swarmer, and we selected stocks that were extra strong and extra prolific queens. And this experiment was tried in one of the greatest swarming seasons we ever saw, and it was a perfect success, as neither of the hives cast a swarm. As soon as we got the stock well to work, there was no trouble about removing brood from one apartment to the other, as the queen passed freely into every part of the hive, of her own accord. By supplying these hives with young queens, and attending to extracting of the honey, we think that swarming would be entirely prevented.

We differ from Mr. Beckford about the early swarms, for this reason: His surplus is probably gathered from white clover—that is, the main supply, while ours is gathered from basswood (which does not come in until July) and fall flowers. Consequently early swarms is what is wanted with us, as we can get them and the parent stock into good condition in time for the harvest.

We have digressed a trifle from our subject. We tried another of our twin hives as a non-swarmer, in this manner; We removed a strong stock, combs, brood and all, into it, and filled up the vacant end with brood from other hives. The queen was an extra prolific one, and kept all the combs occupied with brood. This did not give us room to work our extractor, as we wanted to, and the bees were so numerous that they filled the inside of the hive and both porticos were clustered full, both night and day. (Here was where we wanted the extra twenty-six frames in the cap; but we did not have it fixed for them.) Still there was no disposition to swarm, so we inserted a comb containing a sealed and nearly mature queen-cell, and the following day out came the largest swarm we ever saw. We hived it in a two-story standard hive. (Two of our standard hives, one placed on top of the other, makes a two story hive.) Right here we will state that we have repeatedly brought out swarms by the above method of inserting queen cells. In order to succeed it must be done at a time when the hive is populous with bees and brood, and the bees must be gathering forage rapidly. Many beekeepers now wish to control the increase of swarms, therefore we give our method of doing it.

ELISHA GALLUP.

Orchard, Iowa.

[For the American Bee Journal]

The Queen Bee wiser in her Instinct than Man in his Reason.

We may study out many inventions that look very plausible and reasonable to ourselves; but when we come to apply our reason to the instinct of the queen bee, we find she does not view things in the same light as we do. My opinion is, as well might we undertake to teach a goose and gander to pair successfully forty feet up in the air or on the wing, as to undertake to teach the queen and drone to pair anywhere else than in mid-air and on the wing. They know nothing about performing their nuptial vows floundering about on *terra firma* or in confinement, where they have not plenty of sea-room, or to poise themselves in their flight and come together as their instinct teaches.

My opinion is, the queen and drone are attracted to each other by the peculiar sound of their wings, as well as manner of flight. To illustrate a little, we will take a turkey's egg, hatch it under a common barn-yard fowl, and rear it without allowing it to see any other turkey until the time for it to pair with its mate. If a hen, we will procure a male turkey and place him near the hen, but with a partition between, so that she cannot see him when he struts. The hen will show plainly by her action that she understands the meaning of that strut, although she has never seen one of her species. Now let them together, and watch their manner of courtship. We find it to be the same as in all other birds according to their kind, their own peculiar way. Just so with the queen and drone. They, too, have their own way of courting, which is high up in the air, on the wing, where they will not come in contact with wire screening or other impediments at every turn they make; but where they can sing their love song, and poise and embrace each other, accord- to their own peculiar instinct.

A. BENNETT.

Bennington, Ohio.

[For the American Bee Journal.]

Introducing Queens.

If we had only one race of bees, and if one queen were just as good as another, it would still pay to raise queens to be used in making artificial swarms, as much precious time may be thereby saved to the bees, which would otherwise be lost in raising queens in the height of the honey harvest. But when we are aiming to raise only the best, and to make all the improvement we can, to raise and introduce queens is, to the beekeeper, a matter of very great importance. I do not propose to say anything concerning the best method of raising queens, as that has been fully discussed by many who have more experience than I have. But I wish to call the attention of the readers of the Journal to my method of introducing queens.

To introduce a queen safely, the following points should be attended to:

1. Before liberating the new queen, the bees should have time to become thoroughly aware that their former queen is gone, and that their only hope of an immediate successor is in accepting the imprisoned stranger.

2. There should be time for the new queen to acquire the scent of the hive.

3. The bees should have time to become familiar with her, and accustomed to her presence.

4. She should leave the cage when the hive is closed and the colony free from excitement.

This last item is of great importance. If the bees are excited and alarmed, and there is any lingering odor about the queen which would cause her to be recognized as a stranger, her life would be in peril.

Unless some means are employed to give the queen and the colony to which she is to be introduced, the same scent, I would not risk liberating a valuable queen in less than forty-eight hours. I have one end of my queen cage closed with a plug of wood, having a ⅜ inch hole bored through it, the inner end of which is reamered out in the shape of a funnel, that the queen may the more readily find it. The hole is closed with a wooden peg. In cool weather, I prefer to put the cage down between two combs, and in the centre of the cluster. In warm weather it will do to lay it on the top of the frames, if they be not closed at top, and to cover it with a cloth or a piece of carpet. At the end of the second day, I remove the peg from the hole in the stopper, and stick over it, on the end of the stopper, a piece of paper, or of cotton cloth dipped in honey, leaving the cage in the same position it was before, and close the hive. In performing these latter operations, I disturb the bees as little as possible. The bees will soon remove the honeyed cover, and the queen will, after a time, find her way out and be gladly received.

I have introduced a great many queens in this way, and have never had the bees destroy one so introduced; and I do not believe that there is the slightest danger of queens being destroyed, if this plan is carefully carried out. I have followed it in every month from April to December, and always with the same success.

Last September I introduced a queen on a plan upon which I propose to experiment further. I prepared some sweetened water strongly scented with peppermint, and taking some of it in my mouth, I lifted the combs up one by one, and blew the peppermint water upon them in a fine spray, so that the bees were thoroughly moistened and scented with it. Having completed this operation, and removed the old queen while doing it, I dipped the new queen into the peppermint water and put her on one of the combs. She was received without any demonstrations of hostility, and a week after I found her surrounded by her new subjects and filling up the available space in the hive with brood.

I do not advise any one to risk a valuable queen in this way. The one I so introduced was impure, and I did not care whether the bees should kill her or not. M. MAHIN.

New Castle, Ind. Dec. 6, 1871.

[For the American Bee Journal.]

Introducing Queens.

MR. EDITOR:—In almost every number of the Bee Journal I see the question raised and answered how queens are best introduced?

My experience is nothing new at all, often described by others, and once already by myself. The method is so simple and effective, and just this simplicity may be the reason why our beekeeping brethren don't more generally use it.

I grate two good sized nutmegs, mix them up with diluted honey or sugar syrup (or sugar water) in a tumbler holding one-fourth or one-third of a pint, and set it handy. Then I go to the nucleus, cage the queen I want to introduce, and stick her with cage in my vest pocket. Now I proceed to the hive whose queen I intend to supersede, kill her, or dispose of her to suit myself. I next with a teaspoon pour from the tumbler above described enough syrup between every two frames, so as to wet slightly almost every bee in the hive. I leave enough in the tumbler to give the queen a dive in, take her out with the teaspoon, drop her between the frames, and shut the hive.

I have hardly ever made a miss, with this way of introducing. It is in summer often a loss to have a hive queenless for only two days, but with the above described process the bees apparently do not become aware that a change is made.

In the fall I should prefer introducing queens with the cage, as the absence of a queen for a few days at this season does not make so much difference to the hive, and forage being scarce other bees are easily induced to rob. Yet I have introduced queens with nutmeg successfully in the fall, shutting up the entrance with wire gauze for a few days if necessary to keep out robbers.

Last fall I introduced two queens with the nutmeg process, in the presence of brother Hulman, of Terre Haute, Indiana, when he remarked that if he treated his bees in as reckless a manner as I did mine he should ruin his whole apiary. I wish that Mr. Hulman could have given me a call a few days later, when I could have shown him how my two queens were received.

I have often kept queens caged, together with a few workers, on the top of brood frames, until I could make the proper use of them, the queens would keep alive in some instances for weeks, while the workers generally soon died. But last fall I had a valuable queen killed in the cage on the second day, her legs being bitten off, &c. Brother Hulman suggested that the presence of the strange workers in the cage irritated the bees in the hive and caused them to attack the queen. This is reasonable, and since I cage queens alone when introducing, or when I put them for safe-keeping on brood frames.

C. F. MUTH.

Cincinnati, Jan. 15, 1872.

[For the American Bee Journal.]

An Item on Upward Ventilation.

AN EXPERIMENT IN WINTERING.

About the 20th of November we had a few days of unusually cold weather for the time of year in this latitude. It happened that some two weeks before I had equalized the honey by changing frames in several of my stocks, and had inadvertently left all the holes in the frames open in those hives. In my other hives they had all been closed with small blocks when the honey boxes were removed. On the 1st of December I put my bees in winter quarters. I was surprised to find fewer dead bees in every hive that was thus left with a free upward ventilation than in those that were closed. Noticed also that these hives were perfectly dry on the inside, while in the others, in almost every instance, ridges of ice were plainly to be seen leading from the entrance, showing that condensation had taken place within the hive, and the water had run down the sides and out of the hives.

I have on trial an experiment in wintering. It may not be new to many of your readers. I placed my hives in a double row about twelve inches apart each way, on boards covered three or four inches deep with common prairie hay. I then drove posts in the ground, to which common fence boards were tacked, so as to form a large box entirely surrounding the hives, fixed a six inch board about seven inches above the entrances, in such a way as to prevent the hay from closing the entrances to the hives, then crowded the hay all around and on top of the hives. I left half of the slats open in the frames and filled the caps with hay. Of course the result is about the same as if all my hives were buried in a hay stack with the entrances left open.

I fear that trouble may arise whenever the weather is warm enough to cause the bees to fly, from the fact that many will enter the wrong hives and thus be destroyed. As the double row extends north and south, of course the sun will shine on each row of hives but half the day, and as the rays strike upon but a few inches of each hive, I think there will be but a few days during the winter when the bees will be warmed up enough to cause them to fly.

I have tried to winter a few stocks on their summer stands. Will give you the results of my experiments in the spring.

E. A. GASTMAN.

Decatur, Ills., Jan. 6, 1872.

[For the American Bee Journal.]

On Supplying New Swarms with Ready Made Combs.

Some beekeepers assert that supplying ready made combs to new swarms is a great advantage, while others allege that it is an actual damage. Both parties are right. Allow me to explain. If we have a swarm come out at any time when bees are gathering very little honey, and we supply them with ready made comb, the queen can at once go to depositing eggs as rapidly as she chooses, provided the bees gather just sufficient honey to keep her breeding actively, without storing any in the cells to be in her way. Now we know positively that under such circumstances ready made comb is a great advantage. On the other hand, if we have a swarm come out while the basswood is in bloom, or at any time when the bees are gathering honey rapidly, and we supply them with ready made comb they will fill it so quickly that no room is left for the queen to deposit eggs. The consequence is that the swarm, unless attended to and relieved by means of the extractor is actually ruined, for we have a hive completely filled with honey and no bees in the fall. But if we allow them to build their combs they consume so much honey in the elaboration of wax and manufacturing the combs that it gives the queen a chance to deposit eggs, and the swarm turns out to be a good one. Give us the combs ready made, and we will use it under all circumstances, and with our management and the use of the extractor call it an advantage. In fact we can see no chance for argument on this question when properly understood.

E. GALLUP.

Orchard, Iowa.

[For the American Bee Journal.]

Product of a Swarm.

MR. EDITOR :—The honey season is over and our bees are put up in winter quarters. The past season has been what we here call a very fair one. I wintered seventeen colonies last winter, and increased them to thirty. More than one half of my swarms were natural ones. I aimed to keep my colonies strong, with the hives full of bees; but about the time I got them as wanted, they would swarm. The Italians are given to such tricks. Early in the honey season I selected a strong stock of Italians, to see what I could realize from them. On the 12th of May they cast a large swarm. I put it in a two-story Thomas hive, with nine frames above and below; the lower frames ten inches deep, the upper ones eight inches deep. At the time I hived the swarm, I filled about one-half of the frames with empty combs, putting worker combs in the lower frames, and drone combs mostly in the upper set of frames.

From this swarm I took with the Extractor, two hundred and sixty-one and a half (261½) pounds of nice honey. The old stock was used for box honey. From it I took eighty-five (85) pounds. I did not extract any from this stock, but think I could have taken forty or fifty pounds of extracted honey, and the same amount (eighty-five pounds) stored in boxes.

The eighty-five pounds of box honey taken from the old stock, sold for fifteen cents per pound—making $12.75. The two hundred and sixty-one and a half pounds taken from the swarm sold at ten cents per pound, making $26.15. The two amounts together make $38.90, the swarm was worth $15.00—which, added to the foregoing, makes $53.90; from which deduct the cost of the hive $4.00, and it leaves $49.90, as the net profit of one stock. I know this does not compare very favorably with Novice's three hundred and thirty (330) pounds, but I am only a young novice, while he is an old one. And you, Mr. Editor, can tell Novice that I am going to make a larger hive next year, and go for him again.

There are a great many bees in this county, and honey is very cheap here. I got from thirty colonies one thousand pounds of extracted honey, and six hundred and fifty pounds of box honey the past season.

J. P. FORTUNE.

Bloomfield, Iowa, Dec. 11, 1871.

[For the American Bee Journal.]

Novel Bee Dress.

MR. EDITOR:—On our way to town, last spring, our attention and that of the old mare we were riding was attracted by a strange, grotesque figure moving about on the road, whose manœuvres were occasionally very quick and then again quite slow. As we approached it had somewhat the appearance of the Ku Klux of Robinson's circus, minus the head. Approaching nearer we saw a pair of legs in boots beneath, when any fears we might have entertained disappeared, and we learned what was going on.

A man by the name of Parrish, a near neighbor of Old Reuben Birch, had a swarm of bees come off and pitch upon the back of a *worm* rail fence. Having ineffectually tried to hive them, in doing which the enraged bees had left from ten to a dozen stings with different members of the family, he sent for old Reuben, who never failed, as he always did things according to rules laid down in the Tar river code; and it was he we saw in the road.

Well, Reuben was ensconced in the old woman's *Bal-moral*. The drawstring, instead of being about the waist, was tightened just above the brim and around the crown of an old high top beaver. The forepart of the garment was behind; and the hind part, having a slit down it several inches, was before. The slit being near the face served as a kind of window for Reuben to peep out at. He was also armed with a long-handled broom; and the *gum* was placed on a coverlet on the ground, beneath the cluster.

Old Reuben would open a little crack of his stockade, to ascertain the exact locality of the bees, then close up, and with the broom, sweep, sweep, he would take the cluster, and a cloud of bees would in an instant be on the wing. They went for that *Bal-moral*, but down old Reuben would squat and remain motionless until things became a little settled, then peep out again to note progress. More of them settling again on the fence than went into the gum, sweep, sweep, he would again bring them down; and we had to move the old mare several rods further off as the bees were briskly circling, in search of something they *could* get at.

The KING having gone in after the lapse of about fifteen minutes *hiving*, the workers soon followed, and old Reuben, in triumph, walked to where we were standing, and as he came out from under that *Bal-moral*, the sweat was standing about in pools upon his face. We have often thought since, that we never saw a man sweat in earnest before; and feel sure that twenty minutes, on that day, under that *Balmoral*, was equal to the same length of time in Nero's cave at Naples. H.

Murfreesboro, Tenn., Nov. 20, 1871.

[For the American Bee Journal.]

National Society of Beekeepers.

MR. EDITOR:—I agree with you that, in the absence of jealous care, there is great danger of a national society of beekeepers being so conducted as to subserve the selfish purposes only of a few individuals, whose sole object in being present at such gatherings, is that of advancing their own personal and pecuniary interests. One of the first manifestations of such a tendency, is that of some individual writing and publishing a nicely colored report of all he puts on exhibition, or of what he, or such persons as he uses for mouthpieces, say upon all subjects—a polished report which tends towards building up a prosperous business for himself. At the same time care is taken to fail to report what is either exhibited or said by others, who are not their special instruments of profit;—no matter if what these have said or done be ever so much calculated to promote the general interests of beekeeping throughout the country, far above and beyond anything that such designing persons may have said or done, either themselves or through their satellites.

This matter I thought of when the first move was made towards the organization of such a body, but never resorted to any special means of preventing such a tendency, until the North American Beekeepers' Society was organized at

Cleveland, in December 1871, at which I was a member of the Committee appointed to frame a Constitution for the general government of the society. It was, I think, agreed by all the members of the committee, that the treasury of the society should be kept sufficiently flush with means to enable its members to publish an impartial and complete report of all the proceedings and discussions. In the absence of such a report, it was thought that a national society could not do much towards promoting the general beekeeping interests of the country, and would also fall short even in benefiting its own members to the extent it could if the proceedings were printed in pamphlet form for future reference.

With this object in view, special provision for the accumulation of a treasury fund was made in article 5th, wherein it was stated that each member of the society should pay one dollar at the time of becoming a member, and one dollar annually thereafter, into the treasury. But on presenting the constitution to the society for final adoption, objections were urged against the annual payment of one dollar, and this special provision was stricken out.

Through this amendment I fear that one of the principal supports of the society has been withheld, as it seems quite clear to my mind that in the absence of funds for the special purpose of publishing our proceedings, they will remain unpublished, or be liable to be garbled just to suit designing parties, who may be connected with the organization. Thus the object contemplated, of publishing a valuable pamphlet each year, has been completely thwarted. For there can be but little benefit accruing to the beekeeping fraternity at large, out of the annual meetings of such a society, except through the medium of placing before the masses a true report of their discussions, and of the experience of many beekeepers who may, at such meetings, give a full statement of their different methods of managing bees. If its beneficial results are not to be found in this, then such an organization is not calculated to benefit any but that class of persons who have something to sell to beekeepers; and they, or a portion of them, will not fail to have everything reported in full that is calculated to put an additional feather in their caps.

These matters, as I have stated, were thought of by the committee on permanent organization; and after the means for printing our proceedings in full, were discarded, I took it upon myself to offer a resolution (which was adopted) to the effect that the proceedings of the Indianapolis, of the Cincinnati, and of the Cleveland conventions, be published in pamphlet form. It, of course, remains yet to be seen how full and impartial the report will be. Should it be of such a character as to point out selfishness on every page—such as placing certain persons and their merchandise prominently before the beekeeping public, to the exclusion of others of equal or perhaps much more merit; or placing remarks of some persons prominent before the public, not because they have done or said as much for the benefit of bee-culture as others, but because they are instruments of profit and gain to certain parties; then I shall insist upon either a disbanding of the society, or making provision in our constitution for the publication of full and impartial reports. Should this matter be neglected, the grand object for which such a society should exist will be completely submerged.

Let me say to the Editor, that the JOURNAL is improving with each issue. Long may it live and its subscribers be increased tens of thousands annually.

G. BOHRER.

Alexandria, Ind.

[For the American Bee Journal.]

Super and Nucleus Hives.

DEAR JOURNAL:—On page 154, of the Journal for January, Mr. A. Grimm, gives his methods of managing the "super hive" from which to extract honey. As I have met with the same unsatisfactory results as those which Mr. G. speaks of, in the usual mode of management, I adopted a plan entirely different from those given by him; and where an increase of stock is desired, or new combs are needed (which is often the case), I believe my plan is preferable. It is this: If available, procure a frame of straight comb, or failing in this, lift out an outside frame from the brood chamber, placing it with an empty frame on each side, on one side of the super, adjust the division board, and cover the balance of the brood chamber with a honey-board. The honey-board should be composed of two separate pieces (two widths of weather-boarding answers well), so that when it is necessary to furnish additional frames, the edge of the first may be raised over the second, and slid any required distance.

This plan for many reasons, is much better than the one usually followed, namely, that of opening up the whole super at once; as the small amount of surplus room thus given to begin with, does not tend to produce a discouraging effect on the bees, yet there is room sufficient for the effective force of wax workers to be brought into requisition. Besides, as is well known, by alternating empty with full ones, each comb is built in the frame, without being run over and attached to another, as so often happens when two empty frames are placed in the hive, side by side.

We have put up a nucleus hive *a la mode* Gallup, with not only an entrance at each side, but with a nice little portico at each entrance—painting each a different color. Would it not be an additional feature to make the division of wire cloth, as it would certainly add much to the mutual warmth? We have used such partitions when wintering two small colonies in one hive, with success. Let us have your opinion Mr. Gallup, as we "take stock" on your suggestions, having found but few of them that would not bear a practical test.

RUSTICUS.

Jan., 1872.

[For the American Bee Journal.]

"Triumph" Bee Hive Description.

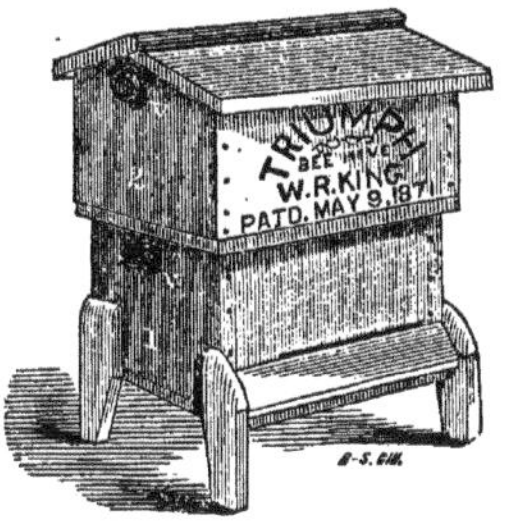

MR. EDITOR, and brother beekeepers:—According to promise, I give you a description of the Triumph hive, with cuts to illustrate it. The above cut represents a front view of the hive, which is 24 inches long, outside measurement, by 16 inches wide and 10 inches deep. The frames are hung either upon the rabbeted edges of the brood chamber, or upon strips $\frac{3}{8}$ of an inch square tacked on the inner edge of the brood chamber $\frac{3}{8}$ of an inch from the top. The frames are hung the narrow way of the hive, instead of lengthwise, as in the Langstroth. The advantage is that in handling new combs filled with brood and honey, there is but little danger of the combs falling out of the frames, as is frequently the case with longer frames. We use from ten to fourteen of these frames, as circumstances require. We have a partition board in either one or both ends of the hive, that fits closely in the chamber, yet is perfectly easy to slide either back or forth, for the purpose of contracting or enlarging at will, the brood chamber. The frames are made of strips $\frac{3}{8}$ of an inch thick. The top piece is $1\frac{3}{8}$ inches wide. We cut three-thirty-seconds of an inch off both edges of this top piece, commencing $1\frac{1}{4}$ inches from each end. This is to let the bees pass into the surplus chamber above. The end pieces are $1\frac{1}{8}$ inches wide, and $9\frac{1}{2}$ inches long. The bottom piece is $\frac{7}{8}$ inch wide. The end pieces of the frame have a little cleat or block $\frac{1}{8}$ inch square and 1 inch long tacked on their bottom edges on both sides. This prevents the frames from touching each other, excepting at these points and at either end at the top. The frames are thus made to fit up close against each other at the points named, yet leaving space for bees to pass above, between, and all around them. We now slide our partition board up against them from either end, placing wedges behind it. The brood chamber is thus formed, and by so arranging it, we secure the frames in such a manner as to be able to ship the hive filled with bees and comb to any part of the United States or Canada, without any danger of the combs being broken down. In November, last, I shipped 43 colonies from Milton, Ky., to this place (over two hundred miles), by boat fifty miles, and by railroad one hundred and fifty, and they were hauled one mile in wagons, and not one comb was broken down; besides. there were not more than one-fourth of a pint of dead bees in all the hives put together. I simply pressed my wedges in tight, putting a nail in each of them to keep them in place. There were no frames to be nailed down. One dozen "Triumph" hives can be prepared for shipping in the same time you would be preparing one of any other kind, differently arranged.

We use the hive both with and without a wire bottom. The wire used is No. 8, and is tacked to the sides and ends of the hive $\frac{3}{8}$ of an inch from the bottom of the frames, covering the whole bottom. Underneath the wire bottom we have a drawer or receiver, to receive all the chippings of comb and filth thrown down by the bees. This drawer has strips of tin, $1\frac{1}{2}$ inches wide, tacked on to its edges all around, extending over the inside. *This is our moth-trap.* Of course there are many worms that pass into this drawer, and unless it is cleansed at least once in ten days, they will accumulate until they fill the drawer to the wire above with web, and then they can return to the brood chamber. I would advise any one who will not look after his bees to use the hive without the wire bottom and drawer; but those that will cleanse it, will find that it is of great advantage, as by means of it we keep the bottom of our hive perfectly clean, without interfering with the bees. We also more successfully ventilate the hive, as will be seen by examining the following cut.

SECTIONAL VIEW.

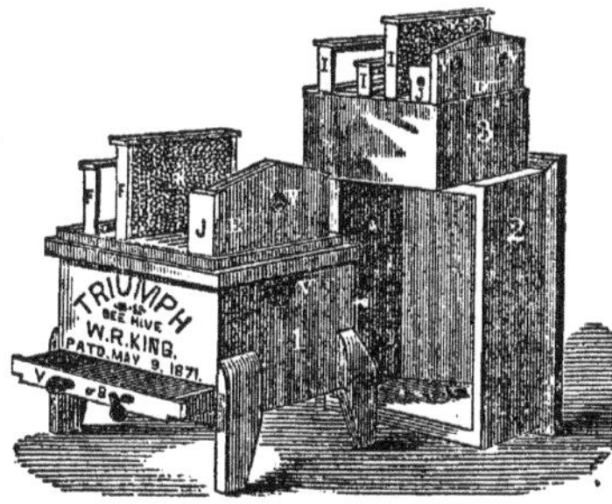

This cut shows a sectional view of the hive with fig. 2, the cap, off. Figure 3, represents the surplus honey chamber resting on the top of the cap, with three of the surplus frames pulled up in it. This chamber has a partition board with wedges. The frames in it are only $6\frac{1}{2}$ inches deep. but are of the same length as those in the brood chamber, and can be used in the brood chamber for feeding purposes. These surplus frames fit closely in the chamber, being suspended on the top edge. We use no honey-board, so-called, *except in winter*.

The patented features in this hive are the *ventilators* and the *perforated division boards*, which are used in a large hive not represented in these cuts, but which I will explain hereafter. The claims as granted read thus: *First*, the *air spaces*, *W, W*, and *ventilators, Z, Z, arranged in either end of the hive, with air space W, and ventilator Z* of the upper chamber substantially as *herein set forth*. *Second, the perforated division boards H, H, arranged on either side of the centre of the chamber A* (brood chamber) *cut-off, I arranged to operate as and for the purposes set forth*. In the first claim the objects *set forth* are that we may *effectually* control the *ventilation* of the hive, and at the same time we prevent others from securing frames in the hives in like manner. The air spaces W, W, spoken of, are the space between the partition boards and the ends of the hive, both in the brood chamber and surplus honey chamber. The perforated division boards are used in a hive 40 inches long, outside measure, and exactly of the same depth and width as the one above described. This hive has three entrances, one in the centre, and one six inches from either end. We form our brood chamber in the centre of the hive by putting in 14 brood frames.

For further particulars, address

W. R. KING.

Franklin, Ky.

[For the American Bee Journal.]

Natural, Hardy, Prolific Queens.

MY LAST BLOW.

No doubt it was in order to puff his *reversible, removable, double cased, sectional casket, movable comb hive*, that Mr. J. M. Price, after worrying his brain, found no other way to attract attention than to give a writ of imbicility to all the beekeepers who make artificial swarms or raise artificial queens; claiming that they act against *reason, nature and common sense*.

That theory, respecting natural, prolific and hardy queens, inflated with hyperboles and misstatements, had no more power of resistance than the red inflated balloons of our children. Verity, with one touch of a pin, caused it to collapse completely. Mr. Price, in the American Bee Journal for November, tries to inflate it anew by similar means, adding calumny thereto.

I beg the reader to remember that in the number of the A. B. J. for January, 1871, page 163, Mr. Price says that he has tested his method for *five years*. In the number for November, nearly a year later, he says he has tested it for *two years*. He erred in the first case, or he erred in the second.

In the A. B. J. for September, 1868, and in that for January, 1869, Mr. P. says this experience is to make *ten swarms from one*, and that *every swarm raised its own queen*. In the same Journal for November, 1871, he says that he *never* raised artificial queens in small swarms, but used only his largest and most vigorous stocks. What is that, if not a second error?

Mr. Price cites Gallup as sustaining the same views as himself. Yet I have already pointed out the ideas of Mr. Gallup, such as I find them in an article published by him in October, 1870. He says—"A queen cell built over an egg and fed as a queen from the start, I have not been able to discover why they are not as good as natural queens raised at swarming time." What shall I call such voluntary mistakes of Mr. Price?

Further on Mr. P. asserts that Novice bought twenty-five queens from Mr. Adam Grimm, to replace his queens, because they were too old, after seventeen months. Yet nowhere did Novice say that his queens were too old; but that he replaced hybrid queens. See A. B. J. for November, 1870, page 100. Is not that a fourth error?

I could make more similar quotations, but these are sufficient to show the truthfulness of Mr. Price.

As to the tested queen that Mr. P. did get from me in the beginning of June for six dollars, she was, before leaving Hamilton, one of the most prolific in my apiary. What experiments did he make with her, when she came into his hands? The reader can read partial accounts of these in the A. B. J. for January, 1871. In that number Mr. P. shows that that queen was the first Italian he had ever seen, and that she was also the first he had ever introduced in all his life. He was then so little acquainted with introducing queens that, after he received her, he looked over the back numbers of the A. B. J., to find the way to introduce her. He states that he put her on a comb of sealed brood, without bees, except those that accompanied her, and placed the hive near his stove. Then, after dark he looked her over and concluded to shake the bees off seven stands at the entrance of her hive; and that the second day after, he changed his mind and placed her, caged, in another hive which had the swarming impulse. And he dwells for more than a column on his unskilful precautions, showing his inexperience in the matter.

So, that unhappy queen, wearied by her journey, had to endure being handled and carried from one hive to another, and bear all the bunglings of Mr. Price, together with ill treatment from the bees of seven hives, more or less ill disposed towards her. And, finally, she had to suffer the pinchings of bees under the swarming impulse—which forced her to lead out a swarm 9½ days after her introduction, and *nearly four days before the first queen cell was capped over!*

Is there any queen breeder who would guarantee the prolificness of his queens, knowing them to be in such blundering hands as those of Mr. Price?

So little did I promise to replace her, and so little did Mr. Price believe that I made such a promise, that, when asking from me another queen, he added—"If you can, let me know, *with price*." With this, I enclose to the editor two letters of Mr. P. Indeed, I wrote to Mr. P. that probably the queen would be better in spring. Knowing the dealings of the man, I did hope that before spring, the queen, recovering from maltreatment, would have reinforced her hive, so as to be in better condition.

But was the queen as unprolific as Mr. P.

asserts? Is she dead, as he alleges? The repeated mistatements of that bee bungler give us the right of doubting these allegations.

I never refused to replace her; but I did refuse *to sell a second queen to Mr. Price,* for he had made too much unwarranted fuss about the first.

Mr. Price can, if he chooses, send my letter of refusal to the editor, whom I authorize to publish it, and to treat me as a falsifier if the facts are not as I represent them.

Proposing a theory before having sufficiently tested it, sustaining his ideas by false allegations, and then calumniating his opponent, are means ill calculated to entitle any one to a claim to be considered a true gentleman.

What think you of it, friend beekeepers?

CH. DADANT.

November 3d, 1871.

P. S.—As many beekeepers may not know what I mean by the "pinching of bees during the swarming fever," I wish to give my experience in explanation.

Two years ago, while experimenting with the Quinby queen yard to prevent swarming, the bees of one hive under experiment tried to swarm. The queen, which had her wings cut, could not follow and was kept a prisoner in the queen yard. While the bees were on the wing, I opened the hive and cut out every queen cell. A few days after the bees swarmed anew, and I saw them pinching and biting the poor queen, to force her to follow the swarm. I opened the hive again, and destroyed all the incipient queen cells. The bees swarmed a third time, and I had the greatest difficulty to rescue the queen, and the next night she was killed and cast out of the hive.

During all that swarming fever, the queen, worried by the bees, had deposited very few eggs; and the bees remained idle in the hive. I did not get an ounce of surplus honey from that stock.

I do not present this experiment to help my cause. The editor can read an account of it in the French "Journal des Fermes" for July, 1870, page 307, where I related it.

Similar pinchings were, without doubt, brought to bear against my queen; for she was introduced in a hive during the swarming impulse. In one of the letters which I send to the Editor, Mr. Price says that she was put in a colony he was *experimenting with raising queen cells.* I beg the reader to remark how discordant that word "*experimenting,*" is with his method tested "*five years.*"

Another proof that my queen endured the pinchings of the bees, is, that she led out a swarm four days before any queen cells were capped over. And Mr. Price wonders at the occurrence!

After having swarmed, my queen was not protected against the hardships inflicted on her by her new possessor. He writes, in one of the letters I send to the Editor, that every morning and every evening, for weeks, he removed every comb containing brood or eggs, and replaced them with frames of empty comb—even removing such as she had commenced to lay in. He adds—"At no time did she lay during any twelve hours more than a two or three inch circle could cover. A circle of two or three inches, in diameter, gives nearly three hundred eggs for twelve hours, or six hundred in twenty-four hours, or nine thousand bees in fifteen days. This was in the last fortnight of July, a time of the greatest drought.

A man who wishes to kill his dog gives him a bad name; but the laying of the queen was somewhat better than represented by Mr. P., who had every interest to find my queen less prolific than his; for she was an artificial queen, and he had already proclaimed his theory.

Besides, in the American Bee Journal for January, 1871, Mr. P. says that—"About the first of September she commenced to do a little better." We thus find that that poor queen, so much traduced in words and abused in acts, was not, to sum up all, near so bad as she was proclaimed to be.

I have seen queens, very prolific in April and May, deposit fewer eggs in July, August, and September, than the queen in question. I guess the Editor would be a competent judge in that matter, and likely to think that changing combs every twelve hours, would interfere with the laying while the queen was reconnoitering the newly introduced combs.

I have one remark more to add, and I am done. In his letter, Mr. J. M. Price says that he obtained seven queens "*all good*" and prolific, and in the American Bee Journal he says, that one of the seven was "*wingless.*" Which of these is the true statement?

In all my discussions with Mr. Price, I wrote with proofs in hand. If he does not show *his* proofs against me, I will hold him a calumniator.

C. D.

[For the American Bee Journal.]

A Little Plain Talk.

MR. EDITOR:—Do let me hit Novice just a little, for I want to know what effect it will have. On page 27 of the August number he says: "*Many are working and thinking of a hive with the proper number of frames spread out horizontally, so that no upper story will be in the way,*" and then he mentions me as of that number. When I got up my hive, I sent a description of it to some twenty individuals, whom I knew were using my style of frame, and requested them to try it; and among the rest I sent a very private description to Novice. Well, I received a very short reply, stating that he did not think it would work, the arrangement was too cold, &c., &c. We were perfectly satisfied then, that he had not paid attention enough to our description to understand it; and on reading his arrangement of his eight American hive (which he calls more compact than Gallup's) we felt very much as though we ought to have sent a description of our hive by telegraph to the North Pole (suppose they have a telegraph attached to that pole by this time), so that we could have received the opinion of an Esquimaux or a Kamschatcan, along with Novice's opinion of our hive. Why, Mr. Editor, only think of his comparing our hive to an American hive, and deciding that the latter, as arranged by him, was much the best! We were just as mad as our skin could hold. But to return to our story. His remarks have called out quite a large private correspondence, and it is for the purpose of making some explanations to said correspondents that I commence this article.

The reader will understand that Novice set his two sets of frames in this manner—one set by the side of the other; while we set one set of frames directly in the rear of the other—quite a different arrangement in our estimation. Now any one using the Kidder, Thomas, or almost any square frame can try the experiment with one or two hives; and we are not sure but even the American will work with our arrangement. Make your outer case long enough to hold two sets of frames, one set directly in the rear of the other, and have an entrance in the front and rear ends, just alike. Have the passages through the centre board, between the two sets of frames, clear across the centre and also at the bottom of said centre board. Now, by closing these passages, either end is in the same fix as a single hive, so far as a swarm of bees is concerned; and in fact, if we keep those passages closed, we can work two swarms of bees in this double hive. So we certainly need not throw it away, but keep it as a curiosity, if for nothing more; still, we believe it will work for one swarm satisfactorily. Now as soon as this swarm is populous enough, and the weather is right for storing and extracting, fill up the rear end with worker comb, remove two or three cards containing unsealed brood into the rear end, replacing in the front end empty worker comb. Now, revolve this hive half around, bringing the rear entrance to the front. (Of course the rear entrance has been kept closed up to this time.) Now what was the front has become the rear. Nearly close this end and open the other, and you bring the whole working force into the vacant end at once, instead of waiting for them to take possession of an upper story (as we sometimes have to do). We have, as the little girl says, *foolished* them; and they are not even aware of it, as both ends are exactly alike. Thus we have the novelty of a swarm of bees departing from one end and arriving loaded at the other. Before admitting the bees to both ends, or at that time, we open the centre passages. Now keep the brood about equally divided, part in one end and part in the other, and in the centre of each apartment, with the empty combs at the sides of the hive. If a novice does not know how to get up a good strong stock of bees in the double hive, let him proceed in this manner: Take brood nearly ready to hatch from other stocks, and fill up the vacant end, time enough before the honey harvest commences, to have them on hand to help to store honey. A large colony, in any hive for storing, should have a good, young and prolific queen. It is useless to work a small, weak swarm with perhaps, a worthless queen in a large hive, expecting great results. Now, we do not say that every one will like this arrangement of frames, but we say that, so far, we are very much pleased with it, and from our experiments last summer, we are pretty confident that we can control swarming to suit ourselves, in such hives. Mr. D. L. Adair has worked his sections in this manner for years, if we rightly understood him. We do not advise everyone to go into this arrangement extensively; but make a trial of it at first with a few hives. The only thing that we were disappointed in was this: Some of our queens occupied the entire twenty-six frames with brood, which left very little room to store honey, and this was the very reason why our thirty-two frame hive gave us the best satisfaction. Now, after taking into consideration your honey resources, and trying some few of these hives, take into consideration also the extraordinary yield of honey in this locality, and the enthusiasm of your humble servant. Each individual must judge for himself whether this hive will suit him.

E. GALLUP.

Orchard, Iowa.

[For the American Bee Journal.]

A Few Inquiries.

ED. BEE JOURNAL:—Will you allow me to ask Mr. W. R. King, of Kentucky some questions with reference to his description of the fertilizing house, &c., that he used last summer, and described in the February number of the Journal, p. 177.

1st. Why do you put sweetened water and honey into old honey combs and place them on a shelf in the house (fertilizing room) if the workers are not permitted to fly in the room?

2d. Is there no danger of the queens entering the wrong hive, fertilizing box, and destroying each other when they return from their wedding flight, if several are in the house at the same time? And if so, how can it be prevented?

3d. Must the top of the house be *dark* colored and why?

Brown muslin would be more durable and it could be painted, which would make it still better to turn the rain.

And now, Mr. Editor, I intend to construct a fertilizing house next summer upon Mr. King's plan. I failed with N. C. Mitchell's plan, but it might have been my own fault. I will try it again, if I live. I like the Journal *first-rate*, having been a constant reader for five years; I would not take five times what it costs for the knowledge that may be gathered from its pages.

I wish that the Journal would make its visits oftener than it does. Say semi-monthly. I for one will be willing to pay double the present price. Will Novice please tell me where he gets his glass honey jars or cans, I want the best and handiest kind. Put me on the *track*.

JOHN GARDNER.

Mt. Gilead, Ohio, February 15, 1872.

[For the American Bee Journal.]

Italians in Supers.

Mr. Editor:—In the November number of the Bee Journal the report of the Michigan Bee-keepers' Convention makes me say that "Italian bees could not be made to work in boxes. This is a great mistake. Thanks to Mr. Grimm for expressing his doubt in the January number of my being the author. I suppose the large amount of box honey made by Italian bees which he saw at my home apiary a few years ago is his reason for the doubt.

Any one having the proper knowledge can get more box honey from any Italian bees I have seen yet than from black bees. I can get all the extracted honey taken out of the hive put back again in boxes if desirable. All beekeepers should acquire the knowledge to manage any stock or variety of bees in any condition, so as to have all the different departments of labor carried on with perfect success. If any colony need wax it can be supplied by causing them to secrete it. The cappings of the honey combs, wax standing in the sun partially melted, and melted wax cooled off with sugar grains, to keep the particles of wax separate, can be used as a substitute in a hurrying time. Of course none but experts will know when it is needed, or how it is used.

It has yet to be satisfactorily proven by disinterested apiarians that the light colored, "beautiful, gentle Italian bee that does not sting" will not secrete as much or more wax, or not work in boxes as well as the dark Italians or the black bees. The common reason why some fail to get the Italians to work in boxes as well as the blacks is they work earlier in the spring, later in the fall, and in cool atmosphere, when the blacks do not. The nights being cool, and few bees in the hive at the time, they store the honey in the centre of the hive. If the honey is extracted at the right time, or the combs changed with the cold blooded blacks it will benefit these as well as the Italians. The extracted honey will be clear gain.

Mr. Grimm says on same page: "box honey is most convenient for transportation to market." This is certainly not the case in this section, as we have to accompany our shipments of box honey and handle with great care to keep it from breakage and stealings. This is not so necessary with extracted. The arctic explorers, or the shippers to cold climates, would surely choose a well cured, good, solid article of extracted honey. All dealers would certainly dispense with boxes and wax if they acquire the knowledge, and more especially in the tropics. How will it be with boxes with wax combs? Does it break in the cold? Or does the moth worm hatch out of wax in hot climates? Saying nothing about packing of boxes of combs for the market, or the rough handling, or the smashing up, or the leaking, or the stealing of the boxes by railroad or boatmen.

Having sold our honey, and owning no right to sell hives, we have nothing in the bee line to sell. Will advertise in the Bee Journal when we do have.

Correspondents sending us questions, when the information requested is all on their side, may send stamp, or we may answer only in the Bee Journal.

J. M. Marvin.

St. Charles, Ills.

[For the American Bee Journal.]

The Monarda-punctata.

Mr. Editor:—You must excuse me for troubling you again about that bee plant the *monarda-punctata.*

I was out again and gathered about three ounces of the seed, which took me about one-half of a day to gather and rub out. I made more particular inquiries about the plant, this time.

It blooms the second year.

Mr. Bailey, who lives in that vicinity, and has kept bees for the last fourteen years, has not lost a swarm in the winter during that time, and attributes his success in wintering his bees, mainly to the monarda-punctata.

He had a swarm come off on the 3d of August, this year, which has filled its hive with comb and honey from this plant, and is in good condition for wintering.

Other beekeepers in the vicinity seem to be equally successful. Inclosed find a sample of honey from this plant, kindly presented by Mr. Bailey; who thinks it is nearly pure, as there were scarcely any other plants in the vicinity from which honey could be obtained.

This plant produces honey in abundance, and is in bloom from the middle of July until frost comes in the fall.

Bees in other localities about here (except where there was buckwheat) have not done so well. From the middle of July they seemed to be falling off in weight, and are not as heavy at the present time, as they were in July. I think that accounts for so many stocks dying in winter, except in the district where the monarda abounds.

I think the name horse-mint will mislead a good many. The horse-mint of this country grows all over the State, even amongst the monarda. It grows about three feet high, and bees do not work on it here. It has only one head on each branch. I think this is probably the horse-balm.

James McClay.

Madison, Wis., Oct. 14, 1871.

☞ The sample of honey from the *monarda*, accompanying this communication, is a beautifully transparent, slightly amber colored, and well-flavored article. The introduction of the plant in suitable soils, would doubtless be advantageous to bee-culture, if it yields honey as abundantly as represented. We should be pleased to receive a specimen of the other plant, called horse-mint in that country.—[Ed.

A Kansas bee tree yielded 300 pounds of honey.

[For the American Bee Journal.]

Non-Flying Fertilization.

MR. EDITOR :—On page 177 present volume A. B. Journal, W. R. King gives his mode of fertilization in confinement, and says make the house eight feet high, board floor and planked up two feet high all round.

I wish to ask Mr. King why he boards up the sides two feet? Would it not be as good only six feet high and cloth from bottom to top, so that two widths yard wide cotton will do. Why the board floor? Would not a smooth dirt or sawdust floor do as well and cost less? Also, why does he put the dark calico over the top? Would not the whole room be better of cotton? If the bright sun rays would attract the bees to the top would it not do to place it under the shade of some thick shady tree. Again, why place the old combs on a shelf filled with sweetened waters? He says there is to be no bees let fly in this house except the queen and drones; were queen and drones ever known to take food away from home? Mr. King please tell us through the Journal—next number—as we want to be getting ready in time.

H. NESBIT.

Cynthiana, Harrison Co., Ky. Feb. 15, 1872.

[For the American Bee Journal.]

A Temporary Bee Room.

Our cellar is a very wet one naturally ; in fact there are two springs in its bottom, from which water rises most of the time during the year. Hence, at first thought one would consider this a rather unfavorable place to rig up for a winter depository for bees. But we had the bottom covered four inches thick, with small stones, and then cemented on top of this so that we have a nice dry bottom now—the water passing off to the drain between the rocks, which afford complete drainage. It was not convenient to have a room partitioned off permanently in our cellar, as it would be very much in the way during summer ; so we have made one temporarily, as follows : We put down scantling, one inch by three, on the cement, where we wanted our partition, and on this we set our posts (joists 2x2), and nailed them to the sleepers above ; then "too nailed" them to the scantling at the bottom, leaving space for door at one side. On these posts we nailed pieces of 1x3 scantling, one piece at the bottom the whole length, and 2 feet 9 inches above we nailed another piece of the same, and so on to the top. We then put on heavy untarred sheathing paper, three feet wide, tacking it to the pieces of scantling at each edge, just enough to keep it from falling. When all was on, we went over it and tacked on laths lengthwise where each two sheets met, which holds it firmly in place. The door to close the entrance, is a scantling frame covered with the paper, like the walls. A wooden tube lets in air from outdoors, while an eight inch funnel (made by bending a piece of the same sheathing paper up, and securing it in place by driving small tacks through the paper into a narrow strip of wood along the inside,) passes from the bee-room up into the room above, and connects with the flue of a chimney. Shelves are arranged in the inside, on which our bees are passing the winter in perfect quiet, and enjoying a clear, dry and wholesome atmosphere. A man will take the whole thing down in two hours in the Spring, and pack it away for another winter.

COST OF THE STRUCTURES.

20 yards of paper..................	75 cents.
50 feet joist and scantling..	75 "
1 day's work of man..............	1 50
	$3 00

G. W. P. JERRARD.

Levant, Me., Dec., 1871.

[For the American Bee Journal.]

Answer to A. Grimm's Puzzle.

Sometime last August I removed a fertile queen from a nucleus for the purpose of rearing another from a cell which I had ready to insert. Next day I opened this nucleus to insert a cell, and found the bees all quiet. I had not then time to ascertain the cause of this quietness, but inserted the cell. Two days after I opened the nucleus again to see whether this cell had hatched. The cell was destroyed, and the bees were all quiet. I then made an examination, and on the second frame found a well known queen with defective wings laying profusely. I knew at once where this queen came from. Four feet directly in the rear of this nucleus stood another, with a defective wing queen that could not fly. As she was a fine and large one I hated to kill her, and while thus hesitating Mr. W. R. King visited my apiary. I showed him this queen, and told him my intention to kill her. He, however, advised me not to do it, but to pile saw dust around that nucleus, or spread a cloth around if I had not the saw dust. I did the latter, and missing the queen from the nucleus I immediately inserted a cell in it, thinking that she was lost. But I was glad to find her again and fertilized.

I had a few days previously received some drones from Mr. Nesbit, and distributed them among these nuclei. This queen must doubtless have met the drones on the ground, for I pitched her up in the air to show a company of visitors that she could not fly. I have her now in a full stand, and saw her last week all right. The queen I took out of that nucleus was sent off.

R. M. ARGO.

Lowell, Ky., Jan. 9, 1872.

The Michigan farmer, who, in addition to his profits from produce, made this season, three thousand dollars by the sale of his honey, has derived as much income from mere *beeing* as from actual doing.

THE AMERICAN BEE JOURNAL.

Washington, March, 1872.

Death of Samuel Wagner.

Readers of the Bee Journal:—Your dear old friend, the honored editor of the American Bee Journal, is dead. On Saturday, February 17th, he awoke early, partially dressed himself, and was talking pleasantly with his wife, when he was suddenly seized with shortness of breath, soon became unconscious, and in less than fifteen minutes breathed his last. The physician pronounced his disease to be aneurism of the heart. He had complained for more than a year of pain and numbness, interfering greatly at times with the use of his pen.

A noble, unselfish, good man has fallen. In the full vigor of his intellect, with judgment unimpaired, and memory wonderfully tenacious. Nearly seventy-three years old! How few of the readers of the Journal could have imagined that its vigorous editorials and wise management were the products of a man who had reached an age when most men are comparatively useless.

If he could have chosen for himself, it would have been to die thus with the harness on; to pass by the shortest transition from useful happy work to the better land.

Few know how much Mr. Samuel Wagner has done for the promotion of bee-culture in America. Being able to read the German fluently*—indeed, until he was nearly ten years old he spoke no English—he had taken all the numbers of the Bienenzietung and other German bee journals, from their origin. His library is unquestionably the choicest repository in America, of German bee literature, and probably the fullest in this department, of any private library in the world. Better acquainted with the history and literature of bee-culture than any man in America, perhaps than any living man—seldom if ever forgetting a single fact once lodged in his extraordinary memory; he was so modest† and reserved, that only those who knew him well, understood the wide range of his reading and investigation.

Unselfish to an unusual degree, he cared comparatively little for money or applause, but kept steadily in view the advancement of the true interests of bee-culture, making his varied information contribute to the wider diffusion of all that pertained to the true theory and practice of his favorite pursuit. While specially familiar with everything pertaining to this subject, he was well versed in the civil history of his country, and intimately with the ecclesiastical history of the German Reformed Church, in which he had served for many years as an honored elder. There were few subjects, indeed, on which he could not converse with ease, and by the extent, variety and *remarkable accuracy* of his information, he was one of the most delightful companions to all who enjoyed the pleasure of his acquaintance.

It is very difficult to realize that all these stores of instructive and entertaining knowledge lie buried in his tomb, and nothing but a firm belief in the wisdom and goodness of that merciful Father, in whom he trusted, can reconcile us to his loss. He who hath brought "life and immortality to light in the Gospel," knows best when and how to summon his children to their unclouded splendor.

L. L. Langstroth.

* We forgot in the February number of the American Bee Journal, to give the proper credit to Mr. Wagner for his translations from the Bienenzietung, given in the article on the Berlepsch frames.

† It is with deep regret that we announce that no likeness exists of our venerable friend. He shrank so instinctively from everything having the least appearance of personal display, that he could never be prevailed on to allow his portrait to be taken.

☞ Samuel Wagner was born at York, Pennsylvania, August 17th, 1798. His father was at that time pastor of the German Reformed Church in that borough. Having accepted a call from the German Reformed congregation at Frederick, Maryland, he removed there. Mr. Wagner there attended the parochial school attached to the church. In 1810, his father resigned, owing to ill health, and returned to York, where he shortly after died. Mr. Wagner was then sent to the York County Academy, where he received his education. After leaving the academy, he engaged for some years in mercantile pursuits. In 1824, he purchased the York Recorder. In 1829, he sold the York Recorder to Mr. T. C. Hamley, and removed to Lancaster, where in 1830, he established the Lancaster Examiner. Receiving the offer of the cashiership of the York Bank, he sold the Examiner to Hammersley & Richards, and returned to York, holding the position of cashier till April, 1862. In 1863, he accepted the position of disbursing officer of the Senate. Resigning this position in 1868, he, for the few remaining years of his life, devoted all his energies to the editing and management of the American Bee Journal, which was to him a labor of love.

Accident to Rev. L. L. Langstroth.

On Friday, January 26th, Mr. Langstroth fell and had his left foot severely injured by the wheel of a street railroad car. He was on his way to my father's house, and was at once brought here by the superintendent of the railroad. At first, it was feared that all the toes except the large one would have to be entirely amputated, as the bones of all of them were broken; the small toes were deeply lacerated by the flange of the wheel, and several bones on the instep broken. From the first, however, he has suffered comparatively little pain from so severe an accident, and the wound has healed so favorably, that no operation will be needed. A very heavy boot alone saved his foot from being crushed to a jelly.* The articles from Mr. Langstroth's pen, written while confined to his bed, will be gratifying to our readers, and we cannot but esteem it providential that he was here when my father died, and able to prepare the obituary which appears in this number.

G. S. WAGNER.

To the Friends of the American Bee Journal.

It is hardly necessary to say, that the American Bee Journal will not die with Mr. Wagner. He was maturing a plan for illustrating it largely, so as to place it in the very front rank of progress and improvement; and was promising himself the pleasure of relief from the mere drudgery of business details, while he devoted himself more exclusively to his work as editor. His journal will continue to be conducted in the interest of no hive or clique, but will be the same honest, intelligent and reliable publication that it has been from the commencement, its pages open to every man who has any decent utterance for or against any hive or any theory in bee-culture—such a publication, in short, as the intelligent beekeepers of America demand and will have.

The readers of the American Bee Journal, who have so often feasted on its treasures, and who feel how much they are indebted to it for success in their favorite pursuit, will doubtless be anxious to know how they can best show their appreciation of the pre-eminent services which the late Mr. Samuel Wagner has rendered to the cause of bee-culture. Friends, rally round the Journal! Let all arrearages be promptly paid up, and let every one try, with that hearty determination which commands success, as soon as possible to remit money for new subscribers. That you may be the more zealous in so doing, bear in mind, that for a considerable time Mr. Wagner published this journal, not only without any remuneration for his services as editor, but at a considerable pecuniary loss. At last it has become more than self-supporting; its list of subscribers has grown more rapidly of late than ever before, and is one of the most permanent of any periodical in the land. Not by puffing and other more questionable methods so widely practiced by papers which have no real merit, but by honest, persistent, intelligent *work*, he had reached a point, where it seemed that his largest expectations would be fully realized; that the American Bee Journal would not only do a great work for the beekeepers of this land, but would afford him a support in his old age, and be a valuable property to be bequeathed to his family.

I know too well the large number of generous men who appreciate this journal, to doubt that they will now come forward with new zeal, and will, both as a duty and a labor of love, do all that needs to be done to carry out his plans, and thus continue to make Samuel Wagner's American Bee Journal the highest standard of authority in everything pertaining to practical and scientific bee-culture.

L. L. LANGSTROTH.

Washington, Feb. 22, 1872.

* Mr. Langstroth has for years when travelling purchased tickets of the Railway Passengers Assurance Company. He did so on this trip, which entitles him to thirty dollars a week while he is laid aside from attention to his business.

Sugar Syrup Dysentery and the Hruschka.

Novice's observations, shown to me by Mr. Wagner, that bees when wintered on sugar syrup, in their first flight do not discharge fæces like those fed on honey, is entirely new to me. I have repeatedly wintered stocks on sugar syrup, having in one very poor season fed it to nearly one hundred colonies, which, in the month of September, had only a few weeks' supply of food on hand. If properly prepared and seasonably fed, it seems to answer, to say the least, as well as honey. Both Mr. Wagner and myself have this winter had numerous letters, informing us that the mortality among bees from dysentery has been unusually severe. Several persons have attributed it to the large quantities of new cider stored up by the bees. In many localities, large quantities of very thin honey were gathered too late to be thickened or sealed over by the bees. This thin honey in cold weather soon becomes thinner still, and then by fermentation sours, and is almost sure death to bees, especially if they are entirely confined to their hives. I believe that the Hruschka will probably afford us an effectual remedy against this cause of dysentery; for all this thin honey can be emptied, and if the bees have not sufficient winter stores, it may be replaced with sugar syrup. The thin honey may be reduced by heat to a proper consistency, to be used as spring food, or perhaps at once safely fed to the colonies from which it was taken. There is often enough of this late gathered honey to injure, if not entirely destroy a colony which has enough winter food without it.

L. L. LANGSTROTH.

NOTE.—It seems to me that Mr. Gallup, or some other correspondent of the Journal, has emptied the thin honey to protect their bees from dysentery, but I cannot refer at this time to their communication.

☞ We hope shortly to present to our readers translations of some unedited letters of Huber, which are full of interesting facts relating to the experiments of that great apiarian. They will be accompanied with notes by the Rev. L. L. Langstroth.

Mel in ore, verba lactis,
Fel in corde, fraus in factis.
Mediæval Latin.

With honeyed lips and creamy words,
His heart is gall, and all his acts are frauds.

Personal—'Homer A. King,' the Eminent Apiarian.*

Those of my readers who saw the American Bee Journal for April, 1871, are aware that in stating the matters at issue between Mr. King and myself, I used no language in the least derogatory to his personal character, or that by the severest construction could be deemed lacking in courtesy towards him. Had he chosen to carry on in the same spirit, the controversy as to the validity of the Langstroth patent, and his alleged infringement upon it, nothing would have appeared in the columns of his paper or of the American Bee Journal which might not properly have been said by Christian gentlemen. So soon, however, as Mr. Otis refused to listen to his propositions for compromises, and I assured him personally that nothing short of a legal decision sustaining or invalidating the Langstroth patent would ever satisfy the beekeeping public, he began to assail me and the late Samuel Wagner, who had so ably exposed the worthlessness of his patents, with the most bitter personalities; to represent me as the mere introducer of foreign inventions, and as sustained by Mr. Wagner in patenting them as my own, in order to deprive others of the honor which was their due. In the December number of his paper, these attacks were brought to a focus, intended if possible to consume us. Not contented with assuming that the works of Debeauvoys, Munn and Berlepsch had fully anticipated all my claims, he suggested that I had procured the re-issue of my patent through a purchasable patent office examiner, and that Mr. Wagner had aided me by his knowledge of German beeculture, to patent a foreign invention as my own. He even went so far as to insinuate that I was acquainted with one Backhaus, to whom Berlepsch says he sent some hives with frames in 1851, thus endeavoring to strengthen the conjecture of the Baron, that I copied my invention from his.

"Cœlum non animum mutant qui trans mare currunt."

The same unscrupulousness which he has shown in all this controversy in this country, he carried with him over the ocean, and by the grossest misrepresentations, induced an honorable man to assail publicly one who had always spoken of him with respect.

"Alas!
Some minds improve by travel—others rather
Resemble copper wire or brass,
Which gets the *narrower* by going farther."

If, in his abuse of a man who less than a year ago he professed to love almost as well as David loved Jonathan, he had ventured to insinuate that I had something to do with the loss of his stolen documents, it would not have surprised me, for this would have been mild compared with his attempt to fasten upon me the brand of perjury, bribery, subornation of perjury and swindling; perjury, in swearing to the invention of another as my own; bribery and subornation of perjury, in purchasing of a sworn official a reissue to which I was not entitled; and swindling, in selling to the public a patent to which I had no valid title.

When this December number came to my house, freighted as it were with maledictions, aimed not merely at my property and rights, but at my reputation, and that of the most noble and generous of friends, I was laid aside from all ability to use either mind or body to any advantage; suffering from a cruel malady, to which I have been subject from my college days, and which has caused the loss of more than one-half of my time for the last twenty or more years—when this deadly missive came to my house, my family hesitated for some time to put it into my hands, dreading its effect upon me in my suffering condition. Deciding at length that it would be wrong to withhold it, it was given to me for perusal. Thank God! instead of harming me, it proved the very best of tonics; nay, rather like an *electric shock*, it raised me from my torpor, set my mind almost instantaneously to work, and shortened by months the usual length of my attacks, so that soon, pen in hand, I was devising what reply ought to be made to its many misrepresentations.

Could I for a moment forget that less than a year ago, this Homer A. King, professed, *after notice had been served upon him of the Otis suit*, the most unbounded friendship for me; that I had published nothing which might not have been said against the most honorable opponent, and that when he found that I would not impede the efforts of Mr. Otis to test the validity of my patent—"only this and nothing more"—he fell upon me with fury, and in almost every number of his paper sought to consign me to "the bottomless pit of public condemnation." (See June, 1871, No. of his paper). No! I could not forget, that to these charges I had made no reply, and that his audacity seemed to be increased by my silence. It was under these circumstances that I still determined to deal as little in personalities as possible, but by adhering strictly to the facts, to protect my legal rights and the rights of those who had purchased under my patent. After doing this in as courteous a manner as seemed possible, I closed my article in the February number of the American Bee Journal with these words:

"Does Mr. King, when suggesting that I might have bribed the patent office examiner, or that I might have conspired with Mr. Wagner to patent a foreign invention as my own, suppose that the beekeepers of this country will consider him as using the legitimate weapons of an honorable warfare, or that they will ever give credit to such unworthy insinuations?"

Since this article was written, Mr. Samuel Wagner has died, and I know that his many

* See Fowler's Journal of Phrenology, Feb., 1871, p. 123.

friends will insist that the man who has heaped upon him such shameful misrepresentations and slanders, shall be shown in his true character. Other facts also have come to light, and I feel it is no longer possible for me to hold any terms with a man so steeped to the lips in falsehood, slander and hypocrisy as is Homer A. King. However strong are my provocations, I believe that I shall not only say nothing which is not strictly proper, but I *know* that if the public could be made acquainted with the true history of this man in his relations to bee-culture, they would see *that I have still kept back some* TREACHERIES *which would be more damaging to him than any which I have yet given to the public.* When the beekeepers of this country have before them the evidence that this man scruples at nothing that he thinks can be made to promote his purposes, I have no fear that they will blame me for at last speaking with a plainness that cannot be misunderstood, or that they will fail to see that in self-defence I have been driven by Mr. King himself to expose the duplicity which has marked his conduct since he first declared war against Mr. Wagner and myself.

In the November number of his paper, Mr. King has the following characteristic utterance: "We hope no one will accuse us of electioneering for office this year. We shall not be a candidate, neither shall we help to elect a man for president, as we did last year, merely to confer an honor upon him, and who has boasted that his election to that office was an acknowledgment of his claims." This means that being unanimously chosen president of a convention of beekeepers, many of whom had rival and perhaps conflicting patents, I have been mean enough to abuse their confidence by boasting that it was an admission of the validity of the claims of my patent as against theirs! Let us look at the language I *have* used, and see if it will warrant any such construction. "The generous treatment which I have received from the two beekeepers' conventions at Indianapolis and Cincinnati, has, I trust, put to rest forever all the aspersions which have been heaped upon me by ignorant or designing men, as being the mere *introducer* of a foreign invention, which with some unimportant modifications, I am charged with having patented, and attempted to palm upon an unsuspecting public as my own." If ever those charges are again made by those who know the facts, they must renounce all claims to truth, honor, or even common decency. I shall not insult the common sense of my readers by seeking to show that only the vilest misconstruction of my language could distort it into any such boasting as Mr. King alleges. I was mistaken, however, in supposing that anything could ever put to silence the aspersions of *designing* men. The charges *have* been made again, and by one who, from what he saw in Europe, was better qualified than almost any other man to know the facts, and by making such charges *he has renounced all claims to truth, honor, or even common decency.*

It is well known, that Mr. King was elected secretary of the beekeepers' association which met in Cleveland last December. In the January number of his paper, he has as secretary given the proceedings of that body.

In his report of the proceedings of that body, he gives a description of a certain hive embracing all the features of the hive patented to me in 1852, and says "*he speaks advisedly*" when he declared that these features were invented by Mr. A. F. Moon over thirty years ago.

Did the association authorize this utterance of Mr. King? did they require him to inject it into the body of his report, that it might go as it were by their endorsement to every part of the beekeeping world? Not one word was said about this matter in their public proceedings, and it was left for Mr. King to do the very thing of which he so falsely accused me, viz.: to use dishonestly his position as an officer of the association, to promote his own selfish interests by trying to damage the claims of others!

Those who have read Mr. King's various communications since this controversy began, cannot but have noticed his frequent professions of being governed by high Christian motives, and his assertions, that under the severest provocations "God still gives him grace to love his enemies." Judged from the tenor of such remarks, coupled with the oft repeated affirmations, that "his non-resistant principles would almost compel him to acquiesce in unjust demands," or "to prefer honorable compromise to legal controversy," one need feel no surprise that he should interlard not only his conversations and letters, but even his *telegraphic communications,** with such suspicious religious utterances. If we give full credit to the sketch of his life, published in the Phrenological Journal for February, 1871, we must agree that he is almost worthy to be canonized as a saint.

"Active out-of-door exercise having now restored the health of Mr. King, his impulses of duty again called him to the home missionary field. A peculiarity in his labor was, that he never received any pay for his ministerial work, not even for travelling expenses, when called to journey for the benefit of his fellow men many miles by rail. This has given him great power with skeptical minds, since they could not question the purity of his motives, and the sincerity of his purposes.

"The business, however, to which he gave such impetus, now began to feel the effects of his absence, and yielding to a strong outside pressure, upon mature deliberation, he decided to return to his business, under the solemn vow that he would use all his surplus income to advance the holy work to which he had devoted his youth."

"Alas! however, for the rarity of Christian charity, under the sun!". It is to be feared that this revelation to all the world of solemn vows, which would otherwise have been known only to Mr. King and his Maker, will be regarded by most persons as a positive violation of the command of the Master:

"Therefore, when thou doest thine alms, do not sound a trumpet before thee, as the hypocrites do in the synagogues and in the streets, that they may have glory of men. Verily I say unto you, they have

* One telegram to me begins thus: "I feel to bless and curse not."

their reward. But when thou doest thine alms, let not thy left hand know what thy right hand doeth."

In all sober verity, such parade of almost saintly perfection, is utterly abhorrent to every right minded man.

Dickens, in his *David Copperfield*, which of all his fictions he says he likes best, has painted in colors which can never fade, a certain *Uriah Heep*, who in his career well nigh exhausted all the heights and depths and lengths and breadths of *the humility dodge*. Was it reserved for Homer A. King to put *the religious dodge* to the same varied uses?

The celebrated poet, Thomas Hood, must have been an indignant witness of the painful union of religious professions with very unreligious acts, or his pen could never thus have consigned them to perpetual infamy :

"With sweet kind natures, as in honeyed cells,
Religion lives, and finds herself at home;
But only on a formal visit dwells
Where wasps instead of bees have formed the comb.
Shun pride, O man! whatever sort beside
You take in lieu, shun spiritual pride!
For of all prides, since Lucifer's attaint,
The proudest swells a *self*-elected saint.
A man may cry Church! Church! at every word,
With no more piety than other people—
A daw's not reckoned a religious bird
Because it keeps a cawing from the steeple.
The temple is a good, a holy place,
But canting only gives it an ill savor;
While saintly mountebanks the porch disgrace,
And bring religion's self into disfavor!
Behold yon servitor of God and mammon,
Who binding up his Bible with his ledger,
Blends Gospel texts with trading gammon,
A black-leg saint, a spiritual hedger,
Who backs his rigid Sabbath, so to speak,
Against the wicked remnant of the week,
A saving bet against his sinful bias—
"Rogue that I am," he whispers to himself,
"I lie—I cheat—do anything for pelf,
But who on earth can say I am not pious!"

Some of my readers may question whether I have weighed carefully the risk of exposing a man who has at least two presses under his control, and an organized body-guard of infringers upon my patent to do his bidding. Others may fear lest on the principle of the old law maxim, "*The greater the truth the greater the libel*," even the just severity of my language may recoil upon myself. After his December utterances, however, Mr. King has no valid reason for being surprised at my plain exposition of his apiarian career; those December utterances he must know would be pronounced libellous by any honest court and jury in the land.

If there are any of my readers to whom my language may seem unjustifiably severe, I would say that they will probably think otherwise when facts are presented to them as they must be, still more damaging to Mr. King.

Beekeepers of America! as I think of the late Samuel Wagner, I feel that it was laid upon me as a sacred duty, to expose the man whose calumnies followed him to the very moment when he sank in unconsciousness; and have, even after his death, though this could not have been intended, have been sown broadcast over the land by M. E. Williams, associate editor with Mr. King. Williams' article, as full of baseness as though dictated by King himself, will be given in due season, with suitable comments thereon, to the readers of the American Bee Journal, who will then know more fully under what a sense of moral indignation I have penned this personal.

L. L. LANGSTROTH.

Washington, D. C., Feb. 23, 1872.

[For the American Bee Journal.]

Patented Honey Boxes.

On page 136, of the December number of the Bee Journal, Mr. George T. Wheeler informs us that he has patented a honey box. We mentioned that kind of honey boxes in the "ANNALS OF BEE-CULTURE" for 1870. Mr. William Plocher, of Fairwater, Fond du Lac county, Wisconsin, an intelligent German beekeeper, who has Huber's work and several other German treatises on bees, has used that device for years, and is now using it. What sense is there in running to the Patent office, with every old notion that we have re-vamped?

A friend of ours in Upper Canada, has hit upon the same principle as our new style hive; and he informs me that he has used it the past season with the greatest satisfaction. And we do not know how many more have hit on the same principle. Now, suppose we had galloped off to the Patent office, and paid Munn & Co., or some other Co., a large fee, we could no doubt have succeeded in making a donkey of ourself, just as hundreds of others have done before for themselves, and as many more will probably keep doing. Just so long as our Patent office is managed as it is and has been, you may depend on it there is and always will be a screw loose somewhere.

E. GALLUP.

Orchard, Iowa.

[For the American Bee Journal.]

Bees at Lucknow, Canada.

MR. EDITOR :—In looking over some of the back numbers of the Journal, I saw an account of the reason for bees leaving for the woods, which brought to my mind an incident connected therewith, which was this. I met one of my neighbor's boys one morning, of whom I inquired how his father's bees were doing. He replied, "very well, only we lost one swarm yesterday." Ah! said I, how was that? "Well," replied he, "yesterday was a very hot day, and a fine large swarm came off and lit on a currant bush. Father said it was *too warm* to put *them in a hive then, and he would leave them till evening*; but when evening came, they were gone." Ah! said I, Charley, if you had subscribed for the AMERICAN BEE JOURNAL two years ago, as I wanted you to do, your swarm, to say nothing else, would have been worth the whole price.

Well, I met the father a few days after, and wanted him to let me send for the Journal for him; but, no, he could not afford it! Mr. Editor, this was a year ago, last June. At that time he had three stocks. Now they are like the meat a man was trying to sell. When asked, if he had killed it, he said no! Did it die? No, *it just gin out!* So with my neighbor's bees—they "just gin out!"

I have never known of a swarm of bees, in my experience, to leave without clustering first; and for myself I have had no trouble in getting swarms to stay, when put in a good clean hive.

I made a slight move last summer, in the Italian bee direction; and received a queen from Mr. A. Grimm, and let me here say, that I consider him very prompt in his dealings, as I got a return in one week after sending. Well, I got my queen introduced all right, but in looking through my stocks three months after, I found my treasure dead on the alighting board, and the hive left queenless. So I am set another year behind in Italianizing, but intend to try again next year, if nothing happens to prevent.

My bees are wintering nicely so far, thanks to Mr. Gallup. May his shadow never grow less. How I should like to take a few lessons under his guidance.

Hoping I shall be able to increase your subscription list before long, I remain, yours, &c.

GEO. T. BURGESS.

Lucknow, Canada, Dec. 18, 1871.

[For the American Bee Journal.]

Introducing a queen into a hive that has sent off a prime swarm.

If I remember right it is stated somewhere in the Journal that a fertile queen bee can be successfully introduced into a hive that has given a prime swarm, if this be done at the moment when swarming has ceased. I tried repeatedly to introduce fertile queens three days after swarming, keeping them caged the previous three days; and though I destroyed every queen cell before liberating my queens, I lost them in every instance where I had not removed the parent stock to a new location. Only when I waited till the seventh day after swarming, destroyed all the queen cells, and the queens already hatched, (if any) likewise, and then delayed six hours longer, could I succeed invariably by simply liberating the queen at the entrance of the hive.

Last summer I tried the method claimed to be uniformly successful, and have to report that I failed four times out of six. Only two queens were accepted, and the two stocks that accepted them, proved to be as productive in surplus honey as other strong stocks that had given no swarms; while the four that killed the offered queens and gave no second swarm, gave me no box-honey at all. I cannot estimate the value of a fertile queen thus successfully introduced in the first half of the month of June, at less than seven or eight dollars. But if we should always lose four out of six queens, it would in the end be a poor speculation to introduce fertile queens into hives that have given prime natural swarms. I suspect that others had better success, or they would have reported their failures. I report my experience only to caution others not to risk valuable queens in this manner as I did. I am well satisfied that an apiarian will much improve many of his mother-stocks, by selecting and inserting a sealed queen cell from a hive that has given a prime swarm a week previous and has piping queens. The stocks so treated will not swarm a second time, and have a fertile queen almost as soon as one can be successfully introduced.

ADAM GRIMM.

Jefferson Wis., Dec. 27, 1871.

[For the American Bee Journal.]

Chloroform and "Blunders."

MR. EDITOR:—Have any of the subscribers to the Journal ever used chloroform in handling bees? If so, how does it work? I do not believe it will work well; but one of my neighbors says he will try it next season, if he loses a few swarms by it.*

In my communication in the January Journal, you give the date of my transferring two stocks of bees to movable comb hives as August 21st. It was done August 29th. You also make it read "three hives full," whereas it should be "their hives full." †

Now I want to take up brother Gallup, for he has infringed on my hive, and goes galloping over the description of it as if he was the sole inventor. Now I have been thinking of this kind of hive for the last six months, and in fact my hives for the last year were of the same size, except in length. I only had ten frames instead of twenty-four and thirty-two. Now I have one made with twenty-six frames, and am going to see if I can get fifty (50) gallons of honey from it next season. At all events brother Gallup did not get the dollar from me for a description of my own hive.

I want some Italians next season and shall probably call on brother Grimm, or some other reliable queen raiser for a supply.

With many good wishes for the success of the Journal, I remain, as ever, truly yours,

J. W. CRAMER.

Oneida, Ills.

* A Number of our subscribers employed chloroform successfully and satisfactorily last summer, using one-tenth or one-eighth of an ounce for a dose.—[ED.

† These were typographical errors, which despite of every care, are as apt to occur in our own articles as in those of our correspondents. They are annoying and vexatious, especially when *queen* cells are converted into *green* cells, and *frames* into *franes*. If the *cash* were always forthcoming when the latter metamorphosis takes place, we should incline to cry *eureka* and think the *philosopher's stone* was found at last, for that would indeed be a substantial transformation.—[ED.

AMERICAN BEE JOURNAL.

EDITED AND PUBLISHED BY SAMUEL WAGNER, WASHINGTON, D. C.

AT TWO DOLLARS PER ANNUM, PAYABLE IN ADVANCE.

VOL. VII. **APRIL, 1872.** No. 10.

[For Wagner's American Bee Journal.]

We promised to give our readers, with suitable comments, the attack on Mr. Wagner by Mr. King's associate editor. We shall preface this attack, with an editorial from King's February number, to show that his paper endorsed it.

"Those who have read Mr. Wagner's 'slang' notes about the person who has brought the *facts* to public notice, concerning the invention of movable frames, will discover the fallacy of Mr. Wagner's statements, by remitting 25 cents to Messrs. Moon & Mitchell, for copies of the *National Bee Journal.* For replies by Mrs. E. S. Tupper, send 25 cents to her, Des Moines, Iowa, for copies of the *Iowa Homestead.*"

[For the National Bee Journal.

Sneaking out a Patent.

MESSRS. EDITORS:—To most of the scurrilous attacks and mean insinuations of Samuel Wagner against Mr. King, the latter has not deigned to reply, and to our knowledge he has more than once refused the columns of his journal for these personal affairs, even though written by others in his own defence. We shall not call in question the wisdom of his course, for when contrasted with Mr. Wagner's, even the latter's own friends cannot but admit that it is the wiser of the two. It is generally true that slanderous reports will not injure, unless by combating them we give them standing and character. But there are occasions when "forbearance ceases to be a virtue;" when if a man does not raise his voice in defence of his motives, or character, he will have the one impugned and the other injured by the falsehoods of envy and malice. From our position as Associate Editor of the *Bee Keepers' Journal*, we have had every opportunity of becoming familiar with all the facts of the present controversy, and shall therefore speak advisedly in answering a few of Mr. W.'s "foot-notes" and editorial vents of impotent rage.

We are informed that Mr. W. is an "old man," and this fact is frequently brought forward to excuse his conduct. Were we to judge of his age by these personal attacks on Mr. King, in defence of his hive interests, we should unhesitatingly pronounce him a *very young man*, for they exhibit only the rashness of youth, and not the experience and sober thought of a mature mind. The only way we can reconcile his injudicious course, his "storms of blind fury," with the reports of his great age, is on the supposition that he is now in his *second childhood.*

Mr. W. warns the writer of an article in his last journal, to be on his guard lest Mr. King, whom he courteously denominates "The Great American Humbug inventor," should "sneak out a patent," on something mentioned in his article. We once heard of a man who insanely supposed he was monarch of the whole earth, and who raved incessantly because men did not come and reverence him. Mr. W. is almost *there*, for he arrogantly assumes that all matters pertaining to apiculture must be referred to him, and if a man obtains a patent on any device to advance bee-culture, without his knowledge and consent, he "sneaks it out." This is just what Mr. W. meant by this expression, and we propose to substantiate it, and to show who "sneaks" and how it is done.

By the rules of the Patent Office, no officer, clerk or employee is permitted to give any information concerning the application for a patent, or the proceedings during its examination, except to the inventor or his authorized agent. Yet it has been long reported that Mr. Wagner was intimate with Patent Office officials, and being better posted on bee matters than they, was generally consulted when applications were made for patents on bee hives, and *owning territory in the L. L. patent*, he had always done what he could "thus sneakingly," to prevent the issue of such patents. These reports were recently confirmed by a prominent member of the Cleveland Association, from the South, and there is no doubt of their truth. When Mr. Quinby made application for a patent, he thought of going to Washington himself, but his agent thought there would be no difficulty in securing it, and he did not go. The consequence was his application was rejected "because the device was covered by Mr. Wagner's patent." How was it discovered that it conflicted with Mr. W.'s patent? Wagner's friend, Mr. Bickford, admitted that he (Mr. W.) "happened" to be in the Patent Office when the application was being examined, and was invited into the room to give his opinion on the case.

Thus Mr. Q.'s patent was not "sneaked out," because the "Oracle" had been consulted, but if he had gone there himself and pushed it through, it would have been "sneaked out." These are *facts*. We expect Mr. W. will deny them, for he has done *worse than that*. We don't say that he owns territory in the L. L. patent now. Oh, no!

Last spring, soon after the broadside of Wagner, Otis & Co. (with pigtail illustrations), Mr. King made application for a patent. He soon heard that it was rejected, but believing there was no good reason for rejection, he went down and argued it through, and for Mr. W.'s benefit announced it in the *Journal* as "Patent No. 4." We verily believe that Mr. W. was the cause of the first rejection, and believing that he had given it a *quietus*, had retired to his den, and the first knowledge he had of its successful issue, was when he read it in the *Journal* This explains how it was "sneaked out," and also accounts for the "howl of insane fury" which the great "Oracle" utters in his impotent wrath.

Now, lest future results should seem to confirm the opinion of Mr. W.'s admirers that he is really a prophet, let us explain how he came by his knowledge. Soon after Mr. King's return from Europe, he mentioned, editorially, that his observations during his travels would enable him to perfect certain improvements which would remunerate him for his expense and time, and also be of great benefit to the cause of apiculture in America. While on a tour through the West he incidentally mentioned this to several prominent beekeepers, and among others to the writer of the article to which Mr. W. appends the filthy note from which we learn for the first time that it is possible "to sneak out a patent."

But Mr. W. attempts to avoid the force of the testimony of Mr. Moon and others by asserting that there was "no living principle in any of their devices, and that all were failures." How much such words as "ratiocination," "in terrorem," and comparing all bee hive inventors, except Mr. Langstroth, to skunks—how much these add to the force of his arguments we leave the reader to decide. If there was no "living principle" in their hives, there is none in Langstroth's, for the same principle is involved in both. How could they be failures (through imperfections), and Mr. L.'s a success (because perfect) when the frames of the latter are only a copy of theirs, and when his hive presented *not one additional new feature*, except the moth blocks at the entrance. It is true Mr. Moon did not use the triangular guide, but L. & Co. do not *now* claim that as their invention.

Is there nothing significant in the fact that Harbison, Metcalf, Langstroth and others began to sell hives extensively about the same time? About the same time, too, that reapers, sewing machines and other improvements were rapidly introduced? The times were ripe for these things, and their introduction was a natural result. That one man should, at that opportune moment, seize on the results of other men's experiments and years of deep thought, and by a combination of favorable circumstances, secure the protection of a patent on a set of combinations, is no proof that he invented a single feature of the device. "Success" is not *always* the infallible evidence of success.

Mr. W. well knows why the testimony of Berlepsch cannot be used as *legal* testimony. But the fact that our laws provide that the prior use of an invention in a foreign country shall not invalidate a patent here, unless such invention shall have been patented, or shall have been described in a printed publication, does not affect the *truths* stated in the Baron's oath. In that oath he declares that he used the identical Langstroth frame (more properly the Moon frame) *six years* in advance of Mr. L., and that there are many living witnesses who will attest the truth of his statements. Mr. W. exhibits astonishing zeal in trying to make the American public believe that Langstroth is "the original inventor," and in the face of the testimony of such a man as Berlepsch, asserts that up to December, 1851, "and for many months thereafter, there were no practical frames in use in Germany." We are glad he is drawing nearer the truth, though slowly and cautiously. Ten years ago he said Berlepsch "adopted" the frames in 1855; last spring he dropped off two years, and put it 1853; *now* he says "up to 1851," and the indefinite for "many months thereafter." We hope he has not reached the "minimum," but will yet "drop another cat." Mr. L. himself comes a little nearer the truth, for he says, "after my application had been favorably decided upon, Berlepsch invented frames of a somewhat similar character." But Mr. W. "does not wish to influence public opinion" by publishing the Berlepsch oath. Oh, no! That would be decidedly wrong! Investigation and National Associations were all right last spring; but they are going too far to suit Mr. W.'s ideas of what is right and proper. Credit is given to whom credit is due. Public opinion is changing, and National Associations give expression to public opinion.

But, again, he did not know how much garbling the Berlepsch oath had undergone in Mr. King's hands. He did know that he had "shamefully garbled Mr. L.'s letters to suit his own base purposes."

This is not an "insinuated untruth," but a *positive falsehood*. There is but *one* letter which Mr. L. ever complained of, but Mr. W. says "letters." Let him produce them. The letter in question is now in this office, and that and the Original Berlepsch Oath can be examined by any one wishing to test the value of Mr. W.'s assertions. An extract from the letter was published in the August number of the *Bee Keepers' Journal* for 1870. There were three paragraphs in the letter. The first related to the death of his son, the second concerning persons whom Mr. L claimed to infringe on his patent, and the third related to Mr. K.'s proposition to terminate an arrangement which had existed between them. We reproduce the first paragraph here, italicising the words which were not published in the extract:

OXFORD, O., *June* 27, 1870.

MESSRS. H. A. KING & CO.,

GENTLEMEN:—My son (J. T. L.) died in Massachusetts, on the 14th, just eight days after leaving home. His health had been failing for more than a year, but he continued to do business until the day he left. He had Catarrhal Consumption as well as heart disease. He was fully aware of his critical condition, and entirely resigned to the divine will. *His wife found your letter of May 30th, in his pocket, and says that if he had not been so very feeble he would have called on you when passing through New York.*

Mr. Quinby was in our office a few days since, and the original letter was shown to him, and compared with the extract given above. One error was found. Mr. L. said "catarrhal consumption as well as heart disease." The extract read, "as well as the heart disease." The word "the" was inserted before the word "heart." What base purpose was served in publishing this extract? Mr. King thought it an act of courtesy to Mr. L. to announce the death of his son, and the reception of such a letter by *any* editor, under similar circumstances, would be accepted as a request on the part of the writer to so announce it. The publication of the business part of the letter would have been sadly inappropriate in that connection, and would have caused greater complaint from the "crew" than even what was done.

This, then, is the "garbling" for a "base purpose" of which Mr. King is publicly accused by the "Oracle" at Washington.

Such accusations show to what extremes the jealous rage of the "old man" has driven him in defence of a sinking cause. All of Mr. King's acts are attributed to "base motives," and are regarded as "poisoned arrows, designed to kill." Even Mr. King's efforts in behalf of Mr. Langstroth, through his journal, and at Cincinnati, were rejected with scorn, and Mr. King accused of "publishing Mr. L. as an object of charity." "What were virtues in other men, are in him vices," for he did not publish his appeal in the *Journal* until Mr. Wagner and Mr. Bickford had made an abortive effort; and at Cincinnati he did not inaugurate the movement till L. L. had been consulted, and to his assent, had added the story of his misfortunes.

More anon,
M. E. WILLIAMS.

Much of Mr. Williams' article needs only a brief reply. To those only tolerably well acquainted with Mr. King's course in this bee-hive controversy, the correct application of Mr. Williams' introductory sentiments will intuitively suggest itself.

The charge that Mr. Wagner having a pecuniary interest in the Langstroth patent,* interfered with the issue of other patents, involves the integrity of officials in the office. We give, therefore, the following statement of Prof. J. Brainard, Chief Examiner, in the class to which bee-hives are attached.

"When I rejected Mr. Quinby's application, I was not personally acquainted with the laté Samuel Wagner, and first became aware of his invention, by finding the drawings of his patent for artificial combs, in the portfolio of the office.

"Mr. Wagner never solicited or received any information on the subject of pending applications for patents, so far as I am aware, from this office. He never in any way volunteered to give information, but only gave it when specially requested.

"I deeply regret that his death puts it out of the power of the office, to avail itself in the legitimate discharge of its duties, of his extensive knowledge of the history of bee-culture, and the state of the art in foreign countries. J. BRAINARD."

The following letter of Mr. King, in the March 15th number of the "Indianapolis Journal," which has just come to hand, ought to be published in this connection.

[For the National Bee Journal.]

CORRECTION.

MESSRS. EDITORS:—Having been traveling in the west for a month past, I have not seen the late numbers of your valuable journal; but since my arrival here I learn that one of your correspondents* has given publicity to a report that reflects unfavorably upon the decisions of the examiner in charge of agricultural implements. I first heard the story about a year ago, but the Commissioner of Patents† was the party named, with whom I was not personally acquainted; but I have known Professor Brainard, the examiner, for many years, and I assure your readers, that the report, so far as it reflects on his character, must be false. He was professor of chemistry in the Medical College of Cleveland, Ohio, and when he received the appointment as examiner here, he was placed at the head of one of the most important departments in the Patent Office, namely, Agricultural Implements and Products of Agriculture.

It is a common remark of attorneys here, that Prof. Brainard is one of the most thorough, critical and conscientious men in the office. They say his initials are on most of the drawings in his department, and a case is sure to be lost if there is any evidence of priority of invention in any one of the thousands of applications for patents on agricultural implements in his department. It is possible that some seek to obtain patents with money where their case lacks merit, but none acquainted with Prof. Brainard could believe for a moment, that he could be tempted from the path of duty. He authorizes me to say that while it is true that he has consulted Mr. Wagner in reference to his knowledge of foreign inventions, he has never communicated to him regarding pending applications, nor received from him gratuitous advice relating to official business.

H. A. KING.

Washington, D. C., Feb. 26, 1872.

Mr. King it will be seen, sustains Prof. Brainard against his own associate editor.

"That broadside of Wagner, Otis, & Co., with pigtail illustrations!" Alas! Alas!

Hæret lateri lethalis arundo.

Fixed in the side, the deadly dart remains.

Friend Beadle, how could you have the heart to do it? Never again, we entreat you, hang out from your office windows such ensnaring

---

* Mr. Wagner owned four counties in this patent.

* Does Mr. King mean to say that his own associate editor, the correspondent referred to, wrote without his advice, consent, or even knowledge?

† Does Mr. King wish to make the late Commissioner of Patents, Col. S. S. Fisher, suspected of being a party to *another* conspiracy?

"coats," that childlike innocents are beguiled into purchasing them as "perfect fits," and cannot be prevented from parading about in them, to the vast amusement of an unfeeling public!

Does *Mr. King* desire us to ventilate further, his attempt to make the public believe that he had a patent on a *then unpatented* machine?

We believe that the decision of the United States Courts on the invention of practical movable comb frames, will be more satisfactory to bee-keepers than volumes of controversy between interested parties.

There can be nothing *so* significant in Mr. Williams' assumed fact, that other parties began to sell movable comb hives about the same time with ourselves, as his ignorance of the true history of such hives in this country. Our hives were largely made, used and sold by us, in the spring and summer of 1852, in our native city of Philadelphia. The patent was issued October 5th, 1852, and the first edition of our work was published in May, 1853. Thousands of these hives were widely disseminated years before Harbison, Metcalf, or any one else, took out a patent on hives using movable frames. From 1852 to 1857, the invention, when not denounced by patent hive-mongers as an impractical conceit, was represented as fit only for *amateur* uses; *and only after its success was established*, were other patents (infringements if not duly licensed under that of Langstroth), brought before the public. The second patent on hives using movable frames was granted March 31st, 1857, to Albert Kelsey; the third to Samuel Kelley, Dec. 8th, 1857; the fourth to Kimball P. Kidder, April 13th, 1858; and the fifth to Ebenezer W. Phelps, November 9th, 1858; while Mr. Harbison's did not issue until January 4th, 1858; and Mr. Metcalf's not until July 30th, 1861.

Need we say much more about the *Berlepsch* declaration?* We give entire credit to the Baron's statement that he made frames before us, and not to Mr. Williams' that they were identical with ours, for the Baron himself nearly a year after the date of our application for a patent, discredited his own invention as "*a mere juggle.*"

In the supplement to his December number, the Baron's declaration, with King's preface is published with a great display of head lines.

IMPORTANT TESTIMONY!

THE OATH OF AUGUST BARON VON BERLEPSCH—EXPLANATION.

"In the April number of the *American Bee Journal*, 1871, Mr. Wagner offered Mr. King space in his Journal for three months to come to answer the attack made on him in that number. At first Mr. King did not intend to reply at all, but subsequent to his return from Europe, he forwarded the following document to Mr Wagner, and Mr. Wagner *refused to publish it*, shielding himself behind the poor defence, "that his offer did not remain open indefinitely." The most obtuse observer, after reading the testimony contained in that document, will discover the *real* reason of his declining it. At the request of several eminent apiarians, some of whom have hitherto been advocates of Mr. Langstroth's claims, and in view of the high character of the testimony, we present it to the apiarians of America."

Then follows the declaration. In the January number of the Journal, Mr. Wagner gave some of his reasons for refusing to publish this declaration. Does Mr. King think that any one of ordinary intelligence can see in the *Baron's declaration*, a REPLY to Mr. Wagner's masterly exposure of *worthlessness of the King patents*?

Mr. King makes an evident parade of what he calls "the oath of the Baron," and we are told that the original oath can be examined at his office. We can find no proof that the Baron made *any* oath—he merely asserts before the notary public, "I have only made such statements as I can at any time attest to under oath."*

There is something mysterious about this *second* declaration procured by Mr. King to supply his loss of the first, when the *first* is declared to have been "recorded in the Notary's books, number 1643." Why subject an invalid to the trouble, and himself to the expense of a second declaration, instead of procuring a *certified copy* of the *first?* What a waste was there of time and money upon a document *now* admitted to have no *legal* value in the suit, and which, while in many ways damaging to Mr. King, shows only that the Baron used frames (but did not describe them) prior to ours. Was it merely to prove this, that Mr. King volunteered his services as the jealous defender of the Baron's fame, and scattered his declaration thick as Vallambrosa's leaves? And yet, after all this superserviceable zeal, he makes the Baron August Von Berlepsch play only "second fiddle" to Major Augustus Munn, Ambrose F. Moon, and perhaps to some other persons as *yet* "the great unknown."

When he first shook his magic kaleidoscope of "prior inventors," the face of Major Munn loomed large across the ocean—soon after the Baron's star was revealed, shining however, with a more subdued light—until in a truly auspicious hour, a glorious Moon rises, full-orbed, in our Western horizon, to outshine the first, and antedate the last!

Neither the Baron nor the Major will, I trust, take any serious offence at this good-natured raillery.

When our King crossed the ocean, he probably appeared before each of them in turn, disguised as another "*Queen of Sheba,*" coming from far-distant lands to pay homage to their wisdom. He is a master hand at such enticements.

Would that after a hearty laugh we could stop here. No one who knows us personally, or from our writings for the last twenty years, will think we find pleasure in exposing the faults of others.

* We will publish this declaration in full, if any attempt is made to prove that we have suppressed any essential part of it.

* When our readers learn that the Baron is suffering from partial paralysis, and that he could only *dictate* the declaration, they can readily account for its inaccuracies, nor will the absence of a formal oath induce them to believe that a man of the Baron's high standing purposely misstated facts.

We can say as we did in that April number a year ago, not, we trust, in any spirit of boasting, but as what ought to be known to all who read these personals:

"We can confidently appeal to the bee-keeping public who have known our course, to hear us out in the assertion, that we have never personally assailed any one, but have often under circumstances of great provocation, refrained from using very damaging facts against those who have assailed us."

We could no longer pursue the same course, and now, in vindication of our departed friend, we must show some of the "treacheries" alluded to in the March number.

To obtain a license under our patent—after he had been notified by my son (the late J. T. L.), and myself, that he was infringing on it—Mr. King represented his business as so extensive, that the one-twelfth, which he proposed to pay, of the net proceeds of his sales of hives and rights in our territory, would probably exceed *all* our own. In THREE YEARS we received as our share of his sales, *less than the price paid for some single counties in the Langstroth patent!* and found besides. that we had lost by hampering ourselves in making sales* many times more than the license fees. Some time after we licensed Mr. King to use the notches in his frames, he substituted *mortices* for them, patented these in *combination* with some other devices, and claimed that he could use them without our license.†

By the terms of our license Mr. King was expressly *guaranteed from all our claims for his heavy infringements under his first patent.* Now even if the decisions of the court had sustained his substitution of a mortice for a notch, could Mr. King after all the benefits he derived *at our expense* from the license, have honorably refused to pay the petty fees? After many intimations however, that he no longer felt bound by his license, he at last writes us the following letter:

New York, *May* 30, 1870.

Messrs. L. L. Langstroth & Son,

Dear Sirs:—An apology is due you for delay in replying to your last, which was received during my absence west, but my brother informed me that he replied briefly about our press of business. I still entertain the high esteem for the senior member of your firm, and hope to receive the photograph‡ I once before requested, as I hope to have the privilege of showing in our Journal that we render honor to whom honor is due. In reference to the report, I finally got time or rather took time (a day to look over the books, as we have not trusted to a clerk to record all on a page as in other matters, lest an oversight might occur that you might think intentional), for I am so jealous of my honor, that I have in opposition to my brother, reported for two years under an arrangement that ceased when we ceased to make and sell hives with notches in the top bars, as is proved by several letters of yours which have been forwarded to us without solicitation (only assent).

But he has now met me with a more powerful argument. Heretofore I could say that no change from a notch to mortice was contemplated when the arrangement was made, but now while admitting my answer he says it was understood that others would not be permitted to peaceably infringe upon your patent, but you have permitted them, without molestation, to appoint agents to sell infringing hives in your territory, and this fact discharges us honorably, while the fact that we have for years ceased to use the notch, legally discharges us from the arrangement. I cannot answer this argument and have therefore taken the position kindly but firmly, to cease sending you money for what we do not use. I presume you have too much wisdom and honor to threaten and abuse in a pretended rage, and as I have only now informed you of this position, upon receiving your reply and closing up the arrangement, kindly we will remit for the report made out a few days since to that date.

Yours as ever very truly,
H. A. King & Co.

This letter insulting us by presuming that we had too much wisdom and honor to threaten and abuse in *a pretended rage*, my son—who until the very close of his life sought to stand between me and business troubles—showed only to his mother, and after expressing his views of the writer, said he would try to call upon him in his journey East. My reply to this letter explains why he did not. A detailed account of all the relations between Mr. King and myself would show that it was written under a deep sense of *accumulated wrongs*—it is enough to say that while this last insult to me and my departed son was quivering in my heart, I duly complied with all the forms of courteous address, in what was intended as a last appeal to any sense of honor or justice in Mr. King's breast. I give the letter:

Oxford, Ohio, *June* 27, 1870.

Messrs. H. A. King & Co.,

Gentlemen:—My son (J. T. L.) died in Massachusetts on the 14th,—just eight days after leaving home. His health has been failing for more than a year, but he continued to do business until the day he left. He had catarrhal consumption as well as heart disease. He was fully aware of his condition, and entirely resigned to the divine will. His wife found your letter of May 30th in his pocket, and says if he had not been so very feeble, he would have called on you when passing through New York.

In answer to one remark in your letter I would say, that neither my son nor myself have had the means or health, to prosecute the numerous parties infringing on our rights, and have been compelled to suffer wrong, without any power of redress.

I am too feeble to discuss the question whether under all the circumstances, you ought to account to us any further. At the time of making the arrangement with us, you were aware that your first patent, in which you used the separated frames and shallow chamber, was an infringement on our rights. Bearing this in mind, do what you think to be honorable

* Parties with whom we were negotiating, when they learned that King was licensed in our territory, declined to purchase, or did it only at reduced prices.

† For the facts more in detail, see p. 219 of the A. B. J., April, 1871. We have the best legal authority for the assertion that both slot and mortice are infringements of our patent. *Neither are original with King*—the first having been used in Kelly's patent, December 8th, 1857, and the other, in W. A. Flanders', May 9th, 1867—while King's bears date september 8th, 1868!

‡ No photograph or biography was ever furnished by us. Our friend, Rev. E. Vanslyke, without our knowledge, supplied both.

and just, and even if I differ in opinion with you, I have neither the health nor disposition to contest the matter.

Yours truly,
L. L. LANGSTROTH.

It was to this letter that Mr. Wagner referred in the January No. of his Journal, when he said —"We do know that Mr. King shamefully garbled Mr. Langstroth's letters to suit his own base purpose." Mr. Williams says this assertion about garbled letters is a "positive falsehood," and that "there is but one letter of which Mr. L. ever complained," but Mr. Wagner says "letters." "Let him produce them." Will Mr. Wagner's charge fall to the ground, if Mr. King has garbled only *one* letter? I hoped for many reasons, never to have been compelled to publish that letter, every thought of which only makes a parent's heart bleed afresh—but Mr. King's authorized champion demanded it, and to vindicate Mr. Wagner, I have produced it. On my own responsibility, therefore, I re-affirm the charge, that the letter was "shamefully garbled"—and if I did not suppose that Mr. Williams is very imperfectly acquainted with the wrongs that I have suffered from Mr. King, I would say that the partial extract and comment, designed to show that Mr. King fairly reproduced it, is almost as bad as the original offence. Let it be understood, that my letter was addressed to a man who had appropriated both engravings and ideas from my work on bee-keeping, giving me no credit for the one, and worse than none for the other—who grossly infringed for years on all the essential and patented features of my hives—who after he had secured impunity by the terms of our license, advertised himself not as *licensed* to use *one* feature in our patent, but as having *out of his desire to do justice, purchased a general interest in the Langstroth patent!* Let it be remembered, I say, that this letter was addressed to *such a man*—to whom I had never written a line except on strict matters of business, and in whose paper we had never been willing to insert even a business advertisement—and will it not be judged a *base* act that (omitting the allusion to the sad circumstances under which his letter came to me), he should divide mine into two, and publish the first part of it, as a special letter addressed to himself? How could his readers infer otherwise, than that I must be on intimate terms of friendship with Mr. King, when in my hour of bitterest anguish, mourning over the death of my only son, I unbosomed myself to him! His comments also on this letter make it impossible for any one to think otherwise.

* * * "We were personally acquainted with the deceased, who was the only son of Rev. L. L. Langstroth, and associated with him in business. * * * He was an affectionate son, and we deeply sympathise with his parents and friends in their bereavement, but especially with his noble father, who has been in feeble health for years, and being highly endowed by nature, education and association with the finer feelings, this arrow of affliction will pierce his heart with such anguish as but few can understand."

Could I keep out of my memory as my eye first glanced over these kind *words*, that coarse suggestion that "we had too much wisdom and honor to threaten in a pretended rage?"

I earnestly desire to do no injustice whatever to Mr. King, in the views I cannot but take of this matter. I know that some of my best friends, when they saw this letter to Mr. King in print—knowing our previous relations, felt that disease must have lamentably weakened my judgment or I never could have written it.

Worse yet remains. Let us suppose that Mr. King's sense of honor would not lead him to think that it was anything more than a shrewd business act to publish *part* of my letter as a special letter to himself. What view must we take of the use made of the rest of it? *It becomes a second letter*—and as the first was one of *friendship*, this becomes one of *business*. The following from the August, 1870, number of Mr. King's paper will show how he gave it to his readers:

"We wrote Mr. Langstroth, in May last, offering a small consideration to close up our arrangement, assigning reasons why we were now neither legally nor morally holden, and he replied as follows: "I am too feeble to discuss the question whether under all the circumstances you ought to account to us any further. * * * Do what you think to be honorable and just, and even if I differ in opinion with you, I have neither the health nor the disposition to contest the matter. Yours truly,
L. L. LANGSTROTH.

We made remittance and thus closed an arrangement, the existence of which unprincipled men have used to make the people believe it applied to the use of movable frames, and that our hives could only be used in territory owned by Mr. Langstroth when the arrangement was made."

By comparing the original and Mr. King's version, the reader will be able to see *how* the letter was garbled. He first omits the sorrowful reason given for not prosecuting infringers. Did he wish to conceal from all other patentees of movable comb-hives, whose champion he now claims to be, *that he had asked us to prosecute them?**

He next *suppresses entirely a condition essential to the proper understanding of all that follows*, and uses just enough as a second letter, to suit his selfish purposes! Common decency ought to have made Mr. King ashamed to publish this letter, even if instead of *amputating* and *mutilating* it, he had given it just as it was written—but my allusions to poverty and sickness, seemed to suggest to him only how he might turn them to the best money profit.

*"Movable comb-hives, whether they contain patented features or not, when made without the closed top slot (or morticed frame), to avoid our patents, are sure to infringe on Mr. L's extended patent, and those who use such hives are required to pay dearly for another right, as his patent covers frames having a shallow chamber, or space between the frames and honey board, or even between the top bars, and our patent covers the other kind, where the top bars form a honey board with slots to admit the bees to the honey-boxes." (King's Bee-keeper's Text Book, p. 140,—ed. 1869). And yet Alfred Kelly used just this arrangement on his patent of 1857!

"Come on my confederates!" for this is the interpretation which I cannot help putting upon that "shameful garbling"—" now is the best time to trample on this troublesome old man—for he is already down, and may never rise again! Dejected, sick, poor! What more to our purpose could he admit! and what rights has he now left which we who are strong are bound to respect!"

Am I carried away by some strong delusion? Has "the prejudiced old man" forgotten what an honorable man he thus assails? He! garble my letter? He! suppress one "jot or one tittle" essential to a fair understanding of the whole matter? He! who is "so jealous of his honor," that he must needs vindicate it from the suspicion of an interpolated "the!" Is not this indeed "tithing the mint, and the anise and the cummin—while all the weightier matters of the law are omitted?" This infatuated man! whom I would fain have spared such an exposure, if justice to the dead had permitted—how much longer will he imagine that—ostrich fashion—he can hide his scheming head under the shifting sands of misrepresentations, and yet not reveal the monstrous proportions of his shameful acts?

Fellow bee-keepers—honorable men and women, knowing as you now do, some of the facts about that letter, can you blame Mr. Wagner for asserting that for a *base purpose* it was *shamefully garbled?* At first I was sorry that he alluded to it, but now I feel rather that the hand of Providence guided his pen.

Just one year ago, I was sitting at the same table with my friend, as he was writing that article, which unfolded "the false assertions and baseless claims" of Mr. H. A. King's patents, in language almost as dispassionate as the summing up of an impartial judge—and which he concluded with the following offer:

"And now to avert all misconception or misconstruction, we here offer the columns of the American Bee Journal to the extent of two pages monthly, for three months to come, to Mr. King for anything he may have to say in refutation of our remarks, or in explanation, exculpation or vindication of his course as a patentee, inventor or dealer in bee hives, or articles in connection therewith. And should Mr. King fail to avail himself of this offer, we extend it to any purchaser of territorial rights under him who may feel disposed to undertake the task."

Neither Mr. King nor any one in his interest ever dared to accept this offer—but for months he assailed the motives of Mr. Wagner and myself, neither of us making any reply—until at last in the December No., emboldened perhaps by our silence, he sought to make us suspected of crimes, which if proved, would have consigned us both to infamy, and myself to the walls of the Penitentiary. Had not the time fully come for us to vindicate our characters?

But for Samuel Wagner, and his American Bee Journal, Homer A. King imagines he might have had the same control over the bee interests of this country, that the *Tammany Ring* wielded over the finances of the city of New York—therefore, he misrepresented and slandered the man whose wide and accurate knowledge, incorruptible honesty, and manly courage have so completely baffled his schemes by revealing their author in his true character to a discerning public.

The generous bee-keepers of this great continent will long delight to honor the name of Samuel Wagner, as that of the friend to whose protracted, wise and unselfish labors, they owe a debt of respect, love and gratitude, which they can never hope sufficiently to repay.

Justum et tenacem propositi virum,
Non civium ardor prava jubentium,
Non vultus instantis tyranni,
Mente quatit solida * * *
Si fractus illabatur orbis,
Impavidum ferient ruinae.

Immutable in purpose, the Just Man must learn,
The wrong demands of heated citizens to spurn,
And ne'er from urging Tyrant's frown, dismayed to turn.—
Should earth to fragments dashed, against This Man be hurl'd,
Unfearing, he'll be buried 'neath a ruined world.

L. L. LANGSTROTH.

Washington, D. C., March 1872.

[For Wagner's American Bee Journal.]

Sworn and Unsworn.

"Destroy his fits and sophistries? In vain!
The creature's at his dirty work again."
POPE.

For the amusement, if not the instruction of the readers of the Journal, we give the last King circular which has come to hand.

TO THE BEEKEEPERS OF AMERICA.

On the evening of February first, about six o'clock, Mr. R. C. Otis called at the hotel where I was stopping, and asked me whether I was engaged, stating that he wanted to talk with me. I replied that I had an engagement at half-past six, but could spend half an hour with him, and invited him to be seated. He said we had better go to his room in the hotel where he was stopping. I consented and went with him, and while on the way, and after we reached his room, he spoke of his failing health, of his poverty, and of the poor chance he had for success in our conflict, stating that I had nine chances out of ten for success. Consequently he had looked over the whole matter and concluded to see me and have a talk. He then discoursed eloquently upon my success in life, and present position and prospects, comparing my past success to that of Orange Judd, and said that if I would unite with Mr. Langstroth and obtain the reissue of his patent, we could achieve a vast fortune, or words to that effect. I told him that there was a time when I could have accepted such a proposition honorably, when I was ignorant of the facts lately brought to light by my trip to Europe and investigations in the United States; that now I could not accept such an offer honorably, and would not if a million of money were laid at my feet. He argued that I could take such a course honorably, and buy him out after judgment was rendered against me. I told him that even supposing such a possibility, I had a remedy for every bee-keeper in the United States, and could not without dishonor entertain the thought for a moment, prior to the rendering of such judgment, but that I had no fears of such a result with the evidence lately brought to light. He expatiated on the ability and integrity of my counsel, Hon. A. F. Perry, and said I could influence him, and with his influence and mine, an extension of Langstroth's patent could be got through Congress. If it was not for the influence which I could bring against it, if he had money enough he could procure such extension alone. When he found I would not consent, he tried another expedient, comparing my success to that of Jim Fisk. I told him I knew Mr. Wagner had influenced a few to entertain such views of me, but they *were* few; that I could not take the course he proposed, and could not remain to hear such comparisons; so I bid him good evening and returned to my hotel. HOMER A. KING.

State of Pennsylvania, }
Lawrence County, } *ss.:*

Personally appeared before me, a Notary Public, duly commissioned, Homer A. King, above named, and being duly affirmed according to law, says the facts set forth in the above statements are correct and true.

GEO. W. MILLER,
Notary Public.

G. W. MILLER, }
Notarial Seal. }
New Castle, Pa., Feb 3, 1872.

During the above interview, Mr. Otis stated that he had spoken to Mr. Langstroth over a year ago about getting his patent extended, but Mr. L. wanted the entire interest in it, hence nothing had been done. I infer from this, that Mr. L. has been again compelled to come to Mr. Otis' terms, and the latter is to have the lion's share in the second extension. Having failed to crush me, and then failing to secure my aid, they now propose to have an extension at all events. Mr. Otis says he erred, by the advice of Mr. L., in waiting for results against me before *pushing* others. He says the moth blocks are a good invention, and if he fails to prove my hive an infringement, it does not break the L. L. patent. I infer that he intends to secure an extension, and then push others to the wall. I do not propose to desert the beekeepers of America, nor let Otis shake off my grasp on the throat of this black mailing business. I will stand by any beekeeper whom Mr. Otis may attack (except his own stool-pigeons,) and I ask the beekeepers of America to *act*, not in furnishing me money, but to bring all their influence to bear on Congress to prevent the extension.

Mr. Otis, I believe, is on his way to Washington for this purpose. (Mr. L. is already there.) Let the beekeepers of every community get up petitions *at once*. Have every beekeeper and others interested to sign them and send them *without delay* to Hon. A. F. Perry, Washington, D. C. Men who own rights in the L. L. patent are as much interested in the matter as those who do not. H. A. KING.

SUGGESTIONS.

In your remonstrance give the following reasons, in substance; of course, adding as many more as you please. But express all as briefly as possible.

1. Langstroth's patent has been re-issued and extended, and has been a source of income to him for a period of twenty-one years.

2. Thousands have already purchased a right *twice*, compelled to do so by *first* extension; and many more have quite recently purchased; both of these classes would now be compelled to re-purchase, in the event of a second extension. This extension would be granted only for the benefit of the patentee, and as there are other hives in the market superior to his, this benefit would be obtained almost entirely at the expense of present right-owners, who have invested, and having their bees established in these hives, would have no alternative but to re-purchase, or suffer great loss by precipitately abandoning the hive.*

3. The claims of said patent are now contested in the U. S. Court. There is abundant evidence that these claims are invalid, and the patent should never have been granted.

4. Langstroth preposterously claims *all* that is valuable in a hive, and that all practical movable frames used in other hives are infringements on his. The attempts, successful and otherwise, to extort money from the beekeepers of America, who use other hives, have been numerous and persistent. These attempts and the violent threats of owners of territory in this patent, have done more to retard the progress of bee-culture among us, than all other causes combined.

These are merely *hints;* express them and all others you may add, briefly, obtain all the signers you can, and forward to your representative or senator *without delay*. *This must be done at once*, or it will be too late.

We shall make very short work of all this *stuff*. Nearly a year ago we personally informed Mr. King, that we would entertain no proposition for a compromise before the issue of the suit,—and that Mr. Otis was of the same opinion. We have never wavered in our determination. Mr. Otis neither has nor pretends to have any authority to use our name in connection with any compromise—nor do I believe that he has ever proposed one—nor does Mr. King's affidavit say that he has.

It seems that "a million laid at his feet," cannot *now* tempt a man so enlightened by foreign travel, to think of compromising with evil doers!

---

* Mr. King seems to leave upon everything that he writes "the trail of the serpent." Does he not know that all hives *legally* in use before the extensions are free from any further demands? Will those having them in use, seek to pay another patent fee for *more* of the same kind—when there are "*superior hives*" in the market? Will Congress extend a patent which the courts have pronounced illegal? But enough of this trash.

How changed from the Homer A. King of a year ago, offering to pay thousands of dollars for a license under a patent which he could prove by *foreign testimony* to be invalid !*

Now comes something which is *not* sworn to. Mr. Otis is represented as admitting substantially that if Kings' hives are pronounced by the courts to be no infringements upon the L. L. patent; that patent "still lives." "The moth blocks are a good invention," so Mr. King *infers*, that he intends to secure an extension, and push others to the wall. Strengthened by such a wise conjecture, he can see a little further into this mill-stone of nefarious plots. "Mr. L. is already in Washington, and Mr. Otis is believed to be on his way there, to secure his lion's share of the second extension."

Let us have a few *facts* to set off against so much *inference*. Neither Mr. Otis, nor any one else, will have an interest in any further extension. I have applied for no such extension, nor have I thought of doing so before the suit of Otis against King has been decided.

What a laughing stock has Mr. King made of himself in this whole matter. Scattering his blank petitions against my application—he flies to Washington on the wings of *express steam*, to oppose it in person—rushes almost breathless into the presence of the astonished officials, requesting the sight of that petition, concocted to escape the piercing vision of such a kingly eagle, and lo to his intense mortification finds a new illustration of the Huddibriastic couplet.

"That optics keen it needs I ween,
To see things that cannot be seen."

If Mr. King is confident that my claims will be so ground up in the legal hopper, that nothing but the moth blocks will come out intact, what interest has he or any one else in opposing an extension? Why should he deprive me of what may prove so harmless a plaything for my "second childhood?" Why should not the dull routine of Congressional duties be relieved by such a huge joke, as the play of Hamlet with the character of Hamlet, Ghost, Queen, *King* and company *all* left out? An application for the extension of a patent which after arrogating so much, has so "fallen from its high estate," as to hide itself under a moth trap! Perhaps if I had the true *regal audacity*, I might not think it impossible, even with such shallow pretences, to deceive the willing public, or force them however unwilling to enter my trap. Visions of patent moth traps would flit through my brain, and wounded as I am, would almost make me dance for joy at the thought of my *patent moth trap*—EXTENDED by ACT OF CONGRESS—and all the bee-keepers of the land fluttering around its pernicious light, to have their silly wings singed for my special benefit!

L. L. LANGSTROTH.

* See March No. of A. B. J., p. 196. Had Mr. King contented himself with an honorable defence of his suit, instead of attempting in every way to forestall public opinion, this and other documents so damaging to him—need never have been given to the public.

[For the American Bee Journal.]

Hives at the Indianapolis Convention.

MR. EDITOR:—On page 192 of the February number, Mr. Gallup states that there were any quantity of patent hives at the National Convention at Indianapolis, that were worthless; that is, they were not calculated for the honey extractor. If this be the true interpretation of his language, I beg leave to differ with him; for I do know that he either labors under a mistake, or I do not at all understand when a hive is adapted to the use of the melextractor. Consequently all my efforts, with those of many others, in endeavoring to get a hive adapted to answer this purpose, are simply failures.

I have visited quite a number of apiaries, and consulted many beekeepers of extensive experience, and among them I had a lengthy interview with Mr. Langstroth. In the course of our conversation he stated to me that a hive containing two sets of frames, one set situated directly above the other, and of equal size, would unquestionably procure the largest yield of honey; and my own experience, together with that of all others whom I have consulted relative to this particular subject, agree that Mr. Langstorth's position is true. They also agree that a hive thus arranged is not only adapted, but better adapted, to the honey emptying machine, than any hive containing only one set of frames. For with a two-story hive, properly arranged and prudently managed, we are not troubled with brood in the upper set of frames, as the queen is confined to the breeding chamber below—which should never be resorted to for surplus honey, except in cases where the queen is about to be crowded out of space in which to deposit eggs sufficient to keep up the population of the hive. And in such cases, it is my opinion, that we should be very cautious not to uncap all the cells in any one frame, except perhaps the outside ones; for it may be, and no doubt often is the case that we rob the breeding apartment of all the early gathered honey, which is less diluted with water, than that collected later in the season. Later gathered honey is not so well calculated to winter bees on, as that which is collected during the earlier part of the season. Then, as already intimated, we should uncap and empty out only sufficient honey to afford the queen room, for laying eggs. This may be accomplished by uncapping the cells two-thirds of the way from the bottom of the combs towards the top. The upper set of frames should be of precisely the same size of the lower ones, for the very plain reason and well established fact that bees will not always work in either boxes or shallow frames, when honey is plenty in the fields; and when, consequently, there is no good reason why they should not leave the breeding apartment and go above to store honey. Under such circumstances the apiarian is not left in a helpless condition, if both the upper and the lower frames are of equal size; for in a few moments he can lift one or two frames containing brood together with the adhering bees from below into the upper chamber. The bees will not desert their brood, but will remain by it, and immediately commence constructing comb and storing honey. Whereas, where boxes are used one or two bees will go above on an exploring expedition to day, and to-morrow a few more will go along as company; which manner of proceeding is kept up from day to day for perhaps a week. Then they sometimes go to work, provided the honey season holds out; but if it slacks up, they also slack up. But where frames are used as above described, all this delay is avoided, by at once putting our bees where circumstances demand they should be. Now, there were hives of this kind at the National Convention. The Langstroth hive and the Allen hive (known as the Home of the Honey Bee) are often made to contain both an upper and a lower set of frames of equal size. The former was there as a two-story hive; and it was intended to have it there also in the two-story form, but it was by some means or other detained on the way, and did not reach the Convention in time to be exhibited. Yet it was stated that it was often made on the two-story plan, for the purpose of adapting it to both the use of the melextractor and to procuring the largest possible amount of surplus honey. Now I will say, in conclusion, that if Mr. Langstroth's views, together with those of many other prominent parties, are at fault, I hope Mr. Gallup will correct us, by giving us the right plan of making hives. For it is the true plan we all should seek and impart. I fully agree with Mr. Gallup that small hives are not well calculated to procure a large yield of honey. Sometimes they answer well but fail much more often than the two-story hive.

G. Bohrer.

Alexandria, Ind., Feb. 1871.

[For the American Bee Journal.]

Mr. Grimm gets a Blowing Up!

Mr. Editor:—We have at different times complaints from parties who have received queens from Mr. Adam Grimm. Those parties claimed that the queens received were darker colored than they expected, and consequently were not pure. Now as we do not like to be bothered with other people's troubles, we propose to give Mr. Grimm particular fits.

On the 23d of May last, we received a line from him stating that we must prepare a stock for a queen by removing the old queen, as in about ten days he was going to send us a queen. Mr. Editor, we did not know what we had ever done to him to cause him to send us a queen; but it is said we always like to be on the contrary side, so we did not do as he ordered, for we did not like to have one of our swarms queenless so long. On the 30th of May the queen arrived. We then deprived a strong hybrid stock of all their comb and brood, and killed their queen by crushing her and threw her in among her subjects; having no comb or brood and nothing but a dead queen, they were soon as sorry a set of bees as you ever saw; we then sprinkled them with sweet water until they were completely gorged, dipped the Grimm queen in honey and tumbled her in head over heels; as the bees were gathering honey rapidly we allowed them to build comb, and they filled up their hive with a rush. We kept out cells of brood from time to time to raise queens from, and we also at different times used the extractor on the hive; yet on the 15th of July out came that confounded Grimm queen with a swarm. She was not one of your fancy light straw colored queens, but to all appearance as pure as any imported queen I ever saw. Her workers are all three-striped, not near as light colored as some of my males, and the objection that I have to them is that they are such confounded workers that there is no getting along with them. The queen breeds about as fast as five of some of those eastern bred, extra light colored ones do; so Mr. Editor, we don't like those fellows a particle for finding fault with him. If he sent them such queens as he did us, we would advise them never to send to him for queens again. But if any one should want just as good a queen as they can get direct from Italy, they might try Mr. Grimm. We bred from that queen in preference to any we had in our yard, yet I suppose if Mr. Benjamin had her he would lose considerable sleep for fear she would lay herself to death.

The queens Mr. J. W. Lindley speaks of were mostly reared from one Grimm queen (see January No.). Now Mr. Editor, don't for a moment suppose that Mr. Grimm sent that queen to us for the sake of bribing us to give him a puff; no, not by any means; but we write this article at the particular request of one of those complainants who wishes us to give Mr. Grimm *Hail Columbia* through the A. B. Journal. Now, Mr. Grimm, why in the name of common sense don't you raise some of those extra light colored and harmless bees, so as to suit such customers. You can do it easy enough by crossing some of your queens with black drones, and then breed back to the Italians, always selecting the lightest colored ones to breed from. You would soon have them as harmless as flies, and they would gather about as much honey as some flies, and they would just suit some of your customers.

P. S. If this blowing up don't suit you, do your own blowing up hereafter.

E. Gallup.

[For the American Bee Journal.]

Queens.

My limited experience indicates that artificial queens, or those sent with a few bees are poor property to make honey with. One sent by Mr. Quinby in 1867, and one send by Mr. Grimm in 1870 were both superseded at one year old, and neither of them ever led a swarm, while a queen that came in a full hive in the spring of 1868, from Mr. Quinby swarmed each year, and on the 11th of June, 1870, when three years old, led the earliest swarm ever seen in this cold island. They showed signs of swarming on the 8th of June: two rainy days intervened, and on the 11th, with a little sunshine and cool north-wind, the old queen led out a swarm, or was led out by the swarm, and was lost, the swarm re-turning, after scattering around on fences and bushes awhile; in nine days, June 20th, a daughter led out a swarm, and next day, 21st, another swarm, both between 8 and 9 A. M. I cut out queen cells to prevent a third swarm next day, as they kept on piping after I had removed the old stocks to a new place, and given one comb to second swarm on old stand. These three gave me 173 pounds of honey, while a yearling queen with one swarm gave 100 pounds extracted honey in 1870, making 73 pounds, or at least $24 in one season, in favor of the three year old queen over her own daughters one year old.

The old queen by the middle of May had 26,000, the yearling 15,000 cells of brood; both had been fed. The first week in June, 1870, the yearling had 31,000, and the three year old 39,000 cells of brood, 8,000 ahead; so much for age. The nuclei queens never gave me a swarm, or a box full of honey. I believe the one from Mr. Quinby did give me two boxes part full, in 1868, of basswood honey, while the queen that came in full hive gave me one swarm and five boxes of honey, forty pounds.

A queen raised by me in 1869 in a nucleus from a cell capped over in a swarming-hive, sent in a small box, one was introduced in my brother's apiary in Illinois. In 1870 his son wrote me, "that hive swarmed twice, besides making an unusual amount of box honey. Now the secret of long lived natural queens appeared plain, but in 1871 he wrote me that "the hive swarmed and the first swarm made 3 or 4 caps and swarmed, but I think that queen was superseded in the spring as the hive run into black bees;" so I conclude that queens which have been boxed and caged do not stand on an equal chance of long life with those never deprived of liberty. I have a queen now in her third year, introduced in 1869, in place of a daughter of a nucleus queen by taking a capped cell from a swarming hive and fastening it with a pin to a central comb, after leaving them queenless one night.

H. D. Miner.

Wash. Harbor, Wis., Jan. 23, 1872.

[From the London Journal of Horticulture.]

Are Artificial Queens inferior to Natural Queens?

Mr. J. M. Price, writing in the American "Bee Journal," asserts that he has proved, beyond doubt, that queens raised artificially are worthless in comparison with those raised naturally. From my own experience I am led to differ from him most decidedly. Out of twenty-five stocks, the largest number of colonies I ever possessed at one time, I had not a single queen that was not either artificially raised in a small nucleus box, or was not the descendant of one who was so raised, but I could never discover that my queens were deficient in breeding powers, or, barring accidents, in longevity. In fact, the fecundity of some of these was frequently a subject of surprise and remark; one queen, in particular, seems to stand pre-eminent in these respects.

Soon after the first introduction of Ligurian queens into this country, my own doubts venture having proved unpropitious, my friend, the late Mr. Woodbury, gave me a royal cell, which he cut out of a small nucleus box, from brood of his best yellow queen. This cell I inserted in a brood comb in a nucleus box, with a few adult bees. In a few days she was hatched out, and I was struck with her size and beautiful color. Soon after she had commenced breeding, I transferred them into an eight frame Langstroth box, and gave the bees another sealed brood comb. The stock was not particularly strong at the close of the autumn, and barely managed to hold its own through the winter; but by the end of April it had become so populous as to present the appearance of being ready even then to send off a swarm. A large super was given to the bees, into which they at once ascended, and were so crowded as to make it seem almost impossible for them to work at comb-building. In about three weeks from that time, considerable progress having been made in that respect, and the bees again crowding outside the entrance, a second super was slipped in between the first and the honey-board of the stock-box, which also became at once crammed with bees. Early in July, I removed the doubled super, containing 54 lbs. of honey comb.

The following year this stock also distinguished itself in spring and early summer by the possession of a teeming population, and gave a splendid glass box super of 75 lbs. weight. The next season seemed equally propitious; a super of 50 lbs. was taken, and an immense swarm thrown off, which also, the same summer, gave me a super of 26 lbs. weight. The following spring I examined the queen which had come off with this swarm, and was convinced, in my own mind, from her peculiar markings and appearance, that she was the same queen which had been raised in the nucleus box. That season this swarm became excessively crowded, and I put on a larger super than I ever used before, and it contained, when full, the large quantity of 86 lbs. of the finest possible honey-comb.

The following spring the old queen showed symptoms of having become almost worn out, and was, I believe, soon afterwards superseded by the bees, as I discovered a queen of a very different character at my next inspection of the interior. At the time of the old queen's death, she must have been at least four years and a half of age.

I mention but this one instance out of many which have come before my notice, but it is quite sufficient, in my mind, to establish the truth of the assertion, that artificial queens may and do prove equal in every respect to the best of those raised by the bees for the purposes of natural swarming.

S. Bevan Fox.

[For the American Bee Journal.]

Side-Box Hive Wanted.

MR. EDITOR:—The summer of 1871 was very poor in this section for honey; the months of June and July were too wet; in fact we could not get more than one or two good days out of a week to gather honey. The blossoms do not seem to yield much honey after a day or two of rain; either the water washes the honey all out of the blossoms, or the cool nights after a rain are not favorable for the secretion of honey; at all events the bees were very cross for a day or two after a storm, then they would seem to enjoy it better for a day; then another rain, and so it kept repeating during the months of June and July.

The consequence of this was, the bees were confined to the hive so much and had so little comb occupied with honey, that they produced an immense amount of brood and bees; so that we were obliged to increase more than we intended and more than we should have done had the honey yielded more steadily.

August and September were so dry and cool that bees gathered no surplus from the buckwheat blossoms, although stocks that were nearly destitute gathered enough to winter on in the cellar. Considering the season we were satisfied with the result; we increased twelve stocks to twenty and took 455 pounds box honey and a little over 100 pounds machine honey. The box honey was nearly all taken from nine old stocks, as we broke up one stock in May for queen cells and nuclei, and one old queen failed in June (an artificial queen according to Price), and one stock we had in an experimental side-box arrangement (since abandoned), from which we took but little surplus. The machine honey was taken mostly from the nuclei and young stocks.

Now, Mr. Editor, we would like to inquire through the medium of your valuable paper (which we consider to be the exponant of intelligent beekeeping in this country), what is the latest plan to arrange a hive for side-boxes? We have seen considerable said in the Journals lately about side-box hives, but mostly by patent hive men, or those interested in the sale of hives, and we do not always place implicit reliance on the statements of these gentlemen.

We judge, from what we have seen of it that Mr. Alley's is a good hive, but it is most too expensive and is not as easily handled as we could wish. We believe there are those who have had experience with side-box hives, who could give the desired information, if they chose to let their light shine. We do not like to say we will give a dollar a piece for description, lest we should get more descriptions than we have dollars, but would be willing to give 25 cents each for a limited number, say twenty-five or so, by as many different individuals, if they will send the descriptions to the editor for publication. What we want is something that can be worked on the non-swarming or nucleus system of management (for a concise of said system see page 60, present volume A. B. J.). Having practiced that plan successfully the past two seasons, we are satisfied that there is no other system of management where boxes are used that can be as successful in this section for obtaining surplus. The frames should be easily handled, and should be arranged for side boxes exclusively, and we would prefer that it should be worked under the Langstroth patent, believing as we do, that the Langstroth patent covers all the desirable points in the movable frames.

Thinking there is such a hive in existence, and having failed in our own side-box experimental hive, after three years' trial, not through any fault in the principle, however, but probably on account of an improper arrangement of the hive, we are prompted to make this inquiry, as we believe that a side-box hive, properly arranged, would require less reduction by taking away brood, to prevent swarming; because it would give more ready access to the boxes than a top-storing hive, and consequently would employ more bees and give more surplus. We do not care anything about their ability to winter on their summer stands, as we prefer to winter our bees in the cellar. We know that there are many who are interested in this subject and we would those who have had success and have tested a side-box hive, to send a brief description to the Journal. J. P. MOORE.

Binghamton, N. Y., Feb. 3, 1872.

[For the American Bee Journal.]

Basswood beats the World, for producing Honey.

THAT IS SIMPLY GALLUP'S OPINION.

Mr. Hosmer's statement of the immense yield of basswood honey, made at the Cleveland Convention, calls out considerable private correspondence on the subject; as also does Gallup's paper read at the Iowa Beekeepers' Convention. I understand from one of our townsmen who was there, that Mr. Furman stated he did not believe such statements—that they were false, &c.; for the greatest yield he ever had from a single swarm in one day, was only fifteen (15) pounds. The reader will understand that Mr. Hosmer stated that one stock gathered fifty-three (53) pounds in one day. I know that I took out five gallons at about four o'clock in the afternoon from my large hive; and at the same hour on the following day the same combs were again completely filled with honey, fully equal to sixty (60) pounds. But I had then no vessels to put it in, therefore did not take it out till the following day.

On one Sunday morning during this immense yield, I noticed my bees coming in loaded and all smeared over with what appeared to be honey, and I supposed that a wild swarm *somewhere* had either melted down its combs, or their tree had fallen and smashed the honey. But on repairing to the basswood (the nearest clump of trees is within a few rods of our apiary), I found them swarming with bees, and every cluster of blossoms was completely covered with nectar, not only inside but outside also. The bees and other insects, in crawling over them, had completely smeared the whole blossom. Take a cluster of basswood blossoms, dip them in liquid honey, hang them up to drip, and you will have an idea of the state of things as I found it; and every basswood tree I visited, both great and small, was in the same condition. I called the attention of some thirty witnesses to this state of facts; and this condition of the blossoms continned about eight days. Here we have thonsands of acres containing more or less basswood trees, and have two varieties of them—one variety blossoming some ten days later than the other, thus prolonging the season for basswood honey. The weather was hot and moist at the time, and the air full of electricity, with heavy thunder showers both north and south of us; and slight showers here, accompanied by heavy thunder, twice during the eight days (at night). The reader will understand that basswood blossoms being pendant, a slight shower does not wash out the nectar. We have repeatedly seen bees at work on basswood and red raspberry blossoms, when it was raining quite smartly. During this immense yield, the whole atmosphere for miles was impregnated with the scent of basswood honey.

I have seen this same state of things for two or three days in succession; at different times, while living in Lower Canada.

Another matter, which the reader should understand is, that drouth does not effect large trees, deep rooted, in the same manner that it does small plants.

Now I wish to ask the question how many colonies of bees it will take to overstock our basswood orchard, at such a time as the above? I am with our editor about this overstocking. We have a neighbor just one mile from us, who had some ten stocks of bees; and less than one hundred (100) pounds would cover his entire crop of surplus. He was OVERSTOCKED *over-the-left!* E. GALLUP.

Orchard, Iowa,

THE HONEY-BEE GLEANING AFTER THE ORIOLE.—Two little girls, the elder scarcely six years of age, were picking the flowers of the Buffalo or Missouri currant (*ribes aureum*), "to get the honey." They saw honey-bees around the bushes. They observed that many of the flowers had one or two little holes at the base of the calyx tube, and that such flowers were not as sweet as the others. They said the bees had torn them open with their jaws, and sucked out the honey.

For two reasons I have examined large numbers of these flowers in different parts of the village, and found many of them had been torn open. Several times I have seen the Baltimore Oriole rapidly going over the bushes, giving each fresh flower a prick with the tip of his beak. No other birds have been seen doing this; nor have I been able to see a honey-bee attempt to make a hole at the side of a flower. The calyx tube is too long for the honey-bee, so she contents herself with gleaning after the Oriole, selecting the injured flowers, and leaving the fresh ones for birds and humble bees.—W. J. BEAL, Union Springs, N. Y., in the AMERICAN NATURALIST.

[For the American Bee Journal.]

"Cross Bred Bees."—A Reply.

MR. EDITOR:—I find on page 149 of vol. 7, American Bee Journal, an article under the above heading which the writer manifestly intends as a criticism on my article in October No., on "The Coming Bee."

I thank Mr. Mahin for what he has said; what we want in bee matters is facts, or as Goethe has expressed it: "Light, more Light," and in order to receive more light, we must like all lesser, orbs, borrow from more favored ones, that which we lack within ourselves.

So if Mr. Mahin or any other one can illuminate my understanding upon this matter of cross bred bees, I shall be very glad to learn wherein my error lays; for I wish to deal only in facts, and impressions drawn from facts. I shall not stop to question Mr. Mahin's capacity for correct conclusions on the matter upon which he speaks so very positively; for a man, to say the least, when he is so certain somebody else is wrong.

As Mr. Mahin has expressed great "curiosity, to know how we have ascertained that his "*mongrel race*" are greatly superior to the pure Italians in their range of flight and acuteness of scent, "I will say in answer, that I own a farm on the prairie 2½ miles directly east of my apiary. The east side of the farm is upward of three miles from my bees. For the past two seasons, since my attention has been directed to cross bred bees, during the blossoming of the Golden Rod, I have taken special pains to note the distance travelled by my bees, to work upon it, and in *every* instance, have found the *cross bred bees further from home, than any others.* On one occasion I took the trouble to count the bees passed on my way in from the east side of the farm; and on the first quarter of a mile I coun'ed five *cross bred bees* and no *Italians.* After the first quarter of a mile was passed, the Italians began to increase; and at the house, two and a half miles away, they were quite numerous. Possibly you might conclude that I keep more of the *mongrel race* than Italians, but not so; my Italians outnumber them five to one. In regard to their acuteness of scent, I will say that during the past season my attention has been particularly called to it, from the annoyance they frequently gave me, whilst opening hives and handing honey. Whenever the forage failed from any cause, they were sure to be first to show it, by presenting themselves wherever there was the least exposure of honey, in doors or out; even entering a dark cellar to obtain it; and besides they have yielded me, the past two seasons nearly double the honey that any of my pure Italians have.

Mr. Mahin again says. "I have several colonies now, a majority of which are somewhat less than *half Italians.* They have received pure Italians queens this fall, and within a few days the pure Italian in those hives, have been bringing in loads of pollen, procured somewhere, I know not where nor from what, while only now and then does *one* of the *mongrels bring in anything* and yet the latter outnumber the former *perhaps five to one.* This fact, ascertained by *careful observation*, would seem to place *pure Italians* ahead in *acuteness* of scent or range of flight, or in something equally important."

Well done, Mr. Careful Observer; this is certainly a settler; and will doubtless give a quietus to all mongrel pretentions. A force of young frisky Italians, have beaten a whole host of old worn out mongrels—the youngest of which, must have nearly reached the "three score and ten" limit of bee existence. Wonderful! Wonderful discovery! ! !

Look again Mr. Mahin and as you look *try* and think a *little.* If proof was wanting in all other respects, the history of the Italian bee, would of itself demonstrate it, as a *mongrel* breed. From the earliest accounts of it, dating back to the days of the Roman Empire, it was certainly exposed to crosses with the black bee. For not only have we accounts of the two breeds existing together in Italy both now and in the past, but to say that the Alps present an absolute impassible barrier to the flight of the honey bee, is an assertion which possibilities do not warrant. When it is known that General Fremont captured a humble bee on the top of one of the loftiest peaks of the Rocky Mountains, is it too much to say that the honey bee, so recklessly persistent in its course when swarming, might at times cross the less elevated portions of the Alpine range.

I do not say that this Alpine or trans-alpine migration of bees, has really transpired; but I do say that I believe such a thing to be possible even to the crossing of the glaciers. I know from personal experience, that neither the Rocky Mountains or Sierra Nevadas, present any obstacle whatever to the passage of the honey bee. Besides Mr. Grimm if I am not mistaken, reports that in the neighborhood where he procured his queens, in Italy, he saw bees, so very dark, that at first he took them to be genuine black bees, but found upon closer inspection they were old Italians. Now does any one suppose, that so proficient a bee-master as Mr. Grimm would mistake an old Italian bee for a common black bee, unless there was such a blending of breeds as to render it uncertain where the dividing line really was? But a very short while ago the *test* of *purity* for Italians was "*three bright straw colored bands*, and the more docile the purer the *breed.* Now, however, the thing is entirely reversed; the *darker the bands the purer the bees* and besides, they are allowed now to *sting* if they want to, without being discarded as impure. What then are the inferences to be drawn from such facts? Simply that the further we *breed* away from the black bee, after a certain intermixture has been reached; the poorer the breed becomes.

I have not said that the "Coming Bee" is to be produced in "*five generations*" or ten generations, but I do say that I believe that when we can control fertilization successfully, we can produce by crosses a better honey bee, than we are at present possessed of; and thus do away with the necessity of going to Italy every year to keep our *stock good.*

A few words with you Mr. Editor, and I will close. You say in your editorial comments upon Mr. Hewitt's article on the *removal* of *eggs* to *and from queen cells*, "the facts stated have *not we believe been remarked before* by any *observer.*"—I wish to call your attention to Richard Colvin's excellent essay on the "Italian Honey Bee." published in the Agricultural Report for 1863, page 539. In the article referred to, Mr. Colvin says in reference to queen raising:—"The combs containing eggs should hang between two others containing a sufficiency of honey and pollen to supply their wants. These combs however should contain *no eggs*, or grub, *young enough* to be *convertible into queens, otherwise* the bees may select their native or impure eggs or grub for queens; and raise the pure Italians as workers only. This is the more important from the fact, that they sometimes transfer eggs, or grub from one cell to another, or from a worker to a queen cell."

Thus wrote Mr. Colvin ten years ago; so Mr. Hewitt's discovery is "no new thing under the sun."

G. A. WRIGHT.

Orchard, Iowa, January 10, 1872.

[For the American Bee Journal.]

My experience with Hybrid Queens.

MR. EDITOR:—I read an article in your invaluable Bee Journal of October, page 77, on "The Coming Bee."

Having had some experience in rearing hybrid queens is my only excuse for troubling you with this communication, and hoping some person may profit by my mistakes.

About the 19th of June, 1870, I received per express, from Mrs. E. S. Tupper, of Brighton, Washington county, Iowa, two Italian queens. I made swarms and successfully introduced them. Wishing to get all my bees Italianized, and having perfect confidence in their purity as Mrs. Tupper had informed me by letter, "*I send out none but tested queens reared in full colonies.*" In about twelve days I unqueened two colonies of black bees and exchanged their combs with my Italian stands, giving the combs that contained the supposed pure Italian eggs to the black queenless colony to raise queens.

In about ten days I unqueened the remainder of my black colonies, and gave them capped queen cells. All went along well, until the young queens hatched, when I noticed they were smaller and much darker than their mothers; not having had experience, I supposed they would get lighter as they got older. In this I was disappointed.

The worker progeny of the supposed pure Italian queens proved them to be hybrids. The worker progeny of the young queens gave but few marks of any Italian blood.

In September, 1870. I purchased one Italian queen of the Rev. L. L. Langstroth, of Oxford, Ohio, and one of T. V. Brooks, Esq., of Lexington, McLean county, Illinois. Both produced as fine worker progeny as any one could desire.

Late in the fall I purchased several stands of

black bees in box hives. Last spring I had pure Italians, black bees, and a variety of hybrids.

I soon found my hybrids cross, but the hybrids raised from hybrids and impregnated by black drones, possessed all the bad qualities of both parentage and but few of the good, as they were less prolific, and did not gather as much honey as the old discarded black honey bee, while the pure Italian queens were most prolific and gave much the largest yield of surplus honey. I must say I could not make any distinction in the honey product of the half-bloods, as they were as prolific and gave as much surplus honey as the pure Italians.

I had six miserably cross and unproductive stands of my raising breeding downward, which in my opinion gave me a good opportunity to test the doctrine as to the superiority or inferiority of "the coming bee."

Any one keeping hybrids and crossing them with the black honey bee, in my humble opinion will find himself the possessor of a miserable substitute for the good old black honey bee, or their superiors in every particular, the Italian.

I commenced last spring with twenty-nine stands, many weak, mostly in old-fashioned boxes—transferred them to the Langstroth hive. I used the Gray & Winder honey extractor, which is superior in every particular over any I have had the pleasure to examine; took fifteen hundred of what is called slung honey and increased my colonies to fifty-three. I italianized my apiary, discarding hybrids.

Geo. L. Lucas.

Peoria, Ill.

[For the American Bee Journal.]

Removal of Stocks in Summer.

The majority of beekeepers suppose that bees cannot be removed, in summer time, for short distances, without losing the greater part of the old workers, by their returning when loaded to their old stand, though circumstances sometimes make such removal desirable. In such cases it may be useful to the inexperienced to know how I have managed matters, as I have at various times removed stocks from ten to eighty rods with perfect success.

I removed three colonies last June, for one of my neighbors, about eighty rods, in the following manner :—doing it in the middle of the day, when the bees were mostly out in the fields at work quite busily. The first performance is to smoke them sufficiently to stop any more bees from leaving the hive, and then keep doing so, or rapping on the hive for about thirty minutes, at short intervals. Then, if in a box hive, drum out all the bees you can get out, together with the queen into a box ; or, if in a movable comb hive (as those on which I operated were) drum and brush out all the bees into a box. Now carry the bees to where you want to place them, also the hive, comb and brood, and re-hive the bees by emptying them down on a board or cloth in front of the hive, letting them run in, and the thing is done.

In removing the three swarms eighty rods, as above, not more than a dozen bees returned to the old stands, and those were probably out to work and had not returned when the hives were removed. But suppose we had removed them in the usual manner, by fastening up the hive and removing them at night. Nearly all the old workers would have returned to the old stands the next morning, and have been lost to the stocks. I have seen stocks entirely ruined by removing them short distances at night, in the last manner.

E. Gallup.

Orchard, Iowa.

[For the American Bee Journal.]

The Season in Iowa.

Mr. Editor :—I commenced last spring with 132 colonies. They commenced swarming the 30th of May ; I had 98 prime swarms by the 5th of July. Returned 26, had 204 colonies the first day of October ; united the nuclei with the weakest, and put them into winter quarters November 28th. With the extractor, I took from 42 colonies 8½ barrels of honey, averaging 73 lbs. per colony. Of box honey and combs in small frames, I took nearly 2,000 lbs., very nearly 20 lbs. average for the rest of my colonies. I sold my strained honey in Burely for 18½ cents ; in jars, for 20 cents. Box honey from 20 to 22 cents per lb. All this honey was made and taken away before the 20th of July, and is of course number one. This season did not come up to the last with me, but will still leave something for this summer's work. The honey is now nearly all sold. I had to feed some of the late swarms, as the season hereabouts was cut short the latter part of July by the drouth.

By the way, I have made a bee feeder, which is cheap and is O. K., without a patent. Take one or two round oyster cans, empty of course ; take off the top and bottom by holding them over hot coals. The end which is not injured I use for a cover. A tin band is put over the outside to hold on the muslin, the same as a strainer ; the band to be one or one and a half inches wide, hemmed on one side. A tinner will make them from two to three cents apiece. This feeder I place over a hole in the honey-board, where the bees are clustered. There will be a half-inch space between the honey-board and the muslin, the band projecting that far below the muslin. It works well. I believe in feeding bees early in spring to stimulate them to breeding. I double up my colonies if weak in April, it will pay best for increase or for yield of honey. I do not practice artificial swarming—natural suits me best. Where honey is the object, never let a hive swarm but once, and often put back the first swarm, if not an extra one ; but where increase of colonies is required, artificial swarming will do the business. I take all queens' cells from colonies which have swarmed naturally for queen raising, and choose from those who are the best workers and are of color. My half-breeds have, on an average, yielded the most surplus honey in boxes. With the extractor I find no difference, and therefore prefer the more practicable ones for that purpose, and use the double story Langstroth hive, with no honey-board. Still I would not condemn any movable comb hive, when they have no extra moth traps, and the frames are of course movable.

P. Lattner.

Lattner's, Dubuque Co., January 19, 1872.

[For the American Bee Journal.]

On Pure Italian Bees.

Mr. Editor:—On page 149 of the January issue for 1872, Mr. R. M. Argo, asks the following question: Can a pure Italian queen whose progeny for the first few weeks all show three yellow bands distinct afterwards produce workers half black bees. In reply, I would say no, provided the queen be pure, and is fertilized by a pure Italian drone. I have had several such cases as he mentioned in the article referred to, and I have also had queens whose workers during the first three months showed them to be but little if any better in color than such as are commonly termed hybrids; after which they assumed a color almost if not quite equal to the finest specimens of Italians.

I do not in such cases claim that the queen and drone are both pure Italians, as such a state of affairs will never be witnessed except one of the parents be bastardized.

If a pure Italian queen be fertilized by a pure black drone, the worker and queen progeny will both afford unmistakable evidence of impurity from the beginning.

And this state of affairs will continue to exist as long as the queen lives and remains fertile, with little if any perceptible difference in color during the time. Such at any rate is what my experience has led me to conclude upon. But if we have bees that are ever so slightly dashed with blood differing from themselves in variety, we may look for and confidently expect just such occurrences as Mr. Argo has described.

And from what I can learn I am well convinced that he is not the only person who meets with such cases, as they are of frequent occurrence but are seldom reported. To report these occurrences it is too much the custom to think it would injure the sale of Italian bees and queens; when the facts in the case are that eventually all will be forced to occupy the position either that we do not succeed in having perfectly pure bees imported to this country or that they are not an original and distinct variety of bees. The latter position I am disposed to favor, as I have made it a part of my business to search after pure bees, and have found Mr. L. L. Langstroth, Mr. J. T. Langstroth, Mr. A. Gray, and Mr. A. Benedict, in company with myself, to occupy the same position, and time will bring all to the same standpoint, except it be, that we do not, as already stated, have pure bees shipped from Italy. But if it turn out (as I believe it will) that the Italians are not distinct in variety, then the sooner we speak out plainly upon this subject the better. For I am confident that we can by careful breeding improve our Italian bees until any dash of foreign blood that may exist among them will only occasionally make itself manifest. Our Chester white hogs are not an original variety. Neither are our Durham cattle original, yet careful breeding has brought them to such a degree of perfection that time will declare them distinct as they already very nearly duplicate themselves in every instance. Our Italian bees do not as yet maintain this degree of purity except in perhaps a very few cases where parties have selected their finest specimens to breed from and have been exceedingly careful as to what kind of stock they introduce into their apiaries. I will state further in regard to our Italian queens, that I do not regard them as being fully tested, until I have seen a number of their queen offspring; when if they are fair duplicates of their mothers I regard them as being good queens to breed from. All queens who will thus duplicate themselves will show uniformly three banded workers. But a queen whose workers may all appear to be in possession of three bands may lack a few in perhaps twenty thousand workers, and an ordinary inspection will not detect their presence among several thousand three banded bees, hence the difficulty in depending upon this method of testing Italian queens. And the farther the mother queen is from distinctness in variety the more frequently will the error in depending upon three banded test manifest itself.

A dash of impurity does not always manifest its presence, but remains sometimes in a latent state through several generations, and then shows itself to both the surprise and disappointment of the breeder. This fact seems to have been lost sight of by many of our queen raisers. If not, they have been too credulous and have too long regarded the Italians as an original distinct and consequently pure variety of bees. Or it is possible that they overlooked both of these facts; I say facts, because I feel thoroughly convinced that we have no perfectly distinct and pure Italians in this country. Then I would say, let us send competent persons to Italy in search of pure bees if they are to be found. And if procured let us breed them in apiaries entirely isolated and beyond the reach of black bees. And if pure bees, cannot be found let us improve such as we have until they become so nearly distinct as to be depended upon. Then and not till then will we see the Dzierzon theory thoroughly tested in practice, and also the fact fully proving the fertilization of the Italian queen by a black drone will not render her drone progeny impure.

G. Bohrer.

Alexandria, Ind., January 25, 1872.

[For the American Bee Journal.]

Italian Bees at the Cleveland Convention.

While for years various parties in the United States have been raising and selling Italian Queens on their supposed superiority over the common variety, nothing very definite as to their honey gathering qualities has found its way into the journals.

Interested parties have, it is true, sent out large statements and in many instances, claimed that they would gather double the honey from red clover, &c. While this was going forward, various honey raisers were trying the merits of Italian bees as honey producers, but as they had converted all their old stocks into Italians, no comparison could be made or opinion formed as to their comparative merits. Those having them obtained large amounts of honey by their skilful management and modestly gave their Italian bees credit for it. This was very natural, but, as it was the skill of the apiarian and not the *Superior Bee*, which gave the results, their reports gave an erroneous impression, and the traffic went on.

Some tried them and gave them up, as they did not provide enough more honey for the extra trouble, and many went so far as to say they would not work in the boxes nearly as well as the old kind. But I am straying from my subjcet and must return to the convention for my statistics. At the convention, it may be well to say, each member was handed a printed blank on which to carry out the number of bees he had, the number of movable frame hives in use, the amount of honey produced and the price obtained, and the number of Italian stocks.

Men from all parts of the country gave in their reports. No class failed to do this except Italian queen vendors and a few others tooting the Italian horn. None of these "advice to beginner's" men report a pound of honey—a very curious fact.

The honey-raisers' report embraces a few having some Italians and some blacks, and, as I have no means of knowing when they were Italianized I have left out the mixed apiarians entirely, and give only those reports which have no doubt as to which kind of bees stored the honey. Of these seventeen hundred and thirty-one Italian stocks, produced twenty-nine thousand and forty-seven pounds of honey, or an average of about sixteen and three-fourths pounds per hive.

As the old kind were in box hives many of them, and of course not in the hands of the most skilled apiarians—while the Italians were in movable comb-hives, and managed by the very men who can give "advice to beginners," I think the old *fogie brown bees have done well.*

Now, Mr. Editor, as the increase of Italian stocks reported does not differ esstentially from the increase of the blacks reported (nearly doubling), we have what the weather report of the Smithsonian Institute bases its opinion on, as also the Life and Fire Insurance Companies, and all other good business men, that is, we have the average yield over a wide extent of territory, managed in a variety of ways with a wonderfully uniform result. It is encouraging to those about to purchase a yearling Balmoral queen with the prospect of raising from year to year a large number of pure queens to take the place of those having a doubtful pedigree.

When we realize that perhaps queen breeders, who as a rule are or have been patent Bee Hive Vendors, may tell the truth when they say there is no profit in rearing tested queens at two dollars cash, it certainly seems no trifling matter and requiring no small amount of courage to embark in an enterprise promising *sixteen* pounds less honey for every Italian stock wintered, with all the attendant trouble, than they would have had, had they saved their *money* and their *plain beautiful* bees.

We are not entirely dependent on this average yield for the evidence that black bees are vastly superior to Italians. The greatest average yield in any apiary last season was that of Mr. Hosmen, which was black bees. Mr. Quinby, who by the way is a large raiser of Italian bees, also reports his greatest yield of honey from one hive to have been secured from black stock. Mr. Gallup, who has realized Novice's prophecy, of "five hundred" pounds per hive I presume obtained it from his *New Hive* merely, and like Mr. Hazen, will not fail to give it to us in different re-hashes for the next five years.

With the best wishes for the Journal and bee-keepers, I remain, &c., T. F. Bingham.

Allegan, Mich.

[From the N. Y. Sun.]

A Big Frog Story.

How an Old Gentleman's Bee Boxes were Robbed of their Honey—And how an Old Thief got rid of his Pursuers—A Story from a Venerable Clergyman.

To the Editor of The Sun.

Sir :—I read your Staten Island frog story the other day with great interest. I have met with several very singular facts in connection with these amphibious animals in the course of my travels, one of which I will here record. In Jamaica, West Indies, the settlers keep their bees—whose honey, by the way, rivals the famous product of Mount Hybla—in old salt fish boxes. The box is first well soaked in a mountain stream, and then daubed inside with honey. When the bees swarm, the hive is placed handy, and they very soon accept the invitation to new quarters. The box is then placed upon four stones, which elevate it about half a foot from the ground, thus giving the bees air and a way of getting in and out.

An old friend of mine had his house and garden near a small stream, which was the resort of a number of frogs. Some of these fellows were eight inches long and four broad. They would come up to the house every evening, and loaf about watching the children at play. When darkness came on, they were supposed to go to their barracks for the night. The old gentleman had a number of bee boxes. He was fond of honey. He liked honey and he liked mead. When the time came one season to take the honey, he was greatly surprised to find that several of his boxes were almost empty. I was passing the next day and he called me in and told me his trouble. He showed me the boxes.

"Thieves have been at work there," said he.

I agreed with him. He proposed that I should

call on my way home in the evening, and that both of us should sit up and watch. This I acceded to.

The night was calm and beautiful. The full moon seemed to float in a sea of silver. We put out the lights, closed the door, and seated ourselves on the piazza behind, where we could smoke our pipes and converse in an undertone without being observed. All was still around the house. The ripple of the stream, a hundred yards away, was all that could be heard. We had sat thus for about two hours, and had almost come to the conclusion to go to our beds, when my attention was attracted by a dark object about the size of a boy's cap, moving in jerky leaps from the side of the house toward the bee boxes.

"Wallace," I whispered, "what is that?"

Wallace careened over and watched the object earnestly.

"It's a frog," said he at last; "no animal of that size but a frog could take such strides."

In the meantime the frog (for we had agreed it was one) had reached the shade of the tree under which the bee boxes stood. We resolved to watch the midnight promenader. We left the house by the front door, walked round through the bushes, and ensconced ourselves in a shady spot where we had full view of the boxes. Our frog had vanished. Hearing a noise like the cracking of dried leaves, we looked toward the house and saw another frog, as we concluded from its gait, moving from the same side whence the first had come, and following the same direction. While we were gazing on this new prowler, we heard the bees in a box within six feet of us begin to buzz as if in consternation. Presently a stream of them flowed from under the box and spread around. Almost at the same moment we saw a dark object emerge from the box and commence a series of very deliberate hops toward the stream. We stealthily approached, still under shade, however, and discovered a frog, which we no doubt rightly surmised was our first friend, literally covered with bees. Covered is not the word. The bees were piled upon him, and clinging in layers to his sides. A large number also flew around him, and furnished music to the procession.

I turned round to see what had become of our second visitor. There he was moving with joyous leaps toward the bee boxes, followed by at least twenty other frogs. One after another these leaping bandits vanished under the box from which our first friend had just come, with the whole family of bees on his back and sides and about his ears.

We were too much astonished and interested to speak. We slowly followed our frog with his load of bees. He made straight for the river, but at a very slow pace. He carried weight and could not move fast. When he got to the water he plunged right in. That was his way of putting down his passengers.

We then returned to the bee box. Our footsteps amid the dry brushwood must have startled the burglars, for when we reached the tree they were going at full speed for the stream. Next morning we examined the box, and found that nearly all the honey had been stolen. The cells were broken, and the honey was plastered round in every direction. While the decoy had carried off the family to a watering place, their mansion had been thoroughly despoiled by his confederates.

W. A. M.

Correspondence.

My apiary last spring consisted of sixteen colones. My surplus honey from this apiary the past season amounted to nineteen hundred and eighty-six pounds. Seven hundred and sixty-eight pounds of the above was extracted. Nine-tenths of it all was basswood honey. Increase, four new swarms. I use the Langstroth hive. Like some others, have used it in an *improved* style and form, but do not now; cannot bear the improvements any longer. Now use the old form and style.

JAMES HEDDON.

Dowagiac, Mich., Feb. 26, 1872.

Enclosed please find two dollars for current volume of the Journal. You may as well consider me a life subscriber, as the Journal is indispensable; a single number often being worth more to me than the whole volume. This has been a good season for bees, that is until the linden blossoms failed, which was about the 15th of July. All our surplus honey was white clover and linden. In the way of swarming, our bees done fine. My bees are most all Italians and hybrids, and in their winter-quarters in good condition. I have one queen that I got from Mr. A. Grimm of Wisconsin, and I think she is a perfect beauty. With the honey extractor, I took from one of my hybrid stocks 225 pounds of white clover and linden honey. I used a double hive and only extracted from the upper hive. I think 40 pounds was the most box honey I got from any one stock, and that was a hybrid.

UNEXPERIENCED.

West Union, Iowa.

Information Wanted.

I am starting with 12 stands Italian bees and expect to have as many more black bees and wish to Italianize them this spring. I am within 40 rods of heavy timber on bottom land, the largest share of the timber is elm and cotton wood. There is also a large quantity of basswood and maple, hard and soft, some willow and tag-alder. I expect to sow something for bees, but do not know what. Can you tell me if the Rocky Mountain bee-plant is better for bees than Alsike clover, and will it pay to sow sweet clover for bees and is it good for anything except bees? Is there anything preferable to either or all of the above mentioned, for that purpose? I would like to get a honey extractor. Do you know what kind is best? I am prepossessed in favor of the Gray and

Winder machine on account of its being geared, but have never used any kind. Is common elder good for bees, and will it pay to cultivate it? I see there is much said about feeding bees syrup in order to make them more prolific in breeding, but have never seen a receipt for making the syrup. Will you please give me the above instructions, or refer me to some one who will, and oblige NELSON PERKINS.

Houston Co., Minn.

I regard your Journal as invaluable to every apiarian who wishes and deserves success in the management of the bee. I have been a bee-keeper for about twenty years but a new beginner in this latitude. With one year's experience here I find it quite different from central Illinois. Some time in the future I hope to be able to contribute to your columns my success or reverses. Wishing the Journal unbounded success in its laudable endeavors, for I know its efforts are being felt all over this land.

JEREMIAH EWING.

Mont., Ohio.

[For the American Bee Journal.]

Novice.

DEAR BEE JOURNAL :—Once more we meet, but can any one of us avoid feeling the solemnity of the thought that our dear old friend of so many years is among the dead.

The presiding genius of all our disputes, successes, triumphs and sorrows, ever ready to assist and lenient as a kind parent to those who erred ; giving these pages freely to all with the conviction, as he once expressed it, that "Truth is great and will prevail." May his successor, whoever he may be, be an equally good man, is our earnest prayer ; that he may have the skill and experience at once of Mr. Wagner, we hardly dare hope.

Our bees are just on their summer stands. Three colonies are dead and we should have been lamenting their loss severely had not there been a peculiarity in regard to the matter that has made us rather *rejoice* at their loss. We believe we fed the sugar syrup to all colonies except five. These five were the American hives that were used double, and we found plenty of sealed honey to carry them through safely, so that the fullest combs were simply put into one of the hives and they were considered all right for winter.

Now, then, those that were dead were three out of the five and the remaining two were at the point of starvation, with the combs of all literally daubed with the excrement so plainly denoting bee cholera or dysentery.

If Mr. Gallup or any one else can give any other reason than food for colonies equal in number and every other condition (side by side in the house), that we know coming out with bright and clean combs and *not one-half of their sealed combs of sugar syrup* consumed.

We are very much inclined to thank Mr. Langstroth for supplying the only remaining clue to the disease, viz., cider mills. Our bees visited in droves a cider mill less than a quarter of a mile away, and we followed, of course, and found the pomace yellow with countless Italians. Every stock must have stored more or less.

We believe late discoveries in the medical world are showing that this *same cider* and excessive use of fruits in general are almost the direct cause of a long list of diseases in the human system, almost as disagreeable as that under which the poor bees have been suffering.

A friend asks if we are going to recommend the bees a beefsteak diet to secure healthy digestion and development of muscle ; to which we reply that pure coffee sugar syrup seems to be to the bees as sure a remedy as the beef has been to us.

There is one reader of the Journal who we really hope, when he sees these lines will see that it is a positive duty of his to give the world a little more light on a subject that has been a life long study with him, with the aid of all modern appliances of science, most especially the microscope.

Does any one know of mignonette as a honey plant. Nothing under our observation has ever kept Italians so busy from July until late in fall as half-a-dozen stalks of what we purchased as tree mignonettee.

Mr. A. S. Fuller, of Russel, N. Y., wrote us so favorably of it that we half decided to occupy the space between our four hundred basswood trees, ten and a half acres, to see if we could not at least keep the bees busy in the fall, for—

"Satan always finds mischief," etc.

Cider mills, etc., and besides we don't like to trouble our neighbors, even if they do laugh at the Italian capers, a joke, etc.

So Gallup wants to see what Novice will do when hit. Just this, our sincerest thanks and to really hope every other reader will say as frankly just what they think of us and wherein they think our views are contracted, one-sided or conceited, and we promise you we won't quarrel, even if we are right and you wrong.

Mr. Editor or each reader may decide for himself, after our reasons are given, which of us is right, or both, or neither (very likely the latter).

QUESTION.

Can a hive be made that will give as good results with combs spread out horizontally as with two stories, like the usual Langstroth form?

Now we are going to try hard to be frank and not make positive assertions. Mr. Gallup has made an enormous result from his hive. Was it the hive or the season? Could he not have done the same with a Langstroth of sufficient capacity? Hosmer, near him, has also made an enormous result with the American, and why will not the American shape of frame bear comparison with Gallup's?

Our six double American hives were placed side by side, with one entrance like the original hive, and one the opposite way, of course, and we mixed the brood all through, every time we extracted honey and even turned the hives "tother end to," as Gallup does, and for a few days they did go "in one end and out the other ;"

but, as we stated before, they would soon all work over to one side or the other, or just as soon as they could get the brood hatched.

Our greatest objection to the Gallup style is the labor of handling so many small frames. Quinby uses the largest frame we know of and we really like the idea.

Do our readers remember what Gallup once said about brooding sticks in the spring?

Ain't there an awful pile of sticks hoarded, especially in June, in his hive, compared with those of larger frames.

Mr. Gallup, we shall not be astonished if you think us thick headed in this matter, nor should we be *very much* astonished if we really were so, for we can look back and see many times where we have been before.

Lifting off the upper story is quite a task, and we are ready for some improvement that does not give greater disadvantages.

Now, please don't send any of your patent hives to examine, kind friends. Our better half is well supplied with kindling wood for some time to come.

Dr. J. H. Salisbury, opposite Post Office, Cleveland, Ohio, wishes a piece of comb containing genuine foul brood, for microscopical examination. Will those so unfortunate as to have foul brood in their apiaries send him a small piece by mail. (Don't send any to us, we never want any in Medina county.) His large experience with microscopical forms of both animal and vegetable life, we think, will enable him to decide at once if foul brood be either, and very probably he may give us a remedy in any case, or some suggestion in regard to the remedy given by F. Abbe.

He has also promised to aid us by making examinations of drones produced from unfertile queens compared with those from fertile queens, and that we do really want some plain facts without theories and unprofitable argument on this subject is the candid opinion of your old friend, NOVICE.

P. S.—Some one asks in the Journal where we get our jars? Of Messrs. Fahnestock, Fortune & Co., Pittsburg, Pa.; they cost about five cents each, corks, labels and all, for one pound jars. Those for two pounds, about seven cents.

Imported Queens.

We have found by dear experience, that a large number, if not the majority of the Italian queens we have imported have been short lived. Many of them have been superseded the first season, and others early the next. We attribute this to the fact that old queens may sometimes have been sent, but more to the way in which the transport boxes are prepared.

The queens which were sent to Mr. Parsons, in 1859, for himself, and the Agricultural Department, were put in common segar boxes, the combs were wedged into these boxes, and a few slits cut in them for ventilation. I assisted in opening a large number; *all* for the Agricultural Department were dead, and nearly all of Mr. Parsons', besides others which came for another party. Out of fifty or more, I do not think we saved more than half a dozen. Some had starved to death, others were drowned in honey, others smothered, and others still, crushed between the combs, which got loose in the boxes. That same season Mr. Carey, of Coleraine, who had the care of Mr. Parsons' apiary, packed over one hundred to go to California, and only one of the number was lost.

In America we guarantee the safe arrival of our queens. We do not know of any breeder in Europe who guarantees the safe arrival of queens sent to this country. Of this we do not complain, but we cannot help feeling sore when our queens arrive dead, or so exhausted as to be short-lived if not worthless, because after our *repeated remonstrances*, the transport boxes are overcrowded with bees.

We are, therefore, specially glad to learn that Messrs. Gray and Winder have determined to send Dr. Bohrer to Italy, this spring, to make an importation for them; for we believe that the Doctor will not only bring over live queens, but such as will arrive in good condition and give satisfaction. We shall make our own importations this season through them, and only wish it was our good fortune to go with the Doctor, and see the Italian bees in their own homes.

L. L. L.

[For the American Bee Journal.]

The Triangular Comb-guide again.

As we learn that Mr. K. P. Kidder is still demanding money from those using his comb-guide, we shall show from facts that have just come to our knowledge, that the salient angle or beveled edge for a comb-guide, was used in a hive with bars in 1843.

M. Frarière, in a work on bee-culture, "*Traite de l'education des abeilles*," published at Paris, in 1843, gives a wood-cut of a side-opening hive, very much like some of Dzierzon's; with two sets of slats or bars which are thus described:

"Un grillage léger composé de six or sept baguettes triangulaires, dont un des angles sera tourné vers le bas, pour diriger le travail des abeilles." "A light grating composed of six or seven triangular sticks, one of the angles of which is turned downwards for directing the work of the bees."

The Clark patent, under which Mr. Kidder claims the absolute control of the triangular guide in bars or frames, having been issued in 1859, cannot cover the use of a device fully described in 1843.

We have repeatedly called the attention of bee keepers to the fact that the salient angle comb-guide, was described by the celebrated English surgeon, John Hunter, in 1792, and that we made, used and sold this same guide more than two years before Mr. Clark applied for a patent, which alone, according to the law, makes it public property.

Will Mr. Kidder take any notice of this prior use so clearly described by M. Frarière? We hope, at least, that the public will. More, anon.

L. L. LANGSTROTH.

THE AMERICAN BEE JOURNAL.

Washington, April, 1872.

All communications and letters of business should be addressed to

GEO. S. WAGNER,
Office of the American Bee Journal,
WASHINGTON, D. C.

In the next issue of our Journal we will give the first of the series of unedited letters of Huber.

The writer of the amusing adventures of the frogs and bees, p. 233, has probably drawn somewhat largely upon a vivid imagination; but we are disposed in the main to credit his story—but we do not believe that the old frog made himself a voluntary martyr for the public good, he only got ahead of the other thieves.

We feel it due to Mr. T. F. Bingham to give his article, by which he attempts to prove by "figures that cannot lie," that black bees are better honey gatherers than Italians. The columns of the Am. B. J; on this question, as well as all others connected with apiculture, will always be open to fair discussion.

We hope before long to give a monthly summary of the contents of the German, French and Italian Bee Journals, so that our readers may know the course of thought, and progress of invention in apiculture, in all parts of the world.

Our readers will no doubt rejoice to learn that an end has come to the controversy which of late has filled so many columns of our Journal. Circumstances beyond our control made these exposures necessary. We hope now to leave the merits of the matters in dispute to the impartial decision of U. S. District Court.

We have on hand a number of very excellent communications, which it was impossible to get in this number.

PUBLICATIONS RECEIVED.

The Rural Alabama. March, 1872.

J. Cochran, Havana, Ill. Catalogue of Flower and Vegetable Seeds.

L. Prang & Co., Schem's Universal Statistical Table.

From James Vick, Rochester, N. Y., a choice variety of Flower and Vegetable Seeds.

I deeply regret the loss of Mr. Wagner, for though I never had the pleasure of personal acquaintance, I could but regard him as a high-toned honorable man. And surely the American Bee Journal was a model paper. I think it has no peer. The wise discrimination, the high tone, straight forward manner with which it was conducted could but elicit thorough and genuine regard.
A. J. COOK.
Lansing, Mich.

I once visited Mr. Wagner in York, Penna., just after his first importation of Italian queens, and my measure of the man was just as you have given it in the obituary notice. His conscientious thoroughness would have caused him to excel in anything he might undertake.
ERICK PARMELY.
New York.

Your letter informing me of Mr. Wagner's death is just before me. I cannot tell you how deeply I sympathize with you in the loss of your friend. One of the American fathers in bee-culture has fallen asleep. After I had learned to know Mr. Wagner's peculiar temperament through you I learned to appreciate him and to overlook what before I thought a harsh side to his nature.

I always admired him for his rare attainments in our beloved science and for his thorough independence of character. No one was so eminently fitted for the place he so gracefully filled. One of the great men in the theory and practice of apiculture has fallen, and we who have been benefited by his ripe culture should strew his memory with sweet immortelles.
E. VAN SLYKE.
Albany, N. Y.

The last number of the Bee Journal has just reached me, conveying the first tidings of your father's death. It came to me with a shock, for, although so advanced in years, his spirit seemed so youthful and energetic that I never dreamed of his passing away. His enthusiasm in behalf of bee-culture in the United States was of such a noble and pure character, his judgment in these matters so sound, and his influence among the different warring interests (for most of our apiarians seem to partake more or less of the belligerent spirit of their little wards) was so great, that his loss is indeed a public calamity. I have received the Journal from its first establishment and have watched your father's course with the greatest respect and admiration.
T. C. PORTER.
Easton, Pa.

Mr. Samuel Wagner, editor of the *American Bee Journal*, died suddenly of apoplexy, at his residence in Washington on the 17th ultimo, at the age of sixty years. Every reader of his paper, who can but have admired his honest, straightforward, independent course as an editor, his hatred of all shams and humbuggery, and his earnest and intelligent devotion to the science of apiculture, will receive this intelligence with profound sorrow. His paper has ever been regarded as the ablest and most enlightened advocate of its specialty in our country, and we hope the demise of Mr. Wagner will not result in its discontinuance.—*Maine Farmer.*

[For the American Bee Journal.]

Questions Answered by Gallup

About the extractor, &c., it appears that comparatively few have yet learned the use of the extractor, and quite a number of those that already have one scarcely understand its great utility. I have quite a number of letters stating that they had always supposed that their locality was not a good one for surplus honey, but by following my instructions they now readily report surplus by the thousand pounds; and have come to the conclusion that all that is nenessary is the requisite knowledge and practical experience, and I am asked questions by the hundred. Now I shall endeavor to answer some of them through the Journal. One prominent question is: *How much comb is required to give a stock abundance of room to work to the best advantage in a large yield of honey.*

From my last season's operations I have come to the conclusion that it requires just (or thereabout) twice the amount of comb that the queen occupies with brood. For example, a queen that occupied 16 of my combs required 32 combs. One occupying 26 required 52 to work to the best advantage. I had in my yard three New England queens of the extra light-colored variety. They would only occupy six combs, the best I could do for them; consequently my standard hive of 12 combs was plenty large enough and to spare for said stocks. As my combs are small there is but little danger of breaking or cracking them in the extractor; even the newest combs could be handled with proper care without breaking. I do not use anything to keep my frames at the proper distance apart in the hive. They are made so that they hang just where they are placed on the rabbits or cleats, all nails, screws, wire, staples, bits of tin or zinc, or any such contrivances are a perfect nuisance, and in the way when we come to handle the combs in and out of the extractor, and especially when we are in a hurry (and we are sometimes in a hurry when the honey is coming in by the ton).

And again we do not like, and never did, combs fixed at permanent distances in the hive. We like the genuine Langstroth principle of movable combs, because *they are movable* in the fullest sense of the word. Others are only partially movable. Understand, we are now giving our opinion not yours. Furthermore, neither Mr. Langstroth nor any of his agents ever attempted to bribe us to use or recommend his principle of movable combs. (Mr. Editor, we are now answering questions, so you will allow us considerable latitude.) We could empty any comb that had sealed brood in it without disturbing or injuring the brood in the least. There was none of the honey thin enough to sour, either in 1870 or 1871, with us.

Now, here comes a tough one; not a tough one to answer, but a tough one for people to believe. *In a good yield of honey how much will a good swarm store per day?* Now before answering this question I will state that I have sent an article for publication setting forth the facts about our immense yield for eight days the past season, and that was what I call a good yield. I now firmly believe that I can get up stocks in my twin hive or any hive on that principle that will store at such a time from 40 to 60 pounds per day. Now don't call me a liar yet; get up as strong a stock as you ever saw and then place feeders enough in your yard containing liquid honey, all they can carry away, and give the bees abundance of room, without crowding, and abundance of comb to store in and you can form an approximate idea of the state of things for eight days the past season.

Mr. Hosmer at Cleveland gave an account of one stock storing 53 pounds in one day. I saw and became partially acquainted with him at Cincinnati, and I call him as candid and truthful a gentleman as I ever came across. (Mr. Hosmer's statement is included in the list of questions,) and is fully entitled to credit for his statement.

Again, do you believe that Mr. H. can winter a pint of bees and build them up to a swarm in the spring? *I certainly do.* Have I not told you in the back numbers of the American Bee Journal of successfully wintering less than a pint. I think I have. It requires experience and skill. The inexperienced had better not venture too far in that direction. It also requires young bees reared in the fall to winter successfully in such small quantities.

Which is the most profitable—box or extracted honey? I will answer in this manner: Where the main supply is white clover, which comes in gradually and continues quite a length of time, it may be most profitable to work for both box and extracted honey, but here where our main supply is from basswood and it comes with a rush and then is over, we cannot get it in boxes. We will say if from a good stock we get 50 pounds in boxes (that is old-fashioned or standard stock) we can safely get 300 pounds with the extractor or in that proportion, or five to one; now reckoning 60 pounds at 20 cents per pound is $12, and 300 pounds at 10 cents is $30. 15 cents is the lowest we have sold any of our extracted honey. We go in for the extracted honey and the extractor. We also go in for supplying honey *so cheap* that it will no longer be a luxury, but every one can use it. Millions of tons of it are going to waste for the want of intelligent beekeepers to superintend the bees.

E. GALLUP.

SHADING IN THE WINTER.—Mr. Taylor says: —"Where the hives stand singly, I have always seen the advantages of fixing before each a wooden screen, nailed to a post sunk in the ground, and large enough to throw the whole front into shade. This does not interfere with the coming forth of the bees at a proper temperature, and it supersedes the necessity of shutting them up when snow is on the ground. This screen should be fixed a foot or two in advance, and so as to intercept the sun's rays, which will be chiefly in winter towards the west side."

[For the American Bee Journal.]

Foggy.

We notice in our article in the February No., page 187, after reading it carefully, that we left it a little foggy, and with your permission we will try to explain.

We said in our example we should make fifteen or twenty double swarms. This is providing that an increase of stocks is desired; if no increase is desired make only two or three, just to give room to return.

In 1870, we made only six new swarms from 32 colonies; all the rest were returned and the season was not very good, yet most all our returned swarms filled the boxes, and some of them two sets of boxes. But our neighbors that hived their swarms single got no honey, and the young swarms did not store enough to live till spring.

Another blunder. We said every stock in the yard will be storing honey. It should read, "except a few at the end of the swarming season that I had no bees to return back to." I made no count on second swarms. I do not allow any to issue from those I return bees back to.

Thanks to Mr. Grimm, we shall in future adopt his plan of doubling all stocks that remain in our yard after swarming, that we have no bees to send back to, then all will be strong enough to store honey while the clover is in bloom.

In 1871, we made quite an increase in our stock. We had a very serious misfortune or else a very beautiful blunder, we think the latter name the best. It cost us about $3, out. We would not like to tell it just now but sometime will give it in a chapter on blunders.

JOSEPH BUTLER.

Mich., March 4, 1872.

[For the American Bee Journal.]

Queen Raising.

MR. EDITOR:—The demand for Italian queens this coming season seems to be greater than any past season. At least I find it so with me from the way orders come in. There is evidently a growing interest awakened in the culture of the bee.

Would it not be a good thing for the readers of the Journal at present, if the old and most experienced queen raisers, such as Longstreth, Quinby, Alley, Benedict, Mrs. Tupper and others, would give a full and detailed account of their method of rearing queens? Many of them have at various times given parts of their methods, but as the Journal is designed for the education of novices and not graduates they should give full detailed accounts, something like that of Alley on page 100, November No. current volume of Journal. Will Friend Alley have the kindness to complete that account for the next No. of the Journal, by way of answering the following questions:

You say you had two hundred and eighty nucleii (queen boxes), in operation in August, besides the full stands, &c. How many full stands do you generally use to supply that number of nucleii boxes with bees, brood and honey, or do you by *liberal feeding* depend on the nucleii boxes to produce the amount of brood required to keep up their own strength without any aid from the full colonies?

What probable number of black bees are within three miles of you, and how far are the nearest, and are not some of your queens mated with bad drones?

Do you use many black bees for rearing queens, and how early in the spring do you commence in your latitude, &c.?

I generally raise in full colonies, but in summer I use about 20 nucleii boxes the same size as Alley, only I rear my cells in full colonies and introduce them in the boxes on the tenth or twelfth day. I am compelled to reinforce my boxes with young bees from full stocks every three weeks in order to keep them strong.

After writing the above I have just received the February number of the Journal, and while on it, would like to answer a question asked me by S. W. Loud, of Virden, Illinois, on page 184. "Asking me if I kill more bees by my close fitting frames than I do by loose ones." I have only tried one triumph hive the past season, and I do not think I killed as many bees as by loose frames; for the hive is so arranged that if used with care you need not kill a single bee. With the exception of the Longstreth, I never handled another hive, but that would kill five times as many bees.

The distinguishing feature of the February No. now before me, is the good news of the recovery of "NOVICE'S" health. What would the Journal look like without him and Gallup, Grimm and a few others.

I must now close, wishing all the readers of the Journal the greatest success in 1872, and as Novice says "rows of barrels of honey."

R. M. ARGO.

Lowell, Ky., February, 1872.

[For the American Bee Journal.]

MR. EDITOR:—Kind sir, according to promise, please find enclosed two dollars for my subscription for another year to the Journal; the longer we take it the harder it appears to do without it. Mr. Editor. you have been trying to buy some of the back numbers, how you have succeeded I do not know, but one thing I do know, twenty-five cents won't buy any of my back numbers, although it looks like a big price. They are worth as much to me as to any other awkward ignoramus, if I would only obey their teachings better. I sometimes think I know something, and pay dear for finding out I know nothing.

You recollect I told you in the Journal that I had packed my hives away with their backs together, stuffing hay in between and on top, made a tight fence on the north and west sides, covered with boards; the weakest hives containing thirty-five pounds of comb and honey. Now, I thought they were all right, but I did not give them upward ventilation. Thinks I, it is the bee nature to gum and close up tight every hole, nook and corner in the hive above them, and if I let it open they will surely freeze; consequently I lost some three or four stocks in Gallup hives. I do not blame the hive. I blame myself. My neighbor, T. P. Duncan, has an old box hive with a ½-inch hole in the top open all winter, and they are all right this spring. Some of my neighbors have informed me that they had some to starve this winter in old box hives with plenty of honey in the hive but no upper ventilation. I have a few fixed Robert Bickford fashion and they did well.

One of my neighbors, Finley Kruson, informed me the other week that a few years ago his boys went out with a gun, and happening to see some combs on the underside of the limb of a large tree, close to the stem, they shot in and knocked down some nice combs with honey and live bees. This was in the spring of the year, before swarming time, and they had evidently wintered out in the open air, with no other protection but the combs, limb and trunk of the tree. Don't you think they had upward ventilation enough? Who knows a similar case in this latitude?

I have got myself a honey slinger, but have not tried it yet. It is geared and runs nicely. I am also getting my new hives ready for operation when the emigrating season comes.

Fearing I am wearing your patience I will close by subscribing, as ever,

A MILLER,

By occupation, but not a moth miller.

[For the American Bee Journal.]

The "Hazen" Beehive.

On page 143 of January number of the Journal, I see "Novice" refers to Jasper Hazen and his opinion of the Italian bees; and in the same number, Mr. Grimm refers to his beehive.

In September 1867, I made a trip among bee-keepers, and as I had previously, through the columns of the Country Gentleman, had some discussions with Mr. Hazen, about the respective merits of his non-swarming hive and the Langstroth hive, I called upon him.

I found him living in the outskirts of the city of Albany, N. Y., and a much older man than I expected to see; then 76 years of age, but full as vigorous as men will average at that age. I told him I wished to see his much lauded non-swarming hive, about which I had seen so much figuring to prove it the best of all hives made. He took me out to see them. He had five old stocks in the spring; but, as the season advanced, lo, they all cast swarms! I thought he seemed a little annoyed, that after all his puffing, his so-called non-swarmer was a failure. I noticed, however, to my surprise, that he was appropriating Mr. Langstroth's invention, without due credit, and evidently with a disposition to detract from his claims as inventor and patentee.

He showed me, I should think, some four or five hundred pounds of box honey, some of it very nice.

In conversation with Mr. William Stratton, of West Troy, whom I visited the same day, he gave Mr. Hazen the credit of having a good hive for box honey. But although he had one hundred and forty stocks in his apiary, I did not see one of Mr. Hazen's hives among them. Mr. Stratton said it had been the best season for box honey in that locality he had ever experienced.

Mr. Hazen's hive (he then called it the Eureka,) is nothing more *in effect*, than a common box hive, about the size and shape of the one used and recommended by Mr. Quinby, with boxes applied to the top and sides.

D. C. HUNT.

North Tunbridge, Vt., Jan. 5, 1870.

New Mode of Destroying Wasps.

Wasps have been rather plentiful. I have for several years adopted a very simple, yet very effectual plan of getting rid of their nests. When I find a nest, I select the noon of a hot sunny day for my operations. I procure a very strong solution of cyanite of potassium, and I saturate a piece of lint, about three or four inches square with the solution. This lint I quietly place at the hole leading to the nest in the ground, in a bank or elsewhere. Nothing more is requisite. Every wasp that arrives at the hole, on its descent alights on the lint, and after one or two gyrations, drops over the edge of the lint into the hole, dead, or else dies upon the lint—not one escapes. After sitting down by the side, watching the operation for about ten or fifteen minutes at most, the number of wasps arriving home becomes very much lessened, and then only a few odd ones arrive. I then dig out the nest. All are destroyed. There is no fuss, no risk of being stung, as every wasp coming home falls on the fatal lint, and has no escape. The evaporation of the cyanide is very rapid, and the air all around the hole is tainted, and the wasps seem fascinated by it, as I never saw any turn away. They look as if they must settle, and when they once alight they have no power to raise themselves; the use of the wings is gone, and they are soon dead from the inhalation of the cyanide.

This is a very simple way of destroying the nest, because if you do not wish to take the nest you may leave the lint there. It will destroy all the nest, and will do no harm to anything else.

When the nest is in a tree, I generally go in the evening, and hold the lint soaked in the cyanide under the bottom hole. The wasps soon begin to drop out, first one by one, then in a regular shower. Of course caution must be used to avoid the inhalation of the cyanide; but as so little is required, it is not very probable any accident will result from the proceeding.—*Cor. Journal Horticulture.*

Omue Epigramma set instur apis, aculeus illi, sint sua mella, sit et corporis exigui.—MARTIAL.

"Three things must Epigrams, like bees, have all,
A sting, and honey, and a body small."

AMERICAN BEE JOURNAL.

EDITED AND PUBLISHED BY SAMUEL WAGNER, WASHINGTON, D. C.

AT TWO DOLLARS PER ANNUM, PAYABLE IN ADVANCE.

VOL. VII. MAY, 1872. No. 11.

[For Wagner's American Bee Journal.]

Letters of F. Huber.

We have the pleasure of presenting to our readers the first of the promised unedited letters of the world renowned Huber. They were first given to the world in *L' Apiculteur*, the French Bee Journal so ably edited by M. H. Hamet.

These letters will have special interest for those who know how largely bee-culture is indebted to the genius, energy, and wonderful enthusiasm of the blind apiarian of Geneva. Some portions of them give charming glimpses of his inner life. François Huber, as we read them, becomes a name more loved and honored than ever. His cheerful heartiness in promoting the welfare of others; his generous appreciation of merit wherever found; his wise discrimination (so seldom at fault) between facts observed and mere theories or conjectures; his readiness to admit his own mistakes and deficiencies; his genuine modesty and almost child-like simplicity, should be studied carefully by all who aspire to benefit their fellow men by describing the works of the Great Creator.

Reading these letters for the first time, when confined to our bed by a railroad accident, we sometimes felt almost as though Huber was standing before us, and we were about to take him by the hand, and express our affection for the man to whom, in common with the whole apiarian world, we owe so much.

Knowing how difficult it is in our moments of enthusiasm not to overestimate our discoveries and inventions, how often have we wished that we could question the first inventor of a movable frame, to learn from him the practical results which he secured by it in his own apiary; how he obviated what seemed to be its inherent difficulties, and what, if any improvements he made upon it. We expected, of course, no answer to such vain longings, when lo! we have as it were Huber *redivivus*, telling us with his own lips the reasons which prevented him from carrying his speculations into practice—criticizing this and that defect of his hive; suggesting alterations and improvements, which go far to convince us that had he been able to use his own eyes, he would have excelled as much in practical as he did in scientific apiculture.

Imagine Huber in his apiary, with eyes, ministering fully to his wonderfully inquisitive and penetrating intellect, and how many mistakes, compelled by his reliance upon others, might have been avoided? Might he not have given a consistency and practical efficiency to his discoveries and inventions, which we now see ought necessarily to have flowed from them, and yet which were not reached until more than half a century after his first letters were published to the world?

L. L. LANGSTROTH.

[From L' Apiculteur.]

Unpublished Letters of F. Huber.

Under the title of Apicultural Documents, we publish the correspondence of Huber with a distinguished practical beekeeper of Switzerland, C. F. Petitpierre Dubied—who was for a short time, in some measure, a co-worker with the distinguished observer of Geneva. The apiary of Dubied was at Couvet, and was one of the largest in the Canton. Some of Huber's letters were written by himself—others were written by his wife or daughter at his dictation.

OUCHY, October 12, 1800.

SIR:—I have just received your letter of September 15th. It has been nearly a month in reaching me, as you see—having been directed to Pregny, which place I left nearly eight years ago. I am flattered, sir, with the confidence you so freely place in me. My observations in Natural History have disclosed to me a method which may be of advantage to beekeepers. I promised myself to be the first to test it; but the circumstances in which I, as well as so many others have been placed,* have not permitted me to give any consistency to my speculations.

Some persons have given my leaf hive a trial, and because they did not take all the necessary precautions, or were not seconded by the skill of their assistants, it has not proved in their hands as great a success as Burnens found it, and as I was too ready to believe all others would. This method then has certainly the disadvantage of requiring both skill and courage † in those who practice it or to whom it is entrusted. But when these qualities are united I venture to assert that it promises more advantages than any others that have been proposed. I advise those persons then, who have done me

*Owing to the French Revolution of 1789. Ed.

† Huber's original letters suggest very obviously, what this and other remarks to follow, put beyond question, viz.: that he did not know how easily bees could be pacified by a little smoke or sweetened water. With this knowledge, the Huber hive, with its close fitting sections, can be used by any one of ordinary skill and courage, who is willing to devote the extra time required for all manipulations.

L. L. L.

the honor to consult me, and whose assistants possess only ordinary skill and intelligence, to adhere to the hive and system of M. de Gelieu.* With very slight alterations it can be adapted to the formation of artificial swarms. Its construction is very simple, its size handy, and it has this further advantage over mine—that its success has been confirmed by time.

M. de Gelieu can reply much better than I to most of your questions; but since you place some value upon my opinion, I will give it you, asking only a little time for reflection. I only write you to-day, sir, to announce my reply, and to prevent you from deeming me guilty of negligence towards you of which I am innocent. I will do my utmost to prove to you the interest I take in your success. Rest assured of this, sir, and believe in my devotion.

F. H.

P. S. If you have the courage to try the leaf hive, you must first try it on a small scale. It is enough perhaps, for the first year, to have four or five of this style, which will answer for instructing your employees in the necessary manipulations. Experience and observation have compelled me to make two alterations in the construction of this hive. The first does away with the hinges which have a disadvantage which I will explain to you another time. The second is in the entrances which I have placed at the bottom of each leaf. Instead of these you must make one, about an inch longer, in each of the two boards which close the small sides of the hive, fitting to it Palteau's entrance regulator. If you expect to stock five leaf hives next spring, it will be advisable to have ten made this winter. The extra frames, you see, will then answer for alternating empty frames between the full ones. Cylindrical hives would be good if they were not too difficult to make accurately. Therefore, I prefer square frames dovetailed together.

(Translated by Dr. EHRICK PARMLEY.)

* Gelieu published in 1772, a work entitled "*A new method of making artificial swarms.*" L. L. L.

[For Wagner's American Bee Journal.]

Queen Nurseries.

As nothing is said on the subject of queen nurseries in the 3d edition of my work on bees, published in 1869, some of the readers of the Journal may be interested in an extract from the 2d edition (published in 1857), page 237.

"I shall here describe what may be called a *queen nursery*, which I have contrived to aid those who are engaged in the rapid multiplication of colonies by artificial means. A solid block, about an inch and a quarter thick, is substituted for one of my frames; holes of about one and a half inches in diameter are bored through it, and covered on both sides with gauze wire, which should be permanently fastened on one side, and arranged in the form of slides on the other, for convenience in opening. A hole should be made in the wire large enough to admit a worker,* and yet confine a young queen when hatched.

"If the apiarian has a number of sealed queens, and there is danger that some may hatch and destroy the others before he can make use of them in forming artificial swarms, he may very carefully cut out the combs containing them, and place each in a separate cradle! The bees having access to them, will give them proper attention, supplying them with food as soon as they are hatched, and then they will always be on hand for use when needed. This nursery must of course be established in a hive which has no mature queen, or it will quickly be transformed into a slaughter-house by the bees.

"In the first edition of this work (published May, 1853), in speaking of the queen nursery, I remarked as follows: I have not yet tested this plan so thoroughly as to be *certain* that it will succeed. . . . When I first used this nursery, I did not give the bees access to it, and I found that the queens were not properly developed, and died in their cells. Perhaps they did not receive sufficient warmth, or were not treated in some other important respects as they would have been if left under the care of the bees. In the multiplicity of my experiments, I did not repeat this one under a sufficient variety of circumstances to ascertain the precise cause of failure, nor have I as yet tried whether it will answer perfectly, by admitting the bees to the queen cells.

"Since writing the above, I have found that this nursery answers perfectly the end designed, by giving the workers access to the queen cells."

L. L. LANGSTROTH.

* One side might be covered with tin, having perforations just five thirty-secondths of an inch wide. L. L. L., 1872.

[For the American Bee Journal.]

Nucleus Hives.

In reply to Rusticus, on page 204, March No., and also to numerous correspondents, I will give my method of managing nucleus hives. In the first place to stock our nucleus, we select two combs from a populous hive containing mature brood and honey at the top of the comb with all the adhering bees. Be careful not to get the old queen. We do this at the approach of evening. We place these two combs in one apartment; on the following morning we insert a sealed and nearly mature queen cell in one of these combs. The reader will understand *we* prefer raising our queen cells in populous stocks that have abundance of brood and nursing bees. The old workers will be apt to go back to the parent stock, and if this leaves the nucleus too weak before the young workers are hatched out in sufficient numbers, we go to any large and populous stock in the middle of the day, take out combs from the centre of the stock, and shake or brush down the adhering workers in front of the nucleus and let them enter: they will be well received, and in this manner you get all young bees to stock your nucleus as young bees less than six days old will stay wherever they are placed. This is a very good plan for strengthening up any stocks. Now our nucleus having all young bees may not gather anything for a few days, and unless supplied, they sometimes suffer for the want of water, so we keep a piece of sponge saturated with water at the entrance; a piece of old comb or even a cotton rag will contain water for them if attended to. As soon as the young queen hatches, we place an empty frame in the centre of the nucleus between these two full combs, and by this time our little fellows have or are ready to commence operations, and we have any quantity of wax workers and nursing bees, and they will invariably fill this empty frame with nice worker comb. The reader will remember our nucleus hive contains three combs in each apartment, and right here we will state that we stock the four apartments all at the same time. We prefer to give the parent stocks empty combs instead of empty frames, for with an old queen the bees are very apt to build too much drone comb to suit us. If you have understood us thus far, you will perceive, that the removal of our combs containing brood and adhering bees from strong stocks and replacing empty worker comb has not perceptibly injured the stock, from which the nucleus was stocked. We have lost nothing, but have gained a good nucleus. To keep this nucleus in good running order, we extract the honey as it is required, giving the young queen abundance of room to deposit eggs, and the nursing bees and wax workers abundance of employment, and to keep those nucleus strong and numerous, we exchange combs occasionally, as required with strong stocks, giving the strong stock an empty comb or a comb containing eggs and young brood from the nuclei, and giving the nuclei a comb from the strong stock containing mature brood. We think there is nothing gained, but a great deal lost in keeping weak nucleus stocks. In fact we want them fairly overrun with bees. In the description of our nucleus hive we forgot to mention, that there should be an inch hole near the top of each apartment, directly over the entrance, for ventilating in hot weather. This hole can be opened or closed either with a slide or a pine or cork plug. We prefer the plug. It should usually be closed at all times in cool weather or at night. You will now see that if rightly managed, there will be no desertion of queens. Great heat will drive out a swarm from any hive, and so it will from these nuclei, and we have a miniature swarm here, so if we have two queen cells, they are so strong and so numerous, that the first queen hatching will lead out a swarm, therefore we must allow only one cell to mature in the nucleus. If we wish to raise queens in these nuclei, we insert a comb (new combs always preferred) in the centre of the nuclei containing eggs and larvæ just hatched, and either cutting out holes and cutting down cells to the foundation, or trimming up the lower edge of the comb to suit our fancy, as we like to have large cells hanging perpendicular with abundance of food placed in the bottom; therefore, whether nuclei or standard stock for raising *good queens*, the nursing bees must be preparing large quantities of food for larvæ at the time of starting queen cells. We do not like too many cells started, as we think in such cases the nurses are apt to neglect all but a few. Therefore we frequently have worthless natural queens.

Now, Mr. Rusticus, you will see with our ideas and management there is not that great necessity for the wire cloth partition that many suppose. I have never used it, but saw it used in Dr. Hamlin's apiary. We have thought that it might make the bees all of the same scent, and thus at times create a difficulty, but as we have never used it, we cannot speak with certainty.

With our method of stocking nuclei, we never have to place them in the cellar. Recollect we are not giving our instructions to those that know more than we do, but to those that know less. We prefer to leave the young queen in the nucleus, until she has stocked it well with brood and eggs. Before removing her, you will recollect that we stated, we had about 60 pounds of extracted honey and 20 frames filled with nice worker comb from one nucleus hive, last season. Now, if you have understood us thus far, you will perceive that these nuclei thus managed will work just as well in proportion to their numbers, as the strongest and largest stock in your apiary, and we have violated no law *of their nature*, either in raising queens or restricting the production of that queen when she is raised, and we have received a profit in honey and new comb fully equal to the profit of standard stocks, as they are usually managed, leaving out the profit of extra queens raised, &c. You will see in the article giving the description of our hive, how to make a standard stock of each of these nucleus hives in the fall.

ELISHA GALLUP.

Orchard, Iowa, March 15, 1872.

[For the American Bee Journal.]

Bees in Louisiana.

DEAR FRIEND:—After an absence of nearly two years, I have returned to my former home, and much to my surprise, found at the Village P. O. all the numbers of your Journal, from January, 1870. In my late home, my pursuits were of such a nature, that I had but little time to devote to my pets, and therefore did not renew my subscription, which expired with 1869. * * *

Last year I had two colonies of black bees, "a present from an old negro," with which to commence. My limited leisure did not permit much care of them, yet I increased them by artificial swarming to five stocks and secured five wild swarms from the Cypress swamps in the rear of my house. There was but little forage until the month of March, when white clover was abundant. This continued until about June 1st, after which there was but little of anything to be had producing honey. The rains in the spring interfered much with the yield of honey, which was very short; say about twenty pounds to each colony, leaving them an additional supply of about ten pounds. They have wintered well in the open air as is the custom here, and there have been but few days during the entire winter, when they were not flying. * * *

The orange trees will be in bloom next week, and from them the bees gather the most delicate of all honey; then comes the White Clover during three months, and if there is not too much rain, I hope to secure a liberal supply of sweets.

I wish the Journal many years of success,

GEORGE HOWE, M. D.

Parish Plaquemines, Louisiana.

[For the American Bee Journal.]

Non-Flying Fertilization.

MR. EDITOR:—In the February issue of the American Bee Journal, in the article of Mr. W. R. King, on non-flying fertilization, page 178, he says: "Let us now see what we have in these boxes. First, a young, unfertilized queen, six or seven days old, anxious to meet the drone. She passes in and out three or four times a day. Second, we have twenty or more drones that have never flown in the open air. They are not conscious of a larger, brighter world abroad. They fly around and around, and are satisfied; even glad to know that they have such a world as this, free from the fiery old workers. Here they have it all to themselves."

It would have been fortunate had Mr. King told us whether or not the drones passed in and out of the boxes during the day like the queen, or do they fly around and around, and die the first day of their egress. Doubtless in this lies the grand success of non-flying fertilization. The box or nucleus can be kept strong with drones of the right age, by frequently inserting combs with young drones hatching, and the number sufficient to keep up animal heat in the absence of the workers.

Hatch and confine queens in nursery cages until the fifth or sixth day, and when the drones are flying through the fertilizing house, let the queen loose in the house, and if she is immediately fertilized, remove her.

I have completed my fertilizing house for $30. It is permanently framed together, and can be carried wherever desired. If non-flying fertilization is a failure, as some suppose it will be, I will have a good fruit house frame left for my part of the trouble.

A. SALISBURY.

Camargo, Ill.

[For Wagner's American Bee Journal.]

Linden Plantations.

In reading Mr. Gallup's very interesting article in the April No. on Linden honey, I noticed specially his remark that one variety of the Linden near him blossomed some ten days earlier than the other. The European Linden usually blossoms a week or ten days earlier than the American, and a bee farm covered with these three varieties might prolong the bloom for a month. Even this time might be lengthened by a wise selection of other varieties.

Those who are acquainted with the superior quality of the Linden honey, are aware that the time is at hand when large plantations will be made for apiarian purposes. The tree is easily propagated, grows very rapidly, and blossoms quite freely when only a few years old. The wood is extensively used for inside cabinet work, and for all kinds of work requiring material light and springy, and which can be made to take and keep almost any desired shape. In some sections of the country its value for lumber is second only to that of the pine, and if acres of Linden should be set out in such places, they would soon become for this purpose, highly profitable, to say nothing of their value for honey supplies.

The attention of our National and State governments has been called strongly to the dangers which menace the country from the wide destruction of our native forests. Already, they are proposing plans for the encouragement of new plantations, and we believe that aid will soon be offered to enterprising apiarians, in making extensive plantings of our best native honey-producing trees.

L. L. LANGSTROTH.

[For the American Bee Journal.]

Central Iowa Beekeepers' Association.

PROCEEDINGS OF THE FIRST ANNUAL MEETING HELD AT CEDAR RAPIDS, JAN. 18 AND 19, 1872.

The Association met at 10 o'clock A. M., January 18th, and was called to order by the President, W. H. Furman, of Cedar Rapids.

A constitution was presented and adopted.

The Association then proceeded to the election of officers for the next year, with the following result:

President—W. H. Furman, of Cedar Rapids.
First Vice Pres't—W. F. Kirk, of Muscatine.
Second Vice Pres't—D. W. Thayer, of Vinton.
Sec'y and Treas'r—G. W. Barclay, of Vinton.

A committee to prepare subjects for discussion was then appointed, and the Association adjourned to meet at 1½ o'clock P. M.

AFTERNOON SESSION.

The Association met pursuant to adjournment, and commenced the discussion of the

First Question:—"What is the best method of swarming bees artificially?"

Mr. May, Cedar Rapids. Asked how bees could best be swarmed so as not to have them chase a fellow.

Dr. Blakesley, Anamosa. I move a strong old colony to a new place; draw cards of comb with eggs, brood and honey from it; place in a new hive and set the new hive in place of the old one, and when the queen cells are ready, form other nuclei and furnish them with queen cells. Then stock up with cards from other hives. The old hive may swarm after that.

Thos. Hair, Marion. Agree with Dr. Blakesley.

J. H. White, Monticello. Takes frames enough from several colonies to make a new one, and sets it where the best old colony stands. Don't be too hasty in multiplying colonies. I have made six from one in a season, and lost all. Keep colonies strong,

W. F. Kirk, Muscatine. Unless I could

swarm bees artificially, I would not keep them. Take two or three frames and the queen from a good colony, put in a new hive and set it in place of the old one, and so have worker comb in the colony that has no queen. Commence as soon in the spring as the colonies are strong enough, and before they commence queen cells. Keep all colonies strong by giving weak ones comb from strong ones. Have managed five hundred colonies in this way and never lost any.

Wm. Townsend, of West Branch, and J. Lewis, of Cedar Rapids, agree with Kirk's method.

Mr. White. Puts a fertile queen with the colony when swarming artificially; no danger of swarming if you commence early, before queen cells are made. Put on boxes early. Equalize all colonies in the spring and in September, by giving weak ones comb from strong ones.

Mr. Furman. If I had but one stock I would take two or three combs, generally two, with the adhering bees and place them in a new hive; place the new hive in the place of the old one. If I had stocks enough should draw a comb with the queen and a quart of bees from a strong stock, put in a new hive, and set the new hive in the place of some other strong stock. Divide as soon as there is a supply of honey in the spring.

Second Question:—"What is the best method of handling bees so as to avoid exciting their anger?"

Mr. Hair. Bees are like men; some are terribly cross. Smoke such thoroughly. If the colonies are gentle, handle them carefully, and give a little sweetened water, perhaps. For smoking I use mostly rotten wood.

Mr. Kirk. Unless bees have honey to fill themselves with, the more you smoke them the crosser they become.

Mr. May. I want to know of Kirk what the object is in smoking bees. Is it in some mysterious manner to make honey for them?

Mr. Kirk. Bees are like Mr. May. If his house was on fire he would grab all the most valuable things he could leave with, and while loaded down he couldn't fight.

Third Question:—"What is the best method of procuring honey in the comb for market?"

Mr. Furman. Use boxes that will hold from five to six pounds. It is sometimes difficult to get bees to work in them. I put in three guide combs; the middle one to reach from the top to the bottom of the box, and placed right side up. Fasten with bees-wax and rosin. It is essential to have empty comb for this purpose. If you have none, empty the honey from some of your combs and place back in the hive, so that the bees may dress it up. Then cut in strips and put in the boxes.

Mr. Hoagland, Fayette County. Bees will work much sooner in the boxes if guide combs are put in. Put them right side up. Think box honey much the best way to prepare honey for the market.

Fourth Question:—"Do bees gather honey from honey dew?"

Mr. Furman. Think they do.

Mr. Kirk. There were tons of honey gathered from it in our region, and it was not as good as buckwheat honey.

W. S. Goodhue, Lisbon. Where I reside, bees gather honey rapidly from honey dew, and it is of splendid quality.

Mr. White. Have seen bees so thick on white oak that I thought they were swarming, and I believe they were at work on honey dew.

Mr. Peters, Anamosa. I believe the quality depends upon the time the honey is gathered. If gathered early it is white; if later it is dark colored. Sometimes it appears in June, and sometimes in August. Found only in dry, warm seasons.

Fifth Question:—"Will it pay to use the 'Extractor'?"

G. W. Barclay, Tipton. Think it will. It is a great benefit when the combs are loaded with honey. For want of breeding room some colonies become weak. Use the "Extractor" and give breeding room. If put up good and honest, extracted honey will pay better at ten cents per pound than honey in comb at thirty or thirty-five cents a pound. I believe we get more box honey by using the "Extractor;" having more breeding room we have stronger swarms.

Mr. Hodge. I have my doubt abouts the "Extractor" being a benefit or profitable. We can't get box honey when there is room below for storing it. We can sell honey in the boxes when we can't sell extracted honey; for the comb is beautiful, and nice for the table. It attracts attention and comment.

Mr. Furman. I have known of the "Extractor" for five years, and was slow to adopt it. I got one a year ago and I like it. When I came to colonies that were at work in boxes, I let them alone. But I found that where bees were not at work in the boxes, extracting set them to work in them, because the comb extracted from was wet with honey, and they would not deposit honey in it till it was cleaned up. Shall use "Extractor" oftener next year. It saves time and honey. I took 100 lbs. of extracted and 37 lbs. of box honey from one hive, and might have taken more.

Mr. Hair. Some like candied honey best, but comb looks best. People are prejudiced against *extracted* honey, because they have used *strained* honey, which is mixed with bee-bread, the crushed young bees, etc., etc.,

Mr. King. I purchased five swarms last spring and they increased to twelve, and I got 500 pounds of extracted honey.

Mr. Furman. Extracting should be done every three days.

Adjourned to 7 o'clock P. M.

EVENING SESSION.

The Association met pursuant to adjournment, and commenced the discussion of the

Sixth Question:—"Is the Italian bee superior to the native or black, and are hybrids better than the native?"

Mr. Kirk. Italians adhere to combs better than the black; are better workers, and more prolific. These three things make them very much superior to the black.

Mr. Goodhue. The Italian will gather honey where the black will starve.

Mr. Peters. One Italian swarm is as good as one and a half of blacks, for robbing; but they are not as liable to rob.

Mr. Townsend. The Italian queens lay their eggs more compact than the black, consequently, are more prolific.

Mr. Barclay. One stand of hybrids is as good as two stands of the natives.

Seventh Question:—"What is the best method of wintering bees?"

Mr. Hoagland, I stand a row of crotches in the ground and lay on a pole for a ridge pole. I then lay on rails, one end on the ground, and the other on the ridge pole. Then cover with straw and put on about a foot of dirt, make a door at one end, ventilate well and keep entirely dark.

W. M. Lanphere, Benton County.—Put my hives up in the form of a pyramid, and cover same as Hoagland.

Mr. Furman. I winter my bees in my house cellar. It is very important to keep an even temperature. I keep the thermometer at about 40. If it is too warm the bees will crawl out.

Mr. Kirk. A dry, dark cellar is as good as anything.

Mr. White. Have wintered bees in the cellar two winters with good success.

Dr. Blakesley. Keep mine in the cellar and like it. They come out in good condition in the spring. Give good ventilation.

W. Hunt, Center Point. Am strictly successful with Langstroth's system.

Mr. Barclay. Have best success out doors with the cob system. Like prairie hay in the caps.

Adjourned to 9½ o'clock A. M., to-morrow.

FRIDAY MORNING, Jan. 19.

The Association met pursuant to adjournment.

Mr Furman. Said he had succeeded in getting the State Board of Agriculture to offer liberal premiums for the best display of Honey, "Extractors," Bees, etc.

It was voted that when we adjourn, it be to meet at such time and place during the next State Fair, as the executive committee may select. [To meet in Cedar Rapids, if a room can be secured.—SEC'Y.]

Discussions on the

Eighth Question:—"In what way can we best get rid of fertile workers?"

Mr. White. If a queen is successfully introduced she will destroy the fertile workers.

Mr. King. Shake the bees into a new hive in a new location, and let the bees go back to the old hive, and the fertile workers won't be likely to get back into the old hive.

Mr. Furman. Fertile workers lay several eggs in a cell, and skip some cells; but queens lay compact. Agree with Mr. King as to the best method of getting rid of fertile workers.

Mr. Hair. Agree with Mr. King.

Ninth Question:—"Are spiders, wrens and king birds friends of the apiarist, in the destruction of the bee moth?"

Mr. White. I don't want any spiders around my hives. Have killed and opened king birds, and never found any bees.

Mr. Peters. Thought king birds a benefit.

Mr. Heald. Had killed king birds and cut open their crops and found them filled with bees.

Mr. Barclay. Believe the king bird was a friend of the apiarist; but believed the Missouri Fitch would prove more of an enemy to the bee than the bee moth.

Adjourned to 1½ o'clock P. M.

AFTERNOON SESSION.

Tenth Question:—"What is the best manner of rearing queens?"

Mr. Furman. My manner of rearing queens is to form nuclei in the spring by taking one or two cards with bees, eggs and brood from a populous colony and put in a nuclei hive; shut the bees in and set in the cellar for a day or two. Take them from the cellar near sundown and let them fly. When the queen hatches examine her and see that her wings, legs, &c., are perfect. The next day after the queen is taken away insert another queen cell. I keep a record of my doings on the hive.

Mr. White. Experience limited,—raise early in season.

Eleventh Question:—"Can queens be fertilized in confinement?"

Mr. White. Have tried Mitchell's way and failed.

Mr. Furman. I believe it is impossible to do it. At the National Beekeepers' Convention I offered $500 to any man or woman that would come to my apiary and fertilize fifty queens in confinement for me.

On the best time to remove bees from winter quarters, all who expressed an opinion, said: the best time is when there is no more danger of injury by cold snaps.

Mr. Furman. Said he marked his hives from one up, and kept a book with the pages numbered to correspond with his hives, and used a page for each hive.

On spring feeding Mr. Hair said he used dry comb, pouring the feed over it and laying on the honey board or tops of frames. Also, feed rye flour.

Mr. Barclay. Make a feeder six inches square of lath, stretch muslin over the top and put feed on that; the bees will suck it through. I feed rye flour, also.

Mr. Furman. Said he was going to feed all stocks more. It stimulates them and we get strong stocks early. They will brood faster and eat more honey, giving room for breeding. Feed regularly, every day a little at a time.

Mr. White. I fed rye flour to twenty swarms last spring, and they ate about half a bushel.

Mr. May. Said he was aware that men took rye in its liquid form, and could not see how temperance men could conscientiously feed rye to bees.

The following resolutions were adopted:

Resolved, That to allow bees to winter on their summer stands is no better economy than to let other stock go unprovided for.

Resolved, That the American people have been thoroughly humbugged by patent bee-hive vendors.

Resolved, That every bee-culturist ought to take one or more bee journals, to the end that bee-culture as a science may take that elevated position among the industries of the State, that is eminently its due.

Resolved, That the President and Secretary of this Association be instructed to collect statistics as to the rise, progress and success of bee-culture in the State, and as to its value as a source of wealth to individuals and to the State.

The President, W. H. Furman, at the request of the Association, delivered an address on bee-culture,– a copy of which was requested for publication, but Mr. Furman refused to comply with the request.

At the request of Mr. Williams, a committee was appointed to prepare a brief and concise article on bee-culture, to be published by him in a pamphlet he is preparing for gratuitous circulation among the farmers of the State.

The thanks of the Association were tendered to those papers that gave notice of this meeting; to the C. & N. W. and B. C. R. & M. R. R. for reduced fare; to citizens and hotels of Cedar Rapids, for reduced charges; to the City Council for the free use of the City Hall; to the officers of the Association, for their efficient labors; and last, but not least, to the State Board of Agriculture, for offering increased premiums for the productions of the apiary.

There was a large attendance of beekeepers at the Association, and the session was a pleasant and profitable one.

MEMBERS' NAMES.

W. H. Furman, J. M. May, I. J. Rogers, C. C. Williams and Abel Evans, Cedar Rapids; Thomas Hare, Lydia Hare, Ida Hare, Eliza Hare and Louisa M. Downs, Marion; D. W. Thayer, S. A. Thayer and A. S. Charberson, Vinton; Dr. E. Blakesley, Lizzie Blakesley and R. O. Peters, Anamosa; W. M. Lanphear and Mr. Sandsbury, Belle Plaine; W. Hunt and E. D. Hazeltine, Center Point; Ezra Heald and Wm. Townsend, West Branch; A. R. Foster and J. B. Thomas. Mt. Vernon; G. H. White, Monticello; A. J. Langaman, Blairstown; E. A. King, Jefferson; Hiram Hoagland, Douglas; Geo. W. Barclay, Tipton; Dr. M. Chandler, Maquoketa; Dr. A. B. Mason, Waterloo; W. S. Goodhue, Lisbon; W. F. Kirk, Muscatine; James Lewis, Sigourney; J. A. Bartholomew, Western; Sarah A. Dodge, Fairfax.

The next annual meeting of the Association will be held at Cedar Rapids, on the third Wednesday in January, 1873.

W. H. FURMAN, *Pres.*
GEO. W. BARCLAY. *Sec'y.*
A. B. MASON, *Ass't Sec'y.*

In Germany, France and Italy they are settling upon a nomenclature for all matters connected with bee-keeping. Until we have definite terms in English, we shall continue to be diffusive or to "beat the air." L. L. L.

[For the American Bee Journal.]

Italian vs. Black Bees.

It is with profound regret that I read in the March number of the Journal that its honored editor is no more; few men have exerted themselves in the bee interest like him; the first to embark in a disinterested bee journal, wholly for the good of the beekeeping world. I say disinterested, because all or nearly all who followed him with bee publications have axes to grind, and publish their papers for the double purpose of advertising their own stock of trade, and at the same time have others to pay them for doing it. Such men are no public benefactors; the less we have to do with them, the better. I am glad to learn, that although the head is removed, the Journal still lives, and will continue its monthly visits as heretofore. It is, indeed, sorrowful to learn that so honorable a member of the bee fraternity has gone; one upon whom we could rely, whose counsel was always pure and unbiased, and who was so abundantly able and willing to enlighten the great body of apiarians of the land. Personally, I never became acquainted with the deceased, but I have been a constant reader of his journal for several years, and I feel as though one of my nearest relatives had been removed.

On page 209, March number of the American Bee Journal, I find an article by Mr. J. M. Marvin, which is a perfect smasher in the bee line. I knew that bee science was rapidly being perfected, but that article was so far ahead of all I ever read or heard of, that I feel like saying a word; 1st, because the report of a certain bee convention made him say that Italian bees did not work in boxes; that having proper knowledge, more box honey can be got from Italian bees than from black bees, and that he can get the extracted honey all put back again in boxes. If this is so, it is certainly a blessing that few men have got that knowledge, for then surely would the bees suffer. But in my limited experience, I find that neither Italians nor black bees will store honey in supers until the body of the hive is full. I might extract it from the body of the hive as often as I pleased, and give the bees access to it, they would invariably carry it back to the brood chamber again. The instinct of the honey bee is to store its supplies as near the brood as possible.

In the next place, he argues that the common reason why some fail to get the *Italians to work as well in boxes as the blacks*, is because the Italians work earlier and later in the season, and when the weather is cool, and few bees in the hive. I am sorry to say that I could never get either the black or Italian bees to store in boxes under such circumstances, and if he can, I would in connection with a great many other bee men, be much obliged if he would give us his *modus operandi* in the next Journal.

He next jumps into Adam Grimm because he says box honey is more convenient for transportation, and that he, Marvin, is obliged to accompany his box honey to market in order to prevent the railroad or other carriers from stealing, &c.

This is not so necessary in extracted honey. He says: "The Arctic explorers or shippers to cold climates would certainly choose a well cured, good, solid article of extracted honey." Well, suppose they do, is that an argument that box honey is not preferable, and that it should not be made? Is it not well understood that artificial honey is and can be made, and that extracted honey can be and often is adulterated, and that many persons on that account will not buy, much less use it? that extracted honey, even if pure, will not sell near as readily or for as good a price as box honey? Mr. Grimm doubtless understands perfectly well, and probably acts in a great measure upon it, notwithstanding all that Mr. Marvin or other men may say. "All dealers would certainly dispense with boxes and wax if they could acquire the knowledge." (What knowledge?) "And especially in the tropics." I would like the gentleman to explain. Again, he says: "How will it be with boxes with wax comb." I did not know that the bees made any other but wax combs, and as for breaking down in cold weather, and moth worms hatching in warm climates, the former can be remedied by making the boxes of a proper size and secure packing, and the latter is no great evil, as honey hardly ever stands over long enough to be damaged in that way. Upon the whole, I think the gentleman's article is too highly colored, and that very little good is derived by beginners from such writings. I, however, must confess that I am yet a novice at the business, and have much yet to learn. With due regard for all, I hope that I have not offended any one, and sorry, indeed, would I be, if I had. This has been a hard winter in our section. Many bees have died, and I fear many more, if not attended to, will die before the spring arrives. Few bees kept in the old-fashioned way, will get over, and I think such a season as the last, will convince old fogies that luck has little to do with successful bee-keeping, and that good management and plenty of it, alone will prove the best luck.

WM. BAKER.

Milford Station, Pa., March 16, 1872.

Dronings.

Anticipating what some critics may think of my desultory comments and questions, I beg leave to "take out a patent" on the above caption.

1. Would it not be of great service, Mr. Editor, to many of your readers, and especially beginners, if you would give us every month, a brief list of "Hints?" You would in that way save many a tyro from that fearful "too late," which so often throws him back a whole year in indispensable bee work. You may answer that the *latitude* of your circulation is so great that your "Hints" would not suit all, but as your journal is issued with such admirable punctuality, the first of every month, surely within the thirty days, your suggestions would come home to every beekeeper from Florida to Maine.

2. Let me advise my brethren, against transferring from box hives to movable frame hives in April, or at any time before swarming—unless indeed they have some urgent reason—and it must be *very* urgent to compensate for the almost inevitable loss of brood, danger of robbery, and certain delay in swarming, accumulation of honey, &c., &c. Last April I transferred a swarm from an old box hive to one of Alley's, and apparently with great success, but in a day or two, the robbers set in persistently, and I had a long and wearisome fight with them. I conquered them at last, but the bees did not store one pound of surplus until nearly the close of the season. When they did get into the side boxes, they worked splendidly, but I firmly believe that if I had waited until June to transfer them, I should have done greatly better.

3. Wont *somebody* tell us of a *certain* plan for securing straight combs? I have tilted my hives at every practicable angle. I have put in the nicest bits of comb guides. I have used Colvins' separators, and still "one event confounds them all," the obstinate wretches in the majority of cases (like the Irishman's hog, that "ran up all manners of streets") will run every way but up and down; the only guaranty, as far as I know, is to have full sheets of empty comb, to alternate with empty frames.

4. The more attractive we can make our honey, the more salable will it be, obviously. In England (as I find from a recent work of Alfred Neighbour's), it is all the fashion to secure honey in glasses, most of them with flat tops, of various sizes, some of them with apertures of three inches in the tops to allow the passage of the bees to and from upper glasses, they have (in most of them) *ventilating* tubes, which would soon be useless *eo nomine*, on account of propolis, but would answer admirably as *nuclei* for the combs. These glasses need not be of first quality, and if ordered in sufficient quantities, might be furnished (I should think) at such rates as would justify us in using them largely. Nine purchasers out of ten would prefer to pay the additional price, especially for that particular pattern of glass, which being flat topped (and provided with a lid), can be inverted, placed upon the table, and when emptied, could be used until next spring as an ordinary preserve jar. I would cheerfully furnish this book to you, Mr. Editor, if you think well enough of my suggestions to have the illustration of these glasses transferred to the Journal. They could readily be gotten up in time for the honey season.

5. I have heard that the editor of our Journal has translated the full works of Huber, with notes and appendix, bringing the science up to the present day. If so, let us start a subscription list, and *insist* upon the publication. I offer the modest sum of ten dollars to begin with.

B.

In some seasons bees will get very little honey from the white clover, although all the conditions are apparently favorable. In the same way, Italian bees will in some seasons get little or no honey from the second crop of red clover, while in others they will *store* largely from this source, while black bees are losing weight.

[For Wagner's American Bee Journal.]

A Well Assumed Moral Indignation!

That our readers may judge impartially, we insert Mr. H. A. King's reply to our personal of March last.

The Defence Of Mr. L. Against "Misrepresentation."

"Whom the gods would destroy they first make mad."

For more than a year past, we have been the object of the grossest misrepresentations and the vilest insinuations, but up to the time of Mr. Wagner's death, Mr. Langstroth himself had maintained his usual dignified position in this controversy. But "how are the mighty fallen." Scarcely were the funeral services of Mr. Wagner ended, when Mr. L. seized his pen, and descending far below the plane of common respect, gives vent to a tirade of foul aspersions and dark insinuations while under the influence of a well assumed "moral indignation."

For this furious outburst, which he says some of his readers may think is overdone and "will recoil upon himself," he pleads as an excuse, what he calls our "December utterances" against him, and that a sacred duty to the late Mr. Wagner demanded it. Mr. L. must have carelessly neglected the imperative call of duty, or else this is *only* an excuse, for his article contains no defence of Mr. W., nor a reply to anything said against him; and Mr. Fisher, Jr., one of Langstroth & Otis's attorneys, pronounced our December article "a fair and genteel discussion on the subject." We believe it has been Mr. L.'s policy from the first to have *others* keep up a steady fire against us, hoping to secure our defeat, and eventually our service in his behalf. About a year since he said that if he had been connected with a man like us, he would have done well; and not long afterwards, he said to us, "with your energy, you would have made a fortune out of my patent." We replied by telling him that in view of his course, in refusing to compromise, we should give him the benefit of all the energy he gave us credit for.

Our success in obtaining testimony invalidating his patent, caused a change in his tactics. If we could not be forced to capitulate by warfare, perhaps our desire for peace, and supposed love of money might induce us to give them the victory. Hence a share of the spoils, and a union with such illustrious men was tendered to us. The dishonorable terms of compromise to secure a union and an extension were rejected, but the proposition admonished us of our duty in another direction. We acted promptly and energetically, and not without success, as the pen of Mr. L. has well proven.

We believe these are the acts which have driven him to desperation. He has become convinced that the proposed union cannot be effected, and now he "will hold no terms with such a man." There is nothing more to be gained, and as he alone is left, he will have the satisfaction of dealing the deadly blows of revenge, himself. We told Mr. Otis that they had no one to blame but themselves, for they refused to compromise when we could have done so honorably, for then we had not the thousandth part of the evidence we now have, against Mr. L.'s claims, but we *never* could have united with any one to collect blackmail from the honest beekeepers of the land. We would not intimate that Mr. L. himself has ever done this, for we will make no insinuations against his character. Our editorial written at Washington before we had heard of Mr. L.'s accident, or Mr. W's death, closed with the following words:

> But as we said before, so we still say, we have no ill will towards Mr. Wagner, or Otis, and that we have the same kind regards for Mr. Langstroth, that we have ever manifested. And we stand ready, as soon as the conflict is over, to do more for him than we ever proposed to do.

He refuses to give credit to our Christian character and non-resistant principles, and labors to convince his readers, that our heart is full of malice towards him. He says we boast of our religious devotion, and as proof, quotes the following, from a biographical sketch of our life, published in the *Phrenological Journal*, February, 1871, and leaves his readers to infer, that the language is our own:

> Active out-of-door exercise having now restored the health of Mr. King, his impulses of duty, again called him to the home missionary field. A peculiarity in his labor, was that he never received any pay for his ministerial work, not even for traveling expenses, when called to journey for the benefit of his fellow men, many miles by rail. This has given him great power with skeptical minds, since they could not question the purity of his motives, and the sincerity of his purposes.
>
> The business, however, to which he gave such impetus, now began to feel the effects of his absence, and yielding to a strong outside pressure, upon mature deliberation, he decided to return to his business, under the solemn vow that he would use all his surplus income to advance the holy work to which he had devoted his youth.

Mr. L. may well quote;

> Alas for the rarity of Christian charity,

for his whole article—especially at this point—is a sad, but forcible illustration of its truth. It is a common fault of biographers to praise too much, but it is not common for men of Mr. L.'s standing, to wander so far from the subject of controversy to obtain matter to injure the personal character of his opponent. If these are his best weapons, and his cause is to be maintained by poetical quotations, works of fiction and attacks upon our personal character, weak indeed must be his position against those who he imagines are his opponents and maligners.

We thank Mr. L. for his just criticism on our extract from the Cleveland paper concerning Mr. Moon's invention of movable frames. We quoted the report of most of the speeches from the Cleveland papers and put in that quotation without thinking that we were reporting it, officially, as secretary of the North American Beekeeper's Association. Mr. L. is also entitled to our thanks, for calling our attention to our announcement that we should not be a candidate for any office. By the solicitation of friends we concluded to allow our name to be used lest our opponents should claim that our refusal was evidence of fears of the result. We inform Mr. L. that the quotation from our JOURNAL, where we are represented as saying that Huber used the *present style* of frames, is a typographical error, as the context shows that it should read "section style."

The quotation about "bottomless pit," is itself a quotation from one of the attacks made on us a year ago. Mr. L.'s reply to Baron Von Berlepsch we trust will meet a response from that gentleman, and if so, the extent of our influence in the preparation of his "Declaration" will be exhibited, as well as the supposed discrepancies noticed in the *Bienenzeitung*.

Mr. King's complaints of "gross misrepresentations and vile insinuations" unsustained by any facts, come with very bad grace from the man who was the *first aggressor* in this controversy. Not until February, 1871, did Mr. Wagner call attention to the worthlessness of his patents—

while in December, 1870, Mr. King telegraphed to the convention at Indianapolis, these words:

"R. C. Otis, of Wisconsin is publicly making many false statements to defeat union at Cincinnati. Mr. Otis is no true friend to Mr. Langstroth." (See Am. B. J., Feb., 1871, p. 172.)

We call special attention to Mr. King's unqualified admission that up to last March, "Mr. Langstroth had maintained his usual dignified position in this controversy." Our course, however highly appreciated, was no protection against his insinuations of bribery, fraud and personal dishonor; nor from his very *un*-dignified sneers. The public will judge whether we have vindicated our friend by discharging "the sacred duty that was laid upon us of exposing" his calumniators. We have never attempted to influence any one to attack the character of Mr. King.

One year ago, in the presence of one of Mr. Otis' attorneys, we told Mr. King that his hives, in our opinion, had nothing of special value not covered by our patent; and that if at the beginning of his apiarian career he had honestly taken hold of our invention instead of infringing upon it, he might by his energy have made a fortune for us both. We think so still.

As we have never desired any compromise, but have sought in every legitimate way to bring the suit to a trial, our readers will place the proper estimate upon Mr. King's assertions, inferences, and conjectures on this subject.

Strong professions, of a desire to guard the public against "black mail," are suspicious, when made by one who has never remonstrated against the "beveled edge comb-guide" fraud, and who is engaged in selling "*rights*" to a hive which, while claiming to be covered by three patents, uses with some petty exceptions, the patented features of none of them.

Mr. King says that a year ago "he had not the thousandth part of the evidence against the Langstroth patent that he now has;" and yet he *then* informed us that the *foreign* evidence, if put into proper shape, was enough. Discerning men, gauging his necessities in the suit by his "year of toils" in Europe and America, will only laugh when he calls my claims "ridiculous;" they can never believe that he piles such Pelions upon Ossas, in the way of testimony, out of mere zeal for works of supererogation!

We want no charity from Mr. King, but if the courts decide that he has *our* money we shall be glad to get it.

Until Mr. King says that the revelation to the whole world of that "solemn vow" was unauthorized by him, he cannot be acquitted of the charge of violating the Master's precepts.

In the supplement to the January, 1871, No. of his paper, Mr. King *began* this controversy through the press, by devoting nearly three columns to a bitter attack upon the personal and business character of Mr. Otis. He prefaced it with this declaration: "It has been a rule of our life that when we could not speak well of a man, we would say nothing about him. We do not now propose to violate this rule"—and yet he scrupled not to insinuate that Mr. Otis had been guilty of bribery and fraud, and makes this fling at his religious character: "We once reproved him, and should judge from his answer that he formerly belonged to a Christian church, but is now living in a backslidden state." Can a man who with loud professions of lofty morality, thus assails the good name of a business competitor, feel surprised that the purity of his motives should be questioned, or that men should think that while he "prays cream, he lives only skim milk?"

That our readers may see how little of *extract* or *quotation*, and how much of a desire to injure us, there is in that part of his *report* which we criticized, we give the language which he used. After describing "a beautiful honey pyramid which Mr. Moon had placed upon the President's table," he says:

"An article appeared in one of the Cleveland papers next day, to the effect that the beekeepers of America were greatly indebted to Mr. Moon for the first invention of movable comb frames in America, which have been used in various forms since their first invention by him in 1838. Although we did not know of its intended publication there until we saw it in the paper, yet we speak advisedly when we say that the movable frame, with narrow top bars suspended on rabbits, with shallow chamber, etc., should be called the 'Moon Frame.'"

If Mr. King still "thanks us for our just criticism," will he show it by retracting his charge that we violated the generous confidence reposed in us by those two conventions, or must we accept his recognition of our previous "dignified position," as a full withdrawal of all charges up to the date of that March personal?

Mr. King's failure to answer grave charges, while he carefully vindicates his historical accuracy from a typographical error, is very suggestive of that "*interpolated the.*"

We are quite willing to wait for the Baron's explanation of the supposed discrepancies.

"*A well assumed moral indignation!*" Mr. King may yet have occasion to say: "These are a few of the unpleasantest words pen ever put to paper."

Stretched wounded and helpless on our bed, the best of friends had died in an adjoining room: instead of his genial morning salutations, came sudden word that he was dangerously ill, followed in a few minutes by the terrible announcement that he was dead. Mr. King coming (as he himself takes pains to inform the public) to that house of sorrow—need we say unbidden and most unwelcome—learned by his intrusion all these facts from our own lips; was, therefore, personally acquainted with the circumstances under which we wrote—heard that there was no likeness of our departed friend, and that we had not been able to take even a last look at his remains; knew further how soon after that visit there came to that afflicted family the accusations which appeared in the Indianapolis Journal. What need alas! was there on our part of any *pretended* moral indignation? and what a revelation does this man make of himself by his cruel suggestion!

If we did step beyond the limits which we had previously assigned to ourselves in this controversy; if our facts were too strong to require any aid from epithets and comparisons however true and however obviously suggested—let our readers "put themselves in our place," and picture the tragical circumstances under which we wrote.

In all this controversy, *Mr. King has given his readers only his own side;* while we have obeyed the almost sacred injunction "*audire alteram partem*" "to hear the other side," so truly embodied in Mr. Wagner's manly offer, and *have given our readers both sides;* so that if any injustice should be done, the bane and the antidote might go together. Only an honest cause could afford this.

Loathing the necessity which forced upon us these personal controversies, we again express the hope that they may be referred for settlement to the only impartial Tribunal.

L. L. LANGSTROTH.

Washington, D. C., April, 1872.

[For the American Bee Journal.]

Dysentery in Bees.

The winter just closing has been one of the most disastrous to bee-culture ever known in this State. I am of opinion that two-thirds of all the bees in this part of the State have died. Some beekeepers have lost all, and others have lost more than half. I have fared better than most others, having lost only five out of seventeen colonies, and only two of them by disease. The other three were smothered by a heavy sleet on newly-fallen snow. The disease that has carried off so many bees is what is termed dysentery. In most cases plenty of honey has been left in the hives.

I have been of opinion, since the disease first manifested itself, that it was caused by an inferior quality of honey gathered from the honeydew that was so abundant last summer and fall. Honey-dew is produced by several kinds of aphides. That which was so abundant in this part of the country last season was the product of the white cottony looking insects called beech lice. Much of the honey stored from July to November was from this source, for it continued to be abundant even after the first severe frosts. Perhaps, if the winter had been mild like the preceding one, so that the bees could have had a good fly occasionally, they would have lived, notwithstanding the poor quality of the honey. I was confirmed in the opinion that the honeydew predisposed the bees to disease by visiting, on yesterday, a neighborhood where there is no beech timber. There I found that the bees are wintering as well as could be desired, no colonies having been lost, and all seeming to be in a perfectly healthy condition.

If the honey had been extracted from the combs last fall, and the bees fed with sugar syrup until they had enough to winter them, they would, no doubt, have been in far better condition this spring.

M. MAHIN.

New Castle, Ind., March 1, 1872.

[For the American Bee Journal.]

The Winter in Michigan.

The past winter has been very disastrous to the beekeeping fraternity of Michigan, for throughout the State there has been a fearful fatality among the bees.

I have heard from several counties, and from all alike comes the doleful report of dysentery and death. We at the college have lost nine colonies, while many more unlucky still have from forty to one hundred deceased colonies.

The cause generally assigned for this fatality is the unparalleled severity of the winter. But as the symptoms are the same in every case, viz., much thin uncapped honey, sour and otherwise unwholesome to the taste, in all the lifeless hives, besmeared combs, and intolerable stench. We believe the cause to be the same in all cases, and think it as evident that it results from sour honey.

Our bees that have died were fixed for winter quarters the last of October.

We then noticed that there was a good deal of uncapped honey, but as it seemed sweet, we believed it would thicken, and be capped over before we should put them into the cellar.

We took considerable honey away, and were rather careful to take that which was nicely capped over to keep for spring feeding. We have a fine dry cellar, and have always had excellent success in wintering, so we passed the winter away from the college, without the least foreboding as to the welfare of our beautiful three-striped Italians. But a sad prospect awaited our return, our bees then appearing as stated above. Why the flowers of the past autumn should have yielded thin honey, which the bees should regard as unworthy of being capped, I think a mystery. If the season had been wet, instead of unprecedentedly dry, I think it would have seemed more explainable.

Last summer we used the two most excellent honey extractors, the Peabody and St. Charles, Illinois, machine, and extracted, I believe, from seven colonies enough to pay for either machine. If we had thrown out the thin honey in the fall and sold it, buying and feeding coffee sugar, *a la* Novice, I am sure we might still have our bees, thus saving $90. If all our apiarists had done the same, thousands of dollars would have been saved to our State.

Apropos to machines, I would say that no apiarist can afford to be without a mel-extractor. We also found Dr. Davis' queen nursery most serviceable.

I cannot close this article without speaking my commendation of the neat Peabody Extractor, the St. Charles machine, rendered easy to work and admirably by the gearing, and Dr. Davis' queen nursery, which is invaluable in helping us to raise and keep our queens without trouble or danger.

A. J. COOK.

Agricultural College, Lansing, Michigan.

Where did Noah preserve the bees during the flood? In the ark-hives.

[For the American Bee Journal.]

Doctors' Differences—Swarms and Strong Stocks.

The beginner in beekeeping meets with much to perplex him in the contradictory statements of those looked upon as "masters." I had concluded that on hiving a swarm, it was desirable to have it on its stand as soon as possible, otherwise the bees would mark the new location and adheie to it. In February number J. Butler recommends that swarms intended to be returned should be kept hived until after sunset. Will he oblige us by stating why this is necessary, and what is done with them from the time of hiving until they are returned? Will he also state what basket hives are? I have also thought that the great desideratum for safe wintering is strong stocks, but now comes Mr. Hosmer, at the Cleveland Convention, with the theory that all stocks should be reduced to one-quart, preparatory to going into winter quarters. To succeed, I presume this small quantity of bees must have peculiar management.

ENQUIRER.

Carlton, Ontario, March, 1872.

Glycerine as Bee Feed and to Prevent Candying.

MR. EDITOR:—In December numbor you state that glycerine is useful for the above purposes. What should be its price? In one town, I am told, 40 to 75 cents per pound, and am assured that both samples are pure. If glycerine will prevent sugar syrup from candying, might it not be added to the honey for the same purpose? I find that honey heated by being kept in boiling water, does not candy as long as it is kept in a dark vessel, but on its being drawn in glass vessels it candies directly.

ENQUIRER.

Ontario, Canada, February, 1872.

Fertilizing Queens in Confinement.

MESSRS. EDITORS:—You will allow me through the columns of your May number to answer the queries of brothers Nesbit and Gardner, in regard to fertilizing queens in confinement. I would have done so through the April number, but my March number did not come to hand in time, not having received it until the 14th, and you require all communications to be sent in by the 15th. Both brothers Nesbit and Gardner ask about the same questions in substance. 1st. Why do you place sweetened water in old combs on a shelf in the top end of the fertilizing room, if the workers are not allowed to fly? Answer: The drones become weary of flying, and very many of them will alight on this shelf, and there find something to refresh them; we are apprized of the fact that drones are not in the habit of taking refreshments from home. 2d. Why do I plank or board up the sides of the house two feet? Answer: We do not think a house six feet high is high enough; does not give sufficient height for them to fly, unless you run your *tent pole* high in the centre. A smooth dirt floor might do as well as boards; we prefer the boards. 3d. Why do we put the dark calico over the top? Answer: To prevent the direct rays of the sun from creating too great heat upon the nucleus boxes. If the house could be arranged in the shade (not too much) of a tree or trees, common brown cotton may be used. 4th. Is there no chances of queens entering the wrong nucleus, and destroying each other? Answer: We never had one killed in this way; we mark our boxes differently, by painting, or by pieces of different colored paper. Now, Mr. Editor, we have, we believe, answered the Enquirers satisfactorily, and will simply add, that all apiarians who decide to build a fertilizer according to my plan, must carry out the *whole* plan as I have attempted to *fully* describe it through the journals. There is no doubt but some will fail, as I have before stated. Men love to add to or take from what they read; my motto is to fully carry out what I read, and if I fail at first, I consider all the circumstances, and frequently find that I was to blame. We are aware that there are a few doubting Thomas's. We are aware that there are men who will doubt even what their eyes see. Such men are presumptuous, and do not like to admit the fact that other men can experiment and bring new things to light. The world is full of such.

WILL. R. KING.

Franklin, Ky.

[For the American Bee Journal.]

On Sugar Syrup for Wintering Bees.

In March number, page 212, Mr. L. L. Langstroth says: Novice's observation shown to me by Mr. Wagner, that bees when wintered on sugar syrup, in their first flight do not discharge their fæces like those fed on honey, is entirely new to me, &c. Novice, in his article on page 198, says: "We have read in the Journal of some such occurrence, but have always had a little doubt about their first flight in spring not showing some discolored spots on the clean snow, but now we have verified it sure." We were the one that Novice did not believe, or, in other words, the writer that he somewhat doubted. When we made such a statement in the American Bee Journal (we think it was in the American Bee Journal, but are not sure), we expected that but very few would believe us; but it was a fact, and belief or unbelief does not alter facts. The cry now comes up from any quantity of correspondents, that their bees are all dead, or have the bee cholera, &c., &c. The reader is already aware, if he has followed us in the American Bee Journal, that we do not believe that bee cholera, or dysentery as it is called, is a contagious disease. It is caused by improper food and improper ventilation. Remove the cause; allow the bees a purifying flight, and there is no more disease. Last spring was very dry in some localities, and there was large quantities of insect honey dew. In the absence of other forage, the bees stored considerable quantities of it, and in many localities there was considerable late thin honey stored, and again in many cases, the bees were left on their summer stands, improperly prepared for winter, and the winter set in extra cold and early. The hives were filled with frost in every part (except in the cluster of bees), caused by the breath of the bees, and the first moderate weather melts and moistens up the hive, and also the honey to a certain extent.

Now, in reply to the note on page 212, we never tried emptying their honey, only suggested the plan. Our suggestions to correspondents are: If the cholera, or bee disease, as you call it, is caused by the insect honey stored in the hive, the remedy is to watch the sources from which your bees are gathering their supply and extract all this insect honey, and feed either good honey for winter, or sugar syrup. If caused by thin watery honey, extract all and evaporate by heat and feed it back again. I hold that 10 lbs. of good thick honey is better than 30 lbs. of thin, watery stuff; or, in other words, 10 lbs. of good honey, of the proper density, will go further towards wintering a swarm of bees than 30 lbs. of thin, watery honey. We have actually wintered swarms on the summer stands in an open bee shed and in an old-fashioned straw hive, when we lived in Lower Canada, where they were confined to the hive by the weather from the 1st of October until the 20th day of April (nearly 7 months), and at times during the winter the mercury was 40° below zero. Don't tell us that bees freeze to death in cold weather, when they are in a proper condition, for we shall doubt your word after our experience, even worse than Novice doubted ours. On their first flight, the bees did not even speck the snow one particle. We have wintered on the summer stands in Wisconsin, with just as good results in the Dutch hive. Those bees were wintered on good honey. We had no extractors in those days. Honey gathered in good weather, from white clover in June, or from basswood in July, is good enough for bees to winter on provided it is stored by a good strong stock, with plenty of nursing bees or evaporators. For in such a stock it is evaporated sufficiently before being sealed up. The reader will recollect, that with our first season's operations with the Hruschka, we stated that we had two stocks of black bees, and their honey was thin and watery, while honey gathered from the same source and at the same time by the Italians, was extra thick; we hastily and erroneously came to the conclusion that the difference in the breed of bees caused that difference, but another season's operations has convinced us that it is or was the condition that the stock was in at the time of gathering the honey. For illustration, take a large stock of all old bees (a stock that has been queenless for quite a while, and that has but very few nursing bees and no brood), and they will gather honey rapidly in a flush time, but their honey will be thin and watery, or imperfectly evaporated. We occasionally have cool, wet seasons, and none of the honey that is stored is of good quality for wintering purposes. I think it was Mr. Marvin, of St. Charles, Ill., that suggested, or had actually tried the experiment of extracting as fast as gathered, and evaporated by heat. At all events, this experiment should be tried, as it would inincrease the yield of honey per stock wonderfully in time of basswood bloom. In an article on wintering bees on their summer stand, we will give our views on preventing the accumulation of frost in the hive.

ELISHA GALLUP.

Orchard, Iowa.

[For the American Bee Journal.]

The "New Idea" Bee Hive.

Mr. Gallup, in the Journal for March, page 208, in an article on his "Twin Hive," says: "Mr. D. L. Adair has worked his sections in this manner for years, if we rightly understand him." With some little difference in details, I have, and it gives me pleasure to confirm most of the conclusions that friend Gallup has arrived at, but I think I have got the thing a little more perfect than he has. I, as long as two years ago, removed all cross-partitions in the hive, and now have one continuous chamber from 3 to 4 feet long, having discovered that they destroyed the unity of the colony, and that the queen would confine herself to fewer sheets of comb, and at the same time, and be more prolific when she could have it all compactly together. Her brood nest is made to occupy the middle of the chamber, while the ends are filled out with pure solid honey. The centre board or division, I find to be a positive injury, besides which, as Mr. Gallup uses it, it is covered by Albert Kelsey's patent, which I used ten years ago, and discarded on account of this very division board. The hive is simpler without the division, and will be found to work better. Without going into details, I will just say that this arrangement of hive proves with me to be more perfectly adapted to the instincts and wants of the bee than any I have seen. It is the only reliable plan for controlling swarming. It renders the mel-extractor useless for securing the greatest profit, as nearly as much honey can be secured in the comb as can be obtained by the honey machine, and will sell for three times as much per pound. By the use of the continuous chamber, and the unity of the colony thereby secured, I find I can secure three times as much honey as by any arrangement that requires the surplus to be deposited in boxes separated from the brood nest. I have in press a small book, intended to explain the theory on which the "New Idea Hive" is based.

D. L. ADAIR.

Hawesville, Ky.

We learn from several prominent beekeepers that if our suggestions in the last No. about using the *Hruschka*, to empty *thin* honey, in the Fall, could have been made last September, many colonies which have died of dysentery might have been saved. L. L. L.

[For the American Bee Journal.]

Bee Feeders.

I have seen several kinds of bee-feeders described in your Journal, but I think I have the cheapest and the best, and as it will soon be time to set our bees out from their winter quarters and feed liquid sweets for early breeding, I will try to describe my feeder, so that any one can make it.

As I use the Langstroth hive, I will describe it for that kind of hive. Take a bottom board from a common honey box, about 5 by 6 inches square and ⅜ of an inch thick; for the bottom nail blocks ¾ inch high around the entrance in the bottom, then nail on sides two inches high, then run melted beeswax in the joints, to make it water tight, then tack small strips from the top of the blocks around the entrance, slanting back to the bottom for the bees to walk out on, then set it over a hole on the honey board, pour in your feed, lay on a glass cover, so that by lifting the top of the hive, you can see when the feeder is out.

A. M. H.

Adams, Ill.

DEAR BEE JOURNAL:—With sorrow we read the account of the death of that most estimable citizen and naturalist, your founder, Samuel Wagner. Sad news, indeed, the March number carries to the beekeepers of our land. His place will not be easily filled. Not being personally acquainted with Mr. Wagner, little did we think he had lived beyond his three score and ten, for "its vigorous editorials," which were generally short, but pointed and always instructive, did not show a man who had lived beyond his allotted days.

To his energy and intelligence, as much or more than any one man, beekeeping has in a few years been elevated from an uncertain, mysterious and ignorant business to a systematic, scientific, and remunerative occupation.

He was respectful and courteous to those he deemed honest, and his criticisms, though often severe, were just, and although modest, he shrank not to expose, with cutting words, the noisy drones and pretenders in our great human hive. He certainly was a good judge of human nature.

To benefit his fellow men seemed to be the bent of his mind. He did not live for the present alone, and many generations will have come and passed away before the name of Samuel Wagner will be forgotten, but "the silver cord has been loosed," and

"Like crowded forest-trees we stand,
And some are mark'd to fall;
The axe will smite at God's command,
And soon shall smite us all."

W. P. H.

Murfreesboro, Tenn., March 14, 1872.

Italian bees, as a general rule, build more drone or store comb than black bees.

[For the American Bee Journal.]

Wintering Bees.

In reply to Novice, vol. 7, No. 8, p. 180, we did not give that swarm any brood or young bees. It was all the proceeds of one queen, and February 12th, 1872, that swarm is on its summer stand, and the queen is putting in her best licks, considering the season of the year. But comparatively few beekeepers yet know what a queen can do, providing we keep removing the sealed brood to the outside, and give her empty comb at just right intervals in the centre of the cluster for her to breed in. We tried Mr. Hazen's plan of giving brood to make up large swarms *at once*, and we know by experience that if we cannot have our stocks in condition for storing surplus, without that plan, it is an excellent one, for extra large swarms are what we want for storing surplus, whether in boxes or for the extractor.

We are wintering our large hives on the summer stands, and thus far, February 15th, 1872, we are highly pleased with the results. We understand that Quinby & Root, Mr. Hetherington, A. H. Hart, and several other prominent northern beekeepers, have adopted that method, and why should we not?

We have to thank Mr. C. C. Vanduzen, of Sproutbrook, N. Y. (who took the trouble to call on us over a year ago), for valuable hints on that head. Many beekeepers have no good cellars, and it is not always convenient to build special repositories. Then again, if all our bees are in the cellar, and the house takes fire and burns down, away go our little pets. Furthermore, our southern beekeepers must have hives that can be wintered on the summer stand. It is as absurd to tell him (when he has no ice) to put ice in his cellar to keep it cool, as it is to tell a northern beekeeper to rub his hives with peach leaves, to make his bees stay in the hives, when there are no peach trees near him.

ELISHA GALLUP.

[For the American Bee Journal.]

Correspondence.

MR. EDITOR: I have lost seven stocks this winter, by some disease I know nothing about. They died suddenly, with plenty of honey. They were in a warm house, well ventilated. Has it visited the apiaries of any of the readers of the Journal, and, if it has, can they tell me how it can be avoided? there seems to have been an epidemic among bees, this last winter in this district.

C. E. WIDENER.

Cumberland, Md., March 25, 1872.

Bees that were left out of doors have wintered very poorly in this section. One-third have died. Honey was poor. The dysentery affected them badly. March 24th, and it is snowing very hard. Please find enclosed a small amount and continue the Journal. We could not do without it. The sad news that we received in the last number of the Bee Journal of the death of Samuel Wagner was shocking. I could hardly make it appear that it was our old Editor, until I read it over two or three times, but may the Journal prosper as ever.

Minna. W. N. ROWLEY.

I like the *Bee Journal* more and more, it seems as if every number was better. I hope it will still continue to grow in the minds of the bee-keeping public, and that all interested will do all they can to increase its circulation both at home and abroad. Bees in this vicinity are wintering rather poorly. I think a great many colonies are as weak now, in numbers as they have been in former times, the 1st of April. Most of the bees in this vicinity are wintered on their summer stands, with no more protection than in the summer; the consequence is, a great many come out warm days and fall down on the snow and die. I think more bees are lost this way, here, than in any other way, except by foul brood.

Bee-keeping in this vicinity is not progressing any more than it was five years ago. Last September I was traveling in the West. I had the pleasure of visiting the apiary of Mr. Adam Grimm, of Jefferson, Wis. I must say that I never saw a nicer lot of honey gathered from any apiary than that of Mr. Grimm's; and here I had a good chance to see his Italian bees and his method of queen raising and shipping queens, &c.

I also called on Mr. Wolfe and Mr. Adam Furbringer to see their bees and I found none but Italians in my travels around Jefferson, so that all of the queens reared by Mr. Grimm were pure and mated with Italian drones. I saw some of the finest productive Italian queens I ever saw at Mr. Grimm's apiary; full swarms of Italians. If I were to purchase Italian bees or queens, I would as soon get them of Mr. Grimm as to send to Italy. With the advantages he has, I think his queens and bees are equally as pure and productive as any that can be found in any country. I came away well pleased with my visit and was well paid for my journey to Wisconsin, and hope I may live to take another trip out there again. D. W. FLETCHER.

Lansingville, N. Y., March 12, 1872.

The summer of 1871 was the poorest season for bees ever known in this part of the country.

No swarms and very little honey from the black bees. Our Italians swarmed *some* as a matter of course, but had to be *swarmed back again* in the fall or strengthened from other stocks.

We broke up quite a number of black stocks and divided their honey and bees among other stocks that were deficient.

Our bees are in winter quarters yet. We have not been into the cellar since about the first of December.

From appearances they will remain where they are for two weeks yet. G. H. BOWERMAN.

Bloomfield, Ontario, April 1, 1872.

It has been the worst season here in Central Michigan since November last—that I ever knew, and I have not been without bees for three months in fifty-three years. I commenced the winter with 76 swarms, and have lost just one-half that number. Yet I have been more fortunate than most other beekeepers, as some have lost all, while others have lost from 80 to 90 per cent. on their investment. I attribute it to a combination of causes: 1st. Bees filled the body of their hives in June and July with a large amount of honey, leaving no room in the brood comb for their queens to deposit eggs for rearing workers, to supply the loss of superannuated bees. 2d. The weather was so cold for five months, that bees could not fly out at all to discharge the fæces, and consequently many died. This retention of their fæces produced cholera, as was shown by the besmearing of their hives and combs.

Now one word in favor of the Italians. My bees are mostly of that species, having bred from the most undoubted purity, from Mr. L. L. Langstroth, Mr. Nesbit and Mr. J. H. Townley.

My experience teaches me that the Italians are more hardy, more prolific, more easily handled, and will work earlier in the morning, later at night, and make more trips to the same fields in a given length of time than the mulattoes; also, less inclined to rob, beside swarming at least two weeks earlier. Last spring my first swarm came off on the 18th of May and no black bees swarmed till the 8th of June.

As to Alsike clover I think it is better for honey than any other honey producing plant I ever saw; also that it is better for hay or for pasture than any other grass, nor will it wash out on side hills or heave by hard freezing.

Byron, Mich., April 6, 1872. O. E. WOLCOTT.

Bees have wintered rather poorly on their summer stands, specking their hives badly; many dying, many not having an opportunity to fly out from the middle of November until about the middle of February. What are left are very weak, but are getting to work lively now. Mine have been at work on buckwheat flour since the 25th of March. I give them the fine bolted flour, pressed down in small heaps in vessels or on a plank. They waste but very little. My bees took but little notice of the flowers of the Partridge pea. Did not see over 3 or 4 on them throughout the season, yet they were very busy visiting two or three stalks of mother-wort close by; also catmint, portulaca, pansey and buckwheat. Yet the pea is a fine blossom for garden culture, even if bees do not attend to it, so, many thanks to the Commissioner of Agriculture for sending me the seed. I suppose through your agency.

Spring appears to be fairly opened now. Most of the frost is out of the ground and Alsike clover is starting finely. I have over four acres out, sown last spring. Some of it was in bloom by the 1st of July and kept in bloom until frost put a stop to it. I suppose the Journal will go on. We feel very sorry at losing the main leader of the Apiarian cause in America—if not in the world. MOSES BAILEY.

Winterset, Iowa, April 8, 1872.

Gallup Upon H. A. King.

Some of the readers of the American Bee Journal may think that our departed friend, Mr. Samuel Wagner, was too harsh with Mr. King. We ask them to bear in mind that Mr. Wagner, as well as Mr. Langstroth, and some others, was perfectly well acquainted with the man. He knew some of his saintly transactions carried on under the cloak of pretended friendship, and Mr. Wagner despised hypocrisy or rascality under the pretence of religion *so bad* that language failed him to express his honest indignation at such proceedings. I heard Mr. King tell us at the Cincinnati convention of his exceeding great love for Mr. Langstroth, and I thought at the time that I understood that love. It was something similar to the love that the highway robber or pickpocket has for his victim.

We too can read Mr. King, and it is sufficient for us to say, that we have severed all our relations with him. During the time that we were writing for his journal, he tried bribery on us, then flattery and soft soap, and last of all, he tried the driving process, and neither of them worked to his satisfaction. We are not in the market to be bought and sold by any one. Flattery and soft soap always make our bristles stand up the wrong way; and perhaps he thinks that we are too much of a hog to be driven. If he had just asked us at the start, we could have saved him all his trouble. Now, if Mr. King has any doubts about this bribery, flattery, or driving, all he has to do is to just ask for some of his private correspondence to be made public. We are aware that it is not manly to publish private correspondence, therefore we leave this matter with Mr. King, and shall govern ourselves accordingly.

In reply to correspondents who ask us why we did not answer Mr. Quinby's article in Mr. King's November number, we state that Mr. King refused to publish our reply, unless we withdrew all our connections with the American Bee Journal. He gave us his *ultimatum:* if we continued our relations with him, he would publish our article, but if we continued our relations with the American Bee Journal, why, then, all our relations with him were severed. We can assure our readers that it did not take us long to decide. We believe we came to a decision in that case the quickest of any case ever submitted to us. Now we have just said as little about this matter as we possibly could, and shall not mention it again unless Mr. King pitches into us, and then we shall defend ourselves to the best of our ability. So correspondents will please ask us no more questions on the above subject.

Let not the reader suppose for one moment that we bear any personal spite against Mr. King, but when we have once found a man to be of his stripe, we wish to have no more dealings with him. Neither did I wish to mix myself up with the controversy between him and Mr. Wagner or Mr. Langstroth; but his rascally attack on Mr. Wagner, in the National Bee Journal, through his partner, Mr. Williams, I thought called for Mr. Wagner's friends to speak out. I certainly was a personal friend of Mr. Wagner, and whatever others may say, he was unselfish, and had the interest of the whole beekeeping fraternity at heart. The beekeepers of America have met with a loss in his death that can scarcely be estimated.

Mr. King has seen fit himself to show that Mr. Williams' statements about Mr. Wagner improperly influencing the patent office examiner, were falsehoods, and we presume if he had called the whole article falsehoods from beginning to end, he would have come very near the truth.

ELISHA GALLUP.

April 2, 1872.

[For the American Bee Journal.]

Novice.

MR. EDITOR AND BEEKEEPING FRIENDS ALL:—We are just now busy as bees planting out the embryo basswood orchard, and this is the way we work:

After the trees are removed (with a generous quantity of their native soil adhering to their roots) from their native forests, we bring them to our "ranche," as a friend calls it, when the ground is prepared as for planting corn. In order to occupy all the ground, we have them planted in the form of the cells of honey comb, with each tree the centre of six of its neighbors. We believe this the most economical plan to cover the ground with trees of any kind. Twelve feet each way was our first decision, but finally changed to sixteen feet. To get the desired points, we stretched a long line, and on this tie alternate pieces of black and white tape eight feet apart; when a tree is planted at all the white knots, each end of the line is moved to the next row fourteen and a quarter feet nearly, by means of measuring sticks. Now plant a tree on the black tapes; the third row on the white, etc., and you will have regular hexagons, with a tree in the centre.

A smart German with a fork removes the earth, and then *finds*, even if he has to go some distance, a fork full of some nice fine soil to sift over the roots when put in place (by a smart Englishman), while "Novice," Jr. (who thinks this part of the bee business more free from "onpleasant" peculiarities than some other branches), carefully sifts in with the dirt one ounce of ground bone, to give the young trees a start. After the trees were on the ground, the three hands mentioned above (all smart) put out in nice shape five hundred the first day.

As to Novice himself, he and his colt were a part of the time making the ground fine with one of Thomas' patent smoothing harrows, and then for a change, pruning most of the branches (that is, Novice, not the colt, although she seemed quite willing, and undoubtedly professed excellent *taste* for the business) after the trees were planted.

For the first three or four years we expect to give them careful cultivation, and shall this season raise a crop of corn among them, three hills between each two trees; so we have the corn in hexagon also, and intend to cultivate all in three different directions, and if stirring the soil will make them grow, grow they will, undoubtedly. One hundred chestnut trees are to be planted in the centre of the grove, where the apiary is to be located, sheltered by heavy timber from the north and west wind. In answer to many inquiries, we would say that young basswood may be found in any forest where large trees abound and stock has been excluded. Ours range from one to ten feet in height, and no stock has been allowed in the woods for about six years.

We have really been so busy for the past two weeks at the ranche, that we could not even find time to get weighed, but feel so exceedingly well, that we think we must begin to have attained about the solidity of any *other* good honest farmer.

Friend Gallup, we haven't got over that hitting yet, and if it results in anything serious, who knows what may turn up. In fact, we went and bought a whole, nice, smooth pine board to make a Gallup hive, or rather a hive with Gallup frames; we could not yet bear to think of thirty-two such frames, or fifty-six in our hive, but thought to transfer a stock, so you need not say any more, we had not even tried one; but before we could made up our mind to spoil the board (we could have done it awful quick with our pet buzz saw run by the wind mill), we remembered a friend who uses the unadulterated Gallup hive, and we saddled that same colt quick, and rushed through seven miles of mud and snow until we had found our friend, whom we catechized thus:

"Do you really think those small combs, less than a foot square, enable you to build up colonies quicker than the abandoned Langstroth frames?"

"Oh! yes, sir."

"And that the advantage is sufficient to pay for handling so many frames?"

"Yes, indeed."

"How many pounds of honey did you take from six such hives in 1871?"

"Over nine hundred, and almost my first attempt."

"And you used only a single story 20 inches long outside, and containing thirteen combs each, all that each hive had for brood or surplus?"

"Precisely"

"And if you wanted more room, how would you have it?"

"In the second story."

"And not in Gallup's New Idea?"

"No; for I cannot see *how* it could give any greater yield."

"Your hives are plain and simple; do you like the movable bottom board?"

"I do."

"And see no sufficient advantage for making a front portico?"

"No great advantage to the bees, but a great one for the spiders to spin their webs."

Now, Mr. Gallup, if Mr. Penn is right, why don't you use long frames a la Quinby, when your colony is built up, or even eight long combs in the second story in the place of thirteen small ones. Or use a hive two feet long and one broad, small frames on spring, and long ones when we use the honey extractor, set in the hive lengthwise, and thus make available the amount of brooding space occupied with your petition boards, ends of frames, etc.

One frame 11 x 23 inches, would certainly be more convenient for the queen than two small ones with boards and sticks to break the continuity of it.

Where the extractor alone is used, we think perhaps something might be gained by a frame nearer square or a little deeper, but would not Mr. Gallup find his larger number of frames per hive in an apiary of one hundred stocks or more rather tedious? NOVICE.

[For the American Bee Journal.]

How Gallup's Bees Wintered.

MR. EDITOR:—In order to throw some light on this Bee Disease, we propose to answer Novice by giving the results of our wintering both on the summer stands and in the cellar. We started with 10 stocks on the stands, one in the Bay State hive and one in the Diamond hive, one in a standard Gallup hive and seven in the large Gallup. One of the swarms in the large hives lost their queen the first of September, and we introduced a young queen in the first week in October, consequently they had none but old bees and all died the first week in March with dysentery. The stocks in the Bay State and Diamond both died in February with Dysentery, yet they had young queens and an abundance of honey. The cause was evidently attributable to the form of the hive; as in long continued and steadily cold weather in a tall hive, the bees cluster in a few ranges of comb; this brings the mass or cluster in a wrong position, that is, the cluster is tall up and down, the consequence is, the bees at the top of the cluster are unnaturally warm, providing those at the bottom are kept at the right temperature, and dysentery has always been the result with me in extremely and steadily long continued cold weather.

For this very reason I have heretofore cautioned beekeepers against using a tall hive. A medium size is always the best. The 7 other stocks came through in splendid condition. I undertook to explain this at the Cleveland Convention, but was interrupted so much by Dr. Bohrer that I sat down in disgust. Don't understand me as saying that the form of the hive had anything to do with the bees of Novice dying, as they were probably indoors.

In my cellar I had 42 stocks and 5 nuclei. I lost two of the nuclei on account of their being all old bees. The three that wintered had all young bees and came through in splendid condition with the consumption of very little stores and no signs of dysentery.

Bees left to themselves stopped breeding earlier last season than common on account of the drouth. Old queens stopped laying from two to three weeks earlier than young queens; consequently five stocks in the cellar with old queens had the dysentery when I set them out on the 26th of March, and large quantities of dead bees; probably two weeks longer of confinement would have used up the entire five stocks. I discovered that two stocks were queenless in September, and introduced young queens after it was too late for them to breed, hence they had all old bees and all died with dysentery the first week in March. If the weather had been mild enough to have allowed them a purifying flight I could have saved them. Knowing that my queens were stopping their breeding too early, I stimulated the stocks having my Grimm and Hamlin queens and kept them breeding up to the first of October. The consequence was they went into winter quarters with all young bees, and the result was (they were housed in about the middle of November, and taken out the 4th of April) that they remained comparatively dormant all winter, and the consumption of honey was almost nothing, and on their first flight there was no discharge, not even to speck the snow one particle, and a table-spoon would have held every dead bee in both hives. Now you can see that the theory of caging queens in the fall to prevent breeding and the consumption of honey, is a *splendid theory*, but ruinous in practice.

Again, if every thing is all right there is no necessity for carrying out bees for a flight in mid-winter. Our honey was excellent for wintering bees. No fault in the honey whatever. Now don't understand us as saying that all bees everywhere went up on the old age theory. The balance of our stocks came out splendidly.

E. GALLUP.

Orchard, Osage Co., Iowa, April 15, 1872.

Review of Foreign Bee Journals.

In the Eichstadt Bee Gazette for October (this journal has been published twenty-seven years), there is a report of the Beekeeper's Exposition in the Crystal Palace of the Capitol of Bavaria.

This Exposition was a success. "Truly," says Baroness Lina von Berlepsch, in closing her report, "the hearts of all beekeepers ought to be filled with pride at seeing the marvellous results of an enterprise founded by a new born association." Baron von Berlepsch, when asked by Professor Seibold, "Did you expect so much?" could but answer, "No;" so numerous were the products exposed and so superior to all expectations.

The Baron, in an appendix to the report of the Baroness, speaks of the different sizes of the hives exhibited, and insists on the necessity of a uniform size of frames. The importance of such uniformity is increasingly felt in this country. He says further:

There were but two articles that could properly be called new: a *double hive* from Mehring and a model for the wintering of bees in the ground, from Antonio Wagner, of Vibsbiburg.

The great sensation of the Exposition was the artificial honey of Mehring. He exhibited jars containing honey and honey combs, claiming that he had fed bees with a decoction of germinated barley, prepared as by the brewers when making beer, which the bees transformed into honey in their stomachs. He says that each hive can thus be made to yield a yearly profit of twenty-five dollars, as the liquid does not cost more than one-third the price of honey.

I maintain in opposition to this, that bees cannot change into honey any sweet substances, for I have made similar experiments, and they have always produced results the very opposite to those claimed by Mehring. The substances that I presented to the bees always remained unchanged, and were never converted into honey. Among the several experiments that I made with Gunther, in 1854.*

I offered some prepared beet juice to the bees, but they refused to touch it so long as I did not mix it with honey. After adding about one-half honey to it they began to carry it into their cells, but the mixture showed no signs of change. In 1856 I had in Seebach a quantity of *Reine Claude* plums. I extracted the stones, and gave the juice to the bees. The taste was not changed after it was stored in their cells. In 1857 I cooked some very sweet pears and offered the juice to the bees,† they would not touch it until I mixed some honey with it, but it remained only pear juice when stored in their cells. These are my experiments, and they are entirely contrary to those of Mehring. I invite all German beekeepers to make similar experiments, to see whether bees can convert a sweet substance into real honey, or whether, according to my experience and that of Dzierzon, they can only gather natural supplies without changing their taste.

Like many beekeepers present at the Exposition, I am of opinion that Mehring for the pleasure of hoaxing the beekeepers, exhibited real honey as an artificial product.

If his declarations were true, the matter would be of the highest importance. The Association of Nurenberg has promised to experiment in the matter.

C. P. DADANT, *Translator*.

The juice of barley (*wort*) has since been tried by Mr. G. Barbo as a stimulating spring bee-feed. We translate the article from the Italian journal *L'Apicultore*, March, 1872.

CH. DADANT.

* In 1852, the Gilmore patent, with its arrangement for converting cheap *watered* Cuba honey into a splendid marketable article, was in full vogue, and a large apiary was erected in Brooklyn, to show the workings of the system. The cheap food was exhibited, and the luxurious product (gathered, however, by bees from far different sources) was also exhibited. The whole thing soon fell into merited contempt. See p. 331 of the 1st edition of my work (published in May, 1853), for a full exposition of such frauds, and conclusions precisely similar to those of the Baron.—L. L. L.

† Columella recommends feeding destitute colonies with such sweet juices.—L. L. L.

"We invite beekeepers to use barley liquor for bee-food and report their success. In the second fortnight of February I began to give this stimulating food to six colonies. The bees accepted it, although I gave it pure, but took it with greater avidity after a little honey was mixed with it. They left no residue, not even the mealy part with which the decoction was saturated. The barley (*malt*) arrives from Germany already germinated, and costs at the brewery a little over sixteen cents a gallon. The decoction must not be prepared more than four or five days in advance, or it might sour. Four or five gallons of juice are obtained from a gallon of the germinated barley, by boiling it in water two hours, and adding a little honey. This stimulating and economical food has the advantage of not attracting robbers, The feeders should be cleaned (scalded) every four or five days."

A propos to the transmutation of sweet substances into honey, the Rev. Jesuit Babaz published a book in France, in 1869, in which he described his method of feeding sugared water to bees to be transformed into honey. By scenting the feed with vanilla or other aromatics, he succeeds in producing honey of different sorts; but he hopes for a decrease in the price of sugar to make this industry a *paying business!*

My opinion is that the surest and best method of producing honey is to take good care of the bees, that they may be able to gather the millions of pounds of honey now wasted.

CH. DADANT.

[For the American Bee Journal.]

MR. EDITOR:—In the January number of the Bee Journal, Mr. Gallup gives the dimensions of *his* hive, and tells the amount of honey produced by a single colony of bees. Also of the wonderful prolificness of *his queens*, and winds up by saying, "*Let the donkeys bray*."

As none of them have *brayed*, I presume they think of "*Gallup*," as the old Dutchman, "who was breaking a colt," did of his *son*, whom he had placed in the bush to *bah* at the colt, to cure him of being *scarey*. The boy *did bah*, and the colt upset the Dutchman, and run away. "Ah!' says the Dutchman, "*you bah too lout*." Now, old donkey, don't bah so *loud* next time.

Then in the April number, he says: "Mr. Furman stated at the beekeepers' convention, that he did not believe such statements. and that they were false," &c. Now, I suppose Mr. Gallup says this to draw me out, as he did one of the writers of the National Bee Journal. I hope friend Gallup will not be offended because I spoke my mind at the convention. I based my sayings on *figures*. He says in the January number of the American Bee Journal, also in the Iowa Homestead, of Janury 12th, that his wonderfully prolific queens occupied over four thousand cubic inches with brood. (I suppose she was trying to spread herself from Maine to Oregon.) Brood-comb being only seven-eighths of an inch thick, there must be four thousand five hundred square inches of comb; and as there are fifty cells to every square inch of comb, giving two hundred and twenty-five thousand cells. As it takes twenty-one days for the worker brood to hatch, by dividing two hundred and twenty-five thousand by twenty-one, it gives us about ten thousand seven hundred and fourteen, the number of eggs that must be laid in each successive day. Now, is this not pretty lively work for a queen to examine each cell and lay nearly eleven thousand eggs in one day? Does she not need some time to eat and rest? *Will she not* take one-half of the time? If she does, she has to lay about two and a half eggs every second. Oh! Gallup, how I would like to have that queen under my glass for a few seconds, to see her turn somersaults. And where do you leave poor Mitchell, who says he can make one hundred swarms from one in a season? Langstroth says twenty thousand bees is a good swarm. Some European writers estimate that from seventy to one hundred thousand eggs are laid in one season, but Gallup's queen lays two hundred and twenty-five thousand eggs in twenty-one days, or ten thousand seven hundred and fourteen in one day, making a large swarm every two days, saying nothing about what he had over four thousand cubic inches. I wish that I was mathematician enough to figure up *to-night* the number of swarms he could produce in one season with such a queen, supposing her daughters to be equally *prolific*. He said in his letter to the Editress of the Homestead, that he expected some would say that he lied. I judged of the truth of his assertions by figures, and will leave the readers to judge for themselves.

As to the amount of honey his colony produced, it leaves a poor chance for figures. I *did say* I did not believe it, and I *do not believe* it yet. If he will convince me that a queen can lay eleven thousand eggs a day for twenty-one days in succession, I will grant that they can gather six hundred pounds in thirty days. As he said in the Homestead, they did gather twenty pounds a day for thirty days in succession, then he had to *stop* to go to *harvesting his grain*, (what a pity he could not have got some poor fellow to have taken his place in the harvest field, and let him stay by his honey, for who knows what a yield he might have taken?) One of his hives lost its queen during this *great yield* of honey, so the product was small. My experience has been, that by taking the queen away just before the honey harvest, they will produce a *larger* yield instead of a smaller one. To substantiate his assertions in regard to his big yield of honey, he goes on in the April number of the American Bee Journal, and gives us an idea (a small one I suppose) of the amount of honey in his section, by comparing the basswood trees to "blossoms dipped in liquid honey and hung up to drip." If I had been in his place, I would have made *sap* troughs and placed under the trees, and run the honey right into barrels, and if I couldn't have got barrels, I would have run it into my well and cistern, and if they got full, I would have dug more holes in the ground for the honey. As necessity is the mother of invention, I suppose he will invent some *dollar machine* to prevent such a waste of honey this coming season. Since his illustrations in the April number, backed by some thirty witnesses, I am almost sorry for what I said at the convention. In the Iowa Homestead of January 12th, he says it would take too much space to give a full description of his hive. So I suppose he is baiting for the dollars of the Novices of Iowa.

Gallup's blowing Grimm doesn't suit me. After stating that he had received numerous letters from parties complaining of Grimm's queens, he goes on to eulogize Mr. Grimm and his queens. I have also received a great many letters, and seen parties personally who have made complaint of Grimm's queens. I myself have received twenty-one tested queens (so he said) from Mr. Grimm, and not one proved to be what *I considered pure*. And if Mr. Gallup breeds from *such* queens, no wonder he has to *puff* them through the papers. Breeders and managers of large apiaries know that a man cannot succeed in keeping his stocks *pure* with the amount of labor Mr. Grimm reports to the department of agriculture, as used in carrying on his apiary. To affirm that his queens are pure, Gallup refers to one "*Lively*" (a new beginner). Would he, "a new beginner," be considered a good judge of purity? Then he insults every honest apiarian in America by saying to Mr. Grimm that all that is necessary to get high colored queens, is to cross his Italians with black drones, and then breed back to Italians. The brightest colored queens I ever received, I got from Mr. Langstroth, "and they proved the best I ever had." Do you suppose he got them in this way? He says: "Now, Mr. Editor, don't for a moment suppose Mr. Grimm sent these queens to bribe us, for a puff." Why Gallup, you thought you could do enough in this way to pay for the *right* to use the Langstroth hive, but I couldn't see it.

That hive of Gallup's, of which we have heard so much. What is there of it? Gallup inquires of himself, what have I done that all these donkeys are braying at me so? Why, I only made a hive large enough to hold twenty-six frames, and another large enough to hold thirty-two frames, and another large enough to hold fifty-two frames. Why couldn't some one have thought of that before? Now, says he, I will cook up some hash for them that will beat them all. I will cause the Linden to be so laden with honey, that my hive will make such a large return, that they will all be glad to send in their dollar and stop their braying. And I will rear a queen that will spread herself from Maine to Texas, and lay a swarm of bees every day. Oh! what a *great bug* am I!

W. H. FURMAN.

Cedar Rapids, Iowa, April 16, 1872.

Nuclei formed from Italian bees, are not as easily discouraged as those from black bees. The latter are much more inclined to desert their hives, to "*Skedadlle*."

"It may, however, be asked—if the truth on this highest of sciences has indeed been discovered, how is it that mankind have not hailed it with a burst of enthusiastic welcome? that when it has been now for seven years before the world, it is as yet so little known? What, however, is the reception ever accorded to a great and fundamental truth? Is it not, that at first, it is simply neglected because unrecognized? A few earnest minds, indeed, perceive and embrace it heartily; but the majority brush past it, so to speak, unconscious of its presence. When by degrees it makes way and gains for itself a hearing, it is met by a storm of opposition. Some minds simply dislike what is new; others hate to be disturbed in their ordinary modes of thought; the self-love of some is wounded by finding that they know nearly nothing of what has been their life-long study, and they are unwilling to submit to become learners where they have so long been teachers; while others again find their interests or their influence imperilled by the new idea. In the darker ages of the world's history, persecution, imprisonment, or death, was commonly the reward of the discoverer; now it is simply opposition or misrepresentation, when not even calumny. When, at length, its opposers are unable to resist the evidence presented of its truth, they next turn round and say: "Well, granted that it is so, this is not new; it is found in the pages of such or such an author, ancient or modern. And true it is, that those who now in the full light of a truth look back to the earlier ages in search for it, will often detect its first faint glimmerings in the works of those who were utterly unconscious of the scope of the idea that had for a moment flashed across their minds, as quickly disappearing, and leaving the darkness as complete as it had been before. At length, however, the time arrives when the new truth finds its place in the intelligence of the age; it is discussed in philosophical works, set forth in elementary treatises, and finally is adopted as the basis of public instruction, does its discoverer at length meet with the honor due? Rarely, even then. Few know the source whence the idea has been derived. Ask them, and they will answer: "I never thought otherwise; I learned the theory at college; or I derived it from such or such a work."

(Extract from Kate McKean's Preface to her Manual of Social Science, condensed from the writings of H. C. Carey, LL. D.)

Sometimes, as well in summer as winter, the bees take pleasure to play abroad before the hive (specially those that are in good plight) flying in and out, and about, so thick, and so earnestly, as if they were swarming or fighting: when indeed it is only to solace themselves; and this chiefly in warm weather, after they have been long kept in.—BUTLER.

Those that by their lightness you perceive to lack honey, you may now save by feeding, or driving them into others that have store.—BUTLER.

THE AMERICAN BEE JOURNAL.

Washington, May, 1872.

All communications and letters of business should be addressed to

GEO. S. WAGNER,
Office of the American Bee Journal,
WASHINGTON, D. C.

The continued and prompt appearance of the Journal will, we trust, dispel the doubts many have had as to its continuance. No efforts have been spared, or will be spared to make it the most reliable aid to bee-culture in the United States. Beekeepers throughout the country should continue to send us lists of beekeepers in their neighborhood who do not take the Journal, so that it may become known to every beekeeper throughout the land.

Mr. Langstroth's wound is so nearly healed that he expects to be able to return home by the 6th of May.

We have received an article from Mr. J. M. Price, in reply to Mr. Chas. Dadant, which we shall insert in the June number, unless the parties can come to some amicable settlement of their difficulties.

We call special attention to the metal corners of Mr. A. J. Root (Novice). We have seen them, and are of opinion that they will prove a great success.

Accounts of heavy losses from bee dysentery come to us from all sections of our northern and middle States. Thin, late gathered honey souring in the uncapped cells, and long continued cold precluding the bees from a cleansing flight, are supposed to be the main cause of the disease.

CORRECTION.—By an oversight, the following sentence was omitted in the article of Mr. Bingham on "Italian Bees at the Cleveland Convention." It should come in immediately following the amount and product of the Italian bees, and read as follows: "Four thousand six hundred and seventy-five stocks of common or black bees gathered one hundred and fifteen thousand six hundred and seventy-four pounds of surplus honey, or an average of nearly twenty-four pounds per hive."

The day before the death of our beloved editor, the beekeepers of Italy experienced a similar loss. Count Resta, one of the founders, and the president for five years of the association for the promotion of bee-culture in Italy, died on the 16th of February; Mr. Samuel Wagner died on the 17th. To Count Resta, Italy owes much of its progress in bee-culture, just as to Mr. Wagner and his journal the United States are largely indebted. The American beekeepers share the grief of our Italian friends, as we know they will share ours, for the name of our lamented editor was well known and often cited in the columns of the Italian bee journals.

CH. DADANT.

Hamilton, Illinois, April 10.

Since Dr. Blumhoff left Italy, I have tried in vain to make the importation of Italian bees a paying business. The moths, running honey, dysentery, rough handling, delays in custom houses or depots, and foul air on steamers, have always caused me to lose many queens. In one year my net loss amounted to over $200. I am receiving a number of letters asking for imported queens, which I cannot furnish; and the need of such queens is generally felt throughout the country to regenerate the breed of Italian bees.

In order to answer this call for Italian bees, I have planned to go myself to Italy, to procure queens that I can sell at a comparatively low price. My traveling expenses will be paid by the care that I shall be able to give to the packing and transportation of the bees.

I will go in July, because at that time I can buy young queens from second swarms which have been raised in large colonies, and which are consequently better than queens raised in nuclei.

The queens will arrive here in September, after as short a journey as possible. The trip will not take more than seventeen days, and perhaps may be shorter. The bees will be sent to purchasers from New York.

I hope the beekeepers of this country will take this opportunity of renovating their stock of Italians, as they will not probably have as good an opportunity for a long time.

CH. DADANT.

Hamilton, Illinois, April 10, 1872.

[For the American Bee Journal.]

Six Months of Disasters.

On page 286 of last volume, I gave my reports of my last year's result. I wintered forty stocks, losing fifteen from dysentery or consequential desertion, leaving me twenty-five to begin with. I brought these up to number fifty-eight. The month of June was very favorable. I had to use the machine every tenth day. In July I had something more than twenty-four hundred pounds of white clover honey. My swarms were all very strong. I extracted nearly all the honey in the beginning of buckwheat blossoms, of which I had several acres near my apiary. September is always a good month here because of the abundance of fall flowers. I kept two barrels of white clover honey in reserve for an emergency. August was dry and the bees gathered nothing. September followed, and the drought and the inactivity of the bees was worse; every farmer was busy at work in burning stumps and clearing land, so that the air was filled with smoke and no bees were seen. October followed with all its disasters and alarm. The whole forest was one sea of fire. The cedar swamps were as dry as cinders. This was the condition of things on the night between the 8th and 9th of October, when at eleven o'clock in the night a tempestuous south wind blew fiercely; the whole forest ignited and became one sea of flame, whereby hundreds of farms with everything desirable were swept away.

I had to fight the fire on every side; several pine stumps were burning near my dwelling house, and when we had no water, we sought to smother the fire with dirt. In this way with great exertions, I preserved my buildings, while all the rest was burned up. Thus we had to work and fight until the middle of October, when rain and relief came. My bees were forgotten and neglected because of the greatest calamity that ever befell a farming community.

The time now was favorable to look after my bees; I found them all alive, but very poor in honey. I diminished the fifty-eight to forty-five. The honey of the twelve was given with the adhering bees to the forty-five, after smoking them. All went well. None were killed. My stocks were all strong. I fed them about eight hundred pounds of the white clover honey I had in reserve. The nights of October were cold; the honey was very thick, so that I had to warm it. Before I was done feeding, November set in. The last week of November I set my bees in the bee-house, forty-five in number. I found at that time that but one-half of the honey was sealed up. On the last day of December I made an examination of the bee-house. I found the bee-house smelling of dysentery. Some hives had already smeared the upper parts of the frames with fæces. I set my hives, some with the honey board on, one inch open for ventilation, some with the honey board half off, and the rest off.

One week later I found their condition worse. Those having the honey board on, clustered on the under side of it, and the rest, with honey board off, were on the combs, but uneasy. In this state they reached February. From week to week I found their condition worse; the frames were all smeared as if by black paint; the stench was unsupportable; in handling the frames they were sticky and disgusting. On the 10th of February several hives were dead; each hive containing a peck of bees; the frames were filled with heaps of smeared bees. The remaining bees were dying fast. The 18th of February was a very fine day, the thermometer standing at 44 degrees above zero. I had never used a thermometer in regulating the cleansing flight of my bees. I had learned by experience in letting them go too early, and many times I regretted my hasty zeal.

The snow was one foot deep on the ground. I had read in Moore's Rural New Yorker, page 10, of January, that the temperature should not be less than 60 degrees, that at 50 degrees they chilled. I had forgotten where I had seen the statement; I thought I had seen it in the Bee Journal, but so it is, the thermometer stood at 45 degrees at 1 o'clock P. M. I found the day so warm and no wind, that I could retain my patience no longer. I went in the bee-house and brought some of my poorest hives out for a cleansing flight. In thirty minutes they were all flying; though weak and falling upon the snow, they were able to rise again. Finding the temperature all right, I set some more out, so that by 3 o'clock they all stood outside. The weather was very favorable, but bees want two hours before the whole are done their cleansing flight; it wants thirty minutes before they are aroused, so it was too late, the mercury began to sink rapidly; thousands upon thousands came out and fell upon the snow, there to find their graves. In this exigency I had to set them in the house again in a worse condition.

All my best hives were set out last. A large number of them were dead on the snow and the rest had not cleansed. The four weak ones had lost but a very small number; they returned and flew beautifully, yet they were very poor. So with tears in my eyes I had to doom them again to pestilence, because of a false statement in a paper which says it wants 60 degrees instead of 45 degrees. Had I set them out at eleven all would have been well and my bees saved. To-day, the 9th of March, they are all dead but six, who will follow the rest, all dwindled away by dysentery. The honey is mostly all grained hard, the bees are in groups all smeared as if painted. The upper part of the frames are sticky and greasy. If any man has a true love for bees, as I have, he will readily imagine my state of feelings at this moment, and when spring smiles upon us, all is desolation to me. Misfortunes never come singly. I had sent fifteen hundred and fifty three pounds of honey to Chicago, and every one knows the dreary calamity that befell that city. If I were at least so happy as Novice, to have some stocks left with which to build up again my apiary I might rejoice one day, but my bees all gone, being located on a very poor rocky farm, my honey unpaid, and above all, being in debt, is as much as one man can bear. Such is fate.

Now, bee brothers, what shall I do with my four hundred empty frames and my hives? Pile them up and hang mourning veils over them? I wish to add that the honey I fed to my bees was among the whitest I ever saw. It was put up in new white oak barrels weighing about seven hundred pounds each; the rest was set in earthen pots and in combs.

This calamity will teach two things, that is, to have a number of double hives non-swarmers for a provision of sealed honey comb frames for emergencies, so as to avoid feeding liquid honey. Had it not been for the forest fire I should have fed in September, and thus it might have been different. If all the hives had the same size frames like mine and Gallup's, it would do immense good; there would be a trade in sealed frame honey, which cannot be done now.

JOSEPH DUFFIELD.

Rousseau P. O., Brown Co., Wisconsin.

[For Wagner's American Bee Journal.]

Color, in Italian Queens.

I had charge for awhile of the only surviving Italian queen of those brought over by Mr. Samuel P. Parsons, of Flushing, Long Island. These bees came in the original hollow logs or gums, which had been carried on the backs of mules over the mountain passes of the Alps. They were purchased in a district where the Italian variety was believed to be in the highest purity. I transferred the only queen that had not perished from the old log to a movable frame hive, a large colony of black bees having been added to the mere handful of Italians. I saw the first queen that hatched from her progeny, she was very beautiful, but from an adjoining cell emerged a very dark sister. This has been my experience with most of the imported queens. The Italians report the same, and as far as I know they are confirmed by the most reliable breeders in Germany, and other parts of Europe. I never had a queen which would "*duplicate* herself in her queen progeny every time," although I have had some which came very near to doing it, but from such queens if kept for a considerable time, and largely used for queen breeding, I never failed to see, sooner or later, the *inevitable dark lady.*

Some of the drones from this Parsons' queen were beautifully colored, real golden drones, while others were quite dark. At first we condemned this queen as not pure, although it seemed impossible that she should be otherwise, Experience with other imported queens taught us that the sporting in color of her queen and drone progeny was not exceptional, but the general law, and there has been no better stock imported then the Parsons.

From the darkest queen bred from pure Parsons stock, when purely fertilized, I have raised as brilliant queen drones and workers as from the most highly colored queens. Such queens are undesirable, because they are not so easily seen on the combs, and are in my experience, more likely to mate with black drones, the attention of such drones being probably more attracted to queens which so closely resemble their own variety in color, than to those of a more golden hue.

In one of my importations, I had a small queen so poorly colored that few could see in her any traces of Italian blood. After laying a few worker eggs, she became a drone layer and quickly disappeared. I raised only one queen from her; she was large and handsome, and for many generations my son and myself preferred her stock to any in the apiary.

Long before the Egyptian bees were imported into Europe, I noticed that many of the workers of a certain colony had a peculiar yellow tuft on their corselets, the same that I afterwards recognized in the Egyptian bees first imported into this country by Langstroth & Son. Vogel, who first introduced them into Europe, affirms that he has produced the veritable Italian bee from crosses between the black and Egyptian varieties. What would be more natural, we might say more certain, than that the Greeks who had such extensive intercourse with Egypt, at a time when honey was almost the only sweet that could be largely and cheaply obtained, should bring this bee across the short stretch of the Mediterranean, and thus produce a mixture between it and their own native black bee?

The laws that regulate the reproduction of crosses from different varieties, are often seemingly inexplicable. Long after a variety has seemed to assume a permanently fixed type, it will occasionally "breed back" to some older type. Many years ago, a certain breed of swine (called the *Byberry,* I think) was introduced into this country; not answering the expectations of breeders, in time it ceased to exist as a distinct variety. An intelligent breeder informed me that *many* years after, a sow would occasionally produce a litter with one original, veritable, Simon Pure Byberry!

Years ago, I call attention in the *Country Gentleman* to the fact that color in Italian queens was a very "uncertain quantity;" that I had often taken two just hatched queens of equal beauty (they may be taken from the same mother), had put one in a full colony or strong nucleus, and removed the other to a cotton or woollen tube placed in a warm room without any attendant bees, offering it at intervals, honey on the head of a pin. While the first queen retains her beauty, the other will often, in a few days, become quite dark! For other facts, proving that beauty of color in Italian queens is often only "skin deep," I must refer the reader to the original article.

It would seem that the Italian bee has not assumed the same fixed type in all the Italian districts where it is considered to be pure. This is precisely what we might expect, if it is not a distinct variety, but a mere cross between the black and Egyptian races. On some queens we cannot find the spots or dots so distinctly seen on the sides of the abdomens of others. The workers from some districts, have light orange rings, while those from others have rings of a dark chestnut or chocolate color.

Those breeders who have made high color of queens the chief desideratum, and have bred "in and in" very closely to secure it, have generally wound up with a weak and degenerate race, beautiful to look at, but very unprofitable for work. My experience is the same with that of Mr. Grimm, on this point. Some years ago, I found that many of the queens obtained from a celebrated European breeder, were very short lived, could seldom keep up the strength of their colonies, and were as a rule, prematurely superseded by the bees. Some of their queens when fertilized, would drop their eggs anywhere; others would pile them up into a few cells, until these cells looked, on a small scale, like measures nearly filled with grain! Such queens seem to be semi-idiotic, resembling much some degenerate specimens of the royal Bourbon families in Europe. I need hardly say that I quickly got rid of that blood.

L. L. LANGSTROTH.

[For the American Bee Journal.]

Will some of the friends of the science of Apiculture and the Bee Journal, have the kindness to respond to the following through the Journal?

Our bees, 60 colonies, were put into our wintering house, nice and dry, about the middle of November, about two weeks earlier than usual, on account of the severity of the weather.

Our wintering house is constructed as follows: It is 28 feet long, 16 feet wide, and 14 feet high, outside measure; having two walls of solid straw 8 inches thick, and one wall of saw dust 8 inches thick between them, on all sides, and top and bottom; a hall across south end 6 feet wide, made by a 4 inch partition of saw dust, sealed on both sides with boards; a board partition through the bee room, lengthwise, dividing it into two rooms, 6 feet wide, and 20 feet long, 10½ feet high, inside measure, two ventilators, one 4 by 3 inches, reaching from floor out at roof, one 6 by 6 inches, reaching from ceiling overhead of bee room out at roof, 4 shelves, making room for 60 hives, or, if put on both sides, 120 hives in each room. On these shelves we placed our 60 colonies, in double hives, that is double case, leaving summer entrances open about 1 inch long, ⅜ inch high, caps off, and honey boards on, but ajar at one end about from ¼ to ½ inch, according to strength of colony. Then a bit of thick rag carpeting over the honey board. The temperature of the house has ranged from 25 to 40 degrees, most of the time stood quite evenly at 36 degrees. Our March was so terrible cold, stormy, windy, snowy and rough, also the first week in April, that we could not remove the bees from their winter quarters until April 5th. At this time only 14 colonies were living, the balance having mostly died, apparently with dysentery; some 5 or 6 perished from want of stores, and, perhaps twice as many more from some cause unknown, as they did not show dysentery. The colonies that survived were all among the weakest colonies put in in the fall; which had been divided and fed with coffee sugar syrup in the fall, some 3 of the strongest colonies showed dampness about mid-winter, and we gave more vent.

Now the question is, did these bees require more vent, or were they too cold? to us it would seem the former. What is the true principle when dampness effects a colony, should they have more vent, or should they be kept warmer? In the warmest summer weather our bees do not suffer from dampness, though all upward vent be stopped.

The long confinement was bad for them, but, we have kept bees confined five months with perfect success in a warm, dry cellar.

We once bought a third swarm, very strong in numbers, but having the hive not more than one-fourth full of comb, and not more than five pounds of honey; we set it in our bee house, a perfectly dark one, covered it with an old carpet, set a quart basin of honey in the hive close up to the bees; we supplied this as often as it became emptied. During the winter this colony filled its hive with comb, and doubled or thribbled its numbers, and did not lose a single handful of bees. It was confined to the hive over 4½ months, swarmed in early May, and gave us 25 lbs. of box honey from apple blossoms in May. This was in the eastern part of Columbia Co., New York, just on the Massachusetts line.

GILES B. AVERY.

Albany Co., N. Y.

[For the American Bee Journal.]

Communication.

"Why don't they stop that pesky Bee Journal? Here it comes the second year, and I haven't got a single new idea, have you?"

"Well, I think I have."

"What is it?"

"Well, you see, I am making the glass honey boxes described by Mr. Worden, and I consider that article alone worth the price of one year's subscription."

"Well, I declare, they are nice, but where do you find the article?"

"In No. —, Vol. —, one of the papers you have been taking, and no better, perhaps, than most of the others you have taken."

The above is the substance of a conversation with one of your subscribers more than a year ago, reminding me of something I read when a boy, about casting pearls before swine.

The last season here was the worst I ever knew for bees. In my home apiary of 145 stocks of bees, I did not have a single swarm, and got but 1,659 lbs. of honey. I have succeeded in wintering most of them, losing but one out of 145; all except 7 were wintered on their summer stands.

I use the Langstroth hive, with frames 11½ by 9¼ inches in the clear, running from front to rear, loose bottoms, and one end to open about ⅝ the distance from the top, and movable partitions.

For surplus honey I use glass boxes of various forms and sizes, and also frames 8⅝ by 5¼ inches in the clear, 1⅝ inches wide, made of two pieces without nails, the top ¼ inch thick; the piece forming the sides and bottom ⅛ inch thick, and cut nearly through with a V in two places for the bottom corners where they are bent at right angles, and fastened to the top by gluing them in a groove. A frame this size weighs 2 ounces, and contains 2½ to 3 lbs. of honey, and is the most salable form I have ever found.

I know not whether the proceedings of the annual meeting of the Beekeeper's Association of Central Illinois have been sent to you for publication, if not, I would say that the *pesky* Bee Journal was commended above all others.

Enclosed find the needful for my own and two new subscribers.

Yours truly,

J. L. WOLCOTT.

Bloomington, March 1, 1872.

AMERICAN BEE JOURNAL.

EDITED AND PUBLISHED BY SAMUEL WAGNER, WASHINGTON, D. C.

AT TWO DOLLARS PER ANNUM, PAYABLE IN ADVANCE.

VOL. VII. JUNE, 1872. No. 12.

Letters of F. Huber, Continued.

OUCHY, *November* 8, 1800.

I thank you, sir, for the many kind expressions contained in your letter. I feel fully the worth of your confidence and hope to merit it, but in matters of rural economy, as well as in others, we must rely upon experience, and therefore I spoke to you of Mr. Gélieu, for whose character and knowledge I have a profound respect, and who has not been so devoted as I have to the theory. But since you are determined to have my opinions I will talk to you about bees as much as you wish, on condition only that you attach no more value to what I say than I do.

Most of the questions you ask me are yet to be solved: We will give them attention in order, and I will give you my ideas (if any occur to me), on the means to be employed to solve them.

I am highly pleased, sir, to learn that you do not entrust the care of your bees to others. The experiments you have made prove that you are fully qualified to handle them with impunity. You are the first to confirm what I have stated. That the only requisite is gentleness, and the firm conviction that the sting is only a formidable weapon to those who treat them roughly, and who make awkward blunders through fear. It also gives me great pleasure to learn that you are prosecuting investigations that I have not been able to pursue. I will assuredly contribute to your success by every means in my power.

The fact that you have noticed is very extraordinary; that queen found dying near your hives and not recognized by any of your bees, might she not have been a stranger queen abandoned, and who came to seek the shelter and the subjects she had lost?

Queens cease laying when they approach the end of their lives; their hive decreases in population daily, and the colony reduced at last to a very small number,* leaves the queen, and never returns to the natal hive; the wokers attracted to happier homes, enter, and are sometimes well received; but the fate of the queen is very different. The bees of the hive she attempts to enter envelope her as you have seen, hug her in their midst, and exhaust her and cast her on the ground, when hunger or the hugging she has received renders her incapable of renewing the attempt.

The beginning of this account is only conjectural. I have never been so fortunate as to be able to follow a queen from her birth to her natural death; neither do I yet know what is the length of the life of a queen.* Probably, you, sir, will be able to tell us that.

This inquiry is useful as well as curious, and I commend it to you. If I have not seen queens die of old age in my own hives, I have often been visited by strange ones that came from I know not where, either alone or poorly accompanied, at the beginning or end of autumn; most frequently these old queens have been found dead at the foot of my hives; at other times I have found them alive on some neighboring stake, having about them fifty or more of their workers. I have seen them pass several days in the open air, and as they also remained there during the night, I may conclude they had no home, and that this small number of workers were all that remained of the family they had presided over.

Only once have we seen the attempt of an aged queen to enter one of my hives succeed. She at first offered herself to others who gave her a poor reception, because they had a queen; but she entered without any difficulty a hive that had lost their queen. Her dark color and the slenderness of her body indicated old age, of which her sterility was a still surer indication. She did not lay an egg in the hive that adopted her at the latter part of autumn, and she died at the end of winter without having laid a single egg, and as queens begin laying the latter part of January, the old age of this one was proven by her sterility. I am more disposed to believe that the queen found at the foot of your hives was a stranger to them, than that she went away from one of those you operated upon October 14th; which even if wounded or dying would not have been unrecognized.

* Huber is speaking of black bees. In my experience the Italians almost always supersede their queen, when her fertility becomes seriously impaired, by rearing another from her worker brood.
L. L. L.

* Huber's fidelity to truth is everywhere apparent. He is never ashamed to confess his ignorance.
L. L. L.

The queen cell found in this hive proves that it had been queenless for some days. Did you discover it on the 14th of October, or later? This circumstance may help to decide the question. The agitation which you noticed would lead one to think that this hive had just lost its queen, and in this case the one you offered, it was not probably the queen it had lost.

To be able to explain a fact in natural history, one must know well the accompanying circumstances, without which any decision is too hazardous. This calls to mind a trait in the fidelity of bees that I must relate to you.

One day I took from a colony a virgin queen that I had given it, to see how the workers would behave under the circumstances. As there was no brood in the hive the loss of the queen was irreparable. I was curious to see what they would do, but I could not perceive any agitation among them, nor anything that led me to suspect that they regretted her loss, or even knew of her absence. I was about to conclude that their indifference arose from her sterility and I found it quite natural that they should have no affection for a mother that was of no use to them; but this human reasoning was not the reasoning of the bees, and I was soon undeceived.

The next day I found the queen numb, from cold or hunger, in the box where I had put her. I therefore placed her in the hive; as soon as they perceived her on the table where she was lying, I saw a few workers range themselves around her, caress her, fawn over her with their proboscis, offer her honey which she did not take, and brush her with their feet; all this was useless; she was dead.

Their care did not diminish from ten o'clock in the morning to eight o'clock in the evening; I then took her away, and without any object in view, placed her on the window sill of my study, in which the hive was. Returning there at ten o'clock in the morning, I was much surprised to find my dead queen surrounded by bees, circling about her in the way you know, and giving to her dead body their customary honor.

The night was not warm, nevertheless the dead queen was not abandoned, and on the morrow I found her faithful guard lavishing upon her the same care they had rendered during her life.

I once more returned her body to the hive and at the same time introduced a young fertile queen, not doubting but that the bees would instantly appreciate the value of my gift, and would prefer the mother I had given them to the dead virgin queen from whom they could expect nothing; another reasoning, also human and quite as pitiable as the preceding. The bees who do not reason, and who perhaps are none the worse for it, treated the strange queen very rudely; they held her in the middle of a mass of bees so that she could not move, and kept her thus over eighteen hours. At this stage the knot of bees reached the entrance of the hive; it was larger than a nut; the bees that formed it imparted to it such a movement, that we saw it roll like a ball which it resembled in form, to the edge of the stand on which the hive rested. Arrived there, a continuation of the same movement caused it to fall on the floor without altering its form; we extricated* the queen just as you did; she had not received a sting but she was very weak; we succeeded in restoring her by returning her to her natal hive.

The bees I have been speaking to you of obstinately cared for the dead body of their queen during two days and a half; I then took her away and gave them young larvæ that they nursed, and from which they procured another queen.

From this and other similar examples, I am inclined to believe the second supposition of no value, and that the queen which was not received by any of your hives was certainly a stranger to them all.

I have dispensed with the hinges of the leaf hive with regret; it is very convenient to open the hive like a book, but when it comes to shutting it up, there is an objection that compelled me to abandon this way. In closing the frames the bees get in the angle formed by two frames, and as the angle grows smaller, one unavoidably crushes those which persist in remaining in this dangerous situation. Burnens, with all his skill, could not avoid often killing them in this way, and it is he who asked me to get rid of the hinges and proved the necessity of it.†

You understand, sir, that you run no risk at all of crushing the bees when the frames are not fastened to each other—you can bring them close together without forming any angle, and can give the bees time to dispose of themselves on the faces of the two combs.‡

The invention you have made for uniting four frames, appears to me excellent; but the leaf hive must have a cover to protect it from changes of wet and dry, which will after a time warp the wood of the frames. It is not then enough, as I have formerly said, to bind together the hive with a cord or twine; such a band is too weak, and does not prevent the hive from bursting open. I might have foreseen this, but can one think of everything?

You will receive in a few days, sir, a small box containing a model of a hive and a little memoir, which I thought to add to this letter, &c. But as the rest is not ready, I cannot longer de-

---

*I have frequently lost a queen by attempting to extricate her—the bees becoming so excited as to sting her. Taught by sad experience, I no longer attempt to separate the bees, but put the ball into a vessel of cold water; they will then very speedily uncluster, and the queen can be safely secured.
L. L. L.

† The generous nature of Huber is no where more apparent, than in his readiness to give to every one full credit for valuable observations or suggestions, "*Suam cuique*"—his own, to each one, seems to have been with him a sacred maxim. L. L. L.

‡ In *Bevan*, on the Honey Bee, 1838, p. 108, may be found *Dunbar's* improved Huber hive. The frames are held together on the front "by *shifting* butt hinges, and at the back by hooks and eyes." To prevent the bees from being crushed, in the manner described by Huber, Dunbar "ploughed out the edges of the frames through their whole extent, to within an eighth of an inch of their outsides."
L. L. L.

lay to reply to yours, and to assure you of my devotion,

I have the honor to be

Yours, very respectfully,

FR. HUBER.

[For Wagner's American Bee Journal.]

Are Artificial Queens Inferior to Natural Queens?

The experience of Mr. L. Bevan Fox, detailed in the article republished in the April No. of the American Bee Journal, from the London Horticultural Journal, is precisely the same with our own. As the subject is one of the greatest importance, both to breeders and purchasers of Italian bees, we shall give our views upon it at some length.*

In 1869, having an unusual number of natural swarms, we determined to secure for most of our stocks, queens bred from what we shall call *swarming queen cells;* so that we could advertise such queens for sale, if we found by experience that they were better than queens bred from non-swarming queen cells. The next season being a poor one, both for swarms and honey, the larger part of our stocks retained these queens, and they remained in our apiary, until in 1871 we superseded them by young queens. Having thus tested such queens for three seasons, and on a large scale, we could not see in them any superiority to queens reared *under favorable circumstances*, from non-swarming queen cells. If any such superiority had existed, we think that it could not have escaped our notice. as we were not influenced by any preconceived theories, and might have sold these queens to better advantage, if we could only have guaranteed their superiority.

We shall now explain exactly what we mean by *favorable circumstances*, so that all our readers may know how to secure them; and thus be able to breed queens from non-swarming, fully equal to those bred from swarming queen cells.†

By favorable circumstances, we mean: 1st. *The proper season of the year.* We have had a queen reared in a full stock in the month of January, when the mercury during the time of her incubation, was once below zero! but while this is possible, the right time for rearing queens in nuclei is, when the season is far enough advanced for the bees to gather freely both pollen and honey, and when drones are beginning to appear, or are nearly matured. From this time until late in September, I have ordinarily found in the latitude of 40 degrees no difficulty whatever in rearing choice queens. 2d. *Abundance of worker bees.* If the nuclei are so small as to become discouraged, the queens being often poorly nourished will be shy breeders and short lived. Not only should there be a generous allowance of bees, but a *large* proportion of them should be *young bees*, or the best results cannot always be secured. 3d. *Abundance of pollen.* If this is deficient the queens not being well fed, will be undersized, or otherwise defective.

We shall here call attention to a marked difference almost always found in the supply of royal jelly given to natural and artificial queens. While the larvæ of the swarming queen cells are usually so *over* supplied that a considerable quantity remains in the cell after the queen has emerged, there is seldom any excess found in the non-swarming cells. Those who have so confidently pronounced all queens reared in non-swarming cells inferior if not worthless, will probably think that these facts prove that the swarming queen cells are well provisioned, while the others are not. But "*enough* is as good as a *feast;*" and enough the non-swarming cells will usually be sure to have, if the breeder understands his business. Why the bees provide an excess for one kind and not for another, may not be apparent, but the former, although "papped, capped and napped in the lap of prodigality," having been "born with a silver"—or judging from the color of the royal surplus—"with a *golden* spoon in their mouths," are not a whit better fitted for the exigencies of life than their seemingly less favored sisters.

4th. *Abundance of honey.* It is desirable that the queen-rearing nuclei should not only be well provisioned, but if natural supplies are not easily procured by them, they ought to be regularly fed in order to keep them at all times in *good heart.* They should not only know nothing of actual scarcity, but should by generous feeding, be saved from even the apprehension of it, and thus made to feel confident in their resources, and ready for all emergencies.

Every experienced breeder knows that he can always have queen cells so largely in excess of his wants, that he need save only such as are perfectly developed. Such cells are usually of good size, and *roughened* all over with ornamentations, as though for some reason the bees felt a special interest in their inmates, while such as are undersized, *smooth*, and blunt instead of having the usual tapering proportions, are much more likely to produce inferior queens.

Under the most favorable circumstances some queens are produced which are so small, or so poorly developed, that the expert destroys them as soon as seen. He who cannot form a pretty accurate judgment from seeing a just hatched

---

* In 1849 we made our first observing hive, and witnessed, almost hourly, all the steps in the process of queen raising from worker brood. So few persons in this country then believed in the possibility of bees producing queens from worker larvæ, that we at one time seriously thought of having the facts *certified* to by Rev. Albert Barnes, and other distinguished Philadelphians, who were eye witnesses to them! How strangely such reminiscences must strike the new generation of beekeepers, to whom, by the aid of movable frames, all the steps in the process of queen rearing are now so familiar.

† If the terms Natural and Artificial queens are used merely to designate queens bred from swarming or non-swarming queen cells, we do not object to them—but we wholly object to using the word artificial to designate some supposed deviation from the laws of Nature, which secures an unnatural and inferior kind of queens. The rearing of queens when bees do not intend to swarm, either to supply the loss of a queen from accident or disease, or to supersede one which is superannuated, or not sufficiently prolific, is plainly a *natural* process.

queen, whether he should preserve or destroy her, is unfit for the business of breeding queens for sale.

L. L. LANGSTROTH.

Dried Cow Dung for Fumigating Bees.

Nearly two thousand years ago, Columella recommended the dried dung of cattle as the best thing for fumigating bees. Learning, soon after importing the Egyptian bees, that the Egyptians made use of the smoke from this substance in all their operations upon their irascible bees, we began to use it largely in our apiary. The smoke from burning cow dung, while very penetrating, is not offensive. It can be blown so as to diffuse itself very quickly through the hive, and yet it does not seem to irritate the bees, and our own experience confirms the very strong commendations of Columella. Wherever rotten wood is not easily procured, it will be found of very great value.

When thoroughly dried, it will burn slowly but steadily; and by slightly dampening the outside after lighting it, a piece not larger than the hand may often be made to last for several hours. It does not always ignite as readily as one could wish. Dr. E. Parmley has obviated this difficulty by dipping one corner in coal oil. The odor is so little offensive that it may be used instead of pastiles in the sick room, a little sugar being sprinkled upon it while burning. Those who know how universally the dung of buffaloes, called *buffalo chips*, is used for cooking purposes on our great plains, will feel no prejudices against this seemingly uncleanly substance. We shall call it *buffalo chips*.

L. L. LANGSTROTH.

Uses of Wool in the Apiary.

For the last four years we have used *wool* quite largely for various purposes in our apiary. We use nothing else for stopping up our queen cages, rolling it for this purpose into a tight wad. The bees cannot gnaw it away, and seldom propolise it. We shut up all our nuclei, when first formed, with wool. It can be crowded into place in a moment, admits air, and is easily removed. If we wish for any purpose to shut up a hive, we use wool. In the working season, we keep one "pocket full of wool," and know nothing of the vexations we experienced when using wire-cloth. Occasionally a few bees are caught in the fibers of the wool, but they are for the most part very shy of it, and are quite indisposed to commit *felo de se*, by hanging themselves in its meshes. Robbers will very quickly retreat from a hive well wooled. If we use the words *to wool* and *unwool* a hive or nucleus, instead of to shut up or open the entrance, our readers will understand what we mean.

L. L. LANGSTROTH.

[For Wagner's American Bee Journal.]

Controlling Fertilization.

The controversy on this subject waxes hotter and hotter, and Mr. W. H. Furman seems determined to secure the services of the most prominent parties who have claimed success, if money can do it. We confess that all our attempts to have queens fertilized in confinement have thus far been complete failures. We experimented upon a large number on the plan detailed by us in the American Bee Journal for May, 1871. We dissected the queens and found that not a single one had been fertilized.

For the benefit of our readers, we explain how we dissect queens. Holding the queen firmly by her head and thorax with the left hand, we pull away the abdomen with the right, quickly crushing her head to put her out of pain. We then press gently upon the lower part of the abdomen until the *spermatheca* appears, which we place upon our thumb nail. If the queen has not been fertilized this organ is rather undersized and seems to be only partially distended, looking somewhat like a small white bead; when pressed it discharges a little fluid as clear as water. If the queen has been fertilized, the sac is larger, is more distended, and has a cream like color—when pressed it discharges a milky fluid, like that which fills the organs of the drones.

Three years ago we devised a plan for controlling fertilization, which we communicated to Mr. Samuel Wagner, Dr. Ehrick Parmley, Mr. W. W. Carey and some others. The plan in substance, was to use a fertilizing house or apartment with one window opening fully to the sun's ray at about 2 P. M.—to keep in it one good stock well supplied with choice drones, and to place in it the nuclei, having young queens to be fertilized. The window was to have wire cloth slides* with meshes fine enough to allow free passage to the workers only. For a large part of the day, the window to be left wholly open; but during the flight of the drones the wire slide to be opened and shut at intervals until the drones become accustomed to have their flight to the window interrupted, both when leaving the hive and when returning to it—the workers also learning the lesson of flying either through the open window or the wire cloth. This window was to be placed *high* up, and the stock and nuclei low down, and as far as possible from the window. The drones and workers from the full stock were to be properly educated before the nuclei were introduced. We hoped that in this way, when the queens took their wedding flight, they would fly about the room and mate with drones that did not feel themselves placed in a strange, and therefore an unnatural condition. We founded our hopes of success on the fact that the intercourse of queen and drone (see

* Instead of the wire cloth, panes of glass might be set in a sash, so that at the top of each glass there would be the 5-32 opening. The window might be made large enough to secure any desirable amount of light.

American Bee Journal, vol. 1, for 1861) was witnessed under the following circumstances: In Mr. S. B. Parson's apiary at Flushing, Messrs. William W. Cary and R. C. Otis saw a young Italian queen leave a small nucleus for fertilization. She returned without success, and as she left a second time, they closed the entrance to be more certain of seeing her condition when she returned. A few drones belonging to the nucleus finding their entrance obstructed, took wing and hovered near the box. The returning queen mated with one of them, which dropped dead instantly, and was picked up and preserved in alcohol. This occurrence proved that fertilization did not *necessarily* take place high in the air. A return of our old malady prevented us from testing this plan, which seems to us more feasible than any hitherto communicated to the public.

It will be observed that we do not share Mr. William R. King's fear of "the fiery workers" interfering with the natural propensities of the drones, for we have seen no evidence of any such fear, until about the time when the workers are intent on driving them from the hive. Up to this time they treat them with great affection, not only cherishing them in the larvæ state, but being always willing to give them honey, when they solicit it.

If this plan should prove a success, the nuclei with their fertilized queens could be removed and others set in their places, so that it would be necessary to keep only a small number in the fertilizing house at any one time.

L. L. LANGSTROTH.

Introducing Queens.

M. M. Mahin, in the March No. of the American Bee Journal, gives his way of introducing queens. He says he has introduced one with peppermint water, but would not advise the plan for valuable queens.

I wish to inform Mr. Mahin that we have been introducing queens in that way for the last four years. It is highly useful for imported queens, as it would be very dangerous to cage such queens for any considerable time, after they have been traveling for from twenty-five to thirty-five days.

My father found this method described on p. 16, vol. 4th, of American Bee Journal. He was so confident of its safety that he at once used it for introducing some imported queens. There was so much peppermint in the original recipe that some of the stocks remained in a state of feverish excitement for several days. We prepare it as follows: In a pint of sugared water, put a teaspoonful of essence of peppermint; open the hive, kill the queen, and sprinkle both sides of the comb, bees and all, with the preparation—then dip the new queen into it and place her on one of the combs. The evening is the safest time to introduce, when almost all the bees are back from the fields. We use a chicken's wing for sprinkling.

We have never lost a queen introduced in this way, although we have used it with hundreds. When we expect imported queens to arrive, we cage beforehand a number of queens, so that we can at once introduce the imported queens. We have introduced as many as fifteen imported queens, within an hour after their arrival.

C. P. DADANT.

Hamilton, Illinois.

[For the American Bee Journal.]

Condensing Swarms.

We have said considerable in the American Bee Journal about keeping bees condensed, or in a compact mass, in order to have them work to advantage, raise brood, build comb, evaporate their honey, &c., but as there are a large number of new subscribers we think it will do no harm to give our ideas on that subject once more, and especially about the management of the extractor.

A friend of ours has lost several stocks of bees this winter and his nucleus swarms. We saw these bees in December last, and could have informed him that they would starve to death before spring, just as well then as we could do after they were actually dead. To begin with his nuclei; he extracted their honey late in the season, and the consequence was they were filled again and sealed up thin, watery honey. They had abundance if it had been properly evaporated, but that not being the case, they were never quiet, and consequently consumed all their stores and starved to death in February. Now it is my candid opinion that if the same honey had been extracted and condensed so as to have one-third the amount, and then fed back to them, they would have had abundance and would have remained perfectly quiet all winter. It is astonishing what a small amount of good honey of the right consistency it takes to winter a stock of bees. Now if his stocks that starved had been condensed by the use of the division board to six or eight combs, they would have evaporated their honey so as to have had abundance to winter on. This condensing must be attended to while the bees are gathering their stores. In using the extractor, we must be very careful not to use it too late in the season; yet honey stored late in the season, if the stock is well managed is just as good for wintering purposes as any. To illustrate this, honey stored in June is always good for wintering, because the weather is warm, and the bees are raising large quantities of brood and the stock is strong in numbers, consequently they get up heat enough to evaporate their honey, and one pound of this honey will go farther towards wintering a stock of bees than three pounds stored late in the fall in the same sized hive. Why? Because the weather being cool, they are rearing but little brood and the stock has only about one-half the number it had in June or July. But condense this stock to one-half the number of combs and we get a good quality of honey for wintering or winter food. Take one of our nuclei with three combs, keep it crowded with bees of the proper age, and they will store as good quality of honey for winter food as the largest stock in the apiary, and when properly ventilated in a special repository will not consume one particle more honey in proportion to their numbers than the large stock. We are not writing theory but actual practice. We have wintered less than a pint of bees and they scarcely stirred all winter. Nuclei and spare queens can be wintered just as successfully as full stocks. If you do not know how to manage them so they can make their own honey, then take combs from standard stocks containing good honey and the necessary amount of empty cells for them to cluster in. Their honey should be above them instead of at the side of the cluster. Six or eight of our combs with empty cells below and honey above will winter our largest stock in the cellar, if of the right quality; while 30 filled with improperly evaporated honey is not sufficient.

In extracting honey from our large hives, we ceased to extract from the end the queen was in as soon as the great flush of honey was over. It is so constructed that as soon as the great breeding is over and the stock decreases in numbers, the bees condense themselves or withdraw to one end. Now close the other entrance and the animal heat is still concentrated the same as in a single hive, yet they have full access to the surplus end as long as the honey harvest lasts, and we can keep extracting from that end without disturbing the other. Not so with a two story hive, for we must take off the upper story in order to condense the bees to the lower story, as soon as the flush of honey is over, or we may get improperly evaporated honey in the brooding apartment for winter food. New beginners must be very cautious about this. We have had a strong swarm of bees come out as late as the 20th of September, and by condensing them in our hive by the use of the division board, they stored an excellent quality of honey for winter, and wintered as well as any stock in our apiary; whereas if we had not condensed them we should in all probability have lost them by their storing improperly evaporated honey. We got bit some 20 years ago by not understanding this, and a burned child is careful of going too near the fire. In a cool, wet season we should not hesitate to extract and evaporate by heat and return to the bees for winter food.

E. GALLUP.

[For Wagner's American Bee Journal.]

Italianzing Black Bees.

MR. EDITOR:—I will give to the American Bee Journal my mode of Italianizing black bees and giving them all good, natural queens of the best grade.

First. I get my Italian stock in a good strong condition. About the last of May or first of June have a good natural swarm to come off Two or three days after the swarm has come off, examine the hive and see how many queen cells you have got.

Seven or eight days after the swarm comes off, make as many artificial swarms as you have queen cells for, cut out your queen cells and put one in each hive, that you have taken a swarm from. They will hatch in two or three days and your hive will have a good natural queen. This I have found to be the best way of Italianizing black stocks. I have on several occasions taken queen cells ready to hatch and put them on the lighting board of a black stand which had their queen, and in a few minutes it would come out of the cell, and the bees would invariably treat her well, and the bees either killed the black queen, or the young queen killed the black queen. I have Italianized several stands of black bees in that way. I have found on a trial of three years, that artificial queens are as a rule but of very little account. Out of 20 queens raised artificially in 1870, 12 died before the first of May, 1871, the balance died during the swarming season.

I have found to my satisfaction that good natural queens are the only safe and reliable ones.

R. MILLER.

Malugin's Grove, Ill.

[For the American Bee Journal.]

The Eureka Hive.

In the American Bee Journal for April, 1872, p. 240, I find a communication signed D. C. Hunt, North Tunbridge, Vermont. He says: "I told him I wished to see his much lauded non-swarming hive about which I had seen so much figuring to prove it the best of all hives made." He had five old stocks in the spring; but as the season advanced they all cast swarms! *Facts*. I had but four colonies in my Eureka hives in the spring of 1867. Three of them were native bees, and one of them Italian. Two of the native colonies gave no swarm; one of these gave 174 pounds of surplus honey, the other 124 pounds.

The Italian colony gave 46 pounds. Its first swarm gave 56¾ pounds, second swarm 40 pounds, amounting to 106¾ pounds. The other native colony gave 36¼ pound. Its first swarm gave 61 pounds; amount from both colony and first swarm, 97¼ pounds. From the two that gave no swarms, 298 pounds. Product of the two that swarmed, four new swarms and 204 pounds of honey. It will be seen from the above how much credit is due to his assertions that I had five colonies in the spring, and that they all cast swarms. He says, "I noticed however, to my surprise, that he was appropriating Mr. Langstroth's invention without due credit, and evidently with a disposition to detract from his claims as inventor and patentee." I believe Mr. Langstroth's liberality in giving to preachers of the Gospel the privilege of using his patent without charge is generally known. Having been in the ministry some fifty-six years, I can hardly see how the use of movable comb frames is "use without due credit," or evinces "a disposition to detract from his claims as inventor and patentee."

He says "Mr. William Stratton, of West Troy, whom I visited the same day, gave Mr. Hazen credit of having a good hive for box honey. But though he had one hundred and forty stocks in his apiary, I did not see one of Mr. Hazen's hives among them." "Mr. Hazen's hive, (he then called it the Eureka) is nothing more in effect than a common box hive, about the size and shape of one used and recommended by Mr. Quinby, with boxes applied to the top and sides.

Mr. W. M. Stratton, to whom he refers, believes it to possess advantages over any hive he has ever seen, in the following particulars: 1st. For approaching the sheets of comb at both sides of the hive and removing them latterally, if movable frames are used.

2d. From the number and arrangement of the surplus boxes securing the greatest amount of surplus honey.

3d. For perfect security of warmth for wintering upon the stand.

4th. From the great simplicity of its construetion. WM. M. STRATTON.

Mr. Quinby writes as follows:

ST. JOHNSVILLE, N. Y., *Sept.* 7, 1868.

"I have visited Mr. Hazen's apiary and examined his Eureka Hive. In the arrangement of the large number of surplus boxes in close proximity to the main body of the hive, I think it greatly superior to any patent hive with which I am acquainted. And if he would apply the movable combs to which it is adapted, and a device to prevent swarms leaving, the principle would be nearer what I want in a bee hive, than any I ever saw."

M. QUINBY.

I wish to add, I am not aware of ever expressing an opinion unfavorable to the rights of Mr. Langstroth in my life, as intimated by Mr. Hunt. I have written that with the Eureka Hive, bars or frames may be used at the pleasure of the operator. I have no patent claim covering either. I think one or the other should be used. For the use of the mel-extractor movable frames are a necessity. If one keeps but a small number of colonies and does not manipulate them, but simply hives them when they swarm, and puts on and removes the boxes when required, bars are probably quite as good as frames.

JASPER HAZEN.

Albany, N. Y., April 16, 1872.

[For the American Bee Journal.]

Malt as Bee Food.

As the season is approaching for feeding bees, I will relate a fact in that connection that may be of some benefit to beekeepers:

In the spring of 1870 I had occasion to visit a distillery, as a part of my duties as United States Assistant Assessor, and knowing that rye was frequently made use of for the purpose of distillation, I applied to the proprietor for a small quantity to feed my bees on. He informed me that he had no rye, but he could furnish me with some ground malted barley which he thought would be preferable, as it contained more sacharine matter. I accepted the offer, and as the weather was pleasant and the bees all out hunting for something to do, I immediately procured a large cheese box top and supplied them with a quart placed convenient to the apiary, and in a few minutes it had disappeared, and in the course of a few hours they had consumed a half gallon more. I had never seen anything to equal it before. They would dive into the flour and roll and tumble until they were filled with it, legs, head, and everything about them, and then crawl to some convenient place, and work it into balls and return to their hives. It reminded me more of a flock of wild pigeons fluttering in water to drink. They will continue to eat it until the fruit blossoms. They will not notice the rye flour so long as there is any barley within their reach.

G. B. LONG.

Hopkinson, Ky.

A Bit of Experience.

MR. EDITOR:—The season of 1871 proved to be a poor one in this vicinity. The white clover yielded an ordinary amount of honey, but the Linden bloom was injured by the late frost, and yielded but a small amount of honey; then followed a month in which the bees gathered nothing. About the 20th of August, what we call the English Smartweed began yielding honey; this plant I consider equal to buckwheat. From this plant my bees obtained their winter supply. The continued dry weather prevented the bees from raising their fall brood, thus leaving the stocks in a critical condition as regards the young bees. I determined to stimulate them up to brooding in order to have them in a proper condition for wintering. Therefore, I commenced feeding them with the poorest quality of honey, making one part water. I fed them thus one week. Some refused to raise brood. I find that every one of those colonies are dead that did not use all the honey.

Out of sixty-eight colonies I have thirty-five good strong colonies. As to the cause of them dying, I attribute it, in a very great degree to the honey. Had I extracted all the unsealed honey I believe they would not all have died, and had I fed the best quality of honey there would have been better results—thus we are all learning dear lessons never to be forgotten.

J. N. WALTER.

Winchester, Van Buren Co., Iowa.

The mortality among bees has been very great this last winter. Many colonies have starved; many have frozen from excessive cold and weakened numbers, and thousands have died from dysentery.

[For the American Bee Journal.]

Rambling Notes.

MR. EDITOR:—Having some leisure, I drop you a few lines from the northwest. It has been a hard winter on bees. So far as I can learn I think that one-half or more of the bees in the west have died, or become so reduced as to be almost worthless so far as surplus honey is concerned.

The majority died apparently of what is known as dysentery. Tall hives have not wintered any better than shallow ones. Some think the losses were occasioned by the long cold winter; others that it was the poor quality of the late honey, and still others that breeding was stopped so early last fall that the bees were too old to winter well. I think the trouble is in all three. Where bees have had care, there has not been much difference in the loss between those wintered out of doors, and those wintered in cellars or buildings made especially for wintering bees. If there was any difference, those in the cellar fared worst. We have had a very long cold winter. The thermometer has not went as low as some other winters, but it has been very steady cold.

Why is it, some of the most practical beekeepers do not write more for the Journal? Is it as some large beekeepers say, if they write others can profit by their experience, and the business will soon be overdone, and they will not get a remunerative price for their honey? Others do not believe in writing for the Journal without getting large pay for what they write. Others do not believe in writing for the Journal, and then have to pay for their own articles, as they think they would rather get all the information from others and give nothing in return.

Now as to the hive question, it looks to me as if there was a great deal more fuss than there is any necessity for.

If Mr. Langstroth's patent is not worth anything as they claim, what is any of their patents worth? If there is not any patent or practical movable frames, then any one of common sense can make a better hive for practical purposes than $\frac{9}{100}$ of the so called patent hives, especially if they are beekeepers.

I will venture to say that there is not one in a hundred who buys a so-called patent hive or individual right, that at the time of purchase knows what the patent covers, and besides some of the patent hive men use the names of practical bee men, as a recommendation of their hives, without the knowledge or consent of the parties. Others will go to some practical beekeeper and leave a hive with him on trial, or if he does not want it, the bee hive vendor will ask permission to set it in the yard until he comes back, as he has only one left in his wagon and he is going after another load, and does not want to haul it around so much. If successful in leaving a hive, he will start off on some other course, and will report that Mr. so and so, giving the name of the man with whom he left the hive, has got one of these hives in his yard, and he thinks it just the hive. In one case I knew of a swindler offering a practical beekeeper $50, to let him set one of his hives in his yard for a short time, but was refused. His hive stood on three legs, with the greatest invention of the age, the moth trap warranted to catch all the larva of the moth in the hive, and let them fall into a tin box and break their necks.

The hive was nothing more than a box hive for two swarms, with a box on top, and side for surplus honey, with an alighting board on hinges, so as to close up every evening and not let any moth get in the hive. You could make, if necessary, the hen roost attachment for closing the hive against the moth.

Then there are some parties in the west who will adopt a common sense independent movable frame hive and recommend it to the public as the best hive in use, but are willing to sell their influence for a mess of pottage, to enable them to gull the unsuspecting public, and to make the sommersault appear all right, they will use a few of the last recommended hives; but go to their apiary in a few years and ask them to show you the practical working of the movable frame hive, and they will almost invariably go to the first hives, or the Langstroth style of frames, or if any other style of frames, one, that has not had a full stock of bees in it over three months, as the others are generally glued shut with propolis, so much as not to be convenient to handle.

I would like to talk a little about the marketing of honey in the Chicago market. Would it not be better for the beekeepers of the northwest to unite and hire some practical man or beekeeper that understands the value of the different grades of honey, to go to Chicago and sell their products for a remunerative price, than to let the commission men and honey houses control the market and dictate the terms. Moreover, by this plan the consumer would get a pure article and not pay full price for a doctored article. To illustrate, you may go to Chicago with a lot of honey; take a sample of nice box honey around among the dealers, the best price they will offer you is 21 cts. You sell your honey, and before leaving the City you see some one with a box of your honey, and ask what they paid for it, the answer will be generally somewhere between 40 and 60 cts. per lb., and if you have extracted honey, the reply generally is the market is over stocked and we do not wish any without you are willing to sell at from 8 to 10 cts. per lb. NORTHWEST.

HOW TO CLARIFY HONEY.—A good way to clarify honey is to add two pounds of a mixture of equal parts of honey and water, one drachm of carbonate of magnesia. After shaking occasionally during a couple of hours, the residue is allowed to settle and the whole filtered, when a beautiful clear filtrate is obtained, which may be evaporated in a water bath to the proper consistency. The only drawback to this method is the length of time it takes to filter the solution; and this may be much abbreviated by taking the same amount of white clay instead of magnesia, when a nearly equally good article is obtained in much less time.—[*Druggists' Circular.*]

[For the American Bee Journal.]

A Large Number of Queen Cells.

In August, 1870, I removed a hybrid queen from a full stock and introduced an Italian. On the twenty-second or twenty-third day after, on opening the hive I found it literally stocked full of queen cells.

A German friend being present suggested we count them. I cut out and removed fifty-four queen cells. What was a little remarkable to me was, they were every one sealed. A majority of them were very large, but some were small. They were on the sides, bottom and edge of the combs. Will some friend tell me why so many, and whether it is common? I ought to say, perhaps, that before removing the hybrid queen—a very prolific one—they had attempted several times to swarm, but were prevented by a Quinby Queen Yard.

Bees seem to be wintering well in this section, so far as I hear. We have had cold weather since December 1st, so that those out of doors, have not been able to fly.

A. C. MANWELL.

Ripon, Wis.

[For the American Bee Journal.]

A Beginner's Experience.

MR. EDITOR:—You request beekeepers to send you an account of their experience in keeping bees, so I thought I would send you mine. I commenced beekeeping in 1866, when I was fifteen years old, by buying an Italian queen of Mr. W. H. Furman, of Cedar Rapids, Iowa, whose advertisement I saw in an agricultural paper.

I put the queen and the few worker bees that came with her, into a large box hive, bought a pound of strained honey and fed them on a piece of tin, and waited with all the patience imaginable for them to go to work, thinking in my ignorance that they would build up a swarm. Well, they stayed there a week or two, built a small piece of comb, and then *swarmed*. Thinking the hive too large, I went to work and made a little one and put them in it. That was the last of them. At the time the queen was purchased, Mr. F. got me to subscribe for the Journal, and I soon saw what a donkey I had been making of myself. So I let the thing rest for a while until I could read and know a little about the business.

In March, 1870, I bought two swarms in old box hives, for twelve dollars ($12.00), one of them one, and the other eight years old. I had heard a great deal said (and almost *sung* sometimes), about the (*Great*) American Bee-hive, so I bought the right (or wrong), and made me some of them, and now I would sell out my right pretty cheap. There, I have put in an *advertisement* Gallup fashion, and I expect somebody will give me fits for it. The season of 1870 was very dry in this part of the country, and but one of my stocks gave me a new swarm, which left the hive just a month later, and tried to enter one of my neighbor's hives, and then there was war. I supposed they were all right, as they were going and coming very briskly, but on looking into the hive after they had left, I found it about half full of nice straight comb but not a drop of honey, and I came to the conclusion that they were starved out, and that I was ten dollars out of pocket. It looked very nice *on paper* to talk about going to a hive full of bees, and open and take out the frames, with all the little scamps coming at you, *sharp end first*. Result of the season, two stocks of bees in old box hives, some empty comb hives, and beekeeper a little down in the mouth.

I didn't like the American hive, so I went to work as all new beginners are said to do, and got up a hive after my own fashion, which I *know* is better than the American. Last year I had better success, for both of my stocks sent off a large swarm each, that filled their hives and gave me several frames, and nearly two boxes full of honey. The swarms came off in the latter part of June, one of them twenty minutes of eight in the morning.

My frames hold twelve pounds each.

In July, with the help of my father and a neighbor, I managed to get the old stocks transferred into American hives. I say managed, for we had an awful time in getting the bees out, as they wouldn't drive for rapping on the hive, or for smoke, so we used brimstone until they were quiet; then went at the hives with chisel and hammer and got them transferred, what there was left of them, for I can assure you, Mr. Editor, that about half of them were quieted, so that they forgot to get up. By grand good luck we didn't happen to kill either of the queens. They gathered enough to winter on with a little feeding at the start. In the latter part of August we got seven swarms given to us, three of them late swarms, and the other four we got for taking the honey from the bees for the owner, who gave us the brood comb to transfer along with the bees. Two of them that were transferred on the 31st of August, filled their hives in fifteen days, about sixty pounds each. We did not use any brimstone on these, but put nets over our heads and gloves on our hands, and *went for 'em*. Mr. Editor, it would have made you laugh to have seen me *light out* for the corn field when my net got loose and the bees got under it. I have got over being afraid of the *sharp end* of a bee, but they will sting for all that, have done it (94) ninety-four times this season, and it *swells* too.

I have handled bees in almost every shape this last season, except introducing queens, and I am going to try that next season. I have made this letter longer than I meant to when I started, but I hope you will excuse me as I am a new beginner.

Brother Gallup, I am going to try some of your frames in my next hives.

Yours truly,

W. M. KELLOGG.

Oneida, Ill., Feb., 1872.

[For the American Bee Journal.]

Will "Novice" or B. Lunderer (blunderer?) state through the Journal how their cloth honey-boards work, as they both spoke favorably of it sometime since, and have now had time to test it thoroughly.

Our bees are in fine condition, having passed through the most severe winter in this section, since 1832. February 15th, we found plenty of eggs, brood in all stages, and young bees; they began about that time to carry in artificial pollen, which we fed them with avidity.

We are reminded by the activity of our pets, that the time is again drawing near to undergo the trial of importing queens, with its expense and usual suspense of waiting and watching to be rewarded by receiving about one-fifth of the number alive that you sent for, and they nearer dead than alive.

We saw Miss Morgan's statement in the Journal about sending for and receiving seven or eight (all she sent for), in good order, and think we can safely say, that it is without a parallel. Those foreigners must be a gallant set, and take extra pains in preparing queens for the fair sex.

But seriously, Mr. Editor, cannot there be some way devised that we can induce these foreign queen-raisers to take more pains in sending queens?

OWEN & LADD.

Brentwood, Tenn.

[For the American Bee Journal.]

Novice.

"Mr. Novice, those American Hives are a perfeet nuisance! 'they ain't good for nothing.'"

TUT! TUT! strong assertions and bad grammar too. Rather say you think they are not good.

"Don't care, they deserve it all. I *know they are not good.* In your absence I have examined ever so many, and they have a miserably small amount of bees and brood compared with one Langstroth hive, and as they have equally good queens and plenty of honey, it must be owing to those miserable side opening hives. I declare, if I were the bees, I would swarm out of every one until you furnished better ones."

"But, what is the reason? are not tall hives better economy than low ones, and are not the flat, 'shallow things' always called bad for building up colonies in spring?"

We opened a bound volume of the American Bee Journal, page 69, vol. 3, where we in 1867, gave our reasons for preferring the American hive to the Langstroth.

"Well, what do you think of that?"

"Just this. I am very sorry to learn that you ever wrote any such foolish stuff. For the past three years the American hive has been far behind the Langstroth, more especially, and for reasons, we don't care for them. You men can spin long theories about rarified air rising and all that, but we *women* take facts as we find them."

"Please do come *now*, Mr. Novice, and look yourself over the thirty American hives and then see the Langstroth, and don't let us argue any more when we can use our eyes so easily."

Well, Mr. Editor, we did examine carefully the thirty tall hives, and then an equal number of the flat ones, and the result was only *much more marked* than we had supposed from observations for the past three or four years.

In the American hive there seems to be a dislike to enlarging the brood circle *downward*, which they must do, as the brood is invariably in spring near the top bars. In the Langstroth hive the brood circle enlarges horizontally and the result decided was to instantly transfer all comb to the Standard Langstroth frames, not only from the American hive, but sundry other patent hives that we have been induced to give a trial; and, Mr. Editor, we have now got it all done neatly, and draw a long breath of relief when we realize that now we shall no more be bothered with close fitting tops and side openers.

We are using one of the Gallup hives, but even at the risk of being called an "old woman," again we must say that we cannot make the queen work down to the bottom of the comb in order to enlarge her circle of brood as readily as we do with the Langstroth hive; yet we selected for the experiment, one of our best queens.

Just imagine an apiary of such system that any frame will go *just right* in any hive with the accuracy almost of American watch work, and you can see what we have been working at for the past few days, and if we don't have something of that kind nearer perfect than we have ever seen, (although many claim it), we shall be much msitaken.

We have several questions in regard to that bee disease.

Mrs. A. D. Morgan, of Pella, Iowa, asks if we consider the honey, taken from stocks that have perished, safe to feed others.

After the bees are out and flying in the spring, we always feed anything they will eat, and have never had any bad results; in fact have never seen any trace of the bee-disease or dysentery, when the weather was such that they could fly.

Will our Western friends who have lost so heavily, please tell us if they are ever troubled *after* the bees are flying in the spring.

In regard to spotting the snow in spring, it pains us to see friend Gallup speak so harshly about his statements not being believed. We may have mentioned in the Journal that we thought some statements were a mistake, but certainly never meant to intimate that any one of our "large family" told a wilful falsehood.

It was not Mr. Gallup's statement that we referred to, but another one, which we have since found, and we only thought that if the writer had looked very carefully he would have found some spots.

Others besides Mr. Gallup have given the theory that when young bees were raised largely in the fall there would be no dysentery, but alas, for theories! the particular stock we wrote about had a drone laying queen and not a bee was hatched after the first of September. We wrote Mr. Langstroth for a queen, which he was not able to furnish us in the fall, and so the drone layer was kept until the latter part of March, when some brood had to be given them to keep them from failing, so that we had all *old bees* and but few in number, yet in flying freely in February no spot was left on the snow *at all*.

Another asks if they all had pollen; to which we reply that we have not been able to find a colony destitute of pollen, even in winter.

In fact, out of the sixty-three stocks we found ample material for studying the subject most thoroughly, which we were compelled to do on account of sharper criticisms than Gallup's, that came from an individual much nearer us.

If anything else besides a pure winter diet of coffee sugar is needed, we shall have abundant opportunity to test it next winter, and will do it. We shall discard every particle of natural honey for winter use; and then if the snow is not discolored and *all* colonies healthy, which we have never had yet, we shall sail all the hats we got, old and new, "better half's," children's and all (just their hats).

Mr. Gallup's article on nuclei's hives, p. 242, we most earnestly commend. If any one thinks his plan too much trouble, we should tell them that we really doubt whether a beekeeper can use his time to any better advantage. The same directions will apply to the ordinary Langstroth hive, with such modifications as any one will readily perceive.

We might here mention that as an experiment, we killed the drone laying queen before alluded to, and allowed the old bees, assisted by a few young ones—less than a teacupful in all—to rear queens. For some time no cells were started, but at length, only two, and then they were quickly capped, as the larvæ was nearly ready to seal over.

One hatched in a very short time after sealing, and our assistants could find no queen, although the cell was opened properly, but we saw her at once, as we knew by previous experience what to look for, viz.: a three banded worker with rather tapering body, shaped like a queen between the shoulders, and of quick, restless movement, unlike a newly hatched worker bee. We killed her and let the other cell hatch. She was much the same, only perhaps a little more queen-like, and we will report if she lays, and how much.

We have had queens when first hatched almost as unprepossessing, that afterward became the mothers of some of of our finest colonies, but not usually. Some have laid only a few hundred eggs or so, and then stopped or become drone layers.

"There, Mr. Novice, is a proof that full colonies are best for raising queens, right before my eyes."

Oh, no! not so strong as that, but so far a proof, that a teacupful of bees, all either *very old* or too young to *fly* in *cool weather* cannot raise a good queen, judging from many careful experiments, we think that one pint of bees of proper age, in warm weather, during a *yield of honey*, will raise as good queens as a two-story hive full of bees."

"But I should prefer being on the safe side." Before answering this we tried to speak mildly, for we always try to speak mildly when an argument comes up; that is, if we don't get too much interested.

"Even to devoting every one of our sixty colonies to queen raising just now, if it was necessary to have sixty queens within a month."

We fear queens would be more than five dollars each at that rate, and we should be very anxious to know whether such a proceeding would really be any safer or produce any better queens.

Our basswood orchard is at this date, May 11th, in our opinion, glorious: Almost every tree has started, and some of them have put out shoots three inches in length.

The chestnuts are also doing their best, and altogether the effect of the thousands with their delicate green round leaves just touched by the rising sun, dew drops and all, is just what we said—"glorious."

That all our bee-keeping friends might stand with us and feel the thrill of pleasure in contemplating the willingness with which old "dame nature" lends her wondrous powers to our guidance, is the wish of your old friend,

NOVICE.

[For the American Bee Journal.]

Transferring Bees.

As quite a number have given their method of transferring bees, and as ours is somewhat different we send it. Our plan is as follows: 1st. We prepare the frames by nailing two strips of wood on each side with one-half inch cleet nails. We then pry the strips loose at one end, on one side of the frame (the strips should run lengthwise on the frame), and turn one strip up and the other down, each a quarter of a circle. We then place the frame bottom side up on a support prepared for the purpose. The frame should be slightly inclined from us.

2d. We prepare the hive by inverting it. Take off one side of the hive that will leave the broad side of the comb towards us. We then place a box over the hive for the bees to go up into.

3d. Transferring. We cut the comb to a measure to fit the frame, and place it in the frame. We then turn the strips to their place and press the nails into place with our thumb; we then place the frame into the hive, and it is done, so far. We have transferred bees from the woods without trouble. Ten or fifteen minutes is long enough to transfer a colony. In transporting a colony we fasten two or more frames together at the end that just fit into the hive; these strips are nailed to the frames.

Will some of the readers of the Journal tell us if it makes any difference if the comb is placed in the frame bottom side up. Some think it does not; we think it does.

SESSAYE.

Rice Co, Minn.

In a word, thou must be chaste, cleanly, sweet, sober, quiet, and familiar; so that they love thee and know thee from all others. BUTLER.

[From the Ohio Farmer.]

The Home of the Honey Bee.

It is said that our honey bee, the *apis mellifica*, originally came from Asia, and that from there it was imported into Europe, and afterward to our country, where it has had so welcome a home and entered so largely into our resources for comfort and revenue.

Though this busy and profitable servant has received many a fatal smoking and robbing as a reward for its labors, yet it has the freedom of our wide domain, and in the deep wilderness, multitudes of swarms live in security, as possessors of all their store.

In this country the bee is considered an amiable insect by its friends, seldom using its sting, except when on the defensive. I have never noticed this amiability, for several times when a boy I received a thrust that seemed to have been given with "malice prepense." Severe as the sting is here (especially when about the eye or lips), I am satisfied that it is much more so in the East. I never was stung while in that country by one, but from the accounts given by the natives, and by foreigners who have suffered from them, I am sure it must be so. I believe that in this country some persons can handle bees with far less danger than others; not because they are more kind and careful, but because they have a natural adaptation to the work; such as Rarey, Magner and Dudley have had to the training of horses.

The Siamese have their beehunters, and they say that "only here and there one can follow the business, because the bees so bite. The bee men, they don't like the smell of, and they bite them but little. They bite very hard and always when they get squeezed."

They never domesticate them in Siam, but hunt for them in the jungle, and when found, always rob them clean. This must provoke the bees, but is not fatal to them, for they live in a country where they have to lay nothing up for winter, and when robbed of what they have on hand, have (*a la* Chicago) only to begin anew.

In this country the wild bees usually seek some crevice or hollow tree in which to spread their wax and deposit their stores. But there I was told they build their combs in the open air, usually selecting as high a point as possible in the tops of some of the lofty trees. The point usually chosen is on the under side of some limb just when it leaves the body of the tree. This is often found fifty or even seventy feet from the ground.

The beehunters have ways of tracing bees similar to those practiced in our country. At a certain point they expose some sweet scented dish, and then trap the bees that gather there, and after a time let one escape. Glad to be liberated, it will rise in the air, and then make a bee line for home. They watch the direction and then follow on. When they need further direction another is let out, and on they go under its lead, and then another, until they find the prize.

But yet they have not the honey in hand. It is full fifty feet above their heads on the lowest limb of some stately tree.

The beeman prepares to ascend. He takes his cord and basket, his knife and resinous torch, covers his body as well as he can with spare clothes of his companions and commences the ascent. When within a few feet of the comb, he lights his torch which he lets drop just below him. This fumigates his person and also puts all the bees on the wing, and they fly around in the greatest excitement and rage. He pays no attention to them, but deliberately throws his basket over the limb, and with his knife cuts off the comb, and by a cord lets it down to his partners below. He then descends and has but few stings to repent.

The quantity usually gathered from any one swarm is not large, for the bee is disposed, with all the rest of the animal creation, to take life easy, in that country, where no winter store has to be laid by, and

> "where everlasting spring abides
> And never withering flowers."

It is said that "every man is as lazy as he can be," and probably the same is true of the "little busy bee," that during one short summer works so faithfully and improves each "shining hour,"

> "And gathers honey all the day,
> From every opening flower."

The honey is never brought to market there in comb, but is always strained. It is not considered much of a luxury, nor very salable as an article of food. It is always very thin and looks more like weak maple syrup than honey. But it has a soft pleasant taste, and if we only could have had some good bread and butter to have eaten with it, no doubt it would have been in greater demand.

From the amount of beeswax that is in market in Bangkok, it must be true that a great quantity of honey is gathered every year from the jungles round about.

[For the American Bee Journal.]

The Extractor.

MR. EDITOR:—We now intend attempting to answer quite a prominent question with correspondents about how to manage with the extractor, extracted honey.

In our large yield, we can work the extractor by the side of the hive that we are operating on unmolested by robbers. But at other times we use a tight box, and as fast as we take out a comb and get off the bees, we place it in the box, shutting down the cover so that no bees can get at it, and continue thus until we have taken out all we wish from that hive. Then close the hive and carry the box containing the honey into a close room, there to extract the honey. We like to keep one set of empty combs on hand to fill the hive at the time. This saves opening again to return the combs. We cut the caps off the cells into a vessel that has a strainer in the bottom, which permits all the honey to drip out.

After draining, these caps are removed to a tight vessel and put to soak with a little water. After soaking the water is drained off and put into the vinegar barrel, and makes excellent vinegar. The comb is then ready to make into wax. Our extracted honey we do not bung up if put in casks, under twenty-four hours. If put in glass jars, we prefer to put it into an open barrel or vessel and let it stand over night, as it goes through a process of working and there is quite a scum raises to the top. This scum goes into the vinegar barrel also. In our first season's operations we put it warm, right from the machine into the jars and closed them up, and we found on selling them this scum did not look well on the top, and on opening them and exposing the honey to the air, it acquired such a disagreeable flavor that it could scarcely be used. It *was terribly annoying to us* to have our customers come to us with such complaints. By running it into an open vessel or barrel, and allowing it to go through the working process over night, then scumming and canning, it is all right. It is also better to allow it to stand awhile before putting it in a barrel. By so doing, if the honey is thinner in some hives than others, mixing brings all right. We put up our honey, the past season in new oak butter casks (heads in both ends), containing almost 150 pounds each, and we have kept them in the cellar. When wanted for use we loosen the top hoops, take out the head and melt it over the fire, as it soon candies or grains solid in the casks. Melting or scalding improves the flavor of late fall honey amazingly. In melting we do not put any water with it. We prefer our honey and water separate.

Here is another question. *How long will extracted honey keep?* It will keep a great deal longer in some families than others. Extracted honey is comparatively a new thing under the sun, and many accuse us and others of making honey out of sugar, &c. We opened one cask of our honey (and we don't know but we sold some of the same sort without opening), that looked very much like sugar. It was coarse grained and the grain looks like the grain of coarse sugar to the naked eye, and if we had not put it up ourself we certainly should have thought it moist sugar. Yet, it was honey for all that, and when melted, of a peculiar rich flavor and of a rich golden color. It was gathered from corn blossoms. We plant a few acres of the white flint or Dutton corn on purpose for our bees. It produces abundance of honey and pollen. Dent, or western corn, produces almost nothing for bees. ELISHA GALLUP.

Orchard, Iowa, April 16, 1872.

In March, when the bees fly, set out rye meal, and see if every colony brings in some. Examine those that do not. Bees with a fertile worker bring in pollen also. Do not take the meal away as soon as pollen is brought in, for weak colonies do not fly far, and often pollen fails again; my bees worked two to three weeks on the meal after the pollen had come in.

HULLMAN.

[For Wagner's American Bee Journal.]

The Bee Hive Controversy.

We reprint Mr. King's reply to our criticisms on the Williams article, and to our vindication of Mr. Wagner. The readers of the Journal will know how to put a proper estimate upon it without a single word of comment from us. We shall republish in a separate pamphlet, as a supplement to the American Bee Journal, the whole of this controversy *(both sides)* as it has appeared in the pages of this Journal.

"Mr. Langstroth's Last Words."

We have too much matter of *interest* to beekeepers, to devote much space to personal affairs merely, hence we shall only glance at the voluminous valedictory of Mr. L.

The terrible "charges," the awful "treachery," the "damaging facts," have now been used as "legitimate weapons of an honorable warfare;" the pent-up, concentrated hate of years has been poured forth, and, contrary to Mr. L.'s expectations, we are not dead yet. It was too bad to keep us in "quivering suspense" for a whole month, before we could know our doom. The broadside has come, and after the smoke cleared up, we not only find ourselves alive, but positively *uninjured.* Should we not be thankful?

From an analysis of Mr. L.'s last two articles, it is evident that he considered *any* weapons he could employ against us as "legitimate" and "honorable," and if he could not kill us with one, he would with another. The awful "treachery" turns out to be only his view of what he supposes to have been our representations, in making a bargain several years since with his son, now deceased. The "garbling for a base purpose" has dwindled down to a mere difference of opinion as to whether the quotation with the omission of a clause which we indicated by asterisks, was garbling or not. He sustains his opinion by repeating the accusation, while we say the omission was made to avoid occupying space in the discussion of another subject which would have been introduced.

The attempt to create a prejudice against us by almost, if not actually asserting that we had asked him to prosecute other hive dealers, is a shrewd one, but in the end, Mr. L. will find that "Honesty" would have been "the better policy." He *knows* that he cannot produce one particle of evidence to prove this inferred charge. That was his son's proposition, made probably to secure as few unfavorable exceptions as possible, and in closing the arrangement we merely reminded them of the fact. We have done more for beekeepers in this particular than all others combined. "Actions speak louder than words," hence we do not fear that Mr. L. will establish much prejudice against us.

As an indication of how thinking men regard Mr. L.'s articles, we present the following extract (not garbled), from a letter we have just received.

"What is the matter with Mr. L.? He goes at you with hammer and tongs in column after column of trash without a single show of anything damaging. According to his own testimony you have done nothing which is not in strict accordance with business principles, and ordinary transactions. I was astonished to find such trivial matters magnified into mountains of sinfulness by one I have for years delighted to hold in grateful respect."

[For the American Bee Journal.]

Natural Prolific and Hardy Queens.

Answer to Mr. Dadant's last blow.

On pages 206 and 207, March No. of the American Bee Journal, Mr. Dadant asks me to answer his article—which should be headed "A Chapter of voluntary mistakes," by Charles Dadant.

For I find it composed entirely of such, and I propose to prove them such.

Voluntary mistake No. 1. On page 206, he says, "yet nowhere did Novice say that his queens were too *old*, but that he replaced hybrid queens."

Voluntary mistake No. 2. On page 206, he says, "so little did I promise to replace her, and so little did Mr. Price believe that I made such promise," &c.

Voluntary mistake No. 3. On page 207, he says, "I never refused to replace her."

Voluntary mistake No. 4. On page 207, he says, "but I did refuse to sell a second queen to Mr. Price."

Answer to mistake No. 1. On page 224, vol. VI, American Bee Journal, April No. 1871, Novice gives his reasons for his purchasing twenty-five queens from Mr. Grimm in these words: "and last fall *so many* of our *old* queens failed, that we purchased twenty-five queens from Mr. Grimm to replace them."

Answer to mistake No. 2: (Extract of letter.)

HAMILTON, ILL., *June* 7, 1870.

MR. J. M. PRICE,

DEAR SIR:—The queen I sent to you is raised from imported stock and is very prolific. *I guarantee her all right.*

In my letter ordering, I not only asked him to guarantee her safe arrival, but that he guarantee her pure—purely mated and prolific, and referred him to my article "All Abroad," and told him that if he thought he had a queen that would be satisfactory, after he had read that article, to send her to me C. O. D.

That I did expect him to replace her is proved by my writing to him, informing him of her unprolificness.

He answered me as follows:

HAMILTON, ILL., *Aug.* 4, 1870.

Mr. J. M. PRICE,

DEAR SIR:—Do not give her up before another season's trial. Yours respectfully,

CHAS. DADANT.

As this was not replacing her, I wrote again. He answered as follows: (Extract.)

HAMILTON, ILL.

Mr. JNO. M. PRICE,

DEAR SIR:—As soon as the bees can raise queens I will send one to you next spring.

Yours respectfully,

CHAS. DADANT.

Beekeepers, have I not proved that he did expect to replace her, and did know that he had promised to do so?

I will give you an extract of his advertisement in the Journal at the time he sent her to me.

Advertisement from April to September, 1870: (Extract.)

"The queens will be sent from here safe arrival guaranteed. CHAS. DADANT,
April, 1870, 6 mos. Hamilton, Ill."

In the spring I wrote him of her condition and received not the queens, as promised, but the following letter:

HAMILTON, ILL., *April* 21, 1871.

Mr. JNO. M. PRICE,

DEAR SIR:—You did so much fuss about the queen I sent you last spring, that I am very little disposed to let you (*have*) any more queens.

Yours very respectfully,

CHAS. DADANT.

Answer to mistake No. 4. His last letter to me before his refusal: (Extract.)

HAMILTON, ILL.

"But I think your best way be to get one or two imported queens. CHAS. DADANT."

Friend Beekeepers:—After reading the above correspondence, and his advertisement, what shall we call his Wilful Voluntary Mistakes? Also under what head shall I class his mode of getting money? But after wronging me out of my money (which is a very small part of the damage that the sending of that worthless queen was to me), is it a sign of an honest dealer to go back of his guarantee on an order, and keep the money that he came into possession of by that guarantee, and after beating me out of my money in that manner? Is it a sign of a gentleman to try and add insult to injury and wrong by his false "Wilful Voluntary Mistakes?"

JOHN M. PRICE.

Buffalo Grove, Iowa, March 10, 1872.

[From Shuckards' "BRITISH BEES."]

Bees.

It is very natural that the bees should interest the majority of us, so many agreeable and attractive associations being connected with the name. It is immediately suggestive of spring, sunshine, and flowers,—meadows gaily enamelled, green lanes, thymy downs, and fragrant heaths. It speaks of industry, forethought, and competence,—of well ordered government, and of due but not degrading subordination. The economy of the hive has been compared by our great poet to the polity of a populous kingdom under monarchial government. He says:—

"Therefore doth Heaven divide
The state of man in divers functions,
Setting endeavor in continual motion;
To which is fixed, as an aim or butt,
Obedience: for so work the honey bees;
Creatures, that, by a rule in nature, teach
The act of order to a peopled kingdom.
They have a king, and officers of sorts:
Where some, like magistrates, correct at home;
Others, like merchants, venture trade abroad;

Others like soldiers, armed in their stings,
Make boot upon the summer's velvet buds;
Which pillage they, with merry march, bring home
To the tent-royal of their emperor:
Who, envied in his majesty, surveys
The singing masons building roof of gold;
The civil citizens kneading up the honey;
The poor mechanic porters crowding in
Their heavy burdens at his narrow gate;
The sad ey'd justice, with his surly hum,
Delivering o'er to executors pale
The lazy yawning drone."—HENRY V, 1, 2.

Nothing escaped the wonderful vision of this "myriad minded" man, and its pertinent application. This description, although certainly not technically accurate, is a superb broad sketch, and shows how well he was acquainted with the natural history and habits of the domestic bee.

The curiosity bees have attracted from time immemorial, and the wonders of their economy elicited by the observation and study of modern investigators, is but a grateful return for the benefits derived to man from their persevering assiduity and skill. It is the just homage of reason to perfect instinct running closely parallel to its own wonderful attributes. Indeed, so complex are many of the operations of this instinct, as to have induced the surmise of a positive affinity to reason, instead of its being a mere analogy, working blindly and without reflection. The felicity of the adaptation of the hexagonal waxen cells, and the skill of the construction of the comb to their purposes, has occupied the obstruse calculations of profound mathematicians; and since human ingenuity has devised modes of investigating, unobserved, the various proceedings of the interior of the hive, wonder has grown still greater, and admiration has reached its climax.

The intimate connection of "bees" with nature's elegancies, the flowers, is an association which links them agreeably to our regard, for each suggests the other; their vivacity and music giving animation and variety to what might otherwise pall by beautiful but inanimate attractions. When we combine with this the services which bees perform in their eager pursuits, our admiration extends beyond them to their great originator, who, by such apparently small means, accomplishes so simply yet completely, a most important object of creation.

That bees were cultivated by man in the earliest conditions of his existence, possibly whilst his yet limited family was still occupying the primitive cradle of the race at Hindoo Koosh, or on the fertile slopes of the Himalayas, or upon the more distant table land or plateau of Thibet, or in the delicious vales of Cashmere, or wherever it might have been, somewhere widely away to the east of the Caspian Sea,—is a very probable supposition. Accident furthered by curiosity, would have early led to the discovery of stores of honey which the assiduity of the bees had hoarded; its agreeable odor would have induced further search, which would have strengthened the possession by keener observation, and have led in due course to the fixing of them in his immediate vicinity.

To this remote period, possibly not so early as the discovery of the treasures of the bee, may be assigned also the first domestication of the animals useful to man, many of which are still found in those districts in all their primitive wildness. The discovery and cultivation of the cereal plants will also date from this early age. The domestication of animals has never been satisfactorily explained, but all inquiry seems to point to those regions as the native land, both of them, and of the *graminæ* which produce our grain; for Heinzleman, Linnæus' enthusiastic disciple, found there those grasses still growing wild, which have not been found elsewhere in a natural state.

Thus, long before the three great branches of the human race, the Aryan, Shemetic, and Turonian, took their divergent courses from the procreative nest which was to populate the earth, they were already endowed from their patrimony with the best gifts nature could present to them; and they were thus fitted, in their estrangement from their home, with the requirements, which the vicissitudes they might have to contend with in their migrations, most needed. They would eventually have settled into varying conditions, differently modified by time acting conjunctively with climate and position, until in the lapse of years, and the changes the earth has since undergone, the stamp impressed by these causes, which would have been originally evanescent, became indelible. That but one language was originally theirs, the researches of philology distinctly prove, by finding a language still more ancient than its Aryan, Shemetic, and Turonian derivatives. From this elder language these all spring, their common origin being deduced from the analogies extant in each. These investigations are confirmed by the Scriptural account "That the whole earth was of one language and of one speech," previous to the Flood, and it describes the first migration as coincident with the subsidence of the waters.

That animals have been domesticated in a very early stage of man's existence, we have distinct proof in many recent geological discoveries, and all these discoveries show the same animals to have been in every instance subjugated; thus pointing to a primitive and earlier domestication in the region where both were originally produced. That pasture land was provided for the sustenance of those animals, they being chiefly herbivorous, is a necessary conclusion. Thence ensues the fair deduction that *phanerogamous* or flower-bearing plants coexisted, and bees, consequently, and necessarily too—thus participating reciprocal advantages, they receiving from those plants sustenance, and giving them fertility.

Claiming thus this very high antiquity for man's nutritive "bee," which was of far earlier utility to him than the silk worm, whose labor demanded a very advanced condition of skill and civilization, to be made available; it is perfectly consistent, and indeed needful, to claim the simultaneous existence of all the bees' allies. The earliest Shemetic and Aryan records, the Book of Job, the Vedas, the Egyptian sculptures and papyri, as well as the poems of Homer, confirm the early cultivation of bees by man for domestic uses; and their frequent representation in the Egyptian hieroglyphics, wherein the bee occurs as the symbol of royalty, clearly shows that their economy, with a monarch at its head, was known; a hive, too, being figured, as Sir Gardner Wilkinson tells us, upon a very ancient tomb at Thebis, is early evidence of its domestication there, and how early even historically, it was brought under the special dominion of mankind. I adduce these particulars, merely to intimate how very early, even in the present condition of the earth, bees were beneficial to mankind, and that, therefore, the connection may have subsisted, as I have previously urged, on the remotest and very primitive ages of the existence of man; and that imperatively with them, the entire family of man, of which they form a unit only, was also created.

In America, where *apis mellifica* is of European introduction, swarms of these bees, escaping domestication, resume their natural condition, and have pressed forward far into the uncleared wild; and widely in advance of the conquering colonist, they have taken their abode in the primitive unreclaimed forest. Nor do they remain stationary, but on, still on, with every successive year, spreading in every direction; and thus surely indicating to the aboriginal red man, the certain, if even slow, approach of civilization, and the consequent necessity of his own protective retreat—a strong instance of the distributive processes of nature. It clearly shows how the wild bees may have similarly migrated in all directions from the centre of their origin. That they are now found at the very *ultima Thule*, so far away from their assumed incunabula, and with such apparent existing obstructions to their distributive process, is a proof, had we no other, that the condition of the earth must have been geographically very different at the period of their beginning, and that vast geological changes have, since then, altered its physical features. Where islands now exist, these must then have formed portions of widely sweeping continents, and seas have been dry land, which have since swept over the same area, insulating irregular portions by the submergence of irregular intervals, and thus have left them in their present condition, with their then existing inhabitants restricted to the circuit they now occupy. That long periods of time must necessarily have elapsed to have effected this by the methods we still see in operation, is no proof that it has not been. Nature, in her large operations, has no regard for the duration of time. Her courses are so sure that they are ever eventually successful; for as to her, whose permanency is not computable, it matters not what period the process takes; and she is as indifferent to the seconds of time, whereby man's brevity is spanned, as she is to the wastefulness of her own exuberant resources, knowing that neither is lost in the result at which she reaches; consuming the one, and scattering broadcast the other, but in unnoticable infinitesimals, she does it irrespective of the origin, the needs, or the duration of man, who can only watch her irrepressible advances by transmitting from generation to generation the records of his observation; marking thus by imaginary stations the course of the incessant stream which carries him upon its surface.

That other bees are found besides social bees, may be new to some of my readers, who will perhaps learn now, for the first time, that collective similarities of organization and habits associate other insects with "the bee," as bees. Although the names of "domestic bee," "honey bee," or "social bee," imply a contradistinction to some other "bee," yet it must have been very long before even the most acute observer could have noticed the peculiarities of structure which constitute other insects "bees," and ally the "wild bees" to the "domestic bee," from the deficiency of artificial means to examine minutely the organization whereby the affinity is clearly proved. This is also further shown in the poverty of our language in vernacular terms to express them distinctively; for even the name of "wild bees," in as far as it has been applied to any except the "honey-bee" in a wildened state, is a usage of modern introduction, and of date subsequent to their examination and appreciation. Our native tongue, in the words "bee," "wasp," "fly," and "ant," compasses all those thousands of different winged and unwinged insects which modern science comprises in two very extensive orders in entomology of the *Hymenoptera* and the *Diptera*,—thus exhibiting how very poor common language is in words to denote distinctive differences in creatures even when the differences are so marked, and the habits so dissimilar, as in the several groups constituting these orders. But progressively extending knowledge, and a more familiar intimacy with insects and their habits, will doubtless, in the course of time, supervene, as old aversions, prejudices, and superstitions wear out, when by the light of instruction we shall gradually arouse to perceive that "His breath has passed that way too;" and that, therefore, they all put forth strong claims to the notice and admiration of man.

It is highly improbable that ordinary language will ever find distinctive names to indicate *genera*, and far less *species*; and although we have some few words which combine large groups, such as "gnats," "flesh flies," "gad flies," "gall flies," "dragon flies," "sand wasps," "bumble bees," &c., &c.; and, although the small group, which it is my purpose to describe hereafter in all their attractive peculiarities, has had several vernacular denominations applied to them to indicate their most distinctive characteristics, such as "cuckoo bees," "carpenter bees," "mason bees," "carding bees," &c., yet many which are not thus to be distinguished will have to wait long for their special appellation.

The first breathings of spring bring forth the bees. Before the hedgerows and the trees have burst their buds, and expanded their yet delicate green leaves to the strengthening influence of the air, and whilst only here and there the whole blossoms of the black thorn sparkle around, and patches of chickweed spread their bloom in attractive humility on waste bits of ground in corners of fields, they are abroad. Their hum will be heard in some very favorite sunny nook, where the precious primrose spreads forth its delicate pale blossoms, in the modest confidence of conscious beauty, to catch the eye of the sun, as well as

"Daffodils, that come before the swallow dares,
And take the winds of March with beauty."

The yellow catkins of the sallow, too, are already swarmed around by bees, the latter being our Northern representative of the palm, which heralded "peace to earth and good will to man." The bees thus announce that the business of the year has begun, and that the lethargy of winter is superseded by energetic activity.

The instinctive impulse of the cares of maternity prompt the wild bees to their early assiduity, urging them to their eager quest of these foremost indications of the renewed year. The firstling bees are forthwith at their earnest work of collecting honey and pollen, which, kneaded into paste, are to become both the cradle and the sustenance of their future progeny.

Wherever we investigate wonderful Nature, we observe the most beautiful adaptation and arrangement; everywhere the correlations of structure with function. In confirmation of which I may here briefly notice in anticipation, that the bees are divided into two large groups—the short-tongued and the long-tongued—and it is the short-tongued which are first abroad, the corolla of the first flowers being shallow, and the nectar depositories obvious, an arrangement which facilitates their obtaining the honey already at hand. These bees are also amply furnished, in the clothing of their posterior legs, or otherwise, with the means to convey home the pollen which they vigorously collect, finding it already in superfluous abundance, and which, being borne from flower to flower, impregnates and makes fruitful those plants which require external agents to accomplish their fertility. Thus nature duly provides, by an interchange of offices, for the general good, and by simple, although sometimes obscure means, gives motion and persistency to the wheel within wheel which so exquisitely fulfil her designs, and roll forward, unremittingly, her stupendous fabric.

The way in which bees execute this object and design of nature, and to which they, more evidently than any other insects, are called to the performance, is shown in the implanted instinct which prompts them to seek flowers, knowing, by means of that instinct, that flowers will furnish them with what is needful both for their own sustenance and for that of their descendants. Flowers, to this end, are furnished with the requisite attractive qualifications to allure the bees. Whether their odor or their color be the tempting vehicle, or both conjunctively, it is scarcely possible to say, but that they should hold out special invitation is requisite to the maintenance of their own perpetuity. This, it is supposed, the color of flowers chiefly effects by being visible from a distance. Flowers, within themselves, indicate to the bees visiting them, the presence of nectaria by spots colored differently from their petals. This nectar, gathered by the bees as honey, is secreted by glands or glandulous surfaces, seated upon the organs of fructification; and Nature has also furnished means to protect these depositories of honey for the bees from the intrusive action of the rain, which might wash the secretion away. To this end it has clothed the corollæ with a surface of minute hairs, which effectually secures them from its obtrusive action, and thus displays the importance it attaches to the co-operation of the bees. That bees should vary considerably in size is a further accommodation of Nature to promote the fertilization of flowers, which, in some cases, none but small insects could accomplish. Many plants could not be perpetuated but for the agency of insects, and especially of bees; and it is remarkable that it is chiefly those which require this intervention that have a nectarium and secrete honey. By thus seeking the honey, and obtaining it in a variety of ways, bees accomplish this great object of Nature. It often, also, happens that flowers which even contain within themselves the means of ready fructification, cannot derive it from the pollen of their own anthers, but require that the pollen should be conveyed from the anthers of younger flowers. In some cases the reverse takes place, as, for instance, in the *Euphorbia Cyparissias*, wherein it is the pollen of the older flower which, through the same agency, fertilizes the younger. In those occasional cases where the nectarium of the flower is not perceptible, if the spur of such a flower which usually becomes the depository of the nectar, that has oozed from the capsules secreting it, be too narrow for the entrance of the bee, and even beyond the reach of its long tongue, it contrives to attain its object by biting a hole on the outside, through which it taps the store. The skill of bees in finding the honey, even when it is much withdrawn from notice, is a manifest indication of the prompting instinct which tells them where to seek it, and is a matter of extreme interest to the observer, for the honey marks surely guide them; and where these, as in some flowers, are placed in a circle upon its bosom, they work their way around, lapping the nectar as they go. To facilitate this fecundation of plants, which is Nature's prime object, bees are usually more or less hairy; so that if even they limit themselves to imbibing nectar, they involuntarily fulfil the greater design by conveying the pollen from flower to flower. To many insects, especially flies, some flowers are a fatal attraction, for their viscous secretions often make these insects prisoners, and thus destroy them. To the bees this rarely or never happens, either by reason of their superior strength, or possibly from the instinct which repels them from visiting flowers which exude so clammy a substance. It is probably only to the end of promoting fertilization by the attraction of insects that the structure of those flowers which secrete nectar is exclusively conducive, and which fully and satisfactorily explains the final cause of this organization.

To detect these things it is requisite to observe Nature out of doors—an occupation which has its own rich reward in the health and cheerfulness it promotes—and there to watch patiently and attentively. It is only by unremitting perseverance, diligence and assiduity, that we can hope to explore the interesting habits and peeu liar industries of these, although small, yet very attractive insects.

Amongst the early blossoming flowers most in request with the bees, and which therefore seem to be great favorites, we find the chickweed (*Alsine media*), the primrose, and the catkins of the sallow; and these in succession are followed by all the flowers of the spring, summer and autumu. Their greatest favorites would appear to be the *Amentaceæ*, or catkin-bearing shrubs and trees; the willow, hazel, osier, &c., from the male flowers of which they obtain the pollen, and from the female the honey; all the Rosacea, especially the dog-rose, and the Primulaceæ, the Orchideæ, Caryophyllaceæ, Polygoneæ, and the balsamic lilies. Clover is very attractive to them, as are also tares; and the spots on those leaves of the bean which appear before the flower, and exude a sweet secretion; the flowers of all the cabbage tribe. Beneath the shade of the Linden, when in flower, may be heard above one intense hum of thrifty industry. The blossoms of all the fruit trees and shrubs, standard or wall, and all aromatic plants, are highly agreeable to them, such as lavender, lemon-thyme, mignonette, indeed all the *resedas*; also sage, borage, &c.; but to mention separately all the flowers they frequent would be to compile almost a complete flood.

Bees are also endowed with an instinct that teaches them to avoid certain plants that might be dangerous to them. Thus they neither frequent the oleander nor the crown imperial, and they also avoid the *Ranunculaceæ*, on account of some poisonous property; and although the *Melianthus major* drops with honey, it is not sought.

Bees may be further consorted with flowers by the analogy and parallelism of their stages of existence. Thus the egg is equivalent to the seed; the *larva* to the germination and growth; the *pupa* to the bud, and the *imago* to the flower. The flower dies as soon as the seed is fully formed, which is then disseminated by many wonderful contrivances to a propitious soil; and the wild bees die as soon as the store of eggs is wonderfully deposited, according to their several instincts, in fitting receptacles, and provision furnished to sustain the development of the progeny. Thus each secures perpetuity to its species, but individually ceases.

[For the American Bee Journal.]

Gallup hits Somebody.

MR. EDITOR:—We have the April No. *all right*. The first on the docket that claims our attention, is Dr. Bohrer. He infers that we disagree with Mr. Langstroth, and condemn the two-story Langstroth hive, because we said there was any quantity of worthless hives at Cleveland. The reader will readily see that we did not say that there was no good hive there. *By no means*. Now, Doctor, never again use such a shallow excuse to get in your F. R. Allen hive. Old birds are not often caught with chaff. The next is T. F. Bingham. He is afraid he will have to hear for the next five years about Gallup's hive. Now the reader knows that Mr. B. has a patent hive, and it galls some of those patent hive fellows *terribly* to think that after all the boasting, THE OLD LANGSTROTH PRINCIPLE IS STILL AHEAD.

Some of them would give considerable, if Gallup and the AMERICAN BEE JOURNAL were dead and buried, but it is our sincere desire that the influence of the American Bee Journal may never be less. Now will the reader please take notice that in giving a description of the hive we use, we have no other motive than to illustrate a principle in beekeeping.

We have already forwarded an article illustrating how to use the Langstroth hive on the same principle. We certainly believe we could have obtained the same results from a regular Langstroth spread out horizontally in such a season as the past. I have already cautioned others not to go into the large Gallup hive extensively, but make one or two for trial. We always prefer a good season for getting a large yield of honey.

This buying up extracted honey and feeding to one or two stocks, so as to be able to report an extra large yield per hive, and thus create a demand for a particular hive, is not what Gallup believes in. *We have no hives for sale, and consequently no axe to grind.*

The next is Novice, and oh how we are going to hit him! He says he really likes the Quinby frame or a large one. Now, Novice, warrant us just such seasons as the past two and we are with you; but how is it in a cool wet season, when our stocks are only medium sized. All of the honey gathered is thin and watery and needs a great deal of evaporation, and we have no extractors, but are compelled to use a hive in which we can condense the bees into a small compass or compact mass; or our honey is sealed up before it is half evaporated, and the consequence is, our bees all die over winter from dysentery. We have paid dearly for our knowledge on this subject. We have seen a number of such seasons in our northern climate. We have always said that a larger frame would be preferable farther south, at least it is our opinion that it would be preferable. We guess you mixed that a trifle, when you said our bees were brooding sticks. The fact is in this cool backward spring, our bees are in the best possible shape for keeping up the animal heat for developing brood, and there is no sticks in the centre of that brood. After our stocks become strong and numerous, and the weather becomes warm or hot, then our sticks or division in the centre of the frame is not one particle of detriment in practice, although it appear to be in theory.

To-day, April 15th, 1872, the spring has come in cold and backward. No natural pollen yet, and no forage from natural sources. Now you know some of our reasons for small combs.

ELISHA GALLUP.

Orchard, Mitchell Co., Iowa.

Dzierzon says, "the first day the bees fly in spring is a day of great jubilee for me;" I trust it is for the many readers of the Journal. HULLMAN.

THE AMERICAN BEE JOURNAL.

Washington, June, 1872.

All communications and letters of business should be addressed to

GEO. S. WAGNER,
Office of the American Bee Journal,
WASHINGTON, D. C.

With this number closes the 7th volume of the American Bee Journal. We think this a fitting occasion to return our thanks to those kind friends who have stood by us, and so efficiently aided us in conducting the Journal since the sudden death of its late editor. Called so unexpectedly to assume the charge of the Journal, and burdened with many other weighty duties, we would have been unable without their aid to conduct it.

The Journal will in the future pursue the same independent course that it has in the past, seeking the true development and improvement of bee-culture in this country; and will continue unhesitatingly to expose whatever it believes to be fraud and deception.

We doubt whether any class of interests have suffered more in this country than bee-culture, from the intrigues and deceptions of designing persons, and the only way to defeat the plans of these persons, is exposure. It is disagreeable, and at times painful, but is nevertheless a positive duty of a journalist who desires the true and complete development of the cause he advocates. Mere personal controversies we deprecate, and shall endeavor to close the columns of the Journal to all who seek to engage in them.

Although the beekeepers of this country have during the past winter sustained heavy losses, it is gratifying to know that few intend to abandon bee-culture. The great majority are going to try again, thinking that they have discovered the cause of their troubles. We trust they have, and will not again be called upon to meet such heavy losses.

The many friends of Dr. Bohrer will be pained to learn of the calamity with which he met when just about leaving for Europe, and which has resulted in his abandoning his trip, and will join with us in hoping that his new venture will prove more successful.

Rev. Mr. Langstroth, we are happy to inform the readers of the American Bee Journal, has safely reached his home in Oxford, Ohio. His foot is healing rapidly, and we hope soon to hear of his being able to throw aside his crutches, and have again the full use of his foot.

The locust trees in this city are done blossoming. While in blossom, they were alive with bees. The linden is just coming into blossom.

A prompt renewal of subscriptions and payment of arrearage, would be of great aid to us at present.

In answer to many inquiries, we would say, that we are unable to furnish complete sets of the present volume of the Journal, the supply of the July and January numbers being exhausted. Having moved from our former residence, we have been compelled to pack up all the back numbers of the Journal, but shall keep a list of those desiring them, and will send them before long.

We will, during the coming month, send bills to all in arrearages, and shall expect a prompt settlement. All subscriptions must be paid in advance; no Journals will be sent after the expiration of the time for which the subscription has been paid.

[For the American Bee Journal.]

Chautauqua Beekeepers' Association.

The 5th semi-annual meeting of the Chautauqua Beekeepers' Association met at the American House, Jamestown, N Y., Tuesday afternoon. J. M. Beebe, President. Notwithstanding the very unfavorable weather, and the almost impassable condition of the roads, a good number of beekeepers were in attendance. The first subject for discussion was wintering bees. As many persons had lost a large portion of their stock during the past winter, they were naturally anxious to learn the cause, and ascertain the proper remedy.

Mr. Beebe stated that he had lost two weak swarms only; had thirty swarms last fall. He had constructed a house to winter his bees in, costing him $110, but he preferred to winter them upon their summer stands. He fed stocks deficient in stores; thought all should have 25 lbs. each to be safe, although the less honey they consume the better. His feed is sugar syrup; to 10 lbs. of coffee sugar add 5 lbs. of water, and let it boil five minutes.

Mr. Cook started with 70 swarms and lost one-tenth. The winter he regarded as a very hard one, owing to the excessive cold, intermingled with frequent warm spells. He fed the same as Mr. Beebe, only he mixed honey with the syrup.

He gave upward ventilation. The most of the swarms he lost, he attributed to honey dew, causing dysentery. There is usually about six weeks of honey season proper, but only four last year. He considered last season as the worst for the beekeepers he ever knew, *but even then the investment paid.*

Mr. Philips lost 44 swarms out of fifty. He wintered a part out of doors, a part in the cellar, and the rest in the kitchen. He lost the most in the kitchen. Gave ample ventilation, had no dysentery or foul brood in his young swarms. All the stocks that died left an abundance of honey. In reply to a question as to the quality of honey in California, where he had resided for many years, he stated that it was as white and nice as here, and that the white mustard was to honey producers there what the clover ishere.

Mr. Joseph Cook lost ten swarms out of 44. He considered the past winter a hard one for the bees. This was the first lost in wintering he had met with, but he attributed it in great measure to his failure to properly care for them.

Mr. Henry Whilford lost eight swarms out of 29. Gave too much upward ventilation. He thought it a good plan to put something inside the hive for the bees to fall on, so they could return to the cluster. In response to a question, he stated that combs moulded in this climate long before the bees perished. He favored wintering bees in a house built for the purpose. The winter was a severe one for beekeepers.

Mr. Beebe stated that he had obtained 216 lbs. of box honey, and a new swarm from one old one, in a single season. He offered to wager that he could in any season make *more net profit from fifty swarms of bees, than could be made in the same season from thirty cows.* He favored Italians to the native black bees. He preferred artificial swarming where increases of stock was desired. Thought natural swarms produced the most honey.

Mr. Campbell had taken 104 lbs. from one swarm, leaving them enough for winter.

Mr. Grout obtained 35 lbs. a week from each hive from each swarm by using the mel-extractor.

Mr E H. Jenner had invested $75 in bees, but had never realized $5 worth of honey. Used the box hive, but should do so no longer. In reply to a question, Mr. Beebe said he would prefer to transfer swarms now, or else wait till 21 days after swarming, because there was less brood at these two seasons. If now, make the transfer in a warm room. There was considerable interest in improved hives, several leading kinds were represented. The Beebe hive was unanimously considered to be the very best hive now before the public. The past winter had firmly established the fact, that it was unequalled for safe wintering bees upon their summer stands. The simple yet efficient arrangement of the comb frames received commendation. Cheapness of construction, perfect adaptation to the wants of the beekeepers, combined with complete control secured over the bees are a few of the superior merits of the bee hive.

After listening with interest to an address by Mr. Albert M. Cook on the History and Use of the Honey Bee, the association adjourned to meet at Mayville, Tuesday, September 3d, 1872.

HERBERT A. BURCH.

[For the American Bee Journal.]

Dr. Bohrer's Trip to Europe.

MR. EDITOR.—Inasmuch as it was announced in the columns of your Journal for April, that I was going to Italy for the purpose of importing Italian queens, and as it is now evident I cannot go, I deem it but justice to such as contemplated obtaining imported queens through me, as well as to myself, to explain why I am not going this season.

On the morning of the 13th of the present month I was about to complete my arrangements for the trip, when the cry of fire attracted my attention in the direction of my dwelling. It was on fire, and was, together with much of my household goods, consumed. This, of course, turned my family into the street, and compelled me to remain at home and rebuild. But if the beekeepers of the country desire it, and will send me their orders by the time the North American Beekeepers' Association meets at Indianapolis, in December next, I will start to Europe about the first of April, 1873, so as to get back to this country by the first of June. I think I can deliver the queens in New York in good order, and send them from there to the end of their journey for $12 each, which is much lower than imported queens usually cost, as they are badly packed, kept long on the route, and are roughly handled, owing to which a large majority of them perish on the way. Aside from this, many of them fall far below the recognized standard of purity, and consequently cannot give breeders or their patrons satisfaction, These difficulties, which are so exceedingly annoying to beekeepers, I propose to remedy, if it is possible to do so, by selecting foreign queens in person, and taking charge of them on their journey as far as New York, at which point they will not be detained but a few hours, as they will be so packed as to be forwarded to their destination without repacking, but will remain in the original packages. The reason why I wish to have the matter determined by the 10th of December is, that it may be announced, and all rest assured that the trip will be made. I wish at least one hundred orders.

G. BOHRER.

Alexandria, Ind., April 21, 1872.

I hope to get up a club for your paper, and the above names are of parties who will be likely to want it. Our county is quite newly settled, but my own and my neighbor's bees did well last season, and I think there is a growing interest in the culture which I should like to see encouraged.

I sowed twelve acres of alsike this spring, and though the old fogies' cry "can't raise it" has been sounded in my ears on all sides, I have the satisfaction of seeing a good stand and the weather most favorable for its growth. I have no doubt that with the addition of this pasturage to that of the wild flowers they will store plenty of honey.

N. H. S.

West Point, Neb., May 13, 1872.

[For the American Bee Journal.]

I promised to report this spring how my bees wintered. It nearly makes me sick to think of the fatality of the past winter among bees in this country. Out of forty-seven strong stocks and one weak one I have but ten left, and some of them very weak. Bee cholera the cause. But I do not feel like giving it up yet, so I have dought some more and am going to try again, and do what I can this season in making up my loss. * * * I was truly sorry to hear of the beath of our editor.

JONATHAN SMITH.

Willow Branch, Ind., April 24, 1872.

Lightning Source UK Ltd.
Milton Keynes UK
UKHW021953190219
337571UK00011B/1960/P

9 781332 249084